Wĭthûr Wē

Wĭthûr Wē

Matthew Bruce Alexander

2010

Dedication

For my boys, Bruce and Will, and for my little one still on the way.

PART I

1

As it had since before the human presence, Aldra II slowly turned on its axis and its sun appeared to sink in the western sky. Land passed into shadow and splotches of artificial light began to glow. On the southern coast of a mountainous northern island, on the twilight border between the light and dark, the city of Arcarius nestled at the base of some foothills.

The day had been warm, but a cool wind now swept through, promising a chill when the forever moonless night fully arrived. In the southeast of the city, encroaching on higher terrain, there sat a sprawling building built piecemeal, giving the impression of a pile of boxes stacked on and around each other. At the front entrance there was a wooden sign as cracked as the street running by it. Suspended at two corners from a warped wooden pole by two lengths of chain, it swung in the breeze with a soft creak. The sign said, "Nigel's" in peeling white paint.

A retractable dome opened up a large dining room and bar to the outside, and in it a party was winding down. Many guests dallied to finish a drink or conversation, and all made sure to have some parting words with Nigel's son, Alistair Ashley 3nn. A tall youth whose large muscles had finished filling out a broad frame, he was obliged to look down when speaking with others. He wore a patient smile on his plain and weary face as he endured pleasantry after pleasantry from well intentioned folk.

"I always make it a point to express my gratitude to our military men and women," said an aunt with a voice quavering with age. "I've always said you give far in excess of the rest of us."

He smiled at her earnest doting. "We appreciate your appreciation."

She grabbed his thick left hand with both of hers and feebly squeezed as she gushed, "Our family is very, very, very, very proud of you, my dear."

"Thank you very much."

Alistair's uncle shouldered in when he decided his wife had used up her allotted time. Roughly shaking hands, he said, "When you have some time, be sure to stop by and tell us some stories."

"I'll do that."

"Absolutely wonderful what you've done," his aunt said as her husband took her by the shoulders and guided her to the exit. When she was gone another filled her spot, but he noted with relief that the procession was diminishing.

"Can't believe you stayed for four cycles," said a young cousin.

"Well, I was learning a lot. And this way I'm no longer eligible for the draft."

"I'm up before the council in two years; maybe I should do what you did."

"Think it through carefully. It's not...it can be hard. I'd look into something else first."

The boy gave him a strange look. "Well...you stayed."

Alistair shrugged. "Yeah...I guess...It's dangerous on Kaldis. Consider all your options first."

His young cousin slowly nodded, his expectation of Alistair's enthusiastic endorsement thwarted, and moved on.

When the adoring children and fawning women and approving men finally left, Alistair made his way to the bar where his father, Nigel Ashley 4xx, was wiping the wood down with a wet rag. The mahogany bar was flawlessly smooth and polished, a distinct contrast with the threadbare carpets, stained walls and cracked doorframes everywhere else. He had paused to admire it when he first entered the dining room, impressed with what his father had installed while he was away.

Nigel gave his son an understanding smile.

"If I made it a small affair, we would have had about three hundred offended friends and relatives," he apologized.

"I'm glad they came," Alistair replied, and as if to prove it he hopped over the bar despite his fatigue. Setting out a tray, he put some mugs on it and filled them with beer. "I'm just on Kaldisian time right now. It's going to take me a while to get used to Aldran time again."

"Is it true they have 25 'time zones' on Kaldis?"

"Yes."

"That has to be confusing."

"Actually, most planets do it that way." His father fixed a somewhat skeptical gaze on him. Alistair chuckled. "I'm not lying to you. Earth has 24 time zones."

Nigel tossed his rag in a pile of dirty laundry on the floor, shaking his head in a noncommittal way. The Ashley patriarch was of average height with a slight build that bent a little more every year. His youngest child was taller and broader than him when he left, but the difference now was astonishing. Though he had not grown taller, he was 18 stone if he was an ounce.

"You sure did grow a body while you were off," he said, laying a hand on his son's shoulder. "You come from your mother's side, I think."

"I don't even know how much of this is me," Alistair mumbled.

Before Nigel could respond, he inclined his head to a poster, tacked to the wall, of a gentleman in military garb. He was perhaps forty cycles and was smiling warmly yet condescendingly at anyone who peered at him. Along the bottom were the words "Warwick for Mayor". As he recalled, the poster would be covering up a stain from water damage.

"I didn't realize you were into politics."

"Oh, that. That's nothing," said Nigel, dismissing it with a wave of his hand. "Actually, you'd probably like him. He's been harping on the bureaucracies non-stop."

Alistair nodded and hummed as he poured but did not commit to an answer.

"Listen, Alistair, your mother and I are going to leave you and your friends alone now. Be sure to shut the roof when you're done. We'll finish cleaning up tomorrow."

"Thanks, Dad."

Nigel gripped his son by the shoulders, still incredulous that his boy was so solid. He gave him a rough, manly hug, a firm pat on the back and then left, supported by a cane. His hip had gone bad while Alistair was off and he was waiting for his operation. As Alistair watched him struggle over the warped wooden floor covered by a lumpy carpet, he frowned with concern but was interrupted by his mother, Mary Ashley 1yt. She placed herself in his line of sight and enveloped him in a hug. He gave her stout form his own embrace and rocked her back and forth. For the tenth time that night, her eyes welled up with tears.

"You stay up as long as you like," she said and pulled him down by his muscled neck to kiss his forehead.

"I'll be along soon. I'm about to fall over as it is."

She inclined her head to be kissed, and he returned her peck on the forehead. She smiled once, looked him up and down yet again, and went off after her husband.

Grabbing the tray of drinks, Alistair made his way to the far end of the dining room. There, by the railing overlooking the hillside and the precipitous drop to the sea, his six closest friends were seated in various positions: along the rail, on the floor, and on a few chairs at the table. Laughing, they moved in that sluggish way of the inebriated. He set the tray down on the table to a chorus of approving sounds. They each grabbed a mug, sloshing a little beer onto the tray, and clanked them together, sloshing a bit more. After the wordless toast, they all chugged. His swallow taken, Alistair licked his lips and sprawled out in a chair, holding his beer on his stomach and struggling to keep his eyes open.

Having downed his mug already, the immense Oliver Keegan 3nn eyed Alistair and said, "I think the man's no good for winger anymore." Alistair smiled back at his rugby mate. "You'll have to come up with me on the line."

Elizabeth, happy and shameless now, leaned forward from her seat on Oliver's lap and poked Alistair's legs, approvingly noting how little give there was.

"Your thighs are enormous. And hard as rocks."

"Have the decency to wait 'til I'm gone," Oliver protested. He bit her on the neck and she squealed and slapped his mammoth chest. "Elizabeth dear," he began in a tone of mock gentility, "if I said you had a beautiful body, would you hold it against me?"

The others politely chuckled, but Elizabeth pouted. "That's been used a thousand times before."

Oliver paused to search for the words which came to him slowly through the vapors of alcohol. "So, my dear, has your body."

An uproar ensued, with Jack losing his balance and landing on the floor. Henry nearly followed. Elizabeth laughed despite herself, though she made sure to give Oliver a good whack on the chest for form's sake. When the laughter died down, no one could think of anything to fill the silence. They shifted their gazes between Alistair and nothing in particular until Gregory softly said, "Four cycles."

"Four cycles," Alistair echoed, nodding.

"Will you go back?" asked Stephanie.

"Absolutely not."

"Didn't like it?"

He opened his mouth but couldn't decide how much he wanted to let out. Finally, he settled for, "I learned a lot. But I'm done with it."

"At least you got to be off," said Oliver. "That's something few people can say."

"What will you do now?" asked Greg.

Alistair leaned back and with a self-satisfied smile said, "I'm not going to do much of anything for a while."

"Unemployment is outlawed," Stephanie reminded him. "Idle labor is to report for duty to the Employment Bureau."

"My dad's putting me on the payroll as an employee. I just don't have any duties for a couple weeks."

"Must be nice!" said Henry, and the others groaned.

Stephanie did not allow the merriment of the moment to stifle a disapproving look. Elizabeth tossed a crumpled napkin at him.

Oliver raised his empty mug and said, "To a long awaited homecoming."

"Hear, hear!" was the general reply.

Later, after the sun finally set, Oliver and Alistair were alone, leaning on the railing and looking out over the city lights and the occasional ship at sea. In the center of the city, emitting a soft and fuzzy white glow, was an enormous sphere: Arcarius' power center, many of whose sections were dark. Dark, too, would be all corresponding sectors of the city. After a time, these dark sections would relight, others would turn off and the pattern of night lights across Arcarius would alter in response to the planned rationing.

The wind was quite strong now, and it brought the smells of the ocean to their nostrils as they heard waves crashing against the cliff face many yards below. Alistair breathed deeply and sighed as he considered the view.

"So what's Kaldis like?"

He turned to his friend. Oliver was so large as to be comical. About twenty-four stone and not far from seven feet tall, he was nearly too large to function in normal society. His face was almost a caricature, with a large nose and wide overhanging forehead, and his thick hands and short fingers hinted at an awesome power.

"Sometimes I can't even remember. I just remember drills and explosions and shooting…I want to think of Kaldis without the warfare but…"

Oliver fixed a pained look on his friend.

"No, it wasn't all bad."

Oliver's expression didn't change.

"There were some good times. And I learned a lot. I'm going to make that count for something."

"Is it really anarchy?"

Alistair snorted. "Hardly. The image you have here is nothing like the real Kaldis."

"Did you keep a diary? Something we can see?"

"I kept a holographic diary. We're going to watch it tomorrow. Come on over and see it with us, if you like."

"If I can make it. Did you image The Ruins?"

"There are a lot of ruins on Kaldis nowadays."

"You know the ones I mean."

Space travel being prohibited, few Aldrans, and next to none who were not military, had ever been to Kaldis to see the famous Ruins. They were the three million year old remains of a small settlement predating the human race, the only proof ever found that non-human intelligence existed in the universe, or at least had existed once.

"That was my number one goal from the beginning. But my 3D imager is being processed right now. I don't think they'll allow me to keep all the images."

Oliver gave Alistair a conspiratorial look. "You smuggled some through though, right?"

Alistair smiled but said nothing. They shared a quiet moment looking out over the city. A burst of fire, small and distant and trailing a long tail, appeared in the sky, streaking from over the ocean towards land, towards Avon on the main continent to the south.

"Smugglers," was Oliver's comment.

"I wonder what they're bringing us," said Alistair as he watched the offworlders begin their illicit landing. He let the cool wind flow against him for a few minutes more as he watched the fireball. Finally, after it disappeared behind a mountain, he stood up and stretched. Oliver took the hint.

"Well, I'll be on my way." They clasped forearms in the standard rugby salute and farewell. "It's nice to have you back, little buddy."

"We'll have to play some rugby soon."

"If you remember how."

Later, when the slow moving roof finally closed, he locked the exit and made his way through the building to the section his family used as a home. His memory alone would have been enough to guide him through the pitch black hallways, but darkness was never a problem for him any more. He let himself in and found his parents sitting by the fire in the living room, enjoying the rare delicacy of a cup of hot chocolate. His father offered him a glass and he took it. Sitting down across from him, he sipped at the sweet, diluted liquid.

"Your buddies really tied one on tonight," his father said in a tone just shy of disapproving.

"They kept it under control."

His father nodded and then shared a glance with Mary. Setting his cup down, Nigel leaned forward, resting his elbows on his knees.

"Your grandfather died."

Alistair confronted the pronouncement stone-faced, the cup of chocolate paused halfway to his mouth.

"We wanted to wait until the party was over to tell you."

"When?" Alistair's expression was still unreadable.

"Two cycles ago," his mother said, her eyes tearing up. "We had no way to tell you."

There was a moment of quiet. Alistair took another sip while the fire crackled and made shadows dance about the room. Then, abruptly, he set the cup down on an end table and stood up. "I need to get some sleep," he announced and disappeared up the stairway.

2

The restaurant Alistair's father owned and operated was bustling with activity, like normal. For those few citizens with a license to open a private restaurant, it was a lucrative business. Not directly operated by a bureaucracy and treated with indulgence by the regulators, they had evolved into the centers of recreation and shopping. Under the pretext of food service, all manner of side activities had arisen to meet the demands of paying customers. The take-out counter for cooked meals had quickly become a grocery store. It was rationalized as uncooked take-out and was usually overlooked by the authorities. Whether or not it was actually illegal was difficult to tell, as the bureaucratic missives passing for law on Aldra were conflicting, but obeisance to the right authority made sure the operation went unhindered.

As Alistair passed by the take-out line, he could not see the end of it. A series of glum and bored faces; of people raggedly dressed in clothes patched many times over; of mothers, fathers and children too accustomed to the waits to be impatient, it wrapped around the street and out of view. On certain days Nigel was allowed to price his food. On other days the Bureau of Agriculture, or any other which decided to involve itself, put a maximum price on food for the benefit of the poorer citizens. Those days when the price was capped, the lines were long; on days when the restaurant owners chose the price, the lines were much shorter.

With a backpack slung over his shoulder, he followed the well-worn street that wound its way to the bottom of the large hill, called Tanard's Mountain, marking the southeastern most point of Arcarius. Near the restaurant lived many of Arcarius' wealthy citizens. Farther down, the same shabby buildings lined the street, shabbier than he remembered.

At the base of the hill, the street led to the Metro station. It was less busy now that the seasonal workers were heading for southern climes, and when he flashed his military ID at the entrance, he was quickly given free admittance, exchanging nods with the two armored Civil Guard who stood watch. After a descent down a flight of escalators, he picked his platform and waited for the car.

Two of the lights over the platform were burnt out. A few of the wall tiles were missing and one still lay shattered where it had fallen. Successive waves of grime and wet filth caked on some areas of the floor, ceiling and wall, and the entire tunnel was filled with a musty and unpleasant odor. While he scrunched his nose in disapproval, he looked about and saw only one other person waited with him. She was an elderly woman, bent over and burdened with a bundle of something.

There was some faded red graffiti sprayed across the wall. It was a short poem, part of which was scratched out. One creative soul had, by the application of some more paint, turned a couple of the letters into a picture of a man and a donkey engaged in an obscene act. A few other mocking comments in black were written around the piece. The result of time and purposeful defacement was that the original writing was hard to decipher, but he could read enough of it to know what it originally said: Solid, Loyal, Red and Blue/ Aldran workers through and through.

The familiar phrase, once ubiquitous, felt as worn as the writing on the wall. Alistair had not heard it since he went off, and for a moment he wondered if some new phrase had replaced it or if it still made the rounds.

A whoosh in the darkness of the tunnel announced the coming of the train. Soon after, its headlights lit the walls. Rounding the corner as it floated a few inches above the ground, it glided to a stop, whipping up a slight breeze to push the discarded newspapers and torn posters across the floor. It was nearly forty yards long and almost a quarter that in width, but it carried only a handful of people.

Taking a seat, he dumped his backpack on the spot next to him as the car began to move, plunging into the darkness of the tunnel ahead but presently emerging from below ground to soar up into the air thirty yards high and trace the outline of Tanard's Mountain. Its path was indicated only by the occasional floating marker, a football-size object glowing bright green. It was a marvelous system of public transportation; too marvelous, notwithstanding the squalor of its stations and carriages, for a city of Arcarius' size. Even in the summer it ran in the red—and during the winter it was a financial disaster—but profit, said the prosperous bureaucrats who ran the city, was not the measure of success.

The car made several stops, including one at the very top of Tanard's Mountain, a spaceport reserved for military and government personnel. It was from there Alistair left Aldra four cycles ago and to there he recently returned. As he traced random patterns with his finger in the film on the window, he wondered if he would ever get back to Kaldis and see Mar Profundo again, though even as he yearned for the city there was a feeling of repulsion mixed in.

The car finally made its way around to the harbor in the southwest. Upon exiting the Metro station, Alistair pulled his jacket tighter about his body and briefly regretted not bringing something heavier. The fall season on Arcarius was not young, and the weather was bringing more and more hints of winter with it. Though the long days could still be warm, despite the artificial cloud cover, the nights were lasting longer and longer at that northern latitude. Even the extra water vapor released into the atmosphere by the deep sea factories couldn't prevent the north from freezing.

The open bay allowed the ocean breeze to sweep through and chill the city, and his skin tightened in response. Resolutely, he stepped from the cover of the Metro entrance and into the wind of the port district. Like many seaports in the galaxy, it was home to society's seedier elements. One could not go far before coming across some miserable soul with a stumbling gait, a distant look in his bloodshot eyes and an unmistakable greenish tint to his skin: a specnine addict. In addition, there were specnine dealers, gamblers, smugglers, prostitutes, the thugs who enforced their own brand of law and the potato vendor, a recent addition to the panoply of lawbreakers. Such a man, as astray as a ballerina in a coal mine, must have felt ashamed to take a place next to the traditional scofflaws, but he was there nonetheless. When a disease borne by insects that fed on potatoes turned into an epidemic, the State outlawed potatoes. The following day, the potato vendor changed his address and set up shop next to the specnine dealer.

Alistair gave wide berth to a hallucinating specnine user. Before long he found himself in front of a ramshackle warehouse long since abandoned by its owner. A couple large, brutish looking men were lounging around, staying just outside the cone of light created by the lamp overlooking the door. As soon as he appeared, their gazes locked on him and never left, and when he strode up to the front door they quickly closed ranks and blocked the entrance, arms crossed over their chests.

They were as large as he, though not so professionally sculpted, and they glared at him as he approached. He met their gazes with a slight blush, but he mustered the will to address them.

"I've got a business proposition for whoever is interested."

"Try the State House."

"I don't think they'd be interested. I need someone with more vision. And more money."

"Why don't you beat it back to your own side of town, tin man?" came a suggestion, using the current pejorative for the Civil Guard.

"No tin here, fellas. I was a marine. Just got back from Kaldis. Now why don't you make a good decision and go tell your boss I've got some Kaldisian goods for him?"

The two suspiciously glared at him and then exchanged glances with each other. Finally, one nodded at his partner who turned and disappeared into the dilapidated warehouse. The remaining guard turned back to Alistair. "You know, now would be a good time to leave if you don't have what you say you have."

"Your advice is duly noted."

The guard pulled a cigarette from a small pack in his pocket and lit up. "Things nice on Kaldis?"

"It's got its good and bad spots, I suppose."

"Same as here." He nodded, as if confirming a notion he had had.

The man no longer seemed interested, so Alistair stood in silence, staring down at the ground. A slig made its slow way across the pavement. Far less bothersome than the mosquito, the slig was a genetically engineered insect that served as bird food in the man-made ecological system on Aldra. When Alistair for a brief period trained on Earth, he discovered how nasty the mosquito could be and took home a new appreciation for the slig, though that did not prevent him from squishing the one presently crawling past him.

The guard's cigarette was long since burnt out and tossed away when his partner reappeared. He fixed his most authoritative and intimidating look on Alistair as he pointed at him with a thick, stubby finger. "Step inside and follow Ritchie. Boss says I get to talk to you if you're wasting his time."

"Don't get your hopes up." He brushed past the tough and entered the building.

Ritchie was a slight and short man with a pockmarked face and two missing front teeth. He was probably in his forties, though it was difficult to tell since men in his station had a tendency to age quickly. He said nothing to Alistair but grabbed the backpack to inspect its contents. Having finished, he turned to lead him through the building.

The warehouse was one large open space. To create the illusion of rooms and hallways, dozens of crates had been stacked together. The only light came from flickering bulbs on the ceiling far above, though as many as half of these were out. The floor was cracked cement, and as plentiful as the cracks were the stains of all shapes and sizes, stains whose origin Alistair was happier not knowing.

After a few turns through the maze, he was led into a "room" with a card table and chairs in the middle. At the opposite end of the table sat a short, thick man with a bald head. His features were sharp, his forearms meaty and his bushy mustache nearly engulfed his lips. Behind him stood two men who might have been clones of the two guards at the entrance.

Ritchie gestured for Alistair to enter and then left him with the three men. Uncomfortable under their gazes, yet not wanting to seem timid, he forced himself to cross the space between them, though his legs felt stiff and awkward, and sat down opposite the bald man. This one glanced at one of his guards and broke into a throaty chuckle.

"OK, kid, you've got a pair. If ya' wanna keep 'em ya' better get me interested in yer proposition."

He had the pronounced accent of a New Bostonian.

"I'm sure you'll like it," said Alistair, struggling mightily to make his voice as solid as his physique. "It's straight from Kaldis."

"Keep talkin'."

"I've got some medicine that'll go for millions on the black market."

The boss leaned forward, resting his elbows on the table. "Now what made ya' think we'd be interested in something illegal like that?" At the same time he snapped and pointed at Alistair and his two bodyguards stepped towards him. They grabbed him, hoisted him to his feet and stripped him. He did not resist, just staring at the floor and blushing down to his chest.

A minute later, he was naked with his hands clasped in front of his groin, a book and some square cardboard pieces from his backpack lying on top of the pile of his clothes. The two guards looked him up and down, pausing to inspect the large and intricate tattoo on his left pectoral, and then nodded to their chief. They returned to his side while Alistair fumbled to put his clothes back on.

"Ya' can call me Mike, by the way," said the bald man with a twinkle in his eyes as he watched Alistair blush.

"Alistair," came the ragged reply. His breathing was suddenly uneven.

"How much of this medicine ya' got?"

"As much as you can make. I have the recipe," he mumbled, hasty to get his clothes back on but not wanting to let on he was discomfited.

"Which medicines?"

"Eight different ones. All chosen for ease and cheapness of production."

"What are they fer?"

"The instructions are all in there. Eridnite is one." Alistair finished with the last button and stood once more fully dressed.

Mike shook his head. "I don't know nothin' 'bout this." Turning to one of his guards, he said, "Go get Jimmy."

"He's asleep by now."

Mike gave him a look.

"He'll be here in ten minutes," the man amended.

As the bodyguard left, Mike turned back to Alistair. "How much will this stuff go fer?"

Alistair sat down again, unbidden. "Hard to say. Some of it's very new. Even the government doesn't have all of it yet."

"How'd you get it?"

"That's confidential."

"Where's the recipe?"

"In a safe place."

"How much ya' want fer it?"

"As much as I can get."

Realizing he wasn't going to get anything more, Mike sat back in his chair with a smirk and waited. "Ya' did well to come to me. You'll be glad ya' did."

About ten minutes later, another rough looking man entered the room. He circled slowly around Alistair, studying him, and finally sat down next to Mike. "You got Eridnite?"

"It's an Eridnite substitute. It's easier to make and about as effective. I've got seven others, three I guarantee you've never heard of."

"What do they do?"

"It's all in the instructions. Let's talk about a price."

"I don't know if I want to pay fer somethin' I don't know what it's gonna do," Mike said with a warning tone.

"I didn't come here to cheat you. I came here to get some money. The truth is, I don't remember all the details. Like I said, it's all in the instructions. I put this together a while ago."

"And how'd you get the instructions past Customs?" asked the man Alistair assumed was Jimmy.

"I'll tell you when I have my money."

Jimmy and Mike shared a look. The former looked somewhat doubtful but eventually shrugged.

"How many Credits ya' want?"

"I don't want Credits. I want gold."

This pronouncement quieted the room. When Mike recovered he leaned forward. "Listen, kid, ya' ain't gettin' gold. My Credits are as good as anyone else's."

"Which is not much." Under the table, Alistair was furiously rubbing his thumbs over his fingers in nervous agitation. "I want gold. Aldran Credits aren't worth the magnetic strips that store them. Besides," he allowed a faint, tremulous smile to creep onto his lips, "the amount of Credits you'd have to give me would get red flagged so even the tin men notice."

Jimmy and Mike gruffly laughed. After Alistair's pronouncement they seemed to relax.

"You know," said Jimmy, "we've done this before. You're not going to be red flagged. We've got ways."

"I don't doubt it. But I still want gold."

"I don't know how long ya' been off," said Mike, "but gold is illegal to possess. Has been fer a while."

"So is what I'm selling you."

"How much?"

"Thirty pounds."

Mike looked at Jimmy in disbelief, but Jimmy kept his gaze fixed on Alistair. Finally, Jimmy leaned into Mike and whispered in his ear. Mike motioned to a bodyguard and when the man bent down, Mike whispered in his ear. The bodyguard nodded and again left the room. Finally, Mike turned to Alistair.

"If I find out you've screwed us—"

"You don't need to make threats."

"How's this going to work?" asked Jimmy.

A bit of tension eased out of Alistair's body, and he tossed the cardboard pieces and book on the table. "The pieces are numbered. Place each piece on the page of the same number and read the words not covered up."

"What did ya' tell customs 'bout these?" asked Mike.

"They were part of a piece of sculpture I made on Kaldis. They thought it was just a piece of amateur art."

This elicited appreciative nods from the other three.

"There's only ten of these pieces," Jimmy commented.

"Those are just the decoding instructions. The real instructions are elsewhere."

"Where?" asked Mike.

Alistair rolled up his left hand sleeve and pointed to a large and oddly shaped mole on his bicep. "The instructions are in the genetic code of this growth on my arm. The decoding instructions are in the book. Get the genetic map to this lump here and you've got yourself a gold mine. Just read the inactive strains of the genome."

"Son of a bitch," breathed Mike. "Is that dangerous?"

"Yep. That's why if you don't take it tonight I take pills to kill it."

"We'll take it tonight," Jimmy said, needing only to lick his lips to complete the perfect image of cupidity.

Hours later, when the sun had long since set and the air grown chill, Alistair labored up the road on Tanard's Mountain, a heavy backpack hanging from his broad shoulders. Upon rounding the last bend in the cracked pavement, he cursed. There was a commotion in front of Nigel's and several Civil Guard were there, complete with a tank—the tin cans referred to in the pejorative—threatening all who would dare cross it. Lights of red and blue and yellow spun and flashed all over the tank and small transport autos. *More than enough lights to announce their presence*, thought Alistair, *but only just enough to satisfy their egos.*

He turned into an alleyway and scanned the area. Finding in the street a grill leading to the sewer, he lifted it and clambered down the ladder, forced to let the backpack dangle from his teeth so he could fit in the cramped space. Halfway down, as his fingers protested at having to grip the frigid metal rungs, he found a small ledge and deposited the backpack there, trying not to gag from the smell. This accomplished, he quickly scurried back up and breathed deeply of the comparatively fresher air.

As he approached the restaurant, a Civil Guardsman, wearing armor more suited to a battlefield, broke away from the rest and approached, his gun not yet raised but in plain view.

"If you're not family you need to leave," the man barked, a microphone in his helmet amplifying his voice enough to awaken any neighbors who weren't already peering out their windows. He had a different accent, which was not uncommon. Most Civil Guard were trans-ferred from their home towns when they joined the force.

"I live here," Alistair mumbled, walking by without sparing him a glance.

His father was next to the tank, speaking to an unarmored officer jotting down notes. Nigel's face was carefully composed, though any who knew him well could see the worry in it. A few of the other Civil Guard stood in a perimeter, some looking bored, some menacing. His brother Gerald was there, and they exchanged grim glances. He sidled up next to his brother near a scorched section of wall with a broken window.

"Molotov cocktail," his brother said and shivered once. His thin, night clothing was little protection from the cold. "The police will probably want to speak to you too."

"Anyone hurt?"

"No. Mom and Katherine are inside. It happened about half an hour ago."

"What the hell is this about?" Alistair was beginning to shake with anger, and he ground his teeth together when he spoke.

"We don't know what it's about."

Alistair spit in the air and his brother gave him an uncertain look. Laying a hand on his forearm, Gerald said, "Just let the Civil Guard do their work, Al."

"If they want to ask me questions they can come find me." Spitting again, he left his brother and went inside.

ॐ ॐ

The highest point of Nigel's restaurant complex was a white dome. It was the observa-tory, a distinguishing aspect of the building. It did not bring in much business, and the little attention it did get was largely from school children whom Nigel allowed to use it for free. Profit had never been his goal; it was a gift for his children, particularly Katherine and Alistair who spent many nights gazing deep into space.

When Alistair entered the observatory, Katherine was leaning back in the high-back chair with her eye pressed to the eyepiece. The room was dark, lit only slightly by some out-side lights streaming in through the opening in the dome. On the computer desk next to him was a portrait of his brother-in-law, Eddy Davidson. His kind, round face tended towards corpulence, and the ever present goofy smile that distinguished him was in full bloom in the photograph. His finger tracing the picture frame, Alistair smiled sadly and wondered where Eddy was, or if he was still alive. Before his and Katherine's first anniversary, he disappeared without a trace.

Pulling out a chair from one of the computer terminals and startling Katherine, he set it next to her. She pressed a button and her own seat slid back into a vertical position while Alistair swung a leg over and sat backwards on his chair. Facing her, he laid his forearms across the back of the seat and let his chin rest there.

"Is mom OK?" Alistair asked.

"No one was hurt."

"I didn't mean physically."

"She's fine. Actually, I think Dad's having a harder time of it. The Guard won't be able to do anything."

"I will."

"Alistair…" There was a stern warning in that solitary word. "Stay out of trouble."

His eyes watered as he glared off into space. Katherine waited patiently, knowing he was working on something. Finally, in a harsh whisper, he managed, "Sometimes I get so mad I can't—" He cut the sentence off and stood up to leave.

Katherine grabbed his forearm.

"Alistair…" she couldn't quite figure out what she wanted to say. "You're…are you OK? You're different since you came back."

"Why should I be the same?" he asked with a challenging tone.

Katherine withdrew her hand from him, like one does from a feral dog. Uncomfortable under her pitying but uncomprehending look, he turned and made for the exit.

"Get a good night's sleep," she said gently. "An inspector's coming tomorrow."

His only response was a snort of derision.

3

Alistair woke long before the others. Now accustomed to a Kaldisian day, he could not remain asleep through the long Aldran night, but the previous one he was unable to get even his usual eight hours. He had a dream he had not had for a couple cycles. One of his first combat operations on Kaldis, before he had been chosen to wear a War Suit, had been to make a sweep through a Mandarin village considered stable. When his platoon entered, fighting erupted. He was escorting a family out of a contested area when his squad met resistance. He left the family in a small alcove and joined his squad in putting it down. It was a matter of a handful of minutes, but when he returned to the alcove where he left the family, all but the father were gone, and he lay on the pavement, blood pooling around him.

That pale, blood-speckled face appeared and reappeared in his nightmares, but by the end of his tour he had nearly forgotten it. It was strange to him that it should come back now, and so vividly. Unsettled, he sat in his bed, staring into the semi-darkness, his thoughts on a dead man whose corpse was buried and rotting on a planet 250 light years away. He concluded he would get no more sleep for a while.

Outside, the wind threw a few raindrops against the walls of the house, and a cold draft seeped inside. He had already sampled the weather a few hours earlier when he ventured into the drizzle to reclaim his backpack, thanking whatever god was listening when he found it undisturbed. After stuffing the bag under his bed, he went to the kitchen, made himself a cup and pondered where to more permanently store the precious metal.

The banks were publicly owned and the government inspected everything put in its vaults. There were certain black market alternatives, but he had no contacts there and did not trust it besides. The best thing to do, he decided, was to convert the gold, purchasing goods from the underground economy. Energy had evolved as a medium of exchange as the government fumbled with the power grid. A hand held device called an enbatt could hold many millions of BTU's of energy and could be plugged into just about anything to transfer or receive energy.

He was sitting at the table, leisurely drinking some sweet coffee and paging through a book when his mother came downstairs, wrapped in her night robe.

"You're getting an early start today," she commented as she gave him a peck on this head.

"I'm still on Kaldisian time."

"Oh, that's right. I keep forgetting what a long day we have."

Mary Ashley set about putting a breakfast together while Alistair continued reading.

"I thought you might like to see Mrs. Durbin's daughter Carrie," she ventured with a tone too light not to be deliberate.

"What do you mean 'see her'? You can show me an image of her if you like. Or do you want me to marry her?"

His mother laughed out loud. "She's not a little girl anymore."

He did not respond.

"Did you find someone on Kaldis?" his mother asked.

He eventually he managed a curt, "Yes."

Recognizing the tenor of his voice, Mrs. Ashley backed away from the subject.

"Well, let me know if you'd like to see her again."

Katherine, Nigel, Mary and Alistair breakfasted together a short time later. Afterwards, as Nigel's employees arrived for the first shift, he took Alistair aside and in a tone both stern and imploring asked him to be on his best behavior for the inspector. He agreed with a sigh.

Gerald arrived right after breakfast, dressed in his finest, most impeccably ironed red and blue Civil Service uniform. Nigel had asked him to come for the inspection, for Gerald held a moderately high post in the bureaucracy. Even had he not asked, Gerald would not have missed it.

The inspector, a short, fat man with a bald dome of a head, arrived and Nigel, with an obsequious bow, invited him in. He and his wife escorted the man directly to a private luxury booth whereupon Nigel's prettiest waitress took his order. Nigel and his family sat with him, speaking in a friendly manner when the inspector was silent, and listening intently when he chose to talk. They laughed at his jokes, they oohed and aahed at the stories he deigned to tell them, they complimented his taste, they thanked him for his time, they wondered at his service to the State and all with toothy smiles. Accustomed to the ritual but unable to conceal his distaste, Alistair maintained a safe distance.

When the inspector had gorged himself on the finest meal the city could produce, he was offered a box of cigars and a brandy which he accepted almost without noting them, as if they had been fetched from his own collection. He lit up a cigar and savored his liquor, permitting himself a refill after the first glass. Nigel offered him free tickets to a concert to be played at the restaurant in the coming week, and these went into his billfold. Mary came by with a freshly baked apple pie. This was acknowledged with a nod. After two hours, the man warmed up to them, and as he smoked his second cigar he regaled them with gossip straight from the highest levels of government. He was brother-in-law to the current vice mayor, and it came out he had studied in Rendral, receiving a degree in philosophy.

And then it was over. Having deduced from his entrance, short trip to the luxury booth and generous breakfast that the restaurant was fit for public enjoyment, he rose with an effort, patted his stomach, and permitted Nigel to shake his hand. Outside, a stinging drizzle still pelted the ground. Mary offered him an umbrella and Gerald held it as they walked. Having done his best to prepare his guest, Nigel deemed it the best moment to broach a delicate topic.

"A Mr. Kevin Wellington is keen to purchase my property," he offered after a small preamble.

"Yes?"

"Indeed. I considered his offer, but I must say I think I prefer to keep the old place."

Alistair directed a curious look at his brother but Gerald avoided his gaze.

"Well, we'll see how it turns out," the inspector carefully said.

Shaking the man's hand again, Nigel said, "If you need anything, be sure to let me know."

Gerald walked with him to his auto, holding the umbrella over his head until he was inside and safe from the rain. He then hurried back to his family and they huddled under it, waving goodbye as the inspector pulled onto the street and headed downhill, disappearing around a bend.

"Did we pass?" asked Alistair as they turned to go inside.

"I think we're alright with the licensing board," his father responded, sounding tired, as if the greater part of his energy had been used up entertaining.

"And the citizens of Arcarius can rest assured this restaurant is safe after a thorough inspection."

No one replied. They shuffled inside, out of the drizzle, one onerous task complete with others still ahead.

4

In the living room, Nigel and Mary Ashley sat next to each other on the couch Alistair's grandfather had built. His older siblings were on another nearby. Alistair knelt in the center of the room and placed an imager there. It was a hand-size device in the shape of a hockey puck, and along its sides were several buttons which he played with.

"OK, turn out the lights."

Gerald hopped up and flipped the switch. The room went dark, and Alistair pushed a final button and retreated to a seat in the corner. A tiny red light blinked on for a second, standing out in the near total darkness, and then the room was lit as if by the sun, with the imager projecting three dimensional pictures on the far side.

There were gasps from the others as a meadow at the foot of some tall hills was projected onto the room. A waterfall could be seen in the distance and in the foreground were Alistair and one of his comrades. The image was still but seemed real, like reality made somehow immobile, a moment in time now frozen for viewing. The sunlight shone and bounced off the water, captured in mid glint. Alistair's friend seemed to be in the room with them, though he was farther back in the picture than the walls would allow.

"That's Ted. Spunk, we called him."

"Where is this?" his mother asked.

"Uh…" Alistair had to look at the screen on his remote control. "Looks like that's just outside the capital. This was early on. I think we were on leave."

"I didn't know Kaldis had a capital. Aren't they anarchists?" his father asked.

"Not even close."

"Where's Ted from?" Gerald asked.

"New Boston. His uncle works up here in the summer, actually."

"Is Ted still on duty?" Nigel asked.

Alistair shook his head, forgetting they couldn't see him. "Ted was shot two cycles in. They shipped him out on a med ship. I never heard what happened to him after that."

This reminder of Alistair's work on Kaldis was a contrast with the idyllic scene before them, and it silenced them. Alistair rotated the image so they could see all three hundred sixty degrees of it and then went on to the next one.

"This was the main square of some little village. I can't remember its name."

"It's pretty," Katherine remarked.

"We came back a year later and wound up leveling the place."

"Oh my god," breathed his mother.

Alistair rotated the image while the others blushed at his blunt comment. Then he went on to the third image.

"That's me and the guys dressed in our war suits."

There were four figures in the picture, all suited up in a sleek looking camouflage out-fit, complete with a helmet. They assumed the largest of the four was Alistair.

"We just ordered one of those for the Civil Guard," said Gerald. "How do they work?"

"Very well. There's an inertial pack on the back—you can't see it here—and it changes colors to blend in if you want. It acts as armor, temperature controlled, night vision, heat vision, muscle support…it's got just about everything you could want."

"Aren't they invisible to radar?" asked Gerald.

"That's why sonar is starting to come back."

"How good's the armor?" asked Katherine.

"I'd've been dead about twelve times over without it."

"Alistair," his mother admonished.

"How many war suits does the army have?" asked Nigel.

"Just over a hundred. But with a war suit, any one soldier is worth a hundred without."

"How'd you wind up with one?"

"I got picked." While they sat impressed, he clicked to the next picture. "Oh, this is from a mountain overlooking Mar Profundo. It's the second largest city on Kaldis."

The image presented to them was of a large metropolis. It was night and the lit city below, each of the thousands and thousands of its lights caught in mid sparkle, spanned the entire stretch of visible land, from left horizon to right horizon, and from the base of the hills on which the picture was shot to the edge of the sea and even beyond into the very waves. The downtown section had buildings a mile high, above the level where the image was taken. A few clouds floated near the building tops, and long, thin tubes in the sky connected many of the large and exotically designed skyscrapers. There were even bubble-covered sections of the city extending into the sea, and the tops of the bubbles just broke the surface while the lights from the buildings below filtered fuzzily through the dark waters. Vehicles in mid-flight were captured in transit between buildings, and hovering advertisements—something quite unfa-miliar to Aldrans—lined the commonly used routes between and above the great buildings. Katherine gasped at the beauty of it.

"I'm surprised they allowed you to return with all this," Gerald said.

"I didn't declare it," Alistair casually replied.

"You didn't declare…" Gerald sighed. "Alistair…"

"They speak a lot of Spanish on Kaldis, don't they?" Katherine asked before a familiar argument could begin.

"Yeah, all sorts of languages."

"Did you learn another language?" his mother asked, as if the thought were a shocking one.

"I learned Spanish pretty well. I picked up some Mandarin and a couple others too. Mar Profundo means Deep Sea in Spanish."

"Did you spend much time there?" asked his mother.

"Almost every leave I had." Alistair stared off into the past as he remembered the city. "Mar Profundo is my favorite city on Kaldis. Or anywhere."

"Why did they build under the sea?" asked Gerald.

"Brings a lot of tourists. Many people prefer living there."

After four cycles, Alistair had taken many images of Kaldis, too many to view in one sitting. He showed them a few more of his favorites and they murmured appreciatively, riddling him with questions, some newly conceived and others stored away for a few cycles. When the show was over, he turned off the imager and put it away. Grabbing a small cloth sack, he rooted around inside while Gerald turned on the light. Producing something that looked a bit like a flashlight, only with a slight bend near one end, Alistair turned to his father.

"I picked this up for you in Mar Profundo. I got you a good supply of batteries, because I don't know if we have anything on Aldra that will work with it."

His father took the proffered item and held it in his hands, smiling in anticipation.

"OK, you got me. What does it do?"

"It's called a *pintador*. A painter. From now on, if you don't want to spend days painting something, you can use this to change the color."

The painter was passed around the room.

"It can also smooth out the paint you already have on, and it applies a gloss to make it look new."

"How's it work?" Nigel asked, a slight smile of awe and surprise still on his face.

"I've got the instructions. They're coming out with a new model that's supposed to be a big improvement but I left Kaldis before it came out."

Gerald was frowning as he gingerly held it in his hands, as if it might contaminate him. "Alistair, I'm pretty sure this is contraband."

"Yeah, I didn't declare it either."

Gerald let out an even louder sigh. "You know I work for the Transportation Bureau."

"This isn't about you."

"No, it's about you and the fact that I am supposed to turn you in for this!" He turned to Nigel. "I think we both know this is a bad idea right now of all times."

The comment provoked a curious look from Alistair. His father wanly smiled.

"Oh…it's a nice gift. I think if we keep it hidden and don't use it out in the open…"

"They're cracking down on this sort of thing now."

"They're always saying that."

Gerald sighed yet again. "This puts me in a bad situation."

"Dad's got a bad hip," said Alistair. "If I want to give him a gift to help him paint the house, I don't see how the government has any business getting involved."

"We don't make laws lightly, Al."

"You work in the Transportation Bureau. You don't make any laws."

"There are good reasons for the things we do in government. How many painters and brush makers and paint makers were unemployed with this?

"You're still on about that?"

"I'll get some drinks for everyone," Mary declared and left for the kitchen.

"Why don't we see what else you have for us," suggested Katherine.

Both of Nigel's sons blushed from repressed feelings as they buried the disagreement. Gerald furiously tapped his fingers on his knee and Alistair turned his attention to his sack as he took out the other gifts he had purchased.

❧◈

The car shifted forward and the final leg of the trip began. Alistair and Oliver had been about the town, visiting a few bars, some familiar sights, seeing things that changed while Alistair was off, and now both were headed back to Nigel's. A young man with a sparse beard, patched clothing and broken spectacles boarded the car at one station and stood at the front facing the other passengers. He introduced himself to his sparse audience and spoke at length about the coming election and why they should vote for Aloysius Warwick.

Prompted by the subject of the man's speech, Alistair asked, "Who are you voting for?"

Oliver snorted. "I'm not. You know they took away your option to write in a candidate?"

Alistair shook his head. "I wasn't going to vote anyway."

"Well, I wanted to pencil myself in. Not that they'd actually count it."

"If they bring back the write in I'll give you a second."

At the front of the car, the campaigner was growing more excited as he gesticulated to an audience that did not appreciate the artistry of the presentation. Oliver and Alistair gave as much attention to the noise of his voice as they did to the whoosh of the air the train stirred up in the tunnels, or the rattle of one of its many loose windows.

"So what is Kaldis actually like? It's not really anarchy, then?"

"It used to be close. Some cities are trying to pass a Constitution. Others are threatening to nullify it, others are going to secede, others are threatening war on those who don't ratify."

"And what the hell are we doing there?"

"Keeping the peace," Alistair said, his voice dripping sarcasm. "Though I must say we entered plenty of peaceful areas and left them smoking rubble."

"Smoking rubble is peaceful."

"We're actually there to reinforce the Neo-Constitutionalists as they call themselves. Every star system in the galaxy has troops there. It's like a party you can't afford not to go to. Everyone wants a new Constitution for Kaldis, and everyone wants to oversee its creation. For the good of all Kaldisians."

"Of course."

The young man at the front finished his speech with a crescendo and a flourish and a few people politely applauded.

"So really, why the hell do we care what Constitution the Kaldisians get?"

"The Solar Empire is there because they are tired of losing emigrants, especially rich businessmen, to Kaldis. We're there because we want to curry favor with the Solar Empire."

"So is it civil war?"

"I don't know what you call it. There are so many alliances. Most of them last less than a week. I met militiamen who didn't even know which side they were fighting on; they just follow their leader. One minute the city of Whitehill is Neo-Constitutionalist, the next minute the whole northern quarter is in rebellion. The next day they are Paleo-Constitutionalists, and then suddenly there's rioting in the streets, only no one can tell what for. Half the planet is peaceful enough; the other half is a mad house. But it's not always the same half from one month to the next."

They reached their stop, and upon exiting they found themselves walking near the young preacher. He approached them with an eager and expectant smile on his face and reached his hand out to Alistair, on the verge of some pleasantry.

"Get stuffed," said Alistair without so much as looking at him.

Oliver stared in amusement; the young proselytizer stared in shock.

"You heard him," said Oliver, perfectly willing to take up the game. "Get to it."

One does not lightly cross men like Alistair and Oliver. The campaigner abruptly turned around and sought friendlier faces.

They reached Alistair's home after a brisk walk, and upon entering Oliver collapsed into a chair in the kitchen. Alistair tossed his coat on the rack, but then caught the sound of voices around the corner. Following the sound, he walked in on his father and mother in the study. There were three men with them, two of whom stood at the sides of another who was seated across from Alistair's parents. The strangers were impeccably dressed in dark colors, their suits the sort only the right connections could procure. Their faces were expressionless. When Alistair appeared in the doorway, the one seated in the middle was calmly adjusting the red handkerchief in the chest pocket of his suit. Whether from the look of suppressed anxiety Nigel and Mary flashed their son, or the body language of the other men in the room, Alistair tensed.

"I just got back with Oliver. Is everything alright?" He folded his arms across his chest and leaned against the doorframe, his dusty workman's clothes a contrast to the elegance of the visitors.

"We were just talking a little business," said Nigel with a lightness in his voice Alistair knew was feigned. He rose wincing, grabbing his hip, and introduced his child. "This is my son Alistair. Alistair, this is Mr. Wellington." He indicated the seated man who slightly nodded at Alistair, still ruffling the scarlet handkerchief. Alistair returned his gaze but not his nod.

"Should I show them to the door?" he asked a bit more loudly than was necessary, and his mother flinched.

"We were just on our way out actually," said Mr. Wellington as he rose. One of his companions pulled his seat back and replaced it when Mr. Wellington stepped away. "We'll leave the rest for another day," he informed Nigel and then brushed by Alistair's cool gaze and also slid by Oliver, whose large frame now took up most of the space behind Alistair. Alistair refused to cede the doorway to Mr. Wellington's large companions, and his companions refused to turn so as to better fit through. This resulted in their shoulders smacking together, a collision all parties pretended did not occur.

When they were gone and the door closed behind them, Alistair turned an inquisitive gaze on his father.

Nigel lifted his hands as if to settle his son down. "Don't get riled up about this, Alistair."

"Is there something to get riled up about?"

"They just want to buy the restaurant."

"And you said no, I take it?"

"Alistair," said his mother as she rose, "let's just forget about this. Oliver, are you staying for lunch?"

"Did you say no?"

"I don't want you involved," said Nigel and he turned and hobbled out of the room.

Following him, Alistair said, "I just want to know what the answer was so I can tell him personally if I ever see him here again."

Nigel turned to face his son. "Damn it, Alistair," he said, but softly, wearily. "I'm not a helpless old woman. And what the heck is the matter with you? You can't pick a fight with men like that."

"I can pick a fight with whoever the hell I want."

"Alistair, what's the matter?"

"You tell me."

"No, with you? What's the matter?"

Looking away, Alistair swallowed an angry lump in his throat. "I'm fed up."

"Well, relax a bit. I can handle negotiations with Mr. Wellington. As much as I appreciate your concern."

With that he gave Alistair a conciliatory smile and left, limping. Alistair noticed his sister at the other end of the hall, looking at him with an ineffable expression. He went to her, sensing she had something to say. Oliver hung back, unsure what to do or where to place himself.

"They want this specific plot of ground for some treatment plant or something," she said softly. "It's right by the spaceport. With rail traffic as backed up as it is…"

Rubbing his chin thoughtfully, he pondered the new information. "Now's the part where you tell me what the government has to do with this."

"Mr. Wellington is threatening to have the property seized and given to him if Dad doesn't sell."

"Does that explain the political poster in the dining room? Dad is counting on Aloysius to win and wants to sidle up to him now?"

Katherine searched for a response. Finally, she said, "That's how the game is played."

"Shitty game." Alistair knew his sister was becoming uncomfortable. In the silence that followed he carefully chose his next sentence. "Katherine, if a government has the power to take your home from you, what can't it do to you?"

"I'm not getting into it right now."

"A government that can take your home could steal your husband too, for instance."

Katherine blanched, set her jaw, and stood up with her back straight and glowered at him. "I have no idea what happened to Eddy, and neither do you."

"He starts a student group criticizing Voluntarist policies. He disappears a few months later. And you think I have no idea what happened to him?"

Katherine's eyes shone with tears she refused to let fall. Rather than fashion a cutting retort, she turned her back and walked away, leaving him to wonder if there was anyone else he could alienate in the next few minutes.

5

The building before Alistair was entirely unremarkable, identical to scores of others scattered throughout the city. It was not just plain: it was dirty and in disrepair. There were State edifices, pristine among the general decrepitude into which Arcarius had fallen, that commanded all the attention and resources, but the present structure was not one of them. To the same degree the Mayor's Palace was maintained, this one was neglected.

He entered through the sagging wooden doorframe and found himself in a waiting room. In the atmosphere of bored disinterest, dozens of patients lounged, few of them with any discernible ailments. Passing through the odor of unwashed bodies and clothes, as well as a whiff of alcohol on someone's breath, he came to stand across a desk from a seated nurse. She was speaking on an old, patched audiphone, her voice bored to match her expression and everyone else's. She did not look up when he towered above her, and went so long without acknowledging him that he was weighing his options of getting her attention when she finally set the device down and directed a quizzical, though still bored, look at him.

"I'm here for Gregory Lushington."

The woman wrote down a number on a ticket and wordlessly handed it to him.

"Actually," he began before she could get lost in another conversation, "I'm not here as a patient. I have something for him."

Sighing as if put upon, the woman languidly lifted open the front cover of a folder and searched through some listings. "Room 234, second floor."

He didn't bother with a thank you or good bye, and she was just as content not to extend the conversation. The elevator was out of order and so he went instead to the stairwell. Braving the moldy smell, he reached the second floor and wandered around before finding a crooked sign directing him to room 234. Its door was open and Gregory, dressed in a white lab coat, was inside with another man with sullied work clothes who sat on the examination bed, leaving dark smudges on the sanitary paper. A nurse stood by Gregory's side looking uncomfortable.

"It seems to me your leg is fine," Greg was saying as Alistair approached.

"Still hurts," the man tersely replied.

"There's nothing physically wrong with your leg. It looks like it has healed quite nicely."

"Still hurts," insisted the patient.

Greg nodded thoughtfully. "I can prescribe you some mild pain killers."

"Can't go back to work with it like this."

"Well, Mr. Adams, your leg is fine. If there is some residual pain I suggest you take something for it, but I can't write you an excuse slip. You've been away from work for seven months now."

"The other doctor gave me a slip."

"You didn't get the other doctor; you got me."

The man stared daggers at Gregory. "I can just get back in line and wait for another."

"Then that's what you'll have to do."

The man grabbed his coat with a fierce movement and stormed out of the room and past Alistair who could not resist saying, "If you limp at least a little it would be more convincing."

The man whirled on him but, upon seeing his size, thought better of it. Greg came out into the hallway and watched him leave.

"He'll have his slip in another eight hours," he sighed.

"You did the right thing."

"Did I?" He paused, then, "What brings you here?"

"Do you have a minute?"

Alistair followed Greg back into the room as the nurse was leaving. "I thought you were a junior surgeon," he commented as Gregory shut the door behind them.

Greg's room was oft used but scrupulously clean. The concrete walls were cracked in spots, and the floor creaked. There were a few stains on the ceiling, and one of the lights had come loose from its moorings and dangled in the air, but the counter tops were clean and dusted. The equipment was neatly and logically put away. The floor was swept.

"I do a shift each week in general practice to relieve some pressure on the waiting lines."

Alistair hopped up on the examination bed. "I need to ask a favor of you."

"Go ahead."

"My dad needs surgery on his hip."

"His operation is in three weeks, isn't it?"

"It just got pushed back half a cycle."

There was silence in the room until Greg exhaled through pursed lips. "Alistair, you're not honestly asking for a private operation?" Alistair said nothing and Greg shook his head. "Out of the question. It's illegal."

"Why should it be illegal?"

"It doesn't matter why, it just is! You can't question these things."

"The hell I can't. My dad's had a bad hip for a cycle. Now he's got another half cycle to wait. At least."

"We're really backed up right now."

"It's the third time his surgery has been postponed."

"Al, I know it's tough. But a bad hip is not life threatening. There are other people who need attention first."

"Greg, do you know how long my father would have to wait for surgery on Kaldis? About two days."

"You're not on Kaldis."

"I'm willing to pay you for the surgery. What the hell does the government have to do with it? If you agree to perform the surgery, and my dad agrees to be operated on, what the bloody hell does the government have to do with it?"

"Alistair," said Greg gently, with infinite patience, "I'm not going to explain our entire government to you. There are reasons these laws are passed."

"That's what everyone always says," growled Alistair. "'I'm not going to get into it with you, Alistair, but there are reasons for these things.' Just once I'd like someone to get into it with me." He fixed a penetrating gaze on his friend. "My dad is in pain and you can help him."

"We have a planet-wide health care system because we as Aldrans decided to take care of all our members, not just the rich. If we let people handle their health care privately, the rich would outbid the poor for all the resources and the system wouldn't work. There, I just got into it with you."

"My dad is living with pain, and is going to have to for another six months. Is your system really working?" With that, he took a small gold bar out of his pocket and laid it on the table.

"I don't want your money," Greg said coldly, in almost a whisper as his body stiffened.

"I know you don't. But the Sisters of Charity Orphanage could certainly use the help."

The look Greg flashed him was coated with anger and trepidation. "They can't spend a gold bar."

"They wouldn't have to. I can convert this to just about anything."

Greg pursed his lips until the blood drained out of them, and his face contorted. He gripped the edge of the examination table until he spat out, "You want to know why I hate your goddamn Free Market? This is it! Damn it, Alistair! If we left everything to individuals this sort of thing would happen constantly."

"What? People offering money for things they want?"

"I'm talking about exploitation! You don't give a damn about the orphanage. You just want to use what I have for your own benefit."

Gregory immediately regretted his harsh words, but he offered no apology. Instead, he released the table and shoved his hands in his pockets, half turning from his visitor. Alistair was silent a moment while he let him regain some composure. When he spoke, his voice was smooth but unyielding.

"It's not true I don't give a damn about the orphanage. But it doesn't matter whether I do or not. You have something I want, and I'm offering you something you want. Whether I hate you or love you, whether I care about parentless children or not, there is a trade here that will be mutually beneficial. You give me your time and talents; I give you something for the orphans."

"I also have to use government property."

"Which was purchased with our taxes. The choice is yours. Turn it down and you're no worse off than if I hadn't made the offer."

He wasn't sure whether Gregory heard him. By degrees he had turned from him until he was now looking in the corner and all Alistair could see was his back. When Gregory spoke his voice was cold and unreadable. "I'll find a good time to get an empty room. I'll recruit a couple assistants. They'll want to be paid."

"I've got more gold where this came from. Gregory…"

Dr. Lushington turned and met Alistair's gaze.

"You're doing the right thing. Thank you."

"You owe me."

"No I don't. That's what the gold is for."

ॐॐ

Alistair left one discussion with Gregory and returned home to another with Gerald. The sun had set, and his family was gathered together in the kitchen, having just finished tea, the fifth meal of the day. His sleeping schedule left him weary again, and with a haggard face and drooping eyelids he dropped his coat on the rack and plopped down on a seat in the kitchen.

"You missed tea," Gerald said by way of a gentle scolding.

"I got it somewhere else. How's your hip, dad?"

"It's OK. It was a little sore this morning."

"I'll bet."

His mother cringed, hearing in his voice that something was coming.

"How much specnine did they manage to seize today?"

Gerald ran his tongue over his teeth, trying to decide whether to engage or ignore. "I work for the Bureau of Transportation. How would I know?"

"I sure hope it was worth it. Lots of other things to be done, but I'm sure it was worth spending time and resources on specnine."

"I'm sure it was."

"At least we got a thorough inspection this morning. The citizens are safe from harm now."

"Alistair, how intent are you on picking a fight? Is there a chance you'll go away if I ignore you, or should I start shouting to get this over with?"

"Don't patronize me."

"Just call me a son of a bitch and get it over with."

"Actually I was always fond of your mother. How about I just call you an asshole?"

The kitchen went silent. Mary rose from her chair and left and Nigel sighed in long suffering frustration.

"Alistair," said Katherine gently, "why don't we save it—"

"I'm not saving anything. It's about time we had it out."

"Let it go, Alistair. You've lived a privileged life. Maybe if you saw a bit more—"

Alistair leaned in so his face was close to his brother's. "Privileged life? Who is this coming from?"

Katherine stepped between them, and Nigel laid a hand on his livid son's shoulder. He was about to speak some soothing words when they were interrupted by an explosion. The house's walls shuddered and a flash of light lit the outside, visible from the kitchen window. After the flash, a softer orange glow flickered and grew.

Alistair bounded out the kitchen and then the front door. He was gone before anyone else reacted.

"Alistair!" his father shouted, but his son would not have stopped even if he had heard.

"Call the Guard!" shouted Gerald and followed his brother. Nigel grabbed his cane and hobbled outside too.

Meanwhile, Alistair, his vision sharp even away from the glow of the fire, caught a glimpse of dark fleeing figures just before they disappeared between two houses across the street. He was after them as fast as his powerful legs would go. When he reached the alley between the houses, he caught another glimpse of a figure disappearing around another corner and he continued his pursuit. In this way he trailed them through the neighborhood—over fences, under bridges, across open lots—and each time he lost sight of them he would round a corner and find himself closer. He was big, fast, athletic and in a rage. They did not elude him for long.

Casting furtive glances over their shoulders, the men, of whom he counted at least four, were running in panic as the large predator closed the distance. One hurled something at him but the marine dodged it without losing a beat. His fingers tingled with anticipation as he closed in on the last in line, and when he was close enough his right hand shot out and hit the man squarely in the middle of the back. He was launched forward and lost his balance. Limbs swinging wildly, he took a couple off-balance steps and then fell forward, landing face first on the pavement.

The other men left their fallen comrade and Alistair let them go, instead launching himself into the air and landing with all his weight on the fallen form. The man gave a pitiable yelp and Alistair punched the back of his head, slamming his face into the pavement. He then grabbed his hair, pulling his head back at an uncomfortable angle.

Putting his lips to the man's ear, Alistair, his spittle spraying the side of the man's head, hissed, "We don't feel like selling."

He flipped him over and slammed his fists into his prey's stomach about a dozen times while the vandal futilely attempted to dislodge his much larger and stronger opponent. Upon finishing the first barrage, Alistair stood up and the man, gasping for air and nearly sobbing, started unsteadily to crawl away. Alistair grabbed him, lifted him up and punched his face. He then lifted the man over his head and threw him into a nearby brick wall. He landed with a thud and lay still.

Alistair's anger abated and, chest heaving from his exertion, he stared down at the man. Glancing around to see if the collaborators were returning, he saw black silhouettes in the windows of the neighborhood. A few people opened their front doors and stood on their porches. He realized how loud his cries of anger had been, and he blushed under the eyes of his audience.

The beaten man stirred and, though too feeble now to rise, dragged himself across the ground. Given something to do other than endure the gazes of the onlookers, the former marine took four giant strides towards his opponent. Grabbing the back of his neck and the belt of his pants, he hoisted the man onto his shoulders, turned on his heel and made his way back to Nigel's, leaving his audience behind but feeling their gazes on his back the entire way home.

6

The door had been hydraulic long ago. Without interruption the power plants supplied it with electricity. The various components were fashioned in diverse factories until finally being assembled and delivered to Arcarius. The inevitable breakdowns were fixed by men trained by the local tech schools; the required spare parts were shipped around the globe. It worked as smoothly as could be expected.

Somewhere, sometime, it was replaced by an ordinary door of metal bars, perhaps because of the increasingly desultory supply of electricity that made the hydraulic door more nuisance than assistance. It might have been replaced when the supply of qualified mechanics was diverted by the government to other purposes. Or perhaps, when the door needed replacing, a bureaucrat several hundred miles away, sitting under a mountain of request slips and guided by a strict quota, could only grant a limited number of the requests. Such a simple thing, but interesting to track the decline of a civilization through the history of a door.

Whatever the reason, the door was now made of crisscrossing steel bars and was opened by hand or, in this case, two pairs of hands. A third pair shoved Alistair through, though he stubbornly resisted the shove, making it quite clear, as he entered the cell, it was by the power of his own legs. He found himself in a spacious and dimly lit holding cell with a low ceiling and about a score of other prisoners.

"Turn around and approach the door," said one guard in a disinterested tone. "Unless you want the cuffs on all night."

Alistair, keeping his mouth shut, walked backwards until his hands hit the door. A guard reached through with a key and released him, then left without comment.

He needed no time for his eyes to adjust to the dim light. The other prisoners eyed him, and he in turn surveyed them, seeing them in multi-tonal shades of gray, much like surveillance equipment. The little visible light interfered with his special vision, but not enough to render it worthless.

Two men lay quivering and drooling on the floor. He did not doubt that much of the powerful smell assaulting him was their doing. A few men sat idly observing the poor addicts, occasionally summoning enough interest to snicker when one was seized by a particularly strong spasm.

Eager to move away from the door and out of attention, Alistair went to the back of the room and made as if to sit down on an open spot on the bench. Immediately, a man of slight build and short stature moved to block him.

"That's my bench," he claimed, jutting his chin out. Timidity did not help a man such as he to survive in the environment from which he no doubt came.

Consumed as always by the blushing and the throbbing pulse in his ears that accompanied public scrutiny, Alistair sought action, having learned that merely standing under many gazes invariably made him look foolish. Grabbing the man by the face, his large hand engulfing it completely, he threw him to the side where he fell and skidded to a stop.

"I'm not in the mood for it," he growled, but he cursed himself when his throat clamped shut on his words, giving them the form of a stutter. There was a general chuckling, but he did not acknowledge their merriment, uncertain whether they were laughing at his clumsy speech or the plight of the man he had sent flying. He sat down on the bench and avoided all gazes, his blush burning his face.

The next challenge came from a larger opponent. Surrounded by his flunkies, an oafish brute, who until recently had been the cell's largest occupant, sat in the corner staring at Alistair from the second he arrived. After a bit of whispering with his mates, the big man got to his feet and approached, his chest puffed out and his shoulders thrown back for effect.

"Find yourself a seat, and find it as far away from me as possible," Alistair suggested before the man got a word out, staring at the floor as he spoke. He kept his voice low, praying he wouldn't attract any more attention, but that was a lost cause from the moment his new adversary stood up.

"I think maybe I need to explain somethin' to ya'," the prisoner began, but Alistair stood up and went nose to nose with him. The man was big but overweight and out of shape, a fearsome foe in a typical bar brawl perhaps, but not a professionally trained fighter like the ex marine he was confronting. All other activity in the cell ceased as the prisoners watched the two big men square off.

"I already said I'm not in the mood for it. Show me you can make a good decision and get back to your little corner over there." His throat constricted on the last few words and he stuttered again.

The big man started to laugh, but the laugh never fully emerged from his mouth. A hand on the chest and a foot behind the heel sent him crashing to the ground. Before the brute had time to blink, indeed almost before his backside hit the floor, Alistair grabbed the back of his head and slugged him three times in the face. There was no wind up, just three short and controlled blows to his nose. When he let him go, his head dropped like deadweight. Rolling over, he clutched his face and moaned while blood streamed onto the floor to merge with the other stains.

"I'm not in the mood for it," Alistair declared for the third time with a look around the cell. The prisoners divided their attention between the victor and the vanquished, and no one moved to dispute him.

As the former marine sat back down, several of the brute's lackeys rushed over to help the beaten man back to his corner. They half carried, half dragged him, giving Alistair furtive glances over their shoulders. For his part, Alistair fought to control his breathing, and his shoulders, thrown out like a male gorilla claiming territory, slumped down to a relaxed position. His face, however, still burned.

"So what are you in for?" asked a man.

Turning his head to get a look at the speaker, Alistair saw several days' growth of beard and some dark bruises on what would be a handsome face. He had curly black hair that was oily, and his clothes, though they looked like they had been worn for a week or longer, were of the highest quality and a bit ostentatious of color and cut. He sat in a relaxed fashion, one leg crossed over the other and gently kicking back and forth, managing, even in those surroundings, to exude a quiet dignity. There was an intelligence in his eyes most of the other denizens of the cell lacked; he held himself erect and with grace.

In response to the question, Alistair inclined his head once towards the spot where his foe had fallen. "That."

The man nodded as he considered it. "At least you've learned your lesson."

Alistair allowed himself a small half smile. "What about you?"

Without answering, the man studied him quizzically for a moment, though the young Ashley could not understand why. With an expression that said "might as well", he finally answered. "All sorts of things. Money laundering, tax evasion, illegal importing, illegal exporting…it's a long list. I'm actually innocent on some counts. Not that it will matter much."

"How long have you been here?"

"I don't even know. We've been fed…I don't know how many times. How dirty do my clothes look?"

"At least a week."

"That sounds about right."

"So what happens to us now? I'm new to this."

"Me too. All I know is we sit here until they get us processed and ready for transport to the main prison. They'll be back to question you before too long."

The man whom Alistair had beaten was upright now and sitting in his spot on the bench. No longer moaning, he was gingerly poking at his tender nose, wincing when he nudged the tender spots a bit too hard. A companion was trying to stop the bleeding with his own shirt, but he was pushed away whenever he got too close. Alistair briefly felt a pang of guilt for his treatment of the thug, but he quashed the feeling. *I didn't go looking for a fight*, he said to himself.

"So who did you thrash?" the man asked. "Were you a tin man?"

"No, I was in the service until recently. The guy I beat set a bomb off at my dad's restaurant. He attacked us first. His buddies got away; he wasn't so lucky." Changing the subject, he continued, "So which of those charges were real ones?"

The man chuckled. "Oh, most of them." He thought for a moment. "Actually, all of them might be. I really don't keep track." He shrugged his shoulders and, with a resigned tone nonetheless tinged with something sounding almost cheerful, or perhaps carefree, said, "I shall be in prison for a very long time." After a pause, the man asked, "You really don't recognize me?"

Alistair shook his head. "Should I?"

An amused expression crossed his face. "Darion Chesterton? Doesn't ring a bell?"

He shook his head again. "I've been off the last four cycles."

"I couldn't decide if you were some inept government agent sent to ply me for information, or if you honestly didn't know who I was."

"The latter."

"He's a damn crook!" spat a man on the far side of the cell. It was not immediately apparent who had spoken.

"He's the biggest thief since…" Whoever the speaker was, he lacked the acuity to complete the thought.

Without acknowledging his detractors, Darion said, "About the time you were joining the armed forces, I was running a smuggling ring. My clients were all over Aldra, and I got them whatever they ordered and made a handsome profit doing it."

One of the prisoners jumped to his feet. "I spent the last two cycles out of work because of scumbags like you!" he shouted, pointing an accusing finger at Darion. "And you sit there feeling proud of your profits! I stole to feed myself; you stole for your fuckin' wardrobe!"

Alistair leveled a steady gaze at the man who had interrupted them. "Why don't you sit down and be quiet before I decide to ask him how he got those bruises?"

The man revealed no fear, but after a dark glare at Darion he was back in his place on the floor. "These fuckin' profiteers," he muttered, the anger still there but controlled now. "You've been gone four cycles? Things have gotten worse since then."

"I'm here for sellin' specnine," another man started slowly, carefully. "Darion and his buddies take all the good opportunities for themselves. The little guy gets left out in the cold while these bastards get rich off the rest of us." The last part he addressed to Darion: "The government's gonna give you what you deserve."

Alistair nodded thoughtfully. "What was the last thing you bought?" he asked the man.

He, caught off guard, seemed suspicious and unwilling to answer at first. Finally, he said, "I got a pair of shoes right before they arrested me."

"How many credits?"

The man snorted. "I traded some potatoes for 'em."

"All right, how many potatoes?"

Shrugging, the man replied, "About thirty. Grew 'em on my roof. What's it to ya'?"

"Would it be fair to say you wanted the shoes more than the potatoes?"

"Obviously."

"Would you say you robbed the shoemaker, or that he robbed you?"

The man looked baffled, like he had gone about as far with the questioning as he was prepared to go. Nevertheless he ventured one last answer: "I already told ya' we traded. I never robbed nobody."

"Darion did exactly what you did. He just did it more often."

There was a general cacophony of protest, and one voice rose above the others. "There's nothing wrong with trading with your neighbors, but he trades away Aldran goods with foreigners!"

"No one needs that much money!" insisted another.

"How can you justify being so rich when some of us are struggling to get by?"

"Every import is a lost job for an Aldran! Not that he cares about any Aldrans other than himself."

The force of their anger was extraordinary, the kind reserved only for those things that threaten what a man holds most dear and sacred. Alistair sighed but did not respond, and a moment later a Civil Guardsman appeared at the door.

"Let's keep it down in here or I'm going to have about twenty sedated prisoners!" he barked, rapping on the metal bars with his nightstick. "Alistair Ashley 3nn?"

Alistair rose and went to the door to have the handcuffs put back on.

ॐ ॐ

To Alistair's surprise his cuffs were taken off before he was asked to sit down at a desk across from an old grizzled officer. The look on the Guardsman's face was pure knowing cynicism, though not necessarily disapproval. When Alistair was seated, the Guardsman pushed some papers across the desk and tossed a pen on top of them.

"Read 'em and sign 'em. Seems we had a mix -up." His tone was as sarcastic as his expression.

"I'm not sure—"

Another Guardsman, standing nearby, cut him off. "The guy cleared it up," he said. Alistair turned to see who addressed him, and the officer gave him a wink. "He told us how you saved him from the men who were assaulting him."

Alistair nodded slowly and turned back around. The graying officer across from him watched the exchange with an expression that might have been amused if he had cared enough to feel anything about it. He scratched at the papers with the pen offered to him. After signing, he was given an envelope containing his ID and other documents he had been forced to surrender. Checking to make sure all was in order, he followed the officer who had winked at him. The man held open the door, and Alistair passed through and left the station, getting a pat on the back as he left.

Outside, Stephanie and Oliver were waiting for him, Stephanie in her Civil Guard uniform and looking as skeptical as the man who had him sign the papers but more judgmental. Oliver sported a grin from ear to ear. The abrupt temperature change from inside the moderately heated Civil Guard station to the outside produced a shiver in Alistair. The wind whipped at their clothes and Stephanie's hair. She had her arms folded across her chest, either as a buffer against the wind or to enhance her disapproving glare.

"Good to see you," Oliver called out and enveloped Alistair in a hearty embrace.

Alistair returned the hug and suddenly had an idea of what had transpired.

"Stephanie," he said by way of a greeting.

"Alistair," Stephanie returned, her expression carefully controlled. "I'm glad you didn't kill anyone."

"No. As it turns out, I saved someone from a deadly assault." He gave Oliver a look out of the corner of his eye.

Oliver chuckled while Stephanie sighed.

"Let's get you home," she said, and the two men walked with her towards the nearest Metro. The darkness of the predawn hours and the chill of the autumn wind made them shiver, and they walked quickly, eager for the relative warmth of the station.

"So, Oliver, you managed this quite well," Stephanie offered.

"I managed nothing, Stephanie dearest," he replied, his voice dripping innocence.

"I'm not talking about the bribery, per se. That's common enough, unfortunately. It's just curious you knew exactly who to bribe and got it done so quickly. And what you said to the young man Alistair 'saved' I'd be curious to hear."

38

With his beefy paw Oliver reached for Stephanie's rough, unfeminine hand and brought it to his lips. "Stephanie, I am truly, truly shocked, and truly hurt you could think such a thing of me."

With a kiss, Oliver let her hand drop and jovially weathered her censorious glare as they reached the entrance to the station.

7

The first snow storm, driven by the gigantic oceanic humidifiers keeping water vapor abundant in the atmosphere, dumped heavy wet flakes over the city which melted on the warmer surfaces. When the long Aldran night came, the water froze and Arcarius was encased in ice. It stayed this way for a week, and then the weather warmed and the ice melted, leaving the citizens waiting for the next storm, the one to last through the cold season. As the popular saying went, *the first snow comes and goes away; the next one all the winter stays.*

That next storm came a week later, on the night of the Debate, the last appearance political candidates were allowed to make before the election. Attendance was mandatory for all citizens, but even absent the legal obligation, Nigel would have been there with his family. The title to his home and business was not, after all, entirely under his own discretion and he knew he would have to put in an appearance. It was while the Ashley's were getting ready that an unenthusiastic Alistair, waiting until the last moment to throw on some clothes, approached his dad with something he discovered in his books.

"Looks like you're exchanging a lot for food right now. Are these rates correct?"

Nigel, trying to remember how to tie a bowtie, didn't look away from the mirror. "They're correct. The official exchange rate is the same, but to get all the food I need, I have to go through the empty shops."

The government gave licenses to practice any sort of business. Many of the men and women granted restaurant licenses were only interested in having them for the food allotments that came with them. An empty shop in the restaurant business meant someone who exchanged for food from the Farm Bureau and turned around and exchanged it with another restaurant.

Nigel continued, "It's the speculators. Empty shoppers are holding food off the market. The government outlawed extortion level exchange rates, but that just means I have to exchange more with enbatts on the side.

"Then it must mean there is less food, or anticipation of less."

"The harvest was bigger this year than any in the last decade. I just saw the report last night."

"Buy preservable food," said Alistair, "and get a good place to store it." He left his father with that bit of advice.

After some imploring, Alistair consented to getting dressed. His family left without him though, since he would be going with his friends and was waiting for them to show up. His father walked without a cane, moving smoothly since his illicit operation. Gerald, noticing his father's unhampered gait, directed a cynical look Alistair's way but said nothing. Through the kitchen window, Alistair watched his father leave and a smile touched his lips.

A light snow fell, a pleasant snow. The city lights lit the air and the gently falling flakes reflected the glow as bit by tiny bit they covered the city and the land around it. The run-down buildings, the roofs in disrepair, the cracked sidewalks, the potholes in the roads…everything was covered with a pristine white powder until the city almost looked attractive. With ruddy cheeks and noses and visible plumes of their breath escaping into the air, Alistair and his friends made their way to the Metro station and there boarded a car for Ewan's Park, named after Arcarius' first mayor.

It was surrounded on all sides by four wide city streets. Forming a perimeter outside the streets were the large buildings of the downtown area, some as high as fifty stories. Most were privately built, but now they were almost all government owned and used by the various bureaucracies.

The windows of the buildings shone with bright colors, and white lights were hung from the tree branches, connecting all the Plaza's trees in a spider web of light. To the north, past the downtown buildings, the mayor's palace rose high above all else. A smooth design with no corners, it also was well lit from its middle reaches to its lofty spires.

The friends drifted here and there, eyeing the attractions, all political in nature. There was music praising the glory of Aldra and Arcarius. Children performed skits of Aldra's history. Would-be office holders and campaign volunteers shook hands and handed out pamphlets. Among the planned revelry a dark rumor was spreading, that New Kensington had been attacked by Kaldis. The details varied from one teller to the next, but they all agreed some sort of bomb attack had occurred, and somehow everyone knew the Kaldisians were the masterminds.

The group separated by degrees until Alistair found himself alone with Oliver on a path around a small pond in the park. They strolled about, nodding at those they knew, Oliver returning appreciative nods to the rugby fans who recognized him. Presently a young woman, probably a student, who carried a rolled up parchment and a pen, accosted them.

"Good evening," she cheerily greeted and continued before they could reply. "I'm collecting pledges."

"Pledges?" asked Alistair.

"Loyalty pledges. You pledge your loyalty to Aldra and then you get to sign your name on the list. We're trying to get everyone to sign."

Oliver and Alistair exchanged glances.

"Has anyone declined?" asked Alistair.

The young woman chuckled, half surprised and half amused by the question. When it became apparent he was indeed waiting for an answer she replied, "No," as if explaining that water was wet and snow was cold.

"What is this loyalty pledge?"

"It's the same one you grew up reciting." A note of perplexity crept into her voice.

"I stopped reciting that when I reached the age of reason."

Her pleasant demeanor became hurt innocence. "It's just showing your support for Aldra. Especially after the attacks."

"I don't care to support Aldra. I am taxed by Aldra. I am forced to serve in Aldra's military. I am regulated by Aldra. I am told what jobs I may perform and for what allotments. I am told what I may do with my land, what I may do with and to my body. All this without so much as a by-your-leave. Frankly, I'm feeling a bit irritated with Aldra at the moment and I don't care to support her."

Had it been able, the woman's jaw would have dropped straight to the ground. As it was, it reached her sternum. She looked to Oliver as if for a translation.

"I'll take a pass as well," he informed her.

As she turned to leave, Alistair said, "Now run along and tell the Civil Guard about the two dissidents."

She nearly flew away.

"One of these times," said Oliver, "we're going to get into trouble for things like that."

"Fine by me."

When they had twice circled the pond and passed many gatherings, listening to all sorts of discourse about the state of Arcarius and ideas for the war with Kaldis, all delivered by the sort of speaker who can feign enthusiasm in front of the most indifferent audience, they decided to look for new ground. After wandering into this fresh territory, Alistair stopped short and put a hand on his friend's shoulder.

"Is that Warwick?" he asked, pointing at the familiar political figure who happened to be speaking to Elizabeth not thirty yards from them. There was a group of eminent dignitaries standing off to the side.

"Flirting with my gal," said Oliver jokingly, but then Aloysius pulled out a rose and gave it to the striking woman whom Oliver called his girlfriend. He gallantly lifted her hand to his lips, lightly kissed her, and placed the rose in her palm. The mayoral candidate returned to his companions then, and Elizabeth raised the rose to her nostrils. Eyebrows raised high, Alistair looked to his friend.

"I'd better go do some damage control," said Oliver with a smile Alistair knew was forced, and as Aloysius walked away, he left to join Elizabeth.

He waited for a moment to watch his friend go and then turned, ducked a snowball fight erupting among some teenagers, and wandered off to see what the rest of the night had in store.

డ్ర-ళ

When the call sounded for the candidates' speeches, Alistair positioned himself at the outer railing of the amphitheater at the center of the park. He could not deny his interest in what was about to transpire, but neither could he bring himself to enter and fully to join the proceedings. Brushing the snow off the stone railing, he leaned sideways against the barrier.

A man had taken position several yards from him. A hard looking man with a prominent scar on his left cheek, he had been in Alistair's vicinity for the last half hour no matter where the former soldier went. Now he stood stock still with his hands in his coat pockets and his collar turned up against the cold. Alistair did not look in his direction, but he never let him out of his peripheral vision.

As the few truly interested parties filed into the amphitheater, Alistair studied them while snow slowly collected on his shoulders. It would not be accurate to say only the rich took interest, but there was a decided shift towards affluence among the attendees. In an economy like Aldra's, wealth came to those with connections, and connections came to those with the interest in making them.

He caught sight of his brother just then. Gerald, at a distance, waved to indicate he had seats for them. Alistair waved him on. Shrugging his shoulders and shaking his head, Gerald turned and entered the amphitheater. Alistair watched his brother go mainly because the view afforded him, from the corner of his eye, a look at the tail. The man was as still as the stone railing upon which Alistair leaned, and he was now half covered by snow on his hat and shoulders.

It was right then that two more men appeared. The tail greeted them with a nod and inclined his head towards Alistair. The two responded with nods of their own and all three moved in on the youngest Ashley. Seeing them coming, Alistair did not move but watched them with an affectation of disinterest and lack of concern, though inside he was tensed and ready to spring. When they reached him they stood close, too close to be polite.

"Alistair Ashley 3nn?" asked one of the newcomers, shorter than his two companions and with thick wavy blonde hair. His breath billowed like a cloud into Alistair's face.

"Alistair Ashley is the name my parents gave me," replied the ex soldier. "3nn is what the government uses to group me. I don't use suffix codes myself."

"I think this one's gonna be disrespectful, Tom," said the other newcomer, a dark haired man with almost shockingly pale skin and sharp features.

"You can feel it coming," the original tail, Tom, affirmed.

Alistair did not reply but he did not avert his gaze either. He stared back at them with a look neither friendly nor unkind. Their talk was quiet, but there was a strain in the air, strong enough to be felt by passersby, to make people furtively glance over their shoulders at the men. As the citizens of Arcarius continued to file in, a bubble of space developed around the four.

"We can't have you harassing people tonight," said the short man.

The left corner of Alistair's lips curled in a faint smirk. His question had just been answered.

"Are you referring to the pledge I refused to sign?"

"So you admit you're harassing people," said Tom.

"I admitted nothing. I asked a question."

"But you knew what we were talking about. Are you going to try to tell us you weren't harassing her?" demanded Tom.

"That's exactly what I'm going to try to tell you," replied Alistair in a tone of voice far too pleasant to be anything but cocky. "You guys seem to have a handle on this conversation, my side as well as your own. Tom, why don't you handle my lines for me? Your two friends can pick up the slack for you and I'll go back to people watching."

"That was disrespectful," said the dark haired one in a flat tone.

"You could feel it coming," Tom reaffirmed.

"We're going to clear this up one way or the other," said the short man.

"Let me guess. One way is I can beg your pardon, preferably with shaking knees to appease your colossal egos, and sign the loyalty pledge. The other way is you can take me away from here and teach me manners with an electric prod in a sound proof room."

"And we didn't even rehearse the scene with him," commented the dark haired one.

"You and Tom aren't the only ones with premonitions."

"But we are going to be the only ones with teeth in our heads in about ten minutes," said Tom.

Alistair broke the cool calm of the confrontation by tilting his head back and laughing. "Gentlemen, did you take a good look at me before you came over here? You knew my name so you must know something about me. Do you have a pretty good idea what I've been doing for the last four cycles?"

Their expressions did not change, but they didn't speak either. Alistair, standing up straight now to lend his impressive height and bulk to his words, continued.

"If you want to take me in and make a scene right here, go right ahead. Put in a call for back up first. I'd say ten more men would be enough. But let me help you out: I'll most likely be alone at some point when I go home. Come for me then. If you were secure enough to take me away for any reason you wanted, you'd have done so with no preamble. So come for me later tonight when I'm alone. But right now I'm guessing you've got nothing but tough talk."

Either a State feels secure enough to openly treat its citizens as property, with no pretense, or it doesn't. Despite his own tough talk, he was relieved with what he got: a quiet retreat. One minute they were in his face, stoic and menacing, and the next they were casually strolling away.

"We'll be looking forward to our next meeting," said the short blonde agent, casting the words over his shoulder.

Alistair could not decide if the looks he received from those who dared come close enough to listen were looks of admiration for a brave man or alarm for a fool. He wished they would find something else to look at. Not feeling as calm and confident as he pretended, he felt his limbs tremble as adrenaline ebbed. Leaning once more on the stone railing to steady limbs he was sure must be giving him away, he turned his gaze to the amphitheater as the candidates came onstage to applause from the crowd.

The applause was as close to thunderous as the size of the crowd and the gloved hands of the audience could achieve. All five candidates for mayor entered from stage right, smiling and waving to the throng as if to old friends. Save for the regal Aloysius, they wore smiles too bright to be genuine.

Four of the five candidates were entirely interchangeable. Only Aloysius Warwick stood out. The others, whose names Alistair either hadn't learned or didn't care to remember, were plain in appearance. SoFeds and Libertarians, they were dressed well but not too well. They moved on stage as if relaxed but not gracefully. They spoke simply. They were common men, or at least that was the image they portrayed, like every other successful Aldran politician.

Standing erect and tall with broad shoulders and nose held high, walking with powerful and confident strides, speaking clearly and commandingly, Aloysius Warwick exuded nobility in the officer's uniform he dared wear to the Debate. His handsome face looked with benevolent superiority at the masses, and Alistair was alarmed by him. Former officers and servicemen had of course run for office, but the Libertarians and SoFeds always affected a more relaxed image. Aloysius, however, was a so-called Realist.

Despite his father's assurances, Alistair disliked Aloysius Warwick intensely and immediately, but what he could not decide was whether he feared him. He was not what a typical Aldran would expect to see in an election, and yet there he was, onstage with the others, the most widely known candidate of the bunch. *What exactly do you mean by coming here looking like a patrician?*

The tone of the debate was kept affable and there were scripted jokes aplenty, with the occasional oblique jab at another candidate. When the time came for speeches, the other four again failed to distinguish themselves. They might have randomly exchanged speeches and no one would have noticed. When Aloysius stepped forward to deliver his speech, the tenor of the evening changed.

It was a call to arms, but the call was not limited to the recent attack by Kaldis. It was a general call to arms, to fight for Aldran greatness. The Kaldisian attack was the clearest rallying point, but was one of many. Military metaphors abounded, and every problem was given a warlike solution, with terms used in the military. Invective after invective was hurled not just at Kaldis, but at any problem, be it poverty, be it shortages, be it influenza. The speech called for a new discipline, a stricter government, and an alert citizenry.

Once the goal was plainly defined, the path leading there was made clear. For too long, according to Mr. Warwick, Aldra had gripped its own economy too tightly. "One does not use an eyedropper to water a garden," he reasoned. "One points a hose and lets physics take over from there." Government would, in Warwick's plan, guide the economy, but the economy must be freed to work. "A bureaucracy is not for making guns and butter," he proclaimed. "It is there to help coordinate the process." Entrepreneurs would bring the economy back to health, they were assured, with the government's guidance and regulation. The excesses of the rich and their constant abuses would be prevented by ubiquitous government scrutiny. Aldra would become strong and proud once again. That was the path; that was the means.

The destination was war.

It was difficult to gauge the crowd's true reaction. There was an excitement in the amphitheater, but how much was due to the men and women Warwick paid to cheer him was difficult to say. His family was rich; he could have filled the entire amphitheater with hired fans. Scanning the crowd, Alistair saw many were not impressed, no matter how good a public speaker Warwick was. *Not enough support*, he said to himself. *No one can win an election in Arcarius with his attitude and rhetoric no matter how much money he has. Not to a post as high as mayor at any rate.*

When the final applause died down, several members of the audience, chosen beforehand, stepped up to a microphone in one of the aisles in order to ask pre-approved questions of the candidates. Alistair saw this and held his breath, struck with an idea, but one that made him weak in the knees. He felt his limbs tremble again, but then he set his jaw and tilted his head forward. He entered the amphitheater and moved towards the microphone, brushing past a handful of people who were exiting. He took the steps two at a time.

"My question," said the first timid speaker, his voice cracking as he spoke in front of the crowd, "is for candidate Aloysius Warwick. Mr. Warwick, we hear our nation has been attacked by the Kaldisians and the next attack may be imminent. What plans do you have for Arcarius as our planet struggles for the war effort?"

As Aloysius accepted a microphone to reply to the question his speech had already answered, Alistair neared the end of the line of questioners. Two armed Civil Guardsmen were coming up the aisle near the line's end. Pausing for a moment, he felt his will drain out of him, but he steeled himself and descended once again. One of the two Civil Guards roughly placed a hand on his chest.

"My question is for candidate Warwick," the next in line stated, her voice also quavering.

"No one else is getting in line," the Guardsman informed Alistair.

"My parents are in the front row," Alistair explained. "I'm just going down to see them."

Dropping his hand from Alistair's chest, the man looked away and nodded almost imperceptibly, already half forgetting his presence. While Aloysius answered the second question, Alistair slipped past the Guardsmen towards the front of the line.

"I also would like to ask a question of Mr. Warwick," said the third in line, an elderly woman.

On stage, Aloysius nodded magnanimously, as if consenting to hear the question were a favor. Three of the other candidates maintained their pleasant smiles while one shuffled his feet.

As Aloysius listened to the question, nodding solemnly, posture always perfect, Alistair noted that every question had been for him. Sitting down in an empty seat, his resolve faded again now that he was near his objective. He nervously tapped his right foot and bit his lower lip. *Do I really want to do this?* he thought, gazing at an audience that now seemed, from the bottom of the amphitheater, to be of immense proportions.

When the fourth and fifth questioner also posed their questions to Aloysius, he was filled with a new determination, in defiance of Warwick's monopoly on the evening. Blushing angrily, he popped out of his seat with a half swallowed growl and grabbed the microphone before it could be handed to the sixth in line.

"I was wondering," he asked in that moment when everyone else around him was frozen in surprise, "if you could leave me out of your plans?"

Aloysius blinked. The other candidates exchanged bewildered looks and the entire amphitheater was silent. For a moment, Alistair fancied the rest of the populace in the park had stopped what they were doing to watch and listen. The thought made him want to throw the microphone away and pull his coat over his head. For all his anger of a moment ago, he nearly turned to run. The blush winter brings to one's cheeks was magnified a thousand times on his visage.

Next to him, the man from whom Alistair stole the microphone cleared his throat. He opened his mouth to say something, but Alistair plunged on.

"What I mean is, can I opt out?" There was motion now among the crowd. The mic man next to him looked around for assistance, and he could hear the whispers and murmurs of the crowd. Aloysius looked around as if someone else might be able to explain this to him. "I'm speaking to you, Mr. Warwick." Aloysius' gaze snapped back to Alistair. "Can I opt out? If I decide I don't want to participate, can I decline your program or am I obligated to go along?"

Seeing no imminent intervention, Aloysius replied, "This isn't a meal at a restaurant, boy. We're talking about running the nation."

One of the other candidates stood up to take advantage of a chance to show leadership. "Can we get some security in here?" he called out in his best version of a commanding tone. He even stuck his chest out for better effect.

"But what if it were more like a restaurant?" asked Alistair. "Imagine a restaurant where one man is elected to choose what everyone will eat, how much they will pay, when they will eat, what they will drink, what they may wear, what music will play…I'm simply requesting the right to order my own meal, or to go to a different restaurant, or perhaps build my own. I do not wish to fight Kaldis, I do not wish to be taxed, I do not wish to be told what I may ingest and what not, I do not wish to be put in a line when I need medical care, I do not wish to be directed as to how I may work and for what wages, I do not wish to be told whom I may hire…" In the middle of his speech, his throat closed up on him and he paused to get himself under control. "I do not wish to be a part of your system." His voice quavered at the end, and he imagined the effect, coming from someone of his size, must have been comical. He fought against his embarrassment and continued. "So my question is, will you let me be to live my life how I want, or are you going to force me into your system? And if you force me into your system, by what right do you do this?"

And then he was seized by several hands and dragged away. Dropping the mic, he allowed himself to be carried along, resigned to whatever sentence he would be given for his display and almost relieved he would soon be safe from the penetrating gaze of the public. He avoided all eye contact with those who watched as he was pulled out of the amphitheater. It was only after he left that he realized the hands pulling him along were not of the Civil Guard, but of his father and brother. They dragged him farther away, to a copse of trees and, with Mary and Katherine not far behind, took refuge in it.

Nigel's face was flushed with fury. "What the hell has gotten into you!?"

"You're a damn fool!" Gerald's outburst followed close on the heels of Nigel's. "What the hell do you think you're accomplishing?"

"I asked a few questions," Alistair said with a feigned innocence that only enraged his brother further.

Gerald lashed out and shoved his younger sibling full in the chest. Though he had not carefully built his body like Alistair, he was still the son of Mary Ashley and was naturally big and strong. Alistair stumbled backwards. Gerald looked ready to continue but Katherine put a restraining hand on his arm.

"Why would you do something like that?" asked Mary of her youngest son, her eyes betraying pain.

"Mom, can't you see what's going on? What kind of world is this where I can't ask questions of the men who run my life? You're scared to death for me because of a few questions!"

"That's right. We are," said Katherine. "For our sake can you avoid trouble for once?"

"Trouble? I just asked a question."

"Drop the act," said Nigel through gritted teeth.

"I'm not acting. Open your eyes! ALL I DID WAS ASK A QUESTION. I'll repeat my last one: what kind of world do we live in where asking a question is dangerous?"

Gerald spun around and walked off muttering, clutching at his head like he wanted to tear through his own scalp. Nigel sighed and approached his son, gripping him gently by the upper arm.

"It's just a question, Dad," said Alistair in the most reasonable tone he could muster. "If our government can't take a simple question, I say we should get rid of it."

"Alistair," said Nigel, his tone as gentle as his grip, "I'm at risk to lose my restaurant. Your brother works for the Transportation Bureau. There are going to be repercussions for what you did tonight if anyone connects us to you. For our sake, stop fighting and just accept things."

It was something he hadn't considered, and his shoulders slumped. His father's words felt like a knee to the gut, and his rebellious spirit fought against a rising tide of guilt.

"We used the same tactic on Kaldis," he said through a mirthless smile. "When we needed to get to someone, we'd kidnap a family member, and we'd publicize it. Then we'd wait, and every once in a while it worked. They'd turn themselves in."

Gerald had managed to calm down a bit and made his way back to the copse of trees. "Aldra did that?" he asked, the surprise of it peeling away his armor and exposing something more vulnerable underneath.

"All it really did was enrage whatever poor city we were trying to control. All it really did was escalate the violence."

Nigel squeezed his son's arm. "Don't be the one to escalate the violence. Not now. For your family, Alistair."

He shook his head in disbelief, but then looked his dad in the eyes. "If they take your restaurant…"

The implied threat hung in the air until Oliver and Henry came running to the copse of trees. They were both breathless.

"You need to leave now," panted Henry, his frail hand grasping Alistair's bicep and tugging at it. "Stephanie told us to get you." Alistair allowed himself to be taken for a moment, and then his instincts kicked in and he took a more active role.

"Walk with me," said Oliver to the Ashley's while Alistair left with Henry. "I'll go with you and maybe they'll mistake me for Alistair."

The five of them began to stroll leisurely in the opposite direction from Henry and Alistair.

"What the hell got into him?" whispered Gerald. The unnecessary whisper was subconscious, a natural reaction when one thinks one is being watched.

"He's had enough," Oliver replied. "So have a few others."

There had been some debate as to the manner in which the Ashley's should return home. Oliver offered to accompany them but Nigel, thanking him, said it would not be necessary. They opted to blend in with the crowd in the Metro. The walk from the station to Nigel's restaurant and the family home was a quiet one. Nigel and Gerald walked in front while Katherine and Mary hung back. Like the expressions on their faces, the thoughts of the four were nearly identical.

"He's an idiot," Gerald muttered, hoping to spark some sort of discussion to crack the silence.

"He's your brother," Nigel answered as if that fact settled the matter. "We're all proud of your work for the Bureau, but don't ever forget your family comes first. Before friends, before your job…before your country. He's headstrong, but he's your brother. Family always comes first."

Gerald considered the words in silence as they neared the dark structure of their house.

৵৽

Oliver was one of the last to return home. He waited around until he found Elizabeth. The Metro car they rode was nearly empty, and the only sound was the soft hum of its machinery. Staring off into space, Elizabeth held against her lips Aloysius' rose, twirling it lightly back and forth. Every so often she would inhale more deeply than normal, and each time Oliver winced.

"I wish you'd get rid of that," said the rugby star for the fourth time.

Elizabeth, bothered out of her reverie, fixed an impatient gaze on him. "Would you forget about it already?"

"It's difficult to forget when you're waving it in my face."

Elizabeth turned away from him with an exasperated groan. "I'm not waving it in your face."

"You might as well be."

"It's a nice gift. I like it. Just let me have it," she pouted.

Oliver leaned forward, fixing his fingers into a steeple that he pressed to his forehead. "Elizabeth, a man does not give a woman a rose without a very specific reason. That is doubly true for someone like Warwick."

"It's a sweet little gift. Stop being so jealous." Her look was almost patronizing. "I'm not interested in him."

"Can you show me that by getting rid of the rose?" She did not respond. "Elizabeth, when was the last time you saw a rose in this city in winter? This is not an innocent flirt."

"Stop being jealous."

"I wouldn't be jealous if I didn't have a reason to be."

Elizabeth dropped the rose in her lap and turned to address Oliver. "Why do you think you get so jealous, Ollie?"

"Stop it," Oliver growled.

"Is it some sort of insecurity from childhood? Or is it just the normal competition between males? Maybe some sort of abandonment issue?"

"You're not a psychologist!" Oliver nearly exploded. "Stop pretending. You didn't even make it into university." No sooner had the words left his mouth than he regretted them. "I'm sorry," he said, his tone of voice much softer, supplicating.

Elizabeth turned back in her seat to face forward, picking the rose up once again, her face a stoic wall threatening to crack under strain.

"Elizabeth, I'm sorry. I didn't mean it—"

"No, you're quite right. I'm not a psychologist and I never will be. I wasn't approved for a university education...like you said." Her voice was as frosty as the winter wind.

Oliver slumped in his seat. "That was a terrible thing to say. I'm sorry I said it. I shouldn't have. But I wish you wouldn't try to analyze every damn thing I do—"

"I think this is my stop," she said, standing up and waiting for Oliver to let her out. When he did, she brushed by without a backward glance and, carrying the rose prominently in her hand, left him in the Metro car.

8

The mountains north of Arcarius were topped with snow all year long, and as winter approached, the snowline descended steadily into the valleys until the island was entirely white. In the sparsely inhabited interior of the island, Stephanie Caldwell lay on her belly in that snow, next to her precinct commander and dressed in white camouflage body armor. As the wind fiercely whipped the frozen precipitate across the ground, she squinted into a pair of binoculars aimed at an innocuous looking log cabin half a kilometer up slope from them. Behind her, at the bottom of the hill and concealed by the natural lumps and divots, were about a dozen Civil Guardsmen, all armed. An operations vehicle sat on the side of the dirt road, its antenna rotating. A few Guardsmen hurriedly rushed in and out of it, purpose in their strides and a glow in their faces the cold weather could not fully account for.

Stephanie lowered the binoculars. "At least a handful of people inside. They're not on to us."

"I agree," said her commander and put his lips, adorned with a thin dark mustache, to a microphone sewn into the wrist of his body armor. "We've got at least three visible targets inside. Targets are unaware, over." The commander paused and listened to the reply in his earpiece. Nodding, he said, "Copy that. On my signal." To Stephanie he said, "We're going in five."

He slid a few feet down slope and then stood up and waded through snow the rest of the way to the operations vehicle. Stephanie raised the binoculars to her eyes and surveyed the wood cabin one last time. From a stone chimney gray smoke issued to be carried away and dispersed by the strong wind. A driveway was not so covered by snow that its form could not be discerned as it wound through the yard and out to the dirt road snaking through the hilly country. The snow covering the driveway showed one set of auto tracks, and at the end of the driveway was a mailbox in good condition, a reminder of the times when mail was still delivered to the interior of the island.

"We're on in three," crackled the voice of her commander in her earpiece. "Find your place."

Stephanie slid down and made her way to the armored carrier rolling up the dirt road to meet her. An officer in the back gave her a hand up and she took her place with about twenty other officers. She was handed a rifle and sat down on a bench along the side while the transport pulled up to the driveway entrance.

"McCartney," she said, "Take your men left. Dillard, you're going right and around the back. Keller, you're coming with me to the front door. When Dillard gives the signal, we'll follow Captain Travis inside. Be ready for anything."

They sat in silence, twenty plumes of visible breath, ten on each side, desultorily puffing out. A soft click announced someone was rechecking his magazine. An officer cleared his throat. Suddenly, the siren wailed.

The wheels of the transport tore into the snow and dirt and it pitched forward as all twenty bodies swayed with the movement. Outside, the hum of gliders, a sort of hover-motor-cycle called a Torpedo, announced the arrival of additional Guardsmen. The transport braked and Stephanie exhorted her troops to move out. She followed, her feet landing in the ankle deep snow and, along with Keller, fell to her belly next to Captain Travis, all three with guns pointed at the cabin. Inside, a face appeared at the window and just as quickly disappeared.

"We're in position, Captain," said the voice in the helmet, and Travis looked at Stepha-nie and nodded.

She, Keller and Travis rose up and, flanked by two men with a hand-held battering ram, approached the front door. The two burly men with the battering ram did not hesitate to smash their instrument into the front door but, to their astonishment, it held. Another blow yielded the same result. Anxiously, Stephanie tapped her finger on her rifle as she pointed it at a front window.

"It's reinforced, sir!" called out one of the men.

"Take out the window!" yelled Travis.

The two men moved to the side and smashed their ram into a front window, shatter-ing it. Travis and Stephanie flanked the window on either side, pointing their rifles inside. Five men stood around a table, having recently been involved in a card game, with their hands raised, their faces looking bewildered.

"Get down on the ground!" Stephanie ordered them. "Face down and hands out! Get down now!" The men hastily complied. "Is there anyone else in the house?" The men looked from one to another and finally one shook his head.

Keller leaped in through the window and, after some deliberation with the locks, opened the door from the inside. Travis, Stephanie and several others poured in. The men were handcuffed and half a dozen officers searched the cabin. Papers and other objects were soon scattered everywhere. Travis grabbed one of the men and, lifting him up, sat him on one of the chairs around the small kitchen table. He took a seat across from him while Stephanie stood at her commander's side.

"Do you want to make this easy on us, or are we going to have to find everything our-selves?" asked the commander, scratching at the black hair of his left sideburn.

The man across from him was dark haired and square jawed. Despite his unshaved beard and generally slovenly appearance, he was handsome. His dark eyes betrayed anger, but not fear, as he faced his interrogator.

"Your boys handled that front door nicely," scoffed the man.

Travis' expression darkened. "Which one of you is Rod Haverly?"

"You're talking to him."

"Rodney, tell me why we're here."

"Roderick, and I didn't invite you, so I don't know."

Stephanie jumped in and said, "You don't look surprised enough to make me believe that. Why bother reinforcing your door like that? Does it buy you a few extra seconds when the Civil Guard come?"

"Wind blows pretty strong out here," Rod answered. "It's a precaution."

An officer tapped Stephanie on her shoulder and she turned her attention to him as Travis continued questioning Roderick amid the chaos of the search.

"They've found a secret chamber in the basement, but it's locked with a steel door," he informed her in a low voice.

Stephanie nodded. "I'll be there in a minute." The officer nodded and moved away while Stephanie relayed the information to Travis.

Nodding and directing a knowing smile towards Rod, Travis said, "It seems you have a vault."

"Are those illegal?"

"Would you care to open it for us?"

"Anything to speed this up."

Escorted by Stephanie and Travis, one on each side firmly holding an arm, he was taken down the rickety steps to his basement and released from his handcuffs. He typed in his code and the door opened with a pop. Two officers rushed into the vault, guns at the ready. They emerged in a moment shaking their heads.

"It's empty," declared one.

"Scan it," ordered Travis, a hint of irritation in his voice. One of the men left and Travis turned on Roderick. "We're going to find anything you have."

"Just so long as you put it back."

"You know how I know you're guilty?" Travis asked him, moving in close to his face, almost nose to nose. "Because you're too good at being interrogated."

"Thank you."

"You can tell a career criminal by how used to questioning he is. How prepared his answers are."

"I have no criminal record, officer."

"For the moment," replied Travis and pulled away from the man. "Take him back up-stairs."

The cabin was invaded by a horde of men and women with all sorts of instruments. Back and forth they went, over the yard, around the basement, under furniture...they found nothing. The five men were finally allowed to sit, though still cuffed, while officers repeatedly questioned them. They shivered in the now freezing cabin, one of them quite violently, but the Civil Guard were indifferent.

Stephanie regarded him with a smoldering anger. She had no doubt he was a specnine trafficker. No one reinforced their front door and kept an electronically operated steel vault in their basement for any other reason. The mailbox out front was also a giveaway. Mail was no longer delivered outside the city, but the mailbox itself could be a convenient signal. He was guilty, living outside the law. He had been given his boundaries, and he had transgressed. *Sit there and shiver*, she thought.

Hours later, as midday approached, Stephanie was still on the scene, sitting in the back of a transport and sharing a smoke with her comrades. The Torpedoes were parked, and the troops who weren't specifically assigned to standing a post were lounging around, waiting for the order to head out. The operations vehicle sat in the front yard, antenna still rotating. Occasionally an officer would exit or enter, but the pace had slowed.

"Fucker should have made his payments," commented one officer as he took a drag on a cigarette and passed it along to his mate.

"Naw, this one never made payments," said another. "He got ratted out by someone who was. That's why we're here."

"That's what I'm saying: fucker should have made his payments."

The cigarette came to Stephanie and she took a puff. It was not something she cared for, but it was a ritual she felt she could not afford to eschew. She inhaled as far as she dared—it would have looked bad to cough—and then passed the precious stick along.

"Talk like that and you'll find yourself before the board in a hurry," said a third man.

Somebody tossed a snowball at him. Stephanie did not react to the talk. It did not concern her and she preferred to ignore it. Captain Travis appeared at the back of the transport and caught her eye. He motioned for her to join him, so she hopped down and walked with her commander across the snow covered lawn, now torn up from hours of traffic.

"There's nothing here. I'm gonna keep interrogating the smart mouth bastard a bit longer, let him freeze a bit, but we're not going to find anything and he isn't going to crack."

Stephanie nodded. "I'll set up a surveillance camera."

"Don't bother. These guys are professionals. They'll find it and disable it. I'm going to give you the job. I want you to form a team, anything you need, and keep your eye on these guys. That'll mean coming out here personally and keeping it under watch."

Stephanie's brows rose in surprise. "What about satellites?"

"Satellites are limited. We'll need a force out here in person. I want these gentlemen in jail before the end of the month."

"Yes, sir."

Travis stopped walking and turned to face her. "They say a lot of good things about you back at the station."

"Thank you, sir."

Travis nodded. "You voted yet?"

"No, sir. I was going to as soon as I'm done here."

"It's about time for siesta."

"In a little bit."

Nodding again, Travis said, "Well, you can head on out of here. Get the teams debriefed and leave a small force with me."

Stephanie nodded and turned to go.

"We're voting Warwick." Travis informed her.

Stephanie stopped in her tracks. "Sir?"

"You know that, right? We're voting Warwick."

Stephanie hesitated, and then tried to nod as confidently as she could. "Yes, sir. That's my understanding." She stood for a moment, staring at her commander who was leveling a penetrating gaze on her. A few strands of hair had gotten out of her helmet and now whipped across her face in the wind. To give herself an excuse to leave, she said, "I'll get the troops dismissed."

"See to it."

ॐॐ

Alistair was reclining in a private viewing booth. It was semicircular, with a small table in the middle, and it faced a screen on which a two dimensional movie was playing. The movie was in black and white, and its reflected glow danced about his features as he watched. The door opened and light streamed in around the hulking form of Oliver. Closing the door quietly, he tiptoed into the room, sitting across from Alistair and setting his drink on the table.

"Voted yet?" the big man asked his friend.

Alistair shook his head but did not look away from the screen. Oliver turned his attention to it for a few moments. A big fat man was walking along at night with a slighter man, while a third, grasping some sort of ancient electronic device, spied upon them. Ducking through iron beams and stepping over obstacles, he trailed their movements while the other two talked, their voices coming through on the receiver in his device.

"How old is this?" Oliver asked when he could feign interest no longer.

"Centuries."

"Their accents are weird. Where is this from?"

Alistair smiled at his companion in friendly toleration. "It was filmed on Kaldis over two hundred years ago."

"Is that the Kaldisian accent?"

"One of them."

Oliver watched for a few more moments. The two men were crossing a bridge. The spy followed along underneath, but as his receiver broadcast the conversation above, it echoed under the bridge and the big man stopped, noticing the echo.

"What's it called?"

"Touch of Evil. It's not the original. As far as we know, that was destroyed during the Second Solar War. This was a recreation by Florentino Amaya. He saw it a few times in his youth, when he studied on Earth, and when it was lost he refilmed it."

"How close is it to the original?"

Alistair shrugged. "No one knows for sure. Amaya swore it was identical. But he was a pretentious bastard."

Oliver watched as the fat man was shot and slowly sank into the river.

"And this was considered fun a long time ago?"

Alistair laughed. "Still is."

Oliver shook his head. "I don't know…two dimensional images are…boring. They don't look real."

"It's the two dimensions that make it so superb," said Alistair with passion. "Representing three dimensions on a two dimensional plane. You can do so much more. Look at the camera angles. Look at the way the camera moves, the way they present the image, the way it's lit."

"You can't even see the whole scene," complained Oliver. "With threedies you can see everything."

"Exactly! There's no artistry to it. With 2D's the director can control what you see and what you don't. He can control the perspective."

"They could at least have filmed it in color." Oliver shrugged, unconvinced, as the credits rolled. "Well, it looks like your 2D is over. The others are just arriving for lunch if you're interested."

"I'll be right out."

Alistair's friends gathered at a large table in the central dining area, and they hailed him and Oliver when they spotted them. Gregory, Elizabeth, Henry and Jack were there, but Stephanie was not. Pulling up a chair, Alistair sank into it and a waitress, a young girl eager to give good service to her boss's son, was immediately at his side.

"Just give me a good beer for now," he said.

"We're out of beer for the next two days," she said with a wince. There were general groans about the table.

"Any juice?"

"A little."

"I'll take whatever we've got."

"And I'll have some red wine," said Oliver.

"I'll see what we have," she replied and hurried off.

"No beer!" groaned Jack. "I had to go straight to whiskey."

"That was probably hard for you," said Henry in feigned sympathy. Jack answered by taking a healthy chug from his glass.

"Did anybody vote yet?" asked Elizabeth.

"Not voting," said Jack, and Henry nodded in solidarity.

"I voted for Warwick," she informed them.

"And I forget who I voted for," Oliver said. "I just made damn sure it wasn't Warwick."

"I voted for Lexington," said Gregory. "I can't stand Warwick. Alistair?"

"Haven't voted."

"But...I imagine you're going to vote for Warwick? Your Dad..."

"I'm not voting for Warwick."

Gregory looked at him as if slightly confused, tilting his head a bit to the side, but he said nothing and neither did Alistair.

Turning to Oliver, Elizabeth said, "Do you really not remember who you voted for?"

"Actually, I think it was Lexington. I didn't really care."

"You shouldn't vote carelessly," she chided and gave him a kiss to soften it.

"I took great care to make sure I didn't vote for Warwick," Oliver insisted and returned her kiss, enveloping her in his left arm.

The waitress reappeared and set down the drinks. Alistair took a sip and then said, "You should have written yourself in."

"They don't allow them anymore," Oliver reminded him and Alistair nodded in remembrance.

"Which party is Lexington?" Elizabeth asked.

"Libertarian," Greg replied.

"They're the ones who...?" she prompted.

"They're the ones who were good a long time ago," Alistair answered. "Before we were born."

The waitress was back with their food, a community stew set in a big bowl with a serving spoon resting on the edge. Steam enticingly rose from the bowl. Oliver grabbed the spoon first, dumped generous servings onto his dish and then passed the spoon to Elizabeth.

"This is what we're all getting?" queried Alistair.

"Menu's a bit sparse today," explained the waitress, and with that she was off to serve another table.

As they served themselves, Stephanie arrived, her cheeks ruddy and her nose dripping. She sat down next to Alistair and greeted her friends.

"Been working outside today?" asked Jack.

"Yeah, ready for some food," she breathed as she set her coat on the back of her chair, revealing her uniform. Oliver tossed her a dish and Gregory handed her a spoon.

"Any word on the election?" Gregory asked the new arrival.

"Warwick's going to win," was her short reply.

Looking about the room, Alistair spotted his brother walking in with an air of searching for someone. A moment later, Gerald spotted the group and came to the table.

"Hello everyone," he greeted them, his manner and tone businesslike. "Alistair, are you free tomorrow?"

"I am not," said Alistair around a mouthful of steaming stew. Gerald seemed put out, though whether it was from the news or Alistair's unhelpful tone and attitude was unclear.

"You're busy all day?"

"Most of it."

Alistair said nothing more and continued eating. When it became apparent he was going to let him stand there, Gregory jumped in.

"Would you care to eat with us, Gerald? We're just getting started."

Gerald surprised his brother by saying yes, and he took a seat next to Stephanie. Alistair stopped eating for a moment to give him a curious look but then went back to ignoring him.

"Everybody voted?" Gerald asked in a tone only Alistair knew well enough to know the question was not innocent.

Oliver pointed out the individual members of the group as he recapped. "No, no, Lexington, Warwick, no, and Lexington I think but anyone but Warwick," he said, finishing with his finger on his own chest. "Stephanie?"

"Not yet, but I'll be voting Warwick," she replied, not looking up from her stew.

"I voted Warwick. That's what the department is doing," Gerald offered and then dug into his stew.

This roused Alistair from his deliberate aloofness. "What did you...the department is...what?" He finally finished with a vigorous shake of his head.

"We're voting Warwick. That's what we're doing this year," Gerald replied and then slurped broth from his spoon. "It's all for the best anyway, because he seems like a suitable candidate."

"We're all voting Warwick too," said Stephanie.

Alistair looked at them like they were crazy. "I'm sorry, that defeats the purpose of voting. Not that I give a shit but…who made this decision?"

"It came down from above," Gerald replied.

"From above? But you don't have to vote for him if you want to pick another candidate."

"That's not…not typically a great idea," Gerald replied.

Stephanie confirmed this with a nod.

Alistair fell back in his chair. "This is unbelievable."

"It's for the best," continued Gerald. "I think an incoming candidate has a right to the support of the bureaucracies he's going to be working with and in charge of."

"There's always some excuse and someone willing to buy it," said Alistair with a shake of his head. "I can't believe you're taking this so…The hell with it. Tomorrow I'm starting the Revolution."

This time it was Gerald's turn to get agitated. He looked around the room for anyone listening to them. "Damn it, Alistair, some time the wrong person is going to hear you say that."

"The wrong people have been hearing me say it all my life. I'm waiting for the right ones."

Gerald's face reddened but he contained his retort and concentrated instead on his stew. The talk eventually turned from politics. When the meal was finished, Gerald excused himself. The others sat around with their drinks until Stephanie excused herself to go vote, and this prompted everyone else to leave too.

Amid the general goodbyes, Oliver turned to Alistair and shook his hand. "I'll be seeing you tomorrow, then?" he asked.

Nodding, Alistair replied, "Tomorrow it is. See you then."

9

Realist Aloysius Warwick ran away with the election, Libertarian Henry Lexington finished a distant second and the vote totals of the others were hardly worth noticing. All over Aldra, from Avon to New Boston, New Kensington to Trenley, Waterdown to Rendral itself, landslide victories were recorded, and the Realists were quick to proclaim the message: the people had given them a mandate. Within hours of being sworn in, the new Realist Parliament appointed General Mortimer Duquesne as Aldra's new President, it's first non-Voluntarist President in a century.

The Realists engaged in the same sort of ancestor worship all regimes find so essential, holding up historical figures as simplistic but shining examples for today's generations, or equally simplistic villains to be denigrated. In this effort the Realists resurrected few unfamiliar ghosts. Instead, they ransacked the Idealist temple and appropriated its idols. It was, for them, the path of least resistance, for the population could go on admiring the same figures, and since most people knew little enough about them to begin with, it was easy to alter perspectives. The result was that the heroes were still the same, they had simply been Realists all along.

Even words sacred to the idealists shifted in meaning and implication. This new breed of Aldran political leader was still strongly isolationist in the Aldran tradition, but isolationism now required foreign intervention. After all, they had been attacked by Kaldis despite their peacekeeping efforts. Isolation at home would be preserved by war abroad. The small peace keeping force had to be expanded.

Such would be the news in the coming weeks when Oliver arrived at Nigel's to pick up his friend. He arrived in a curious vehicle. It was a tiny four wheel apparatus patched together with mismatched parts, as if assembled in a junkyard from bits and pieces meant for diverse other uses. It had a rickety roof, two seats, and sides made from some translucent canvas that opened by way of a zipper. It was drafty, it was uncomfortable, and it was amazing that Oliver managed to fit inside it.

Alistair came out to meet his friend, dressed in home stitched winter clothing so that only a strip around his eyes could be seen. He knew the vehicle and had little confidence in its ability to keep the cold out. Unzipping the side canvas, he got in the passenger seat with a nod to his friend. Oliver pulled the vehicle onto the snow-covered street and slowly drove down the side of the hill, whistling in that cheery way he always did when everyone else found reason to frown.

"There's a heater on the floorboard between us," Oliver told him, and Alistair reached down and flipped it on. "If it needs more juice, I've got a battery behind the seat."

They scampered over the buried streets of Arcarius at a pace only slightly in excess of what Alistair could have achieved with an all out run. It therefore took some time before they left the city and penetrated the surrounding hills on a winding dirt path that traced the low valleys between the hilltops. After they left the city, Alistair reached down and flipped off the heater.

"My feet are sweating," he complained.

"I know. As soon as your face unfreezes, your feet are too hot."

He dealt with the drafts for a while to let his feet cool, and as the sun rose higher and the day warmed a bit, the warmth loosened their tongues and they chatted. Before they realized it, the city of Arcarius disappeared. It took two hours to reach that point, and it took another two to reach their destination. At one point Alistair had to get out of the automobile and push up a steep and icy incline. The heater was turned back on, back off, and then back on again before they pulled into view of their destination.

It was an isolated cabin made of timber. There was a stone chimney, a winding driveway through a spacious yard, and a mailbox out front. Where smooth undisturbed snow should have been, however, the yard had been torn up as if an army regiment had camped there. Alistair spotted several damaged areas of the cabin itself, including a missing front door.

A look of concern on his face, Oliver pulled into the ravaged driveway and up to the house. He shared an apprehensive look with Alistair, and then stopped his vehicle. The two exited slowly, approaching the house like a sleeping dragon. They heard a thud from inside, followed by a curse. Rather than concern Oliver, it put him at ease and he lengthened his stride. Upon reaching the open door, Oliver called out a greeting. Alistair, pulling the ski mask off his head, arrived in time to see a short stocky man with auburn hair approach Oliver and shake his hand.

"What happened—" Oliver began, but the man shushed him. With a wave, he indicated they should follow, and this they did around a corner and down a flight of stairs into a dark basement even colder than the cabin proper.

"I thought I told you not to come," the man said, his smile friendly but his voice betraying irritation. He lit a kerosene lamp in the darkness, and its light was just enough to flicker gently on the basement walls.

"I never got the message," Oliver replied, his breath a great cloud obscuring the space between them.

"Did you check last night?"

"Yeah."

The man shook his head and sighed, and then his gaze found Alistair. "Is this the guy?"

"This is Alistair," Oliver replied, opening his stance to include them both in his speech. "Alistair, this is Kendrick."

Alistair and Kendrick shook hands.

"Well," said Kendrick, "they're no doubt watching the place. That's why I left a message for you not to come. You'll be in their files now."

"Who's watching?" asked Alistair, his voice betraying concern.

"The tin men," Kendrick replied as if Alistair were silly for not knowing. "I haven't seen them since they finished wrecking my place, but since they didn't find what they were looking for..."

"What happened?" asked Oliver.

Kendrick shook his head. "Somebody fingered me...I don't know. A whole battalion showed up here last night and tore the place apart."

"Did they find anything?"

"Of course not. But you two are going to be in their database now. Nothing to be done about it." He shrugged in resignation. "We might as well get this done." He turned a frank gaze on Alistair. "You got payment?"

"I've got payment. You'll see it when I see my order."

"Fair enough," said Kendrick, and he pulled a small communicator from his pocket and spoke into it. "Bring it up, Ryan." So saying, he grabbed the kerosene lamp and left.

"Should we do this right now, with the tin can around?" Alistair asked from his wake.

"They're not going to know anything is going on. And if they try to jump us, your item is in a special container. We'll incinerate it before the tin have a chance to grab it."

"It won't burn," Alistair informed him.

This stopped Kendrick in his tracks. "What?"

"If you got what I asked for, it won't burn."

The black market merchant paused for a second and then shrugged. "Nothing for it now," he said with a sigh and led them back upstairs.

It was only a few minutes later when another man entered the cabin. He was of a stocky build, medium height with medium brown hair and still holding onto his youth. He sported a slash of a scar on the left side of his face. Under his right arm he held a black container in the shape of a briefcase.

"Oliver," the man said with a nod. Oliver returned the greeting with a nod of his own.

"Alistair, this is Ryan Wellesley. Ryan, this is Alistair Ashley, a good friend of mine."

Ryan managed a nod towards Alistair. Then he said, "Oliver, we told you not to fucking come."

"I never got the message."

"What do you mean you never got the fucking message?"

"What I said."

Ryan Wellesley threw his unburdened left arm up in the air. "Can anybody do their fucking job around here?"

"No one, Ryan," said Kendrick. "Just you."

"Don't give me your shit. I'm sick of everybody else dropping the fucking ball." With that, he tossed the container at Alistair, but Kendrick intercepted it.

"If you've got the payment," interjected Kendrick. Then he said, "Hold on a minute."

He went outside and looked around. Still cautious, he returned and took them to a back room cluttered with broken furniture and other odds and ends. "We'll do it in here, and talk soft. Where's the payment?"

Alistair produced a small, solid gold bar from his coat pocket and set it on a broken cabinet resting against the wall. Kendrick's eyes were drawn to it as if by magnetic forces. His face was blank but his eyes glinted.

"We went through a lot of trouble to get this..." he breathed.

"This was the price we agreed on. You're not going to raise it now."

Alistair's stern words snapped Kendrick out of his entrancement. "No, no...I didn't mean...Do you want to examine your purchase?"

Alistair held out his hand and Kendrick passed him the case. From afar it seemed sleek, but now dents and imperfections on its surface were obvious. The lock was even rusted. Something like this, got illegally no doubt, was a difficult and expensive find. It had probably been in use for many, many years. It even looked like the small keypad was not the original. An item like this would be patched and fixed and repatched and refixed until no more use could be squeezed out of it.

On Kaldis they replace these things as soon as the design goes out of style, Alistair remembered.

"44533," Ryan interrupted Alistair's reverie.

After Alistair punched in the code on the keypad, the container snapped open. Inside was a suit of a sleek and thin material, all black. Alistair withdrew it and held it by the shoulders. It proved to be a one-piece suit with a hood, the only apparent opening. The sleeves did not end at the wrist, but flowed into glove shaped endings. The legs, likewise, did not end at the ankles, but formed pockets for the feet, the soles of which were lightly padded and therefore somewhat thicker than the rest of the material.

Tugging at it, Alistair confirmed its considerable elasticity, and when held up to light, nothing reflected off it. The suit was somehow blurry. The material with which it was woven was difficult to focus on. The eyes kept adjusting and readjusting, as if the suit were closer, or perhaps farther, but no clarity was gained, no fine details detected.

"What did you say this was called again?" Oliver asked.

"A Null Suit."

"A fine piece of work," Kendrick commented. And then, picking up the gold bar from the cabinet, he added, "Personally, I'd rather have the gold."

"And I the Null Suit," responded Alistair as he folded it. "That's what made the exchange possible."

Oliver and Alistair shook hands with Kendrick, while Ryan, who was leaning against the wall with his arms folded over his chest, gave them a nod. The two returned to Oliver's jalopy, scrunched inside once again, and Alistair switched on the heater. Oliver, however, paused before he started the engine.

"Do you think we're being observed?" he asked, his eyes scanning the horizons.

Alistair shrugged. "Probably. Someone is out there right now looking at whatever files the tin men have on us."

With a shake of his head and a sigh, Oliver made the engine cough and began the long drive back to the city.

10

After a patch of bad weather, Arcarius almost disappeared, as if someone had pressed a delete key, leaving a blank white page behind. Work crews were sent to fight the blizzard and push the snow back from the government offices, but eventually even these succumbed to the ashen tide. For his part, Alistair was just as happy having snow to cover the eye sores of the city, but he remembered how convenient it had been on Kaldis, most of whose roads and roofs automatically sublimated the snow, with little effort expended by maintenance crews.

The night of the snowstorm, long after Nigel and Mary retired for the night, Alistair stayed up with his sister to watch out the kitchen window as the flakes blanketed the ground. Sipping at steaming drinks, they talked of Katherine's work while one by one the neighboring lights were put out and the snow continued to pile higher and higher. Eventually, it reached and then surpassed the window level, encasing them in a chamber of snow flakes.

It had been a long time since Alistair had spoken so with his sister, and as usual she had more to say than he. He enjoyed listening to her impassioned talk about her scientific work, which currently centered around Flow Theory. It was a scientific field still considered fringe, but the practical applications were staggering should it be proven.

After the storm, Alistair found himself eager to dig Nigel's restaurant out of the white hill around it. He did not realize how restless he had become until he put his muscles to work again. Gerald rushed there from his downtown apartment as soon as the weather permitted and grabbed his own shovel. The new, clean, fresh veneer of the city and the exercise of shoveling combined to lift their spirits, and while they worked they even sang a few songs together, meager voices and paltry sense of melody though they had. Such was the good feeling engendered in Gerald that he did not even blanch when Alistair declined to sing some of the more patriotic songs. Nigel's was back in business before anyone else in the area, these others lacking men as Nigel's sons to excavate their properties.

Later, noses running, cheeks ruddy and palms sore, they went back inside to enjoy some hot chocolate and warm themselves by the fire. As he shared a quiet moment with his brother, sipping away at the chocolate and warming his hands on the hot mug, Alistair felt a sort of quiet peace in Gerald's presence he had not felt since well before he had left for his military service.

He decided one morning to take a walk over Arcarius' new landscape. The city still being buried, and his route taking him through neighborhoods that were empty during the winter, he did not see another soul until he returned. A crowd had gathered in front, and his father was having an animated conversation with one of the men. Quickening his pace, he reached the scene with his teeth clenched and his gaze withering, ready for whatever he might be called upon to do. Though clearly agitated, the crowd hastened to move out of his way, and he soon stood at his father's side.

"…because I'll be damned if you're going to sit on a harvest while my family goes hungry," the man confronting Nigel was saying.

Nigel's expression was not angry; his tone was placating. He held his hands up as if to calm a beast.

"I've got little more than you—" he began but was interrupted.

"Why don't you share what you've got?"

"Why don't you take a couple steps back and guard your tone," suggested Alistair, and the man whirled in anger. When he saw the size of the man confronting him, he reined in his irritation. The crowd hissed and murmured but it did not go beyond that.

"Alistair, I'm Ken Brady," the man grimly, but politely, introduced himself. "I've patronized your father's business for several years now. There's no food in the city. We need what your father's got."

"And I've explained to you we don't have enough to feed half the people here right now," said Nigel. "I have saved a bit for my family and I can't help you."

"There's no food?" Alistair asked without surprise.

"A shipment was due in two days ago," Nigel explained. "When it didn't come, they told us it would be here this morning. It still hasn't arrived."

"What does Gerald say?"

"He's looking into it right now," Nigel said, more to Ken Brady then to Alistair. "There really is nothing I can do for you," he ended with a plea.

"You heard my father," Alistair warned. "Now clear out. And take your mob with you."

"It's not my mob," the man shot back as he walked away. "They're just hungry. If that shipment doesn't come in there's going to be real trouble."

Ken's departure acted as a catalyst, and the crowd dispersed. Nigel shook his head and, placing an arm on his son's shoulder, turned to walk inside.

"The whole city without food?" asked Alistair.

"None that anyone is willing to sell, at any rate. I don't understand it."

"I do," said Alistair in a matter-of-fact tone. "It's happened a million times before in a thousand different places."

"Yeah, I know," his father sighed as they reached the front door. "The State is incompetent."

Once inside, they made for the kitchen where Mary was waiting for them, her expression apprehensive.

"They're gone," said Nigel before she asked.

"Alistair," his mother delicately began, "why don't you stay close to the restaurant for the next few days? Until this blows over."

"That won't be necessary," said Nigel gently and without concern.

"I'll stick around," said Alistair as he sat back in a chair at the table. "I'm not so sure this is going to just blow over."

Nigel joined him as Mary set about preparing a meal now that the crowd was gone. "Why not?" he asked.

"You saw the price of food. The price goes up when demand goes up, or when supply goes down. This particular problem might be due to a mistake at the Transportation Bureau, I don't know. But I can guarantee from what you told me and what I saw in your books that food production is down. The prices the empty shops are charging for food is proof. Did you buy non-perishable food like I told you?"

Nigel nodded. "I bought a whole bunch of spatch," he said, referring to the hard meal made of grain products. First developed for the armed forces, it lasted practically forever and was tasteless enough to mix with anything. Condensed into hard bars, it could be boiled, cooked or eaten raw, and was perfect for storing a lot of calories in a small space. "Cost me an arm and a leg too."

"You'll get your investment back soon enough."

They heard a door open, followed by two feet stomping to shed snow, and a moment later a rosy-cheeked Gerald, his expression as grim as any other, entered the kitchen.

"Damn engines froze on the Metro," he muttered as he walked in and took off his winter apparel. "I had to walk back." He collapsed into a chair with a sigh, leaning his head back and closing his eyes.

"Did you find anything out?" asked Mary.

Gerald prefaced his answer with a another deep sigh. "The shipment is still in Avon. It arrived three days ago and has been sitting there, waiting for a ship with some cargo space." After a pause, he looked at Alistair and said, "I imagine you'll make quite a bit of hay out of this."

"I've got my sickle ready."

"The food will be here by tomorrow. It's a small glitch."

"It's a small glitch for us," retorted Alistair, "because we have food. And we have food because Dad bought some, and he bought some on my advice."

"Should I thank you on my knees?" asked Gerald, putting his head back again and closing his eyes.

"You work at the Transportation Bureau," said Alistair, ignoring his brother's sarcastic remark. "How are shipments handled?"

"What do you mean?" asked Gerald.

"How do you determine what goes where and when?"

Gerald sighed again. "We get request orders from various agencies. We fill out the forms and they go to someone higher up."

"And someone higher up reviews them and plans the shipping schedule?"

"I don't know the details. I imagine it goes something like that."

"Let's assume for a second that civil servants have our good in mind. How do they know where to ship?"

Gerald's voice sounded weary. "Where to ship what?"

"An excellent point! Because there are millions of different things that need to be shipped."

"They can calculate based on their information."

"They collect all sorts of information on the population, don't they?"

"You know they do."

"So they hire lots of workers to collect their data, and they use this to scientifically calculate the population's needs. Then they review the data and review the state of industry… what equipment needs repaired, what needs replaced, who is in possession of what raw materials, who has what partially finished products…and they make decisions for the entire planet, hoping not too many unforeseen circumstances disrupt their plans, like tornadoes, hurricanes, grain rotting, square pegs getting accidentally sent to the round hole factory—"

Gerald lifted his head from the chair and said, "Are you coming to an end?"

"Sounds like a cumbersome, slow system. A businessman just looks at the price of things and he knows what he needs to replace, what he needs to produce…he doesn't have to hire a huge bureau of workers to collect data for him, he just looks at the price. And of course, he doesn't have to calculate how much food it takes to keep a given population alive, he just sells at the market rate to whoever wants to buy."

"It all works so well in theory."

"Now, if we remove the assumption that government is actually full of selfless servants with only the public's good in mind…what if there are people the government doesn't mind starving? What if the government decides to build more guns and make less butter?"

"Then why do people stop using the Free Market if it works so well?"

"People don't discard the Free Market; the State destroys it."

Gerald snorted in derision, but the conversation was ended as Mary set in front of them some steaming plates of spatch of a porridge-like consistency.

"Why don't we eat up and stop the political talk for now," she suggested, sitting down next to Nigel with her own hot bowl. "I added some milk and honey so enjoy it while you can. If that shipment doesn't come in we'll be eating plain spatch until God knows when."

It was amid the occasional slurps of this otherwise silent meal that the door opened once more. Again a pair of feet stomped on the welcome mat in the hallway, and the heavy steps of Oliver were heard, the only non-family member who could, with impunity, enter without a knock.

"My heavens!" gasped Mary when he had entered the kitchen and shown the gash above his left eye. She quickly got up to moisten a towel to apply to his wound.

"Oliver, what happened?" asked Nigel.

"It's a bit rough out there," said the big man with an incongruous grin. "I got stuck in the middle of a food riot." He took a seat at the table while Mary dabbed at his gash with the moist towel.

"I think we should all stay indoors," she said with conviction.

"This is destroying my firm faith in the State," Oliver said with a wink at Alistair.

Alistair grinned and took a bite of spatch while Gerald rolled his eyes.

"Alistair was just saying the same thing," said Gerald. "Would you like some spatch?"

"No thanks," said Oliver, holding up his hands palms out. "I ate recently. I thought I'd drop by to make sure everyone was alright."

"You're the one who looks like he needs help," said Alistair.

"Mean spirited people. Glad I got out of the way before something worse happened."

"I'll get some bandages," Mary said, setting the towel down on the counter and rushing off.

"We had a bit of a rough spot here not long ago," said Nigel. "Alistair showed up just in time."

"The shipment will come in tomorrow and you'll all have forgotten about it in a week," said Gerald. Alistair gave his brother an incredulous look. "Well, maybe Alistair won't forget, but anyone not intent on seeing the down side of everything will."

There was a moment of silence, and then Alistair spoke. "Do you know the Boston Tea Party was provoked by a 2% tax on tea?"

"Never heard of it," Gerald muttered into his bowl.

"It was before the American Empire," Alistair explained. "Great Britain colonized part of North America. They levied a tax of 2% on certain items, and so a few of the colonists crept onto some ships in the harbor and tossed overboard a bunch of British goods subject to the tax. They called it the Boston Tea Party."

"And?"

"About three centuries later the American President signed an order requiring all non-farmers to move into residential zones around the cities. Small villages were leveled, and many people were forcefully removed from their homes."

"What was the point?" asked Nigel.

"The reason they gave was to cut down on oil consumption during the war. That may have been part of it but it also allowed them to register and monitor everyone more easily."

"And what's the relationship with the Boston Tea Party?" asked Gerald with skepticism blatant in his voice.

"In the 18th century a 2% tax caused a rebellion. In the 21st century their descendants were kicked out of house and home and the protests were comparatively mild. It's just interesting to note how constant government oppression can kill people's fighting spirit."

Gerald shook his head and, having finished his meal, got up and set his bowl in the sink.

"But there are limits to what people will stand for," Alistair continued, "when they are faced with starvation."

ॐ ॐ

Stephanie grunted as the man she tried to subdue pushed back into her, squishing her between his body and the brick wall. Reacting without thought, she kicked the back of his knee and, firmly gripping his cuffed hands and seizing the back of his head with the other hand, drove him face first into the snow. He outweighed her and started to come back to his feet, so she grabbed a device from her belt and stuck it in his ribs. The electric shock it produced made his body go rigid and then limp.

She replaced it in its sheath on her belt and lay on top of him, breathing heavily and listening to her heart pound in her ears, feeling the ache of overworked muscles. Then, realizing his face was buried in snow, she grabbed his hair and turned it to the side. Her next act was to fasten another pair of cuffs to his ankles before she rolled him over and flagged down a pair of police officers who were rushing by.

"Give me a hand with this one, will you?" she asked between panting breaths.

"Take a rest, we'll get him."

Grabbing under his arms, the two hoisted him up and took him away. Stephanie sat back in the snow a moment, leaning against the wall, feeling the welt forming on the back of her head from her collision with it a few moments earlier. On the other side of the street, black smoke trickled out of a jagged hole in the brick façade. Two bodies lay still in the snow, waiting to be taken to the morgue. Around one of them the snow was red.

Stephanie came to her feet when Captain Travis approached her. They exchanged nods.

"Did you get a head count?" he asked her.

"Three dead. At least ten seriously wounded."

"I mean on the arrests."

"Not yet, sir. I just finished cuffing one of them."

Travis nodded. "Follow me," he said and walked away.

Stephanie went with him to a tent set up down the street in between a pair of imposing tanks. Inside, the air was warmer and a cuffed prisoner, bloodied, sat in a folding chair in the middle. He was surrounded by at least a dozen large policemen with their meaty arms folded across their chests and their lips curled downwards in disdainful scowls. Stephanie and Travis hung back at the outskirts of the crowd.

"It's just that we were hungry," he was stammering. "When the guy started yelling and throwing bricks...I guess we let it get out of control."

"What happened to this guy?" asked one of the officers.

The man shook his head. "Someone hit him in the face with a brick. He clobbered the guy—he was a huge son of a bitch—I didn't see him after that."

"Did he set off the bomb?"

"I don't know."

Stephanie frowned at this. While the interrogation continued she went to one of the portable computers and accessed the precinct's mainframe. She called up a photograph, printed it, and took it to the man being interrogated, cutting off his interrogator in mid sentence.

"Is this the big guy?"

The man nodded, eager to help out. "Yeah, that's him. That's the guy."

Stephanie took the picture to Travis.

"Have him picked up," he told her.

Stephanie shook her head. "Not yet, sir. I have him under surveillance right now. I'm hoping he is going to lead me to something bigger."

"Why is he under surveillance?"

"He showed up at that specnine house we raided a few days ago. He and a friend."

Travis nodded. "Alright." He took a closer look at the picture. "Wait a minute...Isn't he that rugby player you hang out with?"

Stephanie nodded, blushing. "Yes, sir. I—"

"Stephanie Caldwell," said Travis, tapping a finger on the sheet of paper and using the same voice her father had always used when she was in trouble, "is this something you're up to doing?"

"Absolutely."

"Really? This guy is a friend of yours. Why don't you withdraw from this case and I can give you another."

"That won't be necessary, sir. My duty is to Arcarius and Aldra. If Oliver is breaking the law, he gets no special treatment. You don't need to worry about where my loyalties lie." Her jaw was set and her nostrils were flaring. The blush in her cheeks might have been as much from emotion as from the cold.

Travis gave her a long hard look but eventually nodded. "Keep me up to date," was all he said and then ducked out of the tent.

With her work finished, she declined to return to the precinct headquarters. Instead, she set out for Oliver's apartment but found it empty. This bit of information discovered, she immediately headed for Nigel's. Upon arriving she knocked at the front door and was greeted by Mary Ashley. Following Mary to the kitchen, Stephanie heard voices inside.

"...interesting to note how constant government oppression can kill people's fighting spirit over time." Alistair was saying. As Stephanie rounded the corner, she saw Nigel, Gerald, Alistair and Oliver, his face sporting a recent gash over his left eye, sitting at the kitchen table. Gerald was just getting up to carry his empty bowl to the sink.

"But there are limits to what people will stand for," Alistair continued. "when they are faced with starvation."

"You might just be right about that," said Stephanie as she entered. Everyone turned to face her. Mary started to bandage Oliver's his wound, and Oliver eyed the newcomer apprehensively. Returning his humorless gaze, Stephanie took a seat at the table.

"What happened to your face?" she asked.

"I cut myself shaving," he replied, his usual cheer quite absent. "Are you a tin man investigating or is my friend Stephanie here with me?"

"Your friend Stephanie is an officer. Does this make you nervous?"

Nigel jumped in. "Would you like something to eat, Stephanie?" Without waiting for an answer, he got up and spooned some spatch into a bowl and set it down in front of her.

Stephanie thanked him and ate it with gusto, not having realized how hungry she was, but while she ate her eyes kept drifting back to Oliver and Alistair.

11

The sun set on a dark city conserving energy. The wind swept through the streets, howling and shifting the piles of snow. In a few windows some candles flickered, but no electric lights were permitted save for in some high level bureaus where the government's planners stayed up preparing the future. Only for heating was electricity permitted, and even then there were rolling blackouts lasting for an hour at a time. Still the city went without its shipment of food.

Out at sea, many miles distant, the lights of a ship flickered on the water. Alistair observed it from a window in his father's main dining room, part way up the seaward side of Tanard's Mountain. Alistair's reflection in the window met his forehead as he leaned up against the glass pane, a thin bit of material separating the warmth of within from the chill from without. The room was lit by several dozen candles providing, along with a roaring fire in the fireplace, a soft yet even illumination for the many people now gathered there. As if under the influence of the light, the conversations were in low murmurs so that a steady yet gentle wave of sound permeated the room.

I wonder if our food is coming on that ship, Alistair grumbled to himself as he raised a glass to his lips and tasted his gin mix. Turning from the window, he found the table with his friends and went to it. His father invited guests, including many government officials, for a meal of spatch and odds and ends left over in their pantries. Alistair warned his father against depleting his supply of spatch, but Nigel had made up his mind. Making the most of it, Alistair asked permission to invite his friends, and Nigel agreed, consenting also to allow Gerald and Katherine some guests.

When he got to his seat, Jack, who had imbibed his fair share of the liquor provided, was carelessly gesticulating as he told his friends a story. A bit of his drink sloshed out of the glass and onto the table, but he didn't notice.

"I've never seen anything like it. Listen to this," he slurred. "Oliver and I were assigned to clean up crew—"

"You have to tell them what that is," Henry advised, giving Jack a poke in the ribs.

"Oh yeah. It's…uh…it's clean up crew. When everyone heads south for the winter we have to secure all the equipment and things like that. Anyway, Oliver and I were on clean up crew, and they left us to secure an entire storage facility by ourselves."

"It had already been pretty much finished," Henry interrupted.

Jack made a slow turn to face his companion. "I was going to tell them that."

"Tell them what?"

"What you just said."

"What did I just say?"

"About the storage facility."

"That's what I'm trying to get you to tell them about."

Jack blinked once and shook his head. A couple snickers were stifled as he returned to his tale.

"So the storage facility was left to me and Oliver."

"And it had already been partially prepared," Henry advised.

"Can I tell my story?"

"The facility is too big for you two to secure all by yourselves."

"I know that!"

"But they don't. That's why you need to tell them."

"I'm going to."

"It's like the time I was given a whole file cabinet to organize by that supervisor...you remember her."

Jack's face split into a stupid grin. "Yeah. She was nice."

"I fixed you two up," Henry slyly said with an elbow to Jack's ribs.

Jack smiled again, even more stupidly than before. "I should stop by and see how she's doing." After a moment he popped out of his reverie. "Where was I?"

"I think," Henry said, "you had just got to the part where your supervisor was counting the checks again."

Jack frowned, uncertain, scratching the back of his head as if in an attempt to get his brain working properly. "Was that where I was?"

"I believe so."

"Oh. Well, anyway," Jack resumed, his enthusiasm reduced by a nagging feeling that something was not quite right, "he counted the check receipts again, and we're still three short. And of course mine was one of the ones missing. So I had to wait two extra days before I got paid."

"That's terrible!" said Henry, nearly managing a straight face.

"Actually, my allotment came on time, but the receipt for it got lost. So my money was there, I just didn't know it."

"A beautiful story, Jack," said Oliver, raising his glass as if to toast.

All the friends followed suit, even Henry, who had finally broken into laughter. They touched glasses and sipped their drinks. Setting his back down, Jack suspiciously eyed Henry but said nothing.

Alistair allowed his attention to wander to his father who was busy going from table to table, shaking hands with the bureaucrats and politicians, a smile on his face that never left. Alistair knew what a genuine smile on his father's face looked like, however, and he did not see one at the moment.

"So this event is part charity and part pragmatism," commented Oliver, who was sitting next to Alistair, as he too observed Nigel's efforts.

Alistair just shook his head.

"What I want to know," said Stephanie, attempting to establish a general conversation over the various murmurs around the table, "is what everyone's plans are when they extend the draft." She posed it to everyone, but her eyes were on Oliver and Alistair.

"Let's hope we don't have to find out," said Oliver, avoiding her gaze by taking a chug from his cup.

"Oh, come on. With the Realists in power? You've heard them talking. There's a war on and the draft is going to be extended. In fact, I think everyone is going to be enlisted in the war effort in some fashion."

"Here's to hoping you're wrong," the big man insisted, raising his glass again before tipping it to his lips and draining it.

"You know I'm right. So what are your plans? Alistair? I imagine you'll be in high demand."

At that precise moment, three women and a man entered the dining hall with string instruments in hand. After doffing their winter coats and shaking the snow off, they took their places to the side of the bar, removed their instruments from their cases and softly played. Alistair's eyes wandered from his intent interrogator to the musicians.

"Let's listen to them play," he suggested and turned his seat around, presenting Stephanie with his back.

"I don't want to be shipped off to some other planet to fight a war," muttered Henry.

"You and me and Oliver will be shipped south to work in the mines, I bet," said Jack.

"Don't count on it," said Oliver. "They'll get old folks to do that. We're going to Kaldis to fight on the front lines."

Katherine approached their table. Her smile, as she passed by guests, was a faint imitation of Nigel's as he glad-handed bureaucrats. But whereas Nigel's smile was enough to fool all but those who knew him best, Katherine never managed to erase the worry lines, nor make the stress disappear. When she reached Alistair's table she did not bother with a preamble.

"Mom wants some help serving the spatch." She followed that with, "Hello everyone."

Nodding, Alistair rose from his seat and followed his sister to the kitchen where a large cauldron of spatch was boiling. Mary was standing over it with a paddle-size spatula and stirring in slow circles while Gerald was testing the concoction. Dissatisfied, he grabbed a container and poured in a little more cinnamon.

"Don't add any more," said Mary. "We don't have time." Looking up, she saw her daughter and youngest son joining them. "I hope we have enough," she said, managing a tired smile.

"It's free," said Alistair. "I'll personally deal with anyone who has the nerve to complain about the quantity."

"Perhaps you might care to go easy on certain officials here tonight," suggested Gerald coldly while he put the cap back on the cinnamon container. "Unless you prefer to be homeless."

Alistair opened his mouth to reply but Katherine shoved a tray into his gut with enough force that he might have expelled some air had he a more civilian midsection.

"Let it go. Give everyone a bowl, and then come back for some clean glasses."

Alistair took the tray, stacked some empty bowls on it, and went from seat to seat, setting the bowls down in front of their guests. The atmosphere was buoyed somewhat by the music played by the quartet, and the conversations were growing louder accordingly. Alistair briefly exchanged a few pleasantries with relatives and friends, endured a few introductions to people he did not know, and said nothing at all to the politicians. As he went back to the kitchen for more bowls, his mother came out with some fresh glasses, followed by Katherine with a pitcher of water, their only beverage aside from liquor.

In the kitchen, Gerald was scooping some of the spatch into a smaller kettle. "I'll need your help carrying this," he said.

Alistair stood next to the kettle to wait until Gerald had finished filling it with spatch. "What do you know about the draft?"

Gerald did not divert his gaze from his work but he answered, "As much as you. It's obviously needed for the war. How extensive it will be I don't know. Probably it's coming soon."

"The government can't even feed us adequately and they're ready to send us off to fight a war?"

"Grab the handle on your side and lift together," was Gerald's response.

ॐॐ

When Alistair made it back to his table, Elizabeth was showing off her new firearm. They were outlawed on Aldra without a special permit, a permit everyone understood no ordinary citizen could acquire. Yet there she was, producing from her purse a small, sleek little pistol that fired concussion charges powerful enough to kill a man with no armor on.

Her friends were slack-jawed in shock.

"How the hell did you get a permit for that?" asked Oliver, only just managing to keep his jaw off the floor.

"With the riots and everything I thought I'd need it," she said defensively. "Especially in the winter when the city's practically empty."

"I didn't ask why. I asked how."

Elizabeth passed the gun around, starting with Stephanie. "You just have to know who to ask."

Stephanie held the gun lightly in her hand. She passed it on to Greg with a nod of her head. "That will do the trick. But Elizabeth," she hesitated only a second, "I'm a Civil Guard officer. I have to ask for the permit."

Elizabeth happily complied, proffering it with pride. Stephanie gave it a glance and nodded her head, handing the permit back.

"The gun's yours."

When the gun had been passed around, Elizabeth reclaimed it and put it back in her purse.

"So how did you get the permit?" asked Oliver again. "You aren't that beautiful."

Elizabeth gave him a withering look. "Please, Oliver. I need it for protection. Let it be."

"We could all use one for protection," said Alistair. "You have to be connected to get one, though."

"Aloysius," said Oliver, his hands dropping to the table top with a pair of thuds. His face darkened several shades. "That's how you got it."

Elizabeth didn't react except to blush. Oliver shook his head with a grimace but didn't pursue the inquiry.

Little more was said. Oliver was brooding, and his dark mood infected the others, just as his jovial ones did. After the meal was finished and the guests sat around with a last cup of brandy or other spirit, one of the politicians stood up and proposed a toast. The musicians stopped in the middle of their song, and conversation in the hall died down.

"A toast to a fine evening, with a fine and generous host," he boldly proclaimed, his strong and rich voice just the sort to convince complete strangers he was qualified to run their lives. Nigel smiled, a genuine one, and bowed his head humbly. "And a patriot," the council-man added. "Two of his children work for Aldra, and the third recently returned from a four cycle tour of duty on Kaldis." With his glass, the man indicated Alistair, sitting at the far end of the dining hall. The guests all applauded, but Alistair ducked his head behind Oliver and mutely stared at the table, his cheeks as red as cherries.

As the applause died down, the man continued. "And now Nigel himself is called upon to contribute to our nation." A pause for dramatic effect met with silence. "His restaurant sits on an important location, within easy reach of the mines and not far from the space port. He has been called upon to sell his restaurant to the city, and the deal was authorized this morning."

The politicians and bureaucrats clapped, but few who knew Nigel well did more than lightly touch hands a couple times, their expressions pained. For his part, Alistair sat in shock. He looked for his father and found him, seated with Mary and some relatives. Nigel's expression was a mix of embarrassment, anger and shock; not very different from his youngest son's.

"That son of a bitch," Alistair whispered fiercely, feeling his pulse rise and his limbs shake. He was oddly aware he spit some saliva from his mouth with the force of his curse and it landed on the back of a man sitting in front of him. Oliver grabbed his friend's forearm and held him in his seat. Alistair had not even realized he had begun to stand up. "That goddamn son of a bitch!" he said more loudly, and a few nearby heads turned.

"Save it for later," Oliver cautioned with urgency. "Don't do this now. I'll help you do it later, but right now calm yourself." Grabbing Alistair more firmly, he guided him back to down to his seat.

"He of course will be reimbursed for his sacrifice," the politician intoned. "But we all know Nigel and his dedication. The pride he feels for Aldra I am sure he considers payment enough."

"I am going to slit throats," Alistair quietly raged, his jaw clenched. "This is my goddamn house! I am going to slit throats!" Oliver squeezed his arm again.

"Ladies and gentlemen," concluded the politician, pointing a hand towards the host, "Nigel Ashley. A true Aldran patriot." The politician clapped, and the applause was taken up by the others, though there was no soul in it. Nigel himself rose uncertainly and managed a weak smile. He quickly sat back down—or his knees gave out, the result was the same—and just as quickly the applause died down. Mrs. Ashley pursed her lips and tears threatened to run down her cheeks.

What followed would have been an uncomfortable silence the musicians could have filled with a melody. Most of the guests would have sat quietly for a moment, but eventually would have recovered enough to accompany the music with a bit of conversation. This was not to be, for at that moment there came the sound of an explosion, distant but close enough that the silverware rattled on the table. The crowd gasped in unison and all heads turned to the windows.

Alistair was the first out of his seat and up against the windowpane, but dozens of people followed him. Below lay the cityscape, mostly hidden by darkness save for a spot where a tall building a few miles away had burst into flames. It seemed to have exploded from within, and burning debris was scattered around and threatened to set fire to surrounding structures. The guests, after some initial gasps, watched wordlessly before breaking into various hushed conversations.

The explosion served as a signal the evening was over. Some remained at the window with Alistair, but others made for their coats, planning to get a closer view as they went home. Stephanie was first out the door and headed straight for the scene. Others lagged behind, stopping to say goodbye to Nigel and to thank him for the meal. Gerald also took off, and Alistair considered it but ultimately decided to hang back and wait for news, preferring to be with his parents. Oliver wanted to stick around for a while, but Elizabeth insisted she wanted to go, so he left with her. Jack and Henry also left.

A few minutes and many hurried goodbyes later the room was almost empty. Gregory, Katherine and Alistair sat before the expansive windows, gazing out at the scene as emergency crews responded. Though hidden from view, they could see their red, blue and yellow lights painting the middle and upper stories of the surrounding buildings. Nigel and Mary looked on for a while, quite overcome by the events of the evening, but then turned to cleaning up the mess left behind by their guests. When Alistair, his friend and his sister noticed this, they assisted. Nothing was said. Instead, Nigel moved listlessly about, looking like a man who had lost himself. Mary, an automaton, concentrated on clearing the tables and so managed not to cry. For his part, Alistair wanted to talk to his father, but couldn't think of how to start. He remained silent and, having gathered the last few dirty bowls, entered the kitchen to find Gregory speaking with his mother.

"Thank you for the meal, Mrs. Ashley," he said. "Only you can make spatch taste good."

Mary managed a meager smile.

"I was wondering…the hospital has run out of food. I'm sure I'm going to be called in a few moments…Could I take a few bars of spatch back with me?"

"Oh, of course you can, Gregory," Mary said, patting Alistair's friend on the cheek. "I'll wrap some up for you." With that, she left for the pantry.

Alistair set down the dishes and Gregory turned at the sound. "Alistair." There was a moment of silence. Finally, he managed, "I'm sorry about…about your house."

"I am too."

"Should I say something to your dad?"

Alistair shook his head. "I don't even know what to say."

Gregory lowered his gaze and nodded. "There really isn't much I could say, I guess."

Alistair grimaced. "Saying is for politicians. That's all they're good at and that's all they do. I am so sick of words." Gregory looked sharply at his friend, concerned by his tone. "I think words have no power unless they're untrue. I think words are ignored unless they're convenient. Words are either foul breath coming from a liar's mouth or unheeded noise. Words can wreck a whole planet if they're deceitful enough. I spent four cycles learning how to kill because of someone's words. I've had enough of words and of saying and of talking. I'll fill up your hospital with lying politicians and greedy, jealous, petty men before I try to talk sense to anyone again."

Alistair became aware his chest was heaving. He took a deep breath to calm himself and then turned on his heel and left. Gregory, taken aback by what he heard, and not entirely sure he could write it off as transitory anger, watched his friend leave with a sick feeling in his stomach.

12

Alistair firmly gripped the edge of the roof and hoisted himself up. He stood still for a moment, a black, indistinct figure in his Null Suit. The thin material hugged his form from head to toe, and a mask was pulled down from the hood to cover his face so that not a bit of skin could be seen. Instead of slots for his eyes, there were two small, round caps of a plastic like material opaque on the outside but transparent from the inside. Had anyone looked in his direction, had they been close enough to see in the darkness, they would have seen a blur if they had seen anything at all.

He walked to the other side of the roof, naked under the Null Suit yet perfectly warm. The bitter cold wind blowing all around him, sending snow and bits of ice flying past, did not penetrate the suit. As he came to the edge, he looked out and saw, a few blocks away, the remains of the building blown up earlier that night.

Though it was still smoking, he could see no flames. It remained standing, though the front façade was gone. Parked all around it were tin cans and other vehicles with flashing lights. Dozens of figures moved about, going through the motions of an investigation. Armed men formed a ring around the area, many with scanners. These did not frighten Alistair. He knew no waves would bounce off his suit and return with a signal. Heat detectors would not spot him, nor any sort of movement detector.

He lingered there, surveying the scene, glorying in his invisibility, almost taunting the policemen below. A sneer crept onto his lips and he contained an urge to spit over the edge.

Turning, he raced off into the night, flying over the rooftops, leaping from edge to edge. Then, as suddenly as he started running, he stopped and descended, using the gripping material on the hands and feet to aid him as he clambered down from window ledge to window ledge until once again he stood on the snow covered ground. Looking around, he located the street he wanted and nimbly ran to it, accompanied only by the howl of the night wind. Preferring to remain in the shadows where his suit made him absolutely invisible, Alistair hopped from dark bend to darker corner to darkest alley. For never more than an instant at a time was he to be found in the middle of the street.

And then he arrived. The building before him, ten stories high, was as nondescript as most other apartment buildings. The façade was flat with only the front double doors and windows providing any sort of detail. On the sides there were balconies of respectable size, though during the winter months many were empty. Alistair disappeared in the alley next to it and stopped halfway, looking up at a balcony three stories above.

He strode to it and, grabbing the drainpipe, climbed. He placed his toe in a small crack. He grabbed at an exposed brick where the mortar had worn away just enough to offer a ledge. He leapt into the air and grabbed the railing enclosing the first balcony. In this manner he scaled the side of the edifice; before three minutes elapsed he was standing on the third story balcony. A broken chair lay against the wall at the far end. Cupping his hands around his eyes, an action of habit the goggles of the Null Suit made unnecessary, he pressed his face to the glass and peered into the dark interior.

Satisfied, he reached into a small pouch sewn into the thigh of the Suit and withdrew a device like a hockey puck but half the size. This particular device was reported destroyed in an operation on Kaldis. Placing it flat on the glass near the handle, he slowly traced a circle, leaving a thin line in its wake. He again placed it flat against the glass but this time in the center of the circle he had made. The puck gripped the glass, and when he pulled, it brought the circular portion of the glass with it, cut neatly away from the pane.

Replacing the puck in his pouch and tossing the glass on the snow at his feet, he reached inside, unlocked the porch door and opened it, closing the door after he entered. The wind made a whistling sound as it poured through the newly cut hole, so he grabbed a small pillow off of a couch near him and stuffed it into the opening. The whistling ceased, leaving only the muffled sound of the wind outside.

His heart beating furiously now, Alistair took stock of his surroundings. The building itself was old and showed it. Like the wrinkles and minor infirmities which for a time are marks of respect and wisdom but which, with greater age, pass from respect to pity, and from wisdom to senility, the defects of age in this building had passed from venerable to decrepit. Even so, it was a well-covered decrepitude. In one corner of the room stood a clock as tall as a man, its frame carven oak and stained a robust dark brown. The crack in the wall it covered only just peaked out from the top. A connected room to the left sported a long dining table, also carven of oak and stained. The furniture was generally impeccable, and the worn wooden floors were mostly covered with ornate rugs not so old as to have lost their cushioned fullness and softness.

On an end table by the couch stood a framed picture with a family of five headed by the councilman who had dined on spatch at his father's home and had so praised Nigel for his patriotism while announcing his sacrifice. He briefly considered breaking it.

Moving down a hallway without a definite destination, his footsteps were soft whispers producing no echo to disturb sleeping ears. He entered a study and scrutinized it without disturbing the contents. Finally, he came to a picture on the wall. It was a 2D photo of the capital building in Rendral, at night, in all its ostentatious and many-storied majesty, a capital building designed to impress and to project power. Gently grabbing hold of the frame, he lifted it from the wall and smiled in triumph at the safe behind.

Once more he withdrew the puck-like device from his thigh pouch but this time he placed the thin edge of it up against the safe handle. The metal softened as if melting, but no heat was generated. The handle drooped at its base, still without heat, and eventually he grabbed it and tore it free, sending a few drops of the metal, like melted wax, flying onto other parts of the room.

Now replacing the puck, he withdrew a set of tools and had an easy time opening the safe. No public official in a government such as Aldra's could entrust all his wealth to a bank regulated by the State; they preferred not to have to account for it should they be required. With no other knowledge of him save that he was a public official, Alistair knew the man had this safe. It was only a matter of locating it.

There were gold coins, many of them old and most foreign. He helped himself to these, placing them in a small pouch of thin material. When the pouch was full, he drew tight the drawstrings and put it back in his thigh pouch. There was jewelry as well, and he grabbed those items which he could easily carry. His thigh pouch was nearly bulging with new contents.

It was beyond his ability to castigate in exact proportion to guilt. Probably there was any number of guilty parties whom he would never discover, but he was not going to let his imperfect information, a product of the secrecy with which the State conducted its affairs, absolve guilty government parties of responsibility. That some would go unpunished was not a reason for all to go unpunished. That some might be punished in excess of their culpability in the matter was a risk for which they themselves, because of their clandestine manner of operating, were responsible. It was not as if the theft of Nigel's house and restaurant were the only sin for which they were guilty and indebted to Arcarians in general and Alistair's family in particular.

As he slipped back out the porch door and clambered back down to the street below, his thigh pouch laden with a more suitable down payment for his father's restaurant and his body buffeted by the omnipresent wind, he grimly reflected on how most Aldrans would have labeled him the thief and the councilman the victim.

❧ ❧

Rounding the bend in the road and coming into sight of Nigel's, Alistair suddenly tensed and his heart pounded. He was in the middle of the street, having grown a bit careless as he neared his destination. Candlelight shone weakly from the kitchen window, despite the hour. It was not unlike his mother to rise in the middle of the night to get something to drink, but she did not bother wasting candles for it. His searching gaze, seeing gray where a normal eye would see only blackness, quickly detected the Civil Guard ensconced in shadow, hiding across the street. Though Alistair must have appeared to him only as an indistinct and dark blur, his gaze was fixed on his form. Alistair could even see the squinting eyes and the way he extended his neck to get a better glimpse.

He darted into a side alley between two houses, knowing the officer would be hurrying to the spot where he saw him. Fortunately, the snow covering the street was so densely packed he left no footprints, and as long as he kept to the shadows in the corners, he was confident no one would catch him.

Tracing a path through side streets, he came to the cliff overlooking the ocean to the south. This was prime real estate and politicians and a few business owners owned most of the houses here. He crept through their back yards, following the cliff, until he came to the back of his father's property. From his new perspective he could no longer see the kitchen window, and everything in the back was dark. Pausing a moment to scan the area, his keen vision did not detect anyone else, so he emerged from behind a row of bushes and advanced.

As he neared the wall, comprised mainly of the large window of the dining room, Alistair gained a view of the front and saw two Civil Guard, automatic guns hanging from straps on their shoulders, conferring with one another. The wind covered their words, but he already knew the subject matter. He changed his course and instead went behind the building, between it and the cliff's edge. He passed the dining room and reached the central section where Nigel offered his other entertainments.

The odd construction of the restaurant made his goal easier. He entered a small alley-like opening, the result of two sections built in proximity to each other, and scaled the wall by placing his back against it and using his feet to push against the opposite wall. It was a technique he used many times during his service off, and the Null Suit with its gripping palms and soles made it easier.

He reached the roof of one section in a matter of seconds, and from there he walked to another part, a second story section, and used a similar technique to scale the next wall, although this time the walls were not opposite one another, instead meeting at a ninety degree angle. This was much more difficult, even with the Null Suit, but his finely trained body made the ascent.

Now two stories above the ground, he stood higher than all but the observatory whose hemispherical dome towered before him. This he declined to climb, preferring instead to skirt around it and head for the far eastern section of the complex, which was the Ashley house itself. The going was a bit trickier there, as the roof of the house was slanted and sported some ice, but the surefooted marine made it without incident to his bedroom window.

The lock had broken long ago and never been replaced, so he lifted the window and slipped inside. He did not dare take off his suit in his room, which was no doubt being monitored. Instead, opening his bedroom door, he listened and heard the hum of voices downstairs in the kitchen. As silently as he could, he crept down the upstairs hallway, avoiding the spots he knew would creak, and descended the stairs leading to the family room. The candlelight from the kitchen cast faint illumination, and he hugged the wall to avoid detection. He could hear his mother, father and one other speaking.

"Perhaps if you could tell us why you need to speak to him…" suggested Nigel. There was no answer. "I agree it's strange he's not here…it's not against the law to go out at night. Maybe he just wanted a walk to clear his head."

The conversation continued as Alistair slipped through the family room and down the short hallway that passed the foyer and led to the restaurant. Passing through the double doors, he turned immediately to his left when he detected the soft sound of treading feet coming down the main hallway. He crept back into the smaller side corridor and waited.

A soft glow of light preceded his sister as she held a lit candle in front of her. Her face was tired, her hair disheveled and she wore only a light nightgown. She passed by the corridor without a glance, went into the Ashley house and was gone.

Alistair continued down his corridor until he came to a large metal door locked with an electronic system. He typed in the code and opened the door before slipping into the supply room. After grabbing a length of rope, he left the room and relocked the door. As he made his way back to his room, he heard his sister speaking.

"I can't say for sure he isn't here; it's a big building. But I can't find any trace of him. He's usually in the observatory if he's not watching a 2D."

He ascended the stairs as quickly as he could without compromising his silence. Back in his bedroom, he grabbed his clothes and stuffed them into a sack. Reaching under the bed, he grabbed his precious bars of gold and put them in the sack. He grabbed the gold coins from his thigh pouch, as well as the folded and now wrinkled documents, and tossed them in, as well as some books from his dresser. Then he tied one end of the rope around one of the thick wooden bedposts at each corner of his mattress and chucked the other end out the window.

Once outside and on the ground, he scampered to the cliff's edge and got down on his belly, letting his legs slide over the side. When his searching toes found their familiar foothold, he descended the face of the cliff until, several meters down, he came to a ledge wide enough to stand on. He shuffled east until he came to a cave whose entrance was difficult to detect even in sunlight. It was small, too small for a grown Alistair to fit in comfortably, but it did afford an ideal hiding place for his valuables.

First taking his clothes out of the bag, he doffed his Null Suit and stood naked in the freezing air as he placed the suit in the bag. He paused only a moment to glance at the tattoo on his left pectoral before putting the bag of valuables into the small cave. The tattoo was an ornately drawn circle with eight regularly spaced points around it. Above each point was a small star, also ornately drawn. He considered the tattoo with his usual mix of pride and regret. He had not wanted it, but it was not optional in the program in which he participated.

A sudden gust of wind reminded him how cold it was and he quickly threw his clothes over his freezing skin covered in goose bumps. When he was dressed again, he clambered back up the cliff face and back to the rope hanging from his bedroom window. He blew on his now cold hands before grasping the rope and climbing up. No sooner had he reentered his bedroom and, after untying the rope, tucked it neatly under his dresser than the door burst open and in charged two Civil Guardsmen.

"Alistair Ashley 3nn?" asked the one who had come in first.

Looking past them, Alistair saw the concerned faces of his father, mother and sister still in the hallway. "That's me," he confirmed, fighting to make sure his breathing was steady. "Who else would you find here in the dead of night?"

"Would you mind explaining where you have been?"

"I would actually. It's not really your concern where I was or what I was doing." So saying he tossed his shirt into the corner and, sitting on the edge of the bed, took his shoes off.

"I'm going to leave here either with a good explanation or a prisoner in handcuffs," the officer informed him.

Tossing a shoe into the corner with his shirt, Alistair replied, "I was out doing some exercises. As you may know, I was off for the last four years with the marines on Kaldis. I'm no longer in the service, but I would like to maintain—"

"I know all about your service. Your mother has been explaining it to me for the last hour. I don't believe you were out doing exercises."

Alistair tossed the second shoe at the first and stood up to take his pants off. "You can believe what you like. When I break a law, feel free to come and arrest me. Until then, perhaps you'd care to leave me in peace so I can get a good night's sleep. Why the hell do you care where I was?"

⇔

Stephanie was startled out of sleep by the ring of her communicator. She rolled over in her bed, grabbed it off her bedside table and put it up to her ear.

"This is Stephanie," she said with more of a croak than a voice. She listened without speaking for a moment and then sat up, fully awake now. "What do you mean disappeared?..."

Why the hell did you go in the house?…Because he knows he's being watched now…Did you find anything in his room?…"

Stephanie sighed and got out of bed, setting her feet on the cold floor. "He's obviously smuggled something from Kaldis." She listened for a moment more before grimacing in defeat. "Fine. Keep close watch…it won't be in the house. They'll be moving out soon, so he'll likely try to get it then…No, nothing else. I'll talk to you tomorrow."

Sighing again, Stephanie hung up and tossed the communicator back onto the bedside table. She went to the bedroom window of her tenth story apartment and pulled back the curtain. There, off to the south, was the dark hulk of Tanard's Mountain. The lights from the space port at the top shown several different colors, but no ships were taking off or landing. Below the space port all was darkness. The so-called mountain was discernible mainly by the stars it blotted out from the sky. Somewhere, nearly halfway up and on the far side, was a friend whom she would soon put in jail.

If the thought made her sad or hesitant, her blank expression did not reveal it.

13

When the long awaited supply ship finally arrived, it was with great disappointment that the workers unloading the vessel noted how little food there was. While the ship was docked at Avon, the mayor skimmed off a portion of the cargo. The men doing the skimming had helped themselves as well. When all was said and done, only about a quarter of the food meant for Arcarius actually reached the hungry population.

At the same time, a rumor spread among Arcarians that a great quantity of food was stored at the Mayor's Palace. The source of the rumor was unknown, but it turned out to be true. A large and unruly crowd gathered outside the Palace and grew in size and animosity until the right spark set them off. They stormed the Palace, swept in like a flood and quickly discovered the stored food. What was not immediately consumed was taken. Order was eventually restored, though not without considerable casualties, and ill will festered in the city.

On the national level, it was announced that the draft would be expanded to choose from all able-bodied citizens between the ages of eighteen and fifty-five. The government also announced its privatization plan. Transportation, communication and media, health care, education, law enforcement, national defense, minting and science/research and development would continue under the government's control. Most of manufacturing, agriculture and resource extraction would be privatized with State regulation. Severe penalties were prescribed for any black market activity, and a new secret police force, to be called the Aldran Regulators and Overseers, or ARO, was formed. Those industries too small to come under national control, mainly service providers such as repairmen or landscapers, were left to the cities to regulate. Most of the municipalities created Independent Contractor Guilds, and all independent workers were to register with the appropriate local Guild.

Finally, and perhaps most stunningly, Rendral announced that for the first time in decades, trade with other systems, a supervised trade under strictly regulated terms, would resume. Aldra would trade its surplus for what the planners deemed it lacked. Also, the Incarcerator would be allowed to return to Aldra.

The Incarcerator was a company that ran prison ships that took a planet's hardest criminals and deposited them on Srillium, the prison planet, an unindustrialized world the company made sure stayed that way. President Mortimer Duquesne explained that too many resources went into the prison system, that exporting the prisoners would free up manpower and other resources for the war with Kaldis.

**

"I think these are revolutionary times," Elizabeth declared by way of a summary of the discussion she, Alistair and Oliver were having.

Alistair found himself, for the first time in a long while, in a booth at a restaurant not his father's. Not blessed with the same prime location, it nevertheless had a view of the harbor to its south. On the other side of the restaurant one could see the taller downtown buildings.

The three friends, however, were in the noisy and crowded central section, bombarded by a coarse, electrified music and without a view of city or harbor.

Elizabeth continued, pointing a finger at Alistair, "And I don't care what you think. These are important times and big happenings." She sipped at her drink with a stubborn look on her face.

"What do you mean by that?"

"Oh, you're always a contrarian. You always have some story about how this and that has happened before a dozen times on twenty different planets."

"How could it happen a dozen times on twenty different planets?" asked Oliver.

"You know what I mean," was her response along with a slap on his shoulder.

"Well, this time I agree with you," said Alistair. "Although it has happened before. And more than a dozen times."

"See what I mean?"

"But I agree," he hurried on. "This is, unfortunately, a momentous event."

Elizabeth picked at her food with a self-satisfied expression. "It actually makes sense from an astrological point of view."

"I doubt that very much."

"Still a contrarian. I mean it. I was reading yesterday how…I forget…something about the Terran moon being aligned with one of the constellations or something. Anyway, the last dynasty of the Terran Empire fell during the same alignment."

Alistair snorted. "The Hopfeldt dynasty fell during a currency crisis brought on by decades of inflation brought on by decades of warfare. I don't think the stars—"

"This is exactly what I'm talking about. Stop showing off," she ordered and threw a crumb at him. Oliver laughed. "And by the way, how many times do I have to flick my hair back before you notice my new earrings?"

"One more time, at least."

With an exaggerated sigh, Elizabeth flicked her silky brunette hair back again and exposed the earrings to Alistair's view.

"OK. I noticed them."

"Do you like them?"

"No."

Elizabeth collapsed in defeat and Oliver broke into uncontrollable guffaws.

"Alistair, at some point you are going to have to learn how to please a woman," she admonished.

"How do I please a woman?"

"You can start by complimenting her clothing and jewelry."

"Even if I don't like them?"

"It doesn't matter whether you like them or not. Just say you do."

"If it doesn't matter if I like them, why are you asking my opinion?"

Oliver's laughter redoubled in intensity. Fixing a stern gaze on the jolly giant, Elizabeth warned, "There are consequences for this sort of behavior." She turned back to Alistair. "Be polite and diplomatic for once. Just say they look nice and make me happy."

He frowned as he reconsidered the earrings. Finally, he said, "I think that never in human history has an earring had a nicer place to hang. In truth, if an earring's job is to enhance the beauty of her who wears it, there is very little any earring could accomplish given such a task as these two are saddled with. I pity their inadequacy."

Oliver brought his heavy open palm down on top of the table. "That was excellent! God damn, that was excellent!"

Elizabeth brought her cup to her lips and drank once more. Upon setting it back down, she said, "That will do." She leaned in and gave Oliver a kiss on the lips. "I'm going to leave before he starts showing off again." Elizabeth leaned forward and gave Alistair a kiss on the cheek and then got up and made her way through the rows of tables and booths to the exit. More than a few male heads turned to watch the sway of her hips.

"The only good thing about her leaving is watching her go," Oliver wistfully commented and the two friends shared a chuckle. "OK, you can hide it from her but not from me. What's bothering you, and why are we sitting here in the middle of all this noise?"

Alistair's expression became more serious as well, and he leaned forward on the table to speak with his friend.

"I'm being followed, and I think you probably are too."

Nodding, Oliver replied, "I figured. I haven't caught them yet but—"

"Also…I'm leaving Arcarius."

This elicited a look of stupefaction from Oliver. "What?"

"Tonight. I have to go. I had to hide my Null Suit. That's the reason I know I'm being followed. If I try to get at it again and they catch me I'll be arrested."

"So you're leaving it here?"

Alistair shook his head. "No, Katherine's going to get it for me. I'm going to lose my tail—I hope—get the suit from her and then I'm off."

"How are you leaving?"

"Assuming this noise is covering our conversation and they're not waiting for me at the pier, I've purchased a trip across the channel to Avon."

Oliver leaned back in his seat, his bulk nearly upsetting the table. He regarded his friend with an almost hurt expression. Finally, he nodded. "Stay in touch if you can, little buddy."

"You know I will."

"What are you going to do?"

"Fight. There was almost an uprising here recently. People are fed up with it all. They're myopic, they're ignorant, they're misled…but they still have a sense of when something is this wrong. The food crisis almost got it started. The war is going to make things worse. Somewhere there's a keg of gunpowder that needs a spark."

"Maybe you could do that here."

Alistair shook his head. "It's not going to start here. Even if it does, Arcarius is important for mining, but that's it. No one is going to care. Rendral will just crush it and reopen the mines. No, it has to be done somewhere else, somewhere more central."

Oliver was thoughtful for a moment. "Maybe."

"Anyway, the fewer people who know the better. Wait until I'm gone, and then tell everyone I said goodbye."

"Anything else?"

"Actually, there is a favor I need to ask you."

࿐࿐

A Civil Guard officer sat in the back of a long white van viewing a series of small projection displays. He wore a headset with a small microphone extending over his lips, and a piece in his left ear. The projection displays showed various city scenes, and at the center of each was a plain-clothes officer who, in the display, was no more than a centimeter in height. Though the displays were in true color, a figure in one of the displays glowed red. As that figure left the building he was in—and thus the reach of one projection recorder—he appeared in another display. The next officer trailed the figure but remained always at the center of the display, giving the pavement beneath him the look of a treadmill.

"Red Four, stay with the target until the Laine intersection," he said.

"Laine intersection, copy that.".

When the tailing officer reached the intersection, several meters behind the target, he veered right and was picked up by a vehicle. Meanwhile, another trailer began his pursuit. The officer in the van slid his chair to the right to better observe the target in the new display.

"I'm gonna send Red Four up to the park," said a companion in the van.

"He's really extending our reach."

"If we have to keep recycling tails he's eventually going to notice."

"Maybe."

After another minute or so, the target abruptly turned and entered a small supply store.

"Red Two, continue past. Red One, enter the shop and get in line."

"I'll set up Red Three outside the store," said the companion.

"Use Red Five," replied the officer, obviously the team leader, "Red Three is going to get made if we use him again." There was a moment's pause, then, "Damn it, Red One, get in the shop and give us a visual!"

Moments later the inside of the store appeared on Red One's display, but the glowing figure was not there.

"Maybe he left out the back," suggested the companion.

"There he is," said the team leader as the glowing figure inside the store emerged from the back of the store and made for the shop's entrance.

"He knows."

When the target left the store, he emerged onto Red Five's display and Red Five commenced his pursuit, but something was wrong. The target's gait had changed, and noticing this, the team leader realized the shape of the body was different. Alarmed, he sat upright and gripped the arms of his chair.

"Red Five, take the target. Red Three and Red Six, move in to support the arrest." His companion gave him a look. "It's a different guy. Red One, search the store for the target. He's traded clothes with someone."

On Red Five's display projection, the glowing red figure, though walking forward, appeared to slowly move back into the center of the projection until Red Five accosted him. The officer's attention was interrupted by a report.

"Gold One, the target is not in the store. I think he took a back way out."

"Copy that," said the team leader and cursed. "All vehicles, the target is loose. Search and acquire. Red Five, what's the status?"

"Gold One, we've got a decoy. Said he traded his clothes with the target and didn't ask questions."

"Sure," said Gold One, "the target entered the store, proposed they trade clothes, they went to the back, stripped and got dressed again all in the space of a minute. Horse shit. Take him in for questioning."

"Gold One, this is Red Seven. We've got no sign of the target."

"Keep looking," said Gold One, making it sound like a curse. Tearing his headset off, the team leader tossed it onto the desk in front of him and leaned back in his chair. "Caldwell's going to murder me," he muttered.

&~&

Katherine shivered as she waited on the steps at the front of an abandoned building. Arcarius always had an empty feel in the winter, and now that the entire population was herded into a few city blocks near the center of town, the edges of the city were desolate. She was dressed warmly but had been waiting for a while and made the mistake of sitting on the cold concrete steps. Alistair's bag lay beside her.

She stood up as a figure emerged onto the street and made for her. Without being able to see him clearly, she knew it was her younger brother and felt a wave of relief. When he waved she returned the salute and, picking up the bag, moved to meet him.

"You're late, which is bad enough when it's warm out," she gently chided and gave him a hug. Her red and runny nose gave testament to how long she had been waiting. Alistair smiled and accepted his bag. Katherine's tone became more serious. "And I know you told me not to look in the bag, but I did anyway and I'm not thrilled. Is that a suit made of Steltar?"

"It's a Null Suit. Yes, it's made of Steltar."

"Those are illegal."

"Even worse, this one's imported from Kaldis," he replied with a wry smile.

"Alistair, will you tell me what's going on? If they're following you, how are you going to use it?" He did not respond, but she guessed the answer, perhaps seeing it in his eyes. "You're leaving." He nodded. "When?" Her voice nearly faltered with the question.

"Tonight. In fact, I won't be seeing Mom and Dad before then. You'll have to say goodbye for me."

Against her will, her eyes welled up with tears and she gritted her teeth. "Damn it, Alistair. This is so stupid—"

Alistair put a finger on her lips. "Kath, they've trained me to fight, and that's what I'm going to do."

Katherine could not look him in the eyes, could only shake her head. "This isn't the way."

"The way to what?"

"The way to where you want to go. What are you going to do, take on the whole government? You'll be dead and the rest of us will be exactly where we are now."

"Maybe."

"Maybe?"

"The thought had occurred to me, but obviously I've accepted the risk."

"Accepted the risk, but for what gain? This isn't the way to make things better."

"And what, may I ask, is the way to make things better?"

Katherine set her jaw stubbornly. "Science," she insisted.

"Science? Science is going to help us? And what is science going to do?"

Grabbing her brother's powerful right arm in both her hands, she pleaded, "Alistair, you have no idea. We're so close to so many breakthroughs. It's Flow Theory that I was telling you about. Do you know how many practical applications there are if Flow Theory works out? It's going to be—"

"Katherine," said Alistair gently, sadly, "When was nanotechnology invented?"

She stopped short, surprised by the question. "It goes back centuries…maybe the 22nd century in the Terran calendar?"

"Earlier than that. The foundations for nanotechnology were pursued as early as the late 20th century. By the middle of the 21st, nanotechnology was well established."

"So?"

He disengaged his arm so he could spread both of them wide and turn in a circle, indicating the world around them. "So where are the nanobots?" She did not immediately answer. "Nanotechnology can cure any bacterial or viral illness. It can repair DNA. It can even break down pollution. Yet it never really came into wide spread use until Kaldis was settled. That was over three centuries ago. So where are the nanobots?"

He dropped his arms and when he spoke again, his voice was gentler. "Technology has always outpaced progress. The technology might be there, but it doesn't just appear in every factory ready to go. It needs to be purchased; it needs to be adapted, there needs to be investment…Just because a scientist in a lab discovers a new science doesn't mean it will be widely used.

"We need investment. But how can people invest when government taxes away their wealth? Why work when government will take care of you if you don't, and tax you if you do? Why invest in your business when government may decide to steal it? Why save your money when government will inflate the currency and make it worthless? Why bother upgrading when it costs too much to comply with regulations? Why invent ways to use technology if it will never be profitable? Why work hard to get ahead when a payment to the right politicians will insulate you from any competition?

"It's not science alone that is going to help mankind. It's the Free Market. And the Free Market is sick. Even Kaldis is going to be either a war torn and desolate wasteland or a fascist state. Or both. Somewhere, someone has to stand up and fight for what's right." He ended his lecture and gave his sister a gentle pinch on her cheek. "I'll be in touch," he said, letting his fingers linger for a moment, and then turned to go.

"If you're alive," she somberly said.

"That is a necessary prerequisite," he conceded with a soft grin but was disappointed it did not produce a smile in response. "Kath, it's a done deal. Someday, there will be a world where wives don't have to wonder why their husbands disappeared."

Katherine's eyes welled up, but she could think of nothing to say. Instead, she watched her brother go until he rounded a corner and disappeared behind another empty building.

14

Stephanie Caldwell sat with her hands in her lap while, across the desk from her, Captain Travis examined a report she had given him. He sat erect, his posture perfect as always, his face shaven with the same tiny line of a mustache above his upper lip.

"So you don't know where he is?" Travis said without looking up.

"I don't know where Ashley is. They should be bringing in Keegan shortly. I have men waiting in his apartment."

"You got a warrant?" asked Travis.

"No. You told me not to worry about it after the election."

This startled Travis and he looked up at her, but the surprise was momentary. "That's true." He returned his attention to the report. After a moment more of silent deliberation, he closed the file and tossed it on the desk in front of Stephanie. "Quite right," he said. "The ARO will not be required to go through the standard procedures. Now, how do we find Alistair Ashley 3nn?"

"I don't know that we do. He knew he was being followed and he knew how to disappear. I tried to get his file from the marines to see exactly what sort of training he received but it's classified. I know he was a highly prized, and highly trained, soldier."

"Has he gone through physical enhancement?"

"I expect he has but I don't know for sure. He's…a lot bigger than when he left."

"Well, I doubt very much he'll stay in Arcarius. I'll forward a report to the central ARO office in Rendral. We don't really have much on him other than suspicious behavior. That's enough to bring him in for questioning, but hardly worth pursuing him around the globe."

Captain Travis nodded once, as if settling the matter in his mind.

"Sir, there's another aspect of this I'd like to discuss."

"Go ahead."

Stephanie leaned forward in her chair and folded her hands over her knees. "Alistair's grandfather was one of the last members of The Homesteaders."

"Never heard of them."

"I only have through Alistair. The Homesteaders were a protest movement the government finally stamped out…I don't know…fifty cycles ago. Alistair calls it a forgotten episode in Aldran history. They were around since The Founding. Apparently, many of the original colonists reneged on their agreement with The Founders and demanded more autonomy. There were lots of struggles between Rendral and militant groups who wanted to secede."

"And they called themselves The Homesteaders?"

"Homesteading is when someone moves in on empty land and claims it. The Homesteaders said that's what they were doing when they moved to uncolonized parts of Aldra, so they refused to recognize Rendral's authority."

"But The Founders claimed Aldra before the voyage from Earth."

"The Homesteaders' whole point was that this claim was unjustifiable."

"How quaint. So now…what? Alistair wants to bring The Homesteaders back into existence?"

Stephanie sat back in her chair and folded her arms. "Alistair was always spouting the stuff his grandpa taught him. All anti-government, anti-cooperation. Everybody for himself kind of thing. When I heard Alistair was staying past his one cycle obligation I figured he had finally grown up, but when he came back it was immediately obvious this was not the case. He was still the same, but there was an edge to him. More anger than before. Kaldis definitely changed him, but not for the better."

"You think he poses a danger?"

"I think with the recent bombings that have gone on, and the food riots…I wouldn't be at all surprised if he was involved. At the very least he'll be perfectly willing to use it to his advantage. I know Alistair as well as anybody, I think. He won't spend his life wandering around. He has a goal and he's going to set about attaining it."

Travis had made a steeple with his fingers and now rested his chin on them. "Has there been any activity from the house we raided?"

"Nothing. They moved out soon after. We've got them under surveillance but…frankly I don't think we have enough surveillance for everyone we want to follow. We're seeing evidence of a large network. Every new suspect has thirty contacts, and each contact has thirty more contacts. We'd need to triple our department size to keep track of it all. At least triple."

"So given the situation…how much is it worth to spend resources looking for Alistair?"

Stephanie shrugged.

"Maybe we'll have to wait and see what develops. Don't you work first shift tomorrow?"

She nodded.

"Why don't you head home for the night then?"

Grabbing her report, she left the room and, after a quick stop to file it, she put on her winter coat, hat and gloves and made for the front door of the station. Upon opening it, she was greeted by a blast of frigid air. Her eyes watered, but she plunged into the cold, head forward and face down, and made her way to the Metro station to catch one of the last cars home.

Out in the dark and cold, perched atop a two story building across from the station, Alistair, in his Null Suit, watched Stephanie walk below him. Once again the wind was strong so he could not hear the crunch of her feet on the snow, just the howl of the air tearing through the beleaguered Arcarian streets. The roof he was on was flat with a yard-high brick wall surrounding it, giving him a perfect hiding spot. Next to him was the sack with the precious cargo his sister retrieved for him, as well as another he had brought. The second contained clothing, a toothbrush and other mundane objects, as well as supplies for something else he had planned.

His ship would leave in three hours, giving him a window of opportunity. The captain agreed to smuggle him to Avon, though he would not wait for him. Alistair told him not to look for him; either he would sneak onto the ship or he would not be there. In either case, the captain got the money and his schedule was not interrupted. It was not difficult to convince him, especially when a few gold coins were dropped on the table.

Waiting on the roof for another half hour, Alistair finally saw Captain Travis emerge, bundled up against the cold. Stephanie's boss set the security code, pulled down the metal grating and locked it to the floor. He then went to a small garage at the side of the station and emerged moments later in his auto. Getting out and leaving it running, he performed the same closing procedure on the garage. Either he did not have a remote control, or it was waiting to be fixed. Whatever it was, Travis was forced once more to face the cold before getting back in and driving off, the exhaust from his auto getting snatched by the frigid wind as soon as it emerged from the tailpipe.

Now the area was almost entirely dark. The only illumination came from distant buildings, like the Mayor's Palace, which Aloysius Warwick had taken to lighting all through the night since his election, or from the power sphere not far from it, though this last bit of engineering was not as illuminating as it used to be. The light cast a soft glow on the rooftops; little filtered between the buildings at street level.

With the Civil Guard station empty, Alistair grabbed his belongings and moved along the street by way of the rooftops. When an alley separated buildings, he nimbly sprang from one to the other and so kept his course until he reached the end of the block. Once or twice he landed on a patch of ice, but the treads of his Null Suit handled the smooth material as if it were sandpaper, preventing him from slipping. After a few minutes of progress, the smaller street he followed intersected with Rendral Way, a capacious boulevard with an expansive central island separating the traffic lanes. It ran from the harbor in the southwest, cutting diagonally across much of the city, before ending at the plaza at the Mayor's Palace in the north.

He set his belongings down and produced a length of rope. This he tied to the ends of his two sacks. That finished, he crept to the edge and was about to lower them to the ground when something caught his eye. Forty or so yards across Rendral Way was his target: The Office of National Service. Four stories of weathered bricks and cracked concrete, it was there that Arcarians were registered for the draft.

Someone else was there. The wind prevented him from hearing anything, but he saw a fleeting shadow take off into the alleyway next to the ONS. There were no further signs of movement, but he elected to remain where he was, crouched down, the rope in one hand and the sacks in another, his eyes scanning all along the street. He saw nothing save for the occasional sign blowing wildly in the wind, and the long tails of snow that the wind scooped off the ground and dragged through the air.

And then the ONS exploded.

It exploded with such tremendous force that he was hammered by the might of it and sent skidding across the roof. Dazed, he still sprang to his feet in a crouch, shaking his head to clear it, and returned to the roof's edge. The after effects of the explosion sounded even over the wind, and the ruins of the building were well lit now by various fires. The façade was blown open on the bottom story and most of the second; stray pieces of the structure fell down around the newly created opening. Alistair watched as the entire façade gave way with an impressive din, along with much of the heart of the building. Then he saw a flash of light down the alleyway, like an auto passing by.

Retrieving his belongings, he lowered them to the street below. Not bothering with climbing, he leapt to the ground, landing into a roll. Having sustained nothing more than perhaps a mild bruise, he grabbed the sacks, hoisted them over his shoulder and ran past the ruined building and into the alley where he had seen the figure not long before. Seconds later, he burst onto the next street and took off to his left, towards tail lights many yards ahead, managing to keep pace for a time, hampered as the auto was by the potholes and snow drifts, but the lights disappeared when it made a right turn.

Still running all out, his lungs gulping frigid air that tore at them, Alistair too turned right, hoping to parallel its path for a time. After streaking past building after decrepit building, hollow cadavers left to rot, he darted into the open bowels of a corpse and, kicking through the back wall, came onto another street. The auto was much closer.

Next, he discovered why: it had stopped, though it continued to idle, exhaling its exhaust. His next question was answered when a figure exited the car and held a conversation with another much larger one on the sidewalk. Keeping low and in the shadows, he stole closer, hugging rough brick walls that might have snagged a lesser material, the wind covering the sound of his approach. Upon coming within several meters of the two, just as it looked like they had concluded the conversation and the smaller man was getting back in the auto, he called out, "Oliver!"

The men started, ducking down and pulling guns out. The driver of the auto got out and pointed a gun in Alistair's direction, over the hood of the car, but then Oliver stood up.

"Alistair?" he said, putting his gun away and moving towards his friend.

Alistair rose too and stepped forward, pulling his mask/hood back and grinning as he met his friend with a fierce embrace.

"I thought you were leaving," said Oliver, raising his voice over the wind.

Alistair could tell by the light in his eyes that his friend was smiling under the winter facemask and the frozen bits of breath that condensed on it while he breathed.

"My ship leaves in a couple hours. I was going to board it after I hurled a Molotov cocktail at the ONS."

Oliver threw his head back and roared with laughter. Gripping Alistair's shoulders he shouted, "You arrived a bit too late. Frankly, ours did more damage."

"Why don't you two lovers say your goodbyes and we can get out of here before the tin men come?" called out the driver, and Alistair recognized Ryan Wellesley, his hair getting tousled in the wind.

"Come with us," said Oliver, his eyes gleaming with excitement. "You said the revolution can't start here, but maybe you're wrong."

"Did you guys blow up the last building?"

"We did. Turns out it was…oh hell, we can discuss it later. Are you coming?"

Alistair hesitated only a moment. "I'm coming."

Guiding Alistair with a hand on his back, Oliver indicated he should get in the back. "We're taking this one."

"I don't know about this—" began Wellesley.

"I'm vouching for him," Oliver insisted. "Go ahead and get in," he said to his friend and Alistair, uncertain, entered the back seat. He found himself next to a fellow of forty or so cycles who fixed an unfriendly gaze on him. Oliver closed Alistair's door and got in the front passenger seat.

"We're off," he said and Ryan sped away, leaving the scene of destruction behind them.

15

Oliver chatted as if he didn't notice, but Wellesley and the other rider regarded Alistair with suspicious looks and baleful gazes. Alistair several times caught Wellesley glancing at him in the rearview mirror. It must have been odd for them to have him seated there, he thought, with his blurry Null Suit almost fading into the dark interior of the auto yet his uncovered head clear to see.

When Wellesley finally spoke to him, it was with a flat and guarded tone as he scratched at his scar.

"How's the suit working out?"

"Quite well, thank you."

"My pleasure."

They sped through the empty streets of the west side of the city and into the foothills above it. Winding through, Wellesley eventually turned the auto south, down a snow covered road that sank lower and lower between the hills until it ended at a stretch of snowy beach several miles west of Arcarius. A small boat waited for them, pulled up onto shore just enough so the waves constantly buffeting it did not drag it back into the water.

All but Wellesley got out, and he did not bother with a goodbye but sped off into the hills. The auto's lights disappeared within seconds as the hills closed in around it. Oliver and the other made immediately for the small boat and Alistair followed, his feet crunching on snow that sea spray had partially melted, leaving it to refreeze as ice. Within a few seconds they were in the water and Oliver's companion had the motor running. The sea was rough, but the boat cut through the waves, sending cold ocean spray into the air as they headed into the pitch black ocean.

Alistair was enjoying the wintry air rushing against his face when Oliver leaned over to put his mouth next to his ear and said, "When we get back to the base, let me do the talking." Even so close, his voice was a half shout over the sound of the motor and the wind.

"You always do."

"That's true," said Oliver with a laugh. "But this time it's important. I'm kind of breaking a protocol I was pretty adamant on establishing. Don't worry: they'll accept you. Just let me do the talking."

"Are you running this operation?"

"No, but I'm…let's say in the inner circle."

Alistair nodded and turned back into the wind.

He saw the structure long before they did. It appeared to be a power platform whose square central stage was perhaps two hundred yards on a side. He knew there were several such power platforms in the ocean nearby, each tapping into the heat of Aldra's mantle and beaming the captured power to the main power station in Arcarius, Avon or wherever. The broad central shaft plunging from this particular one, however, was dark and quiet. When the monstrous thing loomed over them, the various sub platforms and metal stairs and walkways and small buildings came into view, as well as perhaps two dozen figures scurrying around.

The driver pulled the boat alongside one of the four colossal tube-shaped legs anchoring the platform to the ocean floor. A set of stairs wrapped around it and ended in a small dock that could be mechanically raised and lowered, though this was a small necessity, as the sun was the only notable tidal influence on Aldra. As they docked, their boat pitching up and down in the waves, two figures came around the bend in the stairs.

"Is that the Medicine Man?" asked one, a short, stout figure with a bushy mustache, as he came down to meet them. He did not seem caught off guard by Alistair's presence.

"Good to see you, Mike," Alistair returned and stood up to dismount onto the metal dock.

Oliver was just jumping onto it himself, and as his bulk left the boat it caused it to pitch to the side. "We met up tonight by coincidence," he explained to Mike. "He was going to hit the same target we did."

Mike nodded. "We'll talk about this up on top." To the driver of the boat, Mike said, "Get it stored away."

The driver nodded and pushed off, restarting the engine while Oliver, Mike, Alistair and the other began to ascend the stairs. With the smooth though aged metal of the support leg on his left and wide open sea on his right, Alistair stared upward and was awed by the massive frame looming high above him. The main platform towered at least one hundred and fifty yards above their heads, and they would have to wrap around the platform's thick leg several times before reaching it, the wind battering at them the entire way.

At the top, now out of earshot of the waves but in near total darkness, they were greeted by about two dozen other men, all rough and scruffy looking with unfriendly gazes. Only one carried a flashlight. Alistair recognized the two guards who had stood watch outside the warehouse the night he sold his information to Mike, along with Ritchie who led him through the warehouse.

"Stop staring and get back to your jobs," barked a breathless Mike, and slowly the men disbanded. The two guards from the warehouse stayed, though, and walked with them as they headed for the main structure, a five story affair at the center of the main platform.

It was Alistair's training that alerted him. He couldn't even say exactly what it was, but his instincts called out a warning. When one of the guards suddenly spun on him with a knife, Alistair reflexively grabbed the wrist, twisted it around behind his back, bent him over with a knee to the midsection, and with his other hand forced his face down into the metal floor of the platform. This was accomplished a split instant before his heart began to race. All the while, he eyed the other guard, ready to spring into action again.

Mike looked at the display and nodded, impressed but still frowning. "OK, you can let him up," he gruffly said, then sighed. "My plan was to scare ya' a bit, see if I could get a confession outta ya'. I guess ya' ruined that."

"I've already vouched for him," Oliver said.

The man whom Alistair bested groaned in the uncomfortable position into which he was forced.

Mike turned his gaze on the big rugby star. "Yeah, well, you and I are going to have a private talk about this."

"It's worth it," said Oliver, indicating his friend and his recent exploit with his hand. "He'll be useful, and he's already a supporter of the cause. You can trust him. I vouch for him. He's a 3nn like me, so I've known him since childhood classes."

Mike frowned for a moment and then looked at Alistair. A gust of wind made his loose clothing snap. "I said ya' could let him up." Alistair complied after a moment's delay. The guard, wincing, got up, rubbing at his shoulder. "Your friend has vouched fer ya'. Ya' betray us, it's gonna fall on him."

"I'm not going to betray you, but the next time someone turns a knife on me, it's going to get sheathed in their midsection."

"The next time someone turns a knife on ya', it'll be a government agent. Stab him wherever you like." To Oliver Mike said, "Give him his quarters," and then he and his retinue left Alistair and Oliver alone.

With a slap on his friend's shoulder, Oliver said, "That went well. Mike's impressed with you." He led Alistair to a smaller one story structure away from the main central one. "Anyone who served off in the marines is useful. And he doesn't realize the full extent of it yet."

"What exactly is the plan here?"

Oliver shrugged. "Rebel. We're fighting the Realist Party, the State…you know. Disrupt. Hopefully, our numbers will swell as things get worse and people see someone's doing something about it. If not…at least we tried."

"How'd you get involved?"

"That's a long story for another time. Right now it's time to get you to your quarters and we can all get some sleep."

The building to which Oliver took Alistair was simply a long hallway with one mess hall and a lot of small quarters with bunk beds. As Alistair entered, he was greeted in the paltry candlelight with stares ranging from cautious to unfriendly. Oliver stopped in the commons to grab a candle which he lit and then led Alistair down the long hallway. As he passed doorway after doorway, he saw men playing cards or engaged in other activities, all abruptly halted when they caught sight of him. Behind him, several heads peeked out from the rooms to observe. Oliver's presence and obvious friendship at least mollified most, but none so much as ventured a smile.

"This is your room, little buddy," said Oliver, stopping halfway down the hall and extending his hand in invitation to enter. "You'll be with Ryan Wellesley."

Alistair moved past Oliver into the room. Oliver spread his arms and put each forearm against one of the door frames as he watched Alistair survey his new surroundings. The room was bare save for a chair in one corner and bunk beds in the other. It was cold but not frigid, body heat having served to make the temperature livable. Alistair tossed his belongings onto the top bunk.

"You can't have the top one. Ryan's very particular about it."

Shrugging, Alistair deposited his sacks instead on the bottom bunk.

"He'll be ornery enough about having a roommate," Oliver continued.

"I need a safe," said Alistair.

"Can I get it tomorrow?"

"No, before I go to sleep I'll need a safe."

Oliver tapped on the door frame for a moment and then finally nodded. "I'll be right back."

When Oliver left, Alistair turned in a circle and considered the room again. Its spartan comforts at least were not filthy. He doffed his Null Suit until he stood naked, and the cold drafts assaulted the body kept so warm inside the Suit. With a shiver, he dug into one of his sacks and pulled out some clothes.

Oliver returned with a small safe as Alistair stood at the window of the room staring out over the dark waters. He bid his friend goodnight while Alistair crouched over the safe, re-setting the lock with a new code. When his more precious belongings, including the Null Suit, were safely stored away, he blew out the candle, lay down on the bottom bunk and listened to the wind outside. It was sometime later when Ryan Wellesley appeared in the doorway, a candle illuminating his cherry red face glistening with ocean spray.

"I just got the best news of my life," he muttered as he dumped a small bag on the ground and blew out his candle.

Alistair briefly glanced at him but declined to respond and not long after they were both asleep on the thin mattresses.

16

Alistair was awakened by fabric landing on his face. He removed it and opened his tired eyes to see Ryan Wellesley standing in the doorway. A weak beam of light was streaming through the window from a sun just creeping over the horizon.

"Time to get up, sweetheart."

Alistair could go from half asleep to up and ready in the time it takes to tell it; he was out of bed and dressing before Wellesley needed to repeat himself.

"Whaddya got in that safe there?" asked Ryan as he folded his arms and leaned against the doorframe.

"Some items of importance," Alistair replied as he pulled a shirt over his head.

"Like what?"

"Books."

Ryan frowned and raised an eyebrow. "Books? Those are items of importance?"

"Value is subjective."

"You can get them at the library."

"Not these books."

"Is that all you got in there?"

"Pretty much," Alistair lied.

After getting dressed, he followed Ryan to the small mess hall where most of the rest of the band were eating a sparse breakfast of bread and porridge. In unison they looked up as he entered, and his ears burned red as he grabbed a plate and sat down next to Oliver. He spooned himself some of the bland porridge from the pot in the middle of the table and grabbed a couple pieces of toasted bread—no butter—and munched quietly on his meal.

"Good morning and welcome to your new life," Oliver said with a cheery grin.

"Good morning," mumbled Alistair, wishing Oliver would not speak as if including the entire crew in the discussion.

"Bob LaSalle," said a voice.

Alistair looked up to see the man across the table holding out his hand. His complexion was a shade or two darker than the others and his hair was black, thick and curly. His features were not entirely Caucasian, with his nose a bit broader and flatter and his lips fuller. Alistair had seen other races on Kaldis and Earth, and knew a few settled on Aldra. Bob LaSalle must have traced part of his lineage to Africa.

Reaching out to shake his hand, Alistair said, "Alistair Ashley. Good to meet you."

The ice having broken, most of the rest of the band introduced themselves. They were an unshaved and unwashed lot, scarred in many cases, but they were not entirely unfriendly now. A couple ignored him, but most offered a welcome of some sort and a few a firm handshake.

"We don't normally allow new recruits onto the base like this," Bob informed him, "but Oliver vouched for you and all."

In response, Oliver shrugged his shoulders and shoveled some more porridge into his mouth.

"Well," Alistair replied, searching for some response, "I hope I don't disappoint."

After breakfast, Alistair accompanied Oliver outside into what proved to be another chilly, windy day. Small flurries of snow were whipped into their faces, and wherever the wind blew into a corner or niche, the flakes piled up and formed drifts. The sky was covered by gray clouds sulking over the sea.

He got his first daylight view of the platform, and it looked like it had been abandoned for many cycles. The rusty metal grating that served as the floor was slick and icy. The massive legs at each corner were spotted with rust. The metal ladders and stairs leading to the upper reaches were in need of replacement, and the walkways and grating above that clustered around the tall machinery towering over the main platform did not look trustworthy either. In one place it had partially fallen and hung suspended in the air, swaying in the wind, a few nuts and bolts preventing a total collapse.

The rebels all had a purpose. Whatever it was they aimed to do, they were taking steps to do it. Men rushed between the central control building and what looked like piles of rubbish kept under tarps tied to the grating. Some carried objects from the piles to the central building, while others were busy repairing the upper reaches, or perhaps dissecting them to use the parts, it was difficult to say. A couple of the men, far, far above at the highest reaches of the platform, seemed to be lookouts, pacing about and peering into the distance.

Following Oliver from the barracks to the central building, he entered through one of the side doors. There was a cacophony inside, with men repairing, dismantling and building all at once. The sound of metal on metal interspersed with barked orders dominated, and so loud was it that the wind outside could not be heard.

"Welcome to the base of operations," yelled Oliver and proceeded to lead him into a stairwell and up to the second story. Once there, with the noise much attenuated, he took him down a hall and into a large room almost empty save for a long table and some folding chairs. The windows had been replaced with plywood so that the room had to be lit with a couple lanterns. It stank of kerosene and unwashed bodies. Mike was there with two other men whom Alistair did not recognize.

"Here's our new recruit," Oliver said and sat down across from Mike at the long conference table, kicking his feet up and resting them on top.

"Get yer damn feet off the table," Mike growled. "I hope that chair breaks underneath ya'."

Oliver smirked but put his feet on the floor.

Mike turned his attention to Alistair, who remained standing. "Alistair, good morning."

"Good morning, Mike."

"Yer gonna learn pretty quick to address me as sir until yer a bit higher in rank."

Alistair hesitated a moment but he finally managed a nod.

"I expect yer used to taking orders, but ya' don't seem to like 'em," Mike continued.

Alistair said nothing.

"Alistair is going to be invaluable," Oliver said. "He spent four cycles on Kaldis; he doesn't need any more boot camp instruction."

Mike spared Oliver a quick glance and then fixed his gaze back on Alistair. "So here y'are. Oliver's vouched fer ya', so do him a favor and don't embarrass yerself. Remember we're glad to have ya' because I ain't gonna tell ya' again. Who'r ya' roomin' with?"

"Ryan Wellesley."

"Fine. Ryan's not paired right now. He'll be yer partner."

"Partner?"

"Questions later. What are yer skills? What can ya' offer us?"

Alistair thought a moment with his cool gaze fixed on Mike. "I can analyze any government program and tell you what sort of market distortions it will produce."

One of Mike's companions chuckled. The other, an auburn haired man a couple dozen cycles older than Alistair, did not react. He leaned back in his chair with one leg draped over an arm.

"Son of a bitch is a bigger smart ass than you are," said Mike to Oliver, who grinned.

"Horseshit," said Oliver. "I'm way more of a smart ass."

"I don't give a damn about yer schoolin'," growled Mike, his attention back to Alistair. "What did ya' learn in the army?"

"I learned how to make war," Alistair replied with a voice cold enough to put out a fire. "If it needs to be demolished, destroyed, dismembered, decapitated or otherwise put out of function, I can do it."

Mike grinned. "Now that's what we need around here."

"But I make war on my own terms," Alistair continued, his voice as firm as he could make it. "I've done plenty of killing and I don't want to go looking for more. At any rate, killing would just play right into the State's hands. I'll recruit, I'll spy, I'll destroy their military equipment, I'll sabotage…but I'm not going to kill unless I have no other choice."

Mike considered Alistair in silence for an uncomfortably long time before he spoke again. "We'll talk about our war philosophies later. Do ya' have any questions fer me now?"

"A couple. What's your ultimate goal? What steps are you taking now to get there? Why are you fighting to begin with? What supplies do you have? What contacts do you have? Are you recruiting? How are you recruiting? How is the recruiting going? Do you have a fall back plan? Do you have another base if this one gets compromised? How much military experience do we have altogether? How many troops do you command? Are you affiliated with other resistance groups? How many and what's their membership?"

Mike gave a throaty chuckle while the auburn haired man let his gaze wander as if bored.

"Supplies could be better. Yeah, we have another base. Plenty, in fact. We're about to abandon this one. Recruiting is slow but I expect it'll pick up. The ultimate plan is to overthrow the government. We're building our supplies right now as ya' may have seen…What were the other questions?"

"Why are you fighting?"

Mike shrugged. "Because now's the time. We're tired of the whole damn thing. We're tired of standing in lines for food that tastes like it came out the backside of a cow. I'm sick of the bastards who run this country and I say it's time to oust 'em. Does that satisfy ya'?"

"Good enough for now."

"So now's my question. Do ya' still have my gold? Is it in that safe?"

"I have none of your gold. I have gold that used to be yours but you transferred to me."

"Details. Here's my problem. We could use it right now. When we paid ya' fer yer information, we didn't realize how bad things were gonna get here. Nobody's got money enough to pay us fer the medicine. People are more likely to die of starvation than some disease. There's just no market it fer it right now."

"There's hardly a market for anything right now. You may have noticed how little my gold can buy. At any rate, we both agreed to the exchange."

"So, how can we convince ya' to spend that gold on our little operation here?"

"As long as we're both fighting the government I'll be happy to spend it on you. In return I want some independence and enough rank to call you by your first name."

Mike chuckled again, unsurprised and, suggested by his gravelly chuckle, impressed. "Done." Mike opened his arms and spoke to the other two. "Boys, here's the new Captain. Just purchased his rank fer thirty pounds of gold."

"I don't have the entire thirty pounds anymore," Alistair answered, taking a seat next to Oliver.

"Lieutenant, then. This is Brad Stanson. This is Johnny Raymond. Clever Johnny as we call him. Now, how exactly do we go about putting ya' to use?"

Brad Stanson, with light brown hair and average height and build, eagerly stood up to shake Alistair's hand. Clever Johnny, a smallish man with the auburn hair streaked with white, did not. He hardly bothered to lift his hand off the table and meet Alistair halfway.

"So now we're five," Mike said. "Maybe with one more brain in the group we can figure out what the hell to do."

"The first thing I would do is get off this rig," Alistair advised. "You're sitting ducks out here as soon as they think to look for you. With a few keystrokes a man in Rendral can aim a satellite, find your heat signatures and let loose a missile. Five minutes later the revolution is over."

Mike turned to Brad Stanson. "Alistair's supposed to be pretty smart too. Got a lot of training in the military; got promoted pretty quickly. Didn't study at university like you, though." Turning back to Alistair, he said, "We were supposed to abandon this place a while ago. Will be shortly. We needed it fer storage. Plus, we knew they wouldn't think to look for a few outlaws way out here. Now that our operations are gettin' bigger, we'll be headin' fer the hills outside Arcarius."

"It would be advisable."

"Apart from our place of residence, we need to decide what the hell to do," Mike continued. "We attacked the draft center. I think that sends a pretty clear message. What next?"

"You can't beat them on a battlefield, so you take advantage of what you do have," Alistair continued. "You form cells and keep only loose ties. You can kill a bear with one shot, but a swarm of bees is harder to eradicate. The movement can't be tied to just one person. It has to be an idea that won't die. The worse things get, the more likely we are to get support. The longer we last and the more we make them sweat, we get even more support."

Brad nodded. "He's quite correct. We need to get the public's sympathy and admiration. On Kaldis there are companies that advertise their product and strive for brand loyalty among the populace. That's what we need. We need an easily recognizable symbol. We can leave it at the location of whatever building we bomb. If there's ever another food shortage—"

"And there will be," interjected Alistair.

"—we need to be there with emergency supplies, courtesy of the revolution, with our symbol marked on the packages of food."

"Fantastic," said Alistair. "The worse things get, the more we can take advantage. But we need to confine our attacks to those who deserve it. We must be able to justify every vengeful act on the State, and we need to match it with charity to the people we are trying to recruit from."

"In any revolution," said Brad, "pamphlets are at least as powerful as rifles. The old saying about the pen and the sword is quite correct. We need to print and distribute pamphlets, thousands of them."

"We point out a code of conduct we believe in," Alistair went on, "and demonstrate how the State has violated it. We follow our ethical code, and each time the State breaks it, we call them on it. Then either we overthrow the masters, or we force them to reform."

Mike shook his head at the last bit. "No reform. We're lookin' to completely overthrow the government. If not fer the whole planet, at least fer Arcarius. Go back to a system of independent city-states like we had a long time ago maybe."

"If the government were to reform, would that not be enough?" Oliver asked.

Mike firmly shook his head. "I'm not in this to get a few concessions from 'em. They need to be crushed. Then we'll take control. I like what ya' said about things getting worse and that being better for us. Let's go down that path a bit."

"Any non market system is going to have difficulty producing and allocating in accordance with what the people desire," said Alistair. "The recent food shortage will be followed by worse ones unless market reforms—"

"No, no," Mike cut him off. "I'm not waiting fer some bureaucrat to make a mistake and cause a shortage. We need to create one and blame it on the government, get people stirred up again."

Alistair shook his head. "It wasn't necessarily a bureaucrat's mistake that caused the last one. It's impossible to centrally coordinate an economy the size of Aldra's, or even one an order of magnitude smaller. Another shortage—of something—is inevitable."

"Fine, but why wait fer it?" asked Mike. "Let's sink the next supply ship that comes in. Make their job harder."

Alistair's faint blush and gritted teeth revealed his feelings for the idea. "Because then we'd be no better than the government we're opposing."

"This is a war."

"I thought we wanted to win the people's hearts."

"It seems to me," said Clever Johnny, speaking for the first time and still casually draped over his chair, "that we are going to be blamed for every problem that occurs anyway. If they are going to blame us for every shortage, why not create more of them?"

"Because then we'll make what the government says true."

"Johnny's right," pronounced Mike with a note of finality. "We steal the food shipments and distribute them and make sure the people know we gave it to them. Failing that, we sink the shipments coming in. We need to make people suffer and then be the only relief they have."

"It seems like a sound plan," offered Brad, with an almost apologetic look to Alistair.

Upon considering them for a moment, Alistair said, "I prefer not to participate in such operations."

Mike fixed a dark look on Alistair. "What operations would ya' prefer to engage in?"

The audacity of Alistair's idea made him hesitate a moment before uttering it. "The prison has recently been filled with a lot of the rioters, a lot of the people who stormed the Palace." Alistair looked at each in turn, as if discerning their attitudes. "I think we can break them out of prison."

☜☞

Mike remained behind to have a word with Clever Johnny and Oliver, while Alistair and Brad left. Outside, Alistair caught Brad's attention and they shook dirty hands again.

"That's a bold plan you proposed," said Brad as they walked together towards the barracks. "This is a group of angry men, and angry men want to fight. Getting them to fight smart is sometimes a chore."

"There's a long history of the State and its dissatisfied customers. We have a lot of lessons to draw from."

"Exactly. What we don't have is a good blueprint for what comes after."

"And what should come after?"

"Government needs to be more responsive to the people. We need to prevent tyrants from getting into authority. We need the right Constitution to make government more efficient, more controlled. We need a lot of things."

Frowning, Alistair replied, "A Constitution is simply words on parchment."

"Well," Brad faltered for a second, "you always have to make sure it is enforced properly."

"How can we recognize a tyrant in time to prevent him from getting into office? How can we be sure a good man won't become one when he tastes power?"

"If we can't find a way then you and I might as well quit what we're doing, because that's the only option we have."

"Is it?"

"When this rebellion finally succeeds—and it will succeed—we'll be in position to make things better for the future."

Alistair was thoughtful a moment. Then he said, "Doesn't it seem government power always—I mean always—gets worse with time?"

Brad nodded after thinking about it for a moment. "It seems that way."

"Doesn't it seem the more power a government gets, the more ruthless is the man at the top?"

"Or woman. Yes it does, I suppose. Just off the top of my head."

"It's almost as if the progression of rising to the top is a weed out process where decent, honest men are discarded in favor of ruthless, power hungry dictators."

As they neared the door to the barracks, Brad said, "That means we need to be on the lookout now. When we seize control, people like you and me need to have the authority."

"I think if you make it to the top, you either are or will be transformed into a man unfit to lead. What if the problem is with the entire concept of leadership and authority itself?"

As they entered the barracks, Brad slowly nodded again and regarded Alistair with genuine interest. "This time will be different," he assured his new comrade.

17

"I hate old people," said Wellesley as he sat across from Alistair in a booth in a dark corner of a near empty restaurant on the fringes of the inhabited part of Arcarius.

He took a sip from his mug and set it back down on the grimy table as a soft tune hummed in the air. There were few staff members there, and fewer patrons.

"They're practically useless. I don't give a damn what they did for society thirty cycles ago. They just sit around and complain about how much their welfare deposit was reduced last month. I'm the one working for it; they should consider themselves lucky they're getting anything. They need to pass a law against old people."

Alistair smiled into his mug as he sipped at his beer. "How about just ending welfare?"

Wellesley just shrugged. "They'll never do that. Were there a lot of old people on Kaldis?"

"A lot more than here."

Wellesley groaned. "Best argument against anarchy."

"Kaldis isn't anarchistic," Alistair corrected, but Wellesley wasn't listening.

"The whole place is up in flames…well hell, *you* know. Everybody runs around wild and look at the mess the place is in. They need someone to impose some order."

"And outlaw old people."

"Hell yeah," said Wellesley and a small grin, defeating him, curled his lips. He took another sip from his beer.

"So let's say we win. We overthrow the government and now we're in charge. What do we do?"

Wellesley shrugged. "Impose some order. Get the trains running on time, make some sensible laws. Common sense stuff."

"And what system would best accomplish that?"

"Oh hell, I don't know. I just know we need a change."

"Is that why you're fighting? For a change?"

Wellesley made a face and nodded slowly as he considered the question. "There's nothing else to do. I repair mining equipment. There's no miners this time of year."

"So start a revolution?"

Wellesley shrugged again. "There's nothing else to do. I've been running specnine for Mike for a while now." After another swig of beer, he continued, "So, how exactly are we going to take this place out?"

Alistair leaned forward with his elbows on the table. "I need to scout it first. I can't do that now because I don't want the surveillance imagers recording me. I'll go tonight and get a basic idea of what we'll need. Nothing too fancy: surprise, brute force, and a quick retreat."

"Do you know what it's like inside?"

"I've been inside."

"I mean…" Wellesley stopped and considered Alistair. "No kidding? You? In there?" He made a face of appreciation. "And here I had you pegged as another clean cut intellectual like Stanson, wet behind the ears. A big clean cut intellectual, but still…well hell's bells."

Alistair chuckled despite himself. "Ryan, where do you think I got to look like this?" He indicated his own physique. "I got quite a bit of experience on Kaldis."

"No, that's not the experience…You know what I mean. On Kaldis, you were on the other side. Now you're a law breaker…what were you in for?"

"I wasn't convicted," he said around a sip of beer. "I was arrested but the victim did not wish to press charges."

"What did you do?"

"He firebombed my dad's place. I ran him down and beat the shit out of him."

Ryan Wellesley gave a low whistle and shook his head. "And he didn't press charges?"

"I think Oliver had something to do with that."

"Son of a bitch," Wellesley grinned. "He bombs your dad's place, so you naturally kick the snot out of him, and you go in the cage. I hate tin men. That's another change we need. When we rule Aldra, no more damn tin men."

"Well, there's plenty to do between now and then."

"Like destroying the local cages and getting some new recruits." Draining the last of his beer, Wellesley reached into his pocket and tossed an iron key onto the table. "That will get you in and out. Just be damn sure to lock it behind you, even if you're inside."

"Will do."

Wellesley nodded, rose, and waddled out of the bar, his belly full of beer and his tab already paid in advance as had become the rule around town. Pocketing the key, Alistair took a last swig and then left his drink half full on the table. He exited the restaurant a few seconds behind Wellesley, but with a different destination.

An hour's walk later, Alistair was at the base of Tanard's Mountain, heading up the winding road leading to the spaceport at the summit. Halfway up he came to a plot of ground he knew better than any other. There were sounds that prepared him for what he was going to see before he rounded the bend. Machinery was running and men were calling to each other over the din.

When he did turn the corner and looked at where Nigel's used to be, an ineffable feeling welled up inside him. Anyone near enough to see the brooding glare he directed at the now empty plot of ground must have shivered from the chill. Where Nigel's had been there was now a crane, a bulldozer and about half a dozen men working on a half finished foundation. There was no sign of the old restaurant and Ashley family home.

"It's not the same without your dad's place anymore," said a voice behind him.

Alistair turned to see a familiar face, a regular at Nigel's and family acquaintance. He was looking apprehensively at Alistair, like one who tries to soothe a tiger. He had a sackful of something he carried over his shoulder.

"I think we'll all miss it."

"It's a shame," the man said, stepping forward to stand next to Alistair. There were icicles dangling from his mustache where his breath had frozen.

"It's an atrocity. A man's home is taken from him without his consent. What gives them the fucking right?"

The man shrugged as best he could with his load. "They're the government. Have they reimbursed your dad yet?"

"It doesn't matter. If they had his consent they could buy it for a single Credit. Without his consent, a million pounds of gold would not be a fair reimbursement."

"Government doesn't need consent."

"Then what good could it ever do us?"

His mouth opened but this time he could not find an answer. Patting him gently on the shoulder, Alistair wished him well and left him and the laborers behind in the long shadows of evening.

The iron key worked, though it required a hefty turn to unlock. Alistair quickly entered the old warehouse and closed the door, making sure to lock it as instructed. The building was not heated, but at least the walls and ceiling acted as shields against the raw Arcarian wind. He grabbed a lantern off the table by the door and lit it, producing a diminutive sphere of dim light and finding himself in an empty room that most likely had been a waiting area. He moved through it and into an office room and past that into the warehouse proper, full of bundles covered in tarps and canvasses, of ropes and hooks hanging down from the ceiling, and of stains on the floor of indeterminate origin. The fishy smell of the wharf was less strong inside the warehouse, but was replaced by the smell of oil and mildew. The uninviting sound of a liquid dripping onto a puddle met his ears.

A well trodden path had sprung up among the covered bundles, and he followed it into the recesses until he detected the glow of another lantern. There, in the back corner, was a small antechamber with several cots. The door to the room was torn off the hinge and dim lantern light filtered from the opening.

Upon crossing the threshold, he saw Oliver sitting at a small desk, his giant form nearly overwhelming it and the chair he sat in. He was furiously writing with a pencil on some parchment, and when Alistair entered he looked up briefly, flashed him a fleeting, humorless smile, and looked back down at his work. Alistair lingered in the doorway for a moment but Oliver, frowning and obsessed with his scribbles, paid him no more heed.

Tentatively, he moved to his cot and removed his shoes. He lay back on the bed with his arms behind his head and closed his eyes for a moment, listening to the sound of Oliver's pencil scratching the paper. He nearly dozed off before he realized the sound had stopped. Opening his eyes, he saw Oliver turned around in his chair with his forearms resting on its back. The giant man said nothing, was not even looking at him.

"Do you want to talk about it?" asked Alistair as gently as he could.

He glanced at Alistair and then back at the wall. "Elizabeth left me."

Alistair sat bolt upright in bed. Swallowing, he tried to think of soothing words, something appropriate, but nothing came out.

"She didn't bother to tell me to my face. I got a letter slipped under my door. When I went to her apartment she wouldn't see me."

Alistair chided himself to say something, but still nothing came out. He swung his legs around to the edge of the bed and set his feet on the floor. Finally, he managed, "Are you writing her a letter?"

"I wrote a letter to her, but she'll never see it. Neither will anyone else."

So saying he opened the portal to his lantern, stuck an edge of the letter inside and, when it caught flame, let the parchment full of his emotion fall to the dirty cement floor. The two friends silently watched as the paper was consumed, leaving behind only the smell of smoke and some ashes that scattered when Oliver kicked them.

"Was it him?"

"Yes."

More silence followed. Unsure if his friend wanted consoling, quiet companionship or solitude, Alistair sat on his cot in indecision, supremely uncomfortable, afraid even to breathe too loudly.

"What do you want to do?" Oliver eventually asked after Alistair had lost track of his breaths. "With your life. You served off on Kaldis; you've got all sorts of technical skills now… what do you want to do? How do you want to live?"

"In an ideal world," Alistair slowly answered, caught off guard by the sudden change in subject, "I think I'd start my own security company." There was a long pause. "What do you want to do?"

Oliver frowned and shook his head. "It doesn't matter." He lifted his bulk off the chair and made for the door. "Are you on tonight?"

"Yeah, I was going to take a little nap until it gets dark out."

"I'll wake you up," Oliver promised and then left.

After blowing out both lanterns, Alistair lay down on his cot, but sleep proved elusive as he thought of Oliver and Elizabeth.

18

Stephanie Caldwell held the parchment and her eyes glided over the writing. It was tinged brown, and thick, rough and uneven, like it was homemade. The original writing, transferred by some method of photocopying, had been in pencil. The officers in the station each had a copy and no one focused on anything else, their mood inclined towards amusement.

*We declare war on the government of Arcarius and of Rendral...For a multitude of offenses...for causing widespread starvation...for numerous prohibitions...a government in need of reform...a return to the early days of Aldra...we will fight until the tyrants are overthrown and a more concerned government rules the land...*At the top of the page, before the ostentatious declaration of war and list of grievances, was a yellow circle with a yellow A inside it, the three points of the A ending at the circle.

"Anyone you know?" asked Captain Travis as he crept up behind Stephanie with a cup of coffee.

She shook her head. "I'm sure I don't know."

"A return to the early days of Aldra. The Republic of Avon. Sounds like your friend Alistair, doesn't it?"

"No, this isn't Alistair. It's similar, but...I definitely wouldn't put it past him to declare war on the government." She let the parchment fall back on the table.

"Are you sure?"

"Yes, sir."

"Stephanie," Travis admonished, his tone just shy of severe, "you wouldn't be shielding him, would you?"

She fixed an incredulous frown on her captain. "I told you, you don't need to worry about that. Alistair is not going to receive favors from me. The law is the law."

Travis nodded. Taking a sip, he said, "What's that symbol for, I wonder?"

Stephanie shrugged. "They're calling for a new Arcarius and a new Aldra. I imagine it stands for one of the two. Or both."

"Even if you're sure it's not Alistair, why don't you stop by the Ashley household and ask around? Let them know Alistair needs our help."

"I don't think there is much help to be had from the Ashley's, but I'll stop by and ask a few questions before I go to the rally."

"You have crowd duty?"

"I signed up for it."

"I'm not surprised." Travis took a sip. "I wonder how Aloysius will handle this," he said, indicating the manifesto.

"I doubt very much he'll mention it. He'd be a fool. It's beneath his dignity. Something like this is best ignored by him and handled swiftly by us."

"Perhaps. But if they blow up any more government buildings he'll have to take notice." When he spoke again, his voice had lost its severity. "Let me know what the Ashley's have to say."

He left before she could reply.

෫෬

Though different interests had conspired to steal Nigel's home and business, the Ashley patriarch was not without recourse. He was, after all, a moderately successful businessman with a daughter who was a respected scientist, a son who was rising through the bureaucratic ranks and another son who had distinguished himself on Kaldis, his recent missteps notwithstanding. Many of the local power brokers spent time at Nigel's and were acquainted with him. The loss of his house was not an act of revenge, for Nigel had no enemies. Rather, he simply owned property deemed fit for better use. *Or rather than owned it,* Nigel thought with a sad smile as he remembered his youngest son, *leased it for a time with the State's permission.* It was a phrase right out of the mouth of his father-in-law the Homesteader.

When Nigel was shown the apartment he, his wife and daughter would be assigned, he was pleased. It was a spacious affair with large bedrooms, a big central area near the dining room and kitchen, a roomy and elegant balcony extending from the central room all along the outside to the master bedroom, and a study/library with a high ceiling and some gorgeous woodwork stained a dark reddish brown. The floors of his new abode did not creak, and the building did not groan when the wind blew against it. Looking out on the downtown from fifteen stories high, it was part of a large building where most of the upper class now resided. Thirty stories in all, the building's foundation was in the shape of a square with a smaller, open square at its center. This area was a courtyard kept safe from the winter weather by a glass ceiling. There was a small garden and a pathway through it, as well as a swimming pool. It had fallen a bit into disrepair, but with such shortages as they had experienced this was understandable. When the compensation for his business and home came on time and in the full amount promised, he made his peace with the State. If they needed his land for the cause, so be it. His living conditions were better than the majority of Aldrans.

As Nigel reclined on a couch in the main room, sipping at a glass of wine before dinner, there was a knock on his door. Rising from the couch, he set the glass down and went to open it.

"Stephanie," he said with a warm smile. "Good to see you."

"It's good to see you, Mr. Ashley," she replied with a smile of her own. "May I come in?"

"Absolutely." He guided her in with a gentle hand on the back. "May I get you something to drink?"

"I can't right now. I actually came to talk to you about Alistair."

"Oh," said Nigel, and his mood became somber. He sat down with an anxious look, indicating with an extended hand that she should also take a seat.

"I'm sure you've heard of the manifesto."

"We did," he said, then hurriedly added, "but we didn't read it. We were told not to read it."

"It's OK. We know people are reading it. Frankly, I think the more people read it the worse off this little revolution will be. It's absurd."

"You think Alistair is involved."

"No I don't. I honestly don't. It's not his kind of…rebellion, I guess. You've heard him talk just like I have. I honestly don't think it's him. I honestly don't. It's similar but…if you have any idea where he is…it looks suspicious. Alistair needs to give us an alibi for a few things. I don't think he's part of this, but he needs to clear his name." There was a moment of silence. "If you knew where he was, would you tell me?"

He did not answer at first. His kind eyes just welled up. "Stephanie…the State comes for my home…that's one thing. If it's what society needs. But this is my son. This is my son."

"We're not looking to arrest him. We just want to help him clear himself of any possible suspicion. I really don't think he had anything to do with the bombings or the pamphlet."

He smiled a smile with the effect of a frown. "If you tell me you don't think he's a part of it, I feel better. If you tell me several times you sound like you can't quite make yourself believe it."

Sighing, she replied, "The best thing for him is to come in and clear his name."

"All I know is what Katherine told me. He's left for Avon and then for who knows where."

She nodded and stood up. "Well, I just wanted to see how things were, let you know we're doing what we can. Are you going to the rally tonight?"

He stood up as well and walked her to the door. "Mrs. Ashley and I are going to spend a quiet evening together."

Stephanie now stood in the doorway. "Until next time."

"Until then," said Nigel and closed the door when Stephanie walked away.

"Maybe we shouldn't be together," suggested Alistair, digging his gloved hands deeper into his coat pockets and hunching his shoulders to keep his hood hanging low over his face.

"We're too bundled up to be recognizable," Oliver replied, giving Alistair only just enough attention to manage a response.

"There probably isn't another couple of men our size likely to be standing together in all of Aldra," Alistair grumbled. "We cannot be found right now." Oliver did not reply. "We have work to do tonight."

The two friends stood on the edge of the crowd that gathered for the rally at the Mayor's Palace. The sky was darkening, and a number of officials stood on the balcony above the double doors of the front entrance. The balcony's colored lights had been lit and shone off the sides of the Palace to impressive effect. In addition, two speakers had been set on either end of the balcony to project the orators' voices.

There were a number of tin men about, and Alistair nervously eyed them. None took any special note of them, but their presence was always a concern. The crowd tittered in its various subdued conversations. Someone emerged onto the balcony and attempted to excite them with a speech, but the cheering and applause was forced, not lasting five seconds past the time the speaker reentered the Palace. There was little to cheer about.

The doors to the balcony reopened, and out walked Aloysius Warwick, dressed in a well decorated officer's uniform. The crowd erupted into applause, this time sincerely. Behind the mayor came an entourage of unnecessary individuals, who, in exchange for making Aloysius look important, got to be seen and imaged with him. They were all dressed splendidly, which is to say their clothing was unfit for the cold in which they found themselves. Elizabeth was among them, dressed most splendidly of all.

She was dazzling. Always a beauty, she stood out even dressed in the rags a miner's daughter managed to put together. Now she was dressed as royalty, wearing an elegant evening gown with a mink coat and make-up expertly applied. She shivered now and then, but it was a sacrifice she no doubt considered worth the opportunity. Her smile was radiant. It was her first public appearance at Aloysius' side and she was clearly enjoying herself. Her smile stood out next to the plastered-on smiles of the local pols, stood out not just for its beautiful splendor but also for its authenticity. Oliver and Alistair could not have been the only ones looking at someone other than the mayor.

The big man stood transfixed, his face nearly cracking at first. He quickly recovered and his expression became stoic and unreadable. When Aloysius spoke, Alistair had no doubt Oliver did not hear him. He was there because he could not resist the torture, and probably would not resist it for a long time. Scanning the crowd, Alistair saw nothing to cause him great alarm. A couple Civil Guardsmen strolled past, but they took no notice of the two.

Aloysius avoided any mention of the leaflet Brad Stanson had written. He talked of the coming war, of the need for social bonding and cohesion, of the need for sacrifice. He spoke of the recent attacks by the Kaldisians, adding to the list the attack on the ONS, and saying how desperate the Kaldisians had proved themselves to be, how afraid they were that Aldra was to enter the war in force.

Alistair almost allowed himself to focus on the speaker, but he happened to glance down at the crowd and saw Stephanie Caldwell, in full Guard uniform, wandering the perimeter. Cursing himself for relaxing his vigilance, he gave Oliver a nudge in the ribs with his elbow.

"We need to get going. Caldwell's here."

Oliver followed Alistair's gaze and quickly spied their old friend. "Alright," he conceded. He looked once more at Elizabeth before turning to the right and following Alistair through the throng.

Alistair decided to walk into the crowd and out the far side, rather than skirt its edge, hoping this would keep them from Stephanie's notice. He was not willing to take the chance she was unaware of the Civil Guard's surveillance of them.

The crowd separated for them, making a wake as they passed through. Alistair prayed this also went unnoticed as he weaved his way through the bodies, opening a space that widened a moment later to allow Oliver passage. When they emerged on the far side, across from where they spotted Stephanie, they stepped right into the path of a pair of Guardsmen with a canine.

The dog approached and sniffed them. Alistair and Oliver stood still, and the officers stopped moving.

"They need to divide the city into precincts like Avon does," said one Guard to his partner.

The dog finished sniffing Alistair and inspected Oliver. The two officers did not even spare a glance.

"They won't do that because our permanent population is too small."

"Most of the year we've got over two million people. For five months we've got a skeleton crew—"

"So they organize us like a smaller city," finished the first officer as if reciting a refrain, and they both shared a chuckle of resignation.

The dog finished its inspection and the officers moved on. Alistair found himself bristling, but was not sure whether it was due to the invasive inspection by the dog or the cavalier disinterest of the officers, who took as much note of them as a fire hydrant on which the dog urinated.

The officers having moved on, the two companions made for a small alley. They turned to regard the scene one last time: Aloysius on the balcony, framed in lights, his voice booming from the speakers; the crowd attentive, if not overly enthusiastic; the several officers patrolling the plaza, all armed as if for battle. Stephanie was not visible, but Elizabeth was, and Oliver's gaze lingered on her a moment longer before he followed Alistair into the alley.

19

With a nervous breath, Alistair lifted his shirt over his head and stood in only his pants. He dropped the apparel on his cot and breathed in again, the action causing his muscles to swell and ripple across his back and shoulders. Exhaling loudly, as if purging his spirit of anxiety, he dropped his chin to his chest and closed his eyes. Oliver watched his friend's routine in the dimly lit room.

"Nervous?"

"I never had a battle yet where I didn't sweat."

"I've never been in a battle," said Oliver, sitting down at the desk. The chair creaked under his weight. "I didn't know you got a tattoo."

Looking down at it, Alistair traced the drawing with his finger. "My first and last. I got it on Kaldis."

Despite the words, Oliver thought he detected a touch of pride in Alistair's voice.

"If we get captured…"

"We'll be executed. So don't get caught." Alistair shook his head and pursed his lips. "Ah, we're not going to get caught. We'll hit them hard and fast and we'll be out before there's a response."

He unbuttoned his pants, pulled them down and reached for his Null Suit on the cot. The material stretched enough so his lower body fit through the opening at the face and passed into the leggings. He pulled it up his body and stuck his hands into the arms before finally pulling the hood over his head and the mask down, attaching it at the chin. Where Alistair had just been there was now a blurry silhouette in human shape, ready to blend with the shadows.

"I'd hate to be the tin man who comes across that in a dark alley."

"That's the idea." Grabbing a few items and placing them into his thigh pouch, Alistair continued, "Get the men in place. Remember how much is riding on this."

"Don't worry about my end."

Sewn into the Steltar of Alistair's Null Suit, inside the mask and next to his mouth, there was a tiny transmitter. Next to his ear was a receiver. The transmitter would first scramble his vocalizations and then send them to Mike's receiver, which would descramble the message, appearing, they hoped, to any outside party as random static. Once the attack began, the State's forces would not know which frequencies to jam. It was ideal for their purposes, but the rebels possessed only the two Mike and Alistair were using.

Thus Alistair waited again atop a building in the dark Arcarian winter night, his body insulated from the frigid air by the amazing properties of his Null Suit. He crouched at the building's edge, across from the prison's concrete outer wall, which ran flush with the edge of the street and comprised the entire city block. From behind the wall, neither sound nor ray of light issued. There was a tower at the center, the only part of the complex visible from where he was, and there would be Civil Guard posted there. Behind the one-way windows in the saucer-shaped head of the tower, they would be sitting at their stations, relying on computer equipment incapable of detecting him.

There were no street lamps in operation, so no long shadows preceded the arrival of four rebels. Only the desultory echoes of four pairs of booted feet hustling down the street in the still night announced their arrival. When they were twenty yards or so from him, they stopped at the door of a building opposite the prison yard wall, opened it with a key, and filed inside. A moment later, a whistle as if from a bird was heard.

"Alpha Team in position," said Alistair softly into his transmitter.

"Alpha Team in position," said Mike on the other end, his voice as clear as if they were side by side. *"Copy that."*

Grabbing the rope and grappling iron at his feet, Alistair stood up. No such primitive entry was possible on Kaldis, for sensors would detect the hook the minute it touched the perimeter wall, but on Aldra the hook fell into place after a smooth toss and no alarm was raised. Pausing only to heft a small satchel, Alistair clambered down the side of the building, taking with him a small sack of supplies. Aided by the rope, he proceeded to scale the smooth concrete prison wall. In a matter of seconds, he was atop the five yard high barrier and surveying the compound and its three story edifice.

"I've gained the wall," he whispered.

"Copy that. Wall gained."

On Kaldis, Alistair embarked on many missions in solitude, with only his communication system keeping him in contact with his mates. It was a strange thing, especially at night, to be so alone and yet to have a link to companionship, to another's voice. It was no different for him there on the prison wall, as he grabbed hold of his grappling hook and prepared to penetrate deeper into the complex.

Wrapping the rope around his shoulder, he sprinted until he came to an intersection, his footfalls mere whispers in the night. Another wall, running perpendicular, ended at the perimeter wall and separated one courtyard from another. He sprinted along it, heading straight for the central building and its tower. When he neared it, he grabbed hold of the edge, lowered himself down as far as he could, and dropped the rest of the way. Removing an item from his satchel, he attached it to the main building's wall. It was the work of a few moments, and when he finished he pressed a red button and a tiny green light at the top of the device turned on.

"Number one in place."

"Number one. Copy."

He went to the courtyard wall on the other side, with the aid of his hook climbed once again atop it, and repeated the process in the next courtyard. In all, he attached five of the devices to the walls of the prison. From there, he went on to attach five more to the inside of the perimeter wall. There was no indication the prison guards were onto them. All was quiet and still. A couple windows in the complex were lit, but Alistair detected no movement and no sound. With one last scan of the area from atop the perimeter wall, he decided it was time.

"Number ten in place. We are go on my end."

"Number ten in place, copy that," came the reply. *"We're go."*

He dashed along the wall towards the complex. When he was halfway across, the sound of ten simultaneous explosions shattered the night's stillness. He saw bursts of light and bits of brick wall flew into the air. It was as if ten fountains erupted from the complex, except dust and chips of brick and concrete, rather than water, were sprayed.

The explosions were followed by the sound of detritus raining back down to earth. Some of the bits pelted Alistair through his Null Suit but he ignored them as he reached the central complex and vaulted onto the roof above. A short-lived quiet reigned. Then, from inside the complex underneath him, came frantic shouting and officers barking orders.

As fast as his legs could take him, Alistair flew towards the tower's base. Upon arriving, he saw bundles of equipment running up and down it, along with long tubes of plastic and a ladder on the north side. He hopped onto this ladder and climbed, the rope and grappling hook still wrapped around his left shoulder, his satchel abandoned.

From below came the sounds of gunfire and shouting voices. Mike's frenetic voice, not speaking to Alistair, broke in intermittently. There were the isolated snaps of the rebels' rifles mixed in with the crackle from the automatic weapons of the Civil Guard. The sounds grew fainter as Alistair climbed all the way up the tower, coming at last to the part underneath the floor of the command room. There was a hatch there, but it would be locked and was not the best way for him to enter anyway.

Once again grabbing his grappling hook, he snagged a railing running underneath the tower and, after testing the weight carefully, let go of the ladder and dangled many yards above the roof of the complex. As he inched his way out to the edge of the tower room, he looked below his hanging feet and saw dozens of points of light burst into fleeting existence. Like fireflies, the flashes from the gunfire lit the courtyard below like a meadow on a spring night, but the crackle of gunfire and the shouts of men in battle were a reminder that below was no innocuous rustic scene.

"To the left! To the left!" Mike yelled to someone, his rough, throaty voice rising an octave as his adrenaline took over.

Upon reaching the edge, Alistair hung suspended from the railing by his left hand while his right reached up and found a small ledge. It was iced over, so he was forced to spend a minute clearing it off. Finally, he grabbed hold of it with his right hand, thankful for the extra grip his Null Suit provided and, fighting every instinct nature had given him, let go of the grappling hook. Reaching up quickly with the second hand, he now hung from the tiny ledge encircling the base of the tower room.

The walls were too thick to hear anything inside, and the one-way windows provided no view into the room, but he imagined things must be getting excited inside. The Guardsmen would be too well trained for things to reach a frantic pitch, but they definitely would be distracted. So thinking, he circled around to the other side of the tower. He heard a mechanical noise, like gears moving, coming from above. Suddenly, a deafening blast assaulted his ears, and then another. The ledge from which he so precariously hung vibrated. Below, sections of the courtyard erupted as the projectiles hit. He redoubled his efforts.

Upon reaching the far side, he pulled himself up so his chin reached the ledge, then placed his right forearm onto the small shelf and pushed himself up until his waist reached the edge and both his palms were supporting him. Leaning into the side of the tower room, never more than a couple inches from losing balance and falling, he lifted his left leg and placed it on the ledge. With his left leg and right arm he held himself steady while, with his left hand, he reached into his thigh pouch and withdrew the small black puck he used at the politician's home. The deafening blast from the tower's guns continued unabated.

"Hold steady! Roderick, hold bloody still goddamnit!"

Alistair lifted the puck above his head and just managed to reach the one-way window above. Licking his lips inside his mask, he cut out a small section, withdrew it, and set it next to him on the ledge with the puck. Grabbing onto the newly made hole, he pulled himself up to stand. Squatting down, he retrieved the puck and cut out a bigger section of the window.

Peering into the tower room, he saw two men and two women in the red and blue Civil Guard uniforms. The men were manning two large guns, almost cannons resting on tripods, and the women were at the computers. He waited for a moment, but they were oblivious to his presence.

Once more reaching into his thigh pouch, he produced a black sphere about half the size of a golf ball. He squeezed it once and then tossed it into the room, scooting sideways away from the hole as he did so. After a moment, there was a buzzing noise and he heard the sound of bodies hitting the floor. The tremendous cannon blasts ceased.

"Tower taken out."

"It's about damn time! They're fucking killing us down here!"

"You should be able to penetrate the complex now," he responded as calmly as if they were discussing weather over a cup of tea.

Using the puck and still pressing himself against the one-way window, he opened an even larger hole, tossed the cut off section into the empty space behind him, and entered the tower room. A circular area about fifteen yards in diameter, it was lined with computer stations and had two cannons at each cardinal direction. It was lit by the lights from the computer monitors and buttons on the keyboards, a soft, multi-hued glow creating dozens of indistinct shadows.

From the receiver of one of the women, he heard a voice demanding a response. He plucked the receiver from the unconscious woman's head and tossed it out the hole in the window, then used their own handcuffs to bind them in pairs, back to back and to the seats bolted to the floor. As expected, they wore firearms and he availed himself of these and their ammo.

Next, he went to one of the cannons and, careful not to fire at any individual, kicked up a cloud of debris and dust in one of the courtyards. Bits of pavement sprayed into the air. The gun's kickback rattled his hands and a blast of wind came back at him with each shot. The visceral thrill of firing a powerful weapon reminded him of Kaldis. This reminder was quickly followed by the awful memory of what such weapons had done, and the sick feeling that remained when the thrill waned.

From the computers' heat sensors he determined that the Civil Guard had retreated from the barrage, so he fired into the building itself, toppling a whole section of roof and wall and leaving the way clear for the rebel advance. This process he repeated once more with another section of courtyard but dared stay no longer.

He used the computer to call for the elevator. A conical apparatus, it immediately rose from the center of the floor like the tower of a submarine from the ocean's waves. Alistair stepped inside only long enough to press the emergency button to disable it. That done, he lifted up the hatch next to the elevator and, cloaked in absolute darkness, descended the tower stairs.

He had not been long on the winding stairs when he heard the rumble of footsteps coming towards him. Setting both his feet against one wall and his back against the opposite, he managed to lift himself up to the ceiling. He held this position until the group of Civil Guard passed beneath him, guns drawn, never noticing the shadow above them despite the flashlights attached to their helmets.

"…almost reached the tower level…" one of the three was saying as he passed underneath.

As soon as they rounded the bend, he let himself down and continued to the bottom. When he reached it, he burst into the room with his gun pointed at the two Guardsmen he found. They were startled and did not have their guns ready. He put a finger in front of his mask where his lips were but kept the gun pointed at them.

"If I wanted to kill you, you'd already be dead. But I'm perfectly willing to if you make me."

There was a moment of hesitation, and he saw the startled looks on their faces as they confronted what to them must have seemed an apparition. One officer tried to draw his gun but a shot in the shoulder sent him spinning to the ground. He landed with a groan.

"How about you?" he asked the other and that one raised his hands in the air. "Excellent."

After he crushed their communicators and handcuffed them together, he moved into the complex. As he weaved his way through the hallways, he heard the sound of occasional gunshots inside, and every now and then a shout or two reached his ears with successive echoes, but the sound he followed was the roar of many voices muted by the thick walls. His going was slow and careful. Every corner was carefully investigated before he rounded it and he frequently checked behind. He came across neither officers nor fellow rebels.

He knew he found what he searched for when the sound of shouting grew louder with each step until the corridor reverberated with the echoes of the yelling and hollering of the inmates. By the time the passageway opened up into a gigantic two-story chamber ringed above and below by holding cells, the floor shook beneath him and the din was so raucous it was hard even to think. The prisoners were not just yelling but were stomping their feet, clapping their hands and even hurling themselves against their cell doors in their excitement and fear.

Alistair burst into the chamber with his gun drawn, but there were no Guardsmen. He blessed his good luck and ran to a holding cell. The prisoner inside, a dirty, ragged and withered looking man with several months' growth of beard, regarded him with wide eyes and retreated back into his cell. Realizing how he must appear, he lifted the mask of his Null Suit, giving a clear face to focus on.

"I'm here to set you free. How do I open the doors?"

The man hesitated a moment until the question finally sank in. With a trembling hand, he indicated a direction and Alistair, following it, spotted a control panel. Climbing a short flight of steps onto a dais, he went to the panel and spent a few seconds inspecting it. He found his button, pressed it and the cage doors on the top floor opened in unison. Though it hardly seemed possible, the roar grew in intensity and prisoners poured out of their cells.

Alistair pressed the next button and the doors of the bottom floor opened, followed by the same flood of freed bodies. There was a mad rush to the passageway leading out. A few prisoners slapped Alistair on the back, but most just stampeded for the exit. When they had gone and the roar of their passing retreated down the corridor, there were a few bodies left strewn about the chamber. Some groaned. Others did not move at all.

Unsure what to do, he found one feeble old man, crawling along the ground with his right ankle twisted at a sickening angle, and hoisted him onto his shoulder. He groaned but did not struggle and, brushing the man's beard out of his eyes, Alistair proceeded to follow the sound of the herd of prisoners, figuring they would know the fastest route out. He nearly caught up to the stragglers of the herd when he rounded a corner and was greeted by large, steel double doors blown open by explosives. The herd of prisoners was disappearing into the night while several rebels watched them go in amazement.

"Follow them!" Alistair barked at a few of the men. "Show them where to go!" The men hesitated. "Get to it!" he roared and that served to put them in motion.

"There's no reason to hang around here any longer," said Mike, and Alistair turned to see him approaching with two men flanking him. "Couldn't ya' find anyone more useless to bring home?" he asked, indicating the old man on Alistair's shoulders.

Alistair dumped the man on one of the men flanking Mike. "See that he comes back with us. We'll get him some medical attention." The man looked reluctant but Mike did not contravene the order so he nodded and left by the open doorway.

"What are ya', a Jesuit?" Mike asked.

"I think we should leave now," Alistair informed him, checking his ammunition.

"What did I just say?" asked Mike, irritated. "Alright, men! We're leaving! To yer safe houses!" Mike turned to Alistair as they walked and gruffly said, "Not a bad night's work. Care to come in my auto?"

Before Alistair could answer, there was an explosion and he was flying through the air. He couldn't tell which way was up until his face smashed into the tiled floor and he nearly rolled over on his head, twisting his neck. While his ears rang and his vision blurred, before he even remembered where he was, he instinctively reached for a gun in a holster that was not there. He got to his knees and rubbed his eyes. Not far from him, he saw the gun he had stolen from the officers. He grabbed it, checked it, and crawled along the ground to the doorway.

Outside an auto was obliterated and several bodies lay strewn about. Pulling his mask back down over his face, he scanned the area and then, like a snake, bellied his way across the ground. Then he saw it: the double doors to the perimeter wall opened and a tank blocked the exit. Guardsmen moved into the grounds, swarming in on either side of the tank.

Taking aim, Alistair fired off ten rounds in succession and four Guardsmen stumbled and fell. Amid the shouts of the troops streaming into the courtyard, he crawled along. He fired a few more shots and another officer fell. Discarding the empty magazine and replacing it, he continued crawling, wincing as each movement produced a fire in his ribs.

The tank fired another round into the open doorway and the front wall collapsed. Looking behind him, Alistair saw a yellow A in a circle painted in the quick, furtive strokes of the graffiti artist, but most of it came down with the collapse.

The attacking Guardsmen now reached the carnage, looking for survivors, and Alistair wisely stopped shooting. Relying on his Null Suit, he crawled towards the perimeter wall, but as far from the tank as he could. When he reached the point where the courtyard wall met the perimeter wall, he staggered to his feet, realizing how woozy he felt. Steadying himself, he ran at the corner where the walls met. With a tremendous leap, he was up in the air and hit the courtyard wall with his right foot. He pushed off upwards and to the left and landed his left foot on the perimeter wall, whence he jumped again back to the right. The extra grip of the Null Suit helped him reach the top in this fashion. With a last leap, just as gravity's pull started to defeat his erratic ascent, he reached out and grabbed the edge. He pulled himself over with a tremendous effort and, lying on his belly, rested for a moment.

He heard the tank move into the courtyard, heard the shouts of the Guardsmen as they retook the complex. His chest was heaving, but it must have been more from shock than exertion, or else his conditioning had further deteriorated. He finally forced himself into a crouch and half leapt, half fell to the ground below, landing with a roll that still knocked the wind from him. Staggering again, he managed to cross the street, his lungs gulping oxygen. Just as the sound of sirens presaged yet more reinforcements, he crept into an alley and disappeared into the surrounding forest of buildings whose windows were beginning, one by one, to light up.

20

In the muted light of the warehouse, with only two lanterns in the corner providing illumination, Gregory Lushington leaned over his friend and massaged his ribs.

"Tell me when it hurts."

"It hurts a little everywhere," Alistair responded, lying back on a cot with several coats bunched together at the head so that his upper body was elevated. "It doesn't hurt too much, though."

"You don't need to be tough. If something hurts, let me know."

Gregory moved from the ribs to the neck, carefully tilting Alistair's head first one way, then another, his fingers kneading the flesh. His gentle digits might have put Alistair to sleep if he hadn't had to wince every now and then when the doctor discovered a painful spot.

Oliver poked his head into the room. That part of his expression not hidden in shadow was grim. "What's the prognosis, doc?"

"Not done yet. But there is no serious wound to the neck or body." So saying, he grabbed his penlight and shone it into Alistair's eyes. As if startled, he pulled back and then drew close again, studying the orbs. With a puzzled look on his face, he checked the other eye. Then he dropped his hands and, eyeing Alistair curiously, flipped the penlight off.

"They were altered on Kaldis," Alistair informed him.

"What was altered?" asked Oliver, entering the room and drawing near Alistair's cot.

"My eyes. It was part of the military program I was in."

"Improving your eyesight?" asked Gregory.

Alistair nodded.

"What did they do?" asked Oliver.

Alistair started to shake his head but stopped and winced. "Gave me better vision. Gave me night vision. All part of making me a killing machine."

"Hmmm," said Gregory and resumed his examination.

"What's the status, Ollie?" Alistair asked.

"We won't know who is dead and who is alive for a little while. The men haven't all reported back to their safe houses."

"Is any effort being made to contact the prisoners?"

Oliver nodded. "They don't have anywhere else to go. The ones we have found have been receptive."

"Are you sure you want to talk about this in front of me?" asked Gregory with a disapproving tone in his voice. He stood up from the cot with an air of finality.

"If I thought you were going to turn us in you wouldn't be here," Oliver informed him. "What's the prognosis?"

"Nothing that won't heal. You might want to take it easy for a day or two. And, of course, I doubt you will want to be seen in public unless you have a good story for your face."

So saying, Gregory held a mirror up to Alistair and for the first time, he saw his swollen and discolored nose, far more ghastly than the healing wound Oliver sported above his eye. There were several other less serious wounds and bruises as well.

"Broken?"

"Would you like me to set it?"

Alistair nodded. Gregory held Alistair's head in his hands with his thumbs at either side of his nose. Gregory paused to take a breath, and then, with one decisive movement, cracked it back into place. Alistair could not contain a strained grunt, and his eyes watered.

"It could be crooked when it heals," Gregory informed him, unwinding a stretch of tape with which he dressed Alistair's nose.

"I'll put myself on a surgery waiting list." Alistair's voice was raspy as he squinted against the tears flowing from his eyes. "They'll have it back to normal in ten cycles or so."

With a sigh, Gregory finished the wrap and collected his equipment.

"Thanks for your help, Greg," said Oliver as Alistair closed his eyes and lay back, rubbing his temples to soften the headache assailing him.

Gregory loudly sighed again but did not answer.

Oliver watched him for a moment with a gloomy expression, but the young doctor did not turn to look at him. Giving Alistair a gentle pat on the shoulder, Oliver said, "Just lay back and rest, little buddy."

This produced a strained chuckle from Gregory. "You are the only person on Aldra who could refer to Alistair as 'little buddy'," he said and then shook his head. "Damn it, you two…" With his belongings packed away in his small carrying case, he turned to face them. "I was going to say 'see you soon' but…"

"We'll see you again," Oliver promised.

"I'm sure you'll be begging for more of my services when Rendral puts your rebellion down," Greg returned and slipped out of the room.

"Greg," Oliver called after him but there was no response. "They'll understand soon enough," he said to Alistair. "So how many do you think died?"

His eyes still closed, Alistair replied, "Our guys? I don't know. But Mike is gone."

"Dead?"

"Buried in rubble."

Oliver sat down at the desk. He considered the information. "That is going to have to be dealt with," he said more to himself. "How many prisoners were there?"

"Four thousand at least."

"If we get just half of them…"

"They've got nowhere else to go. We'll get plenty of them, but we need to find them before the tin men do. Listen, Ollie." Alistair sat up and grabbed Oliver's shirt. "You need to personally oversee that aspect. When the new recruits come in, make sure they see you. They need to know your face best."

"What's going on here, Al? You want me to lead the rebellion?"

"Not lead, no, but we don't want everyone looking to Clever Johnny as if he were in charge."

Oliver nodded, understanding. "Power struggle."

"Don't allow them to call any sort of command meeting until I'm up and about. Probably by tomorrow. Where are they right now?"

"I don't know where Brad is. Clever Johnny's here at the warehouse."

"Don't let Clever Johnny give too many orders. Override him a few times, just to flex your muscle. Don't let the men see him in charge and get used to him giving orders. And whatever happens, don't allow them to call a meeting and cast any votes. Brad could fall on Clever Johnny's side. I have to be there with you."

Oliver nodded as he took it all in. "I'll round up a few men right now and get started."

"This doesn't mean you're in charge either."

"Are you a little paranoid?"

"I'll be better by tomorrow," Alistair said, his voice fading to a croak. "Work hard until then. And try to get a feel for the government's response while you're out there."

"Lay back and rest, little buddy. I'll see to it."

Oliver put out one lantern, dimmed the other, and left Alistair to recuperate in the dark room.

21

The biggest initial effect of the attack on the prison was to cause Rendral to officially declare war on Kaldis. Alistair and Oliver, though against the war itself, could not help but feel a certain guilty excitement at the pronouncement, for it meant the bulk of Aldra's military might be directed elsewhere. Warwick declared Marshall Law and the Civil Guard carried out house-to-house searches. A few of the rebels were apprehended on account of their wounds from the fighting. A few innocent men were taken for sporting an injury. The arrested men, innocent and guilty, were thrown together in a hastily erected camp of barbed wire and chain-link fences. There were soon reports that some had frozen to death. Mayor Warwick was said to have shrugged off the news, saying that if they wanted a warmer prison they should not have destroyed the one they were given.

More grim news came to make the rebels rejoice: another food shortage. The mammoth Agricultural Bureau improperly stored the food it collected for the winter. Much of it rotted, and when word got out, most of the rest disappeared as worker theft skyrocketed. Amid promises to double the yield from the areas with a year round growing season, the government reported the food was being recovered even then, the amount of spoilage was vastly overstated and the citizens should not worry.

It was difficult to get a clear picture of the situation from remote Arcarius. Rumors flew about, countered by State media agencies, and one could never know whether their misinformation was farther from the truth than the exuberant exaggerations from the rumor mills. Though the picture was blurred and distorted by distance and uncertainty, one could still see the basic form coalescing on the canvas. The Realists had seized power and were remaking the State, but they grasped at so much from a people already exhausted from carrying the weight of so large a government.

❧❧

Across the street from Oliver, Bob LaSalle leaned against the brick wall of a townhouse, smoking a cigar and seemingly oblivious to the world. Oliver sat on the side of the road, using the tip of his knife to pick pebbles from the treads of his boots. Two other men farther down the street were apparently tightening the lug nuts of an auto. Hardly concentrating on his boot, Oliver peered down the narrow street framed by brick buildings of varying heights, his hand only absentmindedly guiding the knife point. He stopped when a figure appeared from around the corner. Oliver glanced at LaSalle and saw LaSalle looking back at him. LaSalle tossed his cigar into the street.

Upon seeing this, the other two men quickly stopped working, got in the auto, and started the engine. Oliver sheathed his knife and stood up as the figure approached on LaSalle's side of the street. Ducking into the shadow of a doorway, he pulled down the rolled up brim of his mask and peered out from two eyeholes. As the man passed LaSalle, Oliver's partner also covered his visage.

The target was of middle age and sported newly made and expensive winter clothing of a fashion currently popular among the upper class. When he was directly across the street from Oliver, the rugby star walked out of the doorway towards the man, who stopped at a wooden door and was fumbling with his keys. Finding one and placing it in the keyhole, he unlocked the door. When Oliver heard the click, his walk became a run and he barreled into him, slamming them both into the door and flinging it wide open.

The man cushioned Oliver's impact against the foyer wall and, with a groan, sank to the floor while Bob LaSalle followed them inside. The auto with recently tightened lug nuts pulled up front. Oliver grabbed the semi-conscious man he had crushed and one of the others dashed into the house and closed the door, peering around expectantly. Dragging the target into the living room, Oliver deposited him on the floor.

"Found it!" called LaSalle from another room, and Oliver followed his voice into a pantry.

At the end of the narrow, cramped room there was a locked door. Oliver moved past LaSalle, who had to squeeze up against the shelves to allow the big man through, and with one kick splintered the door. He flipped a switch and, when the light revealed a closet stocked with food, loaded his companions with provisions. They carried them out to the auto and Oliver was close behind with a load of his own. Upon returning, the owner of the home was just rising unsteadily to his feet.

"Watch him," said Oliver, pointing at the man and LaSalle moved to him and shoved him onto a couch.

"Just sit nice and quiet," suggested LaSalle, standing over him while Oliver and the other raided the larder once more.

Two more quick trips and the larder was empty. LaSalle wrapped some twine around the victim's wrists and ankles and left him in the middle of his living room floor. An instant later, the men were gone. From where he was, the bound man heard the door slam shut and the auto pull away, but for many minutes he remained unmoving save for his uncontrollable shaking.

かか

The office of the Chief of Transportation of Arcarius was between Gerald's cubicle and the computer room. Since Gerald's office currently had no electricity, he and nearly everyone else at the Bureau of Transportation were forced to do all computer work in short shifts in a designated room. Between putting his name on the waiting list, checking to see how much longer he had to wait and actually using the room, he had been past Leland Maddox's office a score of times. The door was shut for the entire early part of the day, which was not usual. Just as Gerald's first shift was about to end and he was walking by the office yet again, he saw the door was open and a group of three officials dressed smartly in suits were standing there, concluding some final obligatory remarks before leaving. Leland, the droopy features of his face sagging more than usual, stood in his doorway when they left, his left hand scratching the top of his bald head, the right hand plunged deep into the pockets of his trousers which sagged underneath his generous paunch. When he saw Gerald, his features momentarily brightened before returning to their gentle, lazy wilt. He stuffed his left hand into his pocket and said in a voice that somehow was a perfect fit for his face, "It's worse than usual today. Much worse."

He turned to go back in his office and Gerald repressed a sigh. He would be expected to follow.

"You can leave the door open," said Leland as he unhurriedly sat down at his desk.

Gerald stood with his folders in hand, fighting the urge to fidget. Leland let out a long-suffering sigh.

"I just feel," he began with the tone of voice one uses with a psychiatrist, "like whenever they have something that needs done, they bring it to us. It's always something. You don't have to wait for permission, Gerald. Have a seat."

"Actually, I reserved some time in the computer room and I was just hurrying down there—"

"Oh, heck. You can use my computer," said Leland, reaching over to turn it on.

"Your computer works?"

"Oh, yeah. I had to give my room some power when the men came from Rendral."

"Rendral?"

Leland did not immediately respond to the question. Once his computer was turned on, he stood up, hands back in his pockets, and nodded at the chair. Setting his folders on the desk in front of him, Gerald took the seat and logged on while the inevitable monologue came.

"So today is going to be a particularly difficult one," resumed the boss over the clicking of Gerald's typing. He lugubriously paced around the room, sometimes talking towards Gerald, sometimes towards a wall. "I don't even know where to begin. They're going to go ahead and build another underground tunnel from Avon to Arcarius."

This made Gerald pause. "When do they start?"

"Now."

"What!? During the winter!?"

Leland shrugged, clearly pleased to share his misery with someone. "They want to get a steady stream of raw materials from the island for the war effort."

"I thought they decided it was too expensive, that they would just ship the materials by boat over the channel."

"Well, they've changed their minds. They talked about the—how did they put it?—sporadic boat schedule."

Gerald accepted the information and was ready to move on. He began to type again, but Leland was not finished.

"They want a direct line to Avon. The line is going to be used just for shipping raw materials as soon as they are mined. And they want it done yesterday. They were quite adamant about the need for a smooth train schedule. I must say: I got the distinct impression they were implying some criticism, which is more than I should have to bear. Big shots from Rendral haven't spent a day of their lives in the Transportation Bureau. I'd like to see them try to make sense of things from this end."

Gerald made sure to intersperse some "hmm's" and "aah's" while Leland spoke.

"Anyway, the line is going to be built. They want it finished six months from now."

"Six months?"

"Yes indeed. Six months. This is going to mean no end of work for me. Not that I mind doing it; I try to make things work just like anybody. I just know this means I am going to have the bulk of the work put on my shoulders." Gerald continued typing and Leland paused for a moment to watch him. "They're sending the seasonal workers back in."

"When?"

"Now. They want to build up the stock of raw materials while the underchannel line is being built. They'll ship what they can oversea and in the other line, but they apparently believe we'll be able to ship faster than they can mine, which is my assessment as well. Of course, this is supposed to be our slow season…" Gerald continued typing. "And then there's the bad news." Leland paused for effect but was disappointed in Gerald's lack of reaction. Frowning, he said, "This rebel group has attacked the Northern Line."

Gerald stopped typing again, this time his body frozen stock-still.

"Who knows when the repairs will be made," said Leland, pacing again and with more satisfaction. "They bombed it pretty good. Of course, this means who knows how many extra hours making changes in the schedule. Who understands these idiots? I'll tell you right now, there's more than a couple fools out there with enough orneriness to want to make everything harder on everybody else. I don't know what they think they're accomplishing. Just means more work. Especially for me."

"When did they bomb it?"

"Just now. About two hours ago. It will have to be fixed before any materials can be shipped. I suppose they'll just bomb another section later. Who knows how we'll be able to protect so many miles of railway…"

Gerald leaned back in his chair, his task only partly finished. "Leland, I think we should consider turning computer power on for the whole building."

The apartment buildings near the center of the city, where the winter remnant of Arcarius' population were moved, blocked the early morning light from reaching the shabby and icy streets below. The buildings themselves were in little better shape than the streets, with cracked and crumbling façades, boarded windows and warped wooden roofs. Into this quiet slum an auto entered, spewing steamy exhaust from its rear and quietly rumbling. The auto had a large trunk and when it stopped, several figures exited and one opened it. They hurriedly unloaded several crates and set them in the middle of the street, a task that took them all of twenty seconds. Lastly, a parchment was nailed to the top of the pile, a parchment with a short note and a yellow A in a yellow circle at the top.

Before anyone noticed, they were back in the auto. A window opened and a horn emerged, letting out an earsplitting blast before the vehicle was around the corner. A few moments later, windows opened and curious citizens stuck out their heads and found the pile in the street.

Stephanie hesitated for just a second as she crouched next to her comrades in the dark and damp cold of the stairwell. She watched her breath leave as a cloud to dissipate farther out, mingling invisible with the exhalations of the dozen other men and women under her command. She heard the muffled hum of machinery behind the wall on the floor just above her.

Gripping her pistol tightly in both gloved hands, she met the gaze of her second-in-command and nodded. Her second returned the nod and waved forward two men with a small battering ram. They came from farther below, raced past the officers, and charged at a rickety old wooden door that collapsed under the first blow. Stephanie and company were moving before the first shouts were heard. The men with the battering ram moved aside and ten armed and armored Guardsmen flowed into the room, pointing guns and yelling orders.

Stephanie entered to see the tail end of a mad scramble and a piling of bodies. Six Guardsmen were subduing three resistors amid yelling and cursing. Two others were retrieving a fourth rebel from where he had tried to jump out a back window. The last two were moving through the apartment searching for others. In the back corner, the printing press was still humming. Stephanie casually stepped through the pile of bodies and picked up a freshly printed pamphlet. There was a large circled yellow A at the top, followed by some incendiary rhetoric about the abuses of the State. The fresh ink smudged under her gloved thumb. Glancing over it just once, she crumpled it in her hand and tossed it on the floor.

"Just the four of them, sir," said an officer, returning to the front room, and Stephanie acknowledged him with a nod.

The four rebels were cuffed and laid out, bellies down on the bare wood floor. Several knees, hands and elbows pressed on them, keeping them restrained as they grunted and fidgeted. She moved to one and squatted down at his head.

"Did you want to make a statement before we haul you off?" she asked, her voice low and hard.

The man tried to spit at her, but from his position he only managed to drool on his own chin.

"Get them out and ready for questioning."

The men were promptly lifted up and hauled away.

"We're going to leave a few men here and see if any other rebels show up," said Stephanie.

"Yes, sir."

"Leave behind a force of six. Give them provisions for four days; we can't risk relieving them. If they can arrest some more, all the better. If not…" She let the sentence die unfinished. Then, turning on her heel, she marched out of the room, ready to begin an interrogation.

Because her face was covered by a woolen scarf, her head ducked down into her coat's collar and her hat pulled down nearly over her eyes, Katherine did not see the pile of crates in the middle of the street until she almost stepped on one of the broken slats. The hat muffled her hearing, but that she did not hear the throng of people picking through the wreckage was more likely due to her distracted thinking. She stopped mid-stride and looked up to briefly meet the gaze of an old man tossing aside planks to get at anything underneath. He glanced at her only momentarily before, uninterested, he returned to his scavenging.

She was about to move on when she spied a canned good lying amid the wreckage. She was just bending down to pick it up when a child no more than ten cycles old darted in and snatched it up. She did not even look at Katherine before darting off as quickly as she descended on the can. Standing up straight to look around, Katherine saw a couple dozen people hurriedly returning to their homes, newly acquired groceries in hand.

Curious, she picked through the wreckage, but there was only a parchment with an increasingly familiar logo. She snatched it and looked it over. The message was an attack on the State and an entreaty to support the rebellion. In the middle of famine, it declared, the rebellion supplied food when the State could not. The rebellion freed the innocents held in prison for taking the food they earned but which the State hoarded for itself.

She dropped the parchment, resuming her march to the Science Institute, a march necessitated by the fact the Metro was no longer running. Her thoughts did not return to Flow Theory. Now it was the image of her youngest sibling filling her contemplations.

ক্ষ ক্ষ

The four detainees had been placed in separate holding cells with the traditional one-way mirror. Stephanie sat at a desk on the other side of the mirror facing all four prisoners, studying the initial reports. An overhead lamp illuminated the desktop, and a soft glow came out of the holding cells themselves, but the long hallway to either side was quite dark. She heard Travis before he stepped into the sphere of light around her desk.

"Are you conducting this alone?" he asked her, his thin mustache and hair freshly oiled, his uniform impeccably pressed and his black boots shining.

"They're being monitored on the closed circuit system." She stood to greet her boss. He motioned for her to sit back down. "I want them to feel like they're alone."

"When are you going in?"

"In the next few minutes. They've been alone for almost a day with nothing but water and a little bread. We'll see if they're ready to cooperate."

Travis nodded, but by his vacant stare she knew something more was coming.

"The State wants to open the mines for the winter," he started, tracing a slow path around her desk to the other side.

"Yes, sir. I've read about the war plans."

"Which means this rebellion needs to end before it spreads."

Stephanie snorted. "It's not going to spread. The rebels are a few malcontents; real Aldrans obey the law. They would never—"

"There have been food riots in other cities. Including Rendral itself. We're stretched thin right now, with the war, the change-over of power, the new economic plan…don't overestimate how law abiding Aldrans actually are. When your stomach's empty laws mean little enough." He paused a second, and then went on. "The rebels should be executed after questioning," he declared, watching for Stephanie's reaction. She said nothing. "Do you not agree?"

"It's a bit harsh," she carefully ventured. "We're at war with Kaldis. In other times something like this might be…not tolerated, but dealt with less severely. Kindness is not something we can allow ourselves right now, but execution might be…going too far."

"Perhaps," said Travis, returning to the side he had come from, "but if the rebels are dead, then they're not rebelling."

Stephanie made a face. "And if execution creates sympathy, new recruits might more than offset the losses."

"But I thought Aldrans were law-abiding." A ghost of a smile touched the corners of his lips, but then his voice was serious again. "The rebels are Aldrans like anyone else, Officer Caldwell. They weren't born with a rebel gene; they simply reached the limit of what they were willing to endure. And if they rebel, so can others. You are quite correct. The corpses we make may serve as fertilizer for a revolution."

Stephanie nodded slowly, her brow knit in an expression both curious and concerned. "Captain Travis, I'm not sure what your purpose is. I've been given orders to arrest citizens I hear saying what you just—"

Travis tossed his head back and laughed. "Caldwell, you're the most talented officer I've got. If you want to rise higher learn only to appear blindly loyal. Think realistically. You need to look Mayor Warwick right in the eye and tell him how insignificant the rebels are, and how easily they will be squashed. You can both laugh about it later when you're alone. That's how the game is played."

"I'm not playing a game," she said after a deep breath. "I'm surprised to hear you say that."

Travis nodded. "So how are you going to get these men to talk?"

"The same way I always do."

"Will that be enough?"

"Let's hope."

"And if it isn't? How far are you prepared to go? They have information we have to have."

"Are you suggesting…?" There was no need to say the word itself. "I'm afraid that's something I'm unwilling to do. Not to mention it's illegal."

"Against the law." Travis shook his head again. "It's up to them, really. They have information that belongs to us. They will decide what treatment is appropriate by how cooperative they decide to be. The decision is not even ours to make. They are in control of how they are treated."

Stephanie did not know if it was the words themselves or the matter-of-fact tone in which they were delivered that made her hair stand up on end.

Seeing her expression, Travis continued, "You've already half starved them, and they were about half starved when they got here. It's the same sort of thing, just a bit more hands on."

"There's a big difference."

"What's the big difference?"

She floundered for an explanation. "You know it when you see it."

Then Travis shrugged, making as if to leave her. "I can't order you to do something like that. I just figured if you were dedicated to quashing this rebellion as soon as possible…"

Stephanie swallowed and stood up almost at attention. "Captain Travis, I'll find out what they know one way or another."

Looking back over his shoulder, Captain Travis nodded, his expression pleased. "There are high places in the ARO waiting for people like you, Stephanie. You just have to decide to go there."

☙❧

The bureau's official name was The Ministry of Information Collection and Synthesis. It was a newly created bureau that already had a colloquial moniker: The Snitch's Office. Henry Miller had not often been in that part of town and could not say what the building was before, but it looked like a restaurant. He sat almost alone in the reception room for the better part of two hours, scuffing the heel of his boots on some developing holes in the carpet and waiting to be called. While wiggling his frail frame into every position of which he could conceive and still finding nothing to make him comfortable, he noticed a woman enter and with dismay saw her approach and finally sit down next to him. Henry regarded her in shock from his current distorted position.

"The waiting room is almost entirely empty," he said with no introduction.

The woman glanced about the room with a bewildered expression and then nodded, confirming Henry's analysis.

He sat up straight. "They put all these chairs here so we don't have to rub each other while we wait."

The woman just stared at Henry, her lips parted and her eyes wide. Henry growled a sigh and stood up to look for a different seat. Finding one suitably removed, he collapsed into it and resumed his quest for a more perfect position. When the receptionist finally called his name in a bored voice, he popped up and trotted towards her but abruptly changed course halfway when she pointed at the hallway to her right. He discovered a stern and stout woman of about five decades waiting for him.

"Henry Miller?" she asked, her voice as severe as her visage.

"Yes, ma'am," he answered. Though it was not his custom, her severe expression and appearance induced him to so reply.

"Follow me," she commanded and walked away without looking to see if he followed.

When they entered her office, she sat down at her desk and motioned for him to follow suit. In one corner of her desk stood the 3D image of a child but the room had no other adornments, just a few indeterminate stains on the wallpaper.

"Thank you for your decision to help us at the Ministry of Information Collection and Synthesis," she said in a perfunctory tone. "This is your first report?"

"Yes, ma'am," he said, wincing at his second use of the word and resolving not to use it again. "I just signed up last week."

She slid a form and a pen across the desk. "Fill in this form as we go," she ordered and sat back at her desk, hands folded in her lap. "What do you have to report?"

"Well, not too much. I noticed my neighbor has been going outside late at night, presumably for a smoke but—"

"Write his address down on the form. Anything else?"

"I've noticed there has been some talk…some people are grumbling about the food situation. And I've heard a few people say the rebels have been providing more food than the government."

"Write their names down. What more do you have?"

Henry scratched his head, considering the question. "I caught a couple people reading one of the pamphlets the rebels post everywhere."

"Write the names and addresses."

Henry put the pen to the paper but hesitated. "I'm not sure it's worth it."

"We'll decide that."

"I mean, they read it, but then they crumpled it up and threw it out."

"They can tell us themselves if they are arrested. Right now we need to gather information."

Reluctantly, Henry penned a pair of names, omitting a couple friends. The names he wrote were those of a couple men with whom he had quarreled recently. He felt vaguely guilty about it, but he needed the extra Credits paid to him should his information prove useful. He consoled himself with the thought that nothing would come of it anyway, especially if they were really innocent.

"If that is all...?" the woman prompted when Henry paused in his writing.

"That's all," Henry confirmed and stood up.

She fed Henry's report into her computer and a receipt came out the other side. This she slid across the desk to him. Henry nodded and turned to leave. When he was out the door, but before he turned the corner, she called after him.

"Be sure to read the poster by the front door."

"What's it about?"

"Credits to anyone who can infiltrate the rebel force and report on their activity. You can sign up at the front desk. Please close the door behind you."

Henry obeyed her command. When he found the poster with the news, he approached it with his hands in his pockets and his neck inclined backwards to see it. Some tall individual had no doubt been responsible for affixing it there. As he read, his lips parted and a nervous sensation developed in the pit of his stomach. The Credits they offered were substantial, but the danger it presented made him feel queasy merely entertaining the idea. He bit at his lips. So tantalized was he that he hardly noticed the cold as he left the Snitch's Office.

22

It's eerie, Alistair decided as he climbed the steep slope of a hill hidden from view of Arcarius, *how much the still weather feels like the calm before a storm.* The sun's brilliance waned as it sank below the hill's summit, and he found himself walking through deep snow in cold shadow. It felt so nice just to be able to exert himself without suffering headaches, as he had for the last few days, that his mood was a good one despite the gravity of the meeting ahead.

By the time he reached the top, a tree-lined ridge about five hundred yards north to south, he was breathing harder and sweat formed on his forehead. He was losing his peak conditioning. Vowing to train more faithfully, he looked about and spied the large rock of which he had been told and, weaving through the sparse covering of pine trees, made for it. Clever Johnny and Oliver were already there, the former perched on top of the twenty-foot-tall rock eating an apple while the latter, arms folded, leaned against its base. Alistair waved to his friend and called out a greeting.

"We're not talking until Brad Stanson gets here," Clever Johnny informed him, though his attention seemed to be more on the apple than on Alistair.

"Unless you can come down here and shut me up," Alistair replied, "I think I'll say hi to my friend."

"This was your idea," Clever Johnny retorted. "No talking until we are all together. I expect you to stand by it since the rest of us have while you were busy nursing a headache."

Oliver shrugged but said nothing. Alistair folded his arms and stood quietly with his legs apart, irritated with himself for not lashing back, but moved to silence by the logic. For the next minute, until Brad arrived, the three quietly remained in their chosen places. Only the crunch of Clever Johnny biting into the apple and chewing it broke the silence. It seemed the red haired man consumed the apple as loudly as possible, smacking his lips as he chewed and relishing the sound he was making, that he had brought the apple just to have the ability to make noise while they were quiet. When Brad did arrive, Johnny tossed the core off into the trees, wiped his hands on his winter leggings with a self satisfied air, and announced the meeting could commence.

Brad came burdened with a bundle of books and parchments rolled up like scrolls. He kicked at some of the snow under a tall pine tree and set down the load in the space cleared off.

"I've got maps and all sorts of resources here if we need it," he proclaimed, out of breath, and as an afterthought nodded a greeting to the three of them.

"First order of business is to discuss our little food distribution program," Clever Johnny announced.

"It's been successful," Brad asserted. "I think we've created a lot of sympathy for our cause. That with the symbol Alistair thought up—"

"We need to anticipate the reaction," Johnny interrupted him. "We've been breaking into the homes of politicians. The next home we break into is likely to be guarded. Traps are going to be set. We need to evolve before they do."

"Do you have any suggestions?"

Clever Johnny shrugged and leaned back to recline on the top of the rock. "It's hard to suggest things before we know what they are going to do."

"That's not hard to imagine," said Alistair. "They will set traps for us, but the best thing for them to do is to stop doling out food to high-ranking party members in such large amounts and reduce our payoff. That particular avenue is going to get cut off, but it may have already done its job. Now we need to concentrate on recruiting."

"Which raises other problems," said Clever Johnny. "We've proven ourselves enough of a threat that they will try to infiltrate us."

"That was inevitable and we knew it a long time ago," said Oliver. "No new members will be given access to sensitive information. We stay decentralized and loosely coordinated. We pick lieutenants we know we can trust."

"It might also be a good idea to infiltrate them," offered Alistair.

"I was about to bring that up," said Oliver. "Bob LaSalle's got a cousin in the police force. He says he might be prime for the picking."

There was a moment's pause, and then Clever Johnny said, "Move ahead with it and see what he can do. But don't forget he can play us as a double agent."

"Speaking of infiltration," said Brad, "a number of our men have been drafted."

"And?" prompted Clever Johnny, as if he cared not a whit.

"Do we let it happen or what?"

Alistair shook his head. "If they get drafted they either leave the rebellion or go into hiding. There's no in between choice."

"They might be of use in the military," suggested Brad. "Just thinking long term."

"We need them here now," said Alistair. "No military ever participated in a rebellion not led by one of its generals. They'll be little use there, and with full bellies, likely to go over to the other side."

"So we order the men into hiding when they're drafted," Clever Johnny said simply.

"We can't order them to do that," contested Alistair. "If they want to remain, that's up to them."

"The State's ordering them to go, so we order them to stay."

"They're not in the rebellion because they obey orders," Oliver observed. "We can't make them stay; it won't work."

"Even if it did we have no right to do it," added Alistair. "If they go, they go. The rebellion must be voluntary."

Johnny's eyes challenged Alistair through their narrow slits. "We have few enough men as it is."

"Which brings us back to recruiting," interrupted Brad. Alistair and Clever Johnny were still busy with a staring contest, but he continued. "How about another prison break? They're out in the open so it should be easier this time. The last prison break netted us a whole bunch of recruits."

Alistair shook his head. "I can assure you they are prepared for just such an attempt. We can only pull something like that off if we have surprise on our side, and we won't. If we are going to win, it will be by keeping a step ahead of them and biding our time until everyone and anyone is ready to jump on board. At that point, we storm the castle and depose the aristocracy."

"So how do we stay ahead?" asked Brad.

"We pick different targets and keep attacking," said Clever Johnny. "They can't possibly guard everything. And we infiltrate. And that reminds me: isn't your brother a ranking bureaucrat for the Transportation Bureau?"

Slowly, Alistair nodded and said, "That's right."

Johnny made an expectant face, like a teacher waiting for a pupil to catch up. "So... why don't *you* infiltrate?"

Alistair shook his head, caught off guard by the suggestion. "There's plenty of reasons why that's a bad idea."

"Like?"

"I was being followed. The night I used the Null Suit they came looking for me, asking my family where I was."

"It's not against the law to leave without letting them know."

"Not yet anyway," muttered Oliver.

"The night I went out, I robbed a politician's home. They are going to question me about that."

"Homes get robbed. You weren't the only one out that night."

"I was the only one out whose father's restaurant had just been seized by that particular councilman."

"They've only got motive and opportunity."

"I was a highly trained marine in the Elite Corps. They got means as well."

"That's not enough to get a conviction."

"If I even get a trial! Forget it; it's out of the question. There's no way I can go back and not be arrested."

Johnny shrugged. "I just thought you might want to help the cause, but if you don't want to use your brother that way, I understand."

"No, no, no, you're not going to manipulate me like that. Do you think I'm that easy? My brother is a government stooge and a jackass; I have no problem with using him. As for helping the cause, I've done more since I arrived than I've seen you do."

"So you're done, then?"

Alistair cut himself short and glared at Clever Johnny. "That doesn't even deserve an answer."

"If they were going to arrest you for the robbery," continued Johnny, "they would have done it. They had the opportunity. It's not a crime to evade police surveillance, even if it makes you look guilty as hell. They'll probably put you under watch if you go back, but what I want to know is whether your brother can get you into the Transportation Bureau."

Alistair calmed his breathing which, without his realizing it, had sped up. "Yes, he could probably get me in. If I went back. But going back is too risky. I think I can be better used elsewhere."

Johnny made a face of mild disappointment, as if it meant little to him. "I guess we'll go with LaSalle's cousin, then."

The meeting's intensity and focus diminished, and finally they called it quits. On the way back, Alistair found himself walking next to Brad Stanson who was struggling to hold onto the materials that had been of no use.

"Can I help you carry something?" asked Alistair, and Brad gratefully handed over a few things. He had to stop and pick up a few more that fell before continuing. They walked side by side, picking their legs up high as they trudged through the powdery snow.

Alistair decided to pose a question to Brad. "When this is over, assuming we win, what do you see as the ideal government?"

Brad jumped right in with an answer, eager to discuss the topic. "Definitely something more like what we had, with the Voluntary System. We need to keep the elections free and open, and we need leaders who can govern selflessly, who can make decisions for the public good."

"Is that the important thing then? The greater good?"

"Of course," said Brad with a puzzled look.

"Can you know what the greater good is?"

Brad, panting as he tried to keep up with Alistair, motioned that he needed a breather. "It's obvious."

"Is it? What if there is a public debate over a tract of land. Some people want to use it to grow crops; others want it for a new factory. How can you tell which serves the greater good? Do you take a vote? But what if the minority has stronger feelings about it? How can you measure that? How can you tell what serves the greater good?"

Brad nodded. "I see what you mean. There will be some cases that are going to be a judgment call, but a well intentioned governor will make more right choices, on the balance, than wrong ones."

"So your system depends on the good will of the governors?"

"Doesn't any system?"

"Don't you think anytime you create an institution with the kind of powers governments have, you are going to attract precisely the kind of people you don't want using those powers? The power to tax is the power to take the money one man earns and spend it on what you want, not what he wants. The power to regulate means *you* control how a business operates, not the man who actually worked to create it. Government is the power to punish and reward arbitrarily. Why give anyone that kind of power?"

"Government is needed to make sure people stay in line and follow the law, that businesses don't take advantage of people, that order—"

"But who watches the watchers?"

Brad opened his mouth. He shut it again. Alistair turned and began walking again. Hopping through the snow to catch up, Brad said, "No matter what you do, there is going to be someone on top. You have to design government as best you can and watch over it."

"The human element is always going to be what fails. What if there were a self regulating system which didn't rely on human qualities because it's kept in check by other forces?"

"There is no such system."

"No?"

"If there is no one's thought of it. I don't think we're going to happen upon it. But in the meantime, I think you should consider Clever Johnny's idea about the Transportation Bureau."

Alistair took the suggestion but did not comment.

"You could do us a lot of good there. And I don't think you're going to be arrested."

Alistair walked a bit farther before he answered. "I'll think about it."

23

As she propped up her head with her left hand under her jaw, Stephanie found she was able to flick her pencil so that it spun around for up to a dozen revolutions without falling off the edge of her desk. Moreover, she was confident she would be able get as many as twenty with an especially accurate and forceful flick of her finger. The trick was to get it to spin without moving laterally because, if it fell off the table, obviously none of the revolutions counted.

"Is he handsome?" asked a male voice, startling her. Her cheeks blushed.

"What?"

"The guy you're daydreaming about."

"Do you have something for me?"

The officer tossed a folder onto her desk, chuckled with a merry glint in his eye and sat down across from her.

"You're free to go now," she informed him as she opened the folder.

"I think I'd like to help you out," he said with a youthful self-assurance she would have found amusing if he had not just caught her twiddling her pencil.

"I'm quite fine by myself." Stephanie emptied the contents of the folder onto her desk: a computer disk and a parchment with a now familiar yellow symbol. She tossed the propaganda aside and inserted the disk into her hard drive.

"Have you made any headway with the prisoners?" the young man asked her, placing his feet on the edge of her desk.

Stephanie swatted them off. "Are you still here?" Not waiting for an answer, she spun around in her chair to face her computer display.

"I heard they're not talking."

"They don't know anything. Believe me, if they knew something they'd have told me by now."

"So I thought maybe you could use some help."

Stephanie gave an exasperated sigh and spun back. "What's it going to take to get you to leave me alone?"

"Take me on as a partner."

"I don't even know your name."

"You don't remember?" The young man affected mock sorrow. "Ryan LaSalle," he said brightly with a smile that nearly split his face in half, "since you're pretending not to remember. But my friends call me—"

"I'm not your friend. Whoever your friends are, I hate them. I know what you're trying to do: you want to get in on some of the good action for yourself."

"Am I supposed to be embarrassed about that?"

"This is my case, my investigation, my territory. Piss off."

"Are you here to serve your country or yourself?"

"Excuse me? I might ask you the same thing."

"Come on, let's cooperate. I'm pretty smart. I can help you. You know, you're not much older than I am and this is a pretty important case. It doesn't take much to get people talking, and we're all wondering how you convinced Captain Travis to turn this over to you."

Stephanie snorted and turned back to her computer to access the disk. "You're not half as smart as you think you are."

Ryan stood up and walked around to the side of Stephanie's desk. "Come on, no one would blame you. You're doing your best to get ahead, just like me. I think Captain Travis would be more than happy to...oh, I can't think of a delicate way to phrase it."

"Think how jealous he'll be if I make you my partner."

"I'm willing to share if it will make the deal."

"No, Ryan. I want you all to myself." Her tone could not have been flatter and less interested.

Undaunted, he came around behind Stephanie and studied the 3D images being projected. They were landscapes taken from a satellite. The landscape itself was in shades of blue, while little heat signatures appeared in various shades of yellow, red and orange.

"Are you searching for a hidden camp?"

"I'm checking on my real estate investments."

"You're going to wish you were kinder to me."

"Let me count the ways I doubt that."

The imager now projected some 3D shots of the city, but at a greater magnification. There were shots of the rebels' work: food being eagerly collected by the hungry citizens, parchments nailed to wooden posts, vandalized government buildings. Stephanie, having found nothing of a possible rebel camp, was less interested in these shots and went through them more rapidly. Ryan's attention strayed and he picked up the parchment with the rebel manifesto and examined it.

"I don't know what they think they're going to accomplish," he said as he read. He dismissively tossed it back onto Stephanie's desk. "If they get what they want, that A might as well stand for anarchy."

Ryan's words stopped her in mid motion. Cocking her head to the side, she brought a finger to her lips. Slowly, she stood up and faced Ryan, pointing the finger at him and wagging it as if to concede a good point. She seemed to see him for the first time: his wavy and thick dark brown hair, his multiple dark freckles, his wide nose and full lips. She studied him for less time than it takes to tell it, and then abruptly left, leaving him standing at her desk.

Gerald got up to answer the heavy knocks on the door and conversation at the dinner table came to a halt. Mary, Nigel and Katherine heard him open the door but nothing more. Finally, Mary went to investigate. She gasped and rushed forward when she saw Alistair standing there with a sack over his shoulder, in a staring contest with his brother.

Mary embraced her son, cupping his battered face in her hands with a pained expression, and Nigel embraced him when Mary finally left him the opportunity. Katherine also gave her brother a hug, an uncertain though not reluctant one. The embracing done, Gerald settled for a nod and, after a bit of hesitation, a pat on the shoulder.

"We were worried about you," Nigel offered as Alistair was led into the new Ashley residence. Mary made as if to grab Alistair's sack but he gently rebuffed her.

"I'll get it myself, Mom." To his father he said, "I'm sorry to worry you. I wasn't in any danger."

"What sort of trouble were you in?" asked Gerald with a distinctly foreboding tone.

"I wasn't in any trouble."

Gerald made a low noise and then nodded at Alistair's stitches. "And what about those injuries?"

"A group of thugs tried to mug me."

Mary gasped.

"In Avon?" Gerald asked.

Alistair nodded. "Not long after I got there. They didn't get anything, though. Except a sound beating."

"Looks like they gave as good as they got," Gerald remarked.

"You didn't see them afterwards."

"Did you report it to the Civil Guard?" Nigel asked.

"No, he didn't," Gerald answered, "because it would have shown up in the database I have been using to try and find him."

"No," Alistair confirmed, "I haven't reported it. Too late at this point anyway."

"Are you back for good?" asked his mother hopefully. She clapped when Alistair nodded and rushed to hug him again.

"Actually, I was going to talk to Gerald to see if he could get me in at the Transportation Bureau."

The room went silent and all gazes turned to Gerald.

"I'm not going to make a career in the military. My vacation is over. I figured it was time to look for something to keep me busy for the rest of my life."

Gerald regarded his brother with a blank face. Then he sniffed and said, "Let's sit down and have some supper."

An extra place at the table was made for Alistair between his sister and his mother. While he ate, he found himself eyeing the new household. It took his attention from the table, blanketed by an unease no one wanted to acknowledge. They did not ask him about his travels, and he offered nothing. What little talk there was consisted of trivial topics and felt forced, as if spoken words of any sort were required just to help the soft clinking of silverware fill the quiet. It was Gerald who finally brought up the subject of employment again.

"Why exactly do you want to work in the Transportation Bureau?" he asked, staring intently into his bowl of soup.

"To be honest, no particular reason other than that you work there and might be able to put in a good word for me."

Gerald took the information with a nod and sipped at the soup in his spoon. "And what if I can't honestly put in a good word for you?"

There passed a moment of the most acutely uncomfortable silence before Alistair finally responded. "I guess I can look somewhere else, then."

"Gerald…" his mother began with the tone of a mild rebuke.

152

"Your brother's always been a hard worker," said Nigel.

"Philosophically, why would you choose the Transportation Bureau?" Gerald asked, finally looking his brother in the eye. "You hate government. You've made that abundantly clear. Why work for the…how do you call it?…the Leviathan State?"

"A man's got to make his way somehow. There's no point opening a restaurant because it will just get snatched away when someone with better connections wants your land. Even assuming I could get the permits."

"There are all sorts of private opportunities opening up with the Realists. All sorts of manufacturing jobs—"

"Those aren't private endeavors. They may be called private, but—"

"Fine. But why the Transportation Bureau? Why not reenlist? You made a good career out of it to hear tell."

"I'm not going to reenlist," Alistair answered with finality.

"Why not?"

"Because everything…" Alistair's voice choked off and he could not finish his thought. Finally, he managed, "War is the State in full bloom."

"National defense is important."

"Please don't try to convince me the war on Kaldis is national defense."

Gerald reflected for a time before he finally drew in a deep breath and let it out. "Well then, welcome aboard." It was more surrender than enthusiastic welcome, but the tension around the table evaporated. Mary clapped once and Nigel smiled. "You'll have to go through a background inspection by the Civil Guard first."

"I figured as much," Alistair replied, returning his attention to his soup. "I'll get to that tomorrow." At first the words wouldn't leave his mouth, but finally he managed to say, "Thank you."

Gerald almost imperceptibly nodded into his soup and said nothing more.

ॐ ॐ

The next day, before the sun rose for its relatively brief winter outing, Alistair found himself in the Civil Guard station twiddling his thumbs. The large room, full of desks, lamps, cabinets and a hodge-podge of other furniture, was dark as only a couple lamps were turned on. A lone officer sat at his desk in the corner and typed at his computer, paying the visitor no mind.

Alistair rubbed at eyes burning from lack of sleep. He had reacclimated himself to the long Aldran day, but his insomnia was driven by the images he saw when he closed his eyes. Some nights passed by without difficulty, but the previous night passed without sleep. A thousand faces whirled around in his dreams. They were the faces of his fellow marines, of the people he had seen, shot at, killed. One face in particular kept coming back to him, the face of a young woman he had known and abandoned…but he forced himself to think of other things. He would not think of her, and get himself worked up, in public.

A blast of frosty air announced the arrival of a group of Guardsmen dragging a ragged band of four men into the station. The men, dressed in worn clothing ill fit to protect them from an Arcarian winter, were handcuffed and in need of a bath. Two sported scrapes and what would soon become bruises, and one other had recently been bleeding from the nose. After being separated, the men were dumped into chairs and told to sit still. One was seated near Alistair, and as the former marine regarded him he was met with a defiant stare.

"What's your story, partner?" asked Alistair with a manly camaraderie lacking any note of pity. The man's glare quickly dissolved and a wry half smile curled one corner of his mouth.

"Got caught with my hands in the cookie jar," he smirked with a shake of his head. His mouth smiled, but behind his eyes was something less comical. "Buddies and me were figuring to take off. Sick of the climate, sick of the damn winters. I grew up in New Kensington—"

"I figured that already," Alistair said, referring to his accent, and the man chuckled.

"Anyway, we were figuring to leave. Problem is, we're miners and they've got some project planned and they need workers. We were told to stay." He sighed deeply and leaned back in his seat, tilting his head back. "I'm just tired of the damn winters!" He lifted himself back up and sat up straight.

"Anyway, they told us not to go and caught us trying to leave."

"Well, they have to tell you where to go, don't they?"

"I know. I just didn't want another winter, and this one in the mines. They're cold as hell in the summer…"

"I think you misunderstand. I wasn't saying that to chastise you. They have to tell you where to go because they are controlling the economy. They calculate how much of what they want produced, and then they order it done. So they have to force you to stay, and if they get soft, there will be all sorts of defections."

The look the man gave Alistair left little doubt the economics of it had not sunk in. "The Voluntary System was better," he said, searching for some way to respond. "They gave us orders all the time but…nobody cared."

"And that's why it fell apart. If you want to control an entire economy, you have to be willing to take steps to keep people in line. You can't allow them to work where and how they want. You can't allow them to buy what they want, or earn what they want or pay what they want. You can't allow them to start up unapproved businesses. Everything has to follow the plan."

The man's look did not change, and Alistair knew the last bit flew over his head. "Well, I shouldn't have tried to leave…"

"I think you're still misunderstanding me. The State is using you for its plans."

The man nodded, open-mouthed, concentrating as hard as he could.

"Why should it? You're working and paying for this government, why shouldn't *you* use *it* for *your* plans?"

From the expression on his face, Alistair knew neither that idea nor anything similar had ever crossed his mind before. Whether his expression turned into one of a dawning realization or a confused denial he never got to see. Just then, an officer came and lifted the man from New Kensington to his feet and led him away. For his part, Alistair remembered where he was and chided himself to be more careful with his treasonous talk.

A moment later, the officer who first received Alistair returned. He dropped a few papers on the desk as he pulled up a seat with his foot.

"I got the forms to fill out," he informed Alistair, his tone serious, almost hostile. "There are a few questions I need to ask you." Searching around his desk, he found a pencil and readied one of the forms. "Where have you been the past couple weeks?"

Alistair managed to suppress a knowing smirk. "I went to Avon for a few days."

"Are you aware you were under surveillance?"

"By whom?" asked Alistair in a concerned tone.

"The Civil Guard."

He feigned a look of realization. "I knew there was a group following me. I thought it was one of the specnine dealers. That was one of the reasons I left."

The officer regarded him with an incredulous look. "What happened on the night of October the 32nd?"

"That was a while ago—"

"It was the night you disappeared. They were waiting for you when you returned."

"Oh, yeah. I didn't disappear; I just went for a walk."

"You disappeared from the scanners."

Alistair shrugged. "I don't know anything about that."

The officer nodded slowly, scratching his chin with the end of his pencil. "What happened to your face?"

"Got in a scuffle."

"The night of the 32nd of October—the night you disappeared or went for a walk or whatever—a councilman's house was burgled."

"I'm sorry to hear that."

"The councilman had just been at your father's restaurant. He had just announced your father was losing his land." Alistair just looked at the officer, who held out his hands, expecting an answer. "You were out for a walk."

Still nothing from Alistair.

"It looks suspicious."

"I'm sorry. I guess it looks bad...you have opportunity."

"You're an ex Special Forces marine; we've got means and motive. There's quite a file on you in our archive."

"There is?"

"You've been reported several times for incendiary comments. Anti-government comments."

"I was hoping to put that behind me," Alistair said, hanging his head. "I spent four cycles on Kaldis. I served my country, but it was hard. There was a lot of...a lot of bad things. I came back angry..." He blushed slightly, finding it as difficult to force the truths past his lips as the lies. "I just want to get a regular job and do my bit."

The look the officer gave him was both incredulous and slightly frustrated. "Wait here."

Once again, as the sound of the officer's booted feet on the linoleum floor receded, Alistair was left alone with the officer in the corner, whose staccato typing was the only sound. It was some time later when the other returned with an ill-concealed look of triumph on his face.

"You're a 3nn," he informed Alistair as he sank into his chair.

Alistair nodded slowly, arms folded across his chest as he prepared himself.

The officer shook his head and made a face as if he were disappointed. "Well, it seems we haven't received your weekly report in some time."

Alistair blushed in anger. Every citizen was supposed to file a weekly report of his condition, location and work activities. It was a rule no one followed or enforced.

"I was off fighting on Kaldis for the last four cycles," he growled.

"You could have kept a log and turned it in when you got back."

"When was the last time you filed yours?"

"I'm Civil Guard. When I clock in every day that serves as my report. I'm afraid I'm going to have to arrest you."

Alistair gritted his teeth but managed to control his breathing. "I suppose if you pass enough laws, you can get anyone charged with something."

"Put your hands behind your back," was the officer's answer as he stood up and readied the handcuffs.

24

The small viewing room erupted with laughter and applause such that the floor shook. The sound from the 3D projector could barely be heard and the light from the images played off the enthusiastic faces of the Guardsmen and women as they watched with delight the clips collected for them.

Stephanie Caldwell leaned back and watched with her arms folded. There was a protest in a city she did not recognize, and the Civil Guard beat it down. A knight stick smashed the teeth of one protester, and the audience groaned as if in sympathy, but then followed it up with a hearty cheer. Another protest, this time in Rendral, with the awesome State Palace filling the background. A protester was running from the Guard, but they caught him and, with a shove, sent him crashing headlong into the famous statue of Sidney Ecksley, founder and first president of Aldra. The statue's imperial pose mocked the protester whose blood pooled at its base. Another groan and another cheer.

Though Stephanie forced a few smiles, for the most part her expression was blank. She was not disturbed by the violence, but she was bored. Her gaze wandered about the viewing room until she spied Captain Travis' silhouette in the back doorway. He stood almost at attention with his arms behind his back, as if surveying his troops. Though his face was hidden in shadow, she felt he was looking at her. Standing up, she made her inconspicuous way to the back, passing row after row of Civil Guard too enraptured to notice. She saw Travis' head turn to follow her and finally his pleased smile.

"Telepathy must work," he said. "You got my message." With that, he turned and left. She took three quick steps to catch up with him and the two wound their way through the building, which felt empty with all the Guardsmen in the projector room. Their footsteps echoed through the hallways. "Were you not enjoying the news broadcast?" Travis asked when they had distanced themselves from the other guards.

"That won't be on the news."

"It's a news broadcast for the Civil Guard."

"It was…interesting."

Travis smiled. "But not what you saw yourself doing this evening."

"It keeps the troops enthusiastic."

"Bread and circuses. Only bread has been in short supply. Hence our current problems. We are struggling to save the structure the old order allowed to weaken."

"We? Are you a Realist?"

"With a small 'r'? Oh yes, very much so."

"And with a capital 'R'?"

"I'm also practical with a small 'p'. Some of us are having our own little broadcast in a few minutes. A little less entertainment and a little more business." Travis stopped outside a set of double doors and fixed his gaze on Stephanie. "There are those who enjoy a good circus, and there are those who run it."

Stephanie nodded, a bit cowed by his severe expression and unsure how to respond.

"You know your friend Alistair has come back?"

Stephanie's brows shot up in surprise. "Has he? I've been meaning to talk to you about him."

"Save it for later," Travis advised, and with that, he opened the doors and allowed Stephanie to enter. She was met by the stern and grim faces of older, higher ranking officers and politicians, men with thick white mustaches, wrinkled brows and ponderous frowns who sat about a long, mahogany table with rounded corners. She was one of only a few females in the room. Nodding her head to them and getting nothing in return, she self-consciously stood near the doorway, hoping she was not blushing.

After closing the doors, Travis tapped her on the shoulder by way of guiding her to a cushioned chair next to his own. She sat down and took a deep breath, relieved the attention of the august persons in the room turned elsewhere. She felt a hand squeeze her right shoulder and turned to see Travis give her a fleeting smile before turning his attention to the table.

"I think we might begin by—" began a man on the verge of rising from his seat, but he was cut off by the deep and powerful voice of the Mayor of Arcarius.

"I believe we can get on with it."

Stephanie nearly gasped for she had not noticed Aloysius when she entered. The man whom he interrupted blushed furiously but nodded and sat down. Stephanie briefly wondered to what power struggle that little episode belonged, but then the lights were dimmed and a 3D image was projected onto the table. It was the head and shoulders of a military officer, a man of advancing years but still robust of health and severe of countenance. He wore a traditional military officer's hat, dark blue with a red tassel.

"Good evening, gentlemen," began the officer in the flat and nasal Rendralian accent. "The recent weeks have proven to be momentous ones. We are at war with the Kaldisians even while we suppress an insurrection here at home. As always, I will be as brief as thoroughness allows and as direct as prudence dictates.

"We quite frankly are not prepared for a war, but this is a perfect opportunity for us. It is a war of many against one, and a Kaldisian response specifically against Aldra is nearly unthinkable. We can remain at war for as long as we find it useful."

Stephanie shifted uncomfortably in her chair. She glanced at some of the other faces in the room, but they did not respond to the words, though their attention never left the speaker.

"Your roles in Arcarius are going to be crucial to making sure the armed forces are supplied and ready for what is going to be a protracted war. The rebels in your city must be stamped out immediately, before this nonsense can spread to the workers returning to the mines. Take whatever steps you deem necessary.

"I cannot stress this last point enough. The rebellion has begun to spread to the rest of the planet. There is a large minority who are not in favor of the war. We are still struggling to organize the food supply, which is hard enough by itself, but mixed in with the colossal changeover to private control of such a big portion of the economy…you can imagine the difficulties we are having. Expect more food shortages. Many citizens are too hungry to care about fighting for their planet.

"We believe the rebels are making overtures to some disenchanted business interests who got left empty handed when the industrial contracts were handed out. There are many more businesses who feel threatened by their lack of political contacts, and any one of them might be persuaded to provide assistance. This rebellion must be stamped out now!"

For the first time, the flat, clinical tone was replaced with a bark of fury. The general's eyes glowed intensely for a moment, but then his countenance settled back into composure as he continued to recite from his prepared speech. Stephanie, enraptured by what she was now privy to, could not decide if the outburst was all theatrics or not.

"In the meantime, no political debate is to be tolerated. Monitor your citizens; keep them aware that we provide their safety. Divide and conquer when you can, appease when you must, obliterate when necessary. Use the carrot and use the stick. Arcarius will play a crucial role in all of this, and Rendral will give you what backing you need. I regret to inform you the divisions you asked for are not yet ready to deploy. Don't let this stop you from doing everything in your power to end the insurrection."

Nodding at them, the general paused before he ended with, "Good luck. The next briefing will no doubt bring better news."

His image disappeared. There was a moment of silence before Aloysius spoke.

"We are going to end this rebellion before the divisions arrive. Arcarius can take care of its own problems. We are going to search house to house and make arrests. They can prove their innocence later."

"We need to be careful not to generate too much sympathy for them," advised one white haired woman in a military outfit.

"The coming food shortages will do that anyway," Aloysius replied. "We can at least strike before it happens. And we'll continue to connect the rebel acts to the Kaldisians."

Another military man, a younger one, was shaking his head. "With all due respect, sir, the rebels have too much publicity. I'm just being realistic. They have fliers everywhere, and I'm convinced everyone in the city knows someone who is involved. The people know they have nothing to do with the Kaldisians. Frankly, every stash of food they steal from us and give to the populace makes them less likely to pay us any heed."

Another spoke up. "Sometimes force can crush a rebellion. Sometimes it's the fuel that keeps the fire burning."

"The long and the short of it," Aloysius continued, "is that we are out of options. We will use the Civil Guard to squash them. It doesn't matter how much publicity the rebels have, we'll counter it with our own. We will control all information and form all opinions. The rebellion will be put down before the winter mining begins." The last bit was delivered with a finality that did not admit further discussion.

Afterwards, while the officers and political officials mingled, Stephanie sat in her chair, staring straight ahead but not seeing anything. Captain Travis finished a conversation with a local official and sat down next to her. She smiled weakly for a moment, but when the smile faltered she looked at the floor.

"That," he informed her, "is how it is done."

Stephanie, careful in her response, nodded. "I thought it was…brutally honest."

Travis coldly smiled. "This is how laws have always been made. This is how policy has always been forged. No, Stephanie, it's not the ideal we present to the people. Bread and circuses; divide and conquer; fear and suspicion; slogans and national pride…the formula is always the same. The only difference is how much power the government has."

She again nodded carefully. "Is the war really just a tool to…" Officer Caldwell could not find the words to finish the thought. "I guess…" she paused and swallowed, wondering how to phrase it. "I can understand that difficult decisions must be made for the greater good. But…"

"But what?"

She lowered her voice so the general drone of conversation made her words imperceptible to all but Travis. "How do you know how far to go? How do you decide the right thing to do? How do you…"

"How do we justify our acts?" Travis finished for her when she trailed off. Stephanie nodded and he smiled, this time less coldly than before. "I'll let you think about that yourself. How does one justify these acts?"

That said, he stood back up and left her. The room was slowly emptying, and she took the opportunity to leave. After closing the double doors behind her, she pondered Travis' words.

This is how laws have always been made. This is how policy has always been forged. No, Stephanie, it's not the ideal we present to the populace. Bread and circuses; divide and conquer; fear and suspicion; slogans and national pride…the formula is always the same. The only difference is how much power the government has.

She walked home alone in the dark and cold. All she could think about was Alistair, and how he said the same thing to her so many times. So wrapped up was she in her thoughts that when she arrived she did not remember a single step of her trip back.

25

Leland Maddox sat across from Alistair in the dim light of his office. He would have preferred to look down sternly at the applicant, but since the young man was so tall he settled for tucking his chin into his neck and squinting his eyes in an attempt to make his droopy features harsher. Drumming his fingers on the desk, he looked through Alistair's papers, glancing up occasionally as if finding something he did not like, then clearing his throat, frowning a bit, and returning his attention to the file.

Light and fluffy flakes of snow meandered steadily past the window and Alistair studied the glinting sunlight sparkling off their forms while Leland pretended to be otherwise engrossed. A cloud passed in front of the sun and the sparkling ceased. Leland cleared his throat and turned a page.

"You just got out of jail," he noted with disapproval.

"Yesterday," Alistair replied as he tore his attention from the precipitation. "I was in for two weeks."

Leland fixed his sternest gaze on the young applicant. "Mr. Ashley, we do not make a practice of hiring criminals in our Bureau. What were you in for?"

"Failure to make my weekly availability reports."

Leland was startled out of his act for a moment. "They locked you up for that?"

"It was while I was off on Kaldis—"

"You were on Kaldis?"

"—and I didn't turn in my weekly log from the four cycles I was there."

Leland stared at the file in confusion. He looked back at Alistair, then back at the file and finally back at Alistair. "Well that's a hell of a thing…"

"That was my thought as well."

"Well, you just can't start getting nit picky like that with a kid whose been fighting for us on Kaldis. What division were you in?"

"I was conscripted as a marine, but I eventually joined the Elite Corps."

"Conscripted?"

Alistair almost winced. "Well, I mean enlisted," he amended, inserting the approved terminology. "Anyway, I was accepted into the Elite Corps while I was there."

"Did you get to wear a war suit?"

"Many times."

Leland was impressed. He nodded his head as he pursed his lips, but then his demeanor changed and he was the demanding taskmaster once more. "I'm sure your brother has probably told you I run a pretty tight ship here. We're the Transportation Bureau, but we might as well be called Miscellaneous because we get sent things the other bureaus can't handle. It's irritating, but at the end of the day it's a compliment to me and my staff. We maintain high standards. Period. Do you think you can consistently perform at the kind of level we're looking for?"

"I was chosen for the special forces on Kaldis," was Alistair's flat reply.

"Oh…well…" Leland had the decency to blush and he cleared his throat to cover the awkward pause. "Alistair, I think you're exactly the kind of young man we're looking for. When can you start?"

෭ඁ ෨

The interview was followed by a tour of the building which Leland, despite grumbling about his hectic schedule, was kind enough to give, and at a leisurely pace. He showed him the entrance hall where he was to be searched each morning. There were a dozen armed soldiers, their visages hidden behind face plates, and half were either busy searching incoming citizens or waiting to do so.

The procedure was invasive. It began with the man or woman passing under a monitoring device that rendered a 3D image of the subject, naked, on a projection pad. Any detected contraband would show up on the naked image of the person. After the lewd projections, the subject was treated to a thorough pat down before permission to enter was granted.

After this, Leland took Alistair to the reception counter where tickets were dealt and train schedules posted. Three bored ticketers sat slumped behind the barred windows of their counter, their attention more on a projector broadcasting a soap opera of some sort. Leland did his best to make it seem exciting, telling Alistair of the marvelous way it was run in the warmer months when there was a greater volume of passengers. Farther up and back in the building, he was treated to a viewing of the offices of the higher ranking bureaucrats like Leland, a quick glimpse of privilege to induce an appropriate work ethic. The officials there shook his hand and repeated variations on the same pep talk: they were glad to have him and were expecting a lot.

After the luxury offices, Leland showed him the maze of cubicles where the rank and file labored. Each cubicle came with a cot for the midday siesta, a convention adopted to save on transit times. Alistair noted with distress that his body was not going to be comfortable on such a small bed. The time for the siesta was an hour past, yet many workers still lingered on their cots.

"They are going to crack down on that sort of thing," the Bureau head mentioned as they left the cubicle area. "The abuse of the midday siesta, I mean. The Realist regime is more intent on efficiency."

Taking Alistair downstairs, Leland proudly displayed the cafeteria, assuring him that whatever shortages came, there would always be food of some sort for the Bureau workers when they were on the clock. At the moment, a few lingered over steaming hot cups of some dark liquid, talking quietly and joylessly like the rest of the population. Finally, Leland took Alistair to a back set of labs and offices on the same subterranean level as the cafeteria. The room they came to was dark, lit only by the blue glow of a projection computer. There sat a gaunt woman with mousy brown hair and ill-fitting spectacles. Alistair guessed she was 30 cycles, give or take, and she wore a white lab coat to distinguish her from the other workers in the Bureau.

"Alistair, this is Louise. She's going to take you through her department and explain your duties."

Louise looked up and then immediately down at the floor, shyly smiling. She hesitated between standing up and closing the program she was working with before finally opting for the latter.

"I'll leave you in her capable hands."

With that, Leland nodded his goodbye and left. Louise rose from her chair, fumbling to adjust the glasses on her face, and acknowledged Alistair with a nod of her head, though she looked more at the ground than at him. As the sound of Leland's footsteps grew softer, she shuffled her feet, cleared her throat, brushed back her straight, shoulder-length hair, and finally started to speak, staring straight into her computer projection.

"I, uh…"

Alistair held his hand out, "Alistair Ashley."

Louise smiled nervously and held out a limp hand. "Louise Downing…5wr." She quickly withdrew her hand, and then stared at Alistair curiously.

"3nn," Alistair hastened to add.

"Oh." She paused for a moment. "I thought soldiers were always required to give their code."

"I'm not a soldier any longer."

"That's true. After four cycles I figured—"

"So what exactly am I going to be doing here?"

"Oh. Well, this is the Department of Statistics within the Bureau of Transportation. We compile data and analyze it. We hope to refine the performance equations the various Bureaus use and formulate new ones."

"Performance equations?"

"Yes." Louise pushed her glasses back up to the bridge of her nose. "We create equations to predict behavior. Among other things it helps us plan the train schedule. Have you ever used a projection computer?"

Alistair shook his head. "Not this kind."

"Oh." Louise seemed a bit distressed. "How much have you learned about statistics?"

"Next to nothing. I never went to university."

"Oh." Louise frowned. "It's just that…we'll have to start you off small. You see…"

"I'm totally unqualified for any post in this department."

Louise smiled and nervously laughed. "Well…I suppose you wouldn't be the first candidate we'd pick."

"I think my brother put in a good word for me."

"Gerald's word carries a lot of weight here. Especially with Leland." She chuckled again, nervously, then said, "Well, I'll show you the ins and outs of a projection computer."

As she sat down to begin Alistair's instruction, she lost much of her shyness and confidently navigated the computer. Her speech lost its hesitation, its faltering pauses, and her movements were smooth and sure. Only when Alistair leaned close to get a better view and she felt his nearness did she lose her concentration. At those moments she seemed startled, like one who has been speaking to her image in the mirror and is interrupted in mid soliloquy. As the instruction proceeded, Alistair learned to stay back and let her go, saving his questions for later rather than constantly trip her up. Genuinely interested in what she was showing him, Alistair thought the two hours of instruction, passing from initial introduction to flitting down capricious paths of more in-depth knowledge, sneaked by as if they were a handful of minutes.

26

Henry Miller had never been off Arcarius Island, much less off the planet Aldra, so he had not understood Alistair when his friend referred to what he called the Aldran Malaise. There was, Alistair insisted after returning from his tour of duty, a listlessness in the Aldran character quite absent from Kaldisians. Henry shrugged and thought no more of it, but now even he was noticing something strange. Added to the putative indolence was a fearful suspicion expressed by furtive glances at one's fellows and hushed conversations that paused at the passage of a stranger or even a friend. Scratching at the splintered wood of the table before him with a dirty fingernail, Henry pretended to wonder what was the cause of this shift in public attitude even while an image of the Snitch's Office intruded on his thoughts.

Another possible culprit was passing in front of the large window of the bar in which Henry found himself. Painted in the deep blue and red of the Aldran flag, it was a six-wheel windowless automobile with a smooth exterior devoid of distinguishing details. Though its form gave no hint of its function, everyone in Arcarius knew it was a surveillance auto. Inside, a navigator read a computer display of the surrounding buildings and terrain, making windows wholly unnecessary. Inside would be anywhere from two to six other Civil Guardsmen, monitoring conversations.

"Why don't they disguise it?" asked Henry, interrupting the conversation of his three companions. They paused and looked at him oddly until one of them saw what Henry was watching.

"They're not meant to catch criminals," said one, more presentable than the others by virtue of a recently shaved face.

Henry absentmindedly scratched at his smooth cheeks that never needed a shave.

"They have other ways of doing that. These are made to stick out so we know they're listening."

"Intimidation," growled the second man with a voice scorched by alcohol and tobacco.

Henry nodded and stared into his mug of diluted ale. He had taken a couple sips and had no intention of finishing the awful concoction, but it felt familiar to have it in front of him. He scratched again at the splinters.

"So is it almost time?" he sighed, hoping his voice did not betray his nervousness.

"We'll let you know when it's time," the third man, a decade or more older than the others, gruffly said.

Henry took a deep breath and blew it out slowly through rounded lips and puffed cheeks.

"Try to relax," said the first and drained the rest of his ale. He nodded at the second and that one, seated next to Henry, scooted his chair closer to speak in a more conspiratorial manner.

Henry shrank back out of reflex. "We don't need to cuddle," he protested and scooted his chair back to get some distance.

The man stared at Henry in disbelief and then, chuckling, exchanged amused glances with his companions. "OK, no cuddling. My wife would get jealous anyway."

"I just don't like to be crowded."

The man nodded, bemused, and withdrew a small pipe from his pocket. A wick protruded from one end. "I was just trying to slip you this."

"It's time now," said the third.

Henry fumbled at the pipe and finally slipped it into his pocket. With his other hand he grabbed the lighter sitting on the table, put it in his pocket as he spun to face the door, and got up to leave. Feeling like every eye in the bar was on him, he slinked outside and into the windy cold. He ducked his face behind the raised lapels of his coat and pressed into the chill wind streaming down the city street. The bar door opened behind him and he imagined it was the three men he was with. They would be going in the opposite direction but, as instructed, he did not turn to watch them go. Instead, he made for the barricade surrounding the Mayor's Palace.

The road curved to the left before giving into the square around the Palace, and the buildings on both sides of the street were tall and built close together so that the fortified barricade nearly sprang out in ambush on those who rounded the bend. Between Henry and the capital building was a line of tanks around the edge of the square, the statue in the square's middle, Civil Guard like ants all about and long, streaming wisps of snow blown across the open space. The snowfall had ceased hours ago, but now the snow was blown sideways along the length of the ground as the wind from the sea battered the unprotected side of the city and made its way through the maze of corridor-like streets.

Henry was impressed with the impeccable timing of it all. No sooner did he round the corner and take in the view than a commotion commenced to his left. At first barely audible over the wind, it quickly swelled and he saw the Civil Guard turning their attention to it as debris was hurled at them. As he proceeded, the riot nearly turned into an outright battle, the tanks began to move and moments later a hoverplane appeared overhead.

Gritting his teeth, he took out the pipe and lighter and soon had the wick on fire. It fizzled at first and sprayed sparks but then burned strongly. The wick felt like a beacon announcing his intentions to the Civil Guard, and he imagined their eyes on him. Despite a strict recommendation to the contrary, he abruptly broke into a run. As he passed by a tank, he jammed the pipe into the treads and took off as fast as his legs would take him. Imagining every stray shout was an announcement of his discovery, Henry did not dare pause to look back at his handiwork, but he did hear four nearly simultaneous explosions and knew one of them was his.

꒰ ꒱

"The damage was not irreparable, but it has rendered three of the tanks temporarily inoperable," advised an officer as he followed Captain Travis through the many desks in the large office room. "Immediate repairs are recommended for the fourth."

Stephanie had already seen the report. As she trailed the two, walking next to Ryan LaSalle and waiting for an opportunity to speak with Travis, she wondered whether the revolt could be crushed as Aloysius demanded.

"How many tanks does that leave us?" Travis demanded in an icy tone.

"Four are operational, but all are in need of a tune up. There are two others I am told will be out of the shop by tomorrow."

"So six by tomorrow?"

"Yes, sir."

Captain Travis reached the door to his office. He stopped, turned to face the officer, and nodded. "Very well. Is there anything else?"

"No, sir." When Travis nodded he returned the nod and left.

"Ms. Caldwell, I take it by your persistent presence you wish to speak with me." Travis' tone was unrelentingly cold, a manner he frequently used with those below him but almost never with Stephanie.

"If I may. It's important."

Travis' gaze went to Ryan. "And your friend wants to come along?"

"Ryan will not be needed."

Travis opened the door to his office and allowed Stephanie inside, leaving a disappointed Ryan by himself. After closing the door, Travis went to his cushioned chair at his desk and wearily sank into it, rubbing his eyes with the palms of his hands. She did not know how long he had been without sleep, but he had an unheard-of full day's growth of beard. Uncertain, she stood still and quiet in front of his desk.

Finally, Travis sighed and leaned his head back against the headrest of his chair, his eyes closed. "There will be no early, easy solution to the rebels," he finally said. "Aloysius knows it too. He's ready to escalate."

Stephanie nodded but said nothing.

"And back and forth it will go until…until someone comes out on top." He sat up and opened his eyes. "What is it you want to talk to me about?"

"I know where the rebels' symbol comes from."

"Where?"

"I researched it. I thought the A stood for Aldra, or Arcarius. Turns out it's an ancient symbol for anarchy. It first appeared sometime in the 19th century on Earth."

"Interesting."

"This immediately made me think of Alistair. And when you told me he was back in town…"

"You think he's leading this rebellion?"

"I don't know about leading. He has hardly had time since getting back to build a full rebellion. But he was in the Elite Corps. He easily could have worked his way up the ranks."

"Why does this symbol make you suspicious of him?"

"It's an 'A' inside of an 'O'. Its origins are not well known, but it is attributed to Pierre-Joseph Proudhon, a French anarchist. He is supposed to have said that order is the daughter, not the mother, of liberty. Order, as he saw it, springs from anarchy."

Travis snorted in disdain.

"Order comes from Anarchy. O and A. I've heard Alistair blabber on for hours about just that kind of thing. And he's well read enough to have come across it. The fact he is back in town just confirms my suspicion."

"No, it doesn't confirm it. But I agree this is interesting. What do you propose?"

"He's working for his brother in the Transportation Bureau. We need to keep an eye on him."

"If he's a spy, he's not high up in the hierarchy." Travis rubbed his chin in contemplation. "How sure are you he's involved?"

Stephanie considered how strongly to declare her suspicions. "Something's telling me he is."

"Then pull up a seat and we'll discuss what to do."

There was an unmoving body lying in the middle of the street and Henry instinctively knew it was a corpse. Amid the scattered rubble and debris left from a day's rioting, it was left to lie in an impossible position on an amorphous stain of its own blood. A tide of angry citizens had crashed into a wall of Civil Guard and, in the resultant exchange of action and reaction, the whole messy scene carried itself to other parts, losing energy in proportion to the injured who fell from the ranks, or those who were apprehended and taken to the prisoner camp. When the clashing forces swept through this street, passing the Snitch's Office, some man's son, some woman's husband fell, never to rise again.

The corpse wore the ragged clothes of a poor civilian, and the emaciated frame implied an irregular food supply. Staring at it with a reverence he had not known he possessed, Henry felt guilty, though he could not say why. As he walked past the corpse, giving it a wide berth but scrutinizing it, he could not shake that gnawing feeling of culpability.

Upon reaching the other side of the street, carefully ascending and then descending the snow bank framing it, he stopped at the sound of an approaching auto. The engine's hum reassured him there was life and movement still in the city. The government vehicle, a wagon, rounded the corner and came to a stop a few feet from the cadaver. No sooner did it park than out popped two government employees, street workers with thick winter clothing and a patch of the city seal on their backs and chests. One went to the back of the wagon and opened the door while the other went to the corpse and, giving it a callous kick, managed to roll it onto its back.

Henry winced when he saw how the man's face was mangled such that he would be difficult to identify. The two city workers lifted the dead body by the limbs and tossed it into the back of the wagon. One partner closed the door while the other hopped into the driver's seat. When his friend joined him, the auto pulled forward and slipped around a bend and out of sight. Moments later the sound of the engine and the tires tearing through ice and snow also retreated and the street was returned to the silence in which Henry found it.

Leaving the scene, he trudged into the Snitch's Office, lost in thought, his chin tucked into his chest. The building was unlit and still. His footsteps on the linoleum floors echoed in the small hallways as he made his way into the building. Before long, he spied a faint glow which, upon further investigation, proved to be coming from a candle lit office room whose door was left ajar.

Standing quietly in the doorway, he folded his hands in front of him and waited to be noticed. The man inside had a pad and pen and was scribbling something. Though he gave no indication of having noticed Henry, he eventually said, "Come in," without looking up. Henry sat in the chair across from him.

"The rioters knocked out one of the power stations," he explained with a glance at the candles. "Which one are you?"

"Henry Miller 2kj."

"You have something to report then?"

Nodding, Henry said, "I've infiltrated the rebel army." This made the man stop. "I think I've been officially accepted in."

"How?"

"I had to perform a task."

The man looked at Henry with a severe frown. "As a spy you are still bound by the law. You will be held accountable for any illegal acts you commit."

Henry managed not to stammer. "It was nothing like that…I had to deliver some goods is all." The man did not reply. "Anyway, I'm in."

"Very well," said the man with a dismissive tone and returned to his scribbling. "We will look forward to some productive information from you."

Hesitant, Henry lingered in the chair.

"You will be paid when you deliver us information we are looking for," the man informed him without looking up. "Names of the rebels, especially the leaders. Attack plans. Dates and times. Things we can use. You will be paid according to your usefulness and merely enlisting in their ranks does not prove useful to us."

Seeing little point in further conversation, Henry rose hastily left, unsurprised that he would not be paid but still faintly disappointed.

27

The new Ashley apartment was perfectly soundproof so, while Alistair watched a group of workers hammering at a small tower they were erecting, the sound did not reach his ears. The short tower was going up on a small empty plot of ground between two buildings on the other side of the street, though it was not immediately apparent to Alistair what it would be used for.

At the sound of his father entering the room, softly humming an unrecognizable melody, Alistair turned and saw he carried his *pintador*. With a pleasant smile, Nigel stepped onto a stool and, switching the device on, began to change the walls of the room from off white to a deep, reddish tan. It was the third time since Alistair had moved in that Nigel had repainted with his toy.

"Your mother's got me working again," he said to his son with a wink.

"Is that going to go with the furniture?"

Shrugging, Nigel said, "If not, I'll just change it back." His wand slid back and forth in front of the wall which changed hue as the *pintador* passed over. "It makes me wonder how I ever got by with paint and a brush."

Pleased, Alistair smiled and returned his attention to the structure being erected outside. "Do you know what they're building across the street?"

"Surveillance tower."

Alistair's face instantly fell. "Exactly what for?"

He could hear the wince in his father's voice, almost as if Nigel felt he needed to apologize to his son for the government's actions. "They are going to be monitoring conversations. And recording movements."

Alistair did not speak at first. Instead, he pursed his lips and nodded slowly. "This is a sound proof apartment."

Nigel paused and lowered his *pintador*. Not looking at his son, he replied, "They are coming to gut the walls and replace the material."

Alistair nodded again, slowly, but then suddenly his anger bubbled over, surprising even him. "What a shame they haven't placed a chip in our heads. Perhaps they can sit in the room the next time you're in bed with Mom!"

Nigel blanched at his son's words and put out his hands in supplication. "Alistair, I didn't make the decision—"

"I'm not yelling at you," Alistair curtly barked and fell silent. As Nigel went back to painting the room, his little song now forgotten, Alistair regretted his outburst. More slowly than it had come, the anger drained out of him. "I suppose," he said, searching for something to say to break the silence, "this sort of conversation will have to be curtailed. I imagine they use computers with voice readers for monitoring?"

"I have no idea. I thought you were participating in the system now."

Alistair smiled mirthlessly as he gazed at the workers with foreboding. "So the next time a mother complains of her "rebellious" children, will the Civil Guard come breaking down the door?" Nigel did not reply. *Resources are already in short supply*, Alistair thought. *What could have been made with that labor and those materials if they had not been used for these towers?*

"What time were you going to leave for work?"

Alistair glanced at the clock on the wall. "Right now," he replied and reluctantly got out of the padded seat by the window. His father had already finished "painting" one wall and was standing back to admire his work.

"Well, off I go," Alistair said when he was well bundled and already sweating.

"Twelve hour shift?"

"Oh yeah. And an eight hour one after the nap. I'll see you this evening." With a quick goodbye he was off and a minute later was outside the apartment complex and walking in the freezing but quiet Arcarian air.

Before arriving at the grand Bureau of Transportation Building, an edifice mocking the run down peasant homes and shops nearby, he passed by four other towers under construction. His anger waxed and waned in relation to their proximity, like some perverse law of physics. By the time he trudged past the marble pillars at the entrance of the Bureau, he was somewhat relaxed, his thoughts having taken him step by step to other topics. After he went through the invasive inspection at the entrance, he was incensed again.

Heading straight to his locker on sublevel one, he stashed his winter apparel, donned his white lab coat and headed for the computer lab. He wiggled his constricted shoulders as he went, trying to stretch the coat, the biggest they had. When he reached the main office room and its maze of cubicles, he allowed himself a small grin when he compared it to the first day he had been given a tour of the building. Just as Leland predicted, the Realists cracked down on laziness. One day, an official—dressed in an officer's military uniform as all high ranking government officials now were—arrived with a small entourage of Civil Guard, fifteen minutes after the midday siesta. He promptly arrested any worker still in his or her cot and expropriated them for work in the mines. No questions, no hesitating, no appeals and no mercy. The workforce was reduced by a third; the remainder were either busy or looked like it.

Once past that beehive, he took the stairs to the far more subdued third floor. A narrow white hallway of black and white tiles and hazy lights that nearly put one in a trance led him to his lab. As he drew near, he gradually became aware of the voices of his coworkers. Rounding the corner, he was greeted by the increasingly familiar sight of the lab, lit now by natural light and comfortably furnished in grays and dark blues.

Louise was not there when Alistair arrived, but the other three to whom the former soldier was becoming acquainted were: Edward, Annette and Harcourt. Harcourt, all long spindly limbs, sat hunched over his desk, his face typically expressionless, like the numbers he manipulated, and his elongated legs tucked nearly to his chest as he sat on a chair made for a person of normal height. He was perhaps twenty cycles older than Alistair and nearly as many younger than the other two, Annette and Edward, who were pleasantly chatting with each other.

Annette glanced at Alistair and warmly smiled as he walked in but quickly returned her attention to Edward, who was busy relaying some unimportant gossip to which he was privy.

Steeling himself for twelve hours of work he was confident were absolutely worthless, Alistair made his way to his own projection computer, switched it on, and waited for it to warm up.

"There is going to be a formal ball at the Mayor's Palace next week," said Edward as he pulled out a cigar—a rare commodity just then—snapped a match across the table and touched the flame to the end of the cigar. As he puffed hard to light it, he mixed in some speech with the smoke. "The Mayor is entertaining some dignitaries from Rendral. If anyone is interested…" No one answered his offer and Alistair knew Edward did not care. The point was to make the offer while contentedly puffing on a cigar.

"I suppose we may as well get started for the day," suggested Annette and she stood up. "Is Louise here yet?"

"I sent her for supplies," said Harcourt. "She'll be back momentarily."

"Well, then…Edward and I have been talking and we've come to a couple conclusions. Our job is to coordinate distribution. It's quite a task, and we'll be coordinating our efforts with teams from New Boston and Avon." Annette paused a moment to give them a significant look. "Our work will determine whether the economy works or not, will either lead Aldra to victory against Kaldis or defeat. We have a sacred task and you should all be honored to be a part of it."

At that point Edward spoke, though he did not bother to stand as Annette had. "We need to be able to predict what demand there will be and then we need to decide how exactly to organize the whole project so as to most easily implement the plan. What I mean is this: Do we organize a rigid train schedule and force industry to adapt to it, or do we allow industry to make the demands it wants and adapt our schedule? Ultimately, we cannot supply everything to everyone."

"Given limited means and unlimited wants," interjected Alistair, "some type of rationing must be implemented."

A bit startled, Edward turned to consider Alistair, who had never spoken in front of the whole group, and nodded his head. Alistair blushed, nearly regretting his interjection.

"Exactly. How do we apportion the use of our railways, given limited capacity?"

The sound of footsteps outside announced Louise's return with five plastic cups from which steam wafted. As Edward went on, she handed them out, ducking her head to remain inconspicuous.

"Could we not simply set a price?" Alistair suggested, having taken one step and deciding to press forward. "We could raise the price, and thus reduce industry demand, until supply and demand were equalized."

Louise finished handing out the cups and finally sat down next to Alistair. She smiled shyly as he sipped from his cup, but when he returned her smile she averted her gaze and stared at the floor.

Edward grinned and, taking the cigar out of his mouth, used it to point at Alistair. "That's the Realist spirit!" he proclaimed. "Unfortunately, it won't work with transportation. If we want to use prices, we might as well privatize the railroad! Some things are best left to government, some things to private industry. Obviously, leaving everything to private industry would be a disaster, but the Voluntarist pure socialism was a disaster too. The railroad is the merger point where industry and military meet, where private and public join together. We want to get the best of both systems and unite them, seamlessly."

"What we need is to coordinate behavior on both ends," said Alistair. "So there are no shortages, surpluses, overuse, underuse, delays…"

"Exactly," confirmed Edward.

"I can't think of anything simpler than a price," said Alistair. "I can't think of anything other than a price that would have such a far reaching effect and yet be so simple to achieve. What exactly is the reason we don't want to use it?"

"A fair question," said Edward, preparing to launch into an explanation with the patient goodwill of a professor handling a question he has fielded many times before but which is a new concept for the current batch of students. "The war could get unbelievably expensive if we allow it. Price has to start and end somewhere, and we are that point. Now, notice the problem: the State's generals make purchase orders from private industry, which uses rail to transport the purchased products, and rail is controlled by the State. Well, it would just be a way of getting back part of the price of what we have bought by charging them for rail. And the industrialists aren't stupid, they'll simply raise the price of their products.

"Here's the problem with that: competition can be wasteful, and many companies go out of business. We can't afford to have important industries going out of business during a war. So exclusive rights were granted to some industrialists."

"Monopolies," said Alistair.

Edward fixed a disapproving frown on him. "I don't think it's fair to use that word, Alistair. We have simply given them exclusive rights in some areas. The problem is, without the competition from other industries, these industrialists can charge almost whatever they want. So price controls have been placed on finished goods they sell us. With a rigid price control in place, they can't adapt to the prices of the railroad, can't pass the cost on, and could lose money."

"So why not raise the price limit to account for the rail price?" asked Louise.

"But the rail price will fluctuate. Otherwise, what's the point? A fixed price is as difficult as no price. In both cases, the same coordinating message is constantly being sent even though circumstances change. So rail prices must fluctuate to do a price's work, but if they do, then the price limit must fluctuate. But what is the point of a price limit if it is going to fluctuate? That's not a price limit, that's just a price. And many final products are passed along through several different factories before they are finished. Each time, an industrialist would have to include the cost of shipping into his price. When it finally emerged, ready for sale, it would be unbelievably expensive. So we can't let prices float freely or the war will be too expensive, but we can't keep them rigidly fixed against a floating rail price. Therefore, we have eliminated the rail price. Now we need to make it work with the price-controlled industry."

"But each time rail was paid for," said Alistair, "it would be paid to the government. So the final product might be more expensive, but we have collected transportation fees along the way. If transportation fees are what they are passing along, and we've already collected those, then the price for us doesn't go up."

"Excellent thinking, Alistair! But it does go up for the average citizen," Edward reminded him. "There is a sense that…how do I put it…the government is eager to do well by the people. To get their support. If all their products became so expensive because rail became too expensive because of demand during the war..." Edward finished with a shrug of his shoulders.

"But if the price of rail is kept low with a price control, and companies don't have to pass along that cost...won't that encourage more purchasing of whatever that company is producing?" asked Alistair.

"Supply and Demand," said Edward. "This is true."

"And if there is more demand for something, the company making it will demand more from the companies they buy from to get the material and equipment to make their products."

"That follows."

"Then the prices of these secondary products will go up, but the companies that make the final products are stuck with a price control. Isn't that likely to make them go bankrupt?"

Edward coughed into his hand and nodded his head. "Alistair, that's...that's good thinking. Interesting thinking. The thing is—"

"Wouldn't we need to put price controls on these secondary industries too? But then the same thing happens between the secondary and tertiary industries. And I don't see where it would ever stop."

"Well, that's part of what—"

"At the end, the entire economy would have to be price controlled. Wouldn't it be better to let prices float and pay for everything with taxes, if they must?"

"True...I see what you're saying." Edward hesitated while he tried to think of a reply. "I guess there will always be a danger of this sort of thing...we need to rely on...you know... patriotism in the businesses and a bit of government oversight..."

"If that could work, wouldn't the Voluntarist system have worked?"

"The feeling is the populace is unwilling to support a new taxation plan," Annette answered, stepping in for an increasingly flustered Edward. "And a directive has been given to cut back on adding new Credits to circulation. There are some who are worried we've been adding too many and it might be bad for the system."

"Because if they add too many people will abandon the Credit altogether, since there is nothing backing it in the first place."

Annette smiled. "I think that's a worst-case scenario...whatever the reason, the government does not want to tax and spend. The Voluntarists did enough of that. The intent here is to try and control the economy in a more efficient manner without having prices going wild. That is our task here."

Edward, who plainly was not accustomed to being challenged, flatly declared, "We're not using a price system for the rails, Alistair. It's not our call to make. Our job is to solve these problems you are talking about at the point where the lines have been drawn. Manufacturers of final products are subject to price controls, rail transportation has no price. We need to study the data and come up with a solution to coordinate efforts."

Alistair finally nodded, realizing he had taken Edward to the brink and not wanting to push it any farther. "It sounds like having a mix of the two systems is difficult."

There was a general murmur of consent.

"Maybe the best thing to do would be to study other governments that found a way to make it work. We can imitate them."

"Perhaps," Harcourt's stoic, clinical voice cut through the discussion, "you might like to do some research on that yourself."

Alistair nodded. "I would love to. I'll report back to you on my progress."

"So there is our problem: melding the two systems together and avoiding typical inefficiencies that have resulted. We need to create an equation with simple inputs from easy measurements to accurately coordinate behavior. And of course," Annette concluded, "Rendral wants all of this finished yesterday."

☜☞

Many hours later, after long shifts surrounding a four-hour nap, Alistair emerged from the Transportation Bureau Building with a stream of other workers. So much number crunching drained him and he was hungry, but he looked forward to having the next few dozen hours free. As was his custom, he spoke to no one as he left. Gerald passed by a few yards away without seeing him. He briefly considered calling out to his brother but couldn't summon enough desire or energy.

As he drew closer to his father's home, he became more and more isolated until he was alone, walking down a narrow alleyway cutting through to a main thoroughfare. As monotonous as his work, his feet took the ground a space at a time, crunching the ice and snow. He felt a tingle on the back of his neck as he became aware of another presence behind him. Turning to look, he saw a bundled up pedestrian so large and bulky he could only be Oliver Keegan. A smile split Alistair's face and he stopped to wait for his friend.

"I thought I could sneak up on you," Oliver said when he was closer, his cheeks as red as a cherry and his nose dripping onto his scarf. His face was dirty and had gone several days without being shaved, but his grin was large despite the cracked and dried lips.

"Said the elephant with disappointment."

The two friends enjoyed a rough embrace.

"How's the job?"

"Nothing fruitful just yet. I'm just now getting comfortable with the system. And they're just now getting comfortable with me. Have you heard about these surveillance towers?"

The two men walked side by side.

"I don't anticipate them lasting too long," said Oliver with a sly smile. "Listen, I have a couple things to say. First, Stephanie has discovered what the symbol means."

Alistair could not suppress a grin.

"That's not good. She immediately suspected you."

"How do we know this?"

"Bob's cousin is in the Civil Guard. He's working with Stephanie."

Alistair nodded.

"That means you are likely to be scrutinized. Alistair, I'm not sure what made you suggest it…"

"I thought I'd add a little theory and philosophy to a rebellion of malcontents."

"As if using that symbol would make them warriors of principle," sighed Oliver. "Anyway, you did it and now your position might be compromised."

"Then I should come back with you. I'm still not sold on this thing. You're trying to put together an army; use someone else to do your spying; use me to train the army. I'm more use with you than I am here. And I don't want you alone against Clever Johnny."

"I'm hardly alone."

"I think you need me. I don't trust him."

"Well, there is some good information: we have found a source of funds. A rich supporter of the old regime got left out of the game when permits were handed out."

"And he's feeling vindictive."

"Yes he is."

"Very principled."

"Money is money. And we have already put it to good use. There is a shipload of weapons and military equipment due to arrive tonight. If all goes according to plan, that ship is going to fly by the harbor and crash onto shore several miles east. We'll be free to pick through the goodies."

This revelation stopped Alistair in his tracks. "Can you pull it off?"

Oliver shrugged. "If it doesn't happen, it's no skin off our backs. If it does—"

"How much equipment is on that ship?"

"Plenty. And the Realists were kind enough to anger half of their workers recently who now have to work in the freezing mines instead of their cozy offices." Oliver finished with a significant look at his friend. "We've already managed to recruit a few dozen disaffected former pencil pushers."

"If we can get enough weapons—"

"We'll take the city. Can we count on your help tonight?"

"You don't even need to ask. When and where?"

28

Katherine was a frenzied form as she rushed through the snowy streets of Arcarius, skidded down the icy alleyways, burst into the apartment building and tore up the stairs. It was only when she arrived at the front door of the Ashley apartment that she realized how much her thighs hurt and how labored was her breathing. She allowed herself a moment to regain a modicum of composure and breath before opening the door and charging in. Her mother and father, seated at the table and enjoying an evening snack of tea and crackers, were startled by the entry.

"What's the matter?" her mother asked over her father's incoherent exclamation. Their daughter stood in the doorway, sweating profusely. Her hat and scarf were awry and her eyes wide, as if terrified.

"I've got to go!" she wheezed and rushed towards her bedroom. Mary and Nigel caught up with her while she was combing her bedroom in what nearly resembled an effort to pack her traveling cases.

"What in God's name is going on, Katherine?" her mother demanded.

Katherine paused for a second to face her mom. "I'm going to Rendral!" she proclaimed, and only then did her parents realize she was not scared but ecstatic. "I'm going to Rendral to work on a project with the National Academy of Sciences!" She even jumped into the air like a little girl as she clapped her hands together. Nigel and Mary let out a cheer and rushed to embrace her. It was Nigel who cried first, but Mary was hardly about to be stoic about it and followed suit.

"I assume this is good news," said Alistair from the doorway as he rubbed his eyes and yawned. There were lines imprinted on the side of his face from where he had lain on the covers and his hair, no longer as short as during his service, was long enough to be molded into odd shapes when he slept. Laughing, Katherine rushed to hug him and relate the news.

Then, she remembered she was in a hurry and raced around the room again. "I don't have much time," she explained as she frantically grabbed at clothing, tossed it on the bed, turned in circles while clenching and unclenching her fists, spotted the clothes on her bed and picked them up, turned in another circle and tossed them back on the bed.

Mary moved into the center of the room and, grabbing Katherine by the shoulders, guided her to the door. "I'll get you packed. Your father will fix you something to eat before you go."

A half minute later, Katherine was in the dining area eating a sandwich of ham and stale bread with a cup of tea. Nigel and Alistair sat across from her.

"I just got the news a half hour ago," she explained after swallowing a mouthful of her sandwich. "Can we take the auto to the spaceport?"

Nigel nodded with a smile, his eyes still wet and shiny.

Katherine bit off another mouthful and washed it down with another swig of tea. "Our local director was going to go but he couldn't. I don't know why. Someone from the National Academy called me at work and asked if I could come down."

"What are you going to work on?" asked Alistair.

"Flow Theory. What I was telling you about before."

"So what exactly is Flow Theory?" Nigel asked.

Taking a deep breath, Katherine let it out with a whoosh. "Flow Theory is the most exciting—and potentially most important—theory to come out of the physical sciences since Heim Theory back in the Terran 20th century."

"The Dawn of Technology," said Nigel.

"The end of it," amended Alistair. "The Dawn of Technology refers to the period when lone inventors and scientists worked in their basements...that was one characteristic. Burkhard Heim was kind of in a transition period when science was carried out by teams in a laboratory and science started to become ultra specialized. The defining—"

"Alistair, I love you," said Katherine, putting a hand on her brother's shoulder, "but I don't have much time to tell this."

Alistair looked sheepish and she went on.

"Flow Theory is still unproven...it deals with fundamental forces outside the realm of the physical universe, or at least the universe as we know it. Why does our universe have the properties it has? What makes an electron an electron? Burkhard Heim explained this with the geometrization of space, extending the theories of an earlier scientist named Albert Einstein. But why should our universe have developed that way? Why not with a different kind of geometrization? Flow Theory posits what is called an Overlay."

"An Overlay?" asked Nigel.

Katherine shrugged. "No one can really describe it well, but it works like another layer over the same dimensions we exist in, just laid over top of our reality, like a veneer on a table. In the Overlay are particles called Essentials that flow around in a constant pattern. The interactions of these Essentials as they flow through and over and around each other actually cause the properties that cause the properties of our universe."

"And you're going to try to prove this?"

"It makes certain predictions we are going to try and verify. But if it's true, the technology at our command...in time we could reshape the universe. If we alter the flow of Essentials, we conceivably could remake the rules."

At that moment, Mary's stout form came out of the bedroom hallway with Katherine's packed bags. Alistair jumped up to carry the luggage down to the garage underneath the complex and the others followed him. After a tremendous effort at pulling the frozen trunk open, Alistair loaded Katherine's traveling bags and all four piled into the frigid auto and sat shivering on the seats. Mary took her accustomed position at the front of the government-designed and produced auto and squeezed a throttle. In the driver's seat, Nigel pressed the start button and produced only a small cough from the engine.

"Alistair?" Nigel prompted, and his son jumped out and, grabbing the auto at the back, rocked the machine back and forth, mixing the chemicals inside.

After a minute of this shaking, Nigel was able to start the auto. Mary closed the lid to cover the throttle and hopped inside. The fusion engine slowly sipped at the water powering it and the energy lost through inefficiency trailed out the back, creating a wispy tail of a cloud. Before long, they crested Tanard's Mountain and the spaceport, with its many blinking lights, lay before them. The control tower, thirty stories high, jutted into the sky from the center of the complex and was ringed with lights. On the far side were the naval barracks, drab but solid walls encasing a well-lit complex. As they made for the port, a large vessel shaped somewhat like a beehive was slowly rumbling down a lit path towards a landing pad from whence it would fall into the sky. Katherine rode with her faced pressed to the window, watching the ships with fascination.

"I wonder which is mine," she breathed, fogging the part of the window by her lips.

The landing pads were blocked from their view as Nigel pulled the auto in front of the spaceport and into a parking spot near the entrance. The pavement of the long neglected civilian lot was cracked such that it was now halfway to being a gravel lot, but it was paved long ago with a material which melted ice and eventually evaporated it, a precursor to the roads on Kaldis which directly sublimated frozen liquids. This attribute remained in the material despite its condition, so that the parking lot was a square of gray in the midst of a sea of white.

Mary and Katherine rushed across the lot and into the spaceport proper while Alistair, burdened with the luggage, moved at a lesser pace. Nigel hung back with his son. When the two men reached the entrance, Mary was speaking with an armed port official while Katherine, having found a communicator booth, was speaking with Gerald.

Mary gestured for Nigel and Alistair to follow her. She called out to Katherine, who took two steps towards her mother while hurriedly saying goodbye and dropping the communicator without looking to see if she managed to leave it on its hook. She caught up with the others and, panting, set the lead pace as they proceeded down a long tiled hallway. Guards with powerful rifles stood at attention every fifty feet or so on the right side, while on the left a window gave a view of the landing area.

The western sky, its blue now deepening as oranges and pinks streamed over the tops of the mountains framing the western edge of Arcarius, acted as a backdrop for the launch of a vehicle. There was no burst of flame from a rocket, nor did any jets keep it aloft. Instead, the HD Drive whirred to life and converted photons of electromagnetism into gravitophotons, carriers of one of the three types of gravity. There was a moment when the heavy vehicle, though still touching the ground, seemed to be free of it, like when two boats docked side by side happen to touch one another but are not drawn together by any force. Then the ship was moving away from the ground, first slowly but at ever increasing speeds as the gravitophotons made the ship "fall" into the sky at nearly ten meters per second per second. It was not long before the ship was a small dot in the distance.

They came to Katherine's transport. Two guards stood at either side of the exit door while a couple marines were just finishing gathering their belongings. Katherine, Mary and Nigel arrived out of breath, and Alistair was disappointed to realize he too was breathing just a tad heavy. He again made a mental note to exercise. *It's easier to stay in shape than get it back,* he chided himself. *And you may need to be in shape in the coming months.*

Katherine said goodbye to her family as they enveloped her in their heartiest embrace. Nigel was crying once more, and Mary soon did likewise. Katherine's eyes looked wet as she promised to get in touch with them as soon as she could.

"There's no household communication allowed right now," Nigel told her, "so let us know your number and we'll call you when we can."

"You can call me at the Bureau," Alistair told her as he affectionately pinched her cheek.

"Last call!" shouted a voice at the exit.

Katherine gave each another embrace and then jogged towards the door. The two marines in the waiting area made their way outside. The Ashley's moved to the window to watch Katherine go, staying there even after the ship's steps retracted and the doors closed. They were still there when the transport rumbled down the pathway. Though Alistair briefly worried about the hour and his plans, he said nothing, letting his parents watch as the ship fell skywards. Even then he was sure they would have preferred to stay and stare at the spot where the ship disappeared, but a port officer strode past and gruffly informed them they would have to leave if they did not have a ticket.

29

The Aldran night, always dark without a reflecting satellite, was made even darker by the clouds covering the sky so entirely that nowhere could a star be seen. When one turned away from the city, there was only the black sky and the equally black sea melding together into an impenetrable canvas. As Alistair had shut off his enhanced vision, it was like staring into the maw of a black hole. Only the lapping of the waves against the sides of the boats and the occasional stirring of his companions reminded him of where he was. That and the occasional soft snowflake that melted on his forehead, or got tangled in his eyelashes.

Someone cleared his throat and shifted in his seat, groaning as he relieved pressure on one part of his backside. Turning from his perch on the side, Alistair activated his preternaturally keen vision, an action as natural to him as the moving of a finger, and he picked out the others on board: Oliver Keegan, Bob LaSalle, Ryan Wellesley and Brad Stanson, all unshaven and dirty with warm but ragged clothes. He idly raised his right hand and waved it slowly in front of Ryan's face. His partner blinked once but did not otherwise react.

"What time is it?" asked Ryan as he rubbed at his eyes and yawned.

Brad pinched his wristwatch and the display lit up. "13th block just started," he said. "Anytime now."

"My muscles are going to freeze before the damn ship gets here."

"It's impossible to predict exactly when it will arrive," Brad explained in his pacific and matter-of-fact way.

"Why don't we talk a little less?" suggested Oliver from the back of the donated thirty-foot boat, his right hand resting on the antiquated outboard motor. "Concentrate on the horizon."

A series of waves passed through, inclining the boats first one way and then another, and the water smacked against the many hulls.

"Oh, hell," Wellesley dismissively said a moment later, "Alistair'll see it well before we do."

"Not necessarily true," corrected the ex marine. "My vision cannot see around the curve of the planet any better than yours can. Distance here is not what is hiding the ship from our sight."

"Oh, merciful Christ," Ryan moaned. "Why didn't we pair the two professors together?"

Shrugging, Alistair said, "Whom would we teach?" Oliver, Bob and Brad chuckled but Ryan just shook his head and spit over the side.

They fell back into silence, but it was a ponderous silence. Without any particular reason, Alistair knew each of them was focused on the coming task and possible battle, so that when Bob LaSalle finally spoke it was an extension of each of their thoughts.

"Supposing this goes off as it should…what do we do next? Mount a frontal assault or stay guerrilla?"

"It depends on what we salvage," said Brad quietly from his spot in the prow, never taking his eyes from a horizon he could not distinguish.

"We hit 'em hard and crush 'em fast," said Ryan with force. "City's ripe for the picking." He spit once more over the side.

"Is it?" asked Alistair, not really meaning to enter the conversation but everyone stopped and turned in his direction.

"We have someone here who has some experience with rebels and revolutions," said Oliver.

When it was apparent this was not going to be enough of a prompt, Brad said, "Alistair? What do you think?"

"What do I think? I think Aldrans are hungry and that's why they're feisty. I think if you got the power working and brought back the hearty meals and projector programs they'd quiet right down until they missed their next meal."

"Bread and circuses?" asked Oliver.

"Something like that. I think there is little fighting spirit, and even less principle. No living Aldran has ever been free. A cradle to grave government welfare state is all they've ever known, and the government schools make damn sure they don't learn anything else. It was only when the so-called Voluntary System's flaws became intolerable that trouble began. No centrally controlled system can be held together with smiles and promises. It will take the kind of brutality the Realists are quite prepared to use to do that. The problem is there is no competing ideology. When the Realists' system falls apart or people get sick of it and overthrow it, what's going to replace it? Just more of the same?"

"I'm sorry if we're not the principled philosophers you were looking for," said Bob, "but seeing as we're the only revolution around, what would you do?"

"If we get a good harvest tonight, we attack soon. There are rumors of other insurrections and riots across the planet. A resounding victory might just set off a full-scale revolt, and a resounding victory is more than obtainable against the forces currently in Arcarius."

"But there has to be more than that," said Brad. "Millions of discontents need direction, a leader. Someone needs to step forward and be the face of this rebellion."

"A leader is exactly what we don't need," Alistair said, but Wellesley's response overlapped his.

"And who should this leader be?" he asked with a cynical sneer.

"I don't want it, if that's what you mean," Brad replied. "And I don't envy the man it turns out to be. I'd feel much safer being the man who replaced the guy who steps up, or possibly the one who replaces the man who replaces the guy."

"Maybe, maybe not," mused Oliver. He vigorously scratched at his jaw line, covered in stubble and dirt and grease, and then removed his hat to scratch at his scalp. "The State might just be ready to fall. One good push might do it."

"Lights on the horizon," Bob LaSalle proclaimed, jerking upright in his seat.

The others came alert as well. Oliver took out a pocket-size telescope out and scanned until he had the ship in view. They could hear the stirring and whispering of the men in the other boats.

"It's her," Oliver breathed. He retracted the telescope and stuffed it back in his pocket. He then switched on the tiny device nestled around his ear and from which extended a small microphone to his mouth. "Ready your men," he said, though a slight quaver betrayed his anxiety. "On my mark then. Out."

While they waited, Stanson turned on a small light and set it on the floor of the boat. It was weak, but its soft glow allowed them to discern their surroundings. Bob LaSalle stood up and shook his legs and arms. Wellesley followed suit, groaning as his cold frame protested, and Alistair settled for a few stretches. Stanson, who would remain in the boat, did not bother to warm up, and neither did Oliver, who simply sat in the back with an intense glare at the lights of the distant ship.

Oliver eventually ordered the weapons taken out and loaded. When they could faintly hear the sound of the ship tearing through the waves, they took their places, each tying on his head a distinguishing red bandanna. When they could see the ship's spray sent flying up and out to the side, Oliver pulled the rip cord and the engine came to life. The engines from the other boats were soon rumbling as well.

Taking a deep breath of the salty sea air, Alistair, in the prow, focused his mind on the ship as it barreled towards them. It passed the Arcarian port, and though the radio was disabled if all had gone according to plan, it would be obvious to the port authorities that something was wrong. Praying for a slow response from the government, he rechecked the magazine of the handgun and, finding it still in order, slammed it back into place.

The sabotaged cargo ship was of medium size, perhaps eighty yards from bow to stern and less than a third of that in width. Its gunwale rose fifteen yards above sea level, and the bridge rose a few stories to tower above the freight holds and decks below. In front of the bridge a large crane stood above what Alistair knew was the central cargo hold, a large chamber whose retractable roof served as the floor of the main deck. Lights were spaced at intervals along the gunwale, on a special tower in the bow and all over the control tower. Light also streamed from the windows of the control tower, and the ship was close enough now that Alistair's keen vision could see the black forms of the sailors scrambling about, like ants whose home had just been crushed.

The sound of the boat plowing through the waves grew increasingly louder as did the soft sound of the spray it made, like silk on silk. The men sat quietly as the ship headed directly for the spot on the shore that they had planned for. Some, like Alistair, were upright but unmoving. Others, like LaSalle, twitched and shook and bounced their legs up and down.

Then, with a multitude of different and competing noises, all of them thunderous, the ship first tore at the shallow bottom of the sea and then crashed into a small beach. It cut through the short stretch of sand and rock and finally crashed into the cliff face. With the loud groan of metal under stress, the ship leaned to the port side but did not fall. A few rocks, jarred loose by the colossal impact, fell from the cliff, some of them crashing into the ship's deck. The pop and crackle of electricity was heard, and sparks flashed in several spots.

The comparative quiet that followed sent a tingle through each and every spine, and they anxiously waited like a bird dog on a leash. From the ship the men heard wails of pain and anger and confusion carrying through the night across the dark waters. An alarm went off and several rotating yellow and red emergency lights now gave the ship a different hue.

Emitting a loud, baritone war cry, Oliver fired a few rounds into the air and, as most of the men around him imitated his call, squeezed his throttle. The lights of a score of small boats came on and the small regiment was speeding across the distance between them and their fallen prey.

Amid the whooping and exhilaration, Alistair kept his quiet, preparing himself for the skirmish to come as the wind blew in his face. It was his second battle since returning home, and he still felt naked without a war suit. It meant his tactics and technique would have to adapt to his new vulnerability; it meant less bravado and more circumspection. It also meant he might kill again. *When will that counter stop?* he asked himself.

The freighter, with Tessa in white block lettering on the side, rose above them as they drew into its vicinity, motors humming and men shouting, spurred by adrenaline. Oliver veered right as they headed for the ship's stern and eased down on the throttle. Not all the other boats executed their stops as neatly.

One pilot waited too long to pull up and crashed into the side of the Tessa, sending two unlucky men flying into it. Two other boats ran into each other while braking and Alistair heard a couple splashes announcing men overboard. Though it was not clear exactly where they fell in, they gave gurgling, inchoate cries and splashed about in panic as the frigidity of the water seized them.

"This is a goddamn mess!" Alistair cursed with a glare at Oliver.

Oliver looked embarrassed and quickly moved to cover it. Waving down another boat near him he shouted, "Go help Ritchie's boat." The boat operator looked about and then, when he saw what Oliver was pointing at, waved once and made for the hapless vessel.

Glowering at Alistair's rebuke, Oliver guided his craft expertly next to the stern of the Tessa while Alistair readied a length of rope with a grappling hook on the end. He prayed for a decent throw from the other boats, and no injuries, as Brad, Oliver, Bob and Ryan stooped low while the line whizzed over their heads. Finally, he let it fly and it arced over the edge, the hook hitting the deck with a clang. He pulled it back and neatly caught it on the gunwale. Giving a couple of tugs to be sure, he stepped back and allowed the others to clamber up.

"I'm going to help some of these other clowns," he said with a slap to Oliver's shoulder as the big man passed.

The other boats were not faring as well. Most were still attempting to sidle up to the Tessa, either stopping too far short or smacking into it with a bone-rattling thump. They were not spaced particularly well, having bunched together in their rush to arrive quickly. A few managed to dock, but only two of those got their grappling hooks up and over. As it so happened, a boat had drawn up to the Tessa only a couple yards from Oliver's boat and Alistair leaped from his stern to its bow. His landing unsettled it and one unbalanced rebel fell to his knees.

"I'll throw your hook," he announced without ado and seized the rope from the hands of the stunned man who had been trying to get himself disentangled from his first attempt. Confidently, Alistair drew forth a length of rope and whirled it above his head. When he picked up the speed he required, he let it fly and, just like his first throw, it sailed true.

After an insurance tug, Alistair climbed. Passing Oliver and Bob on the way up, he made it to the top of the Tessa only moments after Ryan Wellesley. With his feet firmly planted on the now sloping deck of the tipped ship, he grabbed his handgun, racked the slide, flipped off the safety, and, as the yellow and red flashing lights played over the scene, prepared to advance.

Though he did not realize it, his muscular form, silhouetted against the red and yellow lights with his right arm holding his gun pointed towards the sky, was a moral boost to the haggard and faltering rebel group. There was experience and confidence in his posture, strength and determination in his form. Unbidden, the rebels drew near him, and when he left, several others were right behind. It was the magnetism of poise that attracted them.

Tilted and slippery from the snowfall, the metal walkways forced them to step carefully. Looking always for cover and possible sniper positions, he led his band of men to a locked door with a single, head-size circular glass window. Gun in front, he closed in on the door, his finger on the trigger.

When he reached it, he paused and listened, his left shoulder up against the wall and his gun in both hands. The ship's motor was still running, kicking up water at the stern. The hum from the engine made everyone and everything on the ship vibrate. In the distance, voices were yelling and moaning and Alistair detected a couple screams but nothing immediately on the other side of the door.

As the men behind him breathed heavily, as much from the excitement as from the exertion, he produced a small charge from his pocket that, with some putty, he stuck to the door near the handle. He gave a military signal with his free hand for the men behind him to back up but no one recognized it, so he gave them a more ordinary indication to scoot back. When they were a safe distance away, he grabbed his remote control and detonated the charge.

There was a concussive blast followed an instant later by a deafening clang as a piece of metal was torn from the door and smashed into a wall. The solid iron door now swung loose on its hinges and smoke hung in the air. On the other side, still deep within the Tessa, a surge of new shouts followed the blast. Alistair entered, his troupe not far behind him.

They were in a small hallway lined with doors like the one they had just destroyed. Pausing at each, he listened and put his eye up to the round window to peer into the room on the other side. Most were unoccupied but a mess as the crash scattered objects about. In one room he saw a prone form lying bleeding against a wall. Halfway up the slope of the long hallway there was a stairwell on the right hand side. Spiraling up and down, it presented the men with their first choice. Alistair approached with great care and found it was clear.

"The others will be heading for the cargo holds," he told the men as he turned to face them. For the first time he noticed Ryan Wellesley, eyes wide and exhilarated, mouth open as he breathed. "Let's head up to the bridge. I want to knock out communication."

The men nodded, and Alistair studied them. Many were dirty and wore worn out winter clothes. Their faces were generally unshaved and filthy from living in the surrounding hills. They were breathing hard, flushed with adrenaline, and a few shifted from one unsteady foot to another. They were seven brave men, but he detected the nervousness of the novice.

"Remember," he told them, "we've got the upper hand. They're rattled and unprepared for us. Be careful, but be confident."

More nods from the men and Alistair proceeded to ascend the tilted, narrow metal staircase. A chorus of echoing footsteps preceded them, and the metal even groaned under their weight. When they passed two stories, there came the quick rattle of automatic fire followed by the piercing sounds of the bullets careening off metal walls. The sounds came from behind, at the back of their group.

"Report!"

It was Wellesley, a few men back, who called up. "We saw a couple of 'em running off."

"If they're running leave them be. These are poor bastards caught in the wrong place at the wrong time. If they don't resist, we don't attack."

The men, startled, tensely held their weapons, jerking about at shadows and flickering lights.

There was some murmuring from below. Alistair could not see them as they were hidden behind the curve of the stairs, but finally someone called up, "Yes, sir."

They reached the upper story without further incident. Just to the right of the stairwell was a large set of double doors that Alistair knew would be the bridge. Checking both directions, he sidled up to the thick, steel doors and peered into the room through the windows.

There was a central station with a projection map sputtering like a flame struggling to stay alive. Leaning against its edges were two men, one of whom bore a Captain's insignia. The other, perhaps his first mate, was bleeding down his forehead. Another man sat at one of the stations around the wall with a cloth held to his head. All three were armed.

Alistair signaled that there were three total, all armed, and hoped his men would understand the message. He then fished out another charge and puttied it to the door before moving back to the stairwell. He extended the remote into the hall, pressed the button and once more there was a blast. This time a section of roof was shaken loose and came crashing to the hallway floor.

"Now!" Alistair shouted and he leaped over the wreckage and onto the bridge. "Don't move!" he bellowed, his voice strong and commanding as he had been trained.

The wounded man who had been sitting down was now fumbling for his gun while the captain was sprawled out on the floor, shaking his head to clear it. The first mate was down on one knee but reaching for a weapon. There was some indecision on their faces, but when seven more armed rebels poured through the doorway the choice became easy.

"No one needs to die here tonight," said Alistair, his voice dropping only a little. "Ryan, take their weapons and get them tied up." Ryan quickly moved to comply. "You," he said with a curt nod at another rebel, "keep an eye out from the windows." The man nodded and moved to the stations to look out at the ship from his high perch. Alistair commanded two others to guard the door and stairwell and then, when the three crewmen were disarmed and bound to chairs, felt a creeping triumph he cautioned himself not to turn into cockiness.

"I need the bill of lading and a schematic of this vessel," he informed the Captain. "And don't play games. We are going to make off with whatever we want; the sooner you help us out, the sooner we'll be gone and you can get medical attention for your men."

The captain's baleful stare did not change, but he said, "It would be quicker if you untied me."

Alistair nodded to the rebel at his side and the man cut the captain loose.

"What the hell did I tie him for?" grumbled Ryan.

The Captain moved to the center projector and typed in a code. A moment later the computer spit out a paper that Alistair snatched up and stuffed into his pocket.

"Get them off the bridge. Put them in another room on this floor," he commanded and the recipient of the order hastened to obey. "And retie the captain, Wellesley."

As the others left, he went to the communication station and set another charge. He set another at the back up station and then spared a moment to scan the horizon from the bridge. The snowfall was gaining in intensity and several flurries battered against the cracked glass, obscuring vision. As far as he could tell, there was nothing yet on its way from the city, whether by air or sea. Temporarily satisfied, he backed out of the bridge where the men were waiting for him.

"Cover your ears," he said and they moved farther away. A moment later, a double blast rent the bridge and the windows shattered outward.

"Are we going to leave them?" asked Wellesley with a nod to the room where they had deposited the captives.

"They'll be rescued soon enough," Alistair replied. "Let's hope it's not too soon. Now get down to the cargo."

The Tessa, once a ship of frantic sailors scrambling to prevent a crash, was now plunged into an even greater state of confusion. As the band descended they heard shouts and gunfire and an occasional explosion. The farther they went, the smokier became the air inside as it filled with the aftermath of the violence. Through the red and yellow tinged smoke they went until finally they emerged from the central tower and onto the main deck.

The wind had picked up and now whipped snowflakes into their eyes. Alistair saw Clever Johnny, flanked by a few others, standing at the edge of the cargo hold door directing men. The sound of desultory gunfire came from the bow, and the muzzle flashes flickered. An occasional form could be seen darting across some walkway or other, occasionally firing at an unseen form somewhere else.

"Orders?" asked Wellesley as Alistair observed the scene with frustration.

"This is going to get out of hand quickly. Yeah, Ryan, let Clever Johnny know he is a sitting duck if someone gets a good sniper position. Looks like he's got someone trying to rig the power box and get the cargo door open. Find out why since we're not using the crane."

Alistair took a moment to scan the horizon but still detected no rescue attempt. Returning his attention to Clever Johnny, he saw Oliver and Wellesley arguing with him. He rushed to their sides.

"We have to have this," Johnny lustfully said.

"You think I don't know that?" said Oliver. "We have to go below, like we planned."

"It was a damn fool decision to use the crane anyway," said Alistair as he approached. "Especially without securing the area first." Clever Johnny glowered under the rebuke but Alistair plunged on. "We head below as planned. Leave six men here on deck to make sure no one follows us below. According to the ship's schematic—"

"We never got the ship's schematic," Clever Johnny insisted almost petulantly.

"—speak for yourself…according to the schematic," Alistair continued, unfolding what he had printed and studying it through the swirling snow flakes, "there is no way to the lower holds from the bow of the ship. If we can keep them holed up there we can concentrate on clearing out resistance below."

"There's a couple guys," said Oliver. "They're armed and there's no getting through them to the main cargo hold."

"Yes there is," Alistair replied in a matter-of-fact tone and he pointed to a group of barrels upended when the Tessa tilted. "Haul a couple of those down with us."

It was only a few minutes later when Alistair, Oliver, Clever Johnny and a few other rebels reached the barricade, whose presence was announced to them by a rattle of gunfire and the sparks of the bullets as they tore into the metal walls. Alistair waited with his back to the wall, inches from the ninety degree turn which would bring him into the fire of the two or three men who guarded their ship's cargo. Oliver and Clever Johnny, both breathless and looking with hope to Alistair, faced him with their backs to the opposite wall, their feet bracing against the incline. He gave an order that was relayed through the ranks and moments later heard the sound of the wooden barrels being rolled through the passageway. The four men rolling the two barrels reached the corner and stopped, looking at Alistair expectantly.

He exchanged a look with Oliver. "Would you like to explain it to them?" Without waiting for a reply he knelt down and affixed the putty and a charge to one end of each barrel.

"This is your last chance to surrender!" Oliver's great voice bellowed through the halls. "You'll not be harmed or even taken hostage. We are getting into the cargo hold one way or another!"

There was a brief pause. "Get stuffed!"

Oliver looked to Alistair who did not bother looking up. "You know your part," said the ex-marine and stood up.

Clearly nervous, Oliver positioned himself behind the first barrel while the others readied their weapons.

"Aim high," Alistair said. "We don't want to take off the top of his head."

"It's too handsome a head to be ruined," Oliver said and managed a smile.

"Go!" said Alistair, and four guns were stuck out into the hallway and began to fire. Oliver had no trouble rolling the barrel and, with a tremendous heave, he hurled it down the hallway, a process greatly aided by the ship's tilt.

No sooner was his job finished than he ducked back into safety around the corner and Clever Johnny set off the charge. The concussive force, contained in enclosed space, hurtled through the hall and knocked a couple rebels to the ground. Alistair, already in position behind the second barrel, rolled it out around the corner. Oliver, Johnny and a few others followed, guns ready. The men fired over his head as they followed him and, half way there, he heaved the barrel forward and then hit the deck. The others followed suit, all covering their ears as Clever Johnny activated the charge and another blast rocked the innards of the Tessa.

Something hit Alistair's skull as he lay face down on the metal flooring and he felt the wet warmth of blood seep through his hair. Ignoring it, he sprang to his feet and charged into the chamber. He entered ready to fire but found he did not need to. Three men were sprawled out on the floor nearly senseless. Holding up a hand to slow down the swarm of rebels who now burst into the chamber, he went to the hatch door and planted another charge. Clever Johnny, meanwhile, had the three prisoners bound and taken.

Alistair cleared the room and detonated the charge. After it went off, he rushed to the steel double doors and quickly threw them open. He shouted at the men to move quickly, and when the designated loaders filed in, he was right behind with his bill of lading, weaving in and out of the wooden crates, searching only for the choicest supplies.

When he found some, and had summarily dismissed a few suggestions from a couple others, he had the men clear a space along the side of the hull. He then set about the delicate task of applying more charges so as to blow an exit hole through which the supplies could be loaded onto the rebel boats outside. First banging the metal siding to determine where the surface of the sea was, he next plotted the positions for his charges, taking care not to place too many lest the resulting explosion spread to the volatile material only a few yards away.

When the charges were placed, he retreated to a safe distance and yet again set them off. He would later reflect that it could have gone worse, but it certainly could have been better. The first result after a hole was blown in the hull was that a piece of metal was shot into the hull of one of the other boats waiting outside. At the same time, water slopped over the bottom edge of the hole and even poured through at times. The hole itself, at least, would be of an adequate size.

"Alright let's move! Move! Move! Move!" he commanded and the men instantly obeyed, instinctively forming a line between the pile of weaponry and the newly formed aperture. He rushed to the opening and waved at the boats outside.

"One at a time now! Form a line. Come on! Let's get this done!"

The process of getting the boats together was not a smooth one and he ached with impatience as he watched them bungle about. The driver of the sinking boat needed rescue, and too many boats banged into each other, the pilots being unused to the fluid movement and lack of brakes that was part of steering a water vessel. With the help of some paddles and ropes they were finally able to get into some sort of order and eventually the goods were moved out.

Alistair helped with unloading the crates for a time before he moved to his next task. A brief search through the stockpile yielded the item he was searching for. He carefully extracted the bomb from its packaging and set it down on a nearby crate. His original intention was to blast a hole in the floor of the hull but that now had a half inch of water. He settled for a smooth corner between the wall and the floor and affixed the bomb to that surface.

"Sir, report from above: skies still all clear," called a voice.

"Excellent! Tell the boats when they're full the crew needs to board and they must leave immediately for their drop point."

"Yes, sir."

With the sound of men grunting and groaning, Alistair prepared the bomb for a countdown. A voice behind him said, "If we set some other explosives near the cargo we can take out the weapons we leave behind." It was Clever Johnny. Alistair turned and, for the first time he could remember, made eye contact with the man.

"And likely the whole crew with it. No, the ship will be disabled enough from the holes in the hull. The extra weapons we'll dump ourselves as much as we can." He turned back around and paid Clever Johnny no more attention. After a moment of silence, Johnny sloshed away through the deepening pool of seawater.

It was a few minutes later, after he went back to the offloading line, when word came down that there were aircraft approaching. The men paused as one.

"How many?" asked Alistair.

"Three that we can see."

"Back to work, men. Fast as you can," he urged them and then made for the stairs to the main deck.

Once up top, he saw unarmed rescue vehicles hovering above the Tessa. They were long, silver and almost featureless cigar-shaped craft with flat bottoms and a small cockpit. Their front and back tapered to a smooth round point, and on their sides they bore the official seal of the city of Arcarius.

Oliver came to stand at his side. "What do we do?"

"The attack craft will be on their way in moments. We need to stop unloading weapons and prepare to make cover for our retreat."

"We're only half finished—"

"It will be enough." Alistair turned and grabbed Oliver by his mammoth shoulders and looked him in the eye. "Head back down to the cargo hold and look for crates with X7-42 on the side. Some will be ammo; some will be the anti-aircraft weapon. Grab two of each and bring them back here. If I'm not here when you get back, unpack them and get the guns loaded. It's an easy process."

"We've got hostages if they try anything," said Clever Johnny, coming up behind them with a small contingent of his supporters, all of whom had guns pointed at the backs of the three men who had tried to prevent them from accessing the weapons hold. Alistair saw their haggard faces, bruised and speckled with dried blood. One man even had a stream still coming down the side of his face. With their hands on top of their heads, they eyed all around them with fear.

"We're not playing hostages," he darkly informed him. "In fact, why don't you let them go back to their buddies over there?" With a nod of his head, Alistair indicated the front structure where their crew mates were holed up.

"Are you joking, Ashley?" Clever Johnny's eyes lit up and he bore his teeth like a wolf. "We've got the national armed forces ready to bear down on us and you want me to give up hostages?"

Alistair felt a sudden surge of adrenaline and he grabbed Clever Johnny behind his head and pulled it towards him so that they touched foreheads. "Violence escalates," he said in a curt and clipped manner. "Get that through your head. If we abuse prisoners, they'll do the same in retaliation."

"Just the same I think I'll hold on to some insurance," Clever Johnny fairly growled.

Alistair released him, exchanged a nod with Oliver who quickly moved off to do his part, and headed for the bridge once again.

Passing the still bound crew members from the bridge, he noticed one was trying to chew threw the bonds of his mate. Like guilty schoolchildren they stopped when they heard him and tried to look nonchalant, but he just ignored them. He burst into the now gusty bridge and, in looking out the window, found himself nearly face to face with one of the rescue craft. He could see the whites of the eyes of the pilot as snowflakes flurried between them.

He searched about for some functioning communications equipment but it was destroyed. Instead, he went to the power switch of a working display and flipped it on and off. The patterns he used were those of the ancient Morse Code, which lingered in use since the Dawn of Technology. They still taught the code to all military recruits, and all pilots were trained by the military.

Men to be rescued in bow. Will not attack rescue craft. He repeated the message twice over until he saw the pilot turn and call back to the other crew members of his rescue craft. Then he turned back around and nodded once to Alistair, a grim nod expressing a reluctant trust. A moment later, the hovering vessel pulled away from the bridge and headed for the bow.

Back out in the hallway, he went to his captives and untied one, ordering him to untie his two mates.

"Your rescue craft are here," he informed them. "You can head to the bow of the boat."

"There might be other injured crew members in this section of the ship," said the Captain while his first mate released his ankles from their bonds. His tone was frank and calm, deliberately so, defiantly without fear yet coolly polite.

Alistair frowned for a moment. "Then search for them and take them with you. Just remember we are armed. No one needs to die here today. Find your men and get out." He gave the men a stern look before leaving them to their own devices.

❧ ⸙

Emerging from the interior of the control center, Alistair stepped onto the deck. The three rescue craft at the far end were hovering over the bow with rope ladders dangling from their undersides. A couple dozen men made their way up the ladders. He looked over the side of the Tessa. The rebel boats were still passing weapons through the hole in the hull. Cursing, he ran to Oliver who was busy loading one of the X7-42's. Clever Johnny was standing nearby, guarding his captives.

"Why the hell are they still unloading crates?"

"We decided to stay just a bit longer," Oliver informed him.

"We need as many weapons as we can get," Clever Johnny said, his voice more controlled now, his tone smooth and dangerous like usual.

"Goddamn it, Oliver. I said to pull out."

"No one voted you in charge, little buddy."

"No, you're right. No one voted me; it just fell to me because I am the only one who knows what the hell he's doing. Now goddamn it, start pulling out!"

Oliver rose and gave Alistair a mock salute. "The weapons are loaded," he curtly said and moved off.

Gnashing his teeth in frustration, Alistair grabbed hold of two men to operate the X7-42's. They were small cannons mounted on a flexible tripod. They fired small, super heated ammo which exploded on contact and melted anything the shards touched. Affixing the tripod feet to the floor, he gave the men a thirty second demonstration on how to aim and shoot before making for the stairs below deck. As he passed Clever Johnny he turned to him and said, "There are at least three men in that section from the ship's crew looking for injured comrades. They will be coming out soon to join their men at the bow. When they come out, let these three go with them."

"This is stupid, Ashley!" Clever Johnny hissed. "Why the hell should we give up hostages?"

Alistair, who had turned from Johnny to head downstairs, spun about now, grabbed the slight man by his shirt, lifted him off his feet and slammed him into the wall of the command structure. "Because I can do this," he hissed. "We don't have facilities to take prisoners and we have no right to imprison them if we did. You have your orders." Releasing the man's shirt, he let him fall to the ground and, not looking back to see the dark look he got, headed below deck.

࿐

The water was ankle deep in the cargo hold when Alistair set the countdown, giving them twenty minutes to withdraw. About two thirds of the boats had already left. Alistair ushered the remaining men out of the hold and told the pilots to pick up their crews at the stern.

Suddenly, he heard the screeching wail of a shot from an X7-42. He winced as he remembered he had not prepared the men for the ear-splitting sound. Several more shots screeched and there was a brief spurt of automatic fire. He rushed back up to the main deck.

The two gunners were firing at some approaching points of light in the sky. Their shots were way off once the glowing bullets dipped, but they gradually corrected for this. The guns continued to scream like a banshee while the rescue craft retreated.

There was a general rush for the stern, but behind the scurrying forms of retreating rebels Alistair saw nine prone forms bleeding on the deck. He recognized the Captain and his first mate as well as the three men taken hostage below deck. Two of the men were still writhing about, but the blood spurting from their wounds foretold a rapidly approaching death.

A thousand images and experiences from his days on Kaldis flashed through his mind. He had been a grunt, outranked and helpless to stop the atrocities, but he was no longer outranked, and as he clenched his fists and ground his teeth he turned with the intention of doing something this time. But he turned right into Oliver's colossal chest.

"Yes," said Oliver, "it was Clever Johnny. Can we discuss it later?"

Alistair shoved his friend in the chest; only he could have forced him three steps back as he did. "I'm going to kill him!" There were tears of rage in his eyes.

"Can we please talk about it later?" Oliver implored him, raising his voice to a shout. They were nearly alone on the deck now; the men had made it to the stern and were scampering down the ropes to their boats. Only the two gunners, whose screeching gunfire continued to rend the night air, were with them.

"That son of a bitch!"

"Alistair—"

"I promised those men safe passage!"

"We'll talk about it later!"

"This is what our government does to Kaldisians, Oliver! Why the hell are we fighting if we're just going to be what we replace!?"

"Alistair, this isn't the time!" Oliver pointed at the approaching attack craft that scattered to avoid the gun fire coming at them. None had yet been hit. "If we're still on this ship in two minutes we're going to be incinerated! WE'LL TALK LATER! You take out Clever Johnny right now and half the men in this rebellion will either leave it or take you out too!"

Both men stood in a ready stance, chests heaving, snowflakes furiously dancing about their forms and in the clouds of their breath.

"I know this isn't what we wanted, but sometimes you have to compromise, Alistair."

The ex marine realized he had raised his fists so he lowered them and he brushed past his friend. The big man sighed in relief, grabbed the two gunners and headed with them to the stern. As they scampered down the ropes, the boomerang shaped aircraft did a flyby, keeping low to the sea as they went. By the time the rebels made it back to their boats and were pushing off each other with paddles, the aircraft had circled back and now peppered them with gunfire.

Splinters and sea spray vaulted into the air. Alistair happened to be looking straight at one man as his chest exploded in a red mist and what remained of him fell limp to the floor. He knew real fear then, not the adrenaline rush that comes from a battle fought from inside a nearly indestructible war suit, but a true, icy fear that comes from the knowledge that any random bullet could end one's life.

"Scatter when you pull out!" he screamed as Brad Stanson and Oliver paddled their way into the clear, past a sinking boat whose members hopped into theirs. Oliver took his seat at the motor and they were on their way, though the laden boat rode low. In all, two boats were left behind at the stern and three others headed for shore, their hulls breached by the gunfire. The rest moved out into the night, scattering in every different direction.

With the wind lashing at him, Alistair unsteadily moved to the front of the boat as it bounced over and through waves. He searched through the store of weapons and found a rocket launcher, but not a rocket. He settled on a powerful semi-automatic hand cannon with a magazine that held eight shots. Hustling to the back of the boat, he knelt down next to Oliver, facing out the back, and spotted an aircraft heading their way. He was dimly aware of the myriad snowflakes stinging the back of his neck as the boat tore through the growing snowstorm.

"Drive erratically. A couple hits and we're finished."

Oliver swerved in an irregular pattern. Alistair sighted the aircraft through his scope and started estimating.

"When the aircraft flies overhead, assuming we're still alive, straighten your course out."

The several other rebels, including Brad Stanson and Ryan Wellesley, sat in fear, tightly gripping the edges of their seats or the side of the boat. All eyes were on Alistair as the aircraft drew near and the water around them shot up spray from the bullets tearing into the sea.

"Straighten out!"

As the craft caught up to them it flew directly overhead. Alistair, balancing as the boat went over waves, pulled on the trigger four times in rapid succession, each shot producing such kickback that only a strong male like him could hope to handle the weapon. The large bullets streaked through the space above the boat, and two flashes announced that a pair of shots hit their mark.

The craft did not go down, but it did pull left. When it turned towards the spaceport at the top of Tanard's Mountain, Alistair breathed a sigh of relief. The others let out a cheer. Seeing the other craft were pursuing other boats, Alistair sank into a seat next to Oliver, allowing himself to relax.

"We have what we need now," Oliver said with a nod to his friend.

"I suppose we do," he responded and laid his head back to watch the snowflakes streak by.

30

It was a phenomenon dating back to the Dawn of Technology: men in tattered clothing huddled around a fire in a metal barrel. In the diffuse light of the cloudy Aldran dawn, their forms cast indistinct shadows on the walls of the three story, U-shaped building behind them. Huddled in the enveloping arms of the edifice, each held a skewered potato over the fire for the flames to caress. Their voices, though quiet, would have echoed in the flagstone courtyard but for the blanketing snow.

The men barely bothered to notice as Oliver and Bob LaSalle walked up to the building, their boots crunching the white blanket. At the end of the left wing was an entrance, and Oliver tugged at the door with one arm, fighting to pull it open against the ice. Yawning, Bob LaSalle covered his mouth and entered with Oliver close behind him. They were at the end of a hallway with a stairway on the left hand side where a man, wrapped up in winter clothes and with a long, ill-kept beard, seemed to be resting.

"Cakewalk," said the large rugby player.

"All clear," the man called out, nodding once.

Above, in the darkness of the stairwell, there was the slight sound of two men sinking back into relaxed positions. Oliver gave the lookout a wink and proceeded to climb the stairs and stride down the third floor hallway. In warmer months, the apartments would teem with seasonal workers but were now officially empty. Two men sat playing dice, a burning pile of something now unrecognizable giving them some meager light and warmth while coating the walls and ceiling with soot. A window was open in a nearby room, and a draft carried some of the smoke out.

"Which one is he in?" Oliver asked.

"Three twenty-two," Bob almost unintelligibly responded through another yawn.

When he came to the indicated door, Oliver made it shudder with a series of knocks. A moment later it opened to reveal Henry Miller. His tired morning eyes took a second to focus on the gigantic form in front of him, but then a bolt of recognition lit his features and his draw dropped.

"Oliver?"

Oliver's wide face split into a grin and he crushed Henry in an enthusiastic hug. Henry permitted the embrace for as long as he could stomach it before bringing all his strength to bear to extricate himself. They moved into the empty, featureless, one room apartment and Bob closed the door. There was a prone form in the unheated room just beginning to stir under a pile of blankets.

"When did you get in?"

Henry, reeling from the surprise, as well as the nervous feeling in the pit of his stomach, struggled to get an answer out. "Rod just brought me last night," he said with a vague gesture in the direction of his roommate. "Didn't tell me the place didn't have heat."

"You'll be in worse places soon enough."

"When did you get in?"

"I've been around since damn near the beginning. I was looking through the recruiting lists and saw your name."

"You've been around…" Henry gave a weak smile. "I guess you outrank me."

"I expect so. Let's take a walk."

Bob moved to sit next to Rod Haverly, who was now sitting upright and rubbing his eyes. He dropped a can and a can opener at his feet and, as he sat down, produced a hunk of bread and cheese from his pocket. Rod opened the can while Bob munched on the bread and cheese.

"We'll be back soon, guys," Oliver said as he and Henry set out at a brisk pace. When he spoke, Henry winced at the booming voice echoing in the bare hallway and clashing with the early hour.

"I was a bit surprised to find you had joined. What brings you to us?"

"Well…" his voice nearly a whisper by comparison, Henry searched for a reply. It was a question whose answer he had rehearsed, but he imagined giving it to a stranger. Somehow, the principled argument he fabricated didn't seem appropriate to give to someone who knew him better. "I guess I just got tired of getting pushed around."

"Was there a specific incident?"

"Not any single incident. I just lost confidence in the State. In the Realists."

"We were a small group for a long time. We sat around making plans and dreaming and not much else." The two rounded the corner that took them from the arm to the central portion of the building. Halfway between them and the far end, the dim hallway opened up into a common room with morning light streaming in, illuminating a great tattered rug on the linoleum floor. A few pieces of furniture were scattered about, mainly wooden chairs the squatters brought. "In the end it was hunger that did it."

"That did what?"

"Overcame apathy."

They reached the common room and Oliver moved to a pair of chairs in the light of a series of small windows. The chair he chose groaned under his weight but held. With his right foot he spun another about so it faced him. Tripping over a tear in the rug, Henry moved to the proffered chair.

"How do you mean, apathy?"

"Inaction. Inertia. It took the prospect of starvation to wake people."

Henry shrugged. "That's the way people are. I was the same, I guess."

"No, Henry, that's not the way people are. It's the way they become. Every creature is born with a spirit to look after itself and the tools to do it with."

"Well…not every creature…Some are born crippled."

"Yes," said Oliver with studied patience, "some people are born crippled. There are exceptions. But by and large we are born with what we need for survival: will and ability.

"There is no law of nature protecting you from harm. Nature is often against you. You must fend for yourself. This doesn't mean you need to go it alone, by any means. Survival is more secure when people work together. But sometime in the distant past, man settled down. The small tribes turned into villages and towns and cities. Protection was no longer every man's concern. There were police and soldiers for that. The relieved citizens could go about their lives and not have to worry about protecting themselves; the State assumed that responsibility."

"Are we fighting to return to a tribal culture?" Henry asked, confused, but Oliver went on as if he had not heard.

"It was not long before our spirit was dampened. If a man witnessed a crime he called the tin men rather than jump into the fray himself. If his property was threatened he looked to men with badges for support, rather than grab his gun and call his neighbors. We became more and more docile. Soon, men were so accustomed to taking orders and being herded they no longer questioned it. We forgot why we created government in the first place. Instead of ruling for us it ruled over us. The few charged with our protection, rather than protect us, controlled us, and we, submissive and tame like sheep, go where they direct and do what they bid.

"But the human spirit cannot be entirely quelled. For centuries different governments have tried to control the human brain. Brainwashing, drugs, operations, mutations, nano-bots…there is nothing that hasn't been tried. No technology has ever afforded a man complete control over another. Free Will is the one thing that can never be taken from us. It can shrink to the size of a grain of salt, but there is always a way to find and awaken it."

Oliver fixed a stern gaze on his friend. "What you are seeing, Henry, is the awakening of Free Will in the people of Aldra. It took starvation to do it, but it's happening."

Henry realized his lips had parted and he shut his mouth. His usually jovial friend had never spoken so eloquently nor so grimly before. Smoldering in Oliver's eyes was a passion he never bothered to consider might be there, and it held him nearly transfixed.

"So what are we going to do?"

"We are going to do what we must always and everywhere strive to do. We are going to refashion this State into something much smaller. We must create a society with the greater good in mind."

"The greatest good for the greatest number of people."

"Can anything possibly make more sense than that?"

"So they're out to remake Aldra."

Oliver shook his head. "Not remotely. Most are here because they're hungry, or angry or both. We promise them a better future and they come along for the ride. But they don't need to be principled vigilantes. As long as the leadership knows where it's going."

Henry blinked and raised his eyebrows. "Are you the leader of the rebellion?"

Oliver gave a half smile and laced his fingers together behind his head. "There is no leader for the moment. That is going to be settled soon."

"…despite advances in communication technology and the ability to collect and sort information, the American experience was much the same. There were misallocations of war supplies all up and down the chain. In order to expedite the shipment of emergency goods, generals were granted the ability to fast track supplies, but every request was fast tracked and the situation did not improve.

"Though each situation has its peculiarities, the fundamentals remain the same. The American Empire, the Sino-European League, the Terran Empire, the Solar Empire...There has, as of yet, been no successful effort to coordinate a war effort—or a peacetime economy— by command and control."

Alistair fell silent and shuffled the papers on the podium in front of him. His presentation over, he was more conscious of the gazes on him.

"Where did you get the term 'command and control'?" Edward finally asked with a frown.

"I...it must have been something I came across."

"I don't much care for it."

"Well, in essence that is what we are trying to do."

"Alistair, there's a difference between guiding and command-and-control," Edward replied with a pointed look.

And there's a difference between guiding and imprisoning for noncompliance, Alistair thought to himself. Aloud, he said, "I guess that's a fair point."

Edward, mollified, nodded and gave him an encouraging smile.

"Tell me, Alistair," said Harcourt from the back of the room, "having done your study, what reasons do you see to be optimistic?"

He could not say why he froze as he looked at Harcourt. The man's small, round glasses reflected back the glow from the ceiling lights so that his eyes could not be seen. His tall, thin frame was perfectly erect and his hands were folded in his lap. His face was like it always was: as stoic as a carved statue, yet he thought he detected a more ominous intent behind the question. He stuttered for a moment but could not invent an answer.

It was Louise who leapt to his defense. "We can use Alistair's research to guide us."

"My question was directed to Alistair," Harcourt cut her off, only his lips moving as he kept his stare on the ex marine. "What reason do you have to be optimistic?"

Scratching his head, Alistair looked down at the podium. He could feel his cheeks burning as what felt like an entire minute passed while he searched for an answer. Looking up, he thought he saw the ghost of a receding smirk on Harcourt's face. His heart pounded as he considered what the sneer meant, for a man in a lie can interpret any innocuous event as a sign he has been caught. His panic turned to anger. His cheeks still burned but with another fuel.

"I suppose the greatest reason for optimism," he evenly replied, trying to make his voice flow naturally as he returned Harcourt's gaze with a direct stare, "is that we have learned a great deal about what does not work; we can rule out tactics we know will fail. Though in my search over several centuries I was unable to find a single instance of a government successfully centrally planning so much as a single sector of an economy, we know at least where the right answer is not."

Harcourt nodded, like a man who has had a suspicion confirmed, or so Alistair imagined. *Maybe it was just a nod,* he thought without conviction.

"Well, Alistair," said Annette as she stood up, "we could have wished your efforts had born more fruit, but the treasure hunter is not at fault if no treasure has been buried to begin with. We're not politicians; we can be honest about the task ahead of us. But we do have to realize how important it is."

It was clear her words were the closing statement, so the others rose and gathered their folders and notebooks and portable computers. Alistair's gaze followed Harcourt as he exited the small conference room, but Harcourt looked at nothing but the path in front of him, his head held high and his posture rigidly perfect.

Moments later, as Alistair walked through the hallways of the Transportation Bureau, he heard footsteps behind him. He intuited that the light, feminine steps belonged to Louise and a moment later was proved right.

Tucking a strand of brown hair behind her left ear, Louise smiled and said, "Annette suggested we all eat lunch together in the south cafeteria."

"I'm sorry, Louise. I'm meeting my brother for lunch today."

"Oh." She stared at the ground for a moment, her strides unnaturally long as she worked to keep up. "Well, it wasn't a big deal. I'll see you in the lab."

"See you then."

When he reached the north cafeteria, he quickly spotted his brother with Leland Maddox who, bent over his bowl, was busy scooping fruit into his mouth with a slow but constant revolving motion. Making his way to the table, Alistair exchanged nods with his brother.

"Good afternoon," he greeted them, dropping his packed lunch onto the table.

"Hello, Alistair," said Leland, sitting up a little straighter to address the newcomer. Gerald just grunted. "Your brother and I were discussing the new economic data." Alistair said nothing as he emptied his little sack of its contents. "It looks like the economy is on an upswing. Quite a nice one, too."

Alistair hummed noncommittally but Gerald said, "Alistair doesn't believe in economic data."

"What's this?"

"I don't mean gathering the data, although he's suspicious of that too. I mean the data itself he thinks is worthless."

Leland looked at Alistair with a slight smile, like he was expecting the punch line of a joke.

Alistair bit into a hunk of bread. "When scientists measure something—anything—they also note the margin of error. I think the same thing should be done with econometric data. No one actually counts every item produced, it is an estimate based on imperfect and incomplete information. I just think they should acknowledge that rather than give the impression they have absolutely accurate data."

"But the data itself isn't worthless," said Leland.

"I don't think it is worthless—"

"I thought I recalled you saying just that," Gerald interjected.

"May I address this without interruption?"

Gerald bit into his wedge of cheese.

"We work to make goods or provide services that make us happy. The problem with counting the number of goods being made and the amount of money circulating is that it is no good for measuring just how much of this happiness, or as economists say, utility, has been achieved. The government may build ten thousand bombs and make the data in its books look good, but are those bombs making us happy?"

"Those bombs are protecting us from Kaldis," Leland said with some conviction.

"I was talking in general, not about this specific case."

Leland frowned as he pondered Alistair's words, his droopy face drooping further.

"And of course production of goods doesn't take leisure time into account. Sometimes what makes us happy is to sit on a couch and do nothing. In this case, by not producing anything we are best maximizing our utility. If the government were to order us back to work, we might produce more goods but have lower utility. A simple figure like the tonnage of goods produced or the amount of money being spent does not tell the whole story."

Leland considered it for a moment. "Well, producing more can't be a bad thing. And someone has to keep track of the statistics."

Alistair repressed a sigh. "I suppose you're right."

Gerald perked up. "Leland! He supposes you're right! I've waited over twenty cycles to hear those words come out of my brother's mouth."

"Why did you invite me to lunch?"

"Oh, relax. We're just having some fun."

"Can you include me?"

"Relax, Alistair. I was just commenting to Leland on what a change you've gone through. I used to not be able to take a sip of tea without getting an economics lecture."

"Well," said Leland, "I just got a lecture a moment ago."

"That's nothing," said Gerald with a dismissive gesture. "Alistair could go on for hours at a time about the Free Market and Subjective Value Theory and...I can't remember what else because I never really listened. But if I mentioned the smallest little government plan he'd quote me a history of its alleged failures. Ensure a dignified wage for workers? No, no, that would unemploy everyone! But now he goes about his business with his head down and his sleeves rolled up. I can visit my parents without taking a sedative. What changed, Alistair? You never told me."

"I told you I wanted to contribute."

"Very noble. Stop obstructing and start cooperating."

"That can be the next State slogan."

"But you can be honest with us, Alistair. There's no litmus test here."

"Yet."

"Do you still believe all that jargon you used to bore us with? Did you have a Road to Damascus Conversion? Or was it bit by bit? Or are you still rethinking things? What was it that made you change?"

"Blow it out your ass." Alistair returned his attention to his food.

"It's OK to admit you were wrong," Gerald said in a matter-of-fact tone. "Sure, government can make mistakes, but the Realists have us on track. Predictable, really. Leland and I were just the other day talking about Reynolds' Survey of Worlds. I don't know if you read it, but it seems the government planned colonies thrived better than the privately founded ones. In fact, Aldra is one of the few privately founded colonies that has endured."

Like a fish swallowing a lure, Alistair could not let the challenge pass.

"The private colonies were few in number and started small. They were also often eradicated by government marines." Alistair realized he was losing his temper but he plunged on. "The Survey of Worlds was a fraud from the moment it was conceived. Reynolds did it while in the employ of the Solar Emperor. It looked only at a few measures of economic output and population growth without taking anything else into consideration. The privately founded colonies always started smaller because they couldn't tax an entire nation to fund the project, but Reynolds simply measured their absolute size at certain intervals after their founding. He also ignored the fact that the best worlds the government claimed for itself; the private ones needed more terraforming. And dozens of government founded colonies devolved into decentralized minimalist states or even anarchist societies. Being founded by the government doesn't change the fact that they were often operating on Free Market principles. Reynolds also fails to consider that when the Heim-Droescher Drive became widely available, the Solar Empire was losing so many citizens, and therefore so much of its tax base, to the freer outlying colonies it chose either to wipe them out, take them over or pressure them into tightening controls to stem the bleeding. Not unlike what is going on with Kaldis right now."

Alistair finished with a glare, but Gerald's shoulders were shaking in silent laughter.

"Listen, boys, I've gotten so much work dumped on me..." Leland stood up, looking uncertain. "I can't afford to take the long lunches you do. Alistair, it was nice to see you again." He quickly left the two siblings to their argument.

"Did you memorize that from a textbook or were you composing on the spot? You should have been a professor, except no one would hire you to teach that kind of thing."

"I know damn well you're trying to bait me; don't think you had me fooled."

"I just wanted to see if the same Alistair was still here. Somehow I figured he was."

"Would you cut it out?" Alistair demanded and he shoved his brother's shoulder. The smile finally disappeared from Gerald's face. "I was doing hard duty on Kaldis while your butt got soft at a desk. I appreciate the job but if you can't leave well enough alone I can eat with someone else."

"Would you relax?" said Gerald, but Alistair stood up and gathered his half finished lunch. "I like you better when you're annoying, not when you're pretending to fit in."

"Whether I fit in or not is none of your concern," Alistair coldly said and turned to go.

"I'll see you at Dad and Mom's tonight. I'm coming over later."

Alistair did not even turn around.

Alistair's fingers, having well learned their way around a keyboard, rapidly typed in the final list of digits. Pausing for a moment to allow himself a stretch, he saved the program and shut down the system. The three dimensional display before him faded and finally disappeared.

"I'll see you all tomorrow," Edward said as he brushed by Alistair to replace his folders in their cabinet drawer.

"It's Tuesday, Edward. Tomorrow's Sunday," Annette reminded him, herself making for the cabinet.

"Of course. See you on Monday."

Alistair waited behind Annette before filing his papers. "I'm sorry I missed the lunch today. I had a prior engagement with my brother."

"You can eat where you want, Alistair."

"No, I mean…weren't we all eating together today?"

"No," she said with a bemused smile and then left him at the cabinet. "Only if you wanted to. See you Monday."

Alistair was just beginning to ponder what that meant when he turned around to see Harcourt having trouble shutting down his computer. The gangly professor had typed in his code twice but, suspended in the air in front of him, a red error warning flashed, accompanied by an electronic beep. He set his fingers to the keypad once again but this time typed in his code number slowly.

2-0-0-3-0-1-0-3-1-4-0

Alistair froze for a second, then turned away before Harcourt could catch him staring. Tense, he grabbed his coat, scarf and hat off the hanger and donned them on the go. Passing Louise on his way out, he did not hear her goodbye. He was out the door, made nervous by the beginning of an idea. He wound his way through the halls and merged with the herd of departing workers, repeating the numbers in his head.

2-0-0-3-0-1-0-3-1-4-0

He repeated the sequence so many times he tripped over it and doubt assailed him. *Were those the ones?* He could no longer clearly picture Harcourt's fingers striking the keys, but he was reasonably sure he had been reciting the same set of eleven numerals. He repeated them a dozen times, and then a score more after that. He used some tricks to make the numbers stick. *Twenty is the number of regular season games in the rugby season. 03, 01, 03. 313…How long ago was the Solar Empire founded? About 380 cycles. No good. Fourteen wins will normally get you into the rugby playoffs, and zero is the number of championships Arcarius has won. 2-0-0-3-0-1-0-3-1-4-0.*

He realized he was walking at a tremendous pace in his adrenaline rush. Slowing down, he looked about and found himself alone and well on his way to his parents' apartment. The frosty night air was especially cold, he realized, and he fixed his hat to better cover his stinging ears. The early northern dusk had darkened to a black night lit only by the faint stars and the rare glow coming from windows in buildings supposed to be empty for the winter. It had been a while since the street lights were in use. Tucking his chin into his scarf and using his breath to keep it warm, he nearly missed the looming hulk in the alley as he passed by. He stopped and waited for Oliver to emerge from the shadows.

"Is this a good idea?"

"Good to see you too," responded Oliver, his usual grin and affable demeanor was back. "You're not being followed. LaSalle's cousin is our tin man. He says Stephanie turned your name in, but her request for a tail was rejected. You're not important enough to warrant the resources."

"Stephanie?" Alistair said, startled. "How 'bout that."

"Don't let it get to you. It's not a surprise."

"How old is that information?"

Oliver shrugged. "A couple days. Why?"

"I think they're on to me at the Bureau."

"Why?"

Alistair shook his head a couple times and frowned. "Just…looks I'm getting. One of my coworkers is acting suspicious. And I ate lunch with my brother today…I felt like I was at a formal inquiry. I'm thinking I might have to pull out."

"Relax a second. It's easy to misinterpret, especially in your position."

"I don't know."

"If you pull out, there's no going back. And I mean not to the job, not to your cozy apartment…you'll be sitting by a fire in a cave somewhere north of the city with a few other rebels who are as unwashed, unshaved and ill-fed as you'll be."

Alistair breathed deeply and started walking. Oliver fell into pace beside him, accompanied by the sound of their feet crunching the paper-thin layer of ice covering the snow.

"I figured you'd want to talk to me about the raid. About Clever Johnny."

"Yeah."

"First of all, thank you for not pursuing it right there on the boat. I know you were angry, but—"

"I'm not angry, Oliver. I'm furious." The proclamation was met with silence so Alistair went on. "I want him brought to justice."

"I think—"

"He did exactly what we criticize our government for. I don't want to hear anything about war and collateral damage."

"I wasn't going to say it."

"I don't want to hear any excuses. He killed innocent men, men I promised protection to. He wasn't in danger, he wasn't driven to do it by anything but…hell I can't even say what drove him to do it."

"You've said it before: war breeds immoral behavior. The chum sitting across from you enjoying a beer can turn into a savage killer on a battlefield. I can't say why he did it. I don't like it anymore than you do—"

"Oliver," Alistair said, grabbing his friend by both shoulders. Having come within sight of his parents' building, he now paused to finish the conversation out of earshot. "I know you hate what he did, but please believe you hate it far less than I do. Do you have any idea what goes on in a training camp?"

Oliver shook his head.

"They spend the entire time trying to singe the humanity out of you. The American Empire fought the Korean War. They discovered that half of their soldiers were purposefully missing their targets when they fired their rifles. Some innate humane instinct pressured them not to kill, even when allowing the enemy to live meant risking your own life. The same held true in other wars, all the way back to the War of Southern Secession. Nearly half of all soldiers only pretended to fire their rifles. Who knows how many more fired high or low on purpose?

"Well good heavens, when the State wants a war they can hardly allow their pawns to make these kinds of decisions. Training tactics changed. After the Korean War the Empire was fighting again in Asia, but this time what they now call the kill instinct was 90%. Since then they have refined their methods. Every military in the galaxy follows it. Over 98% of marines are successfully imbued with the kill instinct. Do you know how they do it?"

Oliver shook his head, his expression properly somber.

"We spend hours repeating killing chants. We pray to be killers before every meal. They start us off torturing and killing animals. Then we graduate to virtual reality humans. Not just shooting but actually torturing. Before we graduate we participate in the execution of criminals. By then most of the recruits can laugh while they kill." The crescendo to which Alistair's voice built cut off and he took a deep breath, finally releasing Oliver's shoulders from his fierce grip.

"I refused to go along. I resisted. I prayed for my humanity to whatever god might have been listening. But I was part of a small, small minority."

Oliver's deep, rumbling voice was compassionate. "How many did you kill on Kaldis?"

"Thirty-six, though my official total was eight hundred and sixteen. I only killed when I absolutely had to. I swear to God I did. I met a man who resisted like me, and he deprogrammed my War Suit. Each suit has a tracking program to measure your effectiveness. He replaced it with a dummy program that recorded non-existent kills. I made it through my tour that way. And yes, some of those I did not kill probably killed my comrades. Do you hate me?"

"Absolutely not."

"You and maybe ten other people on the planet. They say patriotism is the last refuge of the scoundrel. I think it might be worse than that. I didn't want my comrades to die...but we were the invading army. The Kaldisians had the right to fight us."

"Try telling that to the public."

Alistair absentmindedly nodded, staring off into space. "Anyway, I am done with killing. The State must be overthrown, but we will kill only those who directly oppose us, and only if we have to. Clever Johnny is a predator. But then, what right did I have to kill to save myself, especially when I wouldn't do it to save my buddies?" There was a catch in his voice, and he struggled to suppress something.

"I have no idea what to say, Alistair. Why did you stay the extra three cycles?"

Alistair's faint smile was mirthless. "I was stupid. I wanted to learn what they had to teach me, to use it against them. I shouldn't have stayed. It wasn't worth it, but at the time I made the decision I hadn't..." Alistair's trance was broken and he looked his large friend in the eyes. "I think I made a breakthrough today."

"What happened?"

"I might have some access I am not supposed to have. Stay tuned for further details," he finished cryptically, and, giving Oliver a pat on the shoulder, left him staring as he finished his trek home.

31

"All teams in place, lieutenant," said the rough male voice over the communicator.

"Copy. Whenever you're ready, sergeant," Stephanie replied, her eyes glued to the 3D image in front of her. In the back of the command vehicle, lit only by the glow of computer displays, Lieutenant Caldwell sat at the head station, flanked by a handful of others in the dark blue and red of the Civil Guard. A monitor—an insect-size flying surveillance robot—accompanied a team of Guards outside the decaying husk of a factory. The monitor was recording some sort of noise coming from within, but heat sensors picked up nothing because something interfered with the signal.

"How the hell do they have equipment to jam our heat sensors?" grumbled one of the men in the vehicle. "Most of our equipment is on back order."

"Because they're willing to pay what the black market merchants ask," Stephanie replied without taking her eyes off her 3D image. "You get what you pay for." The other officers frowned while she blushed, surprised at what came out of her mouth. She remembered Captain Travis told her that. *Or was that something Alistair said?* It unsettled her to think she could confuse the two.

"They're going in," another officer declared. A blast of condensed air from a handcannon made the front entrance explode into a storm of splinters. A couple more shots were fired and the inside of the factory filled with smoke. The Civil Guard charged in, shouting orders and sweeping their guns. Stephanie was trying to make sense of the cacophony of yells and barked orders in her headset when suddenly there was a flash of light and the 3D image went blank.

"What the hell...?"

"The monitor was taken out," she said with the tone of a curse.

"What was that flash of light?"

While her fellow officers were still looking around in bewilderment, Stephanie hopped out the back door and onto the pavement, a cold wind buffeting her. Though she could not see the factory, she did spy a single cloud of red smoke rising into the air. While her fellow officers joined her, the brisk wind tore the cloud apart. Then the sound of gunfire rang out.

"Back into the vehicle," she commanded. "Put in a call for reinforcements."

There was no knock at the door; the three Guardsmen simply burst through, weapons already drawn. Oliver, relaxed in his padded chair and smoking a cigar, didn't even flinch at the abrupt disturbance, but rather carefully studied the men in front of him. They were beefy and rough, their expressions aggressive and a kind of unfriendly never far from disdainful. Their entry brought in a gust of cold air which carried away the smoke from his cigar. Oliver exhaled through rounded lips.

"We're executing a search of the premises," the first informed him with his Rendralian accent. "Wait outside." His two partners were already moving.

"I'm going to have to ask you to leave," Oliver informed them in a calm tone. "In the future you will knock before entering and enter only when permission is given."

Having already performed two dozen such searches, the men had fallen into a perfunctory rhythm. Oliver's unexpected response was a slap in the face. They stopped and stared.

It was the speaker who recovered first, leveling his gun and an intimidating glare at Oliver. "You lookin' to be arrested?"

"Perhaps I wasn't clear a moment ago," Oliver replied, his voice still steady but now lower and more menacing. "Get out of my apartment."

All three turned to face him, scowls on their angry faces.

"Got something you're hiding, do ya'?"

"Indeed. I've got about ten pounds of specnine in my bedroom I prefer you don't disturb. I sell it and use the proceeds to purchase the illegal arms I donate to the rebel cause. It was these weapons that helped us take down the Tessa, if you remember that. Of course I also purchase explosives, which I made use of during the jail break a few weeks ago."

The trio stared at Oliver. They still had not decided exactly what sort of fool he was when suddenly there were seven guns pointed at them. Men popped out of closets, hallways and from behind furniture, and the Guardsmen were surrounded. A moment later their guns were confiscated and they were handcuffed with their own gear.

❧ ❦

The command vehicle had not come to a complete stop when Stephanie and her fellows hopped out. After the rumbling of the vehicle's engine ceased, the only sound left was the wind, not strong enough to actually moan through the city streets and mountainous crags above, but it tossed a good amount of snow around. There were two bodies lying face down in the parking lot, soaking in their own blood. They had not been there long enough for snow to pile up against them; any meager flakes that might have accumulated were quickly stained crimson and melted. The factory itself seemed from within hit by some concussive force, for every door and what remained of the windows were blown outward. The occasional thin wisp of red smoke still poured out of these.

"Orders?" prompted an officer, much her senior in age though not rank.

"Sweep the area." Then, in a lower voice, "But we're not going to find anything."

The men spread out in formation. As senior officer, Stephanie brought up the rear. Having crept close to the edifice, two men took up positions on either side of the main entrance, backs against the wall. With a mutual nod they signaled each other and a moment later burst through the opening, followed soon after by the rest.

Inside, another body, a Guardsman, lay on the floor, this time on his back but like the others in a pool of his own blood. There was another spot where some blood accumulated but no body lay. The interior of the structure was much like its parking lot: empty save for the occasional rusted metal body stripped of any useful item. The red smoke swirled about in the rafters, occasionally finding an exit and pouring into the atmosphere outside.

They searched and were soon aided by new arrivals, but there was nothing else to be found. Stephanie was walking back to the command vehicle, her cheeks cherry red and her nose a leaky faucet, when the sound of distant gun fire broke out. Everyone froze, heads turned to the west. Stephanie broke into a run, vaulting into the back of the command vehicle.

"Find out what the gun shots are about."

"I'm just getting it now," replied the communications officer, holding a restraining finger up and listening to his headset. Then he said, "The Search & Seizure teams are under attack."

"They were waiting for us. And they have more than one trap ready."

Behind her, the back door opened and another officer stepped up into the vehicle.

"What's going on here?" he demanded to know.

"We're going into battle," was Stephanie's reply.

There had been no recent serious food shortages, a motivation whose absence had concerned Oliver. Nevertheless, something awakened in the populace. Perhaps it was seeing their neighbors fighting back. Perhaps the present SS searches were too intrusive, or maybe too many low level bureaucrats were threatened into voting for a Realist regime they did not desire. The recent experiences with rioting had no doubt left the people less uncomfortable with the idea. Maybe it was the sum of many abuses combined with a general sense that things should be better. Whatever the reason, a long dormant sense of self came to life.

At Oliver's signal the rebels erupted into vindictive violence. The first assault crushed the unprepared Civil Guard who, so used to herding sheep, now had to contend with wolves. There followed a stunned silence while the city collected itself, and then the response came. It was a response the rebels were more than ready for, and when stunned and terrified citizens dared to peek out their windows, they saw a well armed rebel force beating back a Civil Guard they suddenly realized they hated. An entire anti-riot phalanx was mowed down by armor piercing rounds. A tin can was blown to burning bits by a rocket. An attackcraft was hit by some pulse rendering it lifeless and it crashed to the ground, tearing up chunks of pavement until a brick building brought it to a crashing halt.

A mob of citizens formed, unarmed but potent. It swept through the streets, each member emboldened by the safety of numbers, like an army of ants. Where the mob passed they left behind overturned autos, burning buildings and lifeless Guardsmen. A few were brought down, but many more joined the throng. It was then that Aloysius and the governing class felt the second edge of the double blade of Rendralian policy: Civil Guard were transferred to unfamiliar cities so as to be less likely to blanch when brutal action was required. This policy now left the fuming masses with a similar lack of compunction.

With the smell of smoke in the air, Oliver strode through the wreckage of the city, unable to say where all his units were and what exactly was happening. In the distance he could still hear gunfire, but of the forty unit leaders given a rendezvous point to hold, only five reported in and two of those to say the Civil Guard held their point. He could only guess at what happened to the rest.

With the dozen men he pulled from the whirlwind, he marched towards the sound of fighting. A hum of voices became audible under the noise of the bullets and the occasional explosion. When the shattered street he traversed finally dead-ended into a larger boulevard, Oliver looked across the thoroughfare to his right and realized he had come to Rendral Way. A mixed mob of citizens and rebels surrounded the main headquarters of the Civil Guard, a ten-story structure with an ample central courtyard with pillars at the front. It was largely clear save for a few armed individuals hiding behind the pillars and exchanging fire with an unseen opponent trapped in the courtyard.

As Oliver and his cohort pressed into the wind and crossed five-foot snow bank at the median, the mob below was fired upon from windows on the fifth floor. The rebels among them returned fire, as did Oliver and his fellows. *Restraint is something else they need to learn,* he thought as they continued pelting the fifth story long after the attackers retreated. Upon reaching the agitated crowd, he grabbed the first armed rebel he saw and spun him around.

"How the hell did this get started?"

The man, cowed both by Oliver's size and reputation, shook his head. "I just followed along."

Oliver let him go and, crouching low, rushed to the open front section and slid in behind a thick marble pillar. He looked to the man at his right, also behind a pillar, and yelled, "What can you tell me?"

"We've got about two dozen of the bastards pinned down in there," the man shouted. "They're all behind the fountain. We're not letting them—"

There was an explosion and Oliver's face was pelted with small bits of earth and pavement.

"We're not letting them escape!" the man finished.

"Go round up your buddies and get some autos wedged in between these pillars!"

"Yes, sir!"

"Anyone with guns, keep them pointed at the upper windows because they're going to get attacked."

"Yes, sir!"

The man saluted once and, crouching low and keeping directly behind his pillar, moved to carry out the order. Meanwhile, Oliver risked a glance at the courtyard. There was a large above-ground fountain with a statue of a familiar figure whose name he could not recall. It was chipped and cracked from dozens of bullets. The rebels kept a steady stream of pressure on the trapped guards who themselves did little to respond.

A few minutes later, several autos were collected, gears in neutral. Crowds formed behind each and pushed the machines while a few armed individuals moved in step, their guns ready to fire. Enough autos were found to fill most of the openings, which allowed more rebels to take up firing positions. However, when they did, Oliver signaled for them to hold fire, a command that took a half-minute to make it around. This cessation left them in comparative silence, and in place of the cacophony of battle he heard a ringing in his ears.

Boldly, he stood up from behind an auto and addressed his unseen enemies behind the stone fountain. It seemed his voice was strong enough to shake the foundations of the Civil Guard Headquarters.

"We the people of Arcarius declare our independence!"

A cheer went up. Exhilarated, Oliver bathed in the fierce sound of it. When it died down he continued.

"Your incompetence and unconcern for the people you were entrusted to govern will no longer be tolerated! We demand a State for ourselves, a new Republic of Avon. Let this serve as your notice: we will no longer be abused; we will no longer stand for your corruption; we will not accept your ineptitude! You can no longer punch without being punched back. You cannot steal but we will take back what is ours. You will not compel us, and you will not prohibit us anything. We will live as we choose and we choose a new State!"

Another cheer rose from the masses.

"My name is Oliver Keegan! Remember it: I am the voice of the revolution!"

The cheering went on and Oliver's face flushed with victory. A figure stood up from behind the fountain, a female with a head of short blonde hair. Stephanie stared at him in wonderment and he returned the awestruck gaze.

"Leave now!" His voice was angrier than before. "And if you come back, greet us as friends or don't come back at all!"

Amid the gleeful howling of an underdog who has just asserted himself, Stephanie signaled to her troops. Slowly, guns at the ready, they filed away towards one of the entrances. She went in last, her gaze having never left Oliver and his having never left her. When the door shut behind them, the final signal of their retreat, the howling reached an hysterical pitch and Oliver, for all his bulk, was grabbed, hoisted into the air and carried away on the shoulders of his troops.

෮ ෴

The thick stone walls were not enough to keep the rebel cheering from their ears but at least the noise was attenuated. At first the men waited for Stephanie to give an order, but she was too distracted. It was a few moments later when Captain Travis, announced by the click of his impeccably polished boots on the black tile floor, appeared and sent them about their business. Gratefully relinquishing command, Stephanie eased herself into a cushioned bench and leaned back against the wall, sniffing and rubbing at her dripping red nose and staring into space. The Captain, finished delegating, approached her as the sound of the men scurrying off faded away. He stood before her with his arms folded across his chest.

"Oliver Keegan 3nn," she said, unsure whether she said it to herself or to Travis.

"Explain," Travis coolly said, his demeanor, though calm, betraying a hint of his frazzled state.

"He was just outside there. He claimed he was the voice of the rebellion. He claimed he was taking back Arcarius for the people."

"And you know him."

"I grew up with him. He's that rugby player. You already know about him."

Nodding, Travis turned on his heel. "Come with me."

Stephanie, feeling tired and realizing how much her feet hurt, winced once but caught up with her commander.

"Ms. Caldwell, you have been promoted quite quickly through the ranks. I'm sure you know this is my doing, and I'm equally sure you know it was not done on a whim."

"Yes, sir."

"Have you an answer for me?"

"An answer?"

"Yes, an answer," Travis snapped, a rare betrayal of emotion and loss of control. "Oliver Keegan 3nn proposes to secede from Rendral and reform the Republic of Avon. In the name of all Arcarians."

"That is his justification."

"And that was the question I posed to you earlier, was it not? How do we justify what we do? How do we justify what we are about to do to this rebellion?"

Stephanie opened her mouth but only hesitant and tentative sounds came out.

"The people are sick and tired of hunger and war and coerced civic service and a list of other things ten thousand items long. You and I both know full well how the election was won. How do we justify controlling like we do? Mr. Keegan has a point: if the people want to govern themselves why should they be stopped? Why do we get to impose our will on them?"

She still could not answer. Travis stopped and turned to face her.

"I'm waiting for orders. Stay here at Headquarters but get some rest. Stephanie." Officer Caldwell looked her commander in the eye. "I expect an answer from you soon."

Nigel and Mary Ashley huddled together on the living room couch while Alistair stood at the window. An elderly couple, the Chatterley's, sat on another couch and huddled under a blanket. The electricity was off and the heat was cut. They had their own generator but no battery power to run it, so Alistair's parents and their neighbors sat together on the couch under woolen blankets. Alistair, the two longest knives in the kitchen tucked into his belt, stood like a sentry.

A rioting mob had passed right underneath them on the street below. Alistair watched them go, waiting for the sound of intruders in the hallway outside but mercifully none came. The city, now bathed in the ruddy glow of an approaching sunset, was nearly silent. Fires burned but no one came to douse them. There were bodies in the street but no one took them away. He turned from the window and collected the empty teacups on the table between the two sofas. While depositing them in the kitchen sink, he was alerted to footsteps in the hallway outside. Drawing both knives, he placed himself to the side of the front door and coiled like a spring. The Ashley's and the Chatterley's moved into the kitchen.

A key hit the door and Alistair relaxed. He put his knives away when he saw Gerald come through. The two brothers' eyes met and they exchanged slight nods. Gerald shut the door and made sure to lock it. Peeking around the corner and seeing her eldest son, Mary rushed out to embrace him. Everyone else quickly followed.

"What's the news?" Nigel asked.

Shaking his head, Gerald replied, "They're getting ambitious. Mobs rioted all over the city." Gerald looked at Alistair. "I'm glad to see you up here."

"Get off it," said Alistair and went to sit down on a couch.

"I merely meant you were protecting Mom and Dad," Gerald retorted with some heat.

"Alistair's been a savior," said Mary as she took her son by the hand and led him to the kitchen. "Let's not fight. I'll fix you something to eat."

Alistair sat in the living room while his parents and the Chatterley's gathered around Gerald to hear the news. He had few specifics, but he did not let that prevent him from relating quite a tale as if he were privy to the official State report. Alistair stopped paying attention, quickly recognizing his brother knew little of substance. Instead, he went back to the window and looked out at the injured city.

I'm a soldier, not a spy, he thought. It was time to take to the hills, join the guerrillas. Tomorrow, he would use Harcourt's login and, he hoped, find something of value. Either way he would be back with the rebel soldiers by the next sunset. He continued to stare as he mulled his decision, still as a statue. When he finally turned from the window the bloody sun had burned its image onto his retina.

32

In the wake of the riots, Arcarius became a city of isolated communities withdrawn into the interiors of abandoned buildings, fortified like porcupines rolled up in a ball. Defying the government's attempts to consolidate the winter population, unwilling to wait for Civil Guard to quell the violence or afraid of the violence the Civil Guard might commit, extended families and networks of friends staked out their claims. The power having been cut from all but the approved areas, smoke from fires fueled by anything available drifted out of chimneys or makeshift holes in ceilings. Men stood guard at the entrances, armed with homemade weapons.

As Alistair, on his way to the Bureau, passed by these makeshift fortresses, he weathered the gazes of suspicion directed his way. It was difficult to tell how much of the city's population took to these arrangements, nor could he guess how long it would take the Civil Guard to force them back in their designated housing. Perhaps they wouldn't bother at all.

He saw no fewer than three peddlers, men burdened like mules with knapsacks, bags and cases full of items, going from fortress to fortress, hawking their wares. Every neighborhood on Aldra had its craftsmen and peddlers who worked without the benefit of a factory, handcrafting tools and wiring electronics in their living rooms and trading them on the black market. Now they were out seeking opportunity, venturing forth to bring needed supplies to groups of people who preferred not to leave their protective surroundings.

Upon drawing near the Bureau, he spied a young woman in a Civil Guard uniform leaning against the square base of a statue near the entrance. Stephanie Caldwell unfolded her arms and moved to intercept his path. Quelling panic, Alistair scanned the area and, though he could detect no one else, Civil Guard or otherwise, tensed his muscles.

"The Bureau's closed today, Alistair," she informed him when he was within a few feet of her. "You don't look pleased to see me."

"No one is pleased to see someone in that uniform. But good morning all the same." He came to a halt in front of her, legs spread and knees slightly bent, as if awaiting her charge.

"You can relax. I'm not here to arrest you."

He only nodded.

"I know you're a part of the uprising."

"You are incorrect," he managed to say, though it sounded feeble to him. Perhaps he couldn't muster much will to lie when he so strongly desired to spit the truth in her face.

"Don't bother, Alistair. Oliver Keegan 3nn announced yesterday he was the 'Voice of the Rebellion'. I was there to hear it. And if Oliver's in it then you are in it."

"Oliver did what?" he exclaimed, his surprise genuine.

"I said don't bother."

"Well, you do what you have to. I have no idea where Oliver is—"

"This isn't about Oliver. I'm giving you a chance to turn yourself in and avoid some… difficulties. It's either turn yourself in now or be arrested later, and believe me when I say you don't want that."

"There's nothing to turn myself in for," he managed to get through his constricting throat, hoping he wasn't blushing as badly as he felt he was.

"Alistair," she sighed deeply, "this has gotten to the point where the State is not going to be merciful. This will be your last opportunity for clemency. Be grateful and turn yourself in."

"Grateful?" He nodded his head as he considered her words, the corners of his mouth turning down in a bitter frown. "You and I never really were friends, were we? You knew Oliver, and Oliver and I were in the same suffix group. We wound up being in physical proximity…but we never really knew each other. Our paths crossed and recrossed, nothing more. What I knew of you didn't compel me to know more, and I suppose you felt the same way. And now, cycles later, both of us have been pawns for our government, but we have vastly different feelings about it. I can see now what I vaguely felt as a child."

"What did you vaguely feel, Alistair?" she sneered.

"You are part of the State's whip. Don't pretend like you don't know what the State is. What I felt as a child was that flaw in your character that leads you to support it."

"Always paranoid, Alistair. The State is out to get you."

"The State is out to keep me in the herd and fleece me until I'm no longer useful. The State controls everything I do, and everything I don't do, because it has a plan and to hell with mine. Behind every order is a threat to punish me if I don't cooperate. The State exists for its own benefit. Why was I compelled to serve in the military? Because my talents must be at the State's disposal. Why has every nation under invasion forced its citizens to fight and die in defense, even if the vast majority would have been better off under the other government? Because the war wasn't about protecting the people; it was about protecting the State.

"History is one episode after another of a ruling class sucking everything it can from the ruled. But everything it can suck is limited to what the people will allow to be stolen. And so we have parades and anthems and celebrations and holidays and wars and we glorify the military and the Civil Guard and the bureaucrats and we nationalize the schools to teach the proper propaganda, all so the citizens will be more compliant. How do you justify what you do, Stephanie?"

In a taunting, sarcastic tone, which she managed despite the discomfort the question provoked in her, she replied, "But you're not supporting the rebellion, right?"

Alistair, irritated, shifted on his feet and fixed a dark look on her. "There are laws of human nature just like there are laws of physics. Every culture has a sense of what is right and what is wrong. Sooner or later, the growing pressure explodes. Governments always fail, sooner or later. I don't need to participate in the rebellion…it will happen anyway."

Stephanie gave a last mocking smile. "Your last chance is walking away."

Alistair made no move.

Though the Bureau was not open, power was still provided to the various government agencies. At the station where he was required to enter a code before he could pass into the employee section of the building, he made sure to use Harcourt's. He figured if he used Harcourt's code later on without having used it at the entrance, some alarm would be tripped.

He meandered through the expansive edifice, hardly crossing paths with anyone. The heat was turned down and at times he could see his own breath. Deeper into the building he went, seeking solitude with furtive glances over his shoulder, thinking how guilty he must have looked. He could walk casually into a cubicle or office and access the system without the other even knowing something was wrong, but the nervousness building in his stomach prevented him. If he went five seconds without looking over his shoulder, he felt a nagging twinge and was far too tense to effect a casual air. *Better to do this in a dark corner,* he thought, *rather than try to be cavalier and easy about it and get discovered.*

He finally found, on the first sublevel, a large hall of cubicles lit only by the lights from the stairwells at the northeast and southwest corners. Glancing once more behind him as he left the stairwell in the northeast, he moved into the near dark, passing by any number of suitable cubicles but not yet feeling the confidence to take the last step.

Finally, when he reached the center of the hall, where only his artificial vision could perceive, in shades of gray, the objects around him, he sat in front of a 3D computer display. Doffing his gloves and setting them at his side, he fired up the computer and entered Harcourt's login. There was no sense in going back now. The login was recorded and, sooner or later, his break-in would be discovered.

He surfed around the Bureau's network, grabbing a small recorder disk the shape and size of a coin and inserting it into the appropriate slot. He was at the point of starting when something on his 3D display caught his eye. *This has to be some kind of oversight…Harcourt shouldn't have access to this,* he thought as his eyes devoured the information before them.

Then, abruptly, his entire body tensed as he heard footsteps from the northeast stairwell. He admonished himself to relax, that even with his own security code he was cleared to be in this room, but his nervousness did not diminish.

They were two men and they stopped at the bottom of the stairwell. Though they were no longer on a hard tile floor, his keen hearing would have detected the rustling of clothes or even the muffled tread of their feet on the carpet had they continued. He imagined they were staring at the light of his display as it poured out the top of the cubicle. He held stock still, listening, not breathing, not knowing why they were reluctant to enter the room but certain it was his presence that held them back.

And then he heard the click of a gun's hammer being cocked into place.

He was out of his cubicle before the hammer of the second gun was similarly cocked. Ducking down to keep his head below the level of the cubicle walls, he made for the southwest stairwell, winding through the maze as quietly as he could. A different sound alerted him to new developments, and he looked over his shoulder just in time to see a figure clad in black with a ski mask, gun in hand, rise over the cubicle walls as he stood on a desk.

Sinking even lower, he heard the desk creak under the weight of the lookout. He felt a very real terror as he realized the intruder had a clear shot at both stairwells. His fear was unlike any he ever felt on the battlefield, or during the escapade on the Tessa. There, he was subject to chance, to stray bullets and random explosions. Now he was the specific target of two assassins who possessed a tactical superiority. Before his fear rose up to entirely claim him, he forced it back down with an effort, back down to where it was intrusive but manageable.

Slinking into another cubicle, he scanned its contents for something he might use as a weapon. He found nothing better than a ruler which he grabbed before popping back out, moving always farther away from the computer whose light had announced his presence. He moved until he came to a four-way intersection. Holding his breath, he grasped the ruler at its ends and brought it down over his knee, striking the blow diagonally rather than cleanly straight across. There was a snap that, in the quiet of the room, sounded like a thunderclap. Ducking his head as low as he could, he took off. No shot was fired.

These men are experienced, he thought as he sank to the floor with his back to a cubicle wall. *They're not anxious; they're not going to take unlikely shots.* He examined the two halves of the split ruler, reassured to discover each had a reasonably pointy sliver of wood. It wouldn't do to penetrate any thick winter coat or leather, but delivered to the right spot it would make a nasty, perhaps even fatal, wound.

Chancing a cautious peak over the cubicle walls, he saw that one of the assailants was still standing on the desk, gun ready. Sinking back down, he listened for the sound of the man's companion but for the moment there was naught but silence. As he contemplated his circumstances, he realized he was not at such a disadvantage. *Unless they have been given some of the same enhancements, or are wearing special lenses, I can see much better than they can. And I can hear better too. But they must not realize this or they would have turned the lights on. In their dark clothing, they must think they can hide better than me.* Inclining his ear, he could again hear the movements of the second man. He was somewhere in the vicinity of the computer station where Alistair had accessed the network.

Who sent these bastards?

He immediately thought of Stephanie. *What did she say to me? "This is the last chance to save yourself"? Could she be a part of this?* Then the image of Clever Johnny flashed through his mind's eye. He thought of the agents who tried to intimidate him the night of the Debate. Maybe his behavior was reported to Aloysius Warwick. Maybe Aloysius read reports from the Civil Guard, perhaps reports Stephanie filed. *Don't flatter yourself. You're not worth the notice of the mayor. Not yet.*

The lights of the computer display he left running were switched off with a click, and the hall darkened another couple shades. He heard the second assassin moving away from that central cubicle and looked for the best place for an ambush.

He was nimble enough, despite his bulk, to move silently. He proceeded in the general direction of the second assailant, though his route was not a direct one because the cubicles were not laid out in a perfect grid. Eventually, he found an intersection only yards away from the sound of the second man's movements. Approaching one of the corners with the utmost care, he peered around the side and saw the would-be assailant as he moved from cubicle to cubicle, his gun ready to fire.

He coiled himself as the man drew closer, moving from one side of the aisle to the other, unaware his prey was now hunting him. He turned away from Alistair when he checked a cubicle, then turned back when he moved between them. Then he turned away again, and back. Again he repeated the procedure, before coming to the last cubicle before the intersection. One final time he turned his back to Alistair and, with no more announcement than a soft rustle of clothing, Alistair leaped at him.

The man turned to confront his assailant, but Alistair delivered a side-swiping kick with his left foot to the man's forearm and the gun flew from his hand. Having drawn both his hands to his right side, Alistair now sliced his makeshift daggers through the air, aiming for just above the man's beltline. Both wooden points dug into their target and sliced along the midsection. The man gave a stifled groan and Alistair followed with an attempted head butt, but the potentially disabling blow met only empty air. Not pausing for an instant, Alistair delivered another great kick, this one to his attacker's chest. The result was a body propelled several feet through the air before it landed on the ground.

The attack was a matter of no more than three seconds and then Alistair was gone, hidden away in the darkness. No shots were fired and no words were spoken, but when he was again a safe distance away and peering over a cubicle wall, he discovered the first man was no longer standing watch on the desk. Taking advantage of a window of opportunity, he bolted for the southwest stairwell and was soon flying up the steps. He paused only long enough to look at his improvised weapons and saw a piece of cloth pierced by one of them. He examined the fabric and noticed a bit of blood stained it. Tossing the rulers aside, he pocketed the material and made for the exit. Moments later he passed the guards at the front, giving them a hasty nod, and was out under the sun and walking rapidly away, almost jogging. Absent an unforeseen twist of fate, it would be the last time he ever found himself in the halls of the Transportation Bureau.

33

Alistair lay in the snow that formed a mold of his body, nearly as still as the rocks on the hillside around him. Ryan Wellesley, on the other hand, had not stopped digging into the snow and looking for stones underneath to toss down the side of the hill.

"It must be a technical glitch," he muttered for the third time. "You get a new fucking piece of equipment and I think, 'What's the point?' Goddamn thing's broke more often than it works." He tossed another stone. "Most likely a waste of time anyway. The odds they have a satellite trained right on this spot...Hell, Rendral's got hardly any satellites that still work. Rest of 'em are lifeless hunks of scrap metal in orbit."

"I don't mind waiting."

Irritated, Wellesley heaved a stone into a snow bank in response. Just then, in the valley below, a figure emerged from the hill and waved a red flag. Wellesley was on his feet and heading down the hillside with that side-to-side waddle one uses in deep snow. Alistair, hefting his travel sack, was only a couple steps behind. The cave was cloaked from spying technology by a field generator that made the hillside appear to other instruments to be solid all the way through. The problem was, a satellite could still detect anyone walking towards the cave, and if a rebel were to disappear into the side of a hill that was supposed to be solid, it was sure to give them away.

The entrance of the cave was well hidden. Its opening was naturally tucked between folds of rock, and some decoration had further concealed the aperture. The narrow and confined tunnel at the entrance soon opened into a large chamber dimly lit by the blue glow of a dozen or so light sticks set into the cave wall. Much of the cavern was excavated and it was fast losing the normal irregularities of a natural cave.

Alistair spotted three tunnels apart from the one they had come from and a couple men were just getting started making another. They were using a tool he was surprised to see on his home planet. It was a box-shape apparatus about the size of a torso with two large handles on either side. It emitted a beam of red light that softened the stone into the consistency of cream which then poured into a hovering wheelbarrow. It took only a couple minutes to fill the wheelbarrow with the still soft but rapidly solidifying rock.

"It's always good when your enemy has other enemies," said Oliver with a nod at the devices as he approached Alistair and slapped him on the shoulder. His grin was from ear to ear, though his beard nearly covered it, and his skin sported several chapped and cracked areas along with a couple scabs.

"Where'd you get those?" Alistair asked as he gave him a quick and rough embrace. He might have meant the machinery or the sores.

"Kaldis, no less. There are some interests there that think a rebellion on Aldra will keep the Aldran armed forces occupied. We've got foreign sponsors."

"We're official."

By way of guiding him to his quarters, Oliver put an arm over his friend's shoulder. "We've got all sorts of news for you."

"Yeah, I hear the rebellion has a leader now."

Smiling almost sheepishly, Oliver replied, "The rebellion needs a face. I gave it one. Ryan, why don't you hustle off and see if you can make yourself useful?" Wellesley did not bother to hide his irritation but left without a word. Looking carefully around to confirm they were alone, Oliver continued, "And that took the authority neatly away from Johnny."

Alistair nodded in a noncommittal way. "The trick to leading a rebellion is being on top when it's over, not necessarily when it starts."

"Johnny's under control," Oliver assured him and entered a small chamber with a curtain for a door and whose walls, looking like frosting spread on a cake, had obviously been excavated. There was a small desk in the back corner, an octagonal table with four folding chairs, and a couple cots at the far end. It was dimly lit by another light stick ensconced in the wall. "You'll stay with me until we figure out what to do. Hungry?"

"A little." Alistair dumped his travel sack on the floor near the cots. Sitting on one, he asked, "What of the other news?"

"Avon is in revolt. We're pretty sure a few other cities have some activity too, but Avon is on fire. Here." Oliver tossed Alistair a rolled up parchment. The torn and faded paper proved to be a rebel manifesto declaring secession from Rendral and restoration of the Republic of Avon.

"The Republic of Avon? Is this from them or us?

"Them."

"Does this mean they'll want to annex Arcarius?"

"Maybe. If we get to the point where that's a serious problem, I'll be happy."

"And other cities too, you said?"

Oliver nodded. "That's what we hear. News is mainly hearsay, but we've got a few reports I think are reliable." Another smile split the big man's grubby face. "The Empire is cracking."

"Only a matter of time."

"Let's hope."

"I've got some other information you'll be interested in."

"Go on."

Reaching into his travel sack, Alistair fished around for and finally produced a piece of parchment folded over twice. He held it out for Oliver to take and said, "In two weeks time, on the date and hour written down there, a train is coming into Arcarius from the Undersea Tunnel. There are going to be several Apex Committee members on board…as well as President Duquesne."

Oliver's lips parted as he scanned the text.

"They are coming at the head of an army."

Oliver's attention was ripped from the parchment back to his friend. He nodded in understanding. "It makes sense. They need the mines to be operational. A rebellion in Avon is a blow to the war effort, but a rebellion in Arcarius might be lethal. And God forbid we should get control of the mines and set up our own little kingdom."

"Kingdom?"

"Kingdom, Republic…whatever. Don't read into it," he said dismissively and with a hint of irritation. He stared back at the paper. "It looks like we have two weeks to decide what to do next."

"Easy decision: we detonate the mines and keep fighting guerrilla style."

Crumpling the note in his meaty fist, Oliver tossed it back to Alistair and moved to take a seat behind his desk. He scratched at his head and then let both forearms drop down onto the desk.

"I'm thinking it might be time to increase the pressure."

"Oliver, don't get any ideas—"

"Alistair, just hear me out."

Shaking his head like it would keep Oliver's voice from his ears, Alistair said, "Damn it, Oliver, this is the worst time to make a tactical mistake."

"There are things going on—"

"Why don't you listen to someone who has some war experience?"

A knock on the curtain rod interrupted them, and in the following silence they realized how loud their voices had become.

"Come in," said Oliver, clearing his throat.

Two young men entered, one of them pointing at a small crate against the back wall as he looked at Oliver with expectation. Oliver nodded and the two men grabbed the crate and left the room. The big man's gaze followed them and he did not speak until they were gone.

"They have started executing prisoners," he said more quietly. "Suspected rebels are being executed after…let's call it intense questioning."

Shaking his head, Alistair turned and lay back on the cot, lifting his booted feet up like they were weighted down with rocks and easing them onto the foot of his bed. "We have enough fire power now," he said with a despairing sigh, as if he knew in advance his forthcoming advice would be nodded at but not taken. "I could detonate the mines all by myself if you can smuggle the equipment in. Then we sit back and harass as the Empire dissolves in a thousand places at once, like a sugar cube in water. That's all we need to do. And when it happens we'll have our own little island of Arcarius. It doesn't matter what happens anywhere else. We'll have Arcarius and we can be free here. Others can follow our example."

He rolled up onto one elbow to face Oliver. "You want to recruit a proper army, just like a State, and drive them out of Arcarius to take over. Am I right?"

Oliver had the courage to stare his friend in the eye and nod affirmatively. Alistair sighed and returned to his prone position staring up at the cave ceiling.

"The first president of the United States was a dunce named George Washington. When the original colonies revolted against the British Empire, he insisted on forming an army with 'proper' discipline. They surrounded Boston, and a cheap, decentralized rebel movement turned into an expensive, complicated army.

"That's exactly what you are going to be left with if you take Arcarius. A guerrilla army is quick and fleeting. It coalesces and dissipates. Each member supports himself, brings his own food, his own weapons. He comes when he wants to contribute and leaves when other matters call. A guerrilla movement is the way a freedom loving people fight: it can never invade, only defend. Guerrilla warfare is the warfare of freedom; army warfare is the warfare of government slavery.

"This movement was born out of dissatisfaction, nothing more. The Voluntarist System collapsed. We've got an extended empire, we've got hungry and angry citizens, but what we don't have is an ideology. Everyone is fighting what is without a thought to what will be. If you're the face of the rebellion you can give it an ideology, and if you create a regimented army and occupy Arcarius that's exactly what you'll be doing. You'll give it the ideology that brought us the Aldran Commonwealth, and later the Voluntarist System and now the Realists. You'll be giving it the ideology that created the Solar Empire, and the Terran Empire before it. It's the ideology of the Sino-European League, the American Empire, the Soviet Empire, the British Empire, the Roman Empire…it's an ideology that replaces what was with a nearly identical version. Why fight the State just to make the State?"

"You know I respect your opinion, Alistair. I learned a lot from your grandfather, just like you. But the fact is, if we don't take control, someone else will. Someone like Clever Johnny. Who would you rather have at the head of the rebellion, him or me? I believe government is slow and inefficient. I believe there are evil men and they fester in government cabinets and parliaments. I believe good men have been corrupted by working in government. I believe government is unfit to do most things. But I also believe in law and order, and a little government is necessary. It's not fair to say we're fighting the State to make the State. We're fighting to reform the government we have, to make it what it should be. The city is ripe for the picking, and we're sitting here with all the tools and manpower we need. The executed prisoners might just be a perfect catalyst. No more mobs without a goal. This time when we strike, we take the city, and we make government what it should be."

Alistair shook his head again but did not argue. *It's the same damn thing over and over and over and over,* he thought. Out loud he said, "The prisoner execution is likely a response to Clever Johnny's slaughter on The Tessa."

"You might be right. That wasn't my idea."

"I'm not accusing you of anything. But the train with the Realist officials…leave that to me. Take the city if you want—if you can—but leave the train to me."

"What exactly do you have in mind?"

"I'll kidnap Duquesne." The bold pronouncement was delivered in a matter-of-fact tone, and he continued before Oliver could muster a protest. "Let me get a group of men together and we'll get him. He'll be a valuable bargaining token and if we let him live…killing him escalates things again."

Oliver bit at his lip while he thought it over. "And what if, when we're bargaining, they demand the man responsible for the deaths on The Tessa?"

Alistair's words were low and menacing. "I'd turn him over in a heart beat. I don't believe in execution but I'm not going to cry over Clever Johnny. It gets him out of our hair—"

"And alienates a sizable portion of our resistance. Like it or not, this revolution began with underworld elements, and the glue holding it together are the men who've been with it from the beginning…men loyal to Clever Johnny for a long time. Clever Johnny deserves whatever happens to him, but I like to be practical. Turning over Clever Johnny is not. Neither is your plan on kidnapping."

"Just leave it to me."

"No, Alistair. It's too risky when a simple bomb gets rid of him, sends a strong message, and starts the city's conquest off with a bang. Literally. Try to kidnap him and you're as likely to get yourself killed as anything else."

"Bombing the train kills all sorts of innocent rail workers—"

"And keeps you alive and fighting for the cause. People die in war."

Alistair sat bolt upright in his cot and swung his feet over the edge. "That doesn't excuse it! Duquesne is scum, but you don't have the right to indiscriminately bomb civilians, I don't give a damn how convenient it is!"

"Are we going to have this same argument again?" Oliver threw his hands up in the air and let them come crashing down on his desk. The items on top of it rattled from the impact. "What if your death provides the margin the government needs to repress the rebellion? How many more people are going to wish they were dead, or will die some other way, because the Realists are still in control?"

Alistair stood up and loomed threateningly over his friend. "To hell with you, Oliver. I got you this information and we're doing it my way. I'm not arguing about it. My way. Period."

Gritting his teeth, Oliver looked aside and forced himself to breath slowly and deeply until his pulse was under control. "Fine. Your way. Kidnap the asshole. It ought to be easy. I'm sure I'll see you again afterwards."

Alistair sat back down on his cot. "You'd be surprised what sort of things I've been trained to do. I can get this guy if for no other reason than they don't expect anything that sophisticated."

"Well you've got two weeks to prepare for it," Oliver replied and then stood up. "Oh, to hell with it all. Let's get some food."

Alistair nodded and started to rise, but then remembered something. From his sack he produced a piece of cloth with a dried bloodstain and held it for Oliver to see.

"Do you have a somewhere I can store this?"

With the overhead lights turned off, the many colored lights of the computers painted their faces in gentle tones and made indistinct shadows where Stephanie stood looking down into the 3D display. The young cadet at the computer seemed nervous to have her standing over him. During the many moments of down time, when he wasn't relaying a communication or calling up something from the computer files, his fingers moved in the air, as if ghost-typing. Stephanie's own superior sat unmoving in the back corner of the room, and she fancied she could feel his gaze as a tingle on her spine. They were the only souls on the fourth floor of the Civil Headquarters, and the darkness seemed appropriate for their present task.

The 3D display on the computer showed the outline of a building, the corners and edges traced in green and the walls nearly transparent. A section of the street could be seen as well, and the reds and oranges of a human form walked past the building carrying something in its arms. It walked from one edge of the display to the other and then disappeared.

"Just a civilian," said a male voice over the speaker.

"Show me Beta and Gamma sites," Stephanie commanded.

The cadet dropped his fingers to the keyboard and the display blinked off for a fraction of a second before a second display, also a building, came up. There was no sign of life.

"Go on."

The cadet called up another building but it too was lifeless.

"If they don't come soon they're not coming," said the same male voice over the speaker.

Stephanie did not bother to reply. Instead, she grabbed a chair, pulled it next to the cadet and sat down. It had been her intention to stand for the duration—somehow it felt more appropriate with Travis observing—but her feet were throbbing. She decided there was more dignity in sitting than in constantly shifting her weight.

"We've got activity at Alpha."

The cadet brought up the view before Stephanie said a word.

"We see nothing," said Stephanie.

"Nothing from our view, Alpha-1," relayed the cadet.

"The group is still approaching. Six of them, all male."

"Are they carrying anything?"

"One of them has a bundle, it looks like. Hard to say what it is."

A moment later the group appeared on the display. Rising slowly from her chair, Stephanie watched as two stayed near the building while the other four fanned out, doing a poor job of effecting nonchalance.

"Sir, we've confirmed weapons on all six."

"Copy that. Hold your positions."

One of the two near the building's wall went to his knees and worked with an apparatus of some sort. When he finally stood up he faced away from the building and turned in slow semi-circles.

"He's scanning. Tell them to stay still." While the cadet relayed the command, she twisted her torso to look at Captain Travis. "They're better supplied every day." Travis did not respond.

The man with the scanner hopped into an alley and walked to the other side of the building. They could see him through the walls made translucent by their equipment. When he finished a second sweep, his companions rejoined him and one of them picked the lock to a side door. Four entered while two remained outside. The four who went inside immediately separated and spread throughout the four floors, stopping now and then to plant something before moving on. Within ten minutes they were back outside and, without fanfare, departed.

"When they're out of sight, send the team in."

A couple minutes later, orange and red human shapes once again invaded the building, but these moved with more precision and discipline, rifles held at the ready.

"Sir, it looks like we've got audio and 3D video recorders. I don't recognize the model. Probably not Aldran."

"No explosives?"

"Negative. Just surveillance equipment."

Sighing, Stephanie turned to Travis. "I shouldn't have sent them in. Now they know we know."

Travis' response was to turn his hands palms upwards in a resigned gesture. "You need to think quickly, Caldwell."

Stephanie turned to direct her command to the cadet. "Right now they're giving the command to get word to their spy he's been found out. The equipment was planted at Alpha… that means it's…LaSalle." She spoke the name with some regret. "We need to have someone there to arrest them both. Keep the teams in surveillance around the buildings just in case. I'll send relief in a couple hours."

While the cadet was busy relaying her orders, she turned on her heel to leave. Travis was just getting up. He retrieved his hat from the desk nearby, placed it neatly on his head and, posture perfect, fell in stride with her as she walked through the dark hallways of the fourth floor.

"I shouldn't have sent them in," she admitted before Travis could say anything.

"No, you shouldn't have." Stephanie was relieved to hear his voice was not cold. "If they were bombs, they could have been allowed to go off; that area is empty in the winter. But you salvaged what you could from the situation. Hopefully, we can pick up whoever comes to warn LaSalle. Then you and I will handle him personally."

"Yes, sir," she said as they reached the almost pitch black stairwell.

With a polite smile, Travis held the door open and gestured for her to go first. They made their blind way to the bottom floor and there parted. Travis went to the garage and his auto, Stephanie to the front door and a chill walk home.

34

A fierce blizzard enveloped the island and tried to scrub it clean. Alistair's first week in the hills consisted of furiously digging out snow from the cave entrance and long periods of nothing. Rebels huddled in small groups around a heater and listened to the wind outside. They spoke only softly if at all, as if to keep from alerting the storm to their presence in the belly of the mountain. Their beards grew longer, their lips became more chapped and their anxiousness grew.

Before the gusts arrived, there was a window of calm wherein they expected to hear from LaSalle, but they heard nothing from him nor from a team sent to bug a Civil Guard house on LaSalle's tip. No sooner were the expensive bugs in place than Civil Guard picked them clean. Oliver, having been the one to order the operation, took it especially hard. Alistair later told his friend the Civil Guard probably gave different versions of a plan to different suspected spies and waited to see which information was acted on.

Bob LaSalle still did not know, and Oliver was not looking forward to telling him, though he insisted on being the one to do so. The mountainous rugby star spent an entire day brooding, speaking only to Alistair and then just to list the number of ways the whole thing should have made him suspicious from the outset. He was angry enough to launch a full scale assault right then and there and, had the blizzard not decided the issue, Alistair might not have been able to talk him out of it.

The fourth day dawned still and bright. Alistair was the first to burst through the wall of snow blockading the entrance and peer through squinting and watery eyes at the blinding landscape. When his eyes finally adjusted, he saw an unspoiled white wilderness devoid of any other feature than smooth sloping mounds. He allowed himself a minute to survey, and then he and the others got to work, preparing to welcome President Duquesne and the Apex Committee members.

Prisoner cells, torture chambers and the like were always associated with dank and dark subterranean dungeon levels. However accurate this might generally have been, the cells in the Civil Headquarters, reserved for prisoners of special interest, were all on the very top floor. On the off chance a prisoner should actually escape, he had several stories of building to pass through before reaching freedom.

With a precisely regular rhythm, Captain Travis' boot heels clicked cleanly and sharply on the black tiles of the upper story. As Stephanie followed a few paces behind, she stared at his murky reflections on the floor and walls, composed of the same tiles. Travis led her to the center of that story, where the interrogation rooms were. Each was shaped like a circle with a wall cutting through its diameter. The wall was light gray on the side where the room was brightly and harshly lit. On the other, the wall was transparent and the room barely illuminated at all. That half sported a couple computer stations and desks along with some stray chairs, and there

Travis and Stephanie entered. On the other side, a naked Ryan LaSalle sat tied to a chair, his hands behind his back. He looked exhausted and abused.

"We haven't gotten a thing out of him but we haven't tried all that hard," commented the Captain. He turned his hard gaze on his protégé. "You are going to get him to talk."

Stephanie shifted uncomfortably and averted her eyes.

"Yes, Stephanie. You have reached your next step."

Biting her lip, she looked her commander in the eye. "Is this for his sake or mine?"

"Both. And it needs doing. Now."

She braced herself as if for an impact. "I don't feel comfortable with this."

Before the sentence entirely left her mouth, Travis turned from her and went to a computer where, with a grandiose flick of his arm, he threw a switch and turned on the audio to Ryan's half of the interrogation room. The sound of his unsteady, fearful breaths came through.

"I do care about what makes you uncomfortable, Stephanie, but only inasmuch as it is in my interest to cure your discomfort. This is the job, now get used to it." With one hand on his hip and the other supporting his weight on a table near the transparent wall, Travis indicated the door to the other room with a nod of his head. His demeanor, normally controlled and stoic, was flamboyant. Gone was the terribly quiet commander and in his place was a stentorian and dramatic man who unsettled her.

"This is not the job as I understand it," she said as respectfully and firmly as she could.

"I don't doubt that for a second," Travis loudly replied and he paced around her. "You don't understand what the job is. Few people do, but today you are going to learn." Travis stopped in front of her, between her and the viewing wall. "You are going to make that man as miserable as he ever imagined possible, until he tells you anything you want to know. Then you're going to do it some more for good measure. And then you'll take him back to his cell and execute him and have the corpse burnt to ashes. That's exactly what you're going to do because that is exactly your job."

Stephanie actually found herself shaking. Feeling anger well up in her breast, she fought to control her limbs. "This has never been what the job meant—"

"This has always been what the job meant!" Travis resumed his disorienting orbit about her. "I asked you a question a while ago, Ms. Caldwell, and I want an answer. How in God's name can such a thing be justified? How do you justify this?"

"You can't!" she howled, a dam finally crumbling. "He's a traitor and should go to jail. Give him a trial and send him to prison."

"You're as fully aware as I am of what goes on in these chambers. Traitors are captured and tortured everyday. You haven't raised a word of protest until now...now that you are being called on to do your part. You've made a career out of finding traitors and making sure they get their punishment. You know where these people get sent and what happens to them. Don't try to tell me now you don't support it! You may not want to get your own hands dirty, but you've been supporting this government so you DO support it!"

Once again Travis came to a stop in front of her, this time with his arms folded over his chest. Stephanie did not respond.

"How," he asked in a softer tone, "do you justify what you are about to do to that man? The answer is you don't." Stephanie looked sharply at him. "You don't justify it, you just do it. You do it because it needs to be done. Why does it need to be done? Because the State requires it. There has never been a time in human history when some group was not lording it over everyone they could bring under their dominion. It's human nature. There's no God who ordains these things, who punishes wickedness or rewards virtue. There simply is reality, existence, life. There are physical laws governing this universe, but that is all. If there are any moral laws they are undetectable, silent and entirely without effect, so you can either live your life being dominated or you can dominate. As sure as up is up and down is down it's going to happen, and there's no particular reason why it should or shouldn't be you. The ones who control will be resisted, and the ones who resist will either be put down or gain control themselves. Science has progress; history does not. It's a long tale made up of identical chapters. If it's going to happen anyway, then fight to put yourself in a better position. If you don't, then someone no more deserving will do it to you."

Travis was pacing again now. "This is what the State is. It's a collection of people, however keenly or dimly they realize the truth of what I am saying, who have gotten into power. Some feel guilty when they don't become as altruistic as they pictured themselves being. Those were the Voluntarists, and they failed spectacularly. Others act not on a theory but just follow their nature. Some rare few see the State for what it is and know how to use it. The State is not here for the greater good; the State is here for its own good."

"That's not true!"

"The hell it's not!" Travis roared. A single lock of hair fell out of place and hung over his forehead. "On Foundation Day whom do we parade before the citizens? Doctors? Mechanics? Accountants? We give them row after row of soldiers, followed by fat politicians in expensive autos. Steal from your company or your boss and what do you get? A large fine, paid to the State, and a bit of jail time. Steal from the State by not paying your taxes and what happens to you? Twenty cycles minimum. The Voluntarists suspended the death penalty…except for when the victim was a Civil Guardsman, an elected official or a soldier. What was the one other case where even the Voluntarists used the death penalty? Treason. What happens to you if you get in a bar fight and hit another civilian? But hit a Civil Guardsman, even an off duty one, and you get a minimum of one cycle in prison.

"Every penalty, every single solitary punishment, is increased if committed against the State's agents. The State is here for itself, Caldwell, and the citizens are resources. We take the fruits of their labor and spend it on ourselves. We tell them what they may do and what they may not; what they may ingest and what they may not; what they may sell and buy and for how much; where they may live; whom they may marry; where they may educate their children and in what fashion; what they may say; how they may defend themselves; even how they may participate in the government they are being forced to fund, and if they don't do it as we decide we send them to jail. And if for one moment they have the audacity to be less than enthusiastic about our governance, we invent a war to get them begging for our help and we denounce all protesters as traitors.

"This is what government is. It always has been and always will be this way. It is the very nature of the State, and it is the very nature of humans either to create the State or have it forced on them." Travis stepped right in front of Stephanie's face and looked down into her eyes. "Now I am on the verge of being named commander of the Arcarius garrison and head of the ARO. I am going to need good people at my side to keep control of this city. I don't want individuals who obey the State reflexively and support it in the abstract. I want men and women who know what the State is, what it does, and don't flinch when they are called on to do its work. You know now what the State is. You've always known but now it's been made explicit. Can you be the kind of person I need or have I wasted my time with you?"

In response Stephanie, her enervated legs suddenly finding strength, pulled away and flew out the door. Breathing as if in labor, she felt her eyes sting with tears. She got six or seven steps down the hall, trying to swallow a searing lump in her throat, when she stopped. She couldn't say why other than that a vaguely glimpsed image of the end of her present path flashed before her eyes. Behind her, the door burst open and Travis popped out, a look of alarm on his face. When he saw she had stopped, he relaxed. Stephanie twisted her torso around to look at him.

"Will you come back inside with me?" he asked and held out his hand.

Alistair sat slow and unmoving, repeatedly scanning the mostly open stretches of ground around him from the cover of an abandoned railroad car with its roof torn off. It was a bitterly cold morning, and he and his mates were thankful there was no wind. The new fallen snow formed a small hill covering the west side of the tracks, and he wished they could have gotten to the old passenger car without leaving footprints. He sat in one of the doorways and looked at the clear trail they left, feeling exposed. Not wanting to spend much time in a vulnerable and easily detected spot, he arrived with his small and hastily trained troop at the last minute.

"I'm just saying it would cause more trouble than it's worth," Wellesley was saying.

"Naw, it'd be helpful," insisted one of the men. "We've had all sortsa trouble trying to arm ourselves—"

"We've had a steady supply of arms from smugglers for weeks."

"It ain't been steady, and before it was hard going. I'm just saying if they hadn't out-lawed guns, we'd've been armed from the start." The young debater turned to Alistair. "Ain't I right, Alistair? We coulda had more arms from the beginning."

"Are you looking out for Civil Guard?" Alistair asked without looking away from his own post.

"Yeah, I'm looking out. But ain't I right about the guns?"

"If every citizen had a gun they'd be trippin' over 'em left and right," Wellesley said. "More trouble than they're worth."

"Of course it would be helpful if we had guns to begin with," said Alistair, his tone suggesting it was an already settled issue. "All governments prefer to have unarmed citizens. Arms restrictions go back a long, long time. The Qin Dynasty in China, third century B.C., confiscated all weapons for its own use. It wasn't for any other reason than that it gave them an advantage in controlling the provinces. Of course, it didn't work well, but that was their intention."

The men shared surprised glances and then, shaking their heads, snickered.

"Do you do anything other than read?" Wellesley asked.

Turning his head slowly to gaze at his partner, Alistair replied, "What do you think?"

"He reads and he lifts weights," said Kendrick and the men snickered again.

"Where do you learn all that stuff you talk about?" asked another as he tried to recline on an old, torn passenger seat.

"There was a library in Mar Profundo, on Kaldis, where an android reads to you while you lift weights."

There was a second of silence before the men broke into the laughter of one who almost got fooled. Alistair allowed himself a smile.

"How much do you know?" asked Kendrick. "Who was the fifth Governor of the United States?"

"Prime Minister, you jackass," growled Wellesley and the other three hooted and hollered.

"President," corrected Alistair. "And I don't know."

"Oh, we got him! We got him!"

"Who was the best president of the United States?"

"There's no such thing as a good president," Alistair said, and the merriment abruptly halted. "There are mediocre presidents, bad presidents, awful presidents, and unspeakable ones. No good ones."

Wellesley gave a low whistle. "What about Oliver?"

Alistair briefly debated whether or not to answer, but a whistle bursting from the Undersea Tunnel interrupted. Springing to his feet, he reached for his communicator.

"The guests are arriving," he said and waited. There was nothing on the other end. "Dad, do you hear me? The guests are arriving." When there was still no response, he tossed the communicator to Wellesley. "See if you can get that to work," he said and grabbed the detonator. The train whistled again but, hovering over the magnetic rails, it made no other noise to announce its arrival. Scanning the area one more time for Civil Guard, Alistair readied his thumb over the button while his five companions rechecked their weapons. Upon seeing the glow of lights inside the tunnel, he judged the train was at the point of emerging, but before he could blow the track, a great explosion knocked him onto his back. He was shaking his head to clear it when debris started raining down around them, and when he sat up he saw black smoke pouring out of the Undersea Tunnel. A few burning scraps were ejected into the snow. The tunnel itself collapsed and a good portion of the hillside subsided as well, sealing off the Undersea from the island.

Reflexively, Alistair put his hands to his ears but knew there was nothing he could do to stop the ringing. *He betrayed me,* was the only thought he could put together in his head. *He betrayed me.* Turning to the men, he saw their blank, stunned stares, fully as shocked as his. Wellesley had been hit in the forehead by something and a stream of blood was just forging a path around his eye and down his cheek. He turned back to the wreckage and burned with rage.

Wellesley sidled up next to his partner, breathing as if he had just run a mile, and asked, "What do we do now?"

Alistair tossed the detonator into the deep snow outside the car. Gripping his gun, he pulled it from its holster and checked the chamber to confirm the presence of a bullet. "We finish the battle," he said through gnashing teeth.

Having chosen her path, Stephanie walked it with bold strides. It was not for nothing that she so easily fell into command roles, and not for nothing that she caught Travis' attention. Relegating conscience to a back corner of her mind, she threw herself into her assignment.

Nearly every rebel hid his face. When the interrogator entered the cell he would stare at the floor, meekly, and only made eye contact when ordered to do so. Even then it was a tremulous, faltering look turned away at the first opportunity. Ryan LaSalle was no different. The erstwhile jocularity was gone and in its place was shame and terror in equal parts.

"I never need to explain to a traitor why they are guilty," she informed him. "They hide their faces in shame because they already know."

Even such a remark as that did not provoke a response. He was, as she could tell, already beaten, but brutality is not something a successful regime can compromise. The recent Voluntarist collapse was a firm reminder of that. Despite his protestation of ignorance of practically every aspect of the rebellion, and despite the fact Stephanie believed every word of it, Ryan LaSalle was a battered, twisted, bleeding, shattered, quivering body an hour later. His silence was due only to his voice giving out. What once had been a young man's lithe fingers were twisted fragments. Where once an easy, cocky smile had been was now a mouth of shattered teeth and torn lips. The arms that had encircled his mother, his girlfriends, his cousin—the arms which once had wrestled with his father—lay useless on the ground, more like boneless tentacles.

By the faraway stare in his eyes, she figured his mind was shutting out the pain it could not cope with. Her arms tired and her chest heaving, she dropped her hammer onto the floor and glanced at the gray wall where, on the other side, Travis was still watching her, and then back at the body she had broken. Wiping the sweat from her brow with the back of her cleaner left hand, she made for the exit. There was only one thing left to do, but as she reached for the handle her attention was abruptly arrested by the low rumble of a distant explosion.

The Undersea Tunnel ran into Arcarius at the southern part of the city, just east of the harbor, and went north to the main train station at the southern terminus of Rendral Way and the northeast corner of the harbor district. Alistair and his small group followed the tracks from the detonated train to the city's main station, a trip of perhaps two miles. When they emerged from a small cluster of dark and empty worker flats, the station came into view. All was still.

They heard the sounds of a firefight immediately following the detonation of the train. By the time they covered half the distance to the station, the various booms and cracks, at least the nearby ones, had ceased. Now, standing before it, Alistair saw it was perfectly intact. The skirmish did nothing to damage the south side of the structure.

The noises of combat surrounded them on all sides but at a great distance. The lion's share came from the northeast, up Rendral Way, where the Civil Headquarters and Mayor's

Palace were. An occasional flash of light was seen on the hillsides surrounding the city and Alistair's keen vision could make out small groups of men operating light artillery.

"At a run, men," he said and broke into a gallop over the snowy terrain. After a space of a couple hundred yards they reached the platforms and passed into the shadow under the roof perhaps thirty yards above. His head a full foot beneath the platforms, he was unable to see what was above, but there were several streams of blood still dripping a little off the edge even as the red fluid both froze and coagulated. Holding his hand out to slow the men down, he gently approached a set of stone stairs, his firearm at the ready, listening intently for any hint of movement. Slowly he ascended until his searching eyes broke the level of the platform and the sight of several dead bodies greeted him.

The terminal was a spacious area with seven separate platforms long enough that an entire train could shelter underneath the glass roof. Alistair chose the central tracks for the approach on the theory that, running by the largest platform, it would be deemed the most appropriate to welcome Duquesne. He guessed correctly, as there were a couple dozen corpses, killed by gunfire and grenades by the look of them. Some lay peacefully while others were contorted into impossible positions. A few were Civil Guard; most were in civilian clothes. Two station workers had been killed, but they had weapons in their hands and Alistair recognized one as a rebel.

His men picked their way through the carnage of bodies and rent benches and shattered glass. Many were fascinated by the corpses, and one even stooped down to peer into the lifeless eyes of a young woman as she, lying on her shredded abdomen, stared along the platform floor. Alistair remembered his first battlefield, before he was assigned a War Suit, and recalled feeling exactly the same horrible fascination. Such novice feelings were gone now, as was the sick feeling of regret. *No,* he thought, *the regret is not entirely gone. It's buried but not gone. I'll grieve when the battle is over.*

"Staring at the bodies is the surest way to join them," he growled. "Keep a look out and follow me."

He led them down the length of the platform, sweeping his gun back and forth. The sounds of distant battle were all that broke the stillness, that and the occasional sniffle or spit from one of his companions. Passing through the doors at the front of the platforms, he and his men were greeted by the large marble main hall. Lit only dimly by sunlight streaming through the glass front doors and the windows high on the walls, it sported marble staircases in each of the four corners. There were ticket windows, a large, cubical bulletin board in the center that replaced the less trustworthy electric monitors and some abandoned portable stands used by well connected vendors. There was another dead body, a Guardsman, lying spread-eagle and face down with his head pointing towards the entrance.

"I want a gun pointed at each staircase at all times," Alistair informed his team and began to cross the main hall, trusting the men to sort out his order for themselves. They had nearly reached the midway point, a mere handful of yards from the bulletin board, when he signaled a stop, listening for just a moment before hiding behind the board. The others followed suit. Seconds later they finally heard what alerted Alistair: footsteps on the staircase behind them to their left.

236

When the others emerged from the deep shadow of the staircase, it was with slow and fearful steps. The first three were Civil Guard; the twenty or so following were civilians, a few of them ostentatiously dressed. Laying a calming hand on Wellesley's shoulder, Alistair let the party go about halfway from their stairwell to the front doors.

With a whisper so slight it hardly existed, he said, "Stay with me now," and then popped his torso out from the side of the bulletin board.

"Don't move!" he bellowed, and his companions trained their guns on the group.

A collective scream went up from the score of civilians while the Civil Guard, true to their training, hit the deck and aimed their weapons back on the rebels, shouting orders all the while.

"Put your weapons down!" roared Alistair. "You have no cover and we've got you pinned down! Put your weapons down!"

There was another interval of shouting, and finally one of the Civil Guard turned and shouted to his comrades. He raised his weapon towards the ceiling and stood up. The other two did likewise a moment later.

"Keep your weapons pointed right at them," said Alistair and then, sweeping wide to avoid any crossfire, moved out from behind the bulletin board and approached the group.

He was fifteen feet away when he noticed one of the ostentatiously dressed ladies was Elizabeth. He nearly missed a step when he saw her. Her makeup was sullied with tears and several stray strands of her beautiful black hair hung over her face. Her chest heaved in fear but her eyes were fixed on him.

Returning his attention to the Guards, Alistair softly but firmly ordered, "Put your weapons down one at a time. You first…now you…now you. Step away from the weapons and keep your hands above your heads."

With his free hand, Alistair waved his men forward and kicked the weapons to a safer distance.

"You three, get down on your bellies and kiss the floor." They quickly did just that. His companions were at his side a moment later.

"Search the Guards and take anything useful," he commanded, and as they hastened to obey he turned to Elizabeth who was looking at him with a mixture of fear and anger.

"What happened here?"

"What do you think happened here, Alistair!?" She spat his name when she pronounced it.

"Elizabeth, settle down and—"

"Don't tell me to settle down!" she wailed and clumsily drew her arm back and slugged Alistair a blow meant for his face but which connected with his neck. Her body heaved with unsuppressed sobs and the breaths wheezed in and out of her lungs. "They tried to kill us! *You* tried to kill us!"

"Getting worked up isn't going to solve anything."

"Don't give me your logical shit!" Elizabeth's hysterics were creating a stir among the other people in her group.

"Shut that bitch up!" hollered Wellesley.

"SOUND OFF!" Alistair roared and his holler echoed in the marble cavern. Even Elizabeth was reduced to a few quiet sniffles. Summoning his gentlest voice, he said, "Elizabeth, I need you to tell me what happened here."

Through sobs that made her teeth chatter, she gave him the short version. "We were waiting to greet President Duquesne. There was an explosion and then everyone was shooting at us...Alistair they killed Aloysius!" A sob wracked her body. "They killed the mayor!" She broke down into tears again. Supremely uncomfortable and uncertain what to do, Alistair awkwardly placed an arm around her shoulder but she threw it off and retreated into her group of companions.

Sighing, Alistair turned to his fellows. "Have you searched them yet?"

"We got everything."

"Alright. Get out of here," he said and waved them on.

"What the hell?" said Wellesley.

"Get going!" he repeated with a sharp bark that cut through their hesitation. The Civil Guardsmen leapt up and, first at a fast walk and then at a jog, made for the main entrance. The civilians whom they escorted, Elizabeth included, kept pace.

When the rebels were alone again Wellesley sidled up next to Alistair and fixed a disbelieving gaze on him. "They're going to be back in the ranks and rearmed within an hour. We could have saved ourselves the trouble right here. And probably somebody's life."

"They put up their guns and surrendered," Alistair replied without looking at his partner. "I'm not killing anyone in that position. Now let's head up Rendral Way and see what we can see."

His disgruntled men followed him outside, their boots making echoes off the marble of the hall.

‿⸙

Staying in the protection of the narrow alleys and smaller streets, Alistair led his band northeast, parallel to Rendral Way but away from its wide open space. The cacophony of battle persisted, but other than the smoke from fires lit around the city they saw little evidence of it. For several blocks he trekked from alley to alley, pausing to scan when their path crossed another street and then quickly leading his men across. Once, while passing through a neighborhood, he glanced at a window and looked right at a pair of eyes staring back at him. As quickly as he called a halt, the face ducked away into the darkness of the house and Alistair decided it was just a poor woman trying to hide from violence. They hurriedly left the neighborhood behind.

A few blocks later, he once again raised his hand for a halt, listening for a moment. "The battle's moving this way. We're going to camp out in one of these homes and hit them when they come through."

"We could head east and just go around," one of the men suggested, but Alistair was already trudging through the snow of a short front yard. The men followed and caught up as he hopped onto the front porch of the boxlike structure and pounded on its front door.

"What are you doing?" asked Wellesley incredulously.

"Seeing if anyone is home."

Staring ahead at the door in front of him, he did not see the amazed looks of his companions.

"Uh, Alistair…we're in a battle right now. Just kick the door in."

"Property is property."

"OK, but it looks like no one is on this property that is property."

Alistair lifted one massive leg and shattered the wood near the handle with a mighty kick. The door flew inward and bounced back into him as he strode through. Quickly surveying the entrance hall, he crossed over its creaking wood floors to a staircase.

"Make sure the first floor is empty," he commanded without looking back.

With a loud creak at every footstep, he ascended, his gun ready. As his eyes rose above the level of the second floor he saw another hallway as bare as the one below. The house was dusty and had nothing to indicate anyone was living there. He paused at the landing to listen but heard only the battle and the heavy footsteps of his men. Gun first, he quickly checked the half dozen upstairs rooms and found a series of offices with desks, chairs and sagging bookshelves covered in dust. The thick tomes bending the wood of the shelves were tax manuals, all out of date. When he finished checking the last of the rooms and returned to the landing, his men were just coming up the stairs.

"I think this was some kind of accountant's office," said Ryan as he reached the landing.

"That's what I gather. There are two rooms facing the street. We can take up posts there and pick them off as they come through. Is there a side door to this place?"

"East side's got one."

"Good." Alistair pointed two fingers at Kendrick and another man and said, "You two are going to guard our exit. Make sure the next house over is clear. Sooner or later they're going to figure out where we are and we're going to have to move quick. We'll take up positions in the front rooms."

They nodded, faces flushed and eyes wide, a mixture of nervous and eager, and then rushed back down the stairs.

Moments later, Alistair was sitting lookout with Ryan Wellesley. The desk was turned over on its side and placed up against the wall under the window. To its right and up against the wall they stood the bookshelf, bulky manuals still in place, thick and heavy oaken backboard standing as a shield against any bullets to make it through the wall. Alistair was sitting sidesaddle on the overturned desk, eyes scanning back and forth. Wellesley sat behind in one of the padded office chairs, his right knee bouncing up and down and his hands fidgeting with his gun. It was a large firearm, large enough that a smaller person might have used it as a rifle. Wellesley was repeatedly taking out the magazine, flipping the pebble-size round out of the chamber, replacing the round in the magazine, sticking the magazine back in and reloading the chamber. This he did to the rhythm of his bouncing right knee.

"You're likely to have an accident before the battle even starts," said Alistair in a low voice without turning away from his post.

Slamming the magazine back home one more time, Wellesley sighed and laid the gun in his lap. His knee did not stop bouncing. "I'm just sick of waiting."

"We've been waiting about three minutes. It's OK if you're nervous."

"I ain't nervous."

"Of course." After a pause he added, "But if you were, it would be OK."

Another moment passed before Wellesley said, "I think I'd rather be out in the street. We could fire and run. It's too easy to surround us here."

A huge explosion somewhere in the vicinity of Rendral Way threw dirt and chunks of cement into the air. The fighters were close enough that shouts and the occasional scream could be heard.

"The Civil Guard are retreating as fast as they can. The idea is to take a few of them out as they pass by and let our own forces overtake us. Out in the street we'd always be separated from them by a wall of enemy forces."

A few more knee pumps, then, "Do you ever get nervous before a battle?"

"Always."

"You don't seem nervous."

"You learn to control it. My first battle, I was fully half as nervous as you are right now."

Despite himself, Wellesley let out a single suppressed guffaw that sprayed saliva. He wiped his mouth with the back of his hand and his knee calmed down a bit.

"If we were in serious danger I wouldn't be doing this," Alistair assured him. "They are already under fire; they're not even going to realize they're getting hit from our position. By the time they figure out what's going on and where the shots are coming from, they'll be by us. If not, we've got nice brick walls and this furniture as shields. We duck down, head to the side door and we're in the next house."

"And what if we—"

"They're here!" Alistair hissed, his body now tense as he dropped below the desk. Wellesley fumbled for his gun, got it, and slid into place next to Alistair.

A group of Civil Guard came running out of an alley to their left. They crossed the street and took up positions where Alistair and his men could not fire at them.

"It's a revolving retreat," Alistair explained. "One group retreats and takes up covering positions. Then their buddies pass by and leave them in front."

No sooner did he say that than a larger group of Guard came pouring out of the alley. Alistair and Wellesley commenced firing, as did their two comrades. It lasted for just a few seconds and then Alistair grabbed Ryan and they both ducked down below the window sill. It was difficult to tell who had hit whom, but Alistair counted three fallen bodies during their assault.

Crawling deeper into the room to make himself more difficult to see, Alistair surveyed their work. Two Guard were lifting a fallen comrade between them while two others lay still in the snowy street. There were several other trails of blood leading to the south.

"They have no idea where they got hit from," he said and Wellesley broke into a relieved smile. "But I think a tank is coming. Keep your head down." A low rumble had been building for a few seconds and the desultory stream of Civil Guard had stopped. "Be ready to fire."

"At a tin can?"

"At the Guard using it for cover."

A moment later Alistair's prediction was confirmed. The massive yet flexible hulk of a tin can thundered onto the street, its treads tearing up the snow and gripping the pavement underneath. At each corner a small and swiveling automatic gun sat ready to douse a target with its rounds. In the center a larger cannon sprouted from a spherical turret that could point the cannon in any direction. Two Civil Guardsmen lay belly down on either side of the turret, firing their rifles.

Alistair fired off three rounds at the nearer Guard and, after a quick adjustment of his aim, three more at the other. Both men's bodies spasmed as the rounds entered their flesh but almost immediately went slack and stopped moving. The first Guard slipped off the back end of the tank and was crushed beneath the treads. At that moment the tank stopped moving, the mutilated corpse of the Guardsman trapped underneath it, and the abrupt stop caused the second body to slide off the end. Three great booms in rapid succession, accompanied by three fleeting but brilliant flashes of light, rocked the neighborhood as the tank's cannon fired down the alley out of which it had just emerged. Looking out over the roofs of the neighborhood, Alistair saw one quake and then collapse.

And then the turret swiveled and raised the cannon until it was pointed at their hide-out.

"RUN!" Alistair bellowed.

He made it out the door and was vaguely aware that Wellesley was behind him when a concussive force hit him like a wrecking ball. Not for the first time, he was sent flying and lost all sense of up and down until his face scraped along the wooden floor of the hallway and his legs, above his head, slammed into the back wall of the building. He lay there as, by degrees, his hearing returned, bringing the familiar shouting and cracks of gunfire. Trying to move, he realized his right leg had broken through the plaster of the wall and required a strong tug to dislodge it.

After righting himself, he saw Wellesley sitting in the middle of the hall and bleeding from a dozen shallow cuts. He was staring in amazement at the wall in front of him and breathing like he had just run a hundred yard dash. Rising unsteadily, Alistair looked for his gun, finally finding it under a pile of rubble. As he grabbed it a small stream of blood trickled off his nose and splattered on the firearm.

Standing back up he called to his friend, "Ryan, get moving."

Wellesley slowly turned his head to look at Alistair, his jaw hanging open and an uncertain look on his face. A fire burned in the other front room where their two companions were. The cannon round having sliced through the front façade on its way to the other room, it took out the wall at the front of the hallway. Where once brick and mortar had been, he now was staring across the street at another box of a house. Alistair located Ryan's gun and returned it to its owner who was just struggling to his feet.

"Does everything work?" he asked, referring to Ryan's body more than the gun.

Wellesley's lips moved in answer but the sound was buried under a barrage of cannon shots, though the tank was now moving away. Judging his friend to be in fair condition, he grabbed his shoulder and they hobbled down the stairs together. When they reached the bottom, the front door opened to reveal the worried faces of their other companions who had been guarding their exit. They spared a moment to look relieved before Kendrick spoke.

"Donny and Mike?"

Alistair shook his head and the two absorbed the news with a sad, knowing nod.

"Our forces?" asked Alistair.

"They're just catching up to us. The tin men are headed south."

"What do we do now?" asked the other.

Alistair passed by them on his way out the front door. "You guys are free to do what you like. I'm on my way to Civil Headquarters."

35

It is difficult to distinguish between an urban area battered by fighting and one that, the forces which constitute its lifeblood having been strangled, has simply decayed, but this is true only when battle scars are old and settled. In the immediate aftermath of a battle, when the smoke still billows and the flames still angrily flutter; when men still soaked with adrenaline run to and fro shouting; when recently damaged structures suddenly lose their precarious struggle against gravity, there can be no question. Like muddy footprints on a white carpet, the retreating Civil Guard and their rebel opponents left an unmistakable trail through the city. It would have been as easy for Alistair to follow it backwards as follow Rendral Way itself.

As he marched up the city's main street, Alistair struck a contrasting image to the others he passed. They were a flutter of frenzied motion. Groups of rebels ran across the boulevard, destined for some pocket of resistance announcing its presence with gunfire. Once in a while someone would notice him and stop to salute, face flushed, eyes sparkling and mouth split in an exuberant grin. Unaware of just how dour his expression was, he never failed to return the salute but sent them off a bit less enthusiastic.

Upon reaching the Civil Headquarters, he saw a building in ruins. Three of the four walls were standing but the façade and many stories inside had almost entirely collapsed. A fire burned somewhere in the back and let out a thick black smoke while, in the front, several men and women were picking through the rubble. He smelled the unmistakable odor of burnt flesh, and amid the blackened wreckage he spied the odd limb sticking out, or an entire corpse lying prone. Dark stains marked the places where many died.

He left the icon in ruins and followed the boulevard to its terminus. No fewer than three tanks, two of them still burning, littered the rotunda and the courtyard on the far side. When Alistair finally entered the Mayor's Palace, through the grand ornate metal double doors, past merry rebels singing and lounging around the reception chamber with goods stolen from the palace vaults, he caught a glimpse of himself in a large mirror and was startled out of his angry reverie.

Staining his face was a layer of soot with crisscrossing tracks of sweat and water from his sore and bloodshot eyes. There were nicks and scrapes and bruises all about his visage, covering the older wounds not entirely healed, and the aggregate effect made him look like some sort of monster. Before the War Suit he had worn the standard helmet of the Aldran Infantry. After each battle he returned sweaty and disheveled but without grime. *A reminder of the new territory I'm in,* he thought to himself, leaving a smudgy fingerprint on the mirror before turning away.

On the third story of the grandiose structure, he found whom he sought. It was rather like working one's way to the center of a whirlpool. The bodies rushing around and through the palace emanated from a central point. As he got closer the bodies moved faster and grew in number until he burst through a door, nearly knocking over someone he never bothered to look at, and found Oliver Keegan at the center of it all.

Brad Stanson was with him, seated at a desk recently relocated to the center of the spacious chamber. He was nearly hidden behind a pile of books and documents as he tried in his own way to get a handle on the situation, but it was clearly Oliver, towering above Stanson and gesticulating as he circled the desk, who was conducting the chaotic symphony. When one of Oliver's gestures turned his body around so that he caught sight of Alistair, he acknowledged his friend with a grim nod tinged with uncertainty.

"We've still got some pockets of resistance," he said by way of greeting. "If you're interested, we could use some help getting—"

Alistair's right fist smashed Oliver's nose. Not a wild, arcing hook, it had the economy of motion that comes with training and was driven by many pounds of sculpted muscle. Oliver's head snapped back and dragged his body with it, finally coming to a crashing halt on the carpeted floor, a landing which made the room rattle and a pile of papers on Stanson's desk shift and slip to the floor.

The din and movement ceased. The pen cap Stanson was chewing fell from his slack jaws. A pair of rebels, jubilant and laughing, came through the door only to halt and stare at the uncomfortably still scene before them. Oliver let out a groan and rolled to his side, his hands cupping his bleeding nose.

Turning to Stanson, Alistair said, "We need to talk. Follow me out to the hall." He turned to go and Stanson paused only to look at Oliver in disbelief before, half tripping over the chair, he took off to catch up.

"Alistair, I don't understand. We won. We drove the Realists out!"

"I was lied to," Alistair said in a low and hard voice. He moved a few more feet down the hall before he turned to confront Stanson, his voice ominous. "Were you in on the decision to blow the train, or did Oliver ever mention my plan?"

Stanson's look was confused and innocent. "What plan did you have?"

"Never mind. I've got some advice for you; you can take it or leave it. And then I have a question."

"OK."

"Make evacuation plans. You're not going to hold the city against the regular army, and there is no way they are going to let you keep the mines. Retaking this city will be their top priority."

"You haven't seen our defense plans yet."

"I don't need to. This isn't an army; they're guerrillas. You can't fight a standard army on its own terms. Pack provisions and send them to our bases in the hills. Destroy what you can't take with you. When they retake the city—and you'll notice I did not say if—you want to leave them with an empty shell. Set charges in the mines, detonate and leave."

"Alistair, we've had these talks already. I'm sorry you weren't there—"

"You'll want informants among those who remain. Obviously, each man can decide for himself if he wants to risk staying or head for the hills. That's about it: blow the important parts and get out. Unless the entire government falls in the next fifty hours, any rebel left fighting in the city is going to be killed. That's my advice, take it or leave it. Frankly, I don't give much of a damn."

"You're leaving us," said Stanson with a tone of realization.

"You and Oliver are a pair of fools. We're not the first rebellion in history; there are lessons to be learned from the past if you care to study it."

"I'm sorry you feel that way, Alistair. Perhaps you didn't know I went to University—"

"That's a sick joke. If you think you learned more in a State classroom—Oh the hell with it!" He threw his hands up. "I'm finished trying to be heard. I've given you the best advice you're likely to get; take it or leave it. You, Oliver and Clever Johnny are never so dedicated to the rebellion that you don't have the ultimate prize on your minds. You want to replace the State that's going out, and you each have your own plans for running things."

"You're wrong," Stanson said, his eyes flashing anger. He leaned into Alistair and, his voice low, said, "Oliver and I have spoken of this. I'm the perfect man to be an advisor, with my education, and he's the perfect one to be the leader. He's already the face of the rebellion and people follow him naturally. Clever Johnny is out; Oliver and I have already talked about this. Now you can be a part of building a better State."

Alistair laughed because he didn't want to cry. It was a repressed and sickly laugh accompanied by a smile that was more of a grimace. "The lesson never gets learned. We keep doing the same thing over and over and over again. Is there no place I can go to escape the State?"

Stanson drew back, offended. "You think we won't do a better job of it?"

"I think any man who wants the power government has is unfit to wield it. And I think even if it didn't corrupt, it's dangerous to create anything with that kind of power, something anyone might control."

"Alistair," said Stanson with a shake of his head and a tone genuinely sad, "why don't you try to help from within rather than cast yourself out?"

"I hope you listen to my advice. Now, there is a fully equipped Civil Guard station here in the Palace. What floor can I find it on?"

From the safety, if not the comfort, of a ship's deck, Gerald stared over the waves at the city he had just abandoned. Not more than two miles away, it bled dark smoke from its many wounds, and the smoke slowly gathered in a pool above with only the slightest of ocean breezes to carry it away. Gerald solemnly contemplated the day's significance as he watched the black pall and held a blanket tightly around him. There were other refugees with him on the small fisherman's boat, but they had gone below deck for the comparative warmth there. Gerald, driven by a particular foreboding the others had no occasion to share, remained above. He did not turn when he heard footsteps nor glance aside at the man who sat down next to him.

"Leland and Rosalind are going over the archived records," the man said.

"Find anything?"

"Do you expect them too?"

"Yes," Gerald replied with a sigh.

"Looks like Harcourt was surfing around the system, looking into some sensitive information. On a day when the Bureau was closed."

"That's odd."

His companion nodded. "Yes, especially considering he was dead when he did it." At Gerald's shocked expression, the man said, "He was killed in the rioting earlier."

Gerald straightened up and his lips parted. "Ah...so that's it."

"What does that mean?"

"My brother was working with Harcourt," he said and even as he thought it he felt himself grow angry. "He's a bloody anarchist and I vouched for him! He swore he would..." He was too angry to finish the sentence. He grabbed at the back of his head and dug his nails into the skin. "That son of a bitch. That goddamn son of a bitch!" His chest was heaving. He was either on the point of exploding or collapsing.

His companion laid a hand on his shoulder but there was nothing appropriate to say. He lingered only a moment before he rose and went back below deck. Gerald remained where he was. He shivered but welcomed the punishment. It was less than would befall him once official reprimands were handed out. *My own brother,* he thought, deflated, his shoulders slumping and his head falling down until his chin touched his chest. *My own brother assassinated the President!*

☙❧

In the Civil Guard station Alistair found half a dozen rebels. Three were taking stock of the contents, another was seated at a computer station while two others stood over him, giving instructions. He froze when he recognized one of the men at the computer. His pale skin and his raven black hair, together with the sharp features of his face, were distinct and instantly recognizable. He was one of the men who accosted him the night of the Debate.

"So if it ever reads over sixty seven you'll have to use the other program," the pale man was saying, and as he finished he glanced up and saw Alistair. He too froze for an instant but then relaxed, looking back down at the young man sitting at the computer.

"Tom isn't it?" asked Alistair as he approached them.

The man seated at the station stopped and looked up, noticing the tenseness. The other who was standing, a larger man of middle age with reddish brown hair and beard starting to be overtaken by silver, just stared at Alistair.

"Tom was my partner," replied the one with pale skin, his voice as flat and stoic as on the night they met. "But it's nice to be remembered."

"You can probably imagine my surprise to find you here."

"You were a marine, weren't you?"

Alistair nodded.

"Well, I was a Civil Guard."

"But we're both on the same side now." Alistair grinned without humor.

"Welcome aboard, Alistair" the man next to the pale one greeted him, though it felt more like an attempt to establish pecking order. "I'm Clement and this is Cain. The pleasure's ours."

"You knew my name?"

"We did."

"But I didn't know yours."

"Apparently not."

"Gentlemen, there's an excellent reason for that. Don't condescend to welcome me into my own home." Alistair's hard, direct gaze was met with a pair of set jaws and narrowed eyes. "Brad Stanson is on his way to the palace larder. He requires your assistance down there. Feel free to recruit some help along the way…you've got some heavy lifting to do."

Clement's salute was as respectful as if he had spit, and Cain didn't bother with the formality at all. The young man at the computer, who had stared at the confrontation, now avoided Alistair's gaze. Unfortunately, there was nothing for him to do so a second later he stood.

"Perhaps I should help in the larder," he mumbled.

"Have a seat," Alistair suggested with a heavy hand on his shoulder. "What's your name?"

"Dave."

"Dave, I need you to help me with something."

Reaching into a pocket, Alistair produced a rolled strip of leather. When he unrolled it he revealed a piece of bloodstained cloth.

"I need an ID on the DNA in this blood."

Dave nodded and took the proffered cloth, rising from his chair and leading Alistair to a machine in the back corner of the offices. He laid the cloth down flat on the machine's transparent top and positioned what appeared to be a lamp over it, then pressed a button on the side and a red light from the lamp flashed once. He moved to examine a monitor and Alistair peered over his shoulder. There was a flashing code right above a list of names, including his own. The others he did not recognize.

"We got DNA from six subjects," Dave reported. "Including you. I don't know what X-5 means but that's the blood's owner."

"It means he works for the State and we need a special code to see his identity."

"Do we have the code?"

"We do not."

"Sorry I couldn't help," said Dave, taking the strip of cloth and holding it out for Alistair.

"Not done just yet. Come with me." Alistair led Dave to another machine nearby. This one was box shaped like the first but had a small door on the front and on top, instead of a monitor, a 3D display. On the right side there was a seat and a computer with its own smaller 3D display. "Can you operate this?"

"Probably."

"Good. It's a DNA decoder. It can read a DNA sequence of any sort and project a probable image of the subject on the monitor. But it takes a while."

"How long?"

"Maybe a few hours and I need to leave. You stay here and get me an image of this guy." So saying he opened the door and placed the cloth on a small stand inside. Then he closed the door and pressed the ignition.

Dave sat down at the computer and switched on the monitor, taking a second to read the prompts.

"What assumptions?" he asked, his fingers poised over the keyboard.

"Healthy, adequately fed from infancy on. Active lifestyle, no serious diseases. Climate...I don't know. We'll assume he grew up in a temperate climate...it shouldn't matter too much. He's not overweight——"

"Diet?"

"Just give him a standard Aldran diet."

"Age?"

"Forty cycles. Just a guess. When it's finished give me some alternatives too."

Dave finished typing and the scanner ran, spilling a tidal wave of technical readouts onto the 3D display.

"Human," said Dave after a moment of study. On the 3D monitor on top of the machine a generic and featureless humanoid shape in pure white appeared. "Male," he said a moment later as the humanoid shape grew broader shoulders, greater musculature and a phallus. "Caucasian...trace of American Indigenous." The white became a peach color and the skull shape was altered to reflect the new information.

Alistair patted Dave on both shoulders. "Stay with it. I'll be back in a bit."

"Are you going after the resistance?" asked Dave, turning in the chair to look at Alistair. "There are some groups still fighting——"

"I'm going to see my parents. I'll see you when I get back."

36

When Alistair left the Mayor's Palace the sun was nearing the horizon. Someone had thought to douse the flames of the wrecked tanks. There were a few pedestrians about but they moved with less energy than before, and the pockets of resistance were growing fewer in number. Only one distinct gunfight could he hear, and its desultory snap and crackle was a long way off in the eastern part of the city. It could have been mistaken for a distant fireworks display.

He headed due south and found himself in an empty part of the city quite untouched by the day's battle. Absent were the craters where shells hit and exploded, the trails of pockmarks left by bullets on walls, the black smudges where fire had burned. Instead, there were the boarded windows, the foundational cracks in abandoned buildings, the layers of accumulated filth.

There was little wind but as the sun sank a small breeze grew. He tucked his nose under the collar of his coat and his gloved hands into his coat pockets. Oblivious to the world around him, he was likely saved by the vacancy of the area. In a more trafficked street, the footsteps behind him would not have caught his attention.

He turned to see two masked men some yards back. There was a noticeable break in their strides when Alistair turned to regard them. They exchanged glances and he tensed his muscles. When one of the men reached behind his back, Alistair did not wait to see what he was going after.

With no alley nearby, he delivered a powerful kick to a front door which burst inward. A shot rang out as he jumped across the threshold and into the house. His forceful leap carried him into a small foyer and, belly on the floor, into the far wall. He threw up his hands to cushion the impact but still received a good knock on the forehead. With no time to clear his head, he dashed to his right through a dining room and kitchen and into a back living room. Grabbing a chair from the corner of the apparently occupied house, he shattered a back window and jumped through. He heard the simultaneous noises of his clothing tearing on a shard of glass and the footsteps of the assassins gaining entrance to the foyer.

The small backyard was contained by a rusted chain link fence and was bordered by other backyards. Alistair moved right and tried to hurdle the fence, but the soft snowy ground did not provide an ideal launching pad and his feet caught the top as he passed over, sending him headfirst into the snow on the other side. Back on his feet in a flash, he doubled back and came to the street where he first sensed his assailants, darting across it and between two houses on the other side. Just as he passed between them, another shot rang out and the bullet passed through a window. Racing into another backyard, and this time placing his left hand on the fence top, he jumped over another chain link fence into another backyard. He cut left, then right, taking a jagged path until he emerged onto another street parallel to the first.

He cut south to move another house over, and then again passed into a backyard, this time without being shot at. *There's no one in the city who can catch me on foot,* he thought, as much to give himself courage as anything. He reached the next street over, but one of the assailants anticipated his zigzag pattern and, from the other side of the street, fired off a round at him only an instant after he ducked back behind a house.

"He's going south!" the man yelled as the ex marine kicked out a back window and entered yet another home, this one clearly abandoned.

He raced to the front and came out the main door, dashed across the street and repeated the process, thus avoiding the long open lanes of side yards. Finally coming to a street running diagonally alongside a small ravine, he turned southwest, hearing a belated shot ring out as he flashed across the first open lane. Spying a window whose glass was removed, he went to the house preceding it, kicked in its front door and then hauled himself inside the open window.

Once he dropped into the cold empty home, he lay for just a moment to pacify his aching legs before he rose and, finding the stairs, ascended to the second story and found a room with a view to the street in front. He surveyed the ground below, noting the snow around the houses was well enough trodden that he had not left a distinct path. He retrieved his firearm from the under the layers of his winter clothing and loaded the magazine with his few remaining rounds. A moment later, the men emerged onto the diagonal street from different side yards, each pointing a gun. They immediately searched the ravine and began to sweep the area, moving southwest towards Alistair's position. Eventually, they approached the broken front door. Alistair, not wanting to give away his position, elected not to fire.

A minute passed and he wiped away from the window the frozen condensation from his breath. Another passed and the assailants reemerged from the side yard and onto the street. They scanned the area again but less thoroughly. After a brief exchange of words they holstered their weapons and headed northeast. Alistair watched them until they were out of sight, waited another couple minutes and crept out of his hideout, his muscles quivering when relief chased the adrenaline away.

A half hour later, he was ascending the stairs in his parents' apartment building. He saw no one and heard no sound. When no one answered his knock at the door, he let himself in with his key, feeling a growing worry. After stripping off his winter apparel and dumping it on the couch, he heard footsteps in the hallway. Gripping his firearm, he stepped to the kitchen's entrance and waited for the door to open, breathing a sigh of relief when Nigel and Mary entered. Their haggard and fatigued faces came to life when they saw their son, and Mary rushed to hug him.

"Alistair, we couldn't find any of you," she sobbed as she buried her face in her son's chest.

"Do you know where Gerald is?" his father asked, trying to find a part of Alistair he could embrace which his wife had not already claimed. He settled for an affectionate grip on the shoulder.

"I don't know where he is."

"We can't get through to Katherine either," said Mary, finally pulling away from him but still grasping his upper arms.

"All communication is down," Nigel confirmed.

"There's no reason to worry about Katherine," said Alistair. "She's in Rendral...about the safest place on the planet right now."

"And Gerald?" his mother asked.

"Gerald will be fine."

Nigel studied his son a moment and then sighed. "So how mixed up in this are you?"

"I was one of the ringleaders."

"Was?"

Alistair nodded. "Was."

Katherine Ashley was one of dozens in the Great Hall of the Civil Palace in the heart of Rendral, Aldra's capital and largest city. The principally marble hall ran north/south, parallel to the Palace proper, and was open to the elements on its north and south sides. Its eastern façade was checkered with vibrant stain glass windows, all of which were cracked open to admit the warm breeze that, even days after her arrival, she was still thrilled to feel envelope her. The ceiling, decorated with one large mural of the first landing on Aldra and the planting of what would become the Aldran flag, was fifty yards overhead, and the rectangular room alone could have accommodated the entire first floor of the Mayor's Palace of Arcarius. Statues placed in an ordered, rectangular pattern lined the floor of the hall, each twenty yards from its neighbors, and audiphones were installed on the southern wall. As the myriad bureaucrats, Civil Guard, politicians and all other manner of visitor passed by, she stood at one of the audiphones with the receiver in hand.

"Are Mom and Dad still there?" she asked, stress making her voice quaver.

"I'm sure they're fine...but yes, they're in the city."

"What about Alistair?"

There was a pause on the other end.

"I haven't seen him but I think he got out during the fighting."

"If you haven't seen him why do you think that?"

"I'm sure he'll be fine, Kath. And I'm fine. And none of the fighting was near Mom and Dad's."

"Where are you staying?"

"We left on a boat. We were waiting around for a while to see how it turned out but then we made for the main continent. Right now we're in a small town east of Avon."

Katherine sighed and rubbed her knuckles against her forehead. "Will you be going back soon?"

"The talk is the army is going to be sent in soon. I'll be back when the city's secured. Keep trying to call Mom and Dad in the meantime."

"I'll see what I can do. Phone use is restricted right now."

"I know. God, Kath, I haven't talked to you since you left. Is everything going well?"

"The project is great...I don't give a damn about that right now but it's going great."

"Listen, you can't do anything about this in Rendral. You can either worry yourself sick or think positive. There's no reason to think anything bad...there's thousands of people in Arcarius and about a hundred got killed today."

Katherine glanced at the timer on the audiophone. "Listen, Gerald, I'm almost out of time. Keep safe." The clock neared zero so she rushed her last words. "We're running a big experiment next week, when I'm done I'll head back for—"

"Kath, don't let this—"

The phone clicked and the call was cut off. Feeling alone and homesick, Katherine dropped the receiver back in its slot and, barely managing to raise her feet off the polished marble floor, listlessly crossed the Great Hall to the Palace's entrance.

☙ ❧

"...but I don't think they're planning on moving out," said Mary as she whisked through the room, taking empty cups and dishes with her to the kitchen. "But we can't let that stop us. Every time there's a problem here we get left without heat or food or something else. And your father's joints get worse every winter."

Alistair turned his attention from the window and the setting sun and looked sharply at his father. "Are your joints hurting, Dad?"

Nigel dismissed the idea with a wave of his hand. "No more than anyone else's my age."

Mary swept back into the living room and began to replace the pottery and photos on the coffee table. "Don't listen to him. He needs warmer weather. Now that the restaurant was taken from us I don't see any reason to stay here. Katherine's in Rendral, we could go there. Or any place warmer than here."

"Gerald has a job here—" Nigel began.

"Gerald can put in for a transfer," said Mary with a firm tone as she plopped down on the couch next to her husband.

"And that's what we're going to have to do if we want to leave," Nigel reminded her. "Get a permit."

"Oh, we'll get a permit. Goodness sakes. How can they keep an old couple here in the north? It's not as if we're a part of the war effort. Alistair, they'll let us move if we want to, won't they?"

"I'm sure Gerald could see to it if there were any problems. Mom, when you were a kid you didn't have to put in a transfer request when you wanted to move, did you?" Mary shook her head. "Things are different now," Nigel said softly.

"Yeah, they're different now. If what you want doesn't fit in with the State's vision, then your plans have to change." His anger built as he spoke. "Everything else, the propaganda, the brainwashing, the slogans, the bureaucracy...it all grows out of one central fact: someone wants to impose on everyone else, and Dad's joints have to ache because of it."

Alistair sharply turned his head back to face the window and he glowered at the world outside.

"Gerald says they do their best to accommodate requests," said Nigel, his gentle tone a foil to Alistair's heat and anger. "I'm sure they'll allow us to move south."

"You shouldn't have to ask," his son almost whispered.

There was a moment of silence as there always was after Alistair punctuated a discussion with a bit of passion, and then he glanced at the clock on the wall and reluctantly stood up, like one who is awakened too early in the morning.

"I need to head back," he explained and donned his winter apparel.

"Head back where?" his father asked.

"Mayor's Palace. Or what was formerly the Mayor's Palace and will be again in short order. Listen," Alistair looked his father directly in the eyes, "stake out a corner in the building's basement and be ready to head down there at a moment's notice."

"What's going to happen?" his mother asked.

"The army will be sent in to retake the city. I don't expect there to be much fighting in this area…but just be ready. Just in case."

He gave his dad a firm embrace and his mother a pair of pecks on the cheeks before he was out the door, heading down the stairwell, out the entrance hall and into the winter evening. He was considering taking a more direct route back but to the west, somewhere in the vicinity of Rendral Way, he heard what sounded like a large group of laborers. Curious, he decided to head there instead.

When he reached the boulevard, he saw scores of rebels breaking up the road and digging trenches whose edges they lined with anything that would do to stop shrapnel or a bullet. Every thirty yards or so all along the boulevard the trenches were being dug. Not realizing his mouth was open in shock, he regarded the project in silence. He was moved to interfere, to try to impose reason, but finally just shook his head and, with a sigh of equal parts exasperation and resignation, made for the northeast.

He had not gone far when he spotted Henry Miller among the diggers, his slight frame hard at work pitching dirt over his shoulder. Alistair called out to him. Henry stopped and peered around a bit before he caught sight of Alistair. His eyebrows shot up in surprise and, dropping his shovel, he clambered out of the ditch.

"I haven't seen you in forever," breathed Henry. "Did…" Henry stopped, reluctant to speak. "Is it true about you and Oliver?"

"What did you hear?"

"Well…I heard you had a bit of a quarrel."

"A very short quarrel. I socked him one good in the face and it was over."

Henry was at a loss for words.

"Well…all because of the train?"

Alistair glared sharply at Henry. "Who told you that?"

"I talked with Oliver."

Nodding, Alistair looked out over the workers falling deeper into shadow. "This is the most colossal waste of time since the Pyramids."

"We're buildings defenses for the city—"

"You're wasting your damn time. We don't have the men to trench the city, or the time to set our defenses so we don't get flanked. We don't have the artillery to support it all and we don't have the air power to keep from getting bombed half to death before the invasion even starts. There is a long history of guerrilla warfare and it's not a big secret how to do it successfully. If somebody wants to…" He stopped, looked up to the heavens and let out a deep sigh. "Forget it. I'm not going to argue about it. If you're smart you'll come back to the Mayor's Palace with me, grab some supplies and head for the hills."

Before he got anything coherent out of his mouth, Henry started to speak a couple times and looked indecisively between Alistair and his fellows. Finally, he managed, "Alistair...I don't...you're going out in the hills on your own?"

"For now. I'm going to cross the channel as soon as I can and look for something to do on the mainland." He started walking again.

"You're leaving the rebellion?"

"I'm starting my own," he called back, leaving Henry to stare after him for a few moments before, head hanging low and features twisted into a disturbed expression, his friend shuffled back to his trench and grabbed his shovel again.

Midway through his trek back to the Palace, the lights popping on here and there in response to the growing dark suddenly turned off all at once. *Did they even bother about the power generators?* he wondered. Overhead, an aircraft silently hovered overhead. Its body invisible against the black sky, it was like a team of light points circling the city far above, maintaining a rigid formation. *And we are powerless to stop the reconnaissance.*

It was not until he was in the presence of the dark hulk of the Mayor's Palace that Alistair realized what the power outage meant for his DNA test. With a curse he broke into a run, reassured some alarmed guards at the entrance that he was not attacking them, and tore through the Palace until he was back at the station. Most of the Palace was pitch black but some candles were lit and scattered around. Dave was still there, along with one other, and they were both crouching over a piece of equipment in the shape of a box. They turned to look at Alistair as he jogged in.

"I got a generator," Dave explained.

"Excellent work, soldier."

Dave's partner plugged in a wire and, pressing a button, started the generator humming. The DNA constructor came back to life.

"It should automatically save the work as it goes," Alistair prompted.

Dave sat down and replied, "Yeah, it finished about an hour ago. Let's see if I can call up the images..."

He stroked the keys for a moment and tables of information flashed over the 3D pad. Finally, a naked human male appeared. A table of data next to him indicated he was just over six feet tall and weighed about 200 pounds assuming a healthy, lean body weight. His hair was reddish brown and a generous covering of it grew over his arms, chest, belly and legs.

"Give him a short beard and a broken nose sometime in his past. And make him forty five."

Dave typed in the instructions. Rising from his chair then, he came round to stand next to Alistair, as did his companion.

"What is this for?" he asked.

"Something very important, so keep your lips sealed."

"Is that...?" Dave started to ask, pointing at the generated image.

Alistair nodded. "The guy who was in here earlier today? Yes. That's Clement."

37

The dusky interior of the Palace, filled with rebels with the grime of battle, grew more tolerable to smell as the powerless building lost its heat and the seeping cold did what cold always does to odor. With the loss of heat, the squatters in the Palace lost their momentum. They looted what they could, celebrated for a time and now settled down in small camps, waiting for someone else to do something.

One of the few signs of activity was a group of men carrying wounded companions along a hallway. When they passed in front of a ray of light emanating from a room with a generator, Alistair spied Ryan Wellesley struggling with an inert rebel dripping a trail of blood. He hustled to catch up and reached the group just as they entered the Palace's main banquet hall. Wordlessly, he fell into step with Wellesley, shared a nod with him, and halved his burden.

The banquet hall was converted into an infirmary, though not a comfortable one. A couple dozen cots were rounded up, but most of the wounded were lying on the hard floor, on blankets if they were lucky. Despite the dropping temperature the room smelled of many human odors, blood most noticeably. The few bulbs, powered by a dilapidated generator, gave just enough light to turn most forms into silhouettes weaving in and out of long shadows. Like so many miniature geysers, the wounded were lined up on the floor spouting their cloudy breath, and the sundry moans of the conscious reverberated softly throughout.

As Alistair eased his charge onto the bare floor at the end of a row of bodies, he spotted Gregory Lushington in a heated argument with an armed rebel. Gesticulating wildly, the young doctor was a stark contrast to the laconic soldier who merely shook his head every so often, a gesture which sparked a renewed outburst from Gregory. When Alistair drew nearer, dimly aware that Wellesley was tagging along, he could make out the words Gregory flung at the man in a sort of hushed yell.

"…I'm not taking care of a sprained ankle while somebody bleeds to death!" The guard shrugged and looked bored. "I didn't agree to any restrictions when I came here, now give me the supplies!"

The rebel lazily ran his tongue across his bottom row of teeth, pushing his lower lip out, and shrugged again. "Take it up with him," he said, indicating Alistair with a nod of his head before languidly spinning on his heel and walking away.

Gregory turned his head and, seeing Alistair, a relieved expression crossed his face. "They're not letting me treat any Civil Guard," he said, grabbing his friend by the arms. "I've done what I can for the rebels and now they want me applying bandages while the Guardsmen die. There are about a half dozen who are ten minutes from bleeding to death but I might be able to save some if they let me act now. Tell them to give me the supplies to treat them!"

"Ryan, take him to the supplies."

"They're this way," was Wellesley's reply and he set off.

"Thank you," said Gregory with the utmost sincerity and he squeezed Alistair's shoulder before following Wellesley.

Alistair caught the attention of the rebel with whom Gregory had been arguing and called him over with a crooking of his finger. "This place is filling up pretty quickly. Why don't you grab a couple soldiers who can apply a field dressing and get the walking wounded out of here? Find another room for them somewhere else."

"I can't do much more than put a band aid on."

"Buddy, we've got bullets in chest cavities and I count about eight trained medical personnel. Take the ones who can move and treat anybody you think you can help more than harm." The man repressed a sigh but nodded. "And put the safety on that goddamn rifle."

The man stopped and checked his safety, gave a look of unconcerned surprise, clicked the safety into place and nodded his thanks.

Alistair was about to bring some sense and order to the distribution of cots and blankets when a voice stopped him.

"You know, we've only got a limited stock of medical supplies."

Alistair turned to see Oliver, his bulbous nose a ghastly mess and his eye sockets purple patches surrounding blood shot eyes.

"I decided not to use any for an injury I received today."

"You're a martyr for the cause," Alistair replied in a low and even tone, not quite unfriendly. "There are a few train attendants and engineers who are quite beyond any medical attention. You're not getting an apology. I'll deck you a second time long before that happens."

"I don't expect an apology," Oliver responded in an equally even tone. "Look, Alistair, every Civil Guard we patch up is one less of ours we can fix up and one more soldier we have to shoot again. Think of it in those terms. Why the hell would we treat the enemy?"

"Because it feels like the right thing to do," Gregory interjected as he brushed by Oliver with a bundle in his arms. Dumping the bundle on the floor next to an unconscious Civil Guard, he knelt down to attend to him.

"Just stabilize him," Oliver ordered. "This isn't a luxury hospital."

"No hospital is."

"And don't waste your time or our supplies on anyone who isn't ready to die. Or on anyone who isn't going to live."

Oliver waited for a response but Gregory was finished with the conversation. Turning to Alistair, he said, "Can you and I talk for a moment?"

"I think we need to."

"Follow me."

Oliver took Alistair out of the makeshift infirmary, past bored rebels playing cards in the candlelight, to a smaller chamber just down the hall. Lighting a match, he touched it to a candle's wick and closed the door. Alistair's keen night vision scanned the gloom and he saw what must have been some sort of smoking room to judge from the wrecked furniture piled against the back wall. Opulent though it was meant to be, even the ruling class had endured privations of late as evidenced by the handful of accumulated cigarette burns on the old carpet. Oliver set the candle down in the middle of the room.

There was a moment when Alistair thought he felt Oliver soften. Perhaps the big man's shoulders slumped a bit, or his furrowed brow loosened, but the softening proved to be transitory. When he looked into the cold, hard expression of his erstwhile friend he was left with no doubt how Oliver was going to proceed.

"I did what I did for good reason. I tried to tell you before: you are too important to the cause to lose hijacking a train we can blow up and send a stronger message."

"What message is that?"

"That we're not to be trifled with. This is a war and we have to project strength."

Alistair shook his head. "You don't help the cause with acts like that. Right now colonels and generals are gathering in Avon and they're deciding to send the same message and project strength. They'll attack without mercy, and if you survive you'll no doubt decide you weren't hard enough, so the next time you'll be even more vicious. Before long the violence escalates so far, you're stuck in a war with both sides competing to commit the most atrocities. In the meantime you lose the broad support of the people; the general populace views you both as monsters."

"What would you have me do, Alistair? Waste my best soldiers? Let them come at me with all they have and return their punches with a halfhearted slap? You think that's how to win a war?"

"Did you really bring me in here to have this argument?"

"I brought you in here to get your advice. Whatever you think of me, I'm hoping you're still fighting The Realists. So tell me how to fight them." Oliver brought his fists up in front of his chest in a gesture half supplication and half anger.

"I've been giving you advice and you refuse to hear it. If you try and fight like a professional army you are going to get swept off the face of the planet. YOU…CAN'T…WIN… THAT…WAY. This has to be a guerrilla war, and that gives you all sorts of advantages. A guerrilla army costs nothing and requires little organization. They don't have to be housed, trained, fed and paid for. Militias form when they are needed from inspired volunteers and then they disperse when they must, leaving nothing for the State to attack. They can do this because they have the support of the general populace, a support you undermined today. It might be one thing to assassinate a hated dictator, but those innocents you killed have wives, children, family and friends. With every decision like that you erode the support you need to be effective. You shouldn't have done it simply because it was monstrous, but if your conscience isn't enough, at least try to make smarter plays.

"You can start by dispersing. This is the beginning of the war; you won't hold any cities until the end. And blow the mines up to cripple their supplies."

"I don't know if we have enough cloaks to hide in the hills."

"Will you listen to me? I didn't say retreat, I said disperse. Go back to your homes. *You* can't, obviously, and neither can I now, but the rest of the men can take care of themselves. That's the advantage: you don't have to plan a full scale retreat. Decentralize! Let each man take care of himself. If they're dedicated, they'll be back when you need them. A guerrilla army works best when it can't be distinguished from the general populace. So disperse; destroy the mines and disperse. It would be a huge victory so early on."

Oliver studied Alistair for a time. "How will they come at us?"

"I have no idea. If you leave it won't matter. On the way here I saw a reconnaissance craft overhead. They are analyzing our capabilities right now. They may bombard us from the sea while landing paratroopers behind our lines…they could land two forces south and north of the city and slice through us…they may batter us with an air assault first…or they might just try an all out landing on the harbor and run over us. It depends on which General is in charge and what suits his fancy, but even the dimmest plan is guaranteed success. They won't let those mines be taken. And another thing: I'd get the hell out of the Mayor's Palace. The term 'sitting ducks' comes to mind."

"There is some news that might interest you," Oliver said with an air of changing the subject. "We cracked into the Civil Guard's computers. Turns out they have a file on Henry. He is listed as one of their double agents. He's been trying to infiltrate us."

Alistair actually felt as if he had been slugged in the gut. "There's no…no doubt about this?"

Oliver shrugged his shoulders. "There really isn't much he could tell them. That's not what bothers me."

"I've been targeted for assassination," Alistair said in an abrupt change of subject. "The assassins are here with us. I got an image of one from a DNA sample."

"You don't think Henry…?"

Alistair shook his head. "Henry didn't even know we were involved until recently. And he wouldn't do that."

"How sure are you?"

"It's someone else."

"So what do we do about Henry?"

"Keep him. Feed him false information." With that, Alistair moved towards the door, pulling it partially open. "I'm leaving. I'm going to stock up on some supplies and head out. But I am done coordinating with you. Our goals may coincide for the present and we might wind up helping each other, but I'm not fighting this war to put you on a throne."

"That's not what I'm looking for, Alistair!"

"The assassins are Cain and Clement. We used the DNA constructor to make an image of Clement and it's pretty accurate. Let Henry be; the other two I would take out as soon as I could." He took his first step out the door but stopped in mid-stride. "I saw Elizabeth. She was at the train station." Oliver did not reply but his body stiffened. "She's alright. She's mad as hell. I don't know where she's going."

Oliver remained silent and Alistair shut the door behind him as he walked out.

38

Alistair had not gone far when he heard the sound of jogging footsteps and Ryan Wellesley calling his name. Turning, he saw his companion and a tall, gaunt figure accompanying him. He felt a flicker of something he thought might be recognition, and then he realized he was looking at Eddy Davidson. His formerly fleshy body had melted down and his skin looked older and more weathered, but there was no doubt once Alistair made the connection. With a couple giant strides, he rushed to meet his brother-in-law and gripped him by the shoulders.

"Alistair," said Eddy in a whisper and on his lips the ex marine saw a strained version of the affable smile he remembered from years ago.

"Greg recognized him," Ryan said. "Found him in the prison…he said to take him to you."

Eddy had always been corpulent. Just shy of emaciated now, he looked at Alistair with a haunted and distrusting look, a general distrust of the world around him. His thick brown locks were shorn so that he was almost bald, and when he attempted a smile Alistair noticed a handful of teeth were missing or severely chipped. His skin was rough and wrinkles made him look older than he was.

"Have you been here the whole time?" Alistair finally asked. Without precisely knowing what they might be, he felt like there were other things he should have said first, but he felt out of his element. He imagined Katherine scolding him for his awkwardness.

Eddy shook his head as if to say he didn't know. "I've been transported all around but they never let me see where I was. I was drugged—" Eddy's voice caught and his face darkened. "Where's Katherine?" There was a longing in his voice that almost made it crack.

"She's in Rendral."

He let out a sigh of relief that only just stopped from turning into tears.

"She was chosen to work on an experiment for The Science Academy."

A slight bulge in both temples told Alistair that Eddy was gritting his teeth. When he spoke it was an unsteady whisper. "They told me she was…" Swallowing once, Eddy dropped his gaze to the ground and exhaled slowly. "I want to see her."

"I'm going there soon," Alistair told him, making an extemporaneous change of plans and eliciting a sharp look from Wellesley. He patted Eddy's shoulders. "I'll take you down to see her. I'll be taking my parents too."

Looking back up at Alistair, Eddy managed a somewhat brighter smile this time. "My God, you've gotten big. How long has it been?"

"Too long. I was off on Kaldis with the army for…we'll catch up when we have more time. Right now just go back to the infirmary and have a lie down. Get something to eat. I'm going to gather some supplies and see about where we can stay for the next couple days."

Eddy nodded and, shuffling his feet, managed to turn around. "Great to see you, Alistair," he said without looking back, almost too softly to hear.

Alistair watched him shuffle along for a moment and then turned to Wellesley. "What are your plans?"

Shrugging like it didn't matter, Ryan said, "I'll go with you." When Alistair raised an eyebrow he continued, "The idiots running this show are just gonna get everybody killed. What the hell. Never been to Rendral. How we gonna get there?"

Alistair ran his hand through his hair. "I don't know. I may have taken on more than I can manage. With Eddy that weak and both my parents…I don't know…I certainly can't take my parents on the kind of cross country trek I had in mind."

"Just getting off the island is going to be difficult."

"I could do it if I were by myself."

"If it were just the two of us," Wellesley corrected.

Alistair curled up one side of his mouth in an apologetic smile. "We'll cross that channel when we come to it. In the meantime let's stock up on supplies."

They had no problem finding and raiding one of the supply rooms, although it did not yield nearly what Alistair would have liked. Modestly armed, they returned to the infirmary to pick up Eddy. Greg was there waiting for them.

"Alistair, I need your help again. Can you escort a few of the patients to a small clinic on the north side of town?"

"I suppose."

"I'd just feel safer if you were there. I got a hold of a bus we need to put them on. It'll be here any moment." Greg started to turn away and then added, "Henry's driving."

"Henry?"

"He came here looking for you. I asked him to drive the bus. I told him you'd be coming along."

Gregory Lushington was circumspect to a fault when it came to his patients. Alistair had transported many a wounded comrade in arms from all manner of battlefield and knew the basics of stabilization, but he never imagined how meticulously cautious the young doctor could be. He stood around trying not to tap his feet while Gregory took precautions he considered excessive and all the while, like a tingle on the back of his neck, he could feel the inevitable invasion creeping towards them.

It was with great relief that he finally slammed shut the back door of the bus and took his place on the grimy, frozen floor at the back. Stripped of all seats, it now carried ten wounded men, Gregory, an old nurse from Gregory's clinic, Wellesley, Eddy Davidson, Alistair and Henry, who from the driver's seat was trying to catch Alistair's eye.

Henry put the bus in motion and it rumbled over the snowy courtyard in front of the Palace, its one functioning headlight slicing through the dark of night in a lightless city. Wellesley and Alistair rocked back and forth with the rhythm of the bus while Gregory and the nurse were careful to monitor the patients. Eddy curled up with a blanket and was asleep before they went fifty yards. Leaning forward to reach for the window of the back door, Alistair cleared off some frost with a meaty hand, opening a small viewing portal.

As Henry drove and the Palace receded, Alistair contemplated its dark form. The flags at the summit of the mammoth edifice had been struck and the flagpoles torn down. A *symbolic gesture he has time for,* he thought. *But God forbid he should find some personnel to run the power genera-tors.* Suddenly, his body tensed and he sat upright.

"It's started."

Over the hum of the engine and the clunk of the vehicle bouncing, Alistair's soft voice carried only far enough for Wellesley to hear him. His comrade in arms looked up sharply from the floor. Squinting, he could not detect all the details which were plain to Alistair, but he did see points of light hovering over the Palace and slowly descending towards it. Alistair saw the hovering platforms themselves and even the armed soldiers they carried, many taking up positions around the edges.

The platforms descended unimpeded for a time. The Palace was so still, Alistair suspected there was indeed some central command being exerted in restraint. Then, the resistors in the Palace opened fire, causing the force shields protecting the platforms' underbellies to flicker furiously with each projectile turned aside.

Not every bullet was deflected. Sparks and small explosions of light erupted until the space about the Palace resembled a fireworks display and one platform burned. The hovering troop carriers withdrew to a safer distance, save the one on fire. Not rapidly, but in a timely enough manner for a ragtag band of rebels, all fire from the Palace was directed at the damaged platform. It was motionless for a while until, in a single instant, it went from hovering troop carrier to dead weight hurtling towards the earth. It landed with a cacophonous crash and lay burning on the ground.

By now all the conscious occupants of the bus were alerted to the battle. Save for Gregory, who continued his monitoring unperturbed, and Henry, who was forced to mind his driving, the able passengers hastily cleared the nearly opaque frost from the windows of the bus to get a better look at what was transpiring.

"Good heavens," breathed the nurse.

"They're taking it to 'em," said Wellesley with approval. "*We're* taking it," he quickly amended.

From four of the outdoor terraces on the upper levels, there came the larger flashes of a bigger caliber weapon. Portable cannons now bombarded the force fields. There was a general buzz of wonder and approval inside the bus.

"It's not a bad plan," Alistair grudgingly conceded.

"The army doesn't dare destroy the Mayor's Palace," said Wellesley. "And Oliver knows it."

"They didn't come to destroy it, but they will as soon as they decide it isn't worth the trouble Oliver's giving them. At that point they'll fire a missile from a satellite and build a new Palace later. Our boys had better be out before then."

By this point the bus had put some distance between them and the battle and, as it wandered through empty neighborhoods, their view of the fight was increasingly disturbed by houses and other buildings. At one point they could clearly see a second platform crashing down but soon after their view was permanently cut off, though when the nurse cracked open one of the windows they could still hear the battle. They could also hear fighting by the harbor.

Eventually, the bus crawled out of the city proper and into the north foothills. Alistair chafed at the pace but was impotent to do anything about it. The heater finally managed to bring some warmth to the vehicle such that they could no longer see their breath and the frost on the windows melted. The city below, as their ascent slowly revealed it to them, was a display of pinpoints of light. A couple dozen troop transport platforms were in transit above the city. Lines of tracer fire described great arcs in the night sky while the occasional flash of cannon and turret fire mixed with a handful of explosions in the southern part. Like an implacable glacier, the light show moved slowly yet steadily north, pushing rebel resistance back when it did not overtake and surround tiny pockets of it.

"How long until they overtake us, I wonder?" mused Wellesley out loud.

"One way or another we'll be gone before it does," said Alistair. "I'm more concerned about any troops already in the north to trap fleeing rebels."

"We can always ditch our weapons and wait it out in the city."

"That option is not available to me."

When the bus finally pulled into the clinic's parking lot, they were surprised to discover it filled with distraught people. The headlight swept over the crowd as the bus turned in. Many of them were walking wounded, their arms in slings or their heads bandaged, while others were uninjured but wandering aimlessly, perhaps there with a friend or relative or maybe recently made homeless. Several metal barrels held fires around which the cold and weary gathered, and a few munched on some meager rations while a stray snowflake or two floated to the ground.

When Alistair popped open the back door and hopped out, followed closely by Ryan Wellesley, he heard whispers run through the crowd.

"Are the Civil Guard coming back?" asked a voice.

"There's some fighting in the south," Ryan acknowledged while Alistair ducked his head and went to help Gregory unload the injured.

"How soon will they be here?" asked another.

Ryan shrugged while shaking his head and went to assist with the wounded. With the same maddeningly slow pace, Gregory directed them as they carried the injured into the warmth and relative protection of the clinic. When a few of the staff ventured outside to help, the process was accomplished with greater alacrity. After Alistair passed the last stretcher through the entrance, he let out a breath he felt he had been holding since agreeing to help Greg. His relief lasted only until he turned around.

Standing a couple feet away was a slight young woman, her filthy face and gnarled hair lit by the soft glow of the lights at the front entrance. Her nose was red and running, and red streaks crisscrossed over the whites of her eyes. Her mouth was parted as she stared at Alistair. It was Louise Downing.

"Alistair?" she asked as if not comprehending what she was seeing. Her gaze rested for a moment on the many weapons packed around Alistair's person and then her surprise turned to anger.

"You're a rebel!" said the normally diffident girl. "We let you into our lab. You killed the mayor!"

Any argument or protest Alistair might have formed was lost in the furious throbbing in his head. Speechless, he tried to move into the crowd but found that all the stragglers in the parking lot moved swiftly out of his way, denying him refuge. As he went to the parking lot's edge, and to the hillside leading down to the city, Louise followed, relentless in her tirade.

"You murdering bastard!" she cried, tears streaming down her face. "We trusted you and you attacked us. You killed the mayor!" She slugged Alistair in the back and for her efforts received a sprained wrist that made her hiss in pain and cradle the injured part against her chest.

Alistair stepped over the bank of snow created when the parking lot was plowed and, feeling less scrutinized in the dark edge of the crowd, turned on Louise and said, "I didn't know they were going to kill him. In fact I insisted they not do it and I was betrayed."

"*You* were betrayed!?"

"A lot more people than just the mayor were killed," Alistair sternly said, having recovered his composure enough to mount a defense. "A lot more people who deserved it a lot less than he did."

Louise's shoulders dropped. The anguish on her face communicated everything.

"My only fault was to trust some people who didn't deserve it. You are not going to shame me, Louise. I tricked you and everyone else to do what had to be done. Rebellion isn't an act a man commits lightly. Rather than cry for the mayor, ask to what extent he was complicit in the rape of Aldra. How did things get to the point that a rebellion actually became a possibility?"

Louise shook her head and, still cradling her wrist, turned on her heel and left Alistair to stand in the snow. He was so shaken from the unexpected and public scene that he did not notice Gregory follow him as he went to the edge of the hill to stand next to a pine tree and, observing the dark expanse of the city before him, calm himself. He didn't hear Gregory's footsteps in the snow and nearly jumped when the young doctor laid a hand on his shoulder.

"You know her?"

Nodding, Alistair swallowed and said, "At the Transportation Bureau. We were lab assistants."

Gregory handed Alistair a cup of some steaming hot beverage. "She feels betrayed."

"She was betrayed."

"Quite a price to pay. For you and her."

Alistair looked sharply at Gregory, then lifted the cup to his lips and tasted some hot but dilute coffee.

"Thank you for helping with the wounded. I've been told you were itching to go."

Alistair shrugged and took another sip.

They observed what they could of the city. A chill wind blew into them and brought an increasing number of snowflakes. Gregory could see little, but they could both hear violence below, and see occasional flames or flashes of gunfire. Sight and sound, both impeded by darkness and wind and snow, together combined to sketch a vague outline of a city plagued by fighting.

"You were off at the time," Gregory began to say. "I had just started at the hospital. A young woman came in. Pregnant with her first child. And then all of a sudden she takes a bad turn and no one can figure out why. Just inexplicable. The baby died in her womb. She was unconscious when we delivered it, and she never came back. Next day a young man, no older than we are now, had a child and a wife to bury. Just forty hours earlier he was preparing to celebrate the birth of his first born."

Gregory paused to swallow once. "That was three cycles ago, and a not a day has passed since when I haven't thought of it. I don't understand why things like that have to happen, but I'm here to do something about it. They're tragic, but they're mindless and purposeless. With study and work we can overcome them so they never happen again." With a nod of his head Gregory indicated the grumbling city below. "But this nonsense...this is deliberate. How many young men and women are going to be dead when the sun comes up tomorrow? Dead not because some virus got in their system, but dead because someone else, human just like them, decided they wanted them that way."

"I don't have the answer to that, Gregory."

"Is it worth it to you?"

Alistair afforded Gregory a sidelong glance. "When you were starting at the hospital, I was off on Kaldis. I was stationed for a long time in Mar Profundo. It's a gigantic city. On one side is the sea, on the other thousands of miles of rolling hills and dry plains.

"I spent a three or four month stretch out in the drylands to the east. I met a woman there...she was beautiful. I think she liked me...I believe I was falling in love with her. I don't know...I didn't know her long. I still think back and try to sort out what I really felt.

"Anyway, you can imagine how fucked up the whole operation is. Forty systems, almost the entire colonized galaxy, have about twelve millions troops with no clear chain of command. We were never sure from one day to the next who was our enemy and who we would be ordered to fight. Out in the drylands we kind of settled down into a peacekeeping unit and waited for someone else to make a move. Before our commanders got around to noticing our position and deciding what to do with us, a real enemy emerged. I say enemy only because they aimed their guns at us, not because I didn't secretly agree with their goal."

"Which was?"

"Independence. But this group that emerged almost out of nowhere was radical. The Goyistas. They were sweeping through the countryside attacking all offworlders and any Kaldisian who had ever conspired with or might have conspired with offworlders. My unit was only two hundred strong and other units nearby were pulling out. Finally we were ordered out. And then she came to me and begged me to stay, to help her and her family escape. They were going to be slaughtered and they knew it. We weren't allowed to take civilians with us. A few had posed as refugees and managed to bring down some transports, so transporting civilians was strictly forbidden. I would have had to stay and lead them on foot.

"I almost stayed. I swear to you I almost stayed. We would never have escaped with her grandparents and baby cousins and nieces...I knew that. But I almost stayed anyway. My parting image of her..." Alistair's voice faltered, "...was a sobbing, crumpled wreck on the ground as the transport lifted off."

"What happened?" Gregory softly asked, in awe.

"The Goyistas swept through and took the whole continent except for Mar Profundo. We holed up there for a few more months until enough reinforcements were cobbled together to counter attack. I never saw her again. I only had one opportunity to look for her when I got some leave, but her village had been leveled and there was no trace of her. I can't imagine she survived. Probably her last minutes in life included a violent rape…" Alistair fought for composure, "…and a knife being drawn across her throat."

"There was nothing you could do." Gregory felt like the attempted consolation was pathetic. He tried to cover it by asking, "What was her name?"

"I will never say her name again," Alistair replied with force. "But no day goes by I don't think of her, and sometimes wish I *had* stayed. Until the last State is obliterated we will never be free from terror. And people like her and countless billions more will die because some of us are evil enough to try and control the rest."

Gregory was too in awe, both at the story and the normally taciturn man who told it, to think of any appropriate comment. He laid a hand on Alistair's shoulder and finally spoke in a gentle, unhurried voice.

"You were different when you came back. We could tell, but we couldn't really understand why. I guess…Al, I don't know what to say."

Alistair shrugged. "Listening is enough."

Gregory nodded, and his attention was drawn to the clinic some yards distant. "I need to go back inside," he finally said, feeling awkward. Alistair did not respond.

39

Once again smoke rose from Arcarius, rising past snowflakes on their way down. The fires which burned during the night now only smoldered, and the snow, which intensified during the darkest hours, relented and merely sprinkled the earth under the tentative light of the morning sun. A makeshift flagpole displaying a limp Aldran flag was erected at the top of the Mayor's Palace. The great spherical power generator was still standing and, on the outside at least, in good shape. Unharrassed and unhurried, military vehicles roamed the streets of Arcarius, occasionally depositing a load of troops at a doorstep or in a plaza.

Alistair rubbed his eyes and scratched his itching scalp, trying to wake himself up. Having found a razor, he shaved and the morning breeze felt especially cold on his exposed cheeks. He and Ryan spent the evening taking turns on watch. Henry offered to help but Alistair gruffly told him to go to bed. Now he was dragging under the weight of successive nights with little sleep.

Ryan saw nothing during his watches, and Alistair had only once gotten a scare. A patrol craft, hovering over the crumbling roads, passed by an intersection about a hundred yards down hill. It paused in the middle, shining a light down the street it was crossing, the street the clinic was on. Then it moved on, only the quiet hum of the engine giving it away once it passed the buildings lining the cross street. After that there was nothing.

Turning to go back inside and rouse Ryan, Alistair spied Henry's small form trudging through the once again snowed-over parking lot towards Alistair's position.

"Good morning," Henry greeted. The ex marine nodded without comment. "I uh…I decided I want to come with you."

"With me where?" asked Alistair as he moved towards the clinic. Henry reversed his direction to keep up.

"That's for you to decide. Oliver should have taken your advice. Let's head out on our own."

"Hmmm."

"Hmmm, meaning…?"

"You're not a hardy physical specimen, Henry."

Henry frowned at the comment. "I'm not proposing to wrestle the Civil Guard, Al."

"Hmmm."

"Hmmm, meaning…?"

"Hmmm, meaning we're going to be trekking across a lot of countryside, trying to cross the channel, make our way undetected to Rendral and then who knows what from there. All the while, I'm going to have dependents in tow. Is that really what you want?"

Henry's voice got testy and higher in pitch. "You just tried to convince me to come with you last night!"

"Last night plans were different. It's one thing to hide out in the hills around town, it's quite another to do what I have in mind."

"Well I want to come with you."

Having arrived at the door, Alistair paused a moment and turned to face his old friend. "I can't afford to take you with me, Henry. Honestly, your physique concerns me less than you being a government informer."

Henry's face lost its color. Alistair entered the clinic and left him out in the cold.

The rest of the officials were waiting inside a warehouse near the harbor. With the city back under control, it was a matter of waiting for the military to confirm the State buildings were cleared and give the signal to get back to work. While awaiting the imminent go-ahead, a couple warehouses were commandeered, heated, and prepared as lodges for short term use. Gerald, however, did not feel comfortable around his fellows. He chose to prowl around the harbor. With his hands tucked into his coat pockets and his coat collar pulled up around his lips and nose, he watched as snowflake after snowflake fell onto the water's surface and disappeared.

Several small naval vessels were anchored in the harbor and beyond, in the open sea, were a couple dozen larger ones. During the night they were abuzz with activity, occasionally firing rockets into the city. Now, other than the tipping back and forth with the waves, they were still. A few lights shone, a sailor occasionally came on deck, nothing more.

Gerald was startled out of his reverie when a senior official approached and, standing at his side, stared out across the bay with him.

"It's hard to imagine, looking at all that, that the traitors could possibly hope to win," he commented. His unshaven face sported a thin mustache, almost like an outline of the upper lip. The man, whom Gerald recognized from somewhere, used the word traitor, instead of rebel, as directed by the Realist regime.

"They lost," Gerald confirmed. "Who knows what they think or why they think it."

The official softly smiled, but the softness was a thin cushion on top of something far harder. "I've been told your brother worked for a short time at the Transportation Bureau, a job you got for him."

Gerald looked darkly out at the waters, deliberately avoiding the gaze of his superior.

"I also understand he broke into our system with a dead man's code and, not coincidentally, a train carrying some very important personages was destroyed a short time later. A train whose passengers were to have remained a secret to all but a few."

Gerald braced himself. "I was careless to have trusted my brother."

"Careless? He is an avowed anarchist. You were a blithering idiot to have trusted him."

"May I inquire as to your intentions? Have you come here to fire me?"

"No, I am not here to fire you. But I think we can both agree you have some making up to do."

"I believe I do."

"And don't forget it. Greater men than you have lost their jobs and more over lesser oversights than what you are guilty of."

Gerald swallowed once. "How can I be of service?"

"That's quite simple. I should very much like to meet this brother of yours in person."

Despite an effort to steel himself, Gerald could not stop his knees shaking and the color leaving his skin. He stared at the terrible profile framed by the sea and sky behind it, at the unshakably firm and determined expression on the face. "What should I do?" he finally managed.

The other turned his slender body towards Gerald. "Every Civil Guard and soldier you see in this city is now under my command. The mayor has been killed and martial law declared. Find your brother and let me know immediately."

The man, the new commander of the Arcarius garrison and, for the time being, its chief political officer, retraced his steps in the snow. As he watched him go, Gerald looked to the door of the warehouse he had come out of. There were two imposing soldiers waiting for the new garrison commander, and with them he saw Stephanie Caldwell. He made no motion to get her attention and she studiously avoided his gaze. At that moment Gerald remembered who the man was and the realization, not the cold, made him shudder.

‌ঔ৵ঌ

Alistair dared not travel in an auto, and the circuitous route he took around the edge of the city before he found a place where he felt comfortable entering meant he and Ryan did not come to his parents' street until four hours after they left the clinic. When the two rebels, bundled well against the cold, finally reached the snowy avenue, he came face to face with his worst fear. There had been fighting there. The wall of the building across from his parents' had been hit with an explosive and a fire still burned. Several bodies, not all of them in one piece, lay strewn about, some with the uniform of the Aldran military, some in a guerrilla's plain clothing. He stopped and observed the scene for some time, but it was apparent both sides had moved on. Saying nothing, he placed his right hand inside the left side of his coat and gripped the handle of his gun.

They trudged down the vacated street, past dark and empty windows and bolted doors. They did nothing to the bodies save to confirm they were deceased. Next, Alistair went to the damaged section of wall while Ryan checked the last two bodies still in shape enough to possibly be alive. Flames born of the explosion, though dying, still licked at the debris scattered about. Scanning the inside of the building, Alistair saw the twisted and torn remains of some equipment and he grit his teeth.

"There was a surveillance team here."

"How's that?" asked his companion as he jogged up beside him.

With a nod of his head, Alistair indicated the wreckage. "That was surveillance equipment. There was a team here."

"You think they were waiting for you?"

"I can't imagine what else they were here for. The city isn't even completely secured yet and they already have a surveillance team in place, right outside the home of the parents of the man who infiltrated their Transportation Bureau."

"Do they know it was you?"

"They suspect it or they're idiots. Some of our guys must have discovered them." He looked up at his parents' building, to the window he knew was theirs. "I've got a very bad feeling."

Alistair looked down the street the way they had come, and suddenly tensed. Ryan heard nothing but, sensing his friend's uneasiness, had the sense to remain quiet. For a whole minute Alistair was unmoving, and then there was a faint hum in the air that Ryan finally heard too. A hundred yards or so away, a hovering transport craft pulled out onto the street. Alistair took two steps back into the hole in the wall and Ryan quickly followed. Peering out from behind the bricks, Alistair observed as the transport sat in the middle of the road.

If it's a heat detector, he thought, *maybe the fire will cover us.* Another moment or two of quiet, and then the hovercraft pulled forward, crossing the street and leaving their view. Wellesley exhaled the breath he didn't realize he was holding.

"Let's make this quick," said Alistair.

He was just fishing for his key when he saw the gate to the courtyard was bashed in. With a sense of foreboding, he jogged across the relatively warmer courtyard with the glass roof, Wellesley in tow, and came to an entrance to the building itself. This was closed and securely locked, but it was not a solid enough piece to withstand a couple hard kicks from Alistair's mighty legs. The door cracked on the first blow, swung inward on the second and the two rebels were in the rusty stairwell as the echoes from the break-in died down.

Alistair stood listening for some time, hearing nothing and uncertain how to proceed. *They've laid one trap,* he thought as he peered up into the darkness. *Is another still set?* Putting one foot in front of the other with the utmost caution, the two men ascended the stairs at a grand-mother's pace. Each new level, being farther and farther from the window at the bottom, was darker than the previous, a fact which discomfited Wellesley.

Alistair had never realized just how much noise the stairs made until he wanted them to be silent. With every protesting groan under his weight he expected the doors to burst open and Civil Guard to come pouring out. The door to each story passed was a promise of danger that made the skin tingle and the hairs stand up erect, but each promise went unfulfilled.

"Anyone left in the building knows we're here," Ryan muttered after an especially loud creak.

When they finally arrived at the right story, the ex marine opened the stairwell door. The hallway into which they emerged was windowless and, still without power, jet-black. Alistair sensed a stiff reluctance from his companion as he passed into the lightless hallway, but Wellesley said nothing. Seconds later Alistair was knocking at his parents' door. The pounding sent loud thuds through the hallway where the worn carpet was just enough to deaden the echoes. Everything fell silent again and the door remained closed. Upon trying the handle, he found it locked. Producing his key, he opened the door and a faint light from the windows of the living room poured into the hallway.

"Mom? Dad?" he called out as he entered the apartment with Wellesley close behind.

He received no answer and a quick search of the place revealed it to be empty.

"They must have gone somewhere else," suggested Wellesley.

"We'll check the basement."

As they made their way down, Alistair stopped to knock on a few other doors but received no response. This gave him some hope that perhaps the entire population was hiding down in the basement, but when they finally arrived at the musty, subterranean level it also proved to be empty. He stood for a moment with his hands on his hips, looking around as if he might pick up something significant he missed before. Finally, a nervous cough from Wellesley, stuck in the pitch black, interrupted his thoughts.

"I don't know where they could be," he conceded and, biting his lower lip, made for the exit. Once again Wellesley, gripping the back of Alistair's coat for guidance, was eager to follow.

Emerging from the building into the relative brilliance of the early afternoon sun as it shone off the gray bricks of the sheltered courtyard, it occurred to Alistair that this was the best moment to lay a trap. There was no point in going after them in the building, but the courtyard, with its lack of cover and sunlight painful to eyes used to darkness, was a different matter. When he heard the sound of men in the street on the other side of the building, he thought his fears had been realized.

Grabbing Wellesley by his coat, he pulled him close to a wall, waiting for his eyes to adjust. Hugging the rough brick, Alistair moved to a large window of the downstairs lobby and peered through it and another window on the other side to the street opposite. They saw three Civil Guard, two peering about, their rifles hefted, while a third examined a body in the street.

Ryan grabbed for his gun but Alistair dissuaded him.

"There are more nearby. There's another group just down the street. Guaranteed."

Pulling back from the window, Alistair led Wellesley out the back gate of the courtyard from which point they could circle around the patrolling troops and make their torturous way back to the clinic on the north side.

40

At the outset of their return trip, Alistair and Ryan were alert, scanning every corner and window they approached. Giving the squad on the street a wide berth, they left without incident and, when they reached the hills to the east, relaxed somewhat and fell into an easy rhythm. Alistair brooded the entire way, his thoughts on his parents. Wellesley, sensing that this time there was something more to the silence, did not pester him with idle talk.

By the time they were back on the north side, the sun reached its zenith. There was some discussion about how to get to the clinic, with Wellesley preferring one route and Alistair another, but Alistair was not in the mood for a dispute and he muttered an invitation for Wellesley to take any route he wanted while he started down the road of his choice. Wellesley quickly followed and was glad he did when he realized his large companion was correct. Alistair's winding road swept around and between a few hills and left them on a main thoroughfare with the clinic in sight.

They could plainly see as they approached that the parking lot was empty. It had even been cleared of the recent snowfall which still dusted the land with the odd flake. Drawing nearer, they could see the nurses and medical staff through the windows. The clinic had taken in more wounded since they left, and more staff too.

This made Alistair pause, wondering who exactly had been around to drop off the recent batch of wounded and what that would mean for him. Then it struck him as odd that anyone found the time to plow the parking lot the day after the city was invaded. Coming to a dead stop, he put a hand to Wellesley's chest as his companion was about to walk by, chin tucked into his scarf and face down. He came out of his reverie with a start.

"What's the matter?"

Alistair said nothing, but turned around and, walking much faster now, headed for the winding road they had just taken.

"What's the matter?" Wellesley asked again as he jogged to catch up with Alistair.

"Something's not right."

It was then he heard the unmistakable sound of a sergeant's barked orders, the rustle and thumping of hidden troops springing into action and the peel of wheels on pavement. He looked back over his shoulder and saw a platoon of troops pouring out of every nook and cranny. More troops appeared over the top of a nearby hill, and still another squad, complete with two single seat hovercrafts, emerged from the winding road for which they were headed.

Alistair once again stopped dead in his tracks. Wellesley reached for his weapons but Alistair laid a restraining hand on him.

"It's over," he said, his voice equal parts resignation and disbelief.

Wellesley stared at his captors with the wide-open mouth of him who will not believe what has happened. Before commanded to do so, Alistair went down on his knees and raised his hands above his head. A moment later Wellesley did likewise.

"Get down on the ground!"

"Face down! Peckers on the pavement!"

As the Civil Guard advanced, dozens of guns ready to fire, Alistair leaned forward, turning his head to the side, still staring in disbelief. On his cheek he felt the cold wetness of the road, which had soaked up just enough of the sun's rays to melt the bit of ice left on it. He felt the pavement's roughness, even felt the ground vibrate as dozens of tin men approached, their boots pummeling the surface of the street. Then he felt a multitude of knees and shins on his neck and head, several on his back and two on each leg as his arms were twisted behind him and securely bound. He could still feel all this as a black hood was pulled over his head to steal his vision.

ᵒ⁃ᵒ

"Thanks for meeting me," said Clever Johnny as he stepped out from behind a boulder partially blocking the path up the mountain.

Startled, Brad Stanson drew back and nearly dropped the folders he was toting. The lengthening shadows of dusk streaked across the ground, bent this way and that by the shape of the terrain. Brad squinted as he looked at Clever Johnny, outlined by the setting sun.

"I'm not meeting with you."

"You're not meeting with *Oliver*," Johnny informed him, leaning against the boulder and casually picking at his teeth with a toothpick.

"I didn't say anything about Oliver."

Clever Johnny did not immediately reply.

"What the hell do you want? What the hell are you doing here?"

"You're here because I sent you a message you thought was from Oliver," Johnny explained as if bored. "'If you are willing to proceed with the plan against Clever Johnny'—how do I come by these nicknames, I wonder—'meet me this evening by Red One.' And now you've shown up."

"You can imagine my bewilderment when I got the message," said Stanson. "I'm here to find out what's going on."

Clever Johnny nodded as if considering what Brad had told him. "Is that true, Cain?"

"Not bloody likely," said a voice up the slope to Brad's left. He whirled around to peer up at the man Johnny had called Cain, a man with pale skin, jet-black hair and a sharp nose jutting out from his face like a small knife. "When Clement gave him the message he looked like he was expecting it."

"Bewildered is not the word I would use to describe him," said a voice behind Brad.

He whirled again and saw a bigger, burly man with reddish hair and a thick beard. This time he did drop the folders and felt his knees go weak.

"Is it your opinion that Mr. Stanson is plotting against me?" Clever Johnny asked. From his tone he might have been asking Clement his opinion on a rugby match.

"Most definitely."

Stanson was desperate to think of something to say, but his voice failed him and Clever Johnny spoke instead.

"Did you hear that, Brad? 'Most definitely.' He's not just definitely sure about this, he is the most definitely sure that he could possibly be. There is no greater level of definite surety than that which Clement experienced when he handed you the letter."

Stanson stared at Clever Johnny with absolute dread. "Johnny, I don't know anything about a plot. I'm here because I thought Oliver wanted to meet with me. Why the hell would I plot against you?"

"Same reason I'm plotting against you, Oliver and Alistair. Same reason I managed to get Alistair working far away from where he could attend our meetings. Same reason we're all plotting against the State. Same reason Brutus stabbed Caesar."

Brad staggered backwards, his vision becoming fuzzy as his blood throbbed through his head. He barely noticed when Cain leaped from his perch and landed on the path in front of him. Falling to his knees, Stanson cried silently as Cain pulled from his belt a knife nearly a foot in length.

For Cain, the moment before the kill was the most interesting part. The ineffable mix of emotions coursing through his body when he first assassinated another human being—excitement, shock, fear, nervousness and an almost religious fascination—was something he no longer could feel, though he missed it. What was left for him was discovering how the subject would react, because each one was different and there was no way to predict it. He noted with mild curiosity how Stanson behaved and then his hand shot out and he slid the steel between the ribs and into the heart. Stanson lost his strength and slumped, which Cain scarcely noticed as he withdrew the blade, just as he scarcely noticed the faint disappointment he felt at how commonplace it had become.

The strike of the knife was so quick that Stanson's heart was punctured before he felt any pain. When the blade entered his body, when hope was eliminated and the outcome made inevitable, the fear lessened, but the sorrow did not. He had a vague realization the knife must have hit his heart, but he spared little energy on the thought. Rather, he thought of his mother, living far away near New Boston. He thought of the warm, safe, happy times with her, and he yearned to be there and then, away from the unforgiving mountain slope. He thought of the father he had never met, whose identity even his mother did not know for sure. Would he ever know he had a son, that his son had died—been murdered—among the rocks and snow and ice on a frigid island far to the north? Then he thought of his mother again, but by the time his face smacked onto the mountain path, he could no longer feel a thing.

୬∞୧

Alistair's holding cell was as confined as an outhouse and just as comfortable. It was nothing but a metal box about six feet in height with a cramped floor space. A small bench, made of the same metal as the box, afforded him a place to sit, but his captors had neglected to release his bonds. The space was cramped for a normal human; for Alistair it was miserable. Once, when he was roughly stuffed inside, he tested the strength of the box with a couple blows of his shoulders and feet, but to his dismay it was solidly built. He refrained from any further violence in part because it was futile but also because he wanted them to think he had been cowed into submission.

He knew he would be executed. The Realists, little concerned with due process in the best of circumstances, would waste no time in plying him for information and then sending him to the gallows, the guillotine, the chair, the firing squad or to whatever ad hoc apparatus was being used at the moment.

On Kaldis he escorted his share of prisoners scheduled for execution. With few exceptions they became submissive, resigned, accepting their fate regardless of their prior temperament and behavior. The closer they came to execution the more docile they became. The logic of this at first escaped him. At the precise moment when a prisoner has nothing to lose, when he can attack his captors with abandon and, if not free himself, at least sell his life dearly, he becomes meek and pliant. Several cycles of military experience on Kaldis altered his ideas of Man, and he came to realize the key to the seeming paradox. It was not fear of death that intimidated a man into submission, it was authority.

Authority could maintain an empire. It was the glue that held a battalion together, and it made a man compliant, even when faced with his own demise. Especially when faced with his own demise. A soldier, gun in hand, may fight to the death against overwhelming odds, but a man in handcuffs will go mildly to his execution. The reason, as Alistair eventually realized, was not fear; it was because the man in handcuffs was shown to his satisfaction that he was under authority. Demonstrating authority was as key an element of boot camp as any actual training. All the humiliations the recruits were made to suffer were ways to demonstrate authority. When a king wore a crown, he did so to tap into its power. When men must kneel before a king or stand when a judge enters a room, or when nobility dressed differently from serfs, or when generals wore more medals than privates, it was all to demonstrate authority. With authority, a physically frail man such as the first Solar Emperor Yao Sung could be responsible for the deaths of one and a half billion people.

At the same time, Alistair realized something else about authority: it was not a universal force, like gravity; it was a mental construct. The great economist Ludwig von Mises of Austria demonstrated that value was in the human observer. No object had value; it was simply what a person thought about that object. Likewise, authority was not in the person considered to have it; it was in the person who decided to obey. When he comprehended this, authority no longer affected him. He understood authority was his to grant or withhold, and he therefore had no intention of making his execution an easy affair. *I'll die of a gun shot wound on my way to the chamber, but I am not going to stand still in front of the firing squad.*

Thus resolved, he passed the hours in thought in his box. He reflected on the callousness of events, to allow a man to be ripped from his time and place, from his loved ones, and left to die with a life unfinished, eventually to forget he had ever existed. He thought of all the other men and women through time who died unavenged, with lives unfinished, forgotten by time and fate, of all the contributions to the story of humanity whose effects, however slight, were indelible and yet whose authorship, once lost, was forgotten forever. He was about to take his place among the ranks of the forgotten.

A century hence, a millennium hence, a million cycles hence, when people recalled the names of the famous, he would not be among them. At best, his name would be listed in a census file from a dead civilization, one name among millions and billions. Katherine would mourn him; his parents would mourn him; perhaps Gerald would mourn him. Even Oliver might, but he would eventually be forgotten. His grandnieces and nephews would hear a story or two during Foundation Day family gatherings, but their children would not. In a hundred cycles at most he would cease to be even a memory.

He was filled with a desperate anger, and tears welled up in his eyes as he grit his teeth. The injustice of it was nearly unbearable. Only with a great effort did he once again restrain himself from beating on his confining walls. To the extent the six foot box permitted, he stood up and sat down over and over, keeping his muscles loose. He rotated his shoulders, turned his head, stretched his torso…everything he could. He did not want stiff muscles when the cell finally opened to give him one last chance to strike at The Realists.

41

The hamlet tucked away on the edge of a valley stream was illegal. Most of the buildings were cheaply made, for the hamlet could only exist as long as the State either knew nothing about it or did not bother itself with it. There were a couple cabins built before the enforced relocation, and when daring souls ventured outside the city, a few added their hastily constructed edifices to these. There was one street, nothing more than a dirt path presently covered in snow. On either side were a few humble homes, and at the far end, up against the side of the mountain, was a two-story cabin, one of the originals, well built and solid.

It was into this last building that two men carried the scrawny body of a blindfolded Henry. Upon entering, they deposited him on the floor and waited for their leader who sat in a rough-hewn wooden chair in the back corner. Oliver gave the two men a nod and they left as Henry ripped the blindfold from his eyes. In the sparseness of the room—it had only a table and a couple chairs apart from the long unused fireplace—it took but an instant to spot Oliver.

"Good afternoon, Henry."

"Oliver, we gotta talk." Henry's voice sounded desperate. "I know you think I'm a traitor—"

"Who told you that?"

"I talked with Alistair. Listen, my name was on the list of their double agents because I signed up to be one. That was before I knew you were involved." He stepped towards Oliver with his hands turned palms up in supplication. "They were paying for good information and I needed the Credits. But I never gave them any good info. Hell, I didn't have any good info to give. When I talked with you…I just forgot about being an informant and joined the cause. I swear to you I never told them anything. I was fighting against them." A moment passed and Oliver said nothing. "I swear on my soul I never said a thing. You have to believe me!"

"No, I don't have to believe you. Anyone with the power of speech can swear anything they like. If the Civil Guard broke in here right now you would swear you were on their side."

"A real informant wouldn't bother to demand a meeting with you once he knew he had been found out. Oliver, you know me. I didn't give a damn one way or the other. I offered to be an informant because of the Credits. I was…" He shook his head hopelessly. "I was stupid. It was that snitch's program. Anything useful we told them they would pay us for. Then someone suggested I join the rebellion and inform from the inside. But I haven't reported to them for a while. I've been working for the cause because I've seen that it means something. I actually realized you and Alistair were on to something. Oliver, please. I came here to give *you* information."

"What information?"

"They've captured Alistair and Greg. Alistair was leaving for somewhere and I wanted to go with him. Me, Greg and him wound up taking some wounded to a clinic on the north side. But the Civil Guard showed up and arrested everyone."

"But not you."

"They arrested me but my name was on their list…" Henry looked sheepish for a moment but quickly plunged on. "I convinced a commander to let me go, that I hadn't reported because I had been so deep undercover."

"And you gave him information."

"Nothing they didn't already know. They set a trap for Alistair. When he came back they took him." There was another moment of silence. "Oliver, please."

Considering him for a bit, Oliver finally said, "Thank you, Henry. You would have done better to tell me right away you were an informant, but there's nothing to be done about that now."

"Are you going to save him?"

Oliver shifted his bulk. "I doubt there is anything I can do. Most of the rebels have been disbanded for now, and my team and I are moving out of here in short order. As much as I would like to, I don't think I have the capability to help Alistair."

Henry ran a hand through his hair, stumbled and fell into a seated position on the rough wooden floor of the cabin. "He must think I turned him in," he mumbled and surprised even himself when a tear formed in his eye. Struggling to his feet, he grabbed the blindfold from the floor and walked to the door, trudging slowly, as a defeated man. When it slammed shut behind him, Oliver heard a pair of feet treading down the stairs.

"We're moving out, then?" asked the man from the bottom step of the stairs.

"As soon as you can make it happen. Have you gotten a hold of Stanson?"

"Can't find him. He could be anywhere on the island right now."

"Goddamn it," sighed Oliver without any real venom.

"Where are we going from here?"

He rubbed his head with both hands, avoiding his still tender nose. Then he dropped his hands to his sides and took a deep breath. "Gather a force together. As many men as you can. Arm them with whatever we have available."

"Sir?"

"We're going after Alistair."

So well did Alistair's small metal prison insulate him from outside sound, despite the small air vent in the back, that the former marine did not even realize there was anyone outside his cell until the door swung open. Squinting against what seemed to be a bright reddish light, he had difficulty determining how many men were there. Having been trained to fight blind, he prepared to leap from his box and either try an escape or at least crush someone's ribcage with a kick.

"Alistair Ashley 3nn," intoned a man.

"Wrong cell," said Alistair, his voice more of a croak. "My name's just Alistair Ashley."

"Exit the box slowly."

Alistair struggled forward, his muscles tight despite his efforts, and when he emerged, his vision beginning to adjust to what was in reality a low level of light, he despaired at what he saw. He was three stories above the bottom level on a narrow walkway with a grating for a floor. There were several stories above him, and each walkway on both sides of the large prison block was lined with metal boxes just like his, probably a hundred to a level. High above, red tinged lights hung from the ceiling and glowed enough to make it tolerably easy to see.

With him on the walkway were three Civil Guard, one of them a Colonel, and a featureless humanoid form in white. The smooth skin, devoid of any identifying mark, was of a flexible yet durable material. The head was human shaped, with only shallow indentations where eye sockets should be, a gradual and small bump at the nose, and just the smallest indication of lips. It was almost like the face had been washed away. There were no ears and no hair. Female in form, there were small breasts and slightly flared hips but no nipples or naval. It stood about six feet tall and, despite its slender figure, he knew it probably weighed in the vicinity of three hundred pounds. Its presence precluded any possibility of escape.

It was a dreadbot. Outlandishly expensive and complicated to manufacture, they were quite rare on Aldra. Even with the advent of Mechanical DNA, by which nanobots could be programmed to assemble a dreadbot out of raw materials, it was still a lengthy, arduous process, but the results were extraordinary. Dreadbots were inhumanly strong, inhumanly fast, inhumanly quick and as remorselessly lethal as their programmer decided to make them. Even well rested and unbound, he was no match for a dreadbot. His face must have betrayed his disappointment for the Colonel chuckled.

He was a tall man and slender, with dark hair and a thin mustache like a quick trace of a pencil. His chest was covered in metals and insignia of rank and he was flanked by two armed Civil Guardsman whose rifles were leveled at him.

"Alistair Ashley 3nn," said the Colonel with the tone of one who has finally gotten his wish.

Alistair proudly drew himself up to his full height, his cramped back cracking as he straightened it. He suppressed a wince as his shoulders, forced into an unnatural position for so long, protested.

"There is no one here of that name. But you must be deathly afraid of him to spare a dreadbot for escort duty."

The Colonel smiled, his lips as thin as his mustache. "It does not shame me to recognize your physical prowess, Alistair. We know who you are, we know what we trained you to do, and we have no intention of ever letting you slip back into the rebellion. That is why you are going to be executed tomorrow morning."

The Colonel was not telling Alistair anything he did not already know, but hearing the words was different from thinking them. He felt his knees tremble and he fought to keep his composure. The Colonel maliciously smiled.

"You'll be questioned first, of course, and depending on how disagreeable you are we may delay the execution to mid afternoon. It's really up to you, although we both know you won't last any longer than that. But all in due time. Right now, there is something we want to show you."

At that, the Colonel moved past Alistair, confident and unconcerned. Alistair followed, unnerved by the dreadbot, its movements as fluid and graceful as mercury, its footsteps, despite its great weight, almost soundless. The two Civil Guard followed a few paces behind. He could feel a tingle on the two spots on his back where he imagined their rifles were aimed.

Upon reaching the end of the walkway, they descended some stairs, their boots clanking on the metal flooring. He followed the Colonel out prison block and down a brightly lit white hallway before entering a small chamber on the other side of a set of double doors. It was dimly lit and boasted a large window taking up nearly the entire wall on the left side. On the other side of the window was a tiled room with two morgue carts. A figure in white, his face partially concealed by a white surgical mask, stood unmoving with his hands folded in front. On each morgue cart was a white sheet covering a cadaver, the feet of both protruding from the bottom of their sheets.

Alistair was seized by a dreadful premonition and he froze in place. The Colonel gestured to the man in white who proceeded to draw back the sheets. Alistair stared in agony at his parents.

Forgetting all resolve to be proudly defiant until the end, Alistair, like a deflating balloon, sank to his knees with an inchoate cry. The naked bodies of the two who raised and loved him were a hideous sight. Bruises of a sickly blue and purple hue were everywhere. Their faces had been abused, his mother's left hand mangled, and several bullet holes in each chest testified to what finally, mercifully, ended their torture.

His eyes fixed on the almost imperceptible scar at his father's hip where Gregory performed the surgery. It was better than looking at the wreck their bodies had been made into. It was better than seeing the torn and broken digits of the hands that had caressed him as a child, had soothed him to sleep after a nightmare. It was better than seeing teeth protruding through torn lips that had kissed him.

He shook. His chest heaved and his fingernails dug into his palms. With a bellowing roar he came to his feet, but the dreadbot knocked him back against the wall with a shove to the chest. He kicked out with his legs to regain his feet but the dreadbot was standing over him and with another shove it knocked him into the floor. As the air left his lungs, he kicked with his right foot, but the robot caught the leg and threw it back to the floor. Almost before he felt the shock of impact, he was lifted up by his throat. Faster than any snake, the dreadbot drew back its other hand and struck a crippling punch to his face, cracking his nose and making him see stars. It let go and the captive fell to the floor and lay groaning.

"I take it you knew them?" said the Colonel.

When Alistair's senses returned he slowly came to a sitting position, his shoulders throbbing as his arms remained tightly bound. He blew at the trail of blood streaming from his nose to his mouth and a few drops landed on the dreadbot's legs.

"You can't take my hate," he hissed, his voice as unsteady and uneven as his breathing. "My hate is mine and you won't take it from me." More drops of blood spattered the dreadbot.

Around a deep, throaty laugh, the Colonel said, "You can have your hate. We have what we wanted. Now just imagine what will happen when every rebel is faced with the same possibility. You blow up our trains, we'll slaughter your families. I just wanted you to know before we kill you there is no question of the rebellion succeeding. I want you to die knowing you failed."

He left the room then but the dreadbot and the Guardsmen stayed. At a gesture from one of the Guardsmen, the dreadbot, grabbing Alistair by an aching shoulder, hauled him up and marched him back to his cell.

࿊

The room in which Katherine and her colleagues set up the equipment was too small to comfortably accommodate everything. The equipment itself was not ideal, having been assembled piecemeal with parts adapted for new purposes, but the experiment was finally ready.

"This transmitter is not going to hold for long," said one of her fellows as he, sleeves rolled up to the elbows, attempted to connect a part in the innards of one of the lasers.

"We're lucky Dick scavenged this one," commented another as she rolled a pencil back and forth across her desk.

"What happened to the first one we got?" asked the project head, an elderly and bald gentlemen named Lenny.

"War effort," said Katherine.

"What's that?" he asked.

"It was taken for the war effort," she said in a louder voice for his ancient ears.

"So was the mechanic who used to do the assembly," added the first scientist, his upper half inside the open belly of the machine. He withdrew from the apparatus and closed its sliding door, locking it in place with a fork through the handle. "It'll be a miracle if we actually manage this."

"Are we ready?" asked Lenny by way of a gentle order, grabbing his cane and hobbling over to his station. The converted mechanic rolled down his sleeves and they all took up their positions around a small glass sphere suspended above a platform. Inside the sphere was about a liter of water and pointed at it were all manner of machines and devices.

"Commencing," said the woman next to Katherine. The lights dimmed and the automatic doors closed as she typed on her keypad.

"Initiation Sequence," confirmed Katherine as she slipped a ring on her right hand. This hand she thrust into a 3D display to manipulate the virtual controls.

"All systems normal," said the provisional mechanic, and then added, "If you can believe it."

One of the lasers lowered, looking like some strange bird going after prey, until it nearly touched the sphere. A laser on the other side, meant to be matching but due to its makeshift production almost a parody of the first, lowered to the opposite position.

"Are we ready to proceed?" asked Lenny. After a few moments of running over check lists, there was a general murmur of assent.

They didn't have to wait long, and the effect wasn't gradual. One moment there was a liter of water in the sphere, and the next there was a gaseous mix. By stirring the Essentials, they interfered with the 'condensation zones' Burkhard Heim predicted formed the basis for all matter. A jubilant cheer went up from the half dozen scientists and a couple jumped up and down. A pair were shaking hands and slapping each other's shoulders, while Lenny and the mechanic/scientist were staring at the readouts. There was a small commotion and Katherine's attention was turned to the readout display. She and the other scientists gathered behind the mechanic as he studied it.

"There's a…disturbance in the Overlay," he said, not worried but puzzled.

"What sort of disturbance?" asked Katherine.

"Unknown for the moment…"

The group held still for a few minutes, but there was little new information forthcoming. Eventually, the anticipation of discovery ebbed and some drifted away to complete the shut down phase while Lenny and the project mechanic continued to investigate the disturbance. It was nearly a half hour later when Katherine, her duties completed, sat down at her own station to study it herself. As she familiarized herself with the nature of the effect, it began to make sense.

"It's behaving like a wave," she said loudly enough to be heard at the next station.

"That was our thought too," replied the mechanic.

"It's…I think…Lenny," she called, her voice breathless yet uncertain.

"Yes?"

"The frequency is modulating." She let the implication hang in the air. Moments later all the project scientists were gathered around her station.

"Are you saying…an Overlay radio?"

"I say we try to track the source," said Katherine.

All eyes turned to Lenny.

"That would break protocol for the experiment. We take the sensors off and we miss vital data from the sphere."

"We don't move the sensors then we don't find out where this is coming from. Lenny, this looks…like a deliberate signal."

"How could it be a signal? No one's ever manipulated the Overlay before."

Katherine shrugged her shoulders. "I'm not saying it is, it just…if I were trying to send a signal through the Overlay, it would have these qualities I'm seeing."

Lenny at last gave his order: "Use the sensors. Track it."

The mechanic jumped back to his station, and typed furiously. A few minutes later, while the rest ignored their tasks and sat on the edge of their chairs, he said, "It's not local."

"Is it coming from another system?"

"Checking." Another breathless minute was followed by his answer, "Not from a colonized system." This was followed a moment later by, "Not from any system that we can see…" he swept a mystified gaze over them, "…in the Milky Way."

"Are you sure?" asked one.

"Well then, it's coming from a space vessel," suggested the project leader with the confident tone of one who has eliminated all other possibilities. There was a murmur of assent from a few of them.

Leaping up, Katherine exclaimed, "No other system in the galaxy has ever manipulated the Overlay before."

"I'm not so sure anymore," said the other woman.

"If some other system has the capability to manipulate the Overlay," mused the mechanic, "why haven't we heard of it? News like that would spread quickly."

"Perhaps they have only just discovered it themselves."

"Highly coincidental."

"Could this be an endogenous phenomenon in the Overlay?" asked Lenny.

"Sure," said the mechanic, "our understanding is incomplete. To say the least."

"Maybe someone detected our experiment and is sending us a message," suggested Katherine. In reply to their incredulous looks, she insisted, "Why not? That signal arrived only after we ran the test. It makes as much sense as anything else."

"Given the possibility another system has the capability," began the other woman, "they must be farther along than us to be sending signals. But if they can, why wouldn't we already know about it? We are getting a signal from someone who has had Overlay technology for... well, longer than us."

"Kaldis," someone breathed.

Nearly three million of the galaxy's four hundred billion stars had been explored, either by humans or robot drones. Many hundreds of millions more had been examined with remote viewing technologies. Life was found frequently, every time a rocky planet or moon had the right conditions. A fraction of a percent of populated worlds had produced multicellular creatures, and a vanishingly small percentage had animal life large enough to be seen by the naked eye. Nothing like a mammal had ever been found, nor even a chordate, and certainly not intelligent life, but it was known that at least once, before *Homo sapiens*, there was intelligence in the universe. Before *Homo erectus* existed, there was at least one civilization in the galaxy, for the three million year old ruins of an alien race were unearthed on Kaldis.

They were not extensive and existed only in one location. Probably it was an outpost; certainly not the alien homeworld. Allowing for the vast differences which might exist between the species of different worlds, it was estimated no more than a couple thousand lived at the site, and it had only been in use for about a century. That discovery occurred three hundred years ago, and nothing had come after. No one knew what happened to them, nor had signs of any others ever been discovered.

"So are they responding to our experiment?" wondered the other woman out loud.

"Let's not get wild with speculation," urged Lenny. "We still don't know if this is just a natural effect of our manipulation."

"Julie, how fast is the signal traveling?" Katherine asked.

Julie flew to her post and, after a few minutes, she heaved a sigh and sat back in her seat.

"I can't tell exactly how fast it's coming in." She paused a moment, then finally, softly, she said, "But it's faster than the speed of light."

Her statement halted all activity. A few awed smiles were exchanged, a few giggles of anticipation suppressed, and then they were back to work.

"Faster than the speed of light," Katherine heard the man on Julie's other side say. "They detected our technology and they're trying to communicate. They could be a billion light years away and communicating with us as if they were in the next room."

"We don't know anything yet," warned Lenny. "Let's try to act like scientists. Do we have no way of finding the source?"

"Oh, we can find the source," said the mechanic. "With Overlay technology, absolutely. Give me decent funding and the right team and I'll make something in a couple months."

"Alright, just keep recording for as long as the signal lasts. I'm long overdue for a report on the results."

"Talk sweet to 'em."

"Get us some more funding."

Lenny smiled and, pausing to tuck his shirt into his pants, straightened his back as much as his cane would allow and left the room as quickly as his venerable legs would carry him.

42

A hollow metallic pop awakened Alistair from his turbulent slumber. His exhaustion overcame his discomfort and he had nodded off but, as the door opened, the realization of what awaited him swept away all grogginess on a wave of adrenaline. These were to be the last hours of his life.

His eyes watered in protest of the invading light slashing at him. Wincing, he shifted, ready to spring if his captors made the mistake of coming without a dreadbot. The narrow line of sight afforded him by the open door did not yet reveal anyone, so he waited for the other to make the first move.

"You can come on out," said a bored voice.

Alistair struggled out of the box and stood up to his full height. His jailor was sloppily dressed in a Civil Guard uniform, with his shirt untucked, his pants wrinkled and two days' growth of beard. He held a clipboard in his left hand while he yawned into his right, leaning all the while on the door he had just opened. To the jailor's left, far better groomed and impeccably dressed in a high ranking official's Civil Service uniform Alistair knew did not belong to him, was Gerald.

It was almost more than he was prepared to handle. His lips parted in surprise as he met his brother's stoic gaze, but Gerald feigned disinterest.

"Is this the transfer?" the jailor asked.

"I believe this is him."

Holding out the clipboard, which doubled as a computer, the jailor instructed Alistair, "Look into the screen, would ya'?"

He managed to wrest his gaze from his brother's face and glanced at the small screen. A moment later his picture appeared, the one taken the day he enlisted. Next to it was his name and a few vital statistics.

"OK, Alistair Ashley 3nn. You've got the form?"

Gerald handed the man a piece of paper and he, upon glancing over it, frowned.

"This is the old form." Gerald said nothing. "We're not supposed to use the old forms anymore."

"Dear sir," Gerald began in his best tone of bored haughtiness, "you may have noticed we have only just reoccupied the city. We have captains serving as messenger boys, we have cooks acting as nurses, and we don't always have every form we need right at our fingertips."

The jailor was dubious but he accepted the paper, feeding it into the slot on the bottom of his clipboard. "They said these were all going to be electronic soon."

"I think they have other concerns at the moment."

"Greg and Ryan were supposed to be with me," Alistair blurted out, his heart beating furiously. He worried his blushing would give him away, but if he had seen his own filthy face that worry would have been laid to rest. No blush was going to show through the grime and beard.

The jailor regarded Alistair with a raised eyebrow and then turned this look at Gerald. "It's not on the transfer form."

"I didn't put them on because they have already been transferred," Gerald said smoothly, without pause or catch in his voice. Alistair suppressed a sigh of relief as Gerald continued, "Check to make sure, would you?"

"Which prisoners?"

"Gregory Lushington 8tu," said Gerald, "and…I forget the other."

"Ryan Wellesley," Alistair supplied the name, staring at his feet and trying not to sound breathless. "I don't know his suffix code."

The jailor gave a dubious and irritated look but typed the info on his clipboard nonetheless. "Gregory Lushington 8tu and Ryan Wellesley 7aa. Nope. They're still here."

Gerald sighed and rubbed his temples, and for perhaps the first time since he was a little child, Alistair marveled at his brother. It was an impromptu acting job he was sure he could not have pulled off half so well. "I swear to God…Look, just add them to the other form."

"Other form's already been signed."

"And I signed it. So add them to the form. Let's try and cut through some of the crap for once."

The jailor hesitated, so Gerald continued in a louder voice, "Add them to the damn form. I'm not going back to the other side of town to get a new form when we can add them right here. I'm the one who signed the damn thing so stop worrying about it."

"Fine, I'll add 'em," the jailor finally agreed, his irritation finding an outlet when he slammed shut the door to Alistair's former cell. "You need us to transport 'em?"

"You'll have to. I don't have an armed escort to spare right now."

"Fine."

The two brothers shared a furtive glance, and then Gerald was walking back down the walkway. The jailor made a startled sound as he glanced over Alistair's file on his clipboard screen. He turned to Gerald's retreating form.

"This one was due for execution."

"A mistake. Hence my visit," said Gerald without turning or stopping.

"So are the other two."

"Just take care of it, OK?"

Yet another disapproving frown colored the man's face, but he prodded Alistair with the clipboard and they started forward again.

The sensation Alistair felt was indescribable. His face flushed and he felt dizzy. He wanted to shout out to his brother, to thank him, to apologize, to cry that he loved him, to tell him their parents had been murdered…so many things did he want to say and none of them would be uttered. He swallowed a painful lump in his throat and, though it felt unbearable, plodded along.

"What are you moping about?" asked the man as he led Alistair in the opposite direction from his sibling. "You're on your way off this damn rock."

Alistair nearly missed a step. "Off the island?"

"Off. Off the planet." At Alistair's disbelieving look, he went on, "Incarcerator's in town. You'll be taking up residence on Srillium."

He almost staggered when the jailor gave him the news, but it immediately made sense. *He can't leave me on the planet. I have to be gone when the transfer is discovered.* It was a stroke of fantastic luck that The Incarcerator was in the area and Gerald made the most of the situation. He would spend the remainder of his days on a prison planet, living like a Stone Age hunter/gatherer, but he would be alive. And he wouldn't be tortured.

The agony of all the things he would never say to his brother tore at his heart. He already missed him, his sister, even Oliver. He missed his homeland. He thought of what his spying must have done to Gerald, of his callous disregard for his sibling, his easy willingness to use him. He thought of what Gerald had just risked for him. *He'll spend the rest of his life in hiding. They might execute him for this.*

He realized Gerald had upheld his father's principle: family first. He brushed the politics aside and protected his family, just as Nigel Ashley would have wanted. Though the kind Ashley patriarch was forever gone, his influence reached out through Gerald to protect his youngest son. It was more than Alistair could bear. Despite his humiliation, the massive ex-marine broke into tears.

☙ ❧

He was moved to a detention center at the spaceport. It was a simple affair, consisting of a desk and computer station in one corner and a tiled floor taking up the vast majority of the room. He was taken inside, his hands loosely cuffed in front, mercifully relieving his beleaguered shoulders. A few words were exchanged between transporters and security, and then he was led to a spot on the open floor. A guard, one of two, ordered him to stand still and proceeded to type on a keypad sewn into his left sleeve. A few dozen bars of red light appeared and his cell was created. The guard, after taking off the cuffs, walked away and Alistair, stuck in his six by six cell, sat down to await his fate.

He was reclining as best he could when the door to the detention center opened and Henry walked in. With a nervous glance towards Alistair, he spoke to the guards who gestured towards the ex marine, inviting him to do as he pleased. He managed a weak smile and waved as he approached. Alistair sat with his arms resting on his knees and did not respond.

"I found out you were here," he said by way of hello. Alistair still did not respond, but neither did he look away. "Alistair, I wasn't the reason they caught you. I don't know how they found you, but it wasn't me."

"Who are you working for?" Alistair asked in a voice that for Henry was uncomfortably loud.

Sitting on the floor next to Alistair's cell, Henry lowered his voice as if to give him a hint. "It wasn't me. I tried to get Oliver to rescue you. He won't."

"I'm not surprised."

"I just...There's nothing I can do." He hung his head. "This isn't what I wanted."

"This isn't what anyone wanted. The Realists want to impose what they want, the rest of us resist. No one gets what they want."

"I'm on your side, Alistair," he said, leaning in close to the bars and whispering. "I just came to say goodbye. I'm glad they're—"

"I need you to do something for me," Alistair interrupted, showing his first spark of life since Henry had come. "Can you get me a small stasis capsule?"

"A stasis capsule? Alistair, it's hard enough getting my next meal."

"Do it. You owe me. Get a stasis capsule, no larger than a pill, and put…cotton seeds in it."

"Are you out of your mind?"

"I mean it, damn it. Oliver can get one. Don't tell him it's for me. Find a stasis capsule and cotton seeds. Before it's too late. Hurry!"

The commanding tone of his voice had Henry back on his feet. He nodded in wonderment and left the detention center, looking back over his shoulder a couple times as if to reassure himself Alistair was serious. When Henry left, Alistair lay down in his cell, his head in one corner and his feet in the opposite. The hard floor was uncomfortable, but he had been in worse places recently. It was as good a place as any to brood.

By the time Henry was meandering down Tanard's Mountain, he had almost decided the request was too difficult to bother about. He wanted to do something for his friend, but a little voice in his head presented the option of forgetting about it without having to face Alistair afterwards. Hands in his pockets, he sulked as he took the winding road downward. The wind was strong enough to tell a snowstorm was gathering. Far off to the west he could see the clouds, and the handful of snowflakes from the day before had turned into a steady stream, no longer lightly dancing but hurled with some vigor.

The city lay open to his view. He could see the manifold naval vessels out at sea, their lights flashing and whirling as aircraft buzzed around. A few smaller transports were in transit between the harbor and the larger vessels, and he spied what he believed to be a large crowd around the harbor.

"Not taking passengers, eh?" said a voice, and Henry came out of his reverie to notice a family of five loading an auto with baggage. He vaguely knew them from having spent time in the neighborhood.

"Who's not taking passengers?"

"No, I'm asking you," the man said as he lifted a heavy suitcase into the trunk of his auto.

"I don't…Oh! No I wasn't trying to leave."

"Well, I didn't figure you'd be able," said the mother. "Everyone's down at the harbor waiting to get out, but they're not letting hardly anyone. We're going to try."

Henry stared in the direction of the harbor, nodded thoughtfully and turned back to the family.

"Where could I get a stasis capsule?"

They stared at him in surprise. The father shrugged and the mother said, "I'd worry more about your next meal."

"Definitely," he softly said and turned to continue down the street.

"Try the university," said the eldest daughter, a girl of perhaps seventeen cycles.

Henry paused. "We don't have a university."

"University of Avon. They've got a research branch here in town."

Henry's lips parted in a silent, "Ah!" He nodded and waved his thanks, but as he turned for a second time to the downhill road before him, he realized how long the walk would be. Alistair might be gone before he even got there. With trepidation he turned back to the family. It was only a four-door auto, and there were already five of them. The implications of being a sixth passenger nearly sickened him. *Damn you, Alistair,* Henry cursed. *You couldn't ask for...*He couldn't think of an easier request.

Sighing in resignation, he managed to ask, "Might I catch a ride with you?"

❧⨳

"He's been moved."

Oliver was at the point of slamming a magazine into place in his rifle. At the pronouncement from the rebel who had just entered, he let his hand fall to his side.

"What do you mean he's been moved?"

"He was scheduled for execution, now he's not. Being transferred off."

"Off? You mean...?" Oliver nodded in understanding. "How good is this information?"

"I trust it."

"Is he at the spaceport?"

"Yes, sir."

Oliver nodded and waved for the man to leave. Turning to face the other score of men with him in the murky filth of the warehouse, he said, "This could be a trick, put us off his trail until they have time to question him." He punctuated the point by slamming his magazine in place.

Rod Haverly shrugged. "He said he trusted the source."

"Get ready to climb," Oliver gruffly replied and he hoisted a belt of grenades over his shoulder. "We're moving out in five."

Ritchie fell in beside him as he marched for the door. "We get stuck up there and we've got no place to retreat to."

"No one is forced to come. I'll go alone."

Ritchie stopped at the door but Oliver kept going, letting a gust of cold air into the relative warmth inside. Rod Haverly and two others brushed by a moment later. Hands on his hips, Ritchie shook his head, leery, but put up no further protest. Grabbing his own supply of weapons, he was soon out the door in Oliver's wake.

❧⨳

The research branch of The University of Avon was a single, three-story building in the shape of a U surrounding a courtyard. Sidewalks crisscrossed it and a few trees grew, each with a well-weathered bench underneath. The building itself, Henry was disheartened to discover, was not vacant. He expected no one to return so soon. However, this did afford him the opportunity to follow someone into the building and bypass the locked doors. The professor who unwittingly opened the door for him turned for a second to gaze at him, but Henry nonchalantly nodded and the man did not seem alarmed.

Unfamiliar with the layout, he spent some time wandering on the first floor. Passing several different departments, most of them some form of math or science, he saw only wet trails of footprints and nothing suggesting stasis capsules and cotton seeds. *This is ridiculous,* he thought. Pausing to turn in circles, he tried to figure out what to do as the frustration of the task fought with the nervousness of his urgency.

He heard footsteps echoing in the hallway behind him and sprang back into action, feeling he should avoid whomever it was. Now at the base of the U, he hurried forward and rounded the next corner. It was then that he ran into the Agricultural Sciences Department.

Feeling optimistic for the first time, he tried the doors but found them locked. He peered through the narrow window of the entrance door but saw only another short hallway on the other side, so he moved to the next door of the department. It too was locked, but on the other side was a laboratory. There were plants of all kinds growing in rows stacked one above the other, stretching the entire length of the 75 foot room. The plants were not placed in soil, but rather in small containers with holes out of which the roots grew. There was a hovering robot inside, a spherical creation no larger than a poodle, passing down the rows and giving nutrients to the roots as it went.

He drew back a few steps and then rushed forward, delivering as powerful a kick as he could muster. There was a thud and poor Henry bounced backwards, tripping over himself and finally landing on his back with his legs thrown up over his head. Unwinding his tangled limbs, he peered at the door and saw it was unaffected by his assault. With a groan he got back up and, this time removing his right boot, attacked the window, battering it with the heavy heel. He winced at his first echoing blow and looked over his shoulder for signs that someone was alerted. When nothing stirred he tried again. This at first proved as successful as, though less humiliating than, his first assault, but eventually a fracture formed. A couple more hits lengthened the fissure, and then the window broke with a cacophony of glass shards.

Sensing the end of his quest, he rushed through the room and the adjacent chambers and offices until he came across a plant he thought might be cotton. A look at the label confirmed it, though it apparently was some experimental mutant form, and then he realized he had no idea what a cotton seed looked like nor where it was to be found on the plant. With a frustrated groan, he snapped off a portion at the stem and stuffed it in his coat pocket.

After this he began his search for a stasis capsule. Happily enough, the search concluded in the next room, where not only did he find stasis capsules but a large number of them tucked away in a system of drawers containing various plant parts. Ditching the plant he had picked, he rifled through the drawers until he came to one with cotton seeds in it. He lifted a stasis capsule from its slot and placed it in his pocket.

A moment later he was back in the laboratory, making his way to the door. An impish impulse seized him and, perhaps to reestablish dignity after the incident with the door, he let fly another charging kick, this time at the drone hovering a few feet away. There was the pop of a spark as the robot hurtled through the air before landing with a crash on the ground. After rolling into the wall, it lay still. Having made his point, Henry flew out the door, intent on finding a quick ride back to the spaceport.

☜☞

The bars keeping Alistair caged gave off a faint hum. It was hardly noticeable and easily covered up by other sounds, but he lay with his head in the corner and both ears near a bar of light. As the stimulation of his bureaucratic rescue ebbed, he felt again the exhaustion of his many sleepless hours. With the bars softly singing to him, he fell into a trance, an image of his parents the last trace of consciousness to fade out before sleep took him.

He had never been a deep sleeper, so it was something of a surprise to him when a cough awoke him and he opened his eyes to see about a dozen other prisoners, each in his own cage of light. The cages were placed in rows to create a prison block. Rubbing his eyes with the heel of his hand, he sat up and yawned. The man in the cell nearest his was hacking up phlegm while he twitched on the floor, his green tinted skin revealing the nature of his crime. A couple other prisoners glanced Alistair's way as he sat up, and one nodded at him. He nodded back but looked away, preferring to cut off any incipient conversation.

The same two guards lounged in the same corner, occasionally sharing a few quiet words. At times the door to the detention center would slide open and another prisoner, escorted by Civil Guard, would be brought in. In this way new rows were added and the prison block grew larger.

Alistair was at the point of deciding to go back to sleep when the door slid open and Gregory and Ryan were ushered in. As the Guardsmen exchanged the forms for the transfer, Gregory looked about and noticed Alistair, but Alistair signaled him to be quiet. Nodding, Gregory looked away. Only moments later, both he and Ryan were sitting on the floor in their separate cells. Ryan finally noticed Alistair, and Alistair gave him the same sign.

Left with nothing else to do, he surveyed the array of prisoners, discovering it was quite easy to distinguish between the recently arrived and the man who had been in prison for some time. It wasn't that the long-term inmate was more gaunt than the newly arrived one—no one was eating particularly well in Arcarius at the moment—it was the desperation of a man who had been free only hours before which contrasted so distinctly with the bored, cocky, or even excited attitude of a long-term captive who viewed the prospect of a lifetime on the prison planet in an entirely different way. By this way of estimating, Alistair figured more than half of the prisoners were newly captured, probably rebels.

The detention center was nearly full when the communicator on the wall at the guards' station lit up red and emitted a series of beeps. The Guards were startled out of a quiet conversation and one of them rose to answer. Leaning against the wall, he spoke into the communicator for a moment, though Alistair could not make out what he said. He stiffened at one point, nodded once and ended the call. With an air of anxiousness, he whispered a few words to his fellow Guard and quickly exited.

Alistair exchanged glances with Gregory, who also noted the exchange. Wellesley, lying in his cell concentrating on picking his nose, was oblivious. Keeping a look out for further developments, Alistair saw the Guard enter a few moments later and exchange some hasty words with the one who remained. He took off again while his partner tensed, like he was ready to spring into action.

A few more prisoners took notice of events and the soft buzz of hushed conversations died out. They eyed their captor with inquisitive gazes as he sat at his post, no longer slumped over in boredom. When the door to the block opened again one could feel the shared anticipation. Alistair's heart leaped as he saw Henry walk in.

Though he had already passed through one checkpoint just to get inside the spaceport, and yet another to enter the detention center, the Guardsman nevertheless searched Henry by passing a wand over his body, a formality forgone during his first visit. When he finished, he waved Henry on, and all eyes in the room followed him as he made his way to Alistair. The muscular young man wanted to sink into the floor when Henry reached him and he was forced to bear so much attention.

"I got it," said Henry in a whisper.

With the blood raging in his ears, Alistair perhaps did not show the proper appreciation but he did manage a nod. "Send it through."

Sitting down on the floor and trying to effect a nonchalant air, Henry slipped a finger into his left shoe, dug around a bit, and finally dragged the stasis capsule out.

"You put it in your shoe?"

"Why not?" asked Henry in an irritated tone as he passed the capsule through.

Grimacing, Alistair looked for a clean spot on his body to wipe the capsule, but found nothing. Instead, with a wary eye on the distracted Guard, he popped the capsule in his mouth, worked it around to build up saliva, and swallowed it.

"Oh. Sorry."

"You did fine," Alistair managed, accidentally meeting the gaze of a curious prisoner and quickly looking away. "Thank you."

"I hope it helps."

"It will."

The two sat for a moment, but with so many eyes on them there was little either was willing to say. Henry finally collected himself and stood up.

"Goodbye, Alistair."

"Goodbye, my friend."

Henry nodded. As he walked down the aisle of cages, Gregory called out to him, "Henry!"

Henry paused, a look of surprise and then relief on his face. He lifted a hand to wave goodbye and Gregory did likewise, and then Henry was out the door.

It was only a few minutes later when the low muffled rumbling of an explosion reached their ears. The hushed conversations that had resumed were cut off. Prisoners shifted uneasily and the Guardsman grabbed the audiphone. Seconds after he ended the call, the door opened and four Civil Guard marched in, armed and armored.

"What the hell's going on out there?" demanded one prisoner.

One of the Guardsmen, a beefy man with forearms as thick as a normal man's thighs, pointed a short, thick finger in his direction and barked, "Keep your damn mouths shut or you're gettin' a muzzle!" No one said another word.

Another explosion rumbled its way to them, this one close enough that the tremor could be felt. Alistair's keen ears detected what he thought might be gunfire. The prisoners, cowed into silence, had little to do but restlessly stir in their cells, shifting from one apprehensive pose to another. Just outside the door, the sound of dozens of boots stomping the floor in unison was heard, passing from left to right and fading back into silence. Then another explosion hit, this one making the floor rattle.

A moment later the door opened and an officer rushed through. He exchanged words with the others who nodded and turned to the prisoners. "We're gonna transfer you to the ship, now," said one while the officer rushed back outside.

The Guardsmen proceeded to the back corner of the detention block and the original Guard typed again on his sleeve. A section of the floor lowered, forming a ramp leading into a dark lower level.

"Let's make this quick," suggested one of the Guards and they surrounded a prisoner's cell. A few strokes on the keypad and the light bars disappeared. The Civil Guard moved in, handcuffed the man and took him down the ramp and into the darkness, reemerging to repeat the process.

Figuring the process would reveal nothing interesting, Alistair lay down and closed his eyes. He was far too alert to fall asleep, so he listened to the excited stirrings of the prisoners and the occasional sound of troop movements and battle. They would come for him when they came for him, to take him to the last journey through space he would ever take. Until then, there was nothing to do but wait.

ร∽ ∽ร

The gathered crowd of Arcarians at the harbor provided the perfect opportunity for a diversion. With a few men, a large tumult was achieved with a couple shots and a few well timed screams. The Civil Guard did not hesitate to put down the riot and protect the ships in the harbor, and with so many of the forces thus distracted, Oliver struck at the spaceport.

His men were few but well equipped. Having infiltrated the spaceport over the course of an hour or so, in groups small enough to draw little notice, Oliver and half a dozen others arrived in a transport auto filled with the weapons they could not sneak inside. The other three dozen men appeared at the front gates just in time to get their weapons and the well timed though hastily planned assault was on.

It was a move that might not have worked a few days hence, but the State was still grappling to regain control of the city. There were five Civil Guard stationed at the spaceport for every rebel, but they did not come upon them all at once. Instead, they encountered surprised and disorganized resistance in small pockets, and these they swept away with comparative ease.

Now Oliver Keegan 3nn stood in the large, empty hall he knew to be the detention center. Just outside the door lay the two Guardsmen he had shot, but he and his men were alone inside.

"The computers have been locked down, sir," said a man seated at the computer station. "I can't get information."

Oliver gritted his teeth in anger and fired off a few rounds into the far wall. His men hung their heads, hoping his angry gaze would not fall on them.

"We did what we could," he finally mumbled. "Let's commandeer a vessel and get out."

He strode quickly for the exit and the half dozen men with him fell into step behind. Upon returning to the terminal hall, he was met by another of his men.

"The prisoners are being loaded onto a transport," he excitedly said.

"Where?" demanded Oliver, enveloping the man's comparatively frail shoulders in his massive hands and squeezing more than he realized.

"You can see it from the window."

Oliver was only a half step behind him, and when he arrived, anxious hands gripping the rail, he peered out over the landing pads at a trail of prisoners being led up a ramp and into the round, pyramidal form of a transport vessel. They were at least three hundred yards away and guarded by a score of Civil Guard who formed a tunnel on either side of the entrance ramp. Gusts of wind swirled around, carrying snow and lashing at the men.

"We'll never reach them in time," he breathed softly, trying to make out Alistair's larger form but failing to spot him. "Are you sure those are the prisoners?"

"They are." The man waited a moment while Oliver watched the ramp being raised. "Sir?" he prompted.

Shaking his head, Oliver said, "It's time to retreat."

He lingered a moment longer as the ship started to float, no longer secured to the ground by gravity. Then, as if a cord was cut, it soundlessly fell into the sky. Before ten seconds passed it was a small dot, and then it was obscured by clouds.

"Goodbye, Alistair," he said. A moment later he turned from the window and left.

End of Part I

PART II

43

The ride was designed for speed, not comfort. The acceleration of the ship pushed Alistair and the other passengers into the floor. He stood erect at the small circular window, his mighty legs bracing him while the others sank into the floor or the metal benches lining the walls of the twenty-by-twenty holding cell. The benches had straps to hold passengers in place, but with cuffed hands and overfull capacity, and lacking guards who cared enough to strap them in, the two score men and handful of women were left to the mercy of inertia. A couple prisoners groaned against the forces assaulting their bodies but Alistair maintained his silence, watching as the city of Arcarius sank beneath him. Avon would be farther west, probably visible on the other side of the transport vessel. Before long they were above the clouds. The curve of the planet next became discernible and the entirety of the main continent could be seen.

The vast, sprawling city of Rendral and its twenty five million inhabitants came into view, filling Aldra's Birth Crater. Centuries ago, when the emigrant ship reached the system, conditions were unfit for human colonization, and the lengthy process of terraforming was begun. After Aldra was surveyed and its life forms—almost exclusively bacteria—collected and preserved, the first step in the process of terraforming was to wipe the slate clean. Suitable asteroids were found, chosen for size and composition, and impact routes and speed determined after much calculation. Most were directed towards the oceans, creating great clouds of scalding steam to sterilize the planet. One, however, was sent towards land, and it created the Birth Crater, a sort of signature after the lengthy and arduous process of composing their opus. In the Birth Crater the first and capital city of Aldra was founded. Alistair thought of his sister as he stared at its lights, wondering which of them illuminated her.

The blue of the sky faded, replaced by the speckled blackness of space. The circular window darkened against the sun, and thus protected, he stared into Aldra, the G-class star, slightly smaller and much younger than the sun of the human homeworld, with defunct solar power stations in close orbit around it. Craning his neck, Alistair could just make out The Incarcerator as their small vessel approached it. Like most modern interstellar cruisers, it had the shape of a disk and was riddled with miniature lights, some of them constant, others blinking, a few pulsing and whirling.

The pseudo-gravity of their vessel diminished as the ship slowed its acceleration. The low hum of the HD engine ceased when it was switched off. After a few seconds there was no gravity at all and inertia alone carried them forward. With his hands cuffed behind his back, Alistair could do little to keep his position near the window, and when a fellow prisoner, in panic over his first trip into space and squirming wildly, bumped into him he was knocked from the window and lost his view of the great interstellar cruiser.

The looks of panic and awe had only just begun to fade from the faces of the novice travelers when, suddenly, one wall of the cubicle seemed to come at them. Alistair knew it was just the transport vessel turning itself around for deceleration, but his companions did not and a cry of alarm went up from the men as the wall knocked into them just hard enough to stun. Fully aware of what was to come, Alistair kicked his legs like a swimmer to realign his body, but failed to do so before the hum of the engine sounded once again and the ship decelerated. He fell head first to the floor, a short fall and a soft one given that the deceleration was weak at first. This proved quite fortunate as two prisoners fell into him from the ceiling where they had been desperately trying to get some control over their bodies.

Moments later, the deceleration was quite strong and most of the prisoners lay on the floor, subject to a force stronger than the gravity of their homeworld. It was a few minutes later when their deceleration slowed once again and they passed into a large docking bay of The Incarcerator. The ship was immense, half as long and wide as the city of Arcarius itself with a depth about one sixth the length and width. Inside the docking bay, Alistair stepped onto a platform in a field of gravity matching Earth's at sea level, a gravitational field slightly weaker than Aldra's but the difference was almost unnoticeable.

As the noise and the bustle inside the drab, gray docking bay hit him, he looked up to the ceiling many scores of meters above. Dozens of stations and control rooms dotted it, like boxes stuck there, with pedestrian tubes connecting them, leaving the docking bay floor open for ships to land. The strident orders of the armed guards who surrounded them kept the prisoners moving in a single file line towards a cordoned area where a greater crowd of captives gathered. The guards carried no weapons in their hands, but small cannons were mounted on each shoulder. Sensors in their faceplates read the eyes of each guard and the cannons fired at what the soldier was looking at.

Alistair could not find Wellesley or Greg, but received a kick to his shin from one of the guards as he, in Mandarin, yelled for Alistair to face forward and keep walking. When he made it, limping and wincing, to the larger group of prisoners, men and women coming in from all over the planet and in various states of health and abuse, Gregory and Wellesley found him. Their haggard faces showed their fear, but they both took comfort from reuniting with their physically intimidating friend and stopped just short of clinging to him. Alistair said little, obliging questions with begrudging answers of a single word, or possibly just a grunt or nod. Any question whose answer would have necessitated a more intricate response was greeted with a dismissive shrug of the shoulders.

The general mood was hardly conducive to chatter, but the varied accents came to their ears through hushed conversations, brief arguments and complaints that flared up and died out. These conversations rumbled low under the yells and whistles of the guards and under the horns and engines of their vehicles traversing the docking bay. Ringed by armed guards of a decidedly inhospitable demeanor, there were no displays of bravado. No prisoner dared more than glance at his masked captors, and the glances were furtive and fearful.

At the far end was a series of tunnels, and every few seconds a hovering train of carriages emerged whereupon people were herded on. The train then disappeared into one of the tunnels. With the exitus and entrance of prisoners, the crowd was gradually recycled and Alistair and his friends found themselves steadily moving closer to where the prisoners boarded. When they were finally ushered on with a few shoves that did more to display dominance than facilitate the proceedings, they took their seats with about forty others and were soon in total blackness, whooshing through a tunnel and making their way to the cell that would hold them for the trip. Occasionally, a lit station would flash by their eyes for an instant, but most of the trip was in complete darkness with a wind from the tunnel blowing at them.

The jaunt on the transport lasted perhaps two minutes before coming to a stop in another station. They were escorted off and hastily divided into smaller groups sent jogging down one of a series of hallways, always under the watchful eye of armed men. The three companions, managing to stay together, arrived at the same cell and were ushered inside.

The room was almost featureless, consisting of white walls, floor and low ceiling. Its only distinctive features were the small windows lining the walls, windows at approximately face level and ringed by glowing buttons. One of the guards went to one of these windows and pressed some buttons. There was a hiss as a door revealed itself around the window and opened up, unveiling a padded interior almost like a coffin and tilted a few degrees backwards.

A prisoner was grabbed at random and brought to the open door of the hibernation pod. The man, grimy from his imprisonment on Aldra, was shaking as two guards tore his clothes from his body. One guard tossed the clothes into the middle of the room while the other shoved him into the pod and, pressing a couple more buttons, closed it. The lights ringing the window grew active, blinking on and off in a pattern that made it look as if a light were rapidly encircling the window. The man's look of terror abruptly faded and his head settled back.

Hardly bothering to acknowledge it, the guards grabbed another prisoner and she too was stripped naked. When placed in the pod she struggled more than the first, as if overcome by claustrophobia. The door closed on her writhing left arm and the woman screamed as she retracted it. Then the door sealed shut and her scream became almost inaudible, but it made the prisoners restless. A gruff order from one of the guards in heavily accented English was enough to settle them, and a moment later, as the buttons blinked in the same pattern around the window, the woman's head slumped back.

Gregory faced his hibernation with quiet dignity, going so far as to begin to undress as he was pushed in front of his chosen pod. His hands were slapped out of the way in favor of ripping his clothes from his body. When he was placed inside, he closed his eyes, drew a deep breath and swallowed, only his clenched jaw giving away his nervousness. It relaxed when his head settled back.

Alistair betrayed no fear when his turn came. Knowing there was no accountability for the guards during the long voyage in space, he was careful to stare ahead at the wall and give no challenging looks, but he refused to show meekness. His head he held high even as they stripped him naked. A woman was brought next to him as his pod door opened and he noticed she was attractive. As he stepped into his pod—only just able to squeeze inside—he thought grimly of what could befall her during the trip. But the thought was cut short as the door closed. The last thing he saw through the small window, as all sounds from the room were muffled to the brink of vanishing, was Wellesley staring at him with barely restrained fear. Alone with the sound of his own breath, which he could now hear, he prayed Ryan's fear was not a reflection from his own face. Then he lost consciousness.

44

For a moment, Alistair had the delightful sensation of waking up on Foundation Day, wedged in between his brother and sister. They always slept together on Foundation Eve, after the festival and the story telling, and his heart leapt as he thought of the new baseball mitt he would get. Before he had a chance to consider it was odd he already knew his gift beforehand, he lurched forward as two hands yanked on his arms and reality slammed into him. He fell to his knees, naked, remembering the cramped quarters were the walls of the pod, not his siblings, and then pitched forward, falling face first into the floor despite his attempts to stabilize himself. He was vaguely aware of other bodies being dragged out of their hibernation pods and, like him, falling untended to the floor.

Having come out of hibernation before, he knew to lie still until the wooziness and lightheadedness passed. He heard the sound of vomiting and knew someone had tried to rise too soon. He dared not open his eyes. They were sealed shut with sleep anyway, but the light making his eyelids glow was uncomfortably bright and reddish orange, a warning not to expose the sensitive organs. As he lay on the floor he wet himself, helpless to control it. Though he had been in hibernation, he had still aged the equivalent of a day or two, and his weakened body could not hold the urine.

The guard finished his rounds in the room and left, leaving a group of dazed prisoners to lie on the floor in their filth until they could rouse themselves. Outside the chamber he could hear at least two others talking to each other.

Ultimately it was the smell that got him up. He braced his shaky arms against the cold floor and got into a sitting position, leaning back against his pod door until the dizziness passed. He rubbed his eyes, scraping away the sleep from his lashes but not yet daring to test his sight. When he finally did, the light seared him and his vision was blurred. It took several minutes before he could see with any clarity and comfort.

A sprinkler system in the ceiling bathed the filthy prisoners in cold water. A collective groan of distress went up and several prone figures squirmed into a sitting position. Surveying the circular room, Alistair noticed one of the pods was not open, and no prisoner lay on the floor in front of its door. Some, those in ill health, did not withstand long hibernation. It was rare, but possible that he or she died because of this. Despite the safeguards, a blood clot could have formed. It was also possible something was done to him during the trip, either because he angered a guard or because an aggrieved victim bribed one to settle accounts for him.

The thought triggered a memory, and Alistair immediately sought out the attractive woman he saw just before hibernating. He found her lying on the floor in front of her pod, unmoving save for her chest expanding and contracting. There were bruises on her arms not present at the outset of the trip, and there was even a small trail of dried blood on the inside of one of her thighs. Gritting his teeth, he looked away, angry and embarrassed to have seen her in such a state.

The sprinklers switched off and left the prisoners to shiver and drip dry. A few came to their feet, often leaning on the walls for support. Alistair kept his seat, feeling a bit stronger and steadier but seeing little reason to stand. Wellesley was now on his feet but Gregory was still lying on the floor doing naught but breathing. One of the two guards outside, equipped with cannons and faceplate, came in and viewed the convicts.

"Get your buddies on their feet and start filing out."

Alistair caught Wellesley's eye and they both assisted Gregory, who was almost unresponsive. By his arms and shoulders they lifted and supported him as they followed the others back into the hallway they had been in who knew how long ago. When all the inmates who were able left the cell, one of the guards went back in and callously administered a kick to the ribs of any who lingered. He kicked until the pain outweighed the grogginess.

When they trudged down the corridor to what Alistair assumed would be a train station, they merged with other groups and passed by other cells in various states of evacuation. Upon their arrival they were herded with men and women from all over Aldra, all Caucasian, all English speakers. Now they roamed among far greater diversity. Few spoke, but on display were all the pigments of the human race, from tall, blonde and pale Nordics to Africans of darkest ebony. Many displayed no resemblance to any single race, and many possessed a mix of traits. The sharp features of the Mediterranean were softened by the flatter features of the East Asian, or the thick body of the East European was attenuated by the graceful form of the East African. It was a mixing that in truth had been going on since the human race had existed, but whatever divergences had arisen from relative isolation, they were, absent deliberate genetic manipulation, being smoothed over at a faster pace. Wellesley, who had never seen such people as these, stared in wonder.

The bleary detainees stumbled their way down the corridor until they came to another station and the process of shipping them back to a docking bay began. The station was full to bursting, and when the prisoners did not compact their numbers to the guards' satisfaction, they were beaten at the edges until they crammed together in a tighter pack of naked bodies. There was a large window giving a view outside, but it faced away from Srillium and its star and only the speckled void of space could be seen. Alistair stared at it, wondering if any of those speckles were Aldra.

"Are they going to give us clothes?" Wellesley grumbled, his first words.

Alistair shrugged.

"It costs them less not to," said Gregory. "Don't count on much."

"Why the hell did they take our clothes from us?"

"The inside of the pod is designed to prevent bed sores; clothes aren't ," the doctor explained through a yawn.

"Can we at least get clothes on the planet?"

Gregory eyed Alistair, hoping for an answer, but Alistair wasn't speaking. "I don't know what to expect," he finally replied.

As the continuous stream of trains carried away detainees, while others filed in, the three moved inexorably closer to the front. A spark of chatter caught and spread through the crowd until the melodies and lyrics of a hundred languages echoed through the station hall. The babble was doused by the amplified voice of an unseen speaker ordering them to silence.

Their turn finally came. A train sped into the station, abruptly braked and opened its doors. Alistair and his companions hustled in and stood among the crowd. With prisoners from dozens of systems filling the vessel, there was no time to allow sitting room on the carriages. They were tightly packed in and stood chest to back and temple to temple. So teeming with bodies were the carriages that when the train took off, its rapid acceleration hardly moved them and a few poor souls at the back were nearly knocked unconscious from the weight of the rest.

They endured another rapid transit in darkness, blown by the wind in the tunnels, and finally emerged into what Alistair guessed was the same docking bay at which they had arrived. Conical transport ships were landing and taking off a dozen at a time. The train stopped only just long enough for every prisoner to exit and then raced back into the tunnel system, whipping them one last time with a breeze. Then the guards shouted and herded them towards the transports.

An invisible force field prevented the air from rushing out of the docking bay's aperture. The transport vessels were all equipped with a field of their own, the peaks and valleys of whose waves were precisely opposite those of the greater field, so that the two fields cancelled each other out wherever they met, allowing the transports to pass through without allowing air to escape. Through this vast opening the great giant gas planet of Srillium reflected its star's light into the docking bay, rendering it a red hue and casting long shadows. The view was what is properly described as breathtaking, and not a prisoner among them, no matter his worries, entered without gazing out on the stripes and swirls of the planet entirely filling the opening, jaw dropping as far as the tendons would allow.

When Gregory recovered from his awe, his brow furrowed for a moment as a thought occurred to him. "Is that…it's a gas giant. Is Srillium…?"

"Srillium's a moon," was Alistair's reply as he gazed at the planet. Even he was impressed by the majesty of it.

"Where is it?" asked Wellesley.

"Must be on the other side of the ship," said Gregory. "How big is it?"

"Big as Aldra. Almost."

Shuffling ever forward, pressed this way and that by other bodies, Alistair Ashley, Gregory Lushington and Ryan Wellesley approached one of the transport vessels. The guards were going through the crowd, grabbing women and putting them in a different line. A medical team waited at the front of the line, the only staff on the ship whose faces the prisoners could see. They were ringed by a dozen imposing guards, and one by one the women were brought to them. Trembling, each was made to stand with her legs apart whereupon a device was inserted into her vagina. There was a soft buzzing and every one cried out before the doctor extracted the device and a guard sent her stumbling back towards a transport vessel.

"They're sterilizing them!" Gregory hissed, clenching his fists together. "Why the hell are they sterilizing them?"

"They don't want them reproducing," Alistair quietly said, sympathetic, too disturbed by the fact to maintain his terse coldness. "No stable, productive societies can be permitted."

"What the hell do children have to do with a stable society?" said Wellesley, although his normal irritability was tempered by an empathetic somberness.

The women, almost without exception, were inconsolable. The men were silent and stared at the floor, feeling the discomfort of him who wishes to soothe but knows his well-intentioned effort will be rebuffed. Stuffed into their chambers, a few women held each other, strangers suddenly become fast friends, while the men just stood still, too drained to express anything.

Back on a transport, Alistair found his way to the window again, using his bulk to put himself before it and not caring what reaction he received. When the transport fell and left the docking bay, he caught sight of the world that was to be his home and, some day, his sepulcher. It was a blue and green world like all other inhabited planets, more blue than green. Most of what he saw was lit by the sun and the slender crescent of darkness was still faintly aglow with the light reflected from the gas giant. He could see a continent whose center in the northern hemisphere was at about noon. Islands dotted the seas, including an extensive archipelago in the wide-open southern ocean. Any other significant landmasses were on the far side.

The transport took them towards the southwestern section of the continent where it was morning. From the coloration it looked like a land of hills with mountains to the east and west and forests to the north. Farther to the southwest, a peninsula jutted out in the sea, sporting more mountainous terrain as well as a river that ran its length before emptying into the ocean. Some miles south of the peninsula there was an island a small fraction of the size of Arcarius Island.

The transport rotated so that the surface went from being above to being below them and the breaks were applied while flames from the compressed air licked at the window. Since the room was now more crowded than when they first boarded, the landing was even more un-comfortable and there were cries and groans as a pile of bodies formed on the floor. Someone even wailed in genuine pain. Then they felt the soft thud of the landing.

When the door opened, the deep, low hum of a large horn greeted their ears, a hum which would be heard for miles and which they could feel resonate in their chests. Guards awaited them and ushered them down the corridor where they mixed with other prisoners. From there they spiraled downward to the base of the transport at whose center a platform inclined to the ground. Alistair finally set foot on Srillium IIa, in the weeds and mud, as the horn continued to blow.

When all the prisoners were disgorged, the platform was raised. Walking out from un-derneath the ship with Gregory and Wellesley in tow, Alistair took stock of the surroundings. There was a tower about two rugby fields to the north. Made of stone, it stood fifty feet high and was comprised of two levels. The first was a relatively thick base with no visible point of accession, and the second was a narrower part with stairs encircling its perimeter and reaching the top. There was a wooden ladder on the upper section which presumably was lowered to allow admittance to the upper portion. Two men were lounging on top of the base while two others were at the top of the narrower section, one of them blowing into an enormous horn. While Alistair watched, the blower finally paused for breath before blowing again.

The landscape around them was featureless. In the sky far to the east, he could see an-other transport vessel plummeting to earth, preceded by fire and leaving smoke in its trail. Just to their west there was another group of prisoners who arrived before them. Their transport had left but they were still milling around, though a few started walking towards Alistair's group. To the north a group of riders on horseback headed their way and another cavalry was coming from the east. Turning around and peering beneath their transport, he saw a third group coming from the southwest, from the direction of the mountainous peninsula.

"The welcome party," said a man sardonically, his accent one Alistair could not place though he sounded like a native speaker of English. He was Caucasian like they were, probably purely so or close to it. He nodded when he caught Alistair's eye but Alistair ignored him.

At that moment, their transport fell upward. Alistair was surprised to discover his chest was heaving as he watched the cruel ferry take off, abandoning them to their new life.

45

While the three cavalry companies made for them, the two groups of naked arrivals merged together, speakers of like languages mingling. With a last powerful bellow, the man with the horn finally desisted, revealing the rumble of galloping horses. The men from the east reached them first, a mixed lot of about fifty of all races and dressed in primitive animal skins and sporting spears and other weapons of wood and stone. Most were scarred. Not one had a full set of teeth and all had beards in two braids. The naked newcomers regarded them in silent apprehension, each individual standing still so as not to call attention to himself.

A few of the horsemen dismounted to round up the women, unmoved by their cries of protest. One man elected to be gallant and put a hand on one of the horsemen to stop him as he roughly dragged an older woman along the ground. The warrior spun about, sized up the slighter man for a moment, and asked him, "Are you a doctor?"

The question caught the man off guard. "I'm a banker," he replied, whereupon the horseman drew a dagger and plunged it into the banker's lower abdomen. The crowd gasped in unison but the horseman, nonchalant, wiped his obsidian dagger on the earth and resheathed it. Mouth wide open, the banker slumped to the ground while the horseman finished dragging the old woman to dump her among the others. Gregory rushed to the side of the writhing banker.

As the group from the north arrived, a rider from the first group guided his mount towards Alistair and tossed him a bundle of clothes.

"You're welcome to come with us," he said, his voice almost friendly, his accent unfamiliar to Alistair. He was a large man just shy of middle age, with brown skin and principally African features. "I like your tattoo."

Alistair reflexively touched his chest and Ryan, his curiosity piqued, scrutinized the design.

After a moment of consideration, the man reached back and tossed some clothes at Wellesley. "You can come too."

Alistair realized there was little he could do and so began to dress himself in the rough leathers.

"You'll look better in these," said a voice with a thick, Germanic accent and another bundle of clothes fell at Alistair's feet.

Looking up, Alistair saw another horseman, this one sporting green tattoos about every inch of exposed white skin.

"He already agreed to come with us. He won't look good in green."

"He'll look fine," retorted the second. Turning to Alistair, he said, "We've got a larger tribe. With that tattoo you'll be the chief's private bodyguard. Make a good decision."

"He already accepted my invitation."

"You can't invite until we're all here."

"We don't follow those rules no more!"

"Gentlemen," said Alistair quietly, "I'll hold out for the highest offer."

With that, he removed the moccasins he had donned and left both bundles of clothes on the ground. The horseman divided their rueful glances between Alistair and each other. Wellesley, surprised, hesitated only a moment and dropped his clothes as well.

Gregory, as he knelt next to the stabbed banker, was shaking his head and using his hands to staunch the blood flow. The man was moaning, his hands on top of Gregory's. When Alistair was at his side, he looked up at him with an expression part anger and part helpless frustration.

"Lower bowel wound," he muttered. Alistair knew enough about injuries, as well as Gregory's tone, to know there was no hope.

The women had all been rounded up and men from both companies stood guard around them.

"How many females?" asked one of the company from the north, tattooed green like his fellows.

"Forty eight. Times twenty men. Two shipments."

"Any more shipments coming?"

"How would I know? Look up."

The men were being divided into two groups. One had more members but was comprised of smaller men while the other had more athletic, younger and stronger men. Both groups stood still, compliant. A group of horsemen, having dismounted, headed in Alistair's direction. One of the green tattoos grabbed by the shoulder the man with the strange accent who spoke to Alistair right after exiting the transport vessel, and propelled him towards the more numerous group.

"Make your way over there," he gruffly ordered.

"I'm with them," protested the man as he pointed at Alistair with a pleading look.

"Not any more," replied the horseman and as he stood in front of Alistair he put his arms across his chest. "I hear you don't want to get dressed."

"I'll dress when I'm ready."

"Maybe he wants to come with us," challenged another horseman with a braided beard.

"I haven't decided yet."

Ryan put an arm on Alistair's forearm. "Alistair, I wanna get some clothes on."

Alistair considered him a moment and finally shrugged again. "Clothes for the three of us."

"This guy a doctor?" asked one.

"Yes I am," Gregory fairly hissed.

"Well, leave that one. He won't make it more than a few hours."

Gregory stood up and went nose to nose with the man. "I realize that. He won't make it because someone stabbed him for no reason."

The green tattooed man turned away from Gregory. "Three suits," he said, jacking a finger over his shoulder at them. Two warriors brought forth the suits, which were no finer than what a Neanderthal might have worn.

"Make it four," said the other man with the accent, and his look was like a desperate beggar's.

"He's with us," said Gregory with a look at Alistair.

The tattooed horseman impatiently sighed. Turning to Alistair, he put his hands on his hips with a bored expression. "Is this a package deal?"

Alistair finally nodded and started to don the new clothes. The other man rushed over to him and waited to receive clothes of his own.

"I can get used to green tattoos," he said with a chummy smile and a relieved sigh.

A horseman from their newly adopted tribe, without sparing a glance at him, responded, "*You* won't be getting tattoos."

The man regarded him sullenly but said nothing.

By now the final group of horsemen had arrived, distinguishable from the others by the bone earrings and nose rings they sported but otherwise in the same condition: missing teeth, unwashed bodies and multifarious scars. They immediately moved among the new arrivals, inspecting them with an air of experience. A few they grabbed and spun about, but it was a purely physical inspection. They gave the same regard as to a leg of meat at a butcher's.

"How many females?" asked one of the bone rings, his accent revealing him to be a native speaker of English. He had more bones than the others of his group. Many were threaded through his light brown skin at the forearms and legs, while at least ten small bones depended from each ear and softly clinked together with his movements. A large bone pierced his jutting nose, and each eyebrow had a bone threaded through the skin lengthwise. His head sat on a squat, thick neck and his chest was robust and well muscled. His legs and arms squirmed with the flexing of muscles when he moved.

One of the green tattoos answered, "Almost fifty. One's old, though."

"Keep her. She can probably cook."

As the man with multiple piercings moved among the newcomers, he was given a special deference, even by members of the other tribes. It was a begrudging, fearful deference, even from his own men, and by his walk Alistair thought he was quite pleased by it. He came to stand in front of Alistair and looked the former marine up and down, hands on hips.

"You'd do better to come with us."

"How so?"

"He's already picked his tribe," growled a green tattoo.

With a shake of his head, the man said, "Guess I got here too late."

The horsemen set about dividing the females after an intrusive inspection. The men with the bone piercings divided the women into three groups. The other two tribes picked which group would go to the pierced men and then haggled to allocate the rest. It took half an hour to finish, and then the process was repeated with the two hundred men from the less numerous of the male groups. When this second process was finished the more athletic men were given some clothing; the women were given only shoes.

There was an almost palpable sense of relief among the men who came to join Alistair. A few engaged in some lighthearted conversation, but Alistair remained aloof, eyeing the proceedings with distrust. The bulk of the horsemen from the three tribes now encircled the remaining men, several hundred strong but unarmed.

The youngest Ashley felt an alarming presentiment. "I don't like this at all," he softly muttered.

The stabbed banker lay still, moaning only slightly, his hands covered in dried and fresh blood as he clasped his midriff. Gregory, yet to dress and still holding the midsection, softly spoke to him. Alistair could hardly hear them over the chatter of men introducing themselves to their new companions, smiling congratulatory and relieved smiles and shaking hands. The women huddled together, humiliated and silent. Moving to the edge of the group, Alistair clenched his fists as he watched the horsemen. A few of the slighter men, mostly the young, were sent to join one of the three other groups, arriving with the same sense of relief as their fellows. Unlike the women, these men were not even given shoes.

Wellesley came to stand next to Alistair, wearing what looked to be a thin, coarse woolen tunic and leggings with moccasins. They watched as the group of unchosen dwindled. Then the horsemen, the hundred or so not busy sorting out the chosen ones, faced the increasingly anxious older and physically frailer males. There was a moment when the horsemen sat still on their horses, and then, in unison, they quickly and smoothly grabbed their bows.

"No!" yelled Alistair, and Gregory, startled, looked up from his ministrations.

"Keep your mouth shut," growled a warrior and he moved to Alistair to grab him by the bicep.

The horsemen all fitted arrows to their bows. Alistair ripped his arm from the grasp of the man who had accosted him. "Move!" he yelled to the quailing captives.

The arrows flew from taught strings, pierced the flesh of men too subdued and humiliated to resist, and as cries went up blood dripped down. The men were finally moved to action and those not dead, dying or too seriously injured tried to escape. Before they got far a second volley of arrows cut into them, and then a third and fourth, and all but a few fell to the ground. Alistair ran towards the horsemen as the screams and wails of the dying enveloped them all, but the apparent leader of the pierced tribe, as if waiting for this move, rode to intercept him.

"I don't think this one is going to be as useful as we would like," he declared to no one in particular and he dismounted to face Alistair. "Perhaps we should settle things right now."

While a small group of the warriors now waded among the dying men, dispatching them with perfect callousness, a few other horsemen of the three tribes gathered around Alistair and the other, eager for a show.

"Are you a coward," Alistair spat at him, his voice quaking despite his efforts, "or do I get a knife?"

"No," chuckled the man, "we'll do this barehanded."

"Suits me," Alistair shot back, blushing and gritting his teeth, increasingly aware of a developing audience.

Supremely confident, the man removed the bones from his body. A second warrior from his tribe grabbed one of the naked men and tossed him to the ground in front of the leader. The leader held the bones out to the man who quickly understood and accepted them into his trembling hands.

"Away," said the leader with a flick of the wrist after he deposited his collection. He stripped off his animal-skin shirt, revealing a tattoo on his left pectoral. It was the same as

Alistair's, an intricate circular design with eight points spaced evenly around the perimeter. Over two of these points, the one at the top and the one forty five degrees to its right, a small star was tattooed. There was an expectant murmur from the horsemen and the man sported a confident grin.

Alistair stripped off his shirt, exposing the same tattoo, except all eight of his points sported a star. The murmur from the men grew louder and Alistair's opponent's eyes popped open.

"What the hell do you think you're doing!?" he finally snarled, throwing a fist at Alistair and pacing in front of him like a caged tiger. "You think I'm afraid of you? I don't care how many stars you have, I'll tear you to shreds!" He pounded on his own chest with a fist. "You wouldn't be the first son of a bitch and you won't be the last. You try throwing your weight around here and I'll cut you to pieces. You think you can intimidate me? You think you can show me your little tattoo and make me scared? I'll crush you and forget you like all the rest." He held out a forearm and pointed to the holes in his skin. "I'll put your bone in my arm like a thousand others! I'm running out of room but I'll make a space for you! You think you're special? You think you can intimidate me?" He said the last with another thump to his chest and he spun on his heel and left Alistair standing there. "That son of a bitch gets near me, I'll kill him," he swore to his men and then, upon mounting his horse, rode off towards the cluster of new arrivals chosen for his tribe.

The man who held the collection of bones looked about uncertainly and finally decided to head in the direction of his new leader. A murmur came from the horsemen of the other two tribes and one of the green tattoos sidled his horse next to Alistair.

"Nice to have you on board," he said with a smirk. He looked to be a pureblood East Asian and his accent, though slight, sounded it.

As Alistair dressed himself, he asked, "May I inquire as to the purpose of that slaughter?" He was breathing heavily but he kept his tone civil.

The friendly grin disappeared. "Welcome to Srillium. There's not enough food to feed everyone they dump on us. Simple as that." So saying he nudged his horse in the ribs and wandered off.

Wellesley was at Alistair's side a moment later. "What the hell just happened?"

"Pecking order."

The cadavers were skinned and the flesh stripped from the bones. The meat was passed up to the men on the tower, who were joined by a handful of other men, and some supplies were brought out. It looked like they were going to cure the meat. The bones from the bodies were also passed up to the tower guard, as were the skins and the organs. Sitting on the ground among his fellows with his arms on his knees, Alistair watched the process without expression. In the sky a fireball appeared as another transport made its way to the surface, but it would land many miles away.

One of the green tattoos rode up to the assembled recruits to address them. "Congratulations," he said in an unfamiliar accent. "You made it. Some of you have been chosen to take the test to become full warriors of the tribe. Those who don't make it will be servants to

Gamaliel. Some of you will have to proceed without footwear. We were not expecting to have so many of you. You will all be dressed and fed when we make it back to camp, a few hours to the north."

At the mention of food Alistair's stomach gurgled.

"The trek north will serve as your first test. Those who cannot make the trek will be left to die." The man surveyed them from left to right and then nodded. "Move out."

The horsemen from the three tribes went separate ways, though about a third from each tribe stayed behind. This left, in Alistair's tribe, about thirty horsemen leading sixty to seventy warrior prospects, fully clothed; sixteen women, naked with shoes; and about a hundred and fifty entirely naked men. Without any command, the group fell naturally into marching order: horsemen first, followed by new warriors, followed by the women and then by the naked men.

46

"How long were we in hibernation?" Wellesley asked as he stared at his feet plodding along.

The question roused Alistair from his brooding reverie. "Greg, you were clean shaven when we left, right?"

"Close, I think."

"If those are modern hibernation pods…Greg's got about two day's worth of beard… probably two cycles. If the pods are older it was less time."

"Two cycles? So I'm thirty one cycles now? Why does it take so long?"

"All the stops along the way. And your body is still only twenty nine."

"I wonder how your revolution is going," Greg mumbled.

"It might be over by now, for better or worse."

"Revolutionaries, eh?" asked a voice, and Alistair turned to see the one so eager to join them. "They're some of the most common here, they say." He held out a hand which Alistair shook. "Clyde Oliver Jones, Earth. Australia."

"Alistair Ashley, Aldra. Arcarius."

"I'm Gregory Lushington," said Greg, and he stuttered a moment, as if about to say his suffix and then deciding not to. "This is Ryan Wellesley. We're all from Aldra."

"Can't say I've heard of Aldra."

"Aldra's not an important system in the scheme of things," said Alistair.

"What the hell are you talking about?" grouched Wellesley.

"Listen to your mate. No one gives a shit about Aldra on Earth."

"We're fighting the war against Kaldis!"

"You and everyone else. Take it from me, mate, no one knows you're out there. I thought from your accents you might be Canadian or something."

"It's an English-speaking system," said Alistair. "I'm sure some of our ancestors were Canadian."

"What are you here for, Clyde?" Gregory asked.

"Oh, a few crimes I didn't commit. Nothing for it now; just have to make the most of it. What's a guy gotta do to get some clothes around here?"

"Be a soldier or a doctor," Alistair said.

At that moment the horsemen called a halt. Most of the new arrivals, especially those without shoes, sank to the ground to rest, massaging their aching soles. The horsemen pulled off a short distance to confer among themselves, and Alistair warily eyed them as the resting marchers began to chatter.

"We can't get there fast enough," Clyde intoned to no one in particular. "I could eat just about anything at this point."

"Some water would be nice," said another man.

As Clyde chatted in a charismatic way and anyone within earshot leaned in to listen, Alistair eyed his fellow prisoners. They could have wound up there for any number of reasons, whether petty theft, murder, white-collar crimes or getting caught on the wrong side of a political coup. They might have been innocent or guilty, but as he took in their appearance he imagined most were guilty and the traditional lowbrow criminal. Hardened and rough, many looked like men prepared for a fight in any circumstance, ready to provoke one for amusement's sake. They looked at the world without pity or remorse, like they didn't care one way or another about most things, as if nothing could touch them and they were not interested in touching anything or anyone else. The look in their eyes often exuded the flat simplicity of men of low intellect.

There were many exceptions, ones no doubt found guilty of something other than a street crime, or perhaps wrongly convicted. These men, untempered, lacked a shell to hide their nervousness and uncertainty. They pitied their fellows and eagerly sought pity for themselves as compensation. What they attracted was disdain and the attention of brutes looking to flex their muscles.

A few of the clothed warriors-to-be, already feeling full of their new station, now commanded a few of the small, naked men to massage their feet. These slighter men, after some unfriendly prompting, complied with varying degrees of resentment. Alistair looked away in disgust and caught Gregory looking at him. They shared a disapproving look but said nothing.

The horsemen returned from their discussion and passed out some canteens and morsels of cured meat to the newest warriors. These were eagerly and quickly consumed, and while the new warriors ate, the horsemen gathered some of the naked men at the back of the pack and took them off a short distance. Alistair and Gregory shared another look and Alistair came to his feet. A few of the others noticed him and followed his gaze.

"They're going to kill them," Alistair said. "They lied to make them compliant and now they're going to kill them."

"Don't be a goddamn fool," said a man, light brown like so many.

"You wanna bite the hand that feeds you?"

Alistair sat back down but kept his eyes on the proceedings. Once again the group of men was divided, this time in half. While one half was made to kneel the other was escorted a few yards away and then surrounded by the horsemen. The bows came out once more and Gregory grabbed Alistair's arm. Powerless, Alistair watched as the men, compliant as sheep, perhaps incredulous, did nothing to stop their slaughter. After three volleys of arrows, the horsemen waded into the moaning and dying and finished the job with their daggers.

"That will be us after the next shipment," Alistair said softly, his voice unsteady. "We'll be slaughtering helpless men. Unless we do something about it."

"And what are we going to do?" queried a man who sat near them. Of principally African descent, he had been speaking Mandarin with a partner but now addressed Alistair in flawless English and with a hostile tone.

"This is life," said another, a particularly brutish looking thug with scars on his face. He popped a last bit of meat into his mouth and drank from a canteen. "You do what you have to."

Sitting back down, Alistair fell silent and glowered, never taking his eyes from the horsemen who were now skinning the dead. Gregory, moved by events to express his passion in the first way to present itself to him, leaned into Alistair.

"This is why I didn't support your revolution."

Alistair fixed a sharp look on him. "What the hell are you talking about?"

"This is your damn anarchy, Alistair. You take away government and this is what you are left with. This is what men are like."

"You don't know what you're talking about," Alistair sputtered. "You've got prisoners forced onto a…oh, forget it! You have no idea what you're talking about. If this is what men are like then why make some masters over others?"

"If your anarchy could work, why is this always the result?"

"This isn't always the result!"

The sun was almost directly overhead when they started their march. By the time the bodies were skinned and the meat packaged and given to the remaining naked men to carry, it was nearing the opposite horizon. Srillium II's moon had a day about the same length as Earth and Kaldis, which meant it must not have been so close to the gas giant as to be tidally locked. The heat from the sun finally dissipated as their shadows lengthened across the plain. For the lucky ones, now that their bellies had something in them, the march became less trying. For the rest, starving and burdened now with the gruesome flesh of their fellows, the march became nearly intolerable.

At one point Wellesley nudged Alistair and nodded towards the eastern horizon. Peering up, Alistair saw the great body of Srillium II rising into the sky. Only a small part of it was visible; the rest was below the horizon. When it did rise it would be much larger than the sun in the Aldran sky. Its reflected light would bathe the night side in a ruddy hue, possibly providing enough light to read by.

A short time later, when Srillium was half revealed and the sun gone, though some of its light yet lingered, a troupe of horsemen emerged at a gallop from the forest before them. Possessing twice the numbers of their own mounted men, they were just as well armed. They let out a war cry that mixed with the rumble of horses' hooves. The tattooed men pulled up and quickly readied their spears and arrows. The new recruits were pressed into service and Alistair and Wellesley found themselves side by side, the former armed with an obsidian dagger and the latter with a mallet of wood. Gregory was ordered to retreat back to the naked serfs.

"Stay by me," Alistair said, fixing an uncompromising look on his sidekick. Wellesley's frantic nod indicated such a command was unnecessary.

The tattooed men loosed a volley of arrows and half a dozen of their assailants fell from their horses, either because their steeds were struck or because they were. The resulting pile up took out a handful of others, but when the ambushers finally reached the spears of their prey they still outnumbered the green tattoos.

Alistair had trained for hand-to-hand combat, but this sort of battle was unlike anything he had experienced. Bodies thudded together and men grunted, groaned and screamed. He had never smelled the breath of a man he killed in battle, nor been sprayed by his blood as he sank to the ground, nor endured the desperate look in his eyes when he knows he has lost.

He imagined himself weary of battle but hardened by it, but he was unprepared for the proximity and immediacy of what he now confronted. He felt the intense tickle of nervousness in his stomach, as if he were suddenly falling.

One of the mounted attackers broke through the muddle of limbs and bodies. He came out spattered in blood with a great gash on his forehead and he shot the new recruits a wild gaze, baring his teeth and growling. With an imperceptibly fast flick of his arm and wrist, Alistair hurled the dagger at him. The wild look became shock as the dagger plunged into his throat. Clutching at it, he fell from his saddle and landed with a thud on the ground where he lay squirming.

"Finish him, Ryan!" Alistair hissed.

Hesitating only a moment, Ryan ran with his mallet raised high. The man had yet enough sense to defend himself, so instead of a finishing blow to the head Wellesley delivered a crunching strike to his elbow. Before he could act again the rump of a horse backed into him and sent him staggering backwards. He managed to keep his feet but, seeing his target was being trampled by horse hooves, returned to Alistair's side, having managed to hang on to his weapon but leaving the dagger behind.

Alistair now skirted the edge of the throng of warriors. A pair of struggling horsemen were separating themselves from the rest. They each had delivered sundry nicks and blows to the other, but the one with the green tattoo now managed to slice at the neck of the other's horse and the mount, rearing up, threw its rider and galloped off. Without a mount, the man was near helpless to prevent the spear thrust that felled him.

With a running start, Alistair leapt at the victor and wrapped his great arms around his midsection. Leaning back, he pulled the green tattoo from his saddle and they hit the ground, though the man's foot was caught in the crude stirrup. Alistair rolled on top of him, squeezing at his midsection like a python. All the other could do was flail frantically as Alistair, releasing his abdomen, planted both knees on the back of the man's shoulders and reached back to grab the dagger from the man's belt. The horse pulled away, dragging the man with it for a stretch and nearly upsetting Alistair's balance, but the foot finally pulled free and with a flash of obsidian Alistair stabbed through the back of the his neck, instantly ending his struggles.

"What the hell are you doing?" demanded Wellesley who reached him just as the brief struggle ended.

"Get the goddamn horse!" Alistair barked as he came to his feet. "I'll get another one."

Wellesley looked uncertain for a moment but rushed after the horse while Alistair divested the dead man of his weapons. Spear in hand, he turned to survey the battle spreading out over greater territory. Many of the naked servants fled the way they had come, as had many of the new warriors. A few others waded into the battle on foot. Alistair spotted Gregory and Clyde heading his way and giving the battle zone a wide berth and many fearful glances.

When next he spied an opportunity, Alistair rushed at a mounted warrior, leading with the spear and stabbing the man in his side, knocking him from the horse. Gurgling blood, the man fell over, taking the spear with him. One of his brethren noticed the attack and moved in on Alistair, but the ex marine grabbed the fallen man's dagger and flung it at the steed's throat. When it hit, the horse reared back on its hind legs and threw the unprepared rider to the ground.

Panicked, the horse ran off and Alistair charged the fallen man, jumping high into the air and landing atop him, bringing his fist down on his face with a debilitating blow. He availed himself of a new dagger, pulling it quickly from the sheathe and drawing it across the unconscious man's throat. He was sprayed with thick warm liquid which he wiped from his face with his forearm.

Spotting the mount he was after, he made a move for it but quickly fell to his knees as some blood dripped into his mouth. Sickened and queasy, his stomach heaved and he vomited onto the earth. There was little enough in his stomach save bile, and it burned his throat as it passed through. Breathing heavily, he wiped his mouth with the other forearm and, his knees unsteady, rose and stumbled after the riderless horse to grab its reins.

After an unsteady moment between earth and saddle, he got his leg around to the other side and for the first time in his life found himself on horseback. Drawing on vicarious experience from books and threedies, he managed to maneuver it to where Greg and Wellesley were clinging to the back of the other steed. Clyde was shouting instructions, and when he saw Alistair approach he rushed to his side and expertly got himself onto the horse's back.

"Take us out of here!" he bellowed.

They joined the other fleeing convicts but with a distinct advantage. As they headed south, towards the mountains for no other reason than that they were far from the battle, the sounds faded as the number of surviving warriors dwindled and more distance was put between them.

47

They rode their horses hard until the limits of endurance were reached and they were obliged to allow them a rest. Finding a small brook winding through some gentle bumps that fell short of being proper hills, Alistair called a halt. Clyde set about inspecting their steeds with an air of authority while the animals guzzled down water. There was a stout oak near the banks of the brook and Ryan Wellesley immediately stretched out underneath it and closed his eyes. Greg took inventory of what they had, including some items from the saddle-bags, and Alistair went off to attend to private business.

The great planet of Srillium was now half risen in the east, towering over them and dominating the sky. A reddish glow permeated the land. When Gregory found Alistair a little ways upstream, he was squatting down by the water's edge, washing something. At Greg's approach, the muscular Arcarian, looking like a caveman in his animal skin clothes, showed him a capsule.

"A stasis capsule?"

"All the way from Aldra."

"Wash it well," the doctor advised, understanding how Alistair smuggled it. "What's in it?"

"If Henry did as I asked, I expect there to be cotton seeds inside." Alistair stood up and handed the capsule to Greg. "Do we have something that can carry this safely? Without losing it?"

"Other than your intestines? Nothing better than those saddle bags."

Alistair frowned and considered his options. Finally, he shook his head. "I can't lose this." So saying he popped the capsule back in his mouth and swallowed it down. Wincing at the lump in his throat, he crouched down to the water and swallowed a few gulps.

"That's revolting."

"I washed it well."

Returning to the oak tree, Alistair and Greg found the others staring across the plain to the west. Searching for what they observed, Alistair spied a vehicle at the foot of the hills, barely seen by the soft red glow of Srillium, racing across the terrain and heading north. It seemed to be a hovercraft, and as it moved it gave off a barely audible hum only just strong enough to tickle their eardrums. Wordlessly, the four men watched it, their heads tracking from left to right. It finally reached the forest to the north and was swallowed by it.

"I thought…" started Greg.

"There isn't supposed to be any technology here," said Clyde.

The sentence hung in the air while they stared at the spot where they last saw it, as if expecting an explanation to issue from the trees.

Alistair broke the silence. "It doesn't concern us at the moment. Clyde, how are the horses?"

"Well enough. There is a little grain and some jerky in one of the saddle bags. I don't know what animal provided the meat but…"

"Any water?"

"Couple empty skins."

"Fill them, then. We should head out in a few minutes. Save the grain for later."

They spared only another five minutes to rest before clambering back in the saddle, crossing the shallow stream and resuming their trek towards the mountains. Alistair and Greg sat astride one horse while Ryan shared a saddle with Clyde. Their urgency having faded and their energy flagging, they let the horses set a plodding pace and before long Wellesley tucked his chin to his chest and napped.

Srillium rose higher but as they moved the looming hulk of the mountains did not appear to get closer. The stream was long behind them and out of sight, providing proof they were indeed making progress, but the deceptive distance of the mountains would not reveal how far away they were. The plodding of the horses' hooves and an occasional rustle of grass and weeds from a light breeze were all that accompanied Wellesley's snoring. It was some time before Gregory realized the night was still. No crickets chirped and no animals howled.

As if listening to his thoughts, Clyde said, "If you want real desolation, come to Australia. Miles and miles of this in the outback." When no one replied he continued, "What's it like where you come from?"

"Cold," said Gregory.

"We don't have any real mountains, though," Clyde added as he eyed the dark peaks before them.

Unable to pry a conversation out of them, Clyde fell silent for a time. A few minutes later he spoke again.

"They say this was a power colony centuries ago. They gave it up for some reason. The terraforming was done so some investors bought the planet and started shipping criminals here."

No one spoke. This second attempt to start a conversation having failed, Clyde did not speak again. Presently the terrain beneath them sloped upwards, at first imperceptibly but by degrees turning into a hillier country, and now the mountains were noticeably nearer. They came upon a stream and followed it through the valleys of several small hills, winding lazily with it and eschewing a direct route in favor of a flatter one. It was Alistair's plan to camp at the top of a hill in order to be in a better defensive position and spend the morning and most of the day there. Afterwards, under cover of darkness, they would resume their journey.

Upon cresting a hill, they came into view of some bustling activity a few hilltops removed from them. There was a large bonfire on the edge of some trees and figures dancing and gesticulating around it. They appeared as shadows moving in and out of the flames. Alistair could not see much more, as the light from the fire interfered with his night vision, distorting it with something similar to heat waves.

"It's some sort of ceremony…or celebration," he said.

"Should we stay away?" asked Greg.

"Absolutely. For all we know they are waiting for human sacrifices to stop by."

"Are we going to avoid people forever?"

Alistair dismounted. "We'll take turns on watch."

Clyde undressed the horses and, with an item found in the saddlebags that passed for a brush, combed them. Wellesley, having woken up when the horses took the incline of the hillside, stretched out next to Gregory underneath a nearby tree. They both faced the distant bonfire, occasionally closing their eyes for a bit but usually staring at it in fascination. Alistair patrolled in a ring around their campsite, constantly scanning the black crevices and valleys about them. Clyde joined the two men under the tree when the horses had been cared for. He interrupted the quiet only now and then with some commentary or other, never receiving an answer but never discouraged either.

The bonfire burned through most of the night, and all the while the figures danced. Occasionally hints of a chant would reach their ears, and a few times a short, clipped shout was called out, but in between these fits and starts of sound was only quiet. Alistair was the only one who kept strict vigilance, but the other three spent many long minutes staring, usually wordlessly.

After their recent ordeal, they had trouble relaxing into sleep, but when it finally took them it was decisive. When the sun peaked over the eastern horizon, Alistair finally took a rest. By this time, the bonfire was out and the hill, so far as they could tell, vacated. With Wellesley replacing him, he lay himself out on the harsh weeds of the hilltop, his animal skin shirt rolled up under his head and a strip of leather over his eyes, and was soon asleep. When he awoke, they prepared to set out. Their still short beards were a little longer, their eyes red and their faces haggard. One by one they made a trip down to the base of the hill to a small creek to attend to themselves and Clyde readied the horses once more.

"I am really, really hungry," Wellesley groaned as they were finishing up.

"We've got that jerky in the bags," Clyde suggested. "Not much, but enough for a snack."

"What kind of meat is it?" asked Greg.

Alistair went to one of the bags and pulled out a strip of the jerky. Biting off the end with a jerk of his head, he began to chew it. They waited in silence for his judgment.

"Could be human."

"Why do you say that?" asked Greg with alarm.

"I don't recognize the flavor."

Biting off another chunk, he hopped into the waiting saddle.

"I'm not eating…I'm not a fucking cannibal!" yelled Greg.

"No one's forcing you to eat it. It's there if you want it."

Greg was shuddering and his face blushed. "You can't expect me to eat that."

"I expect nothing."

"I won't eat it!"

"Greg, you don't have to eat anything you don't want."

His face contorted, Greg picked a small stone off the ground and flung it at Alistair who deflected it with his forearm.

"There's nothing else to eat, damn it! There's nothing to hunt and nothing to exchange for!" When Alistair did not immediately respond, Gregory's voice grew even louder and he yelled, "Damn you, Alistair, you're the reason I'm stuck here!"

So saying the young doctor fell silent and stared at the ground, his chest heaving and his breath unsteady, like he was stuttering when he inhaled and exhaled. His hands he balled into fists. Uncomfortable, Clyde and Wellesley looked elsewhere.

"There's no point to taboos," Alistair said after a moment, his voice deliberately calm. "Not in a place like this. The savagery of cannibalism is the murder of a human being. I'd just as soon avoid it myself, but the murder has already been committed, assuming this is human meat. Eating it will keep you alive." He turned the horse so it pointed away from Gregory and towards the ashes of the previous night's bonfire. "You're here because you made a choice, just like I did."

Clyde and Wellesley, though uneasy, did not scruple to eat the meat and they chewed at it while they rode. Gregory, unyielding, skipped the meal, but hey left him some in case he changed his mind.

Not long after, they ascended another hill a little ways from their camp. When they crested it they saw the ashes and charred wood from a fire doused with sand. Even now, several hours later, the great fire pit gave off a modicum of heat though no embers glowed.

There were several great oak trees a few yards off, as well as the stump of one thicker than the others. On this stump, which rose three feet above the ground, a man in nothing but a loin cloth sat Indian style with the backs of his hands resting on his knees. His eyes were shut and his graying hair pulled back in a pony tail. The skin of his face was wrinkled and rough, but his posture was perfectly straight. The four men eyed each other uncertainly as they studied him.

"Hello. Might we ask you a question or two?" Alistair finally called out to him.

The man opened one eye to regard them. He closed it a moment later, moving no other part of his body.

"What language do you speak?" Clyde called out but this time the man did not respond at all.

Presently the heads of two others appeared from below on the other side of the hilltop. It proved to be a man and a woman, both of them eastern Asian of ancestry and, no doubt having heard the group as they ascended, they cautiously came up, warily eyeing them. They were dressed like the foursome, with crude animal skin clothes and moccasins for shoes. For a moment no one said a word.

"Will you speak with me?" Alistair asked of them in Mandarin.

"What is your business?" the man asked, his Mandarin tinted with something foreign, Japanese perhaps.

"We're just passing through."

The couple shared a look and nodded. *"We are bringing our offering."* The man raised a woven basket that looked to be filled with fruit and bread.

"Are they going to give us some food?" asked Wellesley with excitement.

"I don't think it's for us, mate," Clyde told him. Then he said, *"Would you be interested in an exchange?"* His Mandarin was perfect without hint of a foreign accent.

"It's our offering," the man insisted, a trifle offended and inclining his head towards the robed man on the stump.

"Bloody idiot," muttered Clyde. "We can take it after they leave."

"Could you direct us to where we can get some food?" asked Alistair.

The man shrugged and pointed to the mountains. "You can get some at Issicroy if you have Right of Passage."

"I didn't recognize that," said Alistair, whose Mandarin was less polished than Clyde's.

"Issicroy. Name of a place it sounds like."

"What's going on?" asked Greg.

"Are you looking for Odin?" the man asked them.

Alistair and Clyde shared a look.

"How did you know?" Clyde asked before Alistair could speak.

"You don't have much time left," the man said and walked towards them. "No time to go to Issicroy." Upon reaching them, with his partner trailing uncertainly behind, he set the basket down and handed out some of the bread and fruit. "We will reduce our offering and say a prayer instead."

"Thank you," said Alistair as he took the fruit and flat, hard bread and put it in his saddlebag.

"Is Odin still in the same place?" Clyde asked, fishing.

"No, no, no. Of course not. Lord Issicroy wouldn't permit it. But he'll find you, I'm sure. If he knows you're coming. If there is room left." The man finished passing out half of his basket of food and looked at them in turn. "Do you have Right of Passage?"

Clyde shook his head. "I don't suppose you can get it for us?"

The man chuckled. "I will say yet another prayer to bless you. We can always hope, right?"

"I never stop."

The man waved goodbye and the silent woman diffidently nodded her head. They went to the man on the tree stump and, after setting the basket down, prostrated themselves and lay there unmoving and spread-eagle.

"Someone has got to tell me what is going on," said Wellesley as he leaned across the gap between the horses and grabbed a pear from the bag on Clyde's saddle. Gregory followed his example and devoured an apple with some of the hard bread.

"I'm not entirely sure," said Alistair. "But it sounds like we might have some tough going in the mountains. And who is this Odin?"

"You know as much as I do," said Clyde.

They left their two benefactors prostrated before the perplexing man on the tree stump. None of the three had moved by the time the foursome dipped below the hilltop.

48

"It must be some kind of religion. The guy stays on that tree stump and people bring him food. He's probably saying prayers or something." Clyde Oliver Jones was gnawing on an apple as his thoughts came pouring out.

"Why the hell would someone give their food away?" asked Ryan with a skeptical tone. "What the hell do they get out of it?"

"Satisfaction," Clyde replied without hesitation. "You'd be surprised what people will do if you throw in the prospect of a deity. You'd be surprised what you can get away with if they think you're a Holy Man."

Gregory directed a dark look at Clyde. "Most people have more needs than just physical ones."

"Don't I know it."

The country they traversed was elevated above the plains. The land and air were clean, possessing a freshness that Aldra, with its neglected and filthy factories, lacked. This crispness became more apparent when the sun approached the western horizon and the warm air cooled.

They zigzagged through gullies and stream valleys where their view was restricted. At these times the only distant objects they saw were the peaks of the mountains. Occasionally they would ascend a hill and a more spacious vista opened before them, and from these points they would plan the next step of their trek before descending again to wiggle through the lower terrain. By the time the sun approached the mountain peaks, swimming in a pool of oranges and purples, they had ascended their fifth hill and caught sight of a lone traveler on the next one over. The man was traveling on foot, burdened by a large pack on his back and accompanied by a pair of goats. A large staff he held in his right hand, planted in the earth in front of him, but the next stride was not taken as he, motionless, regarded the foursome. Alistair finally waved to him and received a small and hesitant wave in return.

Nudging his horse into action, Alistair made for the man and Wellesley followed. They sank into the valley between the two hills and soon climbed to the summit of the next. The man was still there, his gaze not unfriendly but his stance defensive. He made no move to reach for the many weapons they now saw he carried about him, but he left both hands free. He was Caucasian with black hair, snow at the temples, and weathered, suntanned skin. He looked to be fifty though his body was still stout and he stood perfectly erect. His lineage was almost certainly Latin.

"Good evening to you," Alistair called out after the two men appraised each other.

The man nodded. "How did you come by those horses?" he asked. His mild accent was Spanish of some sort but his command of English was deft and relaxed.

"How did you come by those goats?" Alistair deflected the question.

"You are new here, that is why I ask. It is strange you should be riding so soon, and by yourselves."

"How do you know we are new?" asked Ryan, dubious.

"If for no other reason, because you have to ask. Are you passing through?"

"Somewhat aimlessly," said Alistair. "We were pressed into service but our party was attacked. We escaped on these horses. We have no idea what we are doing."

The man shrugged and the pack slid from his back to the ground. "I suppose it is about time to make camp." He nodded his head at their saddle bags. "We can share a meal."

From his pack he produced a bit of rolled cloth and, unrolling it, produced a plank of wood and another stick about the thickness of his thumb. There was some dried grass as well, and the plank of wood had a depression on one side that was blackened like charcoal. He set some of the dried grass in the depression and set one end of the stick in as well. Then, by spinning the stick back and forth between his

hands, he created friction.

Approaching him, Alistair said, "I can handle this if you want to get everything else ready."

The man hesitated a moment but nodded and left Alistair to get the fire started. By the time the stranger stuck two thigh high sticks in the ground, laid another through their forked ends and laid out a crude metal pot and some equally crude and smaller metal bowls, Alistair's brow was sweating. When the man unwrapped some salted meat and sliced a couple potatoes, he was breathing heavy. When some kindling and a log were finally placed on the ground underneath the stick structure and the pot, filled with water, hung from the horizontal stick, he finally produced some smoke in the depression. He gently blew and the dried grass began to burn. This grass was dumped onto the dried grass interspersed with the kindling and the fire spread. He continued creating the friction and more and more grass was lit and added to the kindling. Finally, the log caught fire. From there it was a matter of waiting for the water to heat. When it did, their new companion dumped the meat and potatoes in and sat watching the stew, occasionally stirring, while the others licked their chops. By the time the meal was ready and served in the separate bowls, night was in full possession of the sky and Srillium once again dominated.

"How are your forearms?" asked Greg of Alistair.

After a slurp from his bowl of stew, the big marine replied, "It was a good workout."

"Makes you appreciate matches," Ryan sullenly said as he stared into the fire.

Alistair turned his gaze on their companion, who had said nothing since the preparation began. "Is it taboo to ask where a man is from?"

The man shook his head as he ate. "You can ask where he's from. Don't ask why he's here."

When it was apparent he was not going to offer more, Alistair continued, "Where are you from?"

"Argentina."

"I'm from Australia," offered Clyde with a cheerful tone.

"Where you're from matters very little here," said the man, almost as an admonishment. Having finished his stew, he set the bowl down to tuck into his hard bread. "Since you

329

are going to ask, my name is Santiago. I am on my way to market. You do not have Right of Passage and I am unwilling to sponsor you, so you cannot come with me much farther."

"What should we do?" asked Ryan.

"Make a life. I would suggest avoiding the territory of the tribe you stole the horses from. Your main concern will be food. I am a shepherd and farmer. Most people are if they're not warriors. I am subject to no chieftain; if you survive long enough you might try for your independence."

"We're independent now," Alistair pointed out.

"I hope it lasts."

"Can you tell us a bit about the planet?" asked Greg. "The situation, the politics… anything? Religion?"

"We saw someone on a hovercraft speeding across the plains the other day," said Alistair.

Santiago leaned back until he was lying with his head on his pack. He bit off another chunk of the hard bread and contemplated Srillium in the sky. "This moon produces enough food for a few, yet each year a million more souls are dumped here. The new ones are separated into those who will be useful alive and those who will be useful as a meal. The tribes have a truce near the stone towers where the prisoners are offloaded. They pick from among them.

"The stone towers are the only permanent structures permitted. That hovercraft you saw was Gaian. There is a sect of them here in a forest to the north. They patrol and destroy any buildings they find. The Gaians are charged with guarding the planet and they keep man from dominating it.

"Just southwest of here is a river coming from a lake in the mountains. In the cliffs around the river is Issicroy, one of the few cities here. It is a city built in the caves, and the Lord of Issicroy is higher than any tribal chief. Farther south, on the coast, is Ansacroy, a city on the cliffs facing the ocean. Lords Ansacroy and Issicroy rule because the Gaians permit it. Much of their patrol work is delegated to the Lords, and they rule so long as they please the Gaians. To enter the area around Issicroy and Ansacroy you must have Right of Passage."

"And you have it?" asked Greg.

"To Issicroy. Ansacroy has never concerned me."

"Who is Odin?" asked Clyde.

This query immediately drew a sharp look from Santiago. "How do you know of Odin?"

"Does it matter?"

Santiago shifted uneasily. "Odin is a tribal chief. He is taking his tribe across the sea to an island."

"Why does this man inspire awe from some, make you uneasy, and why would Lord Issicroy be hunting him?" asked Alistair.

Santiago ran his bread around the inside of his bowl and took a bite. "Odin has promised a free island. He has spent two years preaching it. Issicroy and Ansacroy won't allow it. If they can find him they'll kill him. If not…Odin is nearly ready to set out. They say."

"And you packed everything that was important to you in that pack and are going to go along," guessed Greg. This earned him another sharp look from Santiago.

Popping his last chunk of bread into his mouth, the Argentinean laced his fingers behind his head and said, "I was surprised I still had it in me to care. I am ancient by the standards of this damn moon. God made me big and strong, but Time undoes the Lord's work. In another five, maybe ten years I will be dead anyway. Odin's plan is a fool's mission; he'll never make it to the island. But I spend every day growing food so I can eat it. Then I sleep so I can grow some more the next day, and that's about it. I'll trade ten years of that for a fool's hope. At least there is the excitement of the journey, and when we die during it I'll pass from this universe."

"What's so important about the island?" asked Ryan.

Free from pressure," Santiago replied. "No new prisoners are abandoned there, no tribes war across it, no city Lords oppress it. No one needs to die to feed another."

"What about the Gaians?" asked Greg.

"With any luck, Odin will sail to the island and Issicroy will only hear of it later. The Gaians might not care enough to find out. As long as no buildings are constructed I don't see why they should."

"Will you take us to Odin? Can we come with you?" asked Alistair, a restrained intensity evident in his voice.

Santiago sighed. "Why have you been brought to this planet?"

"I thought you weren't supposed to ask," Clyde interjected.

"A rebellion," Alistair said. "Ryan and I were fighting our government. Greg got caught treating some of the injured rebels. We three are from Aldra; Clyde is mum on the subject."

"Fighting your government?" Santiago considered Alistair with a frank gaze, then stared for a time at Srillium, his hands still behind his head. "It's possible Odin will find you useful." He was quiet a moment longer before he closed his eyes. "Yes, I will take you."

49

The next morning, Santiago declined to ride horseback. Alistair proposed a rotation among them but the Argentinean declined. He did consent to loading his gear on the horses, however, and any fears Alistair had about him tiring and slowing them down were allayed as Santiago's trim and fit legs carried him over the terrain with no signs of tiring.

A warm breeze brought dark clouds from the ocean, and by midday the sky was overcast and the heat—not oppressive but, for the three Arcarians, on the mild side of uncomfortable—grew more humid. Not long after, a balmy rain fell and they were thoroughly drenched. Clyde advised them to dismount and proceed on foot rather than allow the soaked saddles to rub raw the horses' skin.

As they plodded along the increasingly soggy ground, the streams they passed swelled and the rain fell harder. There was little wind to drive it into their faces, but falling straight down it almost felt like a waterfall. Alistair was surprised at how long and fierce the storm turned out to be. When they paused underneath a large willow to have a cold lunch, Wellesley plopped on the ground next to him and Alistair knew right away there was something gnawing at him.

"Something you guys said has been bothering me," he announced after a moment or two. When Alistair did not respond he continued, "What do children have to do with developing society? You said they neutered the women to keep people from building a civilization. I would think that without kids people would be freer."

"People with children save more and spend less than people without. They put away money today for their children to use tomorrow."

Ryan shook his head. "That doesn't make sense. How can the economy grow if no one is spending money? Without children civilization would grow faster." He followed this confident pronouncement with a less sure, "Wouldn't it?"

"Spending satisfies your desires for the moment. Saving your money is the same thing as forgoing your consumption for now. If you consume less, less effort is needed for satisfying your present desires and more effort can be put into investing which leads to more growth tomorrow."

Still unconvinced, Ryan shook his head. "Then why was everyone back home…why did the government always try to get us to spend when the economy was bad?"

"Ryan, I have very little understanding of why other people do anything."

Wellesley frowned and fidgeted for a bit, almost as if Alistair placed a burr next to his skin, but he said nothing more. Neither noticed the thoughtful look Santiago gave Alistair.

꙰

The rain proceeding unabated, the men were obliged to continue their trek in it. By this time, the valley floors had turned into bogs and the group traced their path higher on the sides of the hills. The terrain grew ever more elevated as they neared the mountains but the air remained warmish, though after so much soaking they felt a mild chill despite it. They walked with their heads down, taking the beating of the rain drops on the backs of their heads. After an indeterminable length of time spent wading into the downpour, Alistair spotted something as he scanned the hillsides.

"We're being approached by riders," he said, his voice half a yell so he could be heard.

Santiago immediately halted and looked up. After a few moments peering in the general direction of Alistair's gaze, he said, "Your eyesight is good."

"There are five on horseback. Headed our way."

"It's nothing to worry about. Just border guards from Issicroy. We'll keep going until they get here."

When the horsemen reached them they took the slope above and reined in their horses when they closed to within twenty feet. They were some of the most impressive specimens Alistair had yet seen, well muscled, large and imposing, obviously well fed. One of the horsemen rode in front of the others, a man perhaps a few years older than Alistair with clearly expressed West African features on a wide face and his hair formed into dreadlocks. Like his four companions, he had the marks of battle scattered about his body.

"Traveling with friends, Santi?" he asked. His musical accent was also West African.

"They're coming with me to Issicroy," Santiago answered. Both their voices were raised over the cacophony of rain drops.

"What's their purpose?"

"We don't have to answer that and you're not supposed to ask. I'm sponsoring their visit."

"I'm sorry my friend, that's no longer true," replied the black man and he dismounted. The other riders did the same while their leader approached the group. His manner was pleasant, unlike the men behind him who only glowered, and his approach was unthreatening. His speech was unhurried and musical, and he lingered on certain syllables as if tasting them. "Lord Issicroy, Gaia protect him, is concerned about the number of people being sponsored recently. It coincides with the rumors about Odin." Having reached Santiago, the man held out his hand and they gripped forearms. "You yourself have never sponsored anyone before."

"We recently arrived," Clyde interrupted. "Santiago offered to help us out. Said we might be able to settle in somewhere. My name's Clyde."

A warm and pleasant smile on his face, Clyde extended his hand and the other accepted his grasp.

"I am Taribo. Who are your friends?"

Turning to point them out, Clyde responded, "The big one's Alistair. Ryan's that one and Greg is in the back. Greg's a doctor."

Taribo nodded appreciatively. "Doctors are always welcome in Issicroy. Alistair will no doubt be an item of interest."

"I guess I'll just go fuck myself," muttered Ryan.

Taribo laughed without a trace of mocking. "We will see how you fight. Come with us."

They took to their mounts for a short trip back to where Taribo and his men were camped, Santiago climbing up to ride with the West African while his goats followed behind.

The Issicrojan border guards had no defining trait. Taribo himself wore few adornments and no tattoos marked his physique. One of his men was bald, with his entire scalp covered in ritualistic scars snaking about his skull. Two of the scars, where his sideburns would have been, trailed down to touch his jaw. He had a dark black, braided goatee which fell nearly to his sternum. Another man, an East Asian and along with Taribo the only one with a distinct ancestry, sported red tattoos outlined in black covering the entirety of his arms but stopping abruptly at the shoulders. The other two men had no distinguishing features save for two large holes just underneath their bottom lips where Alistair imagined jewelry of some sort had once been placed.

Their camp consisted of two large tents, which, upon their arrival, were immediately struck. Their numbers swelled to twelve, for Taribo had left two men behind. With nine horses and two goats, they set out. The sound of running water was confirmed minutes later when they came to a river, of the many they had seen the only body of running water to be worthy of the name. Upon reaching it they turned west and followed along its banks which cut deeper and deeper into the increasingly mountainous terrain. By the time they plunged into the mountains, the river had carved a canyon into the earth.

It was a magnificent canyon housing Issicroy. Whatever terraforming was done to the moon centuries ago, the presence of liquid water must have long predated it. The river had spent eons cutting through the reddish and orange rock until it had a canyon floor two hundred yards below the surface. It was also nearly two hundred yards wide and the river occupied about a third of that space.

They saw signs of a settlement long before they reached the city, overtaking men on foot heading their way, or crossing paths with those leaving. Once in a while there was a detachment of mounted warriors who exchanged salutes with Taribo and his men. Then they turned a corner and for the first time laid eyes on Issicroy. There were caves from top to bottom on both sides of the canyon, most of them man made or man-altered. Physical structures being forbidden, the Issicrojans had taken advantage of these caves. There were men standing on small rafts, pulling themselves along the river by means of ropes tied to poles. These men were sometimes fishing, sometimes aquafarming and always scantily dressed and well baked by the sun. There were men on the river banks tending to farms on raised mounds of dirt ringed by bricks which, Alistair supposed, were above flood level. Dozens of stands dotted the area where men set about multifarious tasks: tanning, curing, boiling, skinning, hammering, sawing, tying, grinding, gluing, painting...These were small men, more like Gregory in size. Many were hobbled in one way or another; nearly all were missing teeth. There were also warriors on horseback. Larger and well armed, these men rode about in groups and were shown deference by the smaller workers. Spanning the canyon from wall to wall were a few crude rope bridges, little more than planks of wood with a guardrail of twine on either side. A few specks in the sky could be seen making the precarious crossing.

Out of the mouths of the multitude of caves many flags were unfurled, hanging like tongues from open mouths. They were white in color, trimmed in purple and yellow, with the likeness of a tree sewn with purple onto the white background. One particularly large cave mouth near the top of the canyon sported an enormous flag. The only break in the purple and yellow flags was a green one coming from another large cave mouth. Between caves there were occasionally rope ladders, and some had steps carved into the rock, leading from cave to cave or from ledge to ledge. It was difficult to say how many lived in Issicroy, but Alistair guessed it was no fewer than ten thousand.

The faint and muffled roar of falling water was omnipresent, testament to a waterfall somewhere beyond another turn in the expansive rock corridor. It underscored all the other sounds: the thud of a hoe in dirt, the grunt of a man lifting a load, the whoosh of a spear hurled at a fish or the plop as it hit the surface of the river. It was a reassuring sound the waterfall bestowed on the city, for Srillium's moon was a quiet one. No crickets chirped and no wolves howled. A bare minimum of species had been transplanted there—some of them genetically modified—and the resulting silences were disconcerting to those accustomed to nature's hum. The waterfall was a soothing substitute.

"There are many duties for the Lord's warrior," said Taribo to Alistair as their horses plodded along a road which, more than the result of a conscious endeavor, was the byproduct of men and horses moving along the most obvious route and packing the dirt beneath them. "He watches over the workers, he patrols the Lord's lands. Occasionally he must track down a criminal or destroy the Lord's enemies. The greatest warriors become the Lord's personal guards." Alistair said nothing and Taribo cast a careful sidelong glance at him. "I noticed a tattoo on your chest. You will be asked to serve as a personal guard…after a loyalty oath."

"Does it pay well?" Alistair finally mumbled.

Taribo's face broke into a grin. "Better than anything else you'll find. And you live in the Palace."

"The Palace?"

With another nod of his head, Taribo indicated the largest cave mouth near the top of the canyon wall. "More of a cavern, really. But it is the closest thing to a palace you will find on this moon."

"And how are doctors treated," Gregory asked from his seat behind Alistair.

"Two of the doctors are more than seventy years old," said Taribo with reverence in his voice.

Gregory looked at Taribo strangely, not understanding the odd answer.

"It means they are taken care of," the African continued. "Most men, even if they have a tribe, do not live to fifty. You can judge how much a position is esteemed by how many ancients it produces. Your best bet for longevity is as a doctor or one of the Lord's advisors. Some of the warriors graduate to higher positions and live a long time too. So do some of the women."

They veered off to the left, towards the caves, and Taribo and his men bid them farewell for the time being. They passed through a market of tents, ramshackle stands and carts where Santiago advised them to sell their horses. They would fetch a high price at market but were beyond their ability to care for.

The medium of exchange on Srillium's moon was a mixture of iron ore and bolts of tightly woven cloth. Most of the ore was melted into small bars. There was gold, but its value was such that it was inconvenient to use for anything other than large transactions. Several prospective buyers surrounded them when they made their intentions known, and Santiago made sure they got a favorable exchange both for the horses and his two goats. After the sale, burdened now by several pounds of cloth and ore, they followed Santiago to a series of small caves at ground level near the edge of the cluster of cave openings comprising the city.

They rented a small room and stored their earnings. Alistair was leery but Santiago was satisfied their belongings would be well protected and this allayed his fears. Their room was a fifteen by fifteen chamber off a long corridor. Like the other rooms for rent, it was carved from the rock wall. There were no amenities, just the packed dirt floor, but it was cooler and, if nothing else, gave them a place to rest. With little pretense, they lay on the floor and were soon sleeping.

∾ ∿

There is an unmistakable feel of resistance when a sharp object is driven into a body. No one who has ever dealt such a blow could mistake it for the resistance that comes from piercing the ground or some other solid object. When the body is human, when one sees the eyes of one's victim as one feels the impact of the blow, the sensation is indelibly imprinted in the memory. Alistair beheld a spear in his own hands and he snarled as he drove it into a rib cage, but when he felt the disconcerting sensation, the anonymous victim raised her face and he saw his mother, her eyes filled with shock and incomprehension. He sat up suddenly with a sharp intake of breath, then remembered where he was.

There was no light source in their dank room, but in the corridor there were torches and splashes of light made it in to provide some meager illumination. Gregory, Clyde and Ryan were dark forms only barely discernible from the ground they slept on. Santiago was awake and sitting near the open entrance, the weak light dancing lightly on one side of his face as he went over his weapons with a rag of some sort. The Argentinean acknowledged Alistair with nothing more than a glance that did not interrupt his work. He continued in the darkness as Alistair leaned against the rock and ran his hands over his face.

"How long were we asleep?"

"The sun will set soon," Santiago replied in a half whisper without breaking his attention. Alistair expected nothing more in the way of conversation but moments later he said, "Was that your first nightmare since coming?"

"Yes."

"The Gaians here believe your nightmares represent your sins. You will be haunted by the same nightmare until you atone for it."

"I'm not superstitious."

"Neither am I." Apparently satisfied with his small axe, Santiago replaced it in his satchel and took out an obsidian dagger and began to polish it with the rag. "You have some education," he said simply. Alistair did not reply. "Do you plan to stay here?"

"Am I likely to find better prospects somewhere else?"

"No. If you come with me you'll likely be dead soon. There may come a day when that doesn't sound like a bad idea, but I understand you're not there yet. No, stay here. It's best."

"When are you leaving?"

"Tonight. I have a couple things to take care of. I trust you have the wisdom to keep silent about my intentions?"

"You have nothing to fear."

Santiago stuffed his dagger back into the satchel and stood up. "You have a good amount of money. If you save you could probably purchase your own private dwelling. Before I go I will present you and your companions to the Minister of Labor. You can request permission to stay and work here. You will be accepted immediately. So will Gregory."

"And Ryan?"

"Ryan and Clyde…it depends if they need laborers. Ryan might make it as a warrior…" Instead of finishing the thought Santiago shrugged his shoulders.

"What is Lord Issicroy like?"

"He is like any monarch: his first instinct is to preserve his power. His policies are not without wisdom…I suppose he does not act with deliberate malice. Lord Ansacroy is more ambitious. If Issicroy were more like him there would be continuous warfare, but he acts with more care. He rules, of course, because the Gaians allow him to. Many of his decisions are no doubt restricted by his agreement with them. Perhaps that is why so much of his realm is left fallow. The labor force is strictly controlled by Lord Issicroy and his Ministers, but the standard of living here is far higher than among the savage tribes."

When Santiago fell silent, Alistair spent some time considering him. He certainly had been a strong youth. Even now, as old age drew near, he was formidable. Never as large as Alistair, he nevertheless had a stoutness which no doubt allowed him to live on his own to such an advanced age in a hostile place like Srillium. His commentary on Lord Issicroy was frank and keen. It sounded like something he himself could have said. *Am I looking at myself in thirty cycles?* he wondered.

Replacing his dagger, Santiago slung the satchel over his shoulder and stood. "There is an evening worship all must attend. I will be back to take you there." Without another word, he left.

50

Not all men quit their work in unison. Some finished early and looked for a drink while others lingered in the fields and on the rafts, but when the clear baritone horn pierced the air there was no more question of toil. With military discipline all labor and leisure was dropped and every man pointed himself at the cave mouth with the green banner. The young, the sick, the healthy, the bent, the broken, the middle aged…everyone shuffled towards the horn. Some were enthusiastic; others dutifully stoic; all were tired. Hushed exchanges of a handful of mumbled words were the extent of conversation, and Alistair and his group said nothing at all while Santiago led them to the place of worship.

On the ground where they walked were the nearly naked, ill used by time and weather. On the walkways and ledges of the canyon walls were some with white clothing, important persons carried on lecticae and followed by their considerable retinues. Alistair spied, near the top of the canyon walls, some female forms, provocatively dressed, always accompanied by warriors. Across the twine bridges came the population from the other side of the river.

"That is the key to remaining in power," Santiago said after observing the nobility far above them. "Those men being carried along up there. The king must appease his nobles by letting them plunder the people beneath them. He must content them with special privileges and stations. And the powers he doles out to them they in turn must dole out to those directly beneath them so they can plunder what is remaining and be kept content. If the empire is large enough this will continue for several more levels, but always at the bottom there is the mass of people who must be repressed. Their condition is assaulted by plunderer after plunderer and they live in squalor. But the king can do nothing to help them, even if he had a mind to. He must keep his nobles content or he will lose his seat and probably his life."

The words were spoken with no inflection of emotion, as he would comment on the properties of a sheep or goat. Alistair thought he did not say the words for them but merely gave voice to his private thoughts, and he studied Santiago with renewed interest.

Gregory stirred at the words, and feeling compelled to say something he managed, "A democracy allows the people to unseat the king."

"No," said Santiago without conviction but with absolute confidence. "Only the powerful can do that. The powerful must always be appeased by the leader."

When they reached the base of the canyon wall underneath the green banner, they began an indirect ascent, zigzagging up stone stairs and across narrow ledges, occasionally entering a cave to ascend from within. So near to the destination of every soul in the city, they now moved slowly in a swarm. The nobility entering first, the rest of the populace for a time was backed up waiting for their passage before the workers could move forward once again in fits and starts. Nearly an hour passed from the moment the horn announced the service to the point where Alistair and his group stood on the ledge at the mouth of the great cavern, still pressed on all sides by other sweating bodies.

Looking over his shoulder at the expanse of river valley below, the young Aldran exile gazed on a land in deep shadow pricked at various points by burning torches. The land above the canyon being now more open to his gaze from the great height of the cave's entrance, he saw a darkening eastern sky with ruddy Srillium rising up to hulk over it. The sun was entirely absent, but the western sky was yet lit and around a grand peak of the mountain range some light spilled out, bedecking the great mount with purples, oranges and yellows. The majesty of it flooded over and through Alistair, and for a moment he thought of Kaldis, of whose natural wonders he had seen far more than his own planet's. When the throng of bodies, carrying him towards the cave like water to a drain, ripped his gaze away, he almost felt pain.

The expansive cavern was lifted from pitch black darkness to a murky gloom by randomly and sparsely scattered torches held eight feet above the stone floor by slender three legged stands. At the far end of a great open area was a dais with a statue of a tree, ten feet high and inexpertly carved. A dozen or so figures, robed in green with the hoods pulled up, were burning incense and casting the smoke about the tree as the multitude filed in. The nobility were ensconced in private booths higher up in the walls of the cavern. Their retinues knelt around them while the august personages remained on their lecticae, attended to by servants when, with a smooth flick of the wrist, they announced a need. Alistair, flanked by Clyde and Ryan with Santiago and Gregory just in front, knelt on the stone floor in imitation of those around him, a dubious frown on his face. Not a single word was spoken inside. Now that the worshipers found their places and settled down so that the rustling of skin on clothing and stone subsided, the sacred place fell into near silence, the hollow tone of an empty cavern cushioned by the soft bodies filling it. Alistair cast about some searching glances, inspecting the others, but discovered he was nearly the only one with such curiosity. The rest bowed their heads and folded their hands, their postures erect, their lips fluttering in desultory spurts as they breathed their quiet prayers. Santiago dutifully bowed his head, and Gregory was quite contentedly lost in his own prayer. Ryan managed to look both bewildered and bored at the same time and he stared at the front dais without really seeing it, breaking his trance only to wince when his knees protested at their treatment by the stone floor. Only Clyde shared Alistair's eagerness to observe rather than to pray.

There were two enormous horns flanking the dais, held in place by woodwork fixing them to the floor. Without warning the horns emitted their call, an overwhelming hum of deepest bass that rattled the cavern walls and made one's chest cavity vibrate. Taking their cue from the horns, the populace moved from a kneel to a sitting position, their eyes still closed and their heads still bowed. Ryan sighed in relief as he took the weight off his knees. The green robes moved to the front of the dais and cast the smoke of their burning incense out at the crowd. The horns' call never ceased, ebbing and fading in perfect synchronization, one dying out when the other renewed its note. Caressed by the call and swaddled in darkness, Alistair's eyelids grew heavy and he bowed his head only to start and return to wakefulness.

The acolytes in the green robes at last set their incense holders down and moved to surround the statue of the tree. Approaching it on their knees, they enclosed it in a ring and, each man laying hands on the stone bark, languidly swayed back and forth and side to side. In this way they spent the remainder of the worship. Alistair could not guess how long they were there, with the nearly unbroken monotony and the entrancing horns leaving him insensible to the passage of time, but eventually the hum died down, the acolytes rose and the congregation stirred.

As the Issicrojans came to their feet and spoke with one another, Santiago also stood and said to them, "Wait for me here. There is someone you must speak to."

He was gone for no more than a second before Clyde mumbled, "I need to find out more about this," and he too moved off into the crowd.

Gregory was the last to rise; he was the last, in fact, to open his eyes which he did with a slow and deep breath. His expression exuded a calm serenity Alistair recognized but which recent events had extinguished.

"That was...satisfying," he said, his voice barely audible over the echoing of conversation.

"That was a goddamn waste of time," Ryan complained. "Do they do this every night?"

A slight puckering at the corners of his mouth was Gregory's response. "I can hardly imagine a better way to smooth over a hard day's labor. I very much enjoyed it."

Many of the congregation lingered to chat with one another, some of them even conducted business, but just as many left and so the crowd thinned out. Some of the women who had spent the worship in the balconies above now descended to the open area below. Every last one scantily clad, they gathered in groups and waited on the outskirts of the crowd. Occasionally, a man approached to address one. A few words exchanged and then they left through a side tunnel.

"It's a goddamn whore house!" exclaimed Ryan, and a few men nearby cast disapproving gazes on him.

"It's to be expected," Gregory said with a note of sadness.

"Well, hell, we've got money. I wonder how much they cost."

"We're not spending our money on prostitutes," Gregory firmly said. With an inquisitive glance to Alistair he added, "I think I'm right in saying we have greater needs?"

"Speak for yourself."

"We'll talk about expenses later," Alistair impassively replied.

Santiago returned with a few other men. One was Taribo, who greeted Alistair with a nod and grin that threatened to break into a full-toothed smile.

"I have decided to sponsor you, Alistair," he said in his slow, musical accent.

"You must present your petition to a Scribe," Santiago said. "If you wish to stay."

"Tonight?"

"These men will take you. I will be gone before you are done."

He stepped forward and held out his hand which Alistair shook. They looked each other a moment in the eye and nodded but then looked away.

"Good luck with your journey," Alistair softly said.

"On the south coast," Santiago almost whispered. "But...you should not come. It's a fool's hope." He stepped back and nodded once more. "Someone was sent to collect your belongings from the inn. Until we meet again." Santiago finished with a low dip of his head and then left.

Taribo now stepped forward and held out his hand. They gripped at the forearms.

"You will now join us," the warrior proclaimed.

As they followed Taribo and the small contingent of other warriors with him, Clyde Oliver Jones came running to catch up, arriving out of breath.

"You can't imagine what I discovered," he wheezed as they entered a side tunnel and passed through the light of a torch. "You can't imagine."

"What?" asked Wellesley.

"You can't imagine. What are we up to now?"

"We're making a petition to join the city," Gregory replied.

"Ah. Very good."

A winding tunnel led them deeper into the rock and by the time they switched tunnels a couple times they were lost. The dimly lit corridors were artificial, carved from the stone as the majority of the chambers they passed. For having been purposefully carved, it was a decidedly uneven affair, smooth but irregular, with turns and bumps and divots that did not make apparent sense. Finally turning onto a long and straight corridor sloping upwards, they traversed its length and found themselves in another great cavern fully as large as the worship center but with less open space. Like the worship cavern, this one was checkered with stairs and tunnels along its walls, but there were small huts, booths, statues and even a fountain on the lower floor. As the worshippers returned from the service they began to occupy these and activity returned to what Taribo informed them was the Palace. A small cliff separated the front lower level from an upper level one could access by means of walkways that looped around the walls of the cavern and sloped up to the higher floor. Taribo led them to one of these and they made their way to the upper floor, twenty yards above the lower.

The upper floor was empty and had several tunnels in the far wall. The group took one of these and pressed even deeper. The tunnel split on two occasions, other times it crossed other tunnels and once it deposited them in a large hall whereupon they continued with a different corridor. Finally, after a full quarter hour of maneuvering through the tunnel-city of Issicroy, they came to the end of a tunnel and passed through a doorless portal and into a chamber with no other exit. To the left were some shelves with rolled papyrus. Directly in front of them were a tall chair and a desk, tall enough that when a man sat in it, he could stair down at those on the other side of the desk. A small set of steps at the side of the chair's base wound around to the back, giving access to the cushioned seat. On either side of the desk, two three legged stands held burning torches and two guards were just taking up positions there, one under each torch.

A man in flowing robes, well into his sixth decade, emerged from the shadows around the shelves clutching a papyrus scroll while Taribo stopped in front of the desk. From the right a man emerged at a jog and prostrated himself on elbows and knees by the side of the chair. He seemed to be of half Caucasian and half Oriental ancestry, and his body, naked from head to toe, was a well muscled athlete's body. He sported myriad scars as well as many superficial fresh wounds which appeared to have come from a whip. For a moment, while prostrated, the man looked Alistair in the eye, a defiant fury in his gaze, but then stoically stared straight ahead as the man in robes, rather than use the steps built into the chair, stepped on his back to raise himself into the seat. The human stool remained prostrate while, with a soft swish of fabric, the Scribe arranged his robes and sat down, reaching for a plume left in his inkwell.

"Bring the supplicants forward," intoned the Scribe, the light of the torches flickering on his dark brown skin and his sharp features. Alistair guessed he was of Hindu origin.

With a gesture Taribo indicated they should move forward, and so Clyde, Ryan, Gregory and Alistair took two steps. For the first time the Scribe looked at them, his eyelids drooping slightly in an expression of bored pretension. He pointed to Clyde.

"What is your name?" he asked in perfect English, his plume perched over the papyrus.

The Australian stepped forward again, his hands clasped behind his back in what he hoped was a confident but respectful pose. "Clyde Oliver Jones."

"You are from Australia," the Scribe announced.

"Yes, sir."

The soft scratch of the plume tip on parchment mixed with the gentle flutter of the torches' flames.

"How long have you been on Srillium?"

"Not yet a week, sir."

Another pause followed, then, "And your profession?"

"I've done a bit of everything. I've served on fishing boats, I worked on a mining ship in the asteroid belt…I was even a magician."

Nothing of this elicited an expression from the Scribe. When he recorded Clyde's answer, though, he did tilt his head just enough to direct his gaze at the interrogatee.

"Why do you find yourself on Srillium, Clyde Oliver Jones?"

Clyde shifted his stance. "Well…it wasn't anything I had any control over. You see, I was as much a victim as anyone else—"

"For what charge were you found guilty?"

"It was fraud at the end. It was part of a whole pyramid scheme. I was as much taken by it as the people I sold it to. If I had known—"

"Step forward," commanded the Scribe, pointing at Ryan but not looking at him.

Clyde, blushing and gritting his teeth, took a step back as Ryan took one forward.

"What is your name?"

"Ryan Wellesley 7aa."

The Scribe halted his scribbling.

"What is the meaning of 7aa?"

"That's my suffix code. The government gives everyone a suffix code. When it hands out work assignments or living assignments or draft assignments—whatever—it groups people of the same suffix code together. It's for organizational stuff."

"What planet do you hail from?"

"Aldra."

Still engaged with recording the previous answer, the Scribe once again paused before finishing his entry. "I have never heard of Aldra."

"Apparently only Aldrans have."

"Where is Aldra to be found?"

The question flummoxed Ryan. "I don't…well, it's here in the galaxy…I don't really know—"

At this point Alistair stepped forward.

"If I may, sir? The Aldran system is located 434 light years away from Earth along the eleven. It's 12 degrees and 33 minutes above plane."

"An outlier?"

"Yes, sir."

"A new system?"

"No, sir. The Founders went well outside the colonial line of the time."

"Where along the eleven?"

"327 degrees, almost exactly."

"Twenty seven degrees on the eleven," the Scribe said and with deliberate strokes recorded the information, for the first time registering an expression, that of mild curiosity.

Alistair stepped back in line.

After a moment, the Scribe continued, "And how long have you been here?"

"I was on the transport with Clyde," Ryan replied. "All four of us arrived—"

"What was your profession on Aldra?"

"Mining."

"And why were you sent to Srillium?"

"I was uh…" Ryan took another breath. "It was rebellion." Ryan stared at his feet, blushing in embarrassment. "I only did it because I was hungry. The government wasn't getting any food shipments in…a bunch of other things had gone wrong. It wasn't like I—"

"Step forward," intoned the Scribe, pointing at Gregory.

The interrogation proceeded in the same fashion as before. To the final question Gregory replied, "I was healing the wounded. I took care of anyone who needed it, soldiers and rebels alike. The rebels drove the government out of the city and I had an entire clinic of injured men from both sides. When the government retook the city they arrested me for conspiring with the enemy. I suppose that was the charge; it was never formally read to me."

Finally, Alistair stepped forward.

"What is your name?"

"Alistair Ashley."

"And you are also from Aldra?"

"I am."

"What is your suffix code?"

"I don't have one."

"Why were you not given a suffix code?"

"I was given one, but I disavowed it."

"It's 3nn," said Gregory with an exasperated look at Alistair.

"How long have you been on Srillium?"

"A few days, like the others."

"To what did you dedicate yourself on Aldra?"

"My father owned a restaurant," he said, and his voice caught on the word 'father'. After a moment's pause he gathered himself and went on. "On Aldra that's like saying he owned an entertainment park. I then spent four cycles…four years in the marines, most of them on

Kaldis. I was accepted into the Special Forces and…" Alistair grabbed his shirt and pulled aside the part covering his left pectoral. "I completed the Proving."

The naked stool's head, tilted towards the ground, snapped up.

"You wore a War Suit."

"I did."

If it were possible for the Scribe's face to register something like respect and veneration, it did so now with a faint pursing of the lips and a nearly imperceptible nod of the head.

"And for what reason were you brought to Srillium?"

"I fought to overthrow a government."

"On Kaldis?"

"No, on Aldra."

"You fought to overthrow *your* government."

"No. I never consented to the government. I would never enter into any relationship without a way to annul the contract."

To the same degree that admiration touched the Scribe's features before, disapproval now registered.

"A government does not require consent."

"That is why I sought to overthrow it."

"You fought with Gregory and Ryan?"

"No, Gregory did not fight. I fought with Ryan."

"Ryan fought to feed himself. Were you hungry too?"

"No. My father was wealthy and moderately well connected. I never wanted for food."

For a few moments more the Scribe jotted notes on the parchment while the rest waited. Abruptly he dipped his plume one last time in the inkwell, but this time did not withdraw it, and announced, "Your petitions will be duly considered." He descended from the examiner's chair, planting his foot once more on the back of the naked slave, and left the chamber.

"That will be all," said Taribo, his voice oddly soft and somber.

ॐ❧

The naked slave, whom Taribo addressed as Mordecai, was sent to collect their possessions. Taribo himself led them from the Hall of Records, setting a fast pace the others had difficulty maintaining. As the muscled legs of their escort ate up yardage, Alistair got the odd notion that Taribo was not leading them so much as running from them. Almost as if challenged, he kept his own legs pumping and stayed shoulder to shoulder with the other warrior, his movements rough and strong where Taribo's were smooth and graceful.

"From time to time we get political dissidents here," Taribo said after a time. It was some moments before he said anything more so that Alistair thought there was nothing else forthcoming. "There are almost no rebels. They usually are executed. Not worth paying to ship a man to a prison planet when he has committed a capital crime."

"I committed no crime."

Taribo stopped and faced Alistair. "You were not rebelling?" It struck Alistair that Taribo seemed hopeful.

"I *was* rebelling. I said I committed no crime."

With an expression of disgust, Taribo was off again. Clyde and Gregory were breathing heavily by the time he stopped at a curtain drawn across an opening in the wall of the tunnel they were in. He ripped the curtain open and indicated with a curt nod that they were to enter. When Alistair passed him the black warrior would not meet his gaze and, when they were inside, he drew the curtain closed.

As the whispers of Taribo's retreating footsteps sounded outside, Alistair inspected the chamber. Carved out of the rock, it was twelve feet wide and twice that in length, sporting a few wrapped straw bundles on which to recline. The far end was open to the canyon and a cool breeze wafted inside in desultory waves. The sky was now dark and the canyon painted pink from Srillium's light, some of which trickled into their chamber. In the distance, as he stood at the edge and the breeze stroked him, he could hear the soft and continuous rush of the river's waterfall, though the cascade was still unseen.

"It's a nice enough view, I suppose," said Ryan, coming up behind Alistair and gazing out at the land about Issicroy. "I could get used to it."

Gregory was sitting on one of the straw cushions, Clyde was recumbent on his and when Alistair did not respond Ryan retreated from the edge of the cave and went to recline on one of his own. The robust Aldran rebel stood for a few moments more looking out at the scenery before he came to lie down on his own bundle of hay.

"It's not your fault I'm here," Gregory softly said as he stared at the floor between his feet.

Alistair let the waterfall's faint sound fill the intervening moments before answering. "What makes you say that?"

"I made my own choices. What I said was said in anger. It's not your fault."

Alistair managed a slow nod and then, crossing his feet and weaving his fingers together behind his head, he lay on his cushion. Outside the hall a pair of pedestrians padded softly past, their passage causing the curtain to flutter.

"My parents are dead." Alistair made the simple pronouncement with a stoic voice and countenance.

Gregory looked stunned. "How…how do you know? How did it happen?"

"They shot them," he said, the sound coming through clenched teeth and cracking the stoicism enough to hint at a boiling cauldron underneath. When he spoke again it was more controlled. "They tortured them and shot them and gloated over the bodies."

Ryan was sitting upright now. "I'm sorry to hear that, Alistair."

"Alistair, I'm so sorry," Gregory said, whispering lest his voice fail him. There were tears in his eyes. "When did they…?"

"They showed me the bodies right before they meant to execute me. My brother saved us. We were all set to be executed. He doesn't know. I don't know how long we've been gone but he and my sister are probably still wondering what happened to our parents. It feels like it was just earlier this week."

Clyde reached across cushions and patted Alistair's shoulder. "Bad luck, mate," he said, the extent of his ability to console having been reached with something more fit for the death of a pet hamster.

Another group of footsteps delicately announced themselves outside the chamber, and the curtain was presently drawn aside. Three warriors stood outside with Mordecai, still naked and now burdened with their belongings. The warriors said nothing and betrayed no emotion. Without a word the part Caucasian, part Oriental slave entered with the apparent intention of depositing their things.

"They're going to kill you," he whispered as he brushed past Alistair.

The whisper was the slightest of exhalations, barely audible even absent the rush of the waterfall. The speaker himself would have heard it more in his imagination than in reality. Fighting to relax his tense muscles, Alistair realized no one else could have heard the warning. His three companions were no longer comfortably reclining, but that was due to the unfamiliar presence of the warriors outside their chamber. The warriors themselves looked like typical on-duty soldiers: alert but bored.

"I'll return," whispered Mordecai as he moved past Alistair once more, rubbing his nose to cover the movement of his lips now that he was facing the guards. A moment later the curtain was closed and the four visitors were retreating.

Alistair was on his feet a moment later. "We might be in a bit of a predicament."

"What's wrong?" asked Greg.

"That slave gave me a warning."

"How?" asked Ryan.

Alistair went to the curtain, drew it back, and looked both ways down the corridor. Letting the brown fabric fall back into place, he continued, "He said they were going to kill us."

"What?" Greg asked louder than he intended.

"He said he would be coming back."

"Why would he tell us?" asked Ryan dubiously.

"He saw that tattoo on your buddy and wants to be rescued," said Clyde.

Alistair moved to the lip of the cave's entrance and scanned the face of the rock around them. "There'll be no climbing down from here," he pronounced with a grimace.

"I don't know that I want to wait for him to come back," said Ryan, on his feet now and shifting nervously about.

"If he didn't mean to come back he wouldn't have said anything to us," Gregory said.

"It might not be up to him. He may be delayed and come back too late," countered Ryan, "or sent to his cage before he can get to us."

"Why the hell would they want to kill us?" demanded Clyde. "Especially Greg and Alistair?"

"We were rebels," said Alistair, realizing the truth. "This city is ruled by a king and we rebelled against ours."

"Son of a bitch," Ryan hissed. "We should've fucking lied!"

Gregory vaulted out of his cushioned chair and rifled through their belongings. "No weapons."

"We're leaving now," Alistair decided and grabbed a handful of their gear. "Is our money intact?"

"The money is there," said Greg, hoisting a bag himself.

Clyde and Ryan offered no argument, simply grabbing what remained and following Alistair. Since they came from the right, Alistair went left. The particular corridor in which they found themselves was vacant, but it later merged with another more trafficked hallway. Unwilling to turn back, they were taken deeper into the city as the tunnel curved inward. Casting wary glances right and left, they plunged onward, hoping to find a more propitious corridor.

Unable to trust anyone, entirely ignorant of the layout of their present environs, surrounded by thousands who might turn on them in a moment, they might as well have been blind as they went. Whenever a tunnel offered a downhill slope, they took it. Left or right ceased to matter as even Alistair's finely honed directional sense was rendered useless. The only metric to measure their progress was that, the more downward sloping tunnels they took, the more common folk, identified by their coarser dress, they ran into. One cavern housed a tavern emitting from its doorless and windowless openings the sounds of a gay crowd and copious torchlight. Alistair stopped there, peering uncertainly at it, on the point of stopping in to ask directions.

"If you're looking for somewhere to spend your money, my friends and I have just the place," said a woman's voice in fluent English touched by a mild, untraceable accent.

The four men turned to regard the speaker, a stunning woman of no more than 25 years with brown skin, long and smooth black hair, deep brown eyes and full lips. Distant from any torch, her skin nearly blended with the shadows, though her white robes, as fine as could be found on Srillium, stood out. Her arms and shoulders were bare and the robe came down to her knees, leaving the smooth skin of her calves open to view. Barefoot, she leaned against the wall, one ankle crossed over the other and with her head seductively tilted so that she was looking at them from just under her eyebrows. The whites of her eyes, matching the clothing she wore, seemed to glow in the middle of her dark face.

"We don't have any money," Alistair muttered and made as if to move on.

"Men always have money for what I'm offering."

"We're actually a little busy right now," Gregory stammered and shuffled towards Alistair, who was at the entrance of the next tunnel.

"What's the rush?" she said with a playful half smile. "Someone coming to kill you?"

This stopped all in their tracks save Alistair, who did an abrupt about face and charged the young woman, stopping just in time to keep from squashing her against the wall. She started but did not lose her poise, boldly meeting Alistair's gaze.

"What did you say?" he asked, hulking over her with her forehead barely reaching his sternum. The other three crowded around them.

"Mordecai sent me. Well, Mordecai asked me to come; he's in no position to send anything. You remember little naked Mordecai, right?"

"We remember."

"Why don't you come with me and we'll discuss getting you out of here alive?"

"At what price?"

"At whatever price we decide to charge," she said with a smirk and, extricating herself from the narrow space between Alistair and the stone wall, moved towards a different tunnel. "You're not in a strong bargaining position."

As the shadows fell on her, her skin disappeared until only the white robe could be seen, as if floating. Two steps later and her garments too were wrapped in darkness. Alistair paused for a moment, but the issue was a simple one. He entered the tunnel where she disappeared, his companions on his heels.

51

The young woman with the seductive mien glided through the tunnels with the careless ease of one long familiar with them. Alistair could not guess in which direction she led them, but she did so without hesitation. All he could say afterwards was that they were led upwards a bit, but for all the forks they took, turns they made and caverns they crossed he could not say with any confidence that, fifteen minutes of walking later, they were not directly above the very tavern where they met her.

"You never told us your name," said Gregory, moving to her left side.

With expert control she allowed a smile to develop on her lips. "Layla."

"Gregory Lushington," said the young doctor, holding out his head.

"You cannot shake hands with a woman here, Gregory Lushington," she advised him, and she widened the smile when he clumsily withdrew his hand. "Not without paying her first."

"What is your full name?"

"Layla Dubai."

"That's a very pretty name."

"We're taking the right fork," she advised as he, looking at nothing but her, found himself separated from the others by the wedge of stone that created the split in the tunnel. Tripping over himself, he hastened to rejoin the group, but now he found himself stuck in the back with Ryan Wellesley.

"I wish toilet paper were as smooth as you," was his sardonic greeting. "Every shit would be a vacation."

One last tunnel they took, which emptied into a medium size cavern lit by a lone torch. Like most of the others, it was fixed to a tall, three legged stand, this one in the center of the cavern. Some noises issued from somewhere inside, noises composed of hushed human voices, but the people making the sounds remained unseen. At the mouth of the tunnel Layla turned to a small copse of stalagmites.

"They're here," she whispered.

At her words Mordecai, still naked, stepped out from behind a stalagmite and another attractive woman, past thirty years old and dressed like Layla but with lighter skin, stood up behind another.

"Did you bring me clothes?" Mordecai said with a dark look, only just managing to keep his whisper from becoming a hiss. His accent was light but unmistakably Chinese.

"I'm sorry but we didn't have time," said Layla as if the issue were of no concern to her.

In response Mordecai clenched a fist. "This isn't a joke to me."

From the depths of the tunnel came the sound of a giggle and its echoes.

"It's time," said the second woman as she surveyed them. Her accent was familiar to Alistair but he could not place it. Bending down to grab something behind the stalagmite and coming back up with a light ax and a spear, she proffered these to Alistair who took the spear; the ax wound up in Wellesley's hands. Mordecai, after shouldering a couple of bags full of items, grabbed a spear and an obsidian dagger.

"Are we going to fight our way out?" Alistair asked.

"The way out is taken care of," the woman replied, the finger on her lips telling Alistair to be more quiet. Another giggle issued from the cavern. "But we may have to fight later."

Layla took the lead, guiding them towards an outcropping of rock at the far end of the cavern. As they approached, it became clear the voices they were hearing were coming from near it. Layla, Mordecai and the woman stepped gingerly, and Mordecai held his spear so that it did not clack against stone or rub against the straps of the bags he carried. In unconscious imitation, Alistair's group followed, each moving as silently as he could. A low moan that turned into a purr filled the cavern, echoing and reechoing against the stone interior. It was a woman who made the sound.

When they drew near the outcropping, they finally saw the people making the noises, and they saw the reason. Two spears were tossed on the ground next to a pile of leather clothing of the sort Issicrojan warriors wore. A woman, dressed in a white dress of a similar cut to Layla's, sat atop a boulder, her hands supporting her weight as she inclined backwards. Her right leg was splayed out to the side with her foot planted on a stalagmite. Her left leg was draped over the shoulder of a naked man, her thigh and calf running down his back. His head could not be seen but its shape was obvious beneath her dress. His hands pawed at her hips and Alistair, embarrassed and nearly stumbling, saw her wink at him. With a wicked smile she tossed her head back and emitted a loud moan. Whether sincere or not, the outburst covered any sounds they made. Another couple lay flat on the floor, both naked, he on top of her, her enveloping his head in an embrace forcing his face into her chest. The man's movements rocked them back and forth.

For a few moments only did they observe the scene, and then the projection of rock blocked their view and they found themselves at the entrance of a lightless tunnel. It was a jagged fissure in the surrounding stone, as if two puzzle pieces did not fit together properly. Even Alistair's vision could not see far into the opening because the passageway cut left only a short distance from its entrance. Two of their three guides, apparently less familiar with this area, entered with some hesitation, but Mordecai suffered from no such uncertainty and strode into the tunnel and took the lead.

"I'll bring up the rear," mouthed Alistair into Gregory's ear.

The doctor nodded and, hands out in front, lightly touching his companions around him, plunged into the tunnel as more moans covered their exit. Alistair went in last, always with his spear ready. There was never any true danger, but for those who could see nothing it was a harrowing experience, with dangers conjured from their own imaginations. Every echo seemed to reverberate off the walls of an unseen precipice; every trickle of water threatened an underground river; every dip in the height of the ceiling menaced; they were startled by every elevated bit of floor over which they stumbled. In the end the passage was not as long by half as their expectations made it out to be, and they were soon crawling up a cramped incline and emerging from the innards of a hill and into the red tinged Srillium night.

The breeze, first announcing itself while they rested in the chamber on the edge of the underground city, grew in strength to become a proper wind. The long grass on the hillside swayed under its weight and the night was filled with the rustle of grass blades and tree leaves rubbing against one another. When Alistair finally pulled himself out of the shaft, the first thing he saw was the curvaceous body of the second woman, back to him, standing with her legs spread and arms flung out wide, her head thrown back and her dark, curly hair mussed by the wind. Each finger was stretched out as far as it would go, as if she were trying to envelope all of nature with her body.

"Is she praying or can we get started?" Ryan asked.

"Freedom is a thing to be drunk with one's whole body," she replied. "I have not been a free woman for many years."

"And won't be for much longer if we don't start moving," said Mordecai.

With that, Layla reached into a small bag and produced two pairs of moccasins that she and the other woman promptly slipped onto their feet. Mordecai saw this and glowered at them but they, seeming not to notice, started down the hill.

"You said you didn't have time to get me clothes," he called after them, in control of his voice to the same extent a rider controls his mount stung by a bee.

"Our skin is soft, not made for walking around barefoot," Layla informed him without looking back. "You're used to being naked."

With a furious motion, Mordecai grabbed his spear and descended. Alistair and his friends followed, with Alistair moving up to walk next to the woman whose name he did not know.

"It seems we have time for an explanation," he prompted.

"They were going to kill you. We saved you."

From the corner of his eye he fixed an incredulous look on her. "My name is Alistair."

"Giselle."

He gazed at her comely Mediterranean features. Her thick hair was a deep black and cascaded to her shoulders in gentle ringlets which coiled and uncoiled against the bounce of her walk. She was tall enough to reach his chin, and her well toned body had not lost its feminine roundness. Older than he, she still retained her youth but from close range one could detect the beginnings of age's grip on her.

"Giselle…?"

There was a slight hesitation before she answered. "You may call me Giselle La Triste."

"Giselle The Sad?" She did not respond. "And you are from Arcabel, unless I am mistaken." The last comment earned a quick glance from her.

"Yes, Arcabel."

"And what are you getting out of this?"

"I'm sorry?"

"Or what do you expect to get?"

It was Layla who interrupted with an answer. "We are leaving, just like you. It's not an easy life in Issicroy, especially for a woman. We had been planning it for a while. When Mordecai saw your tattoo and heard what you were sent here for…"

"If you think Issicroy is hard for a woman, you should try doing my job for a week," grumbled Mordecai. "Just one week. I'd like to see you do it."

"I rather think you would have a harder time performing ours," Giselle retorted and Layla laughed.

"If I had your equipment," growled Mordecai over their laughter, "I'd consider myself fortunate to live in the kind of luxury you had."

"Oh yes!" said Giselle. "It's such a delight pleasuring all you sweaty, hairy, callused men. I just can't get enough penises inside me."

"And where exactly are we headed now?" Alistair cut in before Mordecai could reply with something as angry as his face looked.

"We were going to travel to the south coast. After that…"

"You are looking for Odin."

There was a hint of surprise in the pause that followed.

"Yes, we are looking for Odin," Giselle confirmed. "And we'll all be executed if we're found."

"I've heard Odin is a risky proposition." This elicited only a shrug from Giselle. "Well, we've got nowhere else to go. A friend of ours left here a little while ago. He is headed that way as well. I don't know what route he would take…"

"If he's on the main trail," said Mordecai, "it's took risky to look for him there. If he's not on the main trail we'll never find him except by accident."

"Do you think they'll pursue us?" asked Alistair.

"It's an absolute certainty," said Mordecai.

"Well, they're as likely to run into us as we are of running into Santiago. Which means if they want a reasonable likelihood of catching us they'll have to send out multiple search parties. And the main trail is as good a place to ambush a search party as anywhere else, correct?"

Mordecai mulled it over for a moment. "Why do we need to find this guy?"

"I think he has a good idea how to find Odin. Besides…he seems like a decent guy. Good head on his shoulders."

Shrugging, the former slave said, "We can probably make the trail before he does. I doubt he left the way we did, and if he wants to use the main trail he's got to travel a ways down the canyon first."

So saying, Mordecai made a slight easterly correction in their bearing. Though the others couldn't make it out, Alistair saw they were headed towards a dark mass of forest. From the way he maneuvered in the dark, he guessed Mordecai possessed sight akin to his own, for the glow of Srillium was partially blocked by clouds, and the landscape so far off was hard to discern. Silent as he pondered their new companions, the ex marine fell in behind Mordecai, using his spear as a walking stick and never ceasing to scan the countryside.

52

As Alistair watched the play of muscles under Mordecai's skin, he concluded he had been, as it was called, enhanced. His physique did not exceed the bounds of what was naturally obtainable, but was beyond what a slave to a semi-barbaric king on a prison planet could have maintained. Beyond what was on his head and perched over his eyes, the half-Caucasian, half-Oriental warrior did not have a hair on his body. Not on his face, which was bereft of not only the shafts of hair but also of the roots which shaving does not remove; nor on his chest; nor where his limbs met his torso. It was a preternatural smoothness interrupted only by the occasional scar, especially on his back.

The two women were content to let Mordecai lead. They walked together a few feet back of the ex slave, never pausing in their hushed conversation for more than a moment or two, but never speaking loudly enough to be heard by normal ears. Gregory, Ryan and Clyde, without having made a conscious decision, clustered around Alistair who walked a few yards back of the women.

The main trail was visible to Alistair each time they crested a hill, a slender line of white wrapping itself about the mounds and valleys of the land before disappearing into the maw of the red-tinged planetlit forest to their south east. As they drew nearer the woods, it sounded as if they approached a violent ocean. The trees themselves danced to the rhythm of the wind, their trunks swaying, their branches fluttering and their leaves frenzied. The shadows of the trees, faint shades cast by Srillium's perfect orb, gesticulated in macabre mockery of the wooden giants, their forms distorted this way and that by the terrain. Upon reaching the summit of the last hill before the forest, the group saw a dark shape moving along the main trail. Human in form and with a long walking stick, the figure was just passing into the trees. Wellesley put his hands to his mouth as if to call out, but Alistair gripped his shoulder, urging him to silence.

"We'll catch up to him soon enough," said the Aldran rebel to his comrade. "If he can hear you, then so can anyone else."

Ryan's aborted call was proved unnecessary a few minutes later as they arrived at the sea of rough, knotted creatures looming above them and still madly dancing. Though shadow hid him from normal eyes, Alistair perceived the form of Santiago several yards within the darkness of the forest floor, leaning against a tree, his arms folded and his spear within easy reach. He raised a hand to salute the Argentinean and got a delayed nod in return. The group stood unmoving at the edge of the forest entrance and finally Santiago grabbed his spear, hefted his pack, and retraced his steps to greet them. His eyes rested on Mordecai.

"You have Issicroy's slave with you. And two women. I would be interested to hear the explanation."

"We decided to rescue Alistair and his friends," Layla said.

"They kill rebels and these three were tired of living there," Alistair added his own answer. "We found each other mutually useful."

"And Alistair claims you can take us to Odin," said Giselle, drawing a finger across her face to capture and remove the hair blown across it.

Santiago gripped his spear with both hands and leaned on it, sighing and saying, "So you find me useful too. But I am not sure what you have to offer me, other than about twenty horsemen who will be looking to take back anyone they don't kill. You, Mordecai," he said, nodding and leveling a severe gaze at the warrior, "will be lucky if all they do is kill you. All I stand to gain is a death sentence if I'm caught with you. I can find Odin easily enough on my own."

"We need you to help us," pleaded Layla.

"This land frowns on needs and charity."

"We spent the night together once," Giselle blurted out.

It was not the introduction to a larger point; she let the sentence, oblique as it was, hang in the air with no follow up. Santiago scrutinized her, his eyes betraying neither agreement nor dispute. His form, without perceptibly altering, yet exuded a sort of acquiescence left behind when his resistance dissolved. Even before he turned to trudge back into the forest, it was understood he would not bicker. Moments later, Alistair and the other six were at his side, moving along the uneven trail that at points had clearly been planned, with flattened ground and rounded stones placed at its edges, and at others seemed like the unintentional result of thousands of feet packing the dirt and beating the life out of the grass.

It was a narrow path, scarcely enough for two riders to traverse while side by side. It looped around hills, it paralleled streams, it passed smaller paths branching off from it. Once it went through a small clearing of tall grass, and the trees ringing it blocked out a good portion of the sky so that Srillium seemed to encompass nearly the entirety of the heavens, staring down at them like an angry eye. When their trail plunged back into the forest, the branches of the trees crowded overhead and blocked the sky once more, leaving them in almost pitch black.

Soon after traversing the clearing, Santiago announced by his actions he would be stopping to rest. He neither invited them to stay nor suggested they continue, but of course they stopped with him. Their little camp was just around a bend in the path. Alistair took up a position near the elbow of the road, next to a tree, to keep watch. The others sank to the ground, save for Mordecai, who fished around in a sack and produced a rolled up length of the weave which passed for money in Issicroy. He dropped it at Giselle's feet as he stood over her, his direct stare unwavering.

"Where did *you* get money?" she asked, unimpressed, or at least feigning it, and not meeting his gaze.

"It's been five years," he said, his voice clear, strong and hungry. It was enough to make the rest of them cringe, for the domineering wooden hulks around them discouraged speech such that only short, whispered phrases passed between them. Mordecai's loud words seemed like a violation. "You want my protection? That should be payment enough. Consider this a tip."

Fury flashed in Layla's eyes. "She doesn't owe you anything and I don't—"

Giselle, with a wary glance at Mordecai, laid a restraining hand on her younger friend. "It's OK," she whispered. Standing up, she held out her hand to the man whose jaw was stubbornly set and whose chest heaved in response to Layla. He had prepared himself for a fight he had no intention of losing, but Giselle's gentle demeanor went a ways to pacifying him.

After Mordecai grasped her hand and was led out of their sight, Gregory stood up and looked at the place where the dense forest swallowed them. Shuffling his feet and fidgeting with his fingers, he next looked to Alistair with an imploring expression. "Well? Are you going to...?"

"To what?"

"Are you going to let this happen?" His voice evinced anger now.

Alistair busied himself with surveying his spear. "She agreed to it. Not my business."

Gregory shook his head but his shoulders slumped in defeat. "Alistair, you're such a goddamn..." The Aldran doctor never revealed what Alistair was, letting his voice trail off to be covered by the rustling leaves.

It was perhaps ten minutes later when Mordecai returned, and Giselle was only half a minute behind. Mordecai slumped down on the ground, his breathing still a trifle elevated. There was a brook on the other side of the trail, and Giselle went to it. The agitation in the trees covered the sounds of her rinsing. No one looked at Mordecai, and no one but Layla looked at Giselle when she returned from the brook. Mordecai and Giselle did not look at each other, the muscular warrior staring off into the trees with a bored but satisfied expression and half closed eyes while Giselle, as if nothing untoward had occurred, resumed a hushed conversation with Layla.

There was an acute discomfort in the air, and when they moved at all it was gingerly, quietly, like small children when father comes home in a foul mood and broods. Things might have remained that way for some time if there were no interruption.

"Riders," Alistair calmly announced. "Five of them."

The others were on their feet, those with weapons hefting them.

"Find a big stick," said Santiago to Clyde and Gregory as he moved past them to take a spot near Alistair. "Move back into the forest a ways and guard the women."

Mordecai was already standing shoulder to shoulder with Alistair in the middle of the trail on the other side of the bend.

"Anyone with night vision?" asked Alistair as he cocked an eye at Mordecai.

The naked warrior returned the same understanding look. "No. These are good soldiers, but not enhanced." Mordecai returned his full attention to the trail. "I'll have clothes soon."

Santiago and Wellesley took up places on either side of the two muscular warriors.

"Issicroy wastes his warriors sending them after us at night like this," said Santiago. "In the forest. How far away are they?"

"Couple hundred yards," said Mordecai.

"Ryan," said Alistair, "hide yourself in the trees on the other side of the bend. Wait until they pass you, and when we attack rush out to one of the horses in the rear and chop off its leg at the knee."

"OK," Ryan nodded, his breathing elevated, like a nervous boxer before a fight.

"Then get the hell back in the forest."

"OK."

"If your axe gets caught in the leg," said Mordecai, "drop it. You're a sitting duck."

"And make sure you get a horse with a healthy rider," warned Santiago. "Don't waste your strike if we've already felled the man in the saddle."

"OK," Ryan nodded once more and moved off to hide behind a tree. He stood with his back against it and gripped his axe like a drowning man grips a life preserver.

Santiago, Alistair and Mordecai, as if they had rehearsed it, moved to the other side of the road, opposite Ryan Wellesley, and sank down behind some bushes and tall grass. Alistair found himself on the right, with Santiago on the left and Mordecai in the middle. For a time he lost sight of the horsemen, but eventually they came back into view, and he watched them in shades of gray, his view impeded by the clumps of grass and small bushes on the forest floor. The riders were moving along at a good trot and sparing little time to search the myriad possible hiding spots they passed. As he studied them, Alistair recognized Taribo riding in the back.

"If we move farther back in the forest they'll ride right by us," he whispered. "They're not even looking."

"But they're bound to turn and come back," Mordecai said. "They might come in daylight. We have the jump on them now."

Alistair hesitated, ground his teeth in indecision. Then he said, "I don't want to do this."

"It's too late," Mordecai shot back in a harsh whisper. "Don't get soft, soldier. These men are looking to kill you. Don't tell me you've never killed a man before."

"Alistair," said Santiago more softly, "it's too late to let Ryan know. These men are trained and ordered to kill; there's no shame in defending yourself."

"I'm rushing the one in the middle," Mordecai informed them. "If both of you aren't at my side when I do it, you'll answer for it."

Alistair's mind whirred, trying to think of a way out, but the riders were approaching fast and he could think of nothing. When they were almost upon them, Mordecai slipped out of his spot in the grass and Alistair's body reacted without conscious direction. The horses whinnied and one of the riders shouted in shock. Alistair stuck his spear in the ribs of his target, the shaved stone of the spear head puncturing the lung. Mordecai skewered another, while Santiago ripped open the belly of the man on the left. Both Mordecai and Alistair's targets teetered in their saddles for a moment before falling over backwards in unison and hitting the ground with a single thud, the spears still protruding from their ribs.

Santiago's man uttered a sick grunt, almost like he was vomiting, and he tried to stab at the Argentinean with his spear, but Mordecai intercepted the weak blow and tugged the spear, pulling the man forward and out of his saddle. Then there was a shriek from one of the horses in the back and the animal tumbled to the ground, tossing its rider to the earth. Only Taribo was left unharmed with an unharmed mount, and the African raised his hands in supplication, dropping his spear as he did so.

"Wait! Wait! Alistair, is that you? Alistair?"

Mordecai made a move towards Taribo's steed but Alistair laid a restraining hand on his shoulder. The wounded and dying moaned as they clutched at their wounds.

"Alistair, hold a moment! I surrender!" So saying, the Issicrojan warrior dismounted, his hands still held aloft in supplication, and he moved into a position where he might defend the one whose horse Wellesley crippled. Over the screams of the wounded animal he said, "Yes, we were sent out to kill you, but I wasn't going to. I didn't expect to find you on this trail. I thought you would stay in the hills. We weren't even searching for you as we went. I swear I had no intention of killing you."

With a groan of tremendous effort, Taribo's comrade extricated himself from the writhing mass of horseflesh, clutching his leg and scooting off to the side of the road and away from the kicking hooves. The injured men lay on the ground, two of them coughing up blood, their chests rising and falling in short, unsteady bursts. Taribo went to the man with the hurt leg and examined the bruised appendage.

"That's a likely story, Taribo," said Mordecai. "But we can't let you go this time. When you return without three of your comrades they are going to know where we are even if you don't tell them."

Taribo snatched a stray spear off the ground and leveled it at Mordecai, but the naked warrior just sneered.

"You're going to fight me in the dark, Taribo?"

"You'd be better off killing this one, Alistair," said the West African, a note of panic evident in his voice. "Issicroy should have executed him when he captured him!"

"They came to kill us," said Giselle, stepping onto the path a few yards behind them. "These men have spent their lives here killing. We're better off without them."

Mordecai stabbed at him but Taribo managed, just barely, to deflect the blow.

"Let him be, Mordecai," said Alistair.

Mordecai stepped back from the reach of the Issicrojan and shot a dark look at Alistair. "This has nothing to do with you. Taribo and I have an unsettled score I'm going to take care of right now."

Mordecai moved back to attack Taribo but Alistair hit the back of his knee with the butt of his spear and the ex slave was forced into a genuflection.

"I said let him be."

With a snarl, Mordecai was back on his feet but this time facing Alistair. Bearing his teeth in a feral scowl, he seemed for all the world like he was going to attack, but the Aldran held his ground with an impassive look, his spear hefted. Mordecai rethought the situation.

"What the hell are we going to do with him?" demanded the former Issicrojan slave.

"I'll come with you," said Taribo, his panic replaced by a desperate hope.

"What about the injured?" asked Santiago, and Alistair was aware of Gregory kneeling by the side of the one he had felled, examining the wound and soothing the man with a few soft words.

In response, Mordecai lashed out with his spear and shredded the throat of the man whom Santiago wounded. The man flailed about with his feet while his hands went to his wrecked windpipe. The move was so fast and so shocking, no one could form words. Only Gregory managed to fling out a hand, as if trying to reach a drowning man, but his cry was inarticulate, emerging before he formed a coherent thought. Taribo responded with an assault on the enhanced warrior, nearly managing to stab the spear in his shoulder before the two came together and, dropping their spears, began to grapple. Spinning about, Mordecai maneuvered them so that Taribo tripped over the dying warrior and they fell to the ground with Mordecai on top. The man with the wounded horse hauled himself to his feet and, as fast as he could limp, made for the fighters. Leaping at the two, Alistair tackled Mordecai, ripping him off of Taribo and Santiago was there to restrain Taribo from taking advantage. Gregory placed himself between the two combatants, both hands outstretched.

"That's enough of this!" the doctor fairly screamed. "Alistair, keep them away from each other!" Mordecai shoved Alistair, who was just at the point of letting him go, and regained his feet but made no aggressive moves. Taribo, chest heaving, arms held from behind by Santiago, never took his gaze off the former slave.

"It was a mercy killing," Mordecai said as if he were talking to simpletons. "He was either going to die in agony over the next two days or…" Mordecai trailed off and let a gesture with his hand, directed at the now still corpse, make his point. "He was never going to survive that wound."

"Alistair," said Taribo with the specious calm of an active volcano not yet erupted, "I implore you: do not trust this monster. He should have died years ago. My Lord's vanity, Gaia protect him, is the only reason he still lives."

"The only reason your Lord still lives is because I couldn't reach him before we had to leave!" shouted Mordecai, thumping his chest with his fist to underscore his point.

"You didn't leave; you ran away like a coward," Taribo retorted, and when Alistair stepped in between him and a charging Mordecai he continued, "Like a sniveling coward!"

"That's enough!" roared Alistair, and he tossed Mordecai back a few feet.

Taribo, gaze locked with Mordecai's, moved to the side of his sole standing companion and helped him to a soft patch of ground off the trail. Mordecai, muttering inaudibly to himself and fiercely scowling, moved to the dead man to strip him. Upon seeing this, Taribo shot up to his feet and was on the point of protesting when Alistair raised a staying hand. Darkly glaring, Taribo consented to remain silent and sat back down.

"Taribo," said Alistair with the stern and commanding tone of a schoolmaster, "can we expect any other search parties to come this way?"

The African shook his head. "We are spread out thin. I doubt we will run into anyone else. Certainly not on this trail."

"Good. We have four horses now. Four of us can remain behind and catch up to the group later. Gregory will want to attend to the injured, and I'm sure Taribo and…"

"Miklos," supplied the other warrior.

"…Miklos will want to stay as well. I'll remain with them and we four will ride and catch up to you when…" Alistair faltered in his speech. "…after it's finished."

"That sounds fine to me," declared Santiago. "And I am going to start moving now."

He quickly gathered what was his, leaving the four stragglers to sort out the new equipment, and headed down the trail again. Layla, Giselle, Wellesley, Mordecai and Clyde, at first startled at Santiago's abrupt decision, scrambled to follow. Wellesley turned once to look at them and raised a hand in goodbye. Alistair returned the salute but was unsure whether Wellesley had the vision to see him or not. A minute later they were around another bend and out of sight.

The crippled horse let out a ghastly screech, and Alistair turned from the ones who had just left. "Let's put it out of its misery," he suggested, but Mordecai was already taking care of it.

53

The gradual advance of day was a nearly imperceptible event in the forest. The thick canopy of leaves allowed only a filtered, attenuated light to leak through such that one realized it had come only well after the process started. In a similar manner to the light's arrival, the lives of the wounded warriors left. Even Gregory, who closely monitored them through the night, could not say with certainty exactly when it happened. The agonizing coughs died out, and the tortured breathing grew shallower and shallower, until its cessation made not the slightest interruption. Gregory knelt and mouthed a prayer, his hands folded and his earnest features tightly wound. Alistair quietly sat and watched over the dying men, at times as unmoving as a statue, whatever thoughts moving in his head effecting no trace of their presence.

Miklos faced the proceedings with an indolent indifference. He sat with his back against a stout tree, his hurt leg laid straight in front of him and his arms, folded to begin, eventually falling to his sides. For brief periods he fell asleep. When he was awake the only indication, apart from his half opened eyes, came from his lips, which he periodically smacked, like a hungry man about to eat only more languidly. His hair was cut short, but unevenly so, as if he had sawed off the longer strands with a sharp flint stone, practical but inartistic. His lightly bronzed skin sported an elaborate black tattoo, an intricate series of vines twisting and turning on themselves, wrapping about every part of his thick body and even reaching up his neck to his jaw where it finally ended in a series of willowy strands. His head was square, tapering off a bit at the top, leaving his jowls thicker than his cranium. Broad and stubby features, well adapted to expressing lethargy, were carved into his face. He had a neck only just enough to merit the name, and from each hand five sausages protruded, stout and indelicate.

Taribo busied himself with preparing the dead horse, starting with the skin. Alistair agreed to clean the skins in the nearby brook, and when Taribo cut the meat into steaks he wrapped them in the skins. Alistair was impressed with how quickly the Issicrojan reduced the steed to neat packages, considering the near total darkness.

"I have no way to preserve it," he said with a shrug. "But we can eat some later today, perhaps."

"I'm not eating horse flesh," said Gregory, interrupting his sullen silence to utter the pronouncement with some disgust.

"You are a recent arrival," Taribo replied. "One soon learns to eat what is available. Worse things than horse flesh will pass your gullet before you expire."

Little else was said. Miklos commented that Taribo had given the horse a more merciful end than Gregory was giving the wounded. The pronouncement momentarily froze the doctor but he did not otherwise respond. When the men passed on, Taribo laid them out on the forest floor in the Gaian fashion, arms at their sides. There they would be, as he put it, reabsorbed into the nature from which they came. Gregory protested what he considered indecency but relented when the African pointed out they were Gaians. With bowed head, Taribo uttered a prayer over their bodies and then they were left to the forest.

It was noon when finally they emerged, sleepy and physically drained, from the cover of trees. The day was a hot one but cloudy, and a light drizzle, of which they had been unaware while beneath the forest canopy, sprinkled the land. The country before them flattened but there were yet some hills and no sign of the other members of the group could be seen. There was no point in stopping simply because the forest had, so they pressed on.

Alistair found himself riding in front with Taribo and managed to rouse himself from his black reverie enough to soften the scowl on his face and ask, "Why are you coming with us, Taribo?"

The Issicrojan was thoughtful for a moment before he responded. "Gaia has dealt me a hand. I can only play with the cards I am given." When Alistair's incredulous look indicated he was not satisfied with the answer, Taribo continued, "There was not much else I could do. You were hardly going to allow me to return and reveal which route you had taken. When I found out you escaped, I tell you sincerely I was pleased. When I was ordered to hunt you down I offered to search the main trail because I could not imagine you would be found there."

"But you're not disappointed you're coming with us?"

"No, I am not. I feel no great loyalty to Issicroy. I mastered the habit of following his name with 'Gaia preserve him', and I learned when to obey orders, but it was a hollow act."

"And your dead companions?"

"They are returning to Gaia," he said in his mellifluous accent, shrugging his shoulders. Alistair's still unsatisfied look prodded a more complete answer from him. "I have been on this planet, this moon, for eight years. Death is not a cataclysmic event here. In any group of ten warriors, one or two will die before the year is out. Things are only a little better in Issicroy. They were out seeking to kill. It seems to me they have no right to complain."

"Do you realize what you're up against if you go with Odin?"

"Better than you do, I suspect. You have no idea what awaits us in the waters between the continent and the island, do you?"

Alistair slowly shook his head, and Taribo grinned.

"If Gaia wishes to take me back, she will take me back." He gave another unconcerned shrug of his shoulders. "But I do not believe she wishes to take me back. If she does, she just missed a good opportunity." Taribo considered Alistair a moment. "And what do you plan to do if we reach the island?"

"The same thing I have always tried to do. Live free." No hollow observance Taribo made to Issicroy ever breathed with the pure sincerity and determination of Alistair's short statement.

Taribo nodded. "They say Odin wants to rule in peace. He wants a stable government—"

"No ruling. No government."

He regarded Alistair with a quizzical arch in his eyebrows. "Odin wants to bring peace," he finally managed in a slow and uncertain tone. "Srillium is like it is because there is no government." Alistair did not respond and Taribo increased the pace of his speech. "We live like this because we have no laws and no way to enforce them. Tribes fight because there are no rules to follow, and no way to make them follow the rules. Issicroy is better because we have a government."

"I will show you laws without Parliament, and justice without government."

Taribo's lips were parted and his brow furrowed. He fell into a confounded silence, shaking his head and pondering the words without finding the sense in them.

The drizzling rain lasted through the afternoon and a good portion of the evening. They stopped once and Taribo, Alistair and Miklos managed, despite the precipitation, to get a fire going, a monumental effort made moderately easier by an apparatus in Taribo's saddle-bag. All the horse meat was cooked and, save for Gregory, they gobbled down much of it. The steaks they did not consume were cooked and repackaged in the skins with the hope it would provide a meal or two more before becoming inedible. Eschewing the meat, Gregory chewed on some bread and cheese.

When the rain stopped and night came, they were met at the side of the road by Santiago. He greeted them with a nod of his head and addressed them.

"There have been developments." He grasped his walking stick and rose to leave, not looking to see if they followed.

He led them half a mile over uneven ground until, upon cresting one last hill, they saw their companions camped at the base below them, well ensconced from any eyes that might be scanning the countryside. A small fire was burning but, hemmed in on all sides by various stacked items, it was visible only from above and its smoke was undetectable at night. Giselle, Layla and Clyde were sitting together, unmoving, packed in a tight group. Their rigid postures and unremitting gazes, fixed on Mordecai, bespoke a controlled tension and even fear. Mordecai, apart from them and with an apparently ravenous appetite, was splayed out over the ground and wolfing down some food, apparently feeling none of the tension reigning on the other side of the fire. Nearby was the bound form of Ryan Wellesley, his arms pulled behind his back and lying belly down on the ground.

"Developments?" said Alistair with a note of irritation.

The riders descended the hillside ahead of Santiago, and Alistair dismounted with a leap and freed Wellesley from his bonds.

Not pausing from his meal, Mordecai said, "If he threatens me again he's getting tied up again."

Wellesley rubbed at his wrists and wiped away some of the mud plastered to the right side of his face. There was a prominent bruise on his left cheek bone, and his upper lip was split and swollen. While muddied rivulets of water from the wet ground trickled down his face, he glared at Mordecai but said nothing, his jaw quivering unsteadily in his anger, his breathing a staccato of unsteadiness. Giselle appeared at his side with a bit of food laid out on a flat tablet of wood. He accepted it and bit into an apple.

"I didn't threaten him," he said around the bite of apple, his voice choked with emotion and humiliation. "We got into an argument and the fucker..." He trailed off and stuffed more food into his mouth. He had the courage to glare down at Mordecai, but that one acted with pure indifference. Shaking his head, Ryan walked away to sit next to Clyde.

For his part, Alistair regarded the scarred warrior, apparently quite free of any remorse, while he ate. *I may find myself fighting alongside him,* thought the youngest Ashley as he weighed his options. There were all manner of things he wanted to say but he held his tongue and when Taribo tossed him an apple he sat down with the rest of the group. They all chose the side of the fire opposite the nonchalant Mordecai.

54

Not long after the sun rose and the members of the group prepared themselves for more travel, Mordecai was once again at the center of an argument. When the time came to resaddle the horses, Giselle suggested using them just for their equipment and supplies while they walked alongside. Mordecai insisted one of the horses was rightfully his and informed her he would be riding it. Neither was ready to back down, nor loathe to engage in a heated argument either, and before long Giselle was nearly screaming curses which Mordecai returned with a lower but more threatening tone. When Mordecai's patience ran out, which did not take long, he grabbed Giselle by the jaw, tossed her back a few yards and onto her backside in the mud, and took possession of the horse. He moved away from the group a few yards to finish fixing the saddle on it.

Unable to compete in physical terms, Giselle immediately turned to Alistair to plead her case, and Gregory and Layla were at her side, turning their indignant looks on the Aldran marine.

"Are you just going to let him take over the group?" Gregory demanded, his eyes flashing. "He just threw a woman down on the ground!"

Layla and Giselle had, presumably, similar points, but in speaking over one another it was difficult to understand what they said.

As Alistair lifted a pack onto one of the saddles for Santiago to tie into place, he said in a quiet voice, "A rattlesnake is best left alone."

This only infuriated the three of them even more, and they shouted back in unison. With a sigh, Alistair finally turned to face them.

"Giselle, what he did was not friendly. It was rude. It was cruel. But as far as his claim to one of the horses goes…he has a point."

"He doesn't have a point!" she nearly screamed, shaking her head as if to rid her ears of the words.

"You decided for the group that we were all going to share," Alistair said simply. "Mordecai doesn't want to."

"You're a son of a bitch!" Layla said, throwing her hands in the air and walking away.

"What the hell is wrong with you men?" Giselle demanded, her hands dramatically held out in front, her fingers gripping, perhaps, or clawing at an imaginary skull. "I was trying to help us out! He doesn't have to throw me to the ground because he disagrees!"

Santiago's smooth voice cut through the screaming match. "There is nothing more pressing right now than to avoid detection. If this discussion cannot be had quietly, perhaps we should table it." He had not looked up from packing his gear and belongings while speaking. His words had their intended effect, and if it did not make the anger dissipate, it dulled its edge.

In the silence that followed, Gregory, having calmed himself, placed his body directly in front of Alistair and gently gripped his larger friend by both shoulders. In a low, flat tone he said, "Alistair, I have been threatened with murder several times in the last week. I've been dumped on a planet where dog eats dog, or literally man eats man. I'm being hunted right now. I know you are the only thing that has kept me alive to this point. Please, I need you to intervene, just a little. Just bare your teeth a bit and show him he's not in control of this group. Please, Alistair. Even if killing the rider makes the horse his, he never could have killed it without you and Ryan and Santiago."

The calm entreaty passed through the shell which was impermeable to screams. Alistair, looking his friend in the eye, paused only a moment before nodding. He patted his friend on the shoulder and then stepped around him to face Mordecai, several yards off and just climbing into the saddle.

"Mordecai," he roared. "Look at me or I swear you're going to have a fight right here!"

Mordecai's posture changed, the nonchalance he so diligently effected was overtaken by apprehension. Waiting long enough to make his defiance clear, he finally turned in the saddle and looked at Alistair with a hard stare.

"We're all walking," the Aldran informed him, his voice still loud and forceful. "Giselle's plan is a good one, and that horse is no more yours than it is mine. If your pride won't let you out of that saddle, you'll have it to thank when I beat the hell out of you!" So saying, Alistair, in an unlikely display for him, yanked his shirt off to remind the ex slave of the tattoo he wore on his left breast. His muscled torso heaved with angry breaths and both fists were tightly balled, making his knuckles livid.

Mordecai, whose knuckles had turned a similar color as he squeezed the reins, finally leapt from the saddle and bounded over to Alistair to stand, as best he could, nose to nose with the taller man.

"I am not a slave!" he yelled. "I never was a slave! Don't think you can order me around and get away with it!"

It was a display of bravado that his pride demanded. In the end, he stuffed a couple more items into a saddle bag and left the camp on foot. Giselle, whose own pride also demanded a display, announced she would be walking in the back, and that Mordecai had better not stray from the front. With that, she dug out a black cloth from her sack and tied it around her jaw and skull so that it covered her head like a nun's habit. Alistair did not know if she was in mourning or what the purpose of it was, but true to her word she kept to the back with Gregory and Layla. Mordecai preceded them all by many yards while Alistair, Miklos, Taribo, Santiago, Clyde and Ryan Wellesley moved in a jumbled bunch in the middle.

By the time the sun asserted itself, the day had become hot. Between the boiling heat and the soggy ground, they were forced to pass through an air so humid they almost had to push at it to move forward. The Arcarians were especially affected, and they swatted at there bodies where trickles of sweat tickled their skin. On several occasions one of them would veer off into a nearby brook and immerse himself in its water, rejoining the group more refreshed, but between the hammer and anvil of sun and earth, no refreshment lasted long. Alistair himself, for all his prodigious stamina, felt his efforts flag as the day wore on. As steps slowed and grew shorter in length, Taribo almost jaunted, taking delight in his superior resistance to the boiling humidity.

The hills were flattening out and the trees grew sparser as they approached the southern coast. In the more open country they feared the greater risk of being seen, but only once did they spot another soul, a ways off to the east and making his way north. If he saw them, he was unconcerned. It was only as evening approached, bringing some relief with a cooler temperature and a gentle breeze, that Alistair, whose slight desire to speak was easily suppressed, found the energy to converse with Taribo. The African, at times still amused by the way the humidity assaulted them, was moving steadily along at his side when Alistair was studying the form of Mordecai far in front of them.

"Mordecai is not a common name," was Alistair's opening sentence.

"No. Mordecai is his assumed name. He was the chief of a tribe. All chiefs take a new name. Odin, for instance, or Mordecai. Our chief was Beelzebub…that was my favorite name. They always choose something they think sounds grandiose. Before Miklos and I worked for Issicroy, Mordecai's tribe slaughtered ours. Miklos and I were the only survivors, and we escaped to Issicroy for protection."

"How did he come to be a slave?"

"He was growing powerful and his tribe was large. But he didn't quite understand how things work here, how to hold on to power. He never got the blessing of the Gaians, and so Issicroy and Ansacroy united to crush him. Issicroy took him as a slave to humiliate him. That was several years ago."

"He slaughtered your tribe?"

"Yes, he did."

"And you don't want to kill him now?"

Taribo shrugged. "Actually, we attacked him. Beelzebub thought he was becoming too powerful. Of course, Beelzebub wanted the same thing. I was a warrior in that tribe for all of six months. It's not like he killed my family. And I was part of the force that crushed him, so I figure we're even."

"And Miklos?"

"Miklos doesn't hold grudges. It's too much work."

The land was streaked by long shadows when Alistair was giving consideration to stopping for the evening. They were approaching a copse of trees offering better cover than anything else he had seen for a while. Suddenly, Gregory fell heavily to his knees and doubled over, vomiting. He had been silent for some time, slowly falling to the back of the group, head tilted downward with a faint frown and Alistair now saw he had mistaken illness for introspection. The group paused and turned to behold the display as a second wave of nausea overcame him.

"He's new," said Layla. "It happens to everyone when they first come here."

Clyde laid a hand on Gregory's back while the doctor remained on all fours, breathing slowly with his eyes closed.

"Something in the water?" asked Alistair.

"I guess."

"Do you want to stop here, Greg?" Alistair asked his friend.

Gregory spit a couple times into the puddle he had made on the dirt trail. Shaking his head, he said, "No, I can...go on...I feel a bit better now."

"It's starting to get dark. I was just thinking this might be a nice place to stop anyway."

Spitting a couple more times, Gregory did not immediately answer. Finally he sat up, his face a sickly gray, and leaned back on his haunches. He let out a deep breath. "I'm fine with what you decide."

"We're only a few miles from the coast," said Santiago, his tone one of subdued impatience.

"Are you supposed to meet someone...how does this work?" asked Alistair of the Argentinean.

"I have to send a signal..." Santiago seemed on the verge of saying more but did not. Finally, he assented, scratching at his growth of beard and saying, "We can camp here in these trees."

"What about Mordecai?" Taribo asked with a nod of his head in the direction of the man who, ignorant of their halt, was still plodding south on the trail.

"He'll notice eventually," said Alistair.

"Fuck him," spat Ryan. "Who cares if he doesn't?"

They made camp in the copse of trees, camp being a simple matter of food preparation and unsaddling and brushing down the horses. Fruit and bread was their meal. The horse steaks were unfit for consumption, but Alistair recommended holding on to them since the flesh could be used as bait for something else. As time passed, it became apparent Mordecai was not going to return, which provoked no great amount of sorrow. Giselle even untied her makeshift habit and, with a trace of self-satisfaction, as if her point was made, stuffed it back in her travel sack.

Clyde was the next new arrival to be overcome with nausea. His attack was not preceded by any indication of illness, but hit him suddenly, in the middle of an offhand sentence, and abruptly he was scurrying for the edge of the copse whereupon he emptied his stomach's contents. Gregory had a healthier aspect by this point, but Clyde, upon crawling back to camp, wordlessly lay down on his side, curled up, and fell directly to sleep, without so much as sparing a glance at anyone.

One by one, the others lay on the soft grass and went to sleep, and before long Alistair and Santiago were the only ones left awake, the first watch having fallen to them without any conscious decision being taken. They exchanged furtive looks as they sat, as if each wished to converse but neither could find any appropriate words to say, so the looks were met with curt nods. Alistair would periodically rise and circle the copse of trees and then return to sit next to his taciturn companion, at which point two more nods were exchanged. This went on past the point where they both felt ridiculous until Santiago finally stirred and came to his feet.

"Mordecai knows how to find them. I will press on tonight."

"What's this?"

"Mordecai was privy to much in Issicroy. The nobility did not guard their speech around him any more than one would in the presence of a rug. He learned much, no doubt, and I think he learned how to contact Odin."

"So let him."

"I don't want him to make contact and tell them he is alone, or that we are in Issicroy's employ and are trying to find him. I will return tomorrow if I am successful. If I am not back, you will find me on the beach somewhere, probably east."

Alistair only nodded, and Santiago, walking stick in hand, left him to his thoughts. Srillium, almost full in the sky, illuminated his departure so that Alistair could see him in red. Santiago never looked back, and finally reached a slight downhill slope and slowly sank into the land until disappearing.

55

Alistair was nudged awake by Miklos' meaty hand on his ribs. The hand lingered a second too long on his side, and Alistair reflexively grabbed the wrist and pried it away. When he opened his eyes to the bright morning light and saw who it was, he relaxed and released the tattooed appendage.

"There's a large group approaching from the south."

On his feet an instant later, Alistair moved out of the copse of trees and onto the trail, squinting as the full strength of the morning sun bore down on him. The earth of the trail had dried out and consequently a plume of dust was being kicked up into the air by about thirty or so figures moving in their direction. Miklos finished trudging out of the trees and came to stand next to him.

"Are they from Issicroy?" asked Alistair, scratching at the unshaven hairs on his face, now almost to the length of a proper beard.

"No way. Ansacroy neither."

"Let's hope they're Odin's men, sent by Santiago. Wake up the others and be ready."

Miklos eyed the oncoming party a moment more and then inclined his face towards Alistair and fixed on him an unreadable stare. "I don't think you really outrank me. Under these circumstances." If he had had pockets, he would have plunged his hands into them and slumped his shoulders.

With little inclination or time to argue, Alistair suppressed a growl of exasperation and went to rouse his friends. Miklos came back a bit later to grab a spear and a dagger while the others, in various stages of waking up, stretched, yawned and rose.

"Are these Odin's men?" asked Greg of Alistair while he scratched at his head.

Alistair only shrugged and grunted. Having armed himself with an axe, he returned to the middle of the trail and stood boldly in its center, weapon prominently displayed. He was followed by an armed Ryan Wellesley, Taribo and Miklos. Greg and Clyde stayed back with the women in the copse of trees.

"I see Santiago," said Alistair, and the announcement did a good deal to relax the tension.

When they were separated by thirty yards, the approaching party stopped at a gesture from the man who walked in front, a short man, only just tall enough to reach Alistair's pectoral muscles. He was shaved but for a reddish brown mustache, the same color as the hair on his head, extending beyond the corners of his mouth and curved down before ending in smaller, upturned points. Srillium's sun, strong at these latitudes, had turned a pale complexion into an unwilling and angry looking reddish bronze. His feet planted in the earth at the width of his shoulders, his hands planted on his hips, he stared down Alistair as if he were seven feet tall. The dozens of faces behind him stared impassively.

"Are you Alistair?" asked the man, his tone the unmistakable accent of the English, which Alistair well recognized from his time on Earth near the metropolis of Londinium. It was not a guttural or cockney accent, but neither was it overly polished, and when he posed his question he raised one shaggy eyebrow.

"Yes. Are you Odin?"

"You can call me Duke. Santiago says you wish to beg for passage to Odin's Island."

Alistair faltered. "I didn't, uh…"

It was Giselle who stepped forward. "We are looking for passage to the island. We are not looking to beg."

Duke directed his attention to the copse of trees from where the striking woman addressed him. "We invite those we wish to come with us. Others must purchase passage. Those without invitation or means must beg."

"Most men count themselves lucky if I go with them," said Layla, stepping forward to be seen.

"Women are always welcome," said Duke, though his formal and somewhat forceful tone did not soften for them.

"Gregory is a doctor," offered Layla, and she grabbed him by the hand and brought him forward so that he could be seen.

"A doctor? Good."

"And these men," said Giselle, smoothly extending her arm towards the four men in the middle of the trail, "are soldiers."

"Santiago told me about Alistair," replied the Englishman and he returned his attention to the large Aldran. With a beckoning wave of his hand and a stern gaze, he commanded, "Come here."

Alistair, self conscious of every step he made, closed the distance between them with a few long, awkward strides until he stood before Duke, staring down at him but feeling as if the man were towering over him. Pursing and twisting his lips and raising an eyebrow, Duke grabbed the animal skin shirt Alistair wore and pulled it aside, exposing the tattoo on Alistair's left pectoral. The Englishman nodded in appreciation, his features softening for just a moment into a more reverent alignment before, with a curt nod and a flick of the wrist, he whipped the shirt back into place.

"Very well. Four soldiers, two concubines and a doctor. But I see an eighth face among you."

"Clyde Oliver Jones, at your service," said the Australian, stepping forward to the side of the women with a short bow.

"What do you do?" demanded Duke, his low tone as cynical and disapproving as his expression had become. His bushy eyebrows crowded close upon his eyes and his hands returned to his hips.

"A bit of a jack-of-all-trades I am," he said with a hopeful smile. "I've worked all over, in all manner—"

"You're here to beg."

Clyde returned to an upright position with a sheepish grin. "I guess I am."

"We have the four horses," Alistair said so only Duke could make it out. "Surely that's worth taking Clyde along."

"We're starting to run short of room," said the diminutive commander and followed the pronouncement with a prolonged, "Hmm. Horses can always be useful, I suppose. Very well." Abruptly turning on his heel, the Englishman marched back the way he came and the men behind him parted like a pair of curtains to let him through and then trailed behind, less meticulous in the rhythm of their marching than their commander. Santiago let the group pass him by so that he was left with the eight he arrived with.

"Thanks for your help, Santiago," said Alistair as their companions moved past them to catch up with the larger group.

A smile showed itself, for an instant, at one corner of Santiago's mouth, and to Alistair it seemed the barrier of cold detachment by which the man kept himself aloof receded only to return in the same interval. Supported by his walking stick, he turned and said, "Let's go." It was a gentle suggestion, almost warm, like the echo of the smile that flitted by a moment before.

ᘒᘓ

The grassy plain spanning the distance between the coast and the hills to the north stretched on for another few miles before the grass thinned out to reveal a whitish sand. Clumps of weeds dotted the landscape but nothing else grew among the pale dunes standing tall before them. At the tops of these, they glimpsed the sea only a few dozen yards distant, but they turned to the west, keeping the body of water on their left. The roar of waves driven by wind was a constant noise in the background. The heat and the glare of the sand beat at them without mercy.

They came across a larger encampment of people, perhaps a hundred strong, nestled in between a series of tall dunes, nearly twenty yards in height. At the top of the dunes were lookouts, lying flat on top of some fabric to protect them from the searing sand underneath. They allowed them to pass without incident, giving salutes which Duke curtly returned, and then the British leader brought them to the five score or so in the sandy and enclosed valley below. He was immediately surrounded by various men with queries, reports, updates and other business.

The faces now surrounding Alistair were sallow, haggard faces. Only Duke among all the men was recently shaved, and no one was washed. Many eyes were shot with blood, and bluish pouches sagged beneath them. No one on Srillium kept the soft and corpulent abdomens comfort and leisure bestow, but these bedraggled folk with sand matted in their hair, grit caked under their fingernails and calluses on their feet, looked as if all those parts of their physiques not entirely indispensable were dissolving away. Not yet emaciated, they resembled the long lines of prisoners Alistair saw on Kaldis, men and women condemned to hard labor and minimal sustenance. They possessed only so much muscle as was required to move without stumbling, to work without collapsing, and no more. Yet for all the privation they were energized, like those who have willingly sacrificed rather than be stolen from, like those who are on the verge of attaining their goal. There was an expectant hope exhaustion could not conceal, rarely seen in a prisoner, and in the acre or so of space between the sand dunes there was much activity.

While Duke was carried away by some, others beset the newcomers, drawing them into the encampment, taking charge of the horses and stock of the new supplies. Alistair was relieved of his weapons and physically appraised by men who regarded him as one might an auto, nodding with an air of expertise and murmuring to each other as they pointed out certain features. The handling was pragmatic and rough, due more to a life and place where gentleness was easily forgotten than to a desire to mishandle. Alistair's tattoo delighted one of them, who explained what it meant to the others who in turn murmured in appreciation. Then, having been separated and swallowed individually by the swarm, the nine were just as quickly brought back together, on the other side of the dune valley, and made to kneel in a row. Duke reappeared and strode up and down the line, inspecting. He finally stepped in front of Alistair, whose head was almost level with his.

"Do you know what we are about?" he demanded to know.

Alistair squirmed as if in extreme discomfort but nodded.

"Do you know what is out there?" Duke twisted his torso to throw a hand out vaguely in the direction of the ocean. "Do you know that many of us will not reach the destination? Speak up!"

"I have no idea," Alistair croaked, his eyes flitting about for a safe place to rest and finally finding the ground in front of him. "I was told it was dangerous."

"Hmph," snorted Duke, but he seemed satisfied. "We accept you. All you need do is swear an oath of loyalty to Odin." Duke looked at them with severity and said, "Well?" This elicited a flurry of nods from the candidates. Duke sharply turned on his heel and was replaced by another man in flowing robes, a Gaian Druid. Shaved bald with a long, gray beard, the brown skinned man glided over to Layla and placed a gnarled hand with throbbing veins and long, twisted, yellowing fingernails on top of her head and croaked a short oath which Layla reiterated. He moved next to Clyde and the process was repeated.

When Alistair's turn came, he murmured the oath with little feeling. The woolen robes, long unwashed, exuded an unpleasant odor, and he lifted his head trying to avoid the smell. The oath finished, the Druid moved on until all nine swore loyalty to the chieftain. They then rose from their knees and were welcomed with a sincere solidarity by their new comrades, but Alistair, when a moment arrived in which he was not being presented to people and giving a short introduction of himself, felt compelled to spit into the sand, as if something had left in his mouth a foul taste.

56

Alistair sat on the sand under the bright, hot sun and considered how much the composition of the men and women under Duke's command was affected by the events which brought them together. They were at the bottom of the social strata, the ones who had little or nothing to lose, the ones whose productivity was consumed by upper classes. The vast majority were peasants, many were Druids and the devoutly faithful. All shone with a jubilant anticipation only faintly marred by a nagging exhaustion.

There was one Beseecher among them, a man whose like they had seen once before. On a rug in the middle of the sand valley he sat, Indian style, with his hands resting on his knees palms up. His eyes were closed and he said nothing, only faintly humming now and then, his lips evincing only hints of speech in the form of faint trembles and quivers that did nothing to form the humming into recognizable vocabulary. He was not an old man, but his Caucasian skin was weathered and well tanned and his unkempt and oily hair, grown long, was a matted mess of knots. His grimy hands sported long and twisted fingernails, as did his callused feet, and his trunk and limbs were slender and sinewy almost to the point of being unhealthy. He was given a space of six feet on either side which no one entered, and none spoke to him, only now and then kneeling down around his halo of undisturbed space to say a prayer and contemplate his sublime meditation.

The ocean of the alien moon beat continually at the sandy shore, the noise rising and falling but never ceasing. Though the oceans of Srillium IIa were shallower than those of Earth and Aldra, the tidal influences were greater, so there was a long stretch of smooth, flat sand with shallow tidal pools which, as night approached, would fill with water. Alistair tried to let the sound of the waves sweep over him, to relax him, to make him forget about the merciless sun on shoulders whose skin was growing pink and tender, to make him forget about the growing sick feeling in his stomach. Ryan had finally vomited not long after arriving at the camp and was even now lying curled up in the sand at the foot of a dune, motionless, with a pitiable expression on his face and occasionally emitting a low moan. Only Alistair awaited his Rite of Passage.

"Odin is out there somewhere," said one of the former peasants who was lounging next to Alistair. He smiled, showing three holes where front teeth were supposed to be. "We're all divided into separate groups, and Odin will join one at the last minute. No one knows which." The man nodded knowingly, then added, "On account of the assassins." He spoke English like one long comfortable with it, but with a touch of a non-native accent. His countenance was comprised of the morphed features descending from all or at least most of the original continents, Africa, Asia, Europe and the Americas, and his skin was the typical light brown of such people.

Alistair did not reply for fear more than words would come pouring out. He instead tucked his head between his knees and waited for his stomach to lose patience and get it over with.

When the length of the shadows of the sand dunes was twice the height of the shifting hills and the brightness of the day lost its edge, a powerful bass note rumbled across the land, coming from the west. Another sounded a short time later, as if in response, this one also from the west but closer than the first. The deep, grumbling notes caused an abrupt change in the encampment. Men moved, several of them converging on a spot of sand to dig, uncovering a large object, easily the length of a man, wrapped in a tarp. Coming to his feet to observe the proceedings, Alistair saw the object being dragged up the side of a sand dune whereupon it was unwrapped and revealed to be a horn. Two men held it upright while a third stepped up to the narrow end, placed his mouth on it and blew with such intensity Alistair half expected to see his ears bleed. The same note was produced and held for as long as the blower had breath to give it.

The horn was then dropped and the sojourners dug into the dunes surrounding them. Alistair and his group moved to lend their help to the endeavor, and soon objects of many sizes and shapes were uncovered and the dunes were steadily wiped away. Boxes with tools were opened while sections of wooden construction were unwrapped. By degrees the work switched from uncovering to dragging the pieces nearer the sea, and finally to assembling. Over the course of a few hours the assembled pieces came to resemble a ship. All of the parts and equipment it required, painstakingly manufactured and buried, finally reached their culmination, so that a population of many thousands, hiding from the other forces of the realm, could disappear across the sea with almost no warning.

"If you don't know what you're doing, have the decency to stay out of the way!" clamored Duke as he moved in and out of different work groups, lending a hand here or a kick in the butt there.

Alistair, having been nudged and bumped and spun about by bodies with a definite purpose, felt like a beach ball on a busy highway. When the simple task of dragging the sections and equipment to the water's edge was complete, the young Aldran found his usefulness was exhausted and decided to extricate himself from the center of the storm, withdrawing to the edge with a small group of similarly ineffectual folk. There they waited with the discomfort of those who want to contribute but are aware that any such contribution will be more hindrance than help. Miklos, having stretched himself out on a soft pile of sand remaining from the now vanished dunes, seemed perfectly content, but the rest kept vigil on the outskirts of the laborers, the moral support their presence lent the endeavor being the extent of their involvement.

The process went as smoothly as could be imagined, and Alistair marveled at the discipline of it. One could turn to make a comment or two to a friend, and in turning back a minute later the ship was noticeably closer to completion. When night eroded the sky until the last sliver of light, clinging to the horizon, finally dissolved and Srillium took its turn over the land, the vessel was completed. It was practical in design, bereft of any ornament, comfort, or feature not necessary in a boat whose only purpose was to travel twenty miles with a crew of six or seven score.

The boat was assembled on top of a long row of logs, former tree trunks stripped of bark and smoothed down. When Duke gave his approval to the completed vessel, a series of levers were placed under the ribs of the frame and over the shoulders of the larger men. Alistair and the others, inactive for a couple hours, quickly volunteered to help. The six score or so labored against gravity and friction and inertia and finally tugged and pushed and levered the boat into a sea that the tide by then had brought much closer to them. Finally, Alistair's own moccasined feet stepped into the cool water of the ocean, and he felt the spray of broken waves on his face and chest, cooling his heated skin which protested at the twisting and rubbing it was made to endure. The spray charged him with an exhilarating freshness and he strained even harder against his lever until finally, with the water now up to his waist, the boat was floating free.

"Man the decks!" cried Duke from the foredeck, and he and the few with him already on the ship unrolled rope ladders over the side.

Most clambered up these but a few, including Alistair and Wellesley, remained in the water, pushing at the ship until it reached their chins and then they too scaled the sides and gained the safety of the craft, arriving in time to kneel down with the others and catch the end of the prayer the Druid was intoning. The Beseecher, placid of expression, was taken to the aft deck and his rug was laid there. He resumed his position of meditation while the oars were put in place and men propelled the boat. Alistair found himself next to Taribo, hands on the same oar, forcing it through the water below.

Taribo fixed a childlike grin on Alistair. "With you and I on this side we will be constantly turning right!" he said and laughed.

Alistair permitted himself a soft smile. Srillium was higher now in the east, its glow shimmering on the black ocean's waves. In the west a handful of stars could be seen in the clear sky. Picking up speed, the boat withdrew from the beach, heading south towards the dark and deeper waters of the channel.

When the shoreline was sufficiently distant, sense of movement diminished. Oar stroke after oar stroke swished through the black waters, but only a faith in physics gave any confidence of forward progress. The prow of the boat dipped in and out of the salty water with that slurp boats make, and occasionally a wave in their proximity would crest and tumble over itself with an accompanying swish, but little else did they hear. The rhythm of their strokes, at first inconsistent with desultory cracks of oars striking, eventually settled into a stable pattern.

Duke, standing on the foredeck and peering at the stars, occasionally muttered something to a man Alistair took to be a lieutenant, and every so often one side of the boat was ordered to skip a stroke to correct the trajectory. Alistair had little confidence in the corrections, for Duke did not convey the relaxed mien of an expert but rather the nervous agitation of an amateur. He checked and rechecked stars with jerks of the head, as if the twinkling points of light might play a prank and reorganize themselves when he wasn't looking. He constantly changed the position and attitude of his hands, and he paced back and forth, often pausing at the gunwale to grip it with whitening knuckles. Had the island not been the size it was, and only as distant as a few leagues, Alistair doubted they would have found it at all.

There were no breaks, for there was no one to relieve them. The ship was large enough that most of the occupants were seated at the benches with their hands on the oars. Almost everyone not rowing was a woman, none of whom was explicitly prohibited from touching the oars but, conditioned as they were by custom, they left the hard labor to the men. These women and perhaps a half dozen men sat in the middle of the boat, a narrow strip of a walkway elevated a couple feet above the rowers but a few feet below the fore and aft decks, to which access was gained by a short flight of steps from the walkway. The animals in their possession were kept on the decks. The spaces beneath them were stuffed with the supplies they were bringing: foodstuffs, seeds, tools and other things packed away in crates and wrapped up in tarps tied together. What supplies could not fit under the decks were distributed among the men and women on the central walkway.

By degrees Alistair grew somber and withdrawn. The tender skin of his arms and shoulders was on fire, and a raging headache beat at his temples and forehead. He said not a word, instead focusing on a point on the wooden floor near his feet as he repeated his oar strokes, passing into an almost hypnotic state. He thought of his parents and his siblings as he rowed in that Srillium night on that Srillium sea. He thought of Oliver and Henry. He thought of Kaldis and many dozens of things so far away.

Taribo, not knowing Alistair well enough to recognize the set of his jaw and squint of his eyes, directed an offhand comment to him but got no response. The African, with a concerned glance, said nothing more. Finally, Alistair emerged from his near catatonic state with an eruption of vomit splattering the water between his feet. Coughing afterwards, he wiped his mouth with his forearm, and spit several times, looking around in embarrassment but only a couple men noticed, sparing him nothing more than a fleeting and indifferent glance between oar strokes. Taribo gave him a sympathetic half smile that he returned with a grim nod, taking hold once more of the oar and putting his strength behind it. He felt a good deal better already.

The vomit, its pungent smell piercing the stench of bodies, made Alistair a bit queasy, but it was diluted by the salt water in the floor of the boat. When this leakage rose to an inch in height men began to mutter uneasily; an occasional splash was heard beneath the groaning of the oars when someone shifted his feet. Duke came down to inspect things but assured his men it posed no real threat. The boat only had to last a short trip, and, he assured them, it undoubtedly would.

Odin's tribe built fifty boats in all, and if everyone followed the plan, all four dozen plus were on the water, drawing nearer to one another as they converged on the island's northern shore. Since it was too dark to see the other boats, it was sound that first indicated this growing proximity, but not a sound any of them was glad to hear. It was at first a great splash, like a large body rising out of the water, but so faint only Alistair and maybe one or two others heard it over the sound of their rowing. It was followed by the unmistakable sound of yelling and screaming. Then came a crash, as of wood being crushed.

Alistair perked up at the sound of the splash, but when the sound of a ship being broken followed, the entire crew, as one, ceased their rowing, startled like a man in a dark room who realizes he is not alone. Straining their ears, leaning towards the sound as if cutting the distance by a few inches would improve their detection, the men listened to the yelling and screaming. There was the sound of a load groan, like some material under great stress, followed by a snap and the flurry of voices became more frenzied. The horror of the unseen menace pressed down on them, and more than a few shivered in the warm air. Another splash was followed by more screams, only faintly reaching their ears from the distance but gaining in terror what it lost in decibels.

"Keep to your rowing, men!" shouted Duke, coming out of a stupor. "There's nothing listening will do for them. Or us."

His bark, so near at hand, was like an electrocution and the men were instantly plying at the oars, redoubling their efforts.

"That's the next ship over," muttered a man in Mandarin. He was one row removed from Taribo and Alistair. *"If it turns our way we're next."*

"What if Odin's in that boat?" asked another.

"If you're talking," shouted Duke, bending over the foredeck and peering into the mass of men at the bottom, "you're not putting enough energy into rowing! Now row!"

The horrifying destruction of the other boat continued unabated. The cracking of wooden beams, the splashing and cries all suggested a terrible scene that each pictured in his head. Those not occupied with rowing were now on either of the two decks, trying to catch a glimpse of the wreckage. Alistair caught sight of Gregory and Layla, kneeling precariously at the top of the pile of supplies on the aft deck, Gregory securing the young woman's waist with his arm. Feeling a real fear take hold of him, almost like a hand trying to crumple his chest, Alistair heaved on his oar. The thought of being in the water, defenseless, while death from the unfathomable depths rose up to devour him, or drag him down to be drowned, was unlike any fear he had ever experienced. The resultant burst of adrenaline was unequaled by any he had ever felt.

The smashing of wood eventually ceased, leaving the desperate cries of men at the mercy of a lethal predator from the deep, and gradually, as the voices were reduced in number, the distant cacophony diminished. Finally there was silence more terrible than any sound that reached their ears. It was interrupted once, then twice, by a scream from a swimmer who had been conserving his energy rather than express his terror to the world, but the scream was short and ended abruptly, as if the vocal tract were flooded with salt water. After the second such scream there were no more interruptions.

A few of the men whimpered, like sympathetic echoes of the carnage just heard. Two lost their composure and were replaced at their oars. On the foredeck above, Duke no longer paced, instead grasping at the gunwale and facing the direction of the attack, straining to catch a glimpse of something in the water, as if his eyes might peel away a layer of darkness if he looked intently enough, as if a forewarning might somehow soften the blow. On Alistair's hands a blister formed and popped, leaving exposed skin to be rubbed raw by the rowing, but he was insensible to this minor ache, so consumed were his thoughts with the silent expanse of water between their ship and the floating debris to the east. Between the wreckage and the negligible protection of their vessel, a large creature, a spawn of the ocean, might be swimming, hurtling towards them with nefarious intent. Or it might be headed away, towards a different ship; either way they had no say in the matter, wretches in the unfeeling hands of fate.

In the dark, over water, there was no way to know, upon hearing a sound, how far away was its origin; nor could they know how fast the invisible menace could swim or if there were others of its kind out there somewhere, waiting to happen upon them. Thus there was no point they could declare themselves safe short of reaching the shores of the island. Every moment of the way they took their fear with them, but there is a difference between acute fright and chronic dread, and men react differently to them. The acute fright they felt when the monster attacked charged them with a powerful burst of energy, but the chronic dread of the ensuing silence lost itself in the monotony, retreated to the subconscious. It was never forgotten, but it did not impart the same frantic urgency to each heave on the oars, did not command such full attention to itself. Alistair noticed the popped blister on his left palm, felt the trembles in his arms which remained when the adrenaline was exhausted. His efforts began to flag.

His slighter companions withstood less than he. Intermittent exhortations from Duke, equal parts encouragement and remonstrance, elicited small responses, miniature replications of the colossal effort provoked by the attack, each one smaller than the previous until Duke could educe nothing more. His pleas lost effect; coordination lapsed; oars once again cracked against each other; limbs trembled; men rested in their efforts, leaving their hands on the oars, but when enough men on the same oar did likewise it became obvious. Rhythm was lost and the boat advanced sporadically.

Duke, with a grimace and a curse, finally called a halt, ordering his men to rest for a few minutes and get their strength back. He assured them the island was only a short distance away now. It was a quick rest before the last bit of the journey, he informed them, but then he looked anxiously over the side of the boat, tapping his left foot and gnawing at his lower lip.

"Sunrise!" called a female voice from the aft deck.

Looking up, Alistair realized it was Layla, still perched on top of the cargo in the back, Gregory at her side. She was pointing behind the ship, which should have been the north.

"We've gotten turned around," muttered Duke and a nervous grumble arose among the rowers. "Just a bit," he assured them. "A couple strokes of the oar and we're back on course. Let's have the…starboard?…let's have the starboard side…come on now, men. Just a couple strokes and we're back on course."

The men on the right side of the ship managed two weary strokes. Duke, peering out at the horizon which showed the faintest signs of illumination, got a few more strokes out of them and the sunrise swiveled around until it was on the port side of the ship and they were facing south again.

"How far off course are we?" demanded a voice from the rowers and more grumbles ensued.

"I see the island!" yelled out one of the lieutenants from the foredeck. "It's directly ahead of us!"

"There it is!" said another in confirmation. "Close at hand now!"

Duke, with rapid but tight, controlled gestures and emphatic cries, spurred the men on, but he need not have bothered, for the discovery of the island was quite enough to get them rowing again. Their arms were still sore but no longer tired, and their hearts furiously beat but for a different reason. Their leader was in the foremost point of the ship, leaning into the gunwale as if his weight could help them slide over the water. He shouted encouragement, turning to pump a fist or wave them on, and by the crescendo of his voice the men in the bottom of the boat could feel themselves drawing near to the island and away from the danger lurking in the sea. The water in the bottom of the boat was reaching their calves, but it was no longer a concern. As the light in the sky spread out slowly and the stars faded, they expected with each stroke of the oars to feel the boat hit solid ground.

And then finally it did.

57

The first indication they were near the shore was when the tips of the oars clipped across the ocean floor. Then there was the rough sound of scraping as the hull of the boat hit rocks rising above the sandy bottom. Finally, the ship plowed into the shallow sand and the crew's momentum pitched them forward; a couple men even fell from their benches. A spontaneous cheer arose and men scrambled over each other to reach the gunwale above and have a look. By the light of the murky early morning, they saw they had not made the beach; their boat ran aground about a hundred yards out.

"You'll have the rest of your lives to stare at the beach, men," said Duke, the attempted gruffness of his tone unable to cover a tone of relief, and perhaps of pride. "We've got unloading to do."

Duke was about to start directing but he found Alistair, who had shouldered his way through the crowd, standing at his side.

"We shouldn't take any chances with this," Alistair said to him. "Why don't you let me take a landing party ashore and make sure there is nothing waiting to ambush us?"

Duke fixed a disapproving glare on Alistair. "I don't even know your name. I've got lieutenants who have been with me a lot longer than you."

"You don't have anybody like me, sir."

The Aldran, whose name Duke knew very well, did not salute, but he was stiffly standing at attention, his ample chest puffed out and his shoulders held wide. His gaze was direct but not challenging and Duke, as he considered the lad, rolled his lips and swiveled his jaw.

"Phrimpong," he barked, and a grizzled man of principally Oriental heritage, with jet black hair but weathered skin that would go better with gray, stepped forward.

"Yes, sir," responded Phrimpong, his rumbling voice even rougher than his skin and his accent British. Had Alistair only heard the voice he would have pictured a brown haired dock worker right off the streets of some English port.

"Take a landing party to the beach and secure the area." With a toss of his head in Alistair's direction he added, "Take this one with you."

Phrimpong regarded Alistair with a deeply skeptical expression, and a challenging one, as if defying the Aldran to protest the fact that a man could be skeptical about him.

The cool water of the ocean reached past Alistair's waist, flooding his moccasins and causing him to wince as the liquid chilled his smoldering skin. Waves rolled past, taking the water to the middle of his back and he tensed his when they did, his sunburn protesting all the while. A spear was shoved into his grasp and, as if it were a rifle to be kept dry, he held it above the surface as he waded towards shore. Feeling the sand of the bottom slide and shift against his leather-clad feet, he moved as swiftly as decorum allowed, leaving a small wake but not splashing, always feeling the menace of the deep water behind him like a prickle at the back of his knees, a tingle blossoming once or twice into a full body shudder.

It was fully three hundred feet from the boat to the shore, and for two hundred of it the water depth remained steady. Finally, at the last stretch, it grew shallow until the twelve warriors, filthy, bedraggled and exhausted, were standing on firm, wet sand as the timid light of dawn expanded. Silently, they faced the willows, birches and oaks that huddled together, regarding the new arrivals. A wave broke on the beach, then another, the water snaking around their ankles. Phrimpong, at the head of the squad, studied the layout, trying to read the secrets of the dense forest before him, his spear gripped tightly and at the ready, his knees bent and his muscles tensed. Somewhere in the distance a bird cawed, and this was answered by another caw farther away.

To the west the beach disappeared around a bend, hiding behind the clustering trees, while to the east it stretched on for miles, more or less straight. Alistair noticed another boat to the east, far enough from them that the peaks of waves in the space between concealed it, but he said nothing for the moment. Apart from the waves and the placid breeze fluttering the foliage, causing it to whisper unintelligible secrets, there was no sound and no movement, just the inscrutable woods.

"Groups of four," muttered Phrimpong and he began to advance.

The dozen men broke into three groups and Alistair chose the one moving west. He fell into place behind them and quietly, eyes always on the verdant mass before them, they swung around the curve, saw an expansive bay on the other side, and crept into the shadowless gloom of the forest. The weeds beneath their feet crackled as the branches hunched over them, blocking out the sky. A bird bolted from the confines of the branches of a willow, startling them before it disappeared. Deeper in, the air was still. Only the crisps and crackles of their companions to the east broke the stillness.

"There is someone else here," announced Alistair, his tone moderate and frank.

"How do you know?"

"Who?"

The young Aldran had leapt onto a boulder and was scanning the ground on the other side.

"There's a path. Beaten down by feet."

"Men or animals?" asked the one nearest Alistair.

Alistair jumped from the boulder to the ground and surveyed the terrain around the path running parallel to the beach to their north.

"Both."

"How can there be men here?" asked one, his voice irritable and skeptical, but he knelt down all the same to inspect the ground.

"It's an animal trail they use for hunting," said another, leaning on his spear.

The man on his knees ran his hand just above the ground, as if he might feel the residue of human presence. "There can't be nobody else on this island," he declared and he glared at the tracks angrily, finally turning his glower on Alistair as if accusing him. "How the hell could they have made it here?"

The Aldran met the glare with a wry look of his own. "We made it here."

"Nobody's ever done what we done," he declared with a wild gesture, sweeping his arm to indicate something or other.

"We bull-rushed the island with numbers," Alistair calmly replied. "Maybe others made it with stealth. Smaller craft."

"Smaller craft get devoured in the ocean."

Alistair shrugged and indicated the path with a nod of his head. "Explaining the presence of humans here is easier than explaining human tracks on a deserted island." His eyes were not on the path but rather were tracking back and forth over the foliage while his companions were distracted by the footprints.

The kneeling man finally rose and shook his head. "There wasn't supposed to be nobody here."

"They don't have to be our enemies," said Alistair.

One of the men grasped Alistair's shoulder and gave it a squeeze of camaraderie. "On this moon, everyone who steps on your territory is an enemy."

Alistair, suppressing a wince from the firm grasp on his aching skin, shook his head firmly. "It doesn't have to be that way."

Having found signs of a human presence, if not the humans themselves, the four men returned to the beach and reunited with the rest. The sun was now over the horizon and their elongated shadows stretched far to the west, as if trying to escape the new land to which they had been taken. The breeze having died, the ocean, the one-way street just traversed, was calm, only small waves lapping quietly at the beach. The beach on the other side, where Ansacroy and Issicroy were, was a thousand light years away. The wooden vessel which bore them across the waters was still run aground, but the others were assembling rafts and forming production lines to whisk the supplies from deck to raft. A few men were already on their way to shore, pushing their burdens over the surface of the water.

When a few supplies were ashore, the famished immigrants opened a crate full of foodstuffs and ravenously tore into it. Alistair's limbs shook. He and his friends, old and new, gathered together and devoured the bread, fruit and dry salted meat passed around. Water was all there was to drink, but this beggar's meal was as succulent as anything he ever tasted. By degrees, as he consumed the food, steadiness returned to his weakened limbs and, the hunger much abated, fatigue made itself felt. As he lay back, his drowsy eyes closed and only the emphatic and strident insistence of Duke and his lieutenants roused him from an incipient slumber. No bed ever felt as soft as the sand on that beach, and no greater effort was ever required to leave comfort and return to work.

The bulk of the party was sent back to the boat to finish unloading the supplies and, later on, to disassemble the ship whose materials would be used on the island. A few other smaller groups, comprised mainly of women with a handful of warriors for protection, were sent out to scavenge while Duke himself, with a select group of men, including Alistair, set out to scout and map the area.

The land around them was flat and verdant, bordering on marshy at times, and their steps often pressed deep into the ground, sometimes emerging with a slurp. The forest was about a mile thick before it thinned into more open territory. Perhaps a mile past that, the land sloped upwards. While there was nothing on the island that could be called a proper mountain, the interior was elevated a few hundred feet above sea level. They came across several more signs of human presence, which greatly displeased Duke, as well as a large pond nestled in the valley of a couple small hills. The unflagging British Captain finally took pity on his troops and allowed them a rest on the shores of the tranquil pond, though he himself scaled the nearest hill and, back straight with one hand over his eyes as he peered into the distance, kept watch over the area.

The seven other warriors relaxed into a familiar camaraderie. Alistair, more reclusive, sat a few feet apart, looking over the surface of the pond, with its lilies and weeds, and a far-away and impassive stare smoothed over his features. He was not seated for more than a minute when, unnoticed by his comrades, he gave a start and perked up, sniffing the air and scanning the shore. A moment later he found what he was searching for and sprang to his feet, spear in hand, and took off. Only then did the others notice and their conversation halted.

Having put several yards between him and the group, some of whom were now uneasily getting up, the Aldran exile finally stopped and knelt down. A moment later he was back on his feet bidding them, with an expansive wave of his arm, to join him. Duke, who descended the hill when he saw Alistair leaving, was just reaching his men.

"Alistair! What the devil's gotten into you?" he demanded, his hands cupped over his mouth.

The Aldran did not speak but just waved them over one more time. With a muffled grumble, Duke snatched up his spear and led his men around the edge of the pond to Alistair's position. As they drew nearer they detected what caught Alistair's attention: the smell of smoldering wood. Pushing through the thigh-high grass, Duke finally stepped next to Alistair and stared down at the charred remains of three logs, still giving off some thin wisps of smoke. The fire was stamped out and the ashes scattered but other than that only footprints and other impressions remained.

"Couple hours," said Alistair. "I think there were three of them."

"Did they hide when they saw us coming?" wondered a man aloud.

Shaking his head, Alistair replied, "When this campfire was being put out we were a couple miles away on the beach. They didn't leave because we startled them. But they may be in the area. Whether they're hostile or not—"

"We're going to proceed on that assumption," Duke interjected, massaging the ends of his long mustache with his grimy fingers. A bead of sweat trickled down his forehead and he wiped it with his forearm. "We need to get back to camp. We'll do more exploring once we're settled in." The note of finality in his voice had his men hefting their spears and turning to go, but before Duke himself left he nodded once to Alistair. "Good work," was all he said.

�� ��

The sun was high in the sky when Duke's group returned to the beach, and the sand had grown uncomfortably hot. Having finished unloading the supplies from the ship, the immigrants brought the various bundles and boxes and crates to the edge of the woods, underneath the cooler shade of the trees. A few were snoozing there, the snoring Miklos among their number, while others were busy disassembling the ship. A few more were separating the supplies by category, though they were in little hurry to finish, spending as much time leaning on the crates and chatting as they did actually dragging the heavy cargo about. Of the group with whom he had traveled, Alistair saw only the tattooed companion of Taribo. He assumed the others were either working on the boat or out foraging.

Though it was not immediately apparent to him, the members of his party were familiar enough with the other crew members to notice there were some new faces in camp. With a hearty and manly greeting, Duke immediately hailed the half dozen newcomers. Their boat, like Duke's, hit shallow waters many yards out and could not be rowed to shore, but there was a large pile of supplies about a mile distant.

It was quickly decided the two camps would merge. Scouts from the other camp had also come across unmistakable signs of a human presence and were no more sanguine about the implications than was Duke. Miklos and the other napping crewmen were roused and sent to help raft the other cargo to their position. By the time the sun was nearing the far horizon and every foot in camp, including Duke's, dragged across the ground rather than lift to take proper steps, the separate pieces of the boat were brought ashore and stacked as a makeshift defensive wall. The population of the camp swelled to nearly three hundred, and Mordecai, it turned out, was one of the new arrivals. Alistair cast a fleeting dark glance in his direction, but the former chieftain did not look at him.

It was not fully dark, and the waning Srillium had yet to rise, when Alistair collapsed into a heap on the grass beneath a willow tree. The evening wind picked up intensity, rustling the leaves and making the waves crash more loudly. Gregory, Wellesley, Taribo, Miklos, Santiago, Giselle, Layla and Clyde, all having reunited, gathered around him, like celestial bodies will accrete around the one with the most gravity. Gregory and Layla quietly conversed as they prepared to sleep, finishing a talk started earlier while they foraged together. The rest fell into exhausted slumber before Srillium made its appearance.

Duke remained alert for an hour, along with a handful of unfortunates chosen for the first watch. When a scout group from a third ship arrived, only they were awake to notice. The scouts brought news of a successful landing and contact with two other ships. They gave their account, took the exchange of information Duke offered, and said farewell, bound to return to the larger camp. The following day, those two camps would merge in the bay. Until then, there was naught to do but rest while some kept watch, wary of the eyes that might be watching them, of the locals who might not be keen to share the island.

58

With the heavy mallet he wielded in his equally heavy hands, Miklos battered the top of a post, lately part of a ship, and drove it into the turf. The man with the multitude of black tattoos and the Greek appellation stood upon a pile of posts so he could reach high enough to hammer the plank downward. Taribo and Alistair held it in place. A few feet away from them, Santiago, Clyde and Wellesley were busy with the same job, working their way towards Alistair. Dozens of cracks rang out across the bay as workers built a defensive fortification in an arc touching the water at two points. Other cracks, distinct from those made at the wall, also rang out, products of tools hacking away at tree trunks, clearing away space inside the embryonic fortress whose curve plunged into the forest.

"They should gather everyone up," Miklos said when, after three powerful blows, he stopped to rest. "There were ten thousand of us, they say."

"There will be less now," Taribo reminded him.

"Yes, but there must still be several thousand. They should gather everyone up and we can build one city in the middle of the island. Ten thousand strong. Do you know why ten thousand, Alistair?"

"The post isn't in yet," the Aldran responded.

Miklos smashed the top of the post again. "Do you know why ten thousand? Because it's the perfect size for a city-state. Plato proved that long ago." Alistair did not respond and Miklos filled the interim with another whack. "Have you read Plato?"

"Yes."

Miklos delivered another blow. "With a wise philosopher-king to lead the government. A great Greek philosopher," he added with a note of pride.

"Miklos, why don't you let me take a turn with the mallet?" asked Alistair, holding out his hand with some insistence.

Miklos plopped down on the ground and dumped the tool in Alistair's hands. Alistair clambered to the top of the pile of posts and began a far more rapid assault on the wood.

"These are things we need to worry about," continued Miklos, his voice louder now to compete with the noise of Alistair's labors. "This is going to be our own nation."

By the time the Greek finished speaking, Alistair, with a rapid barrage, had driven the post far enough to bring it in line with the others. He leaned on it, his chest heaving only a little, and his eyes narrowed as he looked at something at the center of the fortification. Hopping down, he handed the mallet to Miklos.

"I'll be back in a minute," he promised and left his two large companions.

Emerging from the comparatively cool shadows, he passed two dozen women gathered together in a tight group. They spoke softly among themselves while they fabricated nets for fishing and patched clothing. He caught Giselle's eye, but she looked down at the twine she was forming before he could give her a nod of greeting. To his left, in the shade of trees where posts were being roped together, he spied Gregory attending to a handful of ill and wounded, though with scant supplies Alistair was not sure how much he could accomplish apart from a soothing hand on the forehead and an air of calm assurance.

Duke was in the center of the encampment, surrounded by his officers whose postures and poses indicated how important they felt they were. When Alistair approached, he was greeted with unwelcoming gazes tinged with an unease born of the fear a physically inferior creature feels when its station, itself built on force of strength, is implicitly challenged by a more intimidating specimen.

"What's the commotion?" asked Alistair.

"The wall is finished, then, is it?" Duke absently asked, twirling his ample mustache, his concentration on a scroll a young man was busy marking with a quill and ink. Glancing at it, Alistair saw they were forming a rough sketch of the island.

"What's the commotion about?" There followed a long pause in which Duke kept his gaze on the emerging map and the other officers shared looks. "I think I have talents which can be put to better use than building a crude defensive wall," Alistair continued when it became obvious no one wanted to answer him. "So put me to better use."

With an air of reluctance, Duke turned to face Alistair, forced to peer up at him but with a manner that refused to admit a difference in stature. "A scout party was attacked. No one was killed. We're preparing for a larger attack."

Alistair nodded. "I think it is past time I did some scouting."

"What do you have in mind?"

"I'll take a few men with me and find the enemy camp. I'll speak to the chief and see if we can't prevent an all out battle."

"You'll do no such thing. If you find the camp you come straight back to me. The battle started when they attacked us. You go waltzing into their camp with a peace offer and you'll find yourself the main course for a bunch of starving savages."

"I'm not asking your permission," Alistair replied, his voice even and his face carved from stone. "As a courtesy I am letting you know why I won't be in camp for the next few hours, maybe couple days."

"Alistair!" barked the commander, but the massive Aldran had already turned his back and was walking away.

ℚ∿

"What does a government do for society?"

After posing the question, Alistair looked into the eyes of the men around him. They were kneeling down in a small depression near the base of the hill, hidden from view by a few trees and a boulder at the rim. The sun had passed its zenith and a wind rustled the long grass, making swirls here and there. The men considered the question but did not immediately answer, all but Santiago exchanging curious looks with each other. The Argentinean looked at Alistair almost with suspicion.

"It protects people," Taribo finally answered.

"From whom?"

"Criminals," said Miklos.

"Other governments," said Wellesley.

"And who protects us from the government?"

"The Greeks gave us the answer to this," said Miklos. "The men and women in government must be chosen for their wisdom—"

"But what if fools get into government? What if wise men get corrupted by the power?"

Ryan, Miklos and Taribo stumbled for an answer, sputtering and half starting a couple but giving up before a handful of words left their mouths. They seemed bewildered that Alistair should begin a civics lesson at such a time. It was Santiago's calm and confident voice that finally gave a full response.

"Men have struggled with these questions for millennia, Alistair; you can't expect us to give you a short, tidy answer here and now. The question is academic anyway, because what is going to happen is going to happen. People can't conceive an answer so they go on living with whatever government has arisen, however it arose. What is *your* answer?"

"I am going to offer security and arbitration services. I would like you four to join me. We'll protect people's property if they hire us. We'll arbitrate disputes for people. We'll punish criminals and force them to pay restitution. This is what a government does when it does anything useful, but we won't force people to join. And we'll allow them to hire someone else if they prefer." Alistair grew more impassioned as he made the speech. "If two parties with different security services have a dispute, we'll have a contract with them stipulating a third party to mediate. We'll establish common sense laws everyone instinctively feels are right. Differences can be worked out over time. The security firms offering the kind of law enforcement people most agree with will be the most popular, and other firms will have to adopt their law or go out of business."

Wellesley, Taribo and Miklos looked uncertainly at one another. Santiago's face was more impassive, a slight parting of the lips the only concession to the astonishment he felt.

"If a man cannot steal, murder or rape, then no man can," Alistair continued. "All men should be bound by the same law. No one may steal from another, but what is a tax if not taking one man's money whether he consents or not. That's theft or the word has no meaning. No one may murder another, so no one may declare war either. No one may own another, so why do we tolerate conscription? We'll be doing the same things a government does when it does anything useful, but we won't claim a monopoly. We'll work within the market.

"This is the time to do it, before government gets entrenched. I'm going to offer my services to the inhabitants of this island. However many there are, they will be eager for some help against the thousands who have invaded. If we get these inhabitants we'll have some numbers with us. We can take the message to everyone else then. We'll tell them they don't have to bow to a chief. They may feel some loyalty to Odin, or gratefulness perhaps, but these are people who are tired of being slaves. There are many square miles of open land here. We'll tell them to homestead it and be free. We have a real chance here, a chance for a just society with no one dominating another. A real chance for people to be free."

Alistair stopped speaking and observed the effect of his words. It was apparent he had done much to unsettle but little to convince.

"I don't think Duke and Odin will take to this," Taribo finally said.

"What's the point, Alistair?" Santiago demanded, angry.

"What do you mean, 'what's the point'?"

Santiago shook his head and looked away. When he looked back and spoke, there was a passion underneath the words that cracked the stoicism he tried to maintain.

"I wish I could send a message to myself when I was your age. You struggle for a cause, you struggle for other people's benefit and after years of effort you find out they don't care, they never did. There's no point!" The last sentence was sharp, like a dog's bark. "You've got eighty or ninety years to live and then it's over. On this moon you've got less than that. Don't waste years in a futile struggle. Make yourself as happy as you can and let everyone else go hang themselves!" Santiago rubbed his face with both palms and settled himself down a bit. "This is wisdom a young man can't appreciate. Every new generation wastes its youth on idealism and when it grows wiser it's powerless to help the next one."

Alistair let a few seconds pass before speaking.

"If I can convince these inhabitants, will you give me a chance? Will you stand with me?"

Taribo was the first to reply. "Let's see how it goes."

Ryan was embarrassed to have let another beat him to it. "You're fucking crazy but I'm with you."

Miklos shrugged. "Why not. See how it goes. If you can get these others to join."

Alistair turned to Santiago, awaiting a reply. The Argentinean let out a sigh from deep within, and when he spoke all fervor was gone.

"Alright, *Señor Quijote*," he whispered. "Let's attack the windmills."

ൟ ൟ

The day lost the intense brightness of the midday hours. The amorphous clouds in the west were showing a pinkish tint and other colors coalesced near the horizon. Waves lapped at the shore with increased intensity as the wind blew stronger. Around Duke's camp, the workers' zeal abated. After noon they waited out the worst of the heat while taking a meager meal, and for the next couple hours engaged only in light labor until conditions permitted more strenuous activity. The wall was in place as sunset approached, and after a few last hours of hard work the immigrants were easing into the last portion of the day.

There arose a great wail all of the sudden, interrupting the comfortable rhythm of their efforts. It was a long, loud cry with sobs modulating the voice, giving it a vibrato quality. It startled them and when the wail continued hundreds of heads swiveled about, looking for the source of the disturbance.

In the center of camp, a man fell prostrate upon the ground and a circle of spectators, wary but fascinated, formed around him, leaving him with several feet of space on all sides. Duke confronted the occurrence with a frown, and he tucked his chin into his chest with a growl and made for the gathering crowd, pushing his way to the front.

At the moment when Duke reached the interior and spotted the wailer, the man was coming out of his prostrate position, his exposed skin covered in dry sand sticking to the sweat. His hands trembled as he regained his feet, and he grabbed at his head as if trying to wrest it from its neck. The wail diminished to a pitiable moan, and for the first time he became aware of those around him. He reached out with his hands, his eyes wide as if in terror, his mouth open and panting.

"What the Devil's the matter with him?" Duke demanded to know, but none could answer. "Someone fetch the doctor!"

"I saw..." the man ventured to say, his voice feeble and cracked. "...it, it touched me." He grabbed at his own chest, but there was no longer desperation in his movements; he seemed almost relieved. "An R. An R for...Rick? Ron? Raymond?" The man turned to a section of the crowd, to men and women who stared at him in uncomprehending awe, his arms outstretched as if trying to catch them. "Is there a...a Richard? Or maybe Ronald?"

"Reginald?" ventured a timid voice.

The man seized on the answer. "Reginald!" he cried, and he nearly leapt on the man, grabbing him by the shoulders in a fit of passion. "She spoke to me of you, Reginald!"

The man seemed perfectly horrified about what she might have said.

The wailing man clutched at Reginald's chest, where his heart was. "There is so much pain in this heart." Reginald scowled and drew back, but the man stayed with him and his tone was sympathetic and soothing. "So much pain, so undeserving of so much pain. It's a dark secret that brings you to Srillium." The man nodded knowingly, and Reginald blushed a dark red. "But it wasn't your fault, Reginald. I see violence..." the man covered his eyes with one hand while the other reached out, fingers extended to the heavens. "But you were a victim too. It was a violent act."

Reginald was stupefied. "I killed a man." His voice quavered uncertainly. "In a bar fight."

"But you didn't want to kill that man."

Reginald shook his head, his unblinking eyes held captive by the man's intent gaze.

"Reginald wouldn't do that. Not on purpose. It was the pain that moved him."

Reginald did not respond but continued to stare awestruck.

"Reginald deserves to be at peace. His pain drove him, and his pain has been a terrible price to pay. He deserves to be at peace now." There was the faintest hint of mist in Reginald's eyes, and the seer cupped the man's face in his hands. Reginald normally would not let a man touch him in that manner, but his defenses were shattered. "Gaia wishes you to be free, Reginald. I see...I see an instrument. Music. A Piano? Did you play an instrument?"

Reginald shook his head in the negative.

"I'm seeing some sort of instrument...there's music involved. Someone playing something...someone close to you."

"My sister played the violin," he hesitantly suggested.

"That's what Gaia is telling me," cried the seer, exultant. Many of the onlookers murmured. "She made music." He said the words as if they were the most profound and wonderful thing ever revealed to a man. "She made music, Reginald. Perhaps you will make music for Gaia too."

"My sister died..."

"And now it is your turn to play while she is gone. Will give this gift to Gaia?"

Reginald dumbly nodded, a slow nod, his lips parted in religious awe. The seer pulled away and peered into the crowd.

"There is a thief who needs absolution. He took from men what was not his, but he is ready to be forgiven now. There's a...an F. Frank? Fred?"

"His father's name was Fred," said a man, pointing to another.

Fred's son gave his companion a scathing glance, but the seer bounded over to him and held his hands, effecting a look of masculine discomfort on the other's face.

"You have stolen," the seer declared.

"I ain't stolen from anyone," grumbled the man, and he yanked his hands from the seer's grasp.

"You stole from your father."

"My father died a long time ago." The man was growing angry. "I'm here for specnine possession."

"You stole the legacy your father wanted you to leave," the seer corrected him. "You think he is no more because he died? His spirit is a part of everything now. Let yourself be absolved—"

"Bullshit," the man muttered and, turning away, disappeared into the crowd.

"We can all be absolved," the seer announced. "But we must be ready."

"I need absolution," a man timidly said, coming up to the seer and kneeling in front of him.

The seer knelt down as well. "We will be on the same level," he said. "As children of Gaia we will be on the same level."

The crowd drew closer as the seer described to the other what he saw in him. Duke allowed himself to fall back as others pressed in, coming finally to the outer fringe of the throng. His face was impassive and his arms were folded across his chest.

"Another religious man," he pronounced to a companion at his side. He said it with no hint of disapproval, like he would declare that leaves are green.

"Looks like it, sir."

"Do you know him?"

"Not well. He's a new arrival. Clyde I think is his name. Australian."

"Well…listen: don't let this get out of hand. There's a large dose of work left to do. Inform the sentries there's nothing to bother about. Keep watch." So saying Duke retraced his steps back to his command center.

In the middle of the crowd Clyde approached the Druid who regarded him with a look as rough and hard as stone, but Clyde prostrated himself at his feet, in supplication, reaching out to touch his bare toes while he breathed into the sand.

"Gaia's blessing," Clyde begged.

There was only a moment's pause before a dark hand grasped his head. A soft incantation followed, and the Druid bestowed Gaia's blessing on Clyde.

❧ ❦

A sentry guarding a sleeping hamlet spotted a lone figure and called out. The cry did nothing to deter the stranger, nor did the rapid gathering of the other sentries, nor the armed men who came pouring out of the lodges with hefted spears and axes. From the large building at the center emerged a man whose raiment, crude though it was, still was intricate enough to suggest authority. His long dark beard, speckled by gray and separated into two braids, bounced as he hustled to the crowd, slapping men on the backs of their heads and sending them off to fortify other areas lest the man prove to be the first of an assault.

By now the newcomer, a massive man with several days' growth of beard and hair lingering between short and medium, had advanced to within twenty yards. The leader threw out a forewarning hand and commanded him to stop.

"What business do you have here, outlander?" demanded the chief in Mandarin, his strong voice easily heard over the wind. His face was flat and his features, ringed by soft wrinkles, spoke of Mongol heritage.

"My name is Alistair," replied the young man in decent, accented Mandarin, *"and unless I am mistaken, my business is with you."* He stammered a couple times but his speech was understandable.

"You have no business with me, Alistair," insisted the chief, mauling the pronunciation of the name. *"How many are you?"*

"I and four others. We come in peace. We come to talk. I come to make an offer."

"Four others?!" exclaimed the chief, disbelieving. *"You are either lying or a fool."*

"Why don't you let me—"

"Speak Mandarin!"

Alistair nodded, holding up his hands to indicate he meant no offense. *"It doesn't cost you anything but a few moments' time for listening to what I say."* He stumbled through the difficult sentence but managed to get it out. *"If you refuse my offer, I will leave immediately and in peace."*

The chief conferred with some of his men and finally, nodding, he turned around and strode, with steps as large as he could manage, back to the main building from which he had come. One of the men he left behind waved Alistair on. The mob parted to let him through, though more than a few spears were pointed at him. He felt their gazes like he might have felt iron wool on his sunburnt skin, and with every step he thought he might stub his toe and stagger, making himself look ridiculous. His legs obeyed his command like the legs of a marionette obey the string: he felt graceless.

The building, its raw timbers yet to be smoothed over and the gaps between them filled in with mud and straw, lacked a proper door. An animal skin hung like a curtain and he drew it aside and cautiously passed through, his axe still strapped to his back but his hands twitching to grasp it. He stepped into an audience chamber and dining hall. There were two long tables of hewn trees nailed together, and at the other end of the hall, there was a raised dais and a crude throne, its parts also hacked from a tree. Six bodyguards surrounded their chief, standing on the dirt floor at the edge of the dais while the chief himself, going to some lengths to appear at ease, even bored, lounged on his throne, one leg thrown over an arm. The shy Aldran viewed the smaller audience as a welcome relief.

"Say your peace and be gone," was the chief's order.

"I think it is in all of our interests to reach a peaceful agreement. I am going to make an offer to you and the members of your tribe."

"You will make the offer to me. I am the chief of the tribe."

"That would...defeat the purpose of the proposal. I propose to offer my services as..." Alistair struggled with the vocabulary, *"arbitrator and law enforcer. For a fee I will be...available to settle disputes. I will record property and enforce contract...obligations of contract. If necessary I will investigate crimes and see that victims are compensated by criminals. I will enforce retribution for crimes, or for criminal...how is the word?...negligence."*

"We decline your offer."

"Furthermore," Alistair continued unperturbed, *"I and my associates will defend the property of any...subscriber?..."* he hesitated, his tongue tripping up with the language. *"We will defend any member of our services and his property, even with weapons against the people who have come here."*

"You are one of the people who have come here," the chief declared, his condescending attitude having changed to disbelief.

"I hitched a ride on a boat," said Alistair in his native tongue. "I'm not one of them."

One of the guards surrounding the dais cocked his head in the direction of his chief and mumbled a translation.

"You will fight with us?" the chief asked, his tone softer than before but still disbelieving. *"You will join my tribe and fight?"*

Shaking his head, and looking the chief in the eye, Alistair said, *"I am not joining a tribe. I am remaining a free man with no tribe. I am running a business. You are from Earth?"*

The chief nodded. *"Laos."*

"When you wished to buy a meal on Earth, you went to someone who made one and you gave him money for it. He did not have to join your nation or your tribe or anything at all, you just made an exchange. He gave you food; you gave him money. I am offering something similar. I offer protection and arbitration services. I am not joining the tribe, I am offering services."

There passed a good ten seconds before the confused look on the chief's face retreated before a belated understanding.

"A mercenary?"

"I will fight for you if you purchase protection from me, but I am more than a mercenary."

"What are your terms?"

"My terms are less important than my code."

"What is your code, then?"

"Every man has a right to his own body and his own free will. Anything he makes with his body also belongs to him. A man may give away his property by passing the title to another. All who respect the property rights of others deserve to have their own property rights respected. By aggressing against another, a man is saying that such aggression is permissible against him. That is to say, he has given up this right. He is therefore liable to punishment in the form of whatever injustice he committed. Furthermore, he will be monetarily responsible for the pain and suffering and inconvenience he has caused the other."

"And prison?"

"Unless a criminal proves to be a...unless we think he will not correct his ways, there is no reason to imprison him once retribution is delivered and restitution paid. If a man steals a loaf of bread from you, the first thing is that your loaf must be returned to you. If it has been eaten, a replacement must be purchased with the money of the thief. He will also pay a...an amount to compensate you for the time in which you did not have your loaf. The loaf now returned, restitution has been made. However, you will have the option of demanding retribution as well. Because he did not agree to respect your property, you may now treat his property without respect...but to the same degree, no further. The thief must now provide an additional loaf of bread to you, his victim. The criminal will also be made to pay me and my associates for our labor in settling the issue."

"Crime is expensive with you around," the chief chuckled. *"What if this thief attacks me?"*

"He will pay restitution for the damage he has done to you. He will pay me for my services to you. And then, if you choose, you may demand retribution and you may beat him to the same extent he beat you. Or you both may come to an agreement for more monetary damages in exchange for skipping the beating. Or you may hire me to administer the beating on your behalf."

The chief nodded, thoughtful, rubbing his hirsute chin. *"And if he murders me?"*

"If he murders you, he will spend the rest of his days paying restitution to your heirs, whoever you choose to name as your heirs."

"Not executed?"

"No…not executed. There is too much killing already. He will be made to pay for his crimes. Maybe beaten, but there will be no executions."

The chief frowned but it quickly passed from his face. *"That is an interesting code. I will consider it. But mostly I would like to hire you to fight for me."*

"I need to be clearer," said Alistair. *"I am offering these services to anyone who wishes to pay for them. If someone does not want my services, they need not pay for them. But if someone decides they want my services they shall have my protection."* The chief squirmed in his chair but before he could voice his protest Alistair hurried on, *"And if you hire me you shall have the greatest warrior of Srillium to protect you, along with the other great warriors who work for me."*

"Greatest warrior of Srillium?" asked the chief, his eyebrow raised in skepticism.

In response, Alistair pulled aside his animal skin shirt and revealed his tattoo.

.

59

"**M**y main concern is this: there are thousands of people here. How are you going to protect me from all of them if I desert?" It was an older man who asked the question, old at least by the standards of Srillium. He leaned against a tree on the edge of the beach, his arms folded across his chest in an uninviting pose touched by a skeptical frown.

"I don't have to protect you against all of them," Alistair replied. "I don't imagine I'll have to protect you against very many at all. You go off and determine your own future. Do what you wish. If you have property you want protected—your body, your land, your home… whatever—then you register it with me. You may also remain in Odin's tribe and pay Odin's taxes and obey Odin's rules…the choice is yours. Let me ask you this: how do you think a leader is going to be determined?"

"That's yet to be settled. I think we should vote on it."

"And that's exactly what I am offering you. A vote. Only, no one else determines the outcome of your vote. If you wish to hire me, you can hire me. Or you can hire someone else. Or you can accede to Odin's demands. Or you can hire no one and accede to no one. By what right would Odin force you to remain in his tribe?"

"I took a loyalty oath."

"We all took a loyalty oath!" exclaimed another man, one of several who trickled into the discussion. In his incomprehension, he was easily nudged into anger.

"The oath is not valid," declared Santiago, his arms also folded, as he stood at Alistair's side. His voice was stronger than Alistair's. "When you arrived here you were given the choice of a tribe or a grave. Odin has grown wealthy and powerful off an unjust system. You owe him nothing. If you decide to be your own master…then you have the right to be your own master."

"Odin deserves our loyalty for what he done," said another.

"What Odin did, for many years, was exactly what every other murdering tribal chief did. He took warriors, he took slaves, and he killed new arrivals. Killed them, skinned them, and ate them."

"We've all done that!"

Said another, "We done we had to do. Planet won't hold as many as they send. Circumstances are what they are."

"If circumstances can excuse Odin for what he's done," said Santiago with a voice that cut through the angry shouts, "those same circumstances can excuse you from a loyalty oath you took for your own safety, a safety that was compromised, in part, by Odin himself.

"This is what is going to happen next. Odin will either declare himself king or be elected dictator…the details don't matter. He will then begin to rule you. He'll claim the island and dole out parts of it as favors. The people who get the land will be loyal to him, and they will dole out the small favors they can afford to others who will be loyal to them. The rest will be kept in subservience. Then he will tax you. Any man who replaces Odin will tax you. Any dispute you have with Odin, Odin will arbitrate. Who do you think is going to come out on top?"

"How are you guys any different?"

Santiago did not reply, but cast a sidelong glance at Alistair.

"I require no loyalty oath," Alistair began and the men, growing in number, leaned in to hear him. "You can hire me or not. Any dispute you have with me will be solved by a neutral third party we agree on. If you don't hire me, you don't pay me. It's not a tax, it's a membership fee. If you don't like how I do things, you are free to offer the same services and charge for them. And I don't claim to own this island. There is a lot of free, open land out there. You can wait for Odin or Duke to give it to you, if you're that lucky, or you can take land for yourselves, in freedom. A monopoly is when one man, or one company, or one organization is the sole provider of something. He faces no competition nor any prospect of competition. Those who study the Economic Sciences will tell you a monopoly is characterized by decreased output, so the price can be raised, and deteriorating quality of service. Does that not describe every government you ever heard of? Short supply of what matters and poor quality. It describes government because government is a monopoly. I propose to provide you with police and judicial services, but not as a monopoly. My services will be better because they have to be, because if they aren't satisfactory, no one will pay me. I propose we have laws and law enforcement, but that no one be a monopolist. Everything will be based on one simple, unavoidable fact: you are the sole owner of your own person, in perfect equality with every other man and woman in the colonized galaxy."

When he was done speaking, there was a period when the men and handful of women quietly considered his words. A moment later, some of them were slinking away from the gathering, casting furtive and guilty glances. Others remained, but an uneasy whispering arose among them and the space between Alistair and Santiago and their audience widened. Turning, Alistair saw Duke, surrounded by a number of his lieutenants, approaching them with determined steps and a grim expression. Santiago and Alistair faced the imminent assault, standing shoulder to shoulder, their weapons in easy reach.

"Last chance to bow out," muttered Alistair.

Santiago glanced at his friend and one corner of his mouth turned up in a faint smile. "I was exiled to this moon for something much like this," he said, his accent only barely perceptible when he spoke low. "What do you call a man who permits hope to continue to blind him from experience?"

"A sucker."

"I will be a sucker one last time."

Alistair could see Gregory on the outskirts of the crowd, and Giselle and Layla were with him. The young physician regarded him with a disbelieving and worried expression. Giselle and Layla, less concerned for his well being, presented merely skeptical looks. He turned his attention back to Duke as the diminutive commander reached the gathered throng.

"Alistair, you had better have a hell of a good explanation for this."

Though his throat felt parched and his pulse throbbed in his ears, Alistair managed, in a steady voice, to say, "I am selling my services. You are welcome to subscribe if you like."

Duke's mustache jittered as the muscles underneath it trembled in suppressed rage. "I have it from some of my men here that you are planning a mutiny."

"You have it wrong."

"I'm glad to hear it."

"I am offering protection and arbitration services for a fee."

Duke glowered. "What does the word mutiny mean to you?"

"Deposing the captain of a ship. In a metaphorical way it could be used for any sort of rebellion against authority."

"And how exactly is what you're doing not mutiny?"

"I'm selling my services like any businessman."

Duke held out a beckoning hand to Alistair. "Could I have a word with you in private?"

"We prefer the discussion be public," said Santiago.

"Damn it, Alistair! If you want to be a policeman you could have any post you want. With your training? You could have anything just by asking. What the hell is this for?"

"I'm going into business for myself. I don't want to beg for anything. No one has to do business with me if they don't like, and I don't have to do business with anyone if I don't like. I have no intention of doing anyone any harm. I am merely going to arbitrate disputes and provide protection."

"It's purely voluntary," Santiago assured him, raising his voice so it carried over the mob. "Law and its enforcement are too important to leave in any one man's hands. There should be competition—"

"Will you drop this harebrained scheme this instant before I'm forced to do something about it?" Duke was furious enough that he spat as he spoke.

"We have already spoken with the other occupants of the island," Santiago continued. "They were claiming the entirety of it; we dissuaded them from the claim. They have hired us and recognize there are many square miles of unclaimed land here. Our firm will recognize—"

"Your firm?"

"—any homesteaders who want to take land for their own." Santiago turned in a circle now to address every onlooker. "You don't have to wait for scraps from the master's table. You don't have to be a pawn for a tribal leader. You can be free men, free like you've never been before. No taxes, no government, no tyranny. Every thing you do, every relationship you have will be consensual. No one will be forced to do anything, nor prohibited from living how he wants. Answer me honestly: what man or woman would not want to live in such a society?"

"This is enough," said Duke, a finger pointed at the Argentinean. "Another word and you will both be hung for sedition."

"You'd have to take us first," said Alistair, and he hefted his ax with a terrible confidence. "You'll lose the first forty you send my way."

"This is exactly why we need what Alistair offers," proclaimed Santiago. "Look how he reacts to any challenge to his power. Alistair offers you a choice; Duke demands fealty. If you stand with us now you will be free. No laws but the simple few you feel already in your gut. No laws but the ones they taught you as a child: mind your own business and keep your hands to yourself."

At that decisive moment, another broad and muscled form stepped into the open space at the center of the maelstrom. Mordecai, armed and imposing, raised his voice to be heard. There were a number of men with him, men who took to him in the short time he had been there, men who were naturally drawn to the service of bigger, stronger men. "The last thing we need is to live under a tyrant! We have all suffered here on Srillium." He switched to his native Mandarin then. *"I say we live free. No one is bound to serve this man!"* He pointed an accusing finger at Duke.

"There is no need for any violence," said Alistair quickly, for the insistent call of Mordecai rippled through the crowd and provoked a great stir.

"Enough!" yelled Duke as men and women alike took up the argument in a chaotic cacophony, and he, supported by his loyal guards, advanced on Alistair, calling for the rest to join him.

There followed in the breast of every exile a conflict fully as violent and uncertain as what was about to transpire on the beach. Most had been with Odin a short time, and though their esteem of him was high, their first knowledge of him had been as a brutal tribal chief. The serfs who flocked to his banner when he offered them a scrap of dignity felt a passion in defense of the man who delivered them from their servitude, from their slavery. But the same passion was aroused at the thought of owning their own land, forging their own life. Odin was a leader, perhaps, but a leader without the trappings of authority that so impress men. For those who had grown up with and been dazzled by Parliaments, parades, statues, uniforms and every inventible accoutrement of power, Odin could manage only a spear and a headdress. Thus, when Duke called for Alistair's head, and Alistair and Santiago called for freedom, the result was indecision. Most waited to discover which way the wind blew.

They did not have long to find out. Mordecai and his collected band of thugs crashed into the side of Duke's charge and engaged in a furious melee. A few from the crowd joined the fray, but it was not clear whether more joined to protect Duke or to assist Mordecai. One brave man rushed Alistair with a spear, but the Aldran marine soon had the spear out of his hands and, with a moderate blow to the head, sent him sprawling on his back, blinking at the sky. For a few minutes there were grunts of men expending a great physical effort and a yelp or two of agony. Blood spurted into the air on two occasions, speckling those nearby when it came down. Then the battle was over, Duke having retreated to his command center. Three bodies lay unmoving on the sand, dark stains expanding about them. Several others were hobbling or crawling away and Gregory was already taking charge of them.

When Alistair moved to help with the wounded the doctor fixed a disapproving gaze on him. "You saw your chance I guess," he accused. "You finally got a government small enough to take down."

"Where are we taking them?" Alistair tonelessly asked as he hefted the ankles of a man moaning deliriously.

"Where all the others are," muttered Greg, and he lifted at the shoulders.

In the temporary fort, only recently erected, many men milled about. Others gave voice to their passions with whoops and yells and proclamations both cheered and derided. Men came up to Alistair, asking for an audience. One even launched an ill-conceived attack which the Aldran rebuffed in a perfunctory way. When the first was put down with a kick to the chest, two others set upon the assailant and beat him. A restraining hand from Santiago held Alistair back from intervening.

"He tried to kill you," said the Argentinean. "Don't curtail the passions of your supporters when you have only just won them." Alistair hesitated, watching the beating with uncertainty before turning away.

A few intrepid souls needed no more encouragement, and they quickly gathered a few things and trickled out of the fort under cover of confusion. Others would have preferred some time to think it over, but realized a window of opportunity might soon close. They followed closely behind the first group. Yet another group wanting only the safety of numbers took their chance to leave. The fort's wall was disassembled, though not without a number of skirmishes which accounted for two more deaths. There was a great scramble for property, as men gathered to themselves everything they could find. Some set out with what burdens they could manage, many stopping to check with Alistair before they left. He assured them he would be around to register them.

As the encampment disintegrated, as men fought with each other over freedom, loyalty and property, Gregory came to stand next to Alistair while the ex marine observed it all.

"Your great anarchic society," he declared with a hand extended over the chaos. "If only I had thought to warn you a million times all these years."

"Is that what's to blame for this?" Alistair shot back. "Or is it the fault of people like Duke who won't allow men the freedom they were born to? I don't need to argue this with you anymore, Greg. You're about to see what I've been talking about all these years."

60

In the center of the island, near where the hills rose to their highest point, there was a depression in the earth. About one square mile in area and in the shape of an irregular crescent, it was ringed by the peaks and ridges of the rugged terrain, and numerous trees stood as sentries round the body of water in the bowl. In the mornings the lake, ensconced in the earth and shielded from the low light on the horizon, produced a wispy fog that hovered over the waters, sheltered from the night breezes off the ocean, occasionally reaching out a tenuous appendage to caress the trees on the shore. When the sun rose high enough, it eradicated the vapors and warmed the hill tops and the cool air retreated to the shadows in the caves and under the trees.

It was there, at the summit of the highest hill, at the inside nook of the crescent lake, that Alistair chose to build his command center. There the hill rose up fifty meters above the surface of the lake, ending abruptly in a cliff face plunging right to the water below. Elsewhere the ridges around the lake were elevated only a few meters and gently sloped down to the shore, but the location of the command center, nothing more impressive than a crude circular hut, sat as if atop a tower. From there he could see the entirety of the island and out to sea. To the north, past the hills rolling down to the sea and past the sea itself, there was a smudge of something on the horizon, something he knew was the main continent. Behind the shore were the mountains, their snow-topped peaks shining white by day and glowing a faint red by night.

Also to the north was the main encampment of those still loyal to Odin. In the days following Alistair's declaration, there was an exodus from the camps which had coalesced out of the surviving ships and their crews. In all, nearly six thousand men and women reached the island, settling into a dozen camps of several hundred each. After news of the rebellion spread, hundreds and hundreds of individuals set out, often congregating in small communities, occasionally going it alone. However, many stayed with Odin, camped on the northwest edge of the island. At night the many campfires and torches burning in the darkness around the encampment gave the impression of a small city. By day their distant, tiny forms moved like ants about the wide beach and forest where a large wall was still being erected. As of yet no company had issued forth for any purpose, but Alistair still eyed it warily, observing it for signs of imminent aggression.

The hut he and his employees now called home was erected in a short span of time. With no currency circulating yet, he decided to charge labor hours or food. Many hundreds of the population of free men subscribed to his services, making it difficult to record and keep track of them. A pile of rough wood slats with carved notches, organized haphazardly outside the hut, served for their bookkeeping.

The structure of the hut was, at its base, approximately thirty feet in diameter. Access to it was gained by one of three series of stairs comprised of four steps each. The base being raised above the ground, it was ideal for storage and their stock of weapons and food was kept inside. Benches and railing ran around the perimeter of the first story. There were no walls and the ceiling was eight feet above the floor, furnished with a table, some chairs and a desk. All business was conducted there. In the center of the room a spiral staircase wound up and around a central pillar, the supporting backbone of the edifice. This staircase led to the second floor, a less spacious place where Alistair and his warriors slept. It was furnished only with cots, and the central pillar and its stairs continued to the small third story, nothing more than a lookout booth seven feet in diameter. The entire structure was assembled with the rough-hewn logs and branches of the local forests, with the knobs and knots in the wood still to be smoothed out when the proper tools could be produced.

For the most part, when the sun was up, the hut was empty. Gregory moved in with Alistair but spent most of his waking hours traveling from newborn hamlet to newborn hamlet, attending to the medical needs of the community. He never charged for his work, but accepted what was volunteered. Most of the men he treated paid something, even if it was only a token slice of hard bread. Layla went with him, acting as an aide and slowly learning the healing arts. Santiago, Ryan Wellesley and Taribo were too busy recording claims and recruiting new members to have time to relax at the hut, and Alistair himself was busiest of all. There were no serious conflicts for him to arbitrate, but he was constantly consulted and felt nearly overwhelmed with responsibility.

Only Miklos occupied the hut, on the second floor where he lay in a cot with his head wrapped, moaning more loudly when he knew there was someone there to hear. When Alistair and Santiago announced their plans at Duke's camp, Taribo and Miklos went to another nearby to spread the news. A similar fracas ensued and Miklos received a fierce knock to the cranium.

For no reason other than that Alistair and his company took up residence there, several other abodes were erected, or were in the process of erection, nearby. One of them, a large and long structure still to be completed, housed a good number of women who, as a small minority, naturally were drawn to each other. Some of the men, the roughened and crude products of the gutters and penal systems of the scattered human colonies, took to calling it the Whore House, which never failed to elicit scathing looks from the displeased females. Layla and Giselle resided there now, and Gregory was assisting a few other men in its construction when Alistair returned from an assignment.

The sun was low in the western sky and its intensity dulled, though the heat of the day, unopposed by any ocean breeze, still lingered in the air. Profusely sweating, Gregory, when he spotted Alistair, dropped a recently made pole onto the earth at his feet and drew his forearm across his brow, leaving a dark smudge behind. He breathed heavily as he strolled Alistair's way, looking about himself at the progress of their newly born civilization with the air of satisfaction fatigue cannot subdue.

"I haven't seen you since breakfast," said Gregory.

"I haven't eaten since then, either."

"Some of the men took some bread and meat from storage. There's some left if you want."

Alistair abruptly stopped and drew himself up to his full height. "From storage?"

Gregory hastily added, "I told them it was OK."

"I didn't know it was your food to give away."

"Alistair…" Gregory sighed. "Listen, I thought since you had a lot of food saved—"

"I had a lot of food saved for the coming weeks before any crops start to grow and we get sick of eating fish for every damn meal. Assuming we can catch any fish. You think this island came ready made to support several thousand people?" Alistair dumped his burden onto the ground where it landed with a punctuating thump.

Gregory gritted his teeth for a moment but finally relaxed. "You and I have a different idea of what community means."

"We have a different idea of what property means," snapped the ex marine and, grabbing the recently dumped burden, walked away. He spun back around. "It's not that I have a problem with helping hungry people. Can you understand that?"

"Yes, I do."

"I just don't want people taking liberties with what is mine. If it's my food, I should be the one to give it away. If I choose."

"I understand."

"That food was being saved for leaner times, which are coming quite soon. They get used to a free meal any time their stomachs growl and not only will they eat meals today meant for tomorrow, they won't feel the urgency to till the soil or weave the fishing nets they ought to be."

"I get it, Alistair."

"How much goddamn time needs to be spent on the women's lodging, by the way? Is this going to be a luxury hotel?"

"The hotel—" Gregory shook his head. "The…the women's lodge is almost done."

"What are the women doing right now?"

Gregory, having come to the end of his patience, raised his voice and said, "They're making the fishing nets you were just bitching about! Damn it, Alistair, eat a meal and come talk to me when you're less grouchy."

Alistair and Gregory faced each other in silence for a moment, unheeding of the looks they were getting from the other men still working on the women's lodge. Finally, Alistair spoke, his voice lower and his tone friendlier.

"They say you want to build a chapel."

Gregory only nodded.

"When are you going to start?"

"I don't know. Soon I hope."

"You have to eat."

"Obviously."

"You have to drink. To sleep. To clothe yourself. You have all sorts of needs, some of which might come before the chapel. I can't decide for you what you need to do, and you can't decide for me what I need to do."

With a long-suffering tone, Gregory asked, "What's the moral of the story?"

"The moral, Greg, is that I worked for that food and I continue to work for it. It was given to me by people who wanted what I am offering. Now, not only do I have to worry about meals again that much sooner, but a whole lot of time was spent making lodgings far in excess of what anyone else has. The climate is warm and the roof is already built; the girls would be just fine with what was built several days ago. The labor done here today was sustained by my food. Without this food, the men might have decided there were other priorities far more urgent than making the women's bedrooms more comfortable. If the women wanted to work and save up food to pay for this construction, that's their business. But no such saving was done. My savings were used instead, and now my plans have to change. Your chapel sounds like a nice idea, but you have to prioritize. Food and drink. Then shelter. Then clothing. Then...well, you decide." Here Alistair lifted a hand to point at the lodge. "It is impossible to know whether this labor today was well spent because no one was forced to prioritize. With their own savings the women might have chosen something else to pay for instead."

"I won't do it again."

"I know you won't do it again, Gregory. I'm telling you this so you can understand me. My perspective."

"Maybe you might try to understand me some time. I don't want to live like you. You know, for me a community is people sharing. People helping one another without charging for it."

"You can live however you like. But today you forced me to participate in your sharing when I didn't want to. And now my stores are depleted."

Gregory slouched in wordless recognition of Alistair's point. "If it makes you feel any better, I don't think the food had much influence. Those guys are trying to be gallant to impress the women. They'd've done it on empty stomachs."

A chuckle broke free of Alistair's lips despite himself. "That may be true," he conceded.

Before he could turn to go, Gregory said, "Layla wanted to talk to you about something important."

"She knows where to find me."

When he arrived at the hut, Alistair discovered Ryan Wellesley already there. His fellow Aldran was standing at the foot of the stairs and calling up to the second story.

"The meal's ready and it's only going to get colder!"

Alistair trudged up the steps to the first floor and dumped himself wearily into a wooden chair, wincing as a knob on the seat poked the back of his thigh.

"Bring it up to me," called a muffled voice, pathetic in its weakness.

Ryan shared a look with Alistair and shook his head. In his hand he held a rough tablet of wood with a couple strips of dried beef, recently heated, and a hunk of hard, unleavened bread. He dropped the makeshift plate on the table at the center of the room.

"It's down on the table when you're ready," Ryan called up. He was answered by a moan.

Leaning back in the chair, Alistair laid his head back and rested his eyes, feeling the evening breeze as it blew through the open first floor of the hut, stirring the hairs on his arms and causing the slightest of tickles.

"Is there anything left?" Alistair asked.

"I'll grab you something," Ryan promised and exited the hut.

Outside, the brook running from the lake down the side of the hill softly babbled, and waves lapped at the shore. The watery sounds caressed his ear and nearly had him asleep when the labored steps of Miklos as he came down the stairs interrupted. Ryan was just returning with another two tablets of bread and meat. The three converged on the table to eat, Ryan and Alistair side by side across from Miklos. The warrior with the Greek appellation, hunched over his meal, ate with the delicacy of a starving wolf, and the food loudly swished and swirled in his mouth while his jaws pumped away at it. Alistair took little note, but Ryan, in disgust, was finally moved to drop his hunk of bread on the table.

"Holy shit, could you shut up?"

Miklos managed no more response than a quick glance from under his brow, his face still bent down over his food. "This isn't black tie," he mumbled before he shoveled the last strip of beef into his mouth and devoured it with the same racket.

Ryan took another bite of bread and soldiered on for a moment or two before he rose from his seat and grabbed the last bits of food in his hand. "I'm not going to eat my meal next to this," he declared and stomped out of the hut.

"Should have brought my meal upstairs."

"I think tomorrow you'll be with Taribo," said Alistair. "He's going to scout the south side of the island. You'll be gone all day."

Miklos did not reply and a moment later the topic was forgotten as Ryan was replaced with Layla who came and sat next to Alistair. She was wearing the same outfit she wore every day since he first saw her, but now it was showing the smudges and fraying of hard labor, as was her tanned skin.

"Greg said I could talk to you about something."

"Walk with me to the well," said Alistair, wiping the crumbs from his hands and rising from his chair.

The well was a wooden tub salvaged from one of the ships. It held no more than twenty gallons of water when full, which it was not at the moment. Alistair stood over it and cursed.

"This is exactly the kind of shit I am talking about."

Layla shrank away from Alistair. "Greg said you were grumpy tonight."

Sighing, Alistair grabbed the two-gallon bucket next to the tub and began to descend the hill to refill it at the brook below.

"We've got too many people on top of the hill far away from the water and no one wants to take responsibility to refill the bucket," he said to her as she hustled to keep up with his long legs.

"They have as much right to live at the top of the hill as you do."

"That's not what I'm talking about. Everyone insists on having a goddamn community bucket, but because everybody shares the bucket, no one takes responsibility for it, and it needs to be refilled."

"I think they like being next to you. Some people feel safer being close to you and Taribo and the guys."

"Whoever took the bucket from the boat, or took it from the camp—or whatever—should have just kept it for themselves. Anyone who wanted to use it could pay for the water, and if it wasn't worth paying for, they could live closer to the lake shore. That would regulate how many people would crowd onto the hilltop. As it is now, with a free bucket, no one wants to invest in increasing our water supply at the top of the hill. And no one wants to refill the goddamn bucket either. But everybody and their goddamn brother wants to move to the top of the hill."

"You want to charge for a bucket of water? Are you going to charge us for breathing next?"

"Oh, Christ! Never mind. Did you want to talk to me about something?"

"Yes I did." Layla nodded once and swallowed, on the verge of embarking on business she considered important and doing her best to adopt a serious demeanor though she moved downhill at an uncomfortable pace. "The women have had a meeting and we decided we wanted to get a law passed. How exactly does that work in this system?"

"You have to get Parliament to pass it."

"We don't have a Parliament."

"What was that?"

"We don't have a Parliament."

Alistair stopped walking. "Come again?"

"We...don't...have...a...Parliament," she reiterated, bewildered.

"Layla, that's the sweetest music I ever heard." With that pronouncement, Alistair was again setting a fast pace down the hillside.

"So how does a law get passed?" she demanded, hustling to keep the big man within earshot.

"It doesn't."

"What do you mean, 'it doesn't'?" Her breathing was becoming labored. "You have to have a way to pass laws."

"Do you mean Laws with a capital L, or laws with a small l?"

"What the hell are you talking about?"

"Politicians pass laws, small l, and there will be none of those here. Laws, capital L, are discovered, not created, not passed. There is no way to pass a law without a parliament or a king or a dictator, which we won't have. I have offered to enforce Laws, capital L, the ones which have been discovered. These all boil down to not initiating aggression against anyone. Aggression can be murder, rape, theft...assault, fraud...fraud is a type of theft...that's about it. Sometimes the particulars can be tricky, but the basic Laws were passed by Nature, or Gaia, or God, or Allah—whichever one you choose to believe in. There is nothing else to pass."

The look on Layla's face indicated this was so new as to be indecipherable to her, at least when relayed as rapidly and in such a big dose as Alistair delivered it.

"How do you illegalize prostitution, then?"

"Rape is Illegal, with a capital I. Prostitution is not rape."

"But how—"

"You don't. If a man wants to pay a woman for sex, and a woman wants to screw a man for money, that's nobody else's goddamn business."

Layla gritted her teeth at Alistair's rough treatment of her idea, but she calmed herself with an effort and when she spoke, her tone was calm. "Alistair, this is something that maybe you don't empathize with, and that's understandable. You're not a woman, and you haven't been here very long. Women are slaves here. Look around you: there's hardly any of us, and when a woman is sent here she is taken possession of by some chief. Used as a concubine, or a whore. In Issicroy I was a concubine to Lord Issicroy because I was given no other option. It was Giselle who saved me from being a common prostitute, which she spent several years as herself. The other women have had similar experiences, or even worse. This is a new start for us. We don't want prostitution on the island." Her next sentence she pronounced with a solemnity she clearly expected to be convincing. "This is very important to us."

By this time they had descended to the shores of the lake and stood at the mouth of the brook. The sky was darkening and the wind picked up, hurling the waves towards shore with a good deal more force. Every so often a bit of spray from the broken waves was tossed in their faces. Alistair faced Layla Dubai, looked into her alluring face framed by strands of hair bouncing in the currents of air.

"Layla, I have had this same argument with a thousand people in my life. I have convinced maybe five of them, and never on the first go. I don't know why people can't see what I see so clearly. I'll explain it to you as lucidly as I did to them: no one here who purchases my service is going to be coerced into prostitution. If all of you are dead set against being prostitutes, then there is no need for a law to prevent it. But it may be that some women here might wish to choose that profession, or some who are against it now will change their minds later. Their becoming prostitutes does no harm to you, and if they purchase my services they will be protected in their professions as long as they don't cheat their clients."

"We don't want it anywhere on the island."

"But you don't own the island. You may forbid it on any parcel of land you own, no more."

The lower lip of the striking young woman quivered, but the tears welling in her eyes were angry ones, not sorrowful.

"Alistair, I am no longer interested in hiring you for your services," she informed him with a tone that dropped the temperature around them.

If her frigid voice provoked in Alistair any feeling to color his response, it was a slight weariness. "That's your choice. Tell me something, though: how are you going to enforce your law?"

Layla did nothing more than glare at him. Sighing, and having reached the mouth of the stream, Alistair crouched down and skimmed the bucket along the surface of the brook.

"Every law has to be enforced, or what's the point? Say we pass this law of yours and then a man and woman are caught in the act of prostitution. What should we do with them?" He took a long draught from the bucket. Some of the water sloshed out onto his chest. What went in his mouth was not clear, clean water; it had the taste of nature in it, but he was thirsty enough that he didn't care.

"They should get the same penalty," she said with heat. "I'm not trying to blame this all on men. They should both get the same—"

"I'm not saying you're trying to blame it on men," he replied with a serenity that was a foil to her anger. "I'm asking how you plan to enforce your law. What will be the penalty for committing prostitution?"

"That can be decided by a vote. That's not the point—"

"What would your suggestion be? You want to make prostitution illegal, so tell me how this is to be enforced?" He refilled the bucket while she answered.

"It doesn't matter. We can make a jail. We can fine them. We can…I don't know, give them hard labor."

"Let me see if I understand. When a man willingly gives over money for sex, and a woman willingly gives him sex for money—in other words neither party involved disagrees with what happened—you want to kidnap them, which is sometimes referred to as throwing them in jail, or steal their property and call it a fine, or enslave them by giving them hard labor?"

Layla struggled with a response and came up with nothing.

"Would you allow a man and a woman to have sex?"

"Don't be ridiculous!"

"So you would?"

"Of course!"

"But not if he pays for it? It has to be an act of generosity on her part or they both go to jail?"

Layla balled her hands into fists. "I don't know anything about your home world, but every community I have ever seen has set standards. It's called civilization."

"Pointing out that something occurs does not justify its occurrence. In every community I have ever seen there were murders, too. So you want to throw people in a jail if they have sex under terms you disagree with."

"No, not just because I disagree. Just prostitution."

"But you want to throw them in jail."

"I think I already answered that. You said yourself that laws have to be enforced."

"Fine. By what right do you do it?"

"I'm not going to do it."

"But someone has to, and you are going to support them when they do it. By what right does anyone throw someone in jail for what they do with their own body?"

"I said I didn't expect you to understand. You'll never know what it's like to be in that position. We want to prevent this from ever happening here. The idea is that no one has to go to jail because the law is obeyed. And if someone refuses to obey the law, then yes, they might have to go to jail. But that's better for them then prostitution."

"Obviously they don't think so or they wouldn't engage in it. What gives you the right to make that decision for them?"

"A community has a right to set its own standards. No one person's desires trump the entire community."

"So it's not you who has the right to throw the prostitute and her client in jail?"

"Right."

"No one person has this right?"

"The community does."

"But if no one has this right, then how could the community have it? Where would it come from?"

Layla furrowed her brow and shook her head as if helpless. "The same way anyone gets their rights. The community does too."

"A community is just a group of people. There is nothing about it that exists apart from the individuals. An individual has rights because he can conceive of them and respect them in other people. Perhaps you might argue there is no such thing as a Natural Right, but if you do harm to someone, then it follows quite logically that you cannot argue that they cannot do that same harm to you by simply using the code of ethics you chose when you harmed them. The result is most people agree to treat each other decently, and the ones who don't are punished. Even if you don't believe in rights, the final result is the same. This means if you choose to impose yourself on someone else, they can do it back to you. Rights or not, why would you want to behave like that?"

"I told you once," she said with the forcible tone of a final pronouncement. "You'll never understand how terrible prostitution is, and we don't want it here. If that means throwing a couple people in jail as an example, or taking their property as a fine, then so be it. If we take bad choices away, people will only have better choices available to them. We're going to vote it illegal, and you and I will do no further business."

After the argument, Layla turned with a whip of her hair and stormed back up the side of the hill, her movements sharp and angry. Alistair followed behind with casual, lengthy steps and soon caught up to her. The former Issicrojan, still fuming, declined to walk next to him yet lacked the wherewithal to pull ahead. With a groan of frustration, she veered off to the right and took an indirect route back to the top of the hill, leaving Alistair to arrive at the summit first. No sooner had he returned than a small group of men, led by Taribo, rushed to meet him.

"They found something you should see," Taribo informed him, his normally relaxed expression replaced by excitement.

"One moment," said Alistair, and he carried his bucket to the tub and poured its contents in. Thereafter he turned to one of the men flocking around him, a dark skinned man of mixed heritage and hardened features, and asked, "Did you drink any water today?"

The man blinked but nodded yes.

"Then replace it," commanded Alistair, shoving the bucket into his hands. "Make at least one trip and get someone else to do it after you." Alistair ignored the dark look he received as he followed Taribo and the others to the spot of interest. The man waited for a moment, then dropped the bucket by the side of the tub and hurried to rejoin his fellows.

The item of interest turned out to be a hole in the ground, until recently covered by a large rock. It was perfectly circular and in the deepening shadows they saw no bottom. What could be seen of the interior was a smooth, metal wall without seams sporting a row of metal rungs spaced at even intervals of maybe a foot and a half and leading into the impenetrable darkness. The men stood around it with a quiet awe, eyes now on the dark hole, now on Alistair's reaction.

"How deep?" asked Alistair.

"We dunno," answered a man with a musical accent. "Was already dark when we found it."

Alistair got down on his knees and peered into the hole. The faintest trace of a draft of air emanated from it.

"HELLO!" he called down into the shaft. There were the familiar jumbled echoes which faded away by degrees.

"That sounds deep," said Taribo with appropriate respect in his voice.

"Is this the Gaians?" asked one.

"Somebody make a torch," said Alistair, and three men ran off to comply.

A short time later they came back with a tree branch with some grasses tightly woven around the flaming end, lit by the small fire kept alive and burning in the camp. Already the grasses were falling loose as the fire degraded them, but the end of the stick caught flame and continued to burn. The man with the torch passed it to Alistair, reverently, and all three took up positions once again around the shaft. Without preamble he held the torch suspended over the hole for one brief moment before releasing it into the void. The men watched it plunge, its light diminishing to a point a great distance beneath their feet. Once or twice it bounced off a rung or the sides of the shaft and the sounds of the impacts reached their ears ever more weakly the farther it traveled. Finally, the light blinked out, either extinguished by wind or floor, or it was too far away to see. The sense of awe and nervous reverence increased and when at last someone dared to speak, it was in a whisper.

"Who put it there?"

"And where does it go?"

"And why put it there?"

"It's got to be the Gaians."

The contrast of Alistair's response, in a calm voice and a factual tone, startled them. "This is not something I can imagine Gaians building." His voice silenced the whispered discussions and for a time the men did nothing more than stare into the darkness of the shaft. Finally, he ventured another thought. "Before it was a dumping ground for criminals, this moon was a power colony. Work crews came here and built huge Mantle Stations…this was before they had Solar Nets. Once Mantle Stations gave way to Solar Nets, the company here sold the rights to The Incarcerator. All trace of the Mantle Stations was supposed to be eradicated. I'll bet they just missed this."

One of the other men got down on his knees and rapped his callused knuckles on the smooth metal interior. After considering the sound, he said, "Any shaft this narrow what's gotta survive so deep in this place would be made with Herculerium. Anythin' made in the last hunnerd years, least ways. That sure ain't Herculerium. I worked with it for seventeen years an' I'll swear as it ain't. That shaft's real old or whoever dug it ain't got the sense he shoulda been born wit'."

"Over a hundred years old?" asked Taribo.

The man nodded. "Probably a lot older."

"So…what? This goes all the way to the mantle?" asked a man.

"Who knows?" said Alistair. "And right now, it doesn't matter. We've got a lot of work to do before we explore under the surface. To be safe, let's cover the opening and we can worry about this another day."

Alistair took a few steps away from the men before someone called out, "Who owns it?"

"I don't know. If anyone wants to lay claim to it, they may do so. If there is a dispute, you may purchase my arbitration services if you have not already done so. Or you may settle it among yourselves…it's your choice."

It was at that moment that a change occurred. The sun moved an infinitesimally small amount lower on the horizon; the ambient light at the top of the hill diminished to a minute extent; the increase of intensity of the evening breeze would have required sensitive instruments to detect; the actual physical changes were hardly worth noting, but for a group of men standing around the opening of an unknown shaft, it was as if the ground shifted under them. Realization, to an extent at any rate, came to them. There were no magical high priests to make something theirs or to take it away. There never had been; there had merely been charlatans claiming the power. Right and wrong were not malleable according to their sacerdotal whims. Even if a right had no physical impact in the universe, human action did, and human action could be bent, if the actors so chose, in harmony with human rights or at odds with them. There were systems and institutions which, while ostensibly in place to protect rights, by their nature were at odds with them and therefore intrinsically flawed. Other systems were more in harmony with human nature and human rights. Alistair offered them one, perhaps others could be discovered.

Only a glimpse of this did they catch, like a single paragraph read from an enormous tome, and not a one of them could properly have described what it was he saw. But the glimpse was enough to leave an impression, a feeling, and to awaken an instinct. They could not describe what they saw, but they could begin to recognize it.

When Alistair at last returned to the wooden hut, there were men waiting for him in the open first floor. Ryan, Miklos and Santiago were there, along with another whom Alistair did not recognize. He was exceedingly tall, a good deal taller than Alistair himself, with a body that only seemed slender because of his great height. He wore what Alistair took to be an attempt at leather armor, even sporting a wooden helmet with a nose guard, and in his right hand he held a spear that was, for the moment, used as a walking staff. A mallet with an obsidian head was strapped to his back, and a number of small daggers were stowed about his person. He had long black hair pulled into one braid, piercing blue eyes and his skin tone and facial features hinted at a mix of European and Persian heritage. When Alistair ascended the four steps into the hut, he found himself staring into the man's sternum.

"My name is Caleb," he announced, the merest hint of an Eastern European accent in his deep, baritone words.

"He demands an audience with our leader," Santiago announced as he leaned against the writing desk, his arms crossed and his expression skeptical. Ryan and Miklos sat on the common table, their feet on the chairs, a rapt audience. Miklos was slowly consuming an apple with his noisy chewing.

"I am Odin's champion," announced the giant.

"Congratulations," offered Alistair, "but here we have no leader."

"I was told you were."

Miklos' teeth crunched into the apple and tore out a chunk.

"I am the president of Ashley Security & Arbitration. I am no more a leader than any other businessman. I speak for myself and only myself."

There was doubt and incomprehension in Caleb's eyes, but there was intelligence as well. He paused only a moment before asking, "Who will lead you into battle if Odin decides to attack?"

"I will lead some," Alistair admitted.

"Then I will speak with you. Odin wishes to meet with you. He will meet you tomorrow, halfway between here and our city."

"You're calling it a city?" asked Ryan.

"What is the meeting about?" asked Alistair before Caleb could turn on Wellesley.

It was a look of factitious confusion that Caleb gave Alistair. "Odin is going to offer you terms of surrender. It will be easy enough to find him. Just look out over the island tomorrow and you will see his army."

Alistair shared a look with Santiago while Miklos attacked the apple again. "Tell Odin I will be more than happy to meet with him, but not if he comes with an army. There is a wide open grassland between these hills and the forest in the north. If he wants to meet, he can come with a handful of men and plant a flag there. I'll see it and come out to meet him. If he comes with an army, we're just going to prepare for a battle."

"Odin will—" began Caleb with the tone of a protest.

"Those are my conditions. If he wants to see me he will have to meet them. I'm certainly not going to argue about this with one of his underlings. You're dismissed."

Caleb drew himself up to his full height and stared down at Alistair. It was a stare that had melted the resolve of a thousand men, but Alistair met it coolly, unmoving and unmoved. After this mutual measuring process, the tall man with the Slavic accent glided out of the hut on his stilt-like legs, ducking when he reached the edge of the room, went to the edge of the hill's summit and descended. The others did not stir until the tip of his wooden helmet sank below the ridgeline.

"What do we—" began Miklos.

"Spread the word," said Alistair. "All the subscribers agreed to serve as militiamen if the need arises. It looks like the need might arise."

Miklos took one last bite and tossed the apple core outside the hut.

"And we'll be sure to keep a lookout through the night," added the owner of AS&A.

Not waiting for any further response, he climbed the stairs of the central pillar to the lookout perch. Night had arrived, preceding the rising of Srillium by a couple hours, leaving everything around them in darkness. In their camp at the top of the hill a few souls wandered about the dozen buildings in various stages of construction. Three torches had been lit and placed in the ground, and the trio of burning sticks provided a soft, orange light that cast fuzzy shadows in triplicate and left numerous dark corners, niches and alleyways. Beyond that was a sea of darkness infrequently interrupted by torches as the citizens of the newly sprung hamlets created some light to see by. Beyond the sea of dark was a city of torches directly to the north, partially hidden by leaves and branches swaying in the breeze, making the torches appear to flicker on and off. While the wind blew and the grasses and trees rustled and the waves lapped at the shore, the young Aldran stared at his enemies, not concentrating enough to form specific thoughts, but rather just contemplating the scene. Somewhere, in the sea of darkness, a giant messenger was moving, heading towards the city to the north where Odin waited.

Alistair leaned down and rested his chin on the rough wood of the lookout panels, wondering what Odin's response would be.

61

When Alistair awoke the next morning, it was with a profound sense of terror that constricted and threatened to drown him. Of his dreams he remembered nothing, but upon waking his parents were on his mind, and tucked away deep inside him he felt a little child ready to cry. Even his lower lip quivered and his breathing was ragged, but the sensation gripping and squeezing him faded by degrees until he mastered himself. His breathing relaxed and he was left only with the image of his father and mother, like a portrait, staring at him with sad smiles.

The morning air was cool and still. The overcast sky allowed a diffuse light through the open slats of the second floor walls. Somewhere a flock of birds was cawing. The rumbling snores of Miklos filled the cabin but roused none of the exhausted occupants. Taribo lay asleep in peaceful repose, his hands folded on his lower chest like a cadaver, and Wellesley, contorted into an odd tangle of limbs and half coming out of his cot, slept with an open maw that drooled onto the wood floor. Gregory and Santiago's cots were empty.

Leaving the comparative comfort of his wool mattress, stuffed with grasses, and his thin blanket, also wool, Alistair lumbered down the stairs. Santiago, who had taken the last watch, was just coming up the steps from storage with a bit of bread and some half rotten bananas he deposited on the table. His breathing was labored and a sheen of sweat dampened his brow. With a nod to Alistair he sat down and pushed some of the food his way.

Also taking a seat, Alistair grabbed some bread and snapped off a corner. "Jogging?"

Santiago shook his head as he unwrapped a banana. "These things are going to rot, so we might as well eat them now. No, I was...the fire expired last night, so I restarted it."

"They made it too big before."

"I know. This one is smaller. I think we can keep it running without cutting down every tree in the area within a week. I, ah...I told Giselle she could work for us. I think we need another hand around here, someone to handle some administrative duties, organization. Unless you have an objection..."

Alistair shook his head. "That would probably be useful. Have her tend the fire for us and tell her to charge if anyone else wants to use it. And we need to get a water tub of our own and keep it filled. And clean. And we need a...contraption...I want to boil our water, let it evaporate, and then have it condense in another bucket. We can charge for that, too. Clean water."

"I'll mention these things to her."

Alistair paused a moment, then, "Santiago, I'm going to make you an arbitrator. If you want."

"A judge?"

"Whatever you want to call it. You seem to you know what I'm talking about."

Santiago nodded. "I used to write for a number of publications. *Libertad* was the main one. A South American periodical…quarterly publication. That's what made them exile me here."

Alistair said nothing but eyed Santiago with curiosity, not prompting him to speak but not cutting him off either.

"We thought we were stronger than we were. We felt too safe. We put too much confidence in other people. Too much confidence in the strength of ideas." He directed his gaze at Alistair for the first time. "We challenged the authority of the Emperor." Popping a bit of bread in his mouth, he spoke around his chewing with a casual tone, as if the message were of no moment, "A lesson to be learned for us here, perhaps."

They ate their rotten bananas and hard bread in silence until Ryan Wellesley awoke a few minutes later and half tumbled down the stairs. He sat next to Alistair, eyed the few crumbs left from breakfast, and with a groan got back up to grab some food of his own. He returned a minute later with bread and a hunk of cheese and plopped down in a stool next to the table.

"We need to build a barn for Miklos," he grumbled. "I'm not kidding. It took me half the night to fall asleep with that swine snoring like a damn asshole."

"Eat bananas today," was Santiago's response. "They are going to rot soon."

"I'll eat bananas if you make him sleep downstairs."

Without looking up from the tabletop, Alistair mumbled, "He can sleep downstairs from now on. Make it easier on everybody else."

The sound of feet falling on wooden steps alerted him to the approach of another, and he turned to see Giselle, a hesitant look on her face, walking into the hut. She stopped at the edge, hands folded in front of her. Her comparatively finer clothing from Issicroy was gone, replaced by rough animal skins that covered her from knees to shoulders.

"Fix yourself some breakfast," Alistair grunted. "You're hired."

She nodded and allowed herself a smile, recognizing the sincerity in the gruff welcome. A short time later she was sitting at the table with them and Taribo, the next to wander downstairs. They took up a hushed conversation among themselves, and as the overcast day grew lighter there was movement in the young village with its buildings planted helter-skelter about the hut. Someone chopped wood like a drumbeat to mark the rhythm of labor. More percussion joined in as the scuff sounds of tools hoeing the dirt joined the wood chopping, and elsewhere timber groaned as it was bent to the will of workers who made necessarily primitive homes without the benefit of nails.

This sort of workers' symphony was what Alistair listened to as he, having told his men to stay close to camp that day, took up his perch in the top floor of the hut and kept his eyes fixed on the stretch of land to the north. The day was becoming a humid one, with the featureless clouds above blanketing the land, almost smothering it. The sea beyond Odin's camp was smooth and blue, with none of the white caps a wind might have brought, and so the humidity was permitted to hang in the air, causing beads of sweat to form and trickle down his body.

After Miklos finally rose and breakfasted, after those on the first floor dispersed, Alistair heard someone climbing the stairs. He guessed it was Giselle by the weight of the steps, and moments later was proved correct as her head rose above the floor of the lookout booth. She gave him a swift smile and sat across from him, facing south.

"Could you scoot to the side a bit? I need to see to the north."

She smoothly complied, moving around ninety degrees until she sat on the east side.

"Are you sure this isn't going to tip over?" she asked, not particularly interested in an answer but looking for a way to start a conversation. Alistair smiled softly but said nothing. Having tested her voice, she took a deeper breath and said, "I talked to Layla last night." She studied Alistair, waiting for a response but saw nothing other than a slight narrowing of the eyes. "She's rather set on her course. I thought I should...maybe..."

Alistair glanced at her, moving only his eyes. She had never approached anything so gently before, at least not that he had ever seen.

"Is La Triste your maiden name, or your married name?" he asked, returning his unwavering gaze to the north.

"Neither," she replied after a pause. After a second pause she added, "I took that name the day my husband was murdered."

She spoke frankly though reluctantly, and he turned to her, giving her his full attention, but she had nothing else to say.

"What is your real last name?"

"My real last name is La Triste. The name I carried before will never be spoken again."

She waited for him to continue with an almost defiant expression, her head held high and her back straight, almost like a witness being cross examined. Most would have ceased interrogating her at that point, but Alistair, having taken a similar vow before, was intrigued.

"Your husband died here or on Arcabel?"

"He came with me here. He survived for less than ten minutes before some...He was slaughtered and...eaten." She allowed no tears to form in her eyes. "Like all women I was kept alive for other purposes. My husband was eaten. I may have eaten part of him. I ate some meat before I knew what it was...it may have been him. I may have eaten my own husband." Her voice as she told the story was still bewildered after so many years. "I think I was your age when I came here, about ten years ago. Do you remember the Martian War for Independence?"

"Yes. On Aldra they're called the Martian Uprisings. Which one?"

"The third Uprising. I was exiled two years after the Martians were defeated."

The announcement had exactly the effect Giselle anticipated: Alistair's stoic exterior crumbled into a visage of incredulity and his lips parted as his jaw fell open.

"That was...about fifty-five years? How...?"

Giselle shrugged. "I don't know. I don't know what happened. Maybe we were put in storage and someone forgot about us. Maybe the paperwork got lost in some bureau. Whatever the reason, we spent decades in hibernation, but of course I didn't know it when I first arrived. Later on I found out how long I was out. They must have fed us nutrition while we slept or we would have starved long before arriving." She looked him directly in the eyes. "I have lived for about thirty-two Earth years, but I was born maybe ninety years ago. You and I should never have met. I should have finished my life on Arcabel and died about...well, right about now.

"Instead I'm here. I was tasty enough to be kept as the private concubine of a chief. I suppose it could have been worse. When he died, I was passed to the next one, and finally I was sold to Issicroy and lived as a whore until he got a good sample and liked it. I became a concubine again, one of his favorites. And when Layla came I prevailed on him to take her as a concubine so she would never have to be a whore. She was young. Too young to be with any man, but this is Srillium. She's aware of what I did for her...I think she feels guilty because she got off easier than so many others. And now she wants to make up for it. She's doing this for me, Alistair. That's why she wants to outlaw prostitution."

"And what do you want?"

Giselle stared off into space for a moment. "I want some type of friendly resolution."

"People tell me I am too hard; that I don't consider feelings. It's not true, but I don't give feelings more weight than they ought to have. I appreciate you explaining Layla's perspective, but Layla's problems are Layla's problems. I am not going to do that to people, to jail them, fine them, punish them...whatever...because Layla feels guilty about what you did for her. She can take all the votes she likes as often as she wants, but I will not allow anyone purchasing my protection to be punished for prostitution. It simply will not happen. And on another level, I think prostitution is exactly what we need. Last thing we want is several thousand horny men with nothing but each other and a few goats."

Giselle's face split into a grin for just a moment. "You need the magical power of pussy."

Alistair blushed. "Maybe you can tell her you don't need her to do this for you."

"I'm not entirely sure I disagree with her. Prostitution is slavery."

"Not here it isn't."

Before anything more could be said, Alistair stood up, his head nearly slamming against the thatched roof. He lingered only for a moment before, Giselle forgotten, he was spiraling down the stairs to the bottom floor. Giselle, startled, peered out at where he had been watching, finally spotting a group of men traveling over the land between them and Odin's camp. Though she had difficulty distinguishing detail over the distance, she thought she saw a flag tied to the end of a pole.

❧ ❧

Six men came bearing a flag to plant in the earth. Five men came to meet them. As the second group arrived, they closed ranks with Alistair at the front, backed by Ryan Wellesley, Taribo Mpala, Miklos Papadopolous and Santiago Escobar de León. Arrayed in two straight lines awaiting them were the other six, only three of whom Alistair recognized. At the center of the group stood a tall, slender man with hair of a soft golden color. In thick waves it fell down his back, and his beard, streaked with white, fell to his belly. His aging limbs were yet muscular, though his skin bore traces of every ravage life on Srillium had hurled at it. Armed and armored, he looked like he came from some Norse tale, and by his bearing and confident, commanding gaze Alistair guessed him to be Odin.

Flanking Odin was Duke, on his right, and another younger man on his left. Duke was positively dwarfed by Odin's stature while the other, of Oriental heritage with a head that, save for the length of hair allowed to grow from the top and, bound, spill down his back, was bald. Behind these three were three others, one of them being Caleb with two more whom

Alistair had never seen. Caleb towered over the others, even Odin, from his position in the back.

When Alistair's group pulled to within twenty feet, he halted and Odin addressed him.

"I am Odin," he confirmed in a gravelly voice, "of Tirius. My captains are Duke, of Earth, and Wei Bai, of Earth. Caleb I believe you already know, and he comes with two of his men." Odin's accent was Mandarin, incongruous with his Nordic appearance.

"I am Alistair Ashley. I come with Taribo, Miklos, Santiago and Ryan Wellesley. Taribo and Santiago are from Earth, Ryan and I from Aldra, and Miklos is from Arcabel."

"Well met."

"Well met. I was given an ominous message yesterday by your...champion he called himself."

"There are men hiding under your protection who owe their loyalty to me. You owe your loyalty to me, as I believe you swore an oath. I demand you fulfill your oath. If not, my hand will be forced."

"If you wish to press a claim, you may of course present your case in my court. For a fee. There are a few thousand men and women here who are not impressed with your oath and do not consider it binding. Like I said, if you want to press your case..."

"An oath is an oath. An oath is always binding," Odin growled, his eyes narrowing.

"You are welcome to present your case in court."

"Are you aware of what awaits you if you persist?"

"I have a fair idea of what you would like to do, but I don't think you're idiot enough to try it. You want to rule a kingdom, but half the population does not wish to be ruled. I'm guessing another large chunk is kept in your camp by nothing more than fear, and given the right opportunity they'll bolt to live free like the others. I have a feeling you are frightened by this as well, or you would not be parlaying with me right now. Even if you could win, you'd be fighting against men defending their free lives. They will fight to the last man; this is no idle boast. At best you'd be left with a couple hundred men, an empty island and that much more death on your conscience. And all the time you spent eradicating us is time you should have spent planting crops. It would take you months to kill us off, and by then you'd starve. If you're fool enough to engage us, say goodbye to your kingdom, and likely your life. But if you will consent to leave us be—and we will naturally return that favor—you can be free too. I will sell you my police and arbitration services. If you want, you can work for me."

Odin said nothing, but he did not glower in anger. He even seemed a little tired, which condition he expressed with a long sigh.

"This moon is a testament to what men will do when they are not governed," said Odin, not looking at Alistair but gazing out over the land, as if trying to take in the entirety of Srillium he spoke of. "My goal was peace, to unite people under one government, to have one last chance to..." Odin's voice cracked and he stopped speaking.

"We do not need to unite under one government to be peaceful," was Alistair's gentle rebuke. "You may rule anyone who consents to be ruled by you. But out here, away from your camp, we live by a different creed. I do not rule; I offer services, services you are used to being

424

handled by a government. But there is nothing about law or protection that suggests it must be monopolized."

"And yet, you monopolize, just as I do."

"Not true. Anyone who wishes may offer these services, and for all I know others are setting up their own companies right now. Out here, away from your camp, every relationship must be voluntarily agreed to by both sides. I can work for you, you can work for me, we can trade, we can leave each other alone…every man is master of his own fate. This has always been man's dream, at least for himself, but it has also been his dream to take the liberty of those around him. But every once in a while, for a brief interval, a group of people manage to be free. It happened in Ireland for a thousand years; it happened in Iceland for almost four hundred. It happened in the American West and it happened on Kaldis for a long time. Every colony experienced it to varying degrees and time periods, especially in their early years. Now it is going to happen here, at least if we make the right decisions."

Odin's internal struggle created no ripple on his features. After what felt like a long while, his tense posture relaxed and he answered, "I didn't come here for more warfare. We will leave each other be. When the island is properly mapped we can meet to divide it, your territory and mine."

Shaking his head firmly, Alistair replied, "No, sir. That we will not do. I have a small amount of territory already, a tenth of an acre, on the top of the hill." He turned his upper body to the hut, which could just be made out in the distance. "This is the only territory I call my own. I am not the lord of a dominion, I am a businessman. Anyone who is willing to pay may purchase my services, including anyone and everyone in your camp. I tell you this so we do not part with any misunderstandings. On this island there are no rulers."

Odin's eyes hardened again, and he pursed his lips. "There is a great deal of my property taken by these free men of yours."

"There is a great deal of property built by their hands with their tools. If there is something out there that is truly yours, you may purchase my services and file a claim."

For the first time, Odin glanced at his subordinates who could offer him nothing more than a look of peeved bafflement. "Let's go," he softly said to them, and without a word of goodbye or anything to indicate their acceptance or rejection, they marched back to the north.

Alistair's men relaxed; the young Aldran had not realized how tense they were until the tension left. They eased out of formation and Taribo sat down on the long grass of the plain, attempting to root out a pebble from his moccasin. Alistair found Santiago facing him with a thoughtful expression.

"I think we will avoid a war," he decided. "You did well. Firm but not pushing too far."

"Unless I am mistaken, his population is going to trickle out of his camp until he is left with few men at all. At the last his camp will break up and that will be that."

"Let's head back then," suggested Ryan. "And let's get something to eat, too."

62

"The key difference from your perspective is that no one is forced to pay for our services," Alistair explained to Taribo while the latter sat across from him at the table in the hut. "If we don't please people, I go out of business and you lose a job."

"I understand this, my friend," said Taribo with a disarming smile.

"I know you understand, but have you pondered the implications? You told me you were in the military."

"I was."

"Then you need to relearn things. This is not going to be like anything you have ever done or ever seen before."

"How so?"

"Customer service," was Alistair's simple reply. To Taribo's raised eyebrow, he responded, "You have to be polite to people. We have to make people want to hire us, because if they don't want to, they don't have to. Every incident needs to be handled with an eye towards making all parties satisfied with the outcome. It won't always be possible, but that is the goal. Everyone needs to be treated with respect, patience, politeness, and a smile…Everyone is either a customer who deserves our respect or a potential customer who deserves our respect. This isn't a state police force and it sure isn't the armed forces. We don't want to lose anyone's business."

A grin sprouted on Taribo's face, and by the time Alistair finished it bloomed into a full smile accompanied by a delighted laugh.

"Customer-friendly police!" he chortled without derision.

"That's how it has to be," said Alistair, a grin of his own forming.

"I like it. Customer-friendly!" Taribo laughed again. "I will arrest you politely."

"And everything else politely."

"We are the polite police!"

"Can you manage that?"

"They are only one letter different: polite and police."

"Close in spelling," Alistair agreed.

"It was an ironic coincidence until now."

Taribo laughed again, the mirth reaching down into his belly and producing a guffaw. "Polite police." He shook his head in appreciation.

Spying an approaching group of men and women, Alistair remarked, "Here they come. You may get a chance to put your new code into practice."

"I look forward to it."

There were ten who approached the hut. Giselle was there with another woman, while Santiago, Ryan and Miklos were leading five men, one of them a small man of dark coloring, badly beaten and with a foul grimace on his face. Gregory was one of the others, and Santiago was in the forefront, leading them into the hut as Alistair stood to greet them.

"Welcome. I understand there was some unpleasant business last night." There were general nods of assent and a couple forearms drawn across brows to clear away the trickling sweat from a hot, equatorial sun. "We hope to clear that up as quickly and pleasantly as may be done. Santiago, who is the plaintiff and who the defendant?"

Santiago extended a hand to the badly beaten small man and said, "This is Yusuf Hassan, originally of Earth, East Africa. He is the plaintiff." Yusuf managed a nod to Alistair. "This is Bernhard Rachmann, also of Earth, Austria." The second man Santiago indicated was a larger man, balding, with an unfriendly gaze and meaty hands. His lips were curled naturally into the beginnings of a snarl and his ears were pierced and sported small rings and stones from top to bottom. He stared at Alistair as if suspicious. Yusuf looked to be nearing forty while Bernhard was closer to thirty. "Bernhard is the defendant."

"Please have a seat, or a stool as the case may be," bid Taribo, and he bowed as he drew a stool away from the table.

"The plaintiff and defendant may take opposite ends of the table," said Alistair, and both Yusuf and Bernhard seated themselves. Giselle grabbed a wooden block and a small instrument to carve it and sat down next to Alistair, who took a stool at the middle of the table. Gregory took a seat on the other side of Alistair. Miklos, Santiago, Taribo and Ryan remained standing and spread out, while the other three, the woman and two men, sat opposite Giselle, Gregory and Alistair. Holding her tablet in her hand, with the carving knife in the other, Giselle looked at Alistair expectantly. "Let's begin," he said.

"I purchased protection and I want that son of a bitch to get his!" Yusuf exclaimed, as if he had been poised to spring into action at the sound of the starting gun.

Bernhard immediately responded with a diatribe of his own and in an instant there were several speakers proclaiming something or denouncing someone all at once. Alistair let it proceed in this way until Bernhard came half out of his stool with an aggressive gesture. Miklos and Ryan, who were standing in his vicinity, stepped closer to him and, with a wary glance at them, he sat back down. This intervention had the effect of dampening the heated argument.

Using the opportunity to make himself heard, Alistair said, "I appreciate that everyone is upset right now. We are going to try and bring some justice to the situation. Until then, please do not speak out of turn. I'll have some questions to ask and I need clear, lucid answers without interruptions. Everyone with business here will have a chance to speak. Please be patient until it is your time."

His entreaty fell on angry glares the men and woman directed towards each other, but there was no objection.

"Mr. Hassan, what is the nature of your complaint?"

"I was attacked," he replied, his accent thick though he seemed comfortable enough with the language. "What more do you want to hear?"

"Mr. Rachmann, is this correct?"

"Naw," replied Bernhard, as if he were spitting the word. "We got inna fight's all. He lost." Bernhard, despite his Teutonic name and country of origin, spoke English like an American.

"There is a difference between two men getting in a fight and one larger man aggressing against a smaller one," said Alistair. "If two men escalate things to the point of fighting, we might look at it as an implicit agreement to engage in fisticuffs and let the past be the past. But Mr. Hassan is claiming a fight is not what he wanted and that you forced violence on him."

Bernhard's expression suggested he understood little of what Alistair said. "I didn't implicit nothin'," he finally insisted.

"That is exactly what I am saying you stupid ass!" Yusuf jumped off his stool to deliver the pronouncement.

"Please let's relax," said Alistair, making his voice loud but not, he hoped, overbearing. "Mr. Rachmann, Mr. Yusuf claims you threw the first punch." Bernhard said nothing but darkly glared at Yusuf across the table. "Is this true?"

Bernhard pursed and contorted his lips in what he hoped was a fair imitation of boredom. "Yeah," he finally grunted.

"Up to that point, had Mr. Hassan laid a hand on you or was the argument entirely verbal?"

"He didn't touch me."

"How many blows did Mr. Hassan manage to land during the fight?"

"Don't remember."

"Any?"

"Maybe. Don't remember."

"Can you show us a bruise or other mark to indicate Mr. Hassan landed a blow?" Bernhard shrugged.

"How many blows would you say you landed on Mr. Hassan?"

"Don't know."

"More than a dozen?"

"Don't know." Bernhard slumped down in his stool and folded his arms. He gazed at the table and would not look up from it.

"Mr. Rachmann, this is Dr. Lushington. He has given Mr. Hassan a full physical examination so far as current conditions permit. Dr. Lushington, do you have an opinion on the severity of the beating?"

Clearing his throat, Gregory straightened his posture. "I believe the beating was severe but not life threatening. There are contusions in fifteen different locations, some suggesting multiple blunt force trauma. There are lacerations consistent with Mr. Hassan being dragged over gravel, and a patch of chest hair has been ripped from the skin, leaving a welt. Mr. Rachmann has declined to undergo a physical examination so I cannot conclude anything about his condition." Gregory, his manner calm and professional throughout, leaned back in his chair.

"Mr. Wellesley interviewed three witnesses provided to us by Mr. Hassan. Mr. Rachmann, have you brought a witness to testify on your behalf today? Mr. Wellesley indicated you could provide no one at the time he was conducting the interviews."

"Nope," said Bernhard with a sigh.

"Mr. Wellesley, what did the witnesses indicate to you?"

Ryan stepped forward, his hands folded in front of him. "I interviewed six in all, but three of them didn't want to come for the…the thing today. They all backed up what Mr. Hassan said."

"Any discrepancies?"

"Not really."

"I see. Does anyone have anything they would like to declare before I make the pronouncement? Very well. Mr. Bernhard Rachmann, it is my opinion you assaulted Mr. Yusuf Hassan. You turned a heated argument into a physical assault with a smaller man who could not defend himself and who had no desire to engage you in combat. I am declaring you guilty."

Bernhard rolled his eyes.

"Mr. Hassan, do you wish to grant Mr. Rachmann any clemency?"

"What is clemency?"

"Do you wish to forgive all or part of the punishment?"

"I want the full punishment," insisted Yusuf with a defiant look at Bernhard.

"There's not even a jail here," spat the other with dismissive arrogance, and he folded his arms even tighter to his chest.

"Mr. Rachmann, we don't anticipate needing to use a jail very often. We offer a different service here, and now we are going to deliver the justice Mr. Hassan has paid for. First of all, you have physically assaulted Mr. Hassan without his permission. This action on your part is a declaration that you consider such violence permissible. As a first course, Mr. Hassan has the right to do to you what you did to him, or to hire someone to do it. Taribo will be doing the honors today, unless Mr. Hassan wishes to do it himself."

"He's bigger," Yusuf declared with an encouraging nod to the muscular West African.

"Wait a minute…what the hell are you talking about?" For the first time Bernhard's tone betrayed some alarm.

"They're going to beat the hell out of you, stupid ass!" Yusuf barked.

"What the fuck!?" Bernhard yelled, rising from his stool. "You can't do that!"

"Mr. Rachmann," said Taribo, "we regret we cannot allow you to leave now that Mr. Ashley has given the pronouncement. We regret any inconvenience this may cause you and ask you to remain seated until directed otherwise." Taribo finished with an expression of satisfaction.

Bernhard stared for a moment at Taribo's hand which pointed to the stool he had just vacated. Eyes wide with fright and taking rapid breaths, he considered the large men before him, most of them even larger than him, and sat back down.

"It is demonstrably untrue that we cannot beat you, Mr. Rachmann," Alistair said with the flat tone of a lecturer. "Just as you beat Mr. Hassan, we *can* beat you. Whether or not this is a proper course of action is, ultimately, Mr. Hassan's decision, but you certainly have no room to argue you should be treated more gently than you treated Mr. Hassan.

"In our justice system, after a neutral party determines guilt, the aggrieved party determines the punishment, the maximum permissible extent of which the perpetrator himself determines at the moment he commits his crime. You determined the type, intensity, duration and amount of the beating the moment you delivered such to Mr. Hassan. While you wait for your beating, Mr. Mpala will consult with Dr. Lushington so that an accurate punishment may be administered."

In what was a supremely satisfying reaction for Yusuf, Bernhard's lips quivered and his cheeks lost their color.

"But that is just the beginning. We beat you with the permission of Mr. Hassan, a permission he received from you when, by your actions, you declared such things permissible. But when you beat Mr. Hassan, you acted without permission. In other words, our beating is a response and yours was an initiation. The pain to follow is a consequence of your own actions, but the pain Mr. Hassan must endure is unjust, something he should never have had to go through in the first place. You will therefore be made to pay a fine upon which interest will accrue for every moment it remains unpaid. This will be compensation for Mr. Hassan's unnecessary suffering."

Bernhard's jaw, already wide open, threatened to drop to the floor.

"If you refuse to pay the fine, your property will be taken from you and its title transferred to Yusuf until the debt is cleared. If you do not have property enough to settle the debt, and if no one will lend or give you their property to help you, you will be forced to work off the debt. However, in such a case that you refuse to pay the debt on your own, we will be forced to charge you for the trouble of having to force you to work off the debt. This will only make it more expensive, and the accrued interest will be much greater as well. You may at any time, of course, reach an agreement with Mr. Hassan to settle the debt, both the money or property owed and the beating."

It was not entirely clear whether Bernhard fully comprehended what was happening, but he had realized that, short of a sudden desire to be merciful on the part of Yusuf, he was going to be severely beaten and then would have to pay a fine on top of that. The shock on his face morphed into pleading as he looked at a gloating Yusuf Hassan, and then quickly became anger as he gripped the edge of the table and stared down at the floor.

"You can't do it!" he hissed. "I never hired you! I'm not part of your...damn...shit!"

"Mr. Hassan is our client; that is all that matters."

In the end, there was nothing Bernhard could do. He was taken to a holding area next to the hut. He waited there while Taribo spent a few minutes in discussion with Gregory, whose manner and glances towards Alistair betrayed his disapproval. When he felt ready, after Yusuf again declined to forgo the beating in favor of clemency or a monetary settlement, the West African soldier came for Bernhard, guarded by Miklos and Ryan, and led him to a tree with a rope tied around its trunk. A crowd gathered for the spectacle, and excited chatter ran through. There were a few voices expressing disapproval, more that expressed their enthusiasm, but mainly it was a neutral sort of curiosity and excitement.

"If you'd be so kind as to raise your arms," said Taribo as if he were a tailor.

Bernhard, numb with disbelief, raised his unsteady arms and Taribo tied the other end of the rope around his abdomen and then again around the tree, leaving the Austrian firmly secured to its base. The man's stoic visage shattered as fear overcame him.

"It is better to stand still for this sort of thing," suggested Taribo in a chipper tone. "If I miss a target body part because you try and duck, it only means I have to hit you again until I get the target. Are you ready?"

Bernhard was not listening, and when Taribo drew back his hand the man cringed.

"Wait!" he implored Taribo. "Wait! I don't want this. I'm sorry I...I didn't mean it."

"We understand this is unpleasant for you," Taribo said in a voice to calm a crying child. "We wish there were another way, but we have to remind you that Mr. Hassan did not want to be beaten either. Hopefully, in the future, this sort of thing will be unnecessary."

With the terror still shining in Bernhard's eyes, Taribo readied himself to commence. The crowd, tense like fans before a kickoff, hung on his drawn fist. Bernhard gritted his teeth to stop the chattering, looking helplessly for support from the onlookers. Then, the first punch landed like a blow from a sledgehammer. The resultant cry of pain was cut short by a left to his midsection, and the beating was under way. It was a methodical and precise beating, controlled, with Taribo taking care to position himself just so, or to turn Bernhard's head or lift his arms so that all blows landed on their targets. By Taribo's furrowed brow one could see him counting punches, checking off body parts that received their due and proceeding to the next. A rough piece of stone was scraped over Bernhard's left side, from his ribs to his ankles, and in the end Taribo grabbed hold of his ample chest hair and ripped it from his body, finally leaving him slumped and nearly senseless, held up only by the rope binding him. When this was untied, Bernhard fell to the ground where he weakly moaned.

"On behalf of Ashley Security & Arbitration, I would like to say that we hope no such action will be required in the future," said Taribo, breathless, as he rubbed at his sore knuckles. His chest heaved from the exertion and sweat drenched his body and soaked his clothing, but he was nonetheless exhilarated. "Furthermore, we must warn you against any reprisal against Mr. Yusuf, on whose behalf we have acted with justice today." Taribo paused to gulp in some more air. "We'd like to offer you our services which, you must agree, are quick and effective. We aim to make any violation of our customers' property rights an unthinkable proposition, and we encourage you to take advantage of our protection. Your score with Mr. Hassan is well on its way to being settled and, that being the case, we can accept you as a client with the full right of property like anyone else. Your fee for service will be higher than others, of course, due to this precedent and the increased likelihood of intervention it entails." Bernhard could only moan in response. Surveying him for a moment more, Taribo at last added, "Alistair will be by momentarily to settle the property debt owed to Mr. Hassan." The speech delivered, Taribo left Bernhard, the radiance of an irrepressible smile emanating from him.

"That was barbaric," said a voice at the inner edge of the crowd. Alistair, his arms folded as he impassively watched the proceedings, turned to see Gregory.

"Was it?" he asked. "I'll bet barbarians had low crimes rates."

"How can you can stomach it? It makes me sick. I don't know that I want to be a part of this anymore."

"Gregory, why don't you shed a few tears for the victim? Was it any less barbaric when Bernhard decided to kick the hell out of Yusuf? Why should he get to do that and not have to experience it himself?"

Gregory only shook his head and walked away.

63

In her left hand Giselle held a sheaf of brownish papers, and in her right a pencil. In truth the papers were hardly worthy of the name, but someone had managed to grind up some wood into a soupy mulch and beat it down into some brittle sheets that, when dry, were given to crumbling. The pencil was similarly crude, consisting of a carved wooden holder into which a lump of something Giselle suspected was clay mixed with charcoal could be secured. They were rudimentary writing supplies, but they were far preferable to the notches she had been carving on wooden tablets. She could record faster now, and store the recordings in a far smaller space. Working assiduously, she transferred their entire archive from tablet to parchment.

Alistair's hands were free and he had them placed now on his hips as he stood with an open stance, staring down into the recently discovered shaft. Five other men also stood around the hole, staring into it as if waiting for it to reveal a secret. Absentmindedly, one kicked a stone into the shaft and it plummeted, ringing off the sides of the shaft before leaving earshot.

"We wanna claim it," one of the men finally said. "We found it, we explored it. We stake the claim to it right now."

Alistair nodded. "What does it lead to?"

The men shifted uncomfortably. One of them finally answered, "We don't know. Tashiro went farther than anybody else. Didn't see nothin'." The man said this with a toss of his head in the direction of the smallest man among them, a slender and short Japanese man of perhaps forty years. Tashiro picked up the story in accented English.

"I went down…very far. I must be below the level of the sea. Much farther. It got cool where I was. But nothing change except temperature. The tunnel is always like this in wideness…always with a smooth side and always with the ladder. It was too dark to see if anything was written, but from the touch I could feel no change. And smell too. Nothing changes but temperature."

"What's down there?" asked a man of no one in particular.

"Can we own it?" asked one.

"Provisionally, yes," Alistair replied. "Whoever built this is the owner, or whoever paid the builders."

"But this thing is hundreds of years old," one pointed out.

"And abandoned," added Tashiro.

"That is why I am, provisionally, going to record and recognize your claim."

The men broke into satisfied grins.

"But remember, this is essentially a gamble. We don't know if the title to this property is yours or not. Someone may come one day and demonstrate they are the proper owner."

"Well hell," began one, a bit frustrated. "I mean…doesn't property become abandoned…you know…centuries later."

"Every case must be decided on its own merits, but the principles remain the same. Once something is yours, it remains yours until you transfer it, abandon the title, or you can lose the title in payment of a debt. If the original owner passed it on to his heirs, and they to theirs…I just want you to be aware. Someone may come with a good claim to the property. Claiming this is a gamble, as is any property claim. We will recognize it as yours until someone demonstrates it is not."

The men looked thoughtfully at the opening in the ground, and one of them, tapping his finger to his lips while he considered what Alistair said, spoke up. His voice and measured speech carried hints of a greater intelligence than the others. "What if someone comes claiming it was their great-great-grandfather's and that it has passed down to them?"

"If they can show the proper documentation proving it was transferred to them, it is theirs."

The man nodded at this and tapped his lips once or twice more. "What if the title was never officially transferred, but they claim by custom property passes down from parent to child, and their great-great-grandfather never renounced the property, so it would have to have become theirs?"

"Well that's a different…case. In that instance…we would…" Alistair faltered, realizing he did not have a ready-made answer. "I honestly can't give you an answer right now. If such a case were to arise, we would listen to arguments on both sides and try to find the correct answer using logical principles. We would try to establish the correct precedent." Alistair shrugged. "I don't know. I've never encountered that question before."

"Well," said the interrogator, "that's good enough for now. We would like to lay official claim to the tunnel down to as deep as we have explored."

"Giselle will record the claim."

The business with the five men being concluded, Alistair took his leave with Giselle scurrying after, attempting to write and walk over uneven ground at the same time and accomplishing it surprisingly well. The summit of The Great Hill, as it was becoming known, had an expanse of flat ground the approximate size of a rugby field. It was a short walk back to the hut, where Santiago was waiting. Sweating profusely from a long hike over the island's terrain, he was reclining on a stool, his back to the table, sipping at some water from a wooden cup. He made no move to acknowledge them when they arrived, but he had laid out a large and heavy tan parchment over the table, its corners weighted down by rocks. In charcoal a map of some sort was traced, with dark smudges and marks over its surface from the charcoal-stained hands that had grasped it.

Leaning with his hands on the table, Alistair eyed the map. "It's finished?"

"It is finished," confirmed Santiago and downed the rest of his water. He rose from his stool, set the cup on the table and laid his hands on it to lean on, regarding the map which was, to him, upside down. "It is not the most precise map humans have labored to produce, but it is reasonably accurate."

There were no political lines on the map, nothing to indicate settlements, population and territory. Any such markings would have doomed the map to become out of date in a short period of time, for the island was undergoing a rapid transformation. The tools brought over from the main continent hacked at tree trunks, dug up hard ground, sliced through plants, peeled away bark, sawed through wood, broke up rocks and fashioned more tools. There was squabbling over ownership of these instruments, but Alistair and Santiago managed to settle the issues amicably. Most of the population were generally satisfied with the outcomes and, equipped with an increasing stockpile of tools, went to work on the raw resources the island afforded them.

It was almost miraculous how the inhabitants set about their own tasks with little regard for or information about what anyone else was doing. Despite this, the entire scattered and diversified affair was exceptionally well coordinated. These prisoners, living for so long as savages, quickly remembered their roots and divided their labor. One day people were building homes, preparing fields and piecing together fishing nets on their own, and the next individuals were making surpluses of a small number of goods and trading the excess for whatever they lacked.

In short, an economy sprouted on Odin's Island, as it came to be called. It was an uncontrolled and vibrant economy, and with the scraps of knowledge of superior technology Alistair knew existed among them, and with each man free to pursue his ends as he saw fit, he had little doubt they would advance by leaps and bounds, far surpassing in rapidity of development their ancestors of thousands of years ago, at whose level they now lived.

When he was done admiring the map, he instructed Giselle to store it within easy reach, an action which she carried out with her customary punctiliousness. The life she lived on Srillium had not done more than roughen her edges and harden her shell; she preserved a core of a sharp mind, a perceptive eye, a fabulous memory, and a unique thoughtfulness that sought solutions to minor problems often before Alistair was even aware of them.

In the mornings, Alistair rose early to exercise. When he returned Giselle was there, preparing them for the day's business. The next few hours were generally spent traveling, and she packed well for the trip. Occasionally business took them a few miles away and kept them overnight, but he never found himself wanting for something forgotten. Upon returning, they would have a small supper, dispose of business arising in their absence, and then she would retire to the women's lodge.

He was at first uncomfortable with his new companion, being naturally reticent to open up to people, and the fact Giselle was an attractive woman a few years his senior doubled his discomfort. When he walked, he felt as if he went on stilts. He found himself clearing his throat before he spoke so his voice did not crack. He stubbed his toes on obstacles more often than he thought appropriate. However, he eventually grew accustomed to her presence and relaxed; his voice grew steadier and his toes were given a reprieve. He could stretch out on the ground without worrying about whether the position of his arms made him look silly. Her conversation ceased to fluster him. In one instance, upon suggesting to Giselle that they make for the west coast the next day to settle a dispute about property boundaries between two groups of loggers, she remarked that they could then hitch a ride on the logs to the southern part of the island to attend to other business down there.

"A girl needs a good log between her legs now and then," she said with the hint of a smile and a raised eyebrow.

Alistair spluttered, nearly asphyxiating on his own saliva, and blushed a deep red even after his airway cleared.

"I'm sorry," she said with an air of supreme satisfaction. "At my last job that sort of talk was considered appropriate. It was expected, in fact."

He only blushed more, but time and conditioning harden even the most innocent. Her quips and puns, in truth less vulgar than the speech of his fellow marines on Kaldis but which had the distinction of being delivered by a good-looking female, soon produced no more effect in him than a chuckle and shake of his head.

If her risqué speech affected him less, her physique affected him more. Like anyone would, he recognized at first glance that Giselle was beautiful, but he noticed it with all the attention of a preoccupied man. He noted she was attractive like he noted the height of a tree, or the distance of a road, until he began to spend most of his waking hours with her. There was no moment he could point to as his awakening, the moment when her beauty was among his foremost thoughts. It was as if the realization, buried in his subconscious, came loose and floated to the forefront of his brain, crossing no line and experiencing no defining moment, but by degrees growing in prominence.

Her skirt of animal skin came down to the middle of her thighs. A single strap over her left shoulder held it up, leaving her arms and a good portion of her chest bare. A pair of sturdy moccasins adorned her feet. The ensemble left much of her body exposed, and Alistair discovered that in quiet moments, when he was planning and she writing, for instance, his eyes were drawn to her. She was not a pampered princess in an affluent society. Her grooming consisted of a swim in the lake and a good scrubbing without soap to be followed by running a makeshift comb through her shoulder length hair. Her hair did not shine like silk, though she managed to keep the tangles out of it. Her leg was well shaped but not entirely smooth, as a sparse but detectable growth of dark hair arose in the absence of razors and a decidedly thick patch of hair grew underneath each arm where it joined the body. But these niceties of a comfortable culture didn't matter on Srillium, and he grew more and more intoxicated with her, eyeing the outline of her thighs, glancing at the shadows underneath her skirt, studying the shape of her buttocks as it pressed down on a seat, or her solid back and shoulders when the muscles flexed. His admiration for her body joined with his admiration for her ability.

The same continuing proximity which allowed Giselle's charms to enchant Alistair eventually swayed Giselle. He was not especially handsome, and his immensely powerful body, his one trait that did impress some women, was far bigger than she usually preferred. But his work and the ideas which had given birth to it, having first confused and unsettled her, now astonished her. His encyclopedic knowledge of abstruse topics impressed her when she grew more accustomed to it. She discovered a gentleness lingering beneath the surface of his impassive and unyielding logic, a clumsy, guileless desire to be tolerant of the symbolism, spiritualism and irrational emotions he did not comprehend. Furthermore, when she remembered the great gap between what she told him of herself and what he told her of him and decided to press him for information, she saw an ache in him, something more than what the ordinary prisoner feels on being exiled to Srillium. There were places in his memory he would not yet take her but still stared at with haunted eyes, and no woman is entirely immune to a man with emotional pain.

What played the largest role in securing her affection for and attraction to Alistair was her discovery of his feelings for her. Every human is a balance of ego and sympathy that at least responds to the interest of another and often winds up reciprocating. Though Alistair—open, honest, blundering Alistair—thought himself sly and imagined that, when he stole glances at her, she was ignorant of his attentions, she instantly recognized what was going on. Even before he himself fully realized how often he watched her, she was flattered and secretly smiling at his consideration. For all the shaggy, unkempt hair dominating his head and face, she began to return his looks with some appreciative ones of her own, though he never noticed.

Only one dispute threatened to ruin things, and it involved Layla. She came charging into the hut one morning, Giselle in tow, claiming her finely woven cloth, which served as currency still, had been stolen and insisted that, inasmuch as she had paid for his services despite her declaration of firing him, Alistair find the culprit.

"But I already know who did it," he said with utter nonchalance. Too shocked to respond, Layla only stared. "*I* took it."

The former concubine could only utter a couple sounds that, though intended to be words, came out more like strangled coughs.

"Does this bother you?"

"You're a son of a bitch!"

Alistair only shrugged.

Layla collected herself and, through clenched teeth and in a low, deadly tone, said, "Give me my cloth back."

"No."

She hissed like a serpent. "I said give me my cloth back. You've got no right to take it."

"I'm surprised to hear you using that argument, Layla. I'm not claiming I had a right to take it, but rights are ethereal things. Just ideas, really. Entirely without physical effect, unlike, say, gravity. Your right to the cloth did not prevent me from taking it. I concede I had no right to take it, but you must concede I did have the ability. Not only that, but you do not have the ability to take it back."

She brought her hands up in front of her face and her fingers bent like talons. "I am so fucking furious right now," she spat, sounding almost shocked at her own anger, and her voice shook as if to confirm it. "I swear I'm going to gouge your eyes out."

"I really don't think you'll be able to."

"Give me my damn cloth back!"

"I already told you I'm not going to do that."

Her enraged screams attracted the attention of onlookers, and a small crowd gathered around the hut, staying at what they considered a safe distance.

Layla, looking around helplessly, grabbed at her scalp and looked ready to cry.

"Would you say I should not have done that?" asked Alistair with feigned innocence.

"You're a son of a bitch! What the hell do you think?"

"I'm asking *you*."

"Of course you shouldn't have taken it. IT'S…MY…CLOTH!"

Alistair shrugged again. "But when we talk about should and shouldn't…a rock neither should nor shouldn't fall. It will or it won't; there's no choice to be made in the matter. Should holds no such power as gravity. Or electromagnetism. Or any universal force."

"What the hell are you babbling about? The cloth was mine and you took it!"

"So what bothers you is that I imposed my will on something that was your property. And you think I should not have done it…in other words that I didn't have the right to do it."

"You're the one who's always preaching about property rights, you arrogant bastard! Practice what you preach some time!"

"Layla if you are going to get your cloth back, you're going to have to convince me. It's quite clear you won't get it back unless I decide to give it to you. And if you want to convince me you'll have to calm down."

She sat down across from him and lowered her voice, though a string is no less taut when plucked lightly. "We should have let Issicroy execute you. Give me my damn cloth back. Now."

"Are you saying people do not have the right to impose their control over others' property?"

"Yes! Yes! YES!" She accompanied her frenzied answer by pounding her fists on the table.

"But how can that be true in one case and not in another?"

Layla started. Her lips parted and her tirade halted. Somewhere in her brain she made a connection, a vague connection she would not have been able to describe, but nevertheless she had a glimpse of what Alistair was going after.

"Alistair. Please. You should not have taken my cloth. I want you to give it back." The storm having spent itself, her voice was firm but calm.

Alistair nodded towards the stairs in the center of the hut. "The cloth is underneath the bottom step there." When Layla rose to search for it, he continued, "But I like your idea of keeping your hands off other people's property. I like it so much I intend to follow it as a principle from now on. Without exceptions."

"Go fuck yourself," she muttered. Cloth in hand, she stormed out of the hut and passed through the throng outside.

Santiago sat quietly through the entire outburst, his legs propped up on the rail at the edge of the hut, carving a stick with some sharpened flint chips. He only spoke once Layla was gone. "I wonder how many customers that is going to cost us."

Alistair moved only his eyes to glance at Santiago and did not otherwise respond. Of Giselle he asked, "How is the anti-prostitution bill coming along?"

"It has the support of precisely none of the men and only about half the women. Some of the girls are already amassing private fortunes with their pussies."

"I expect some of the wealthiest individuals on this moon will be prostitutes."

"But, Alistair…" Giselle hesitated a moment. "I don't understand this little demonstration. Layla isn't proposing to steal people's property…she wants to prohibit prostitution."

"But what will she do to those who flout her law?"

Giselle responded merely by chewing at her lower lip while she considered the point.

The evening after the argument there was a momentous turn of events on the land bearing Odin's name. Before the sun disappeared, there was a large disturbance in the forest where Odin and his remaining followers were camped behind their timber walls. It was impossible to say what was going on other than a general commotion, but by nightfall the camp was ablaze, giving the northern horizon an orange glow as if the sun were setting there. The inhabitants of the Great Hill gathered to watch the fire, while Miklos, Alistair, Santiago, Ryan, Taribo and Giselle all crowded into the third story tower of the hut, bodies pressed together, fascinated by what it might mean.

Alistair sent Taribo and Miklos to scout around, and they returned with tales of a plague that decimated the population. Though there had been a constant trickle of men and women escaping from the military-style camp, there yet remained a great number of them, densely packed together at Odin's orders, for defensive purposes. It was these tight living quarters which allowed some communicable disease to engulf them, and when Odin would not permit them to disperse, an insurrection broke out.

The next day, Alistair left his camp, passing by Gregory and Layla and the dozens of sick and injured whom they were tending to, and set out through the hills, heading south. Giselle he left back at the hut. Alone, he roamed the hills for several hours, finding a couple camps but not the one he was looking for. Finally, hours after his last meal and just as the sun was beginning its final approach to the horizon, he came upon a group of diggers tunneling into the side of the mount. He called to them and waved and was greeted in return.

When he was within a few yards of the men, who had not stopped their labors while he approached, he said, "I'm looking for one of my new clients. Darion Chesterton."

Still the men continued their labor, save for one covered in dirt and grime so thick one could be forgiven for thinking him to be of another species. He dropped his crude pickax and, white eyes staring out from a face black with dirt, took a few steps in Alistair's direction.

"I think we met once," Alistair said. "In a prison in Arcarius."

"I remember. It was during my first life."

"What are you doing in this one?"

The men were close enough now that they shook hands, each feeling an inexplicable yet warm camaraderie with another he hardly knew.

"I'm going to be rich again," Darion replied and laughed.

"Speaking of wealth," said Alistair, and from his pocket he produced a translucent capsule containing some bits from a plant. "I have a business proposition for you."

64

Mordecai found it easy to shatter the power structure above him, the hierarchy of Odin and his immigrants. This was the part that had most worried him and yet other actors created such a condition that only a small nudge on his part, at the right time, was sufficient to cause a chain reaction. All order collapsed and authority dissipated. He delighted in what appeared to be his good fortune, never imagining the second part, the recreation of a hierarchy with him on top, the part he imagined would naturally follow the first, would elude him.

Within hours of being on the island, Mordecai attracted to him a gang of belligerent malcontents, as he always did; men who recognized a malignant hostility more imposing than theirs and who secretly hoped proximity and obedience to it would amplify their own. He led and they followed, instinct conferring on him more authority than voting does in democratic systems, but after the fall of Duke's authority his power did not grow as he expected it to. With dismay he watched as men and women flowed right out of Duke's camp and spread over the island, uncontrolled, distance attenuating his influence. Like a man grabbing at rocks in a landslide, he collected a few but could not prevent the avalanche.

With his numbers increasing to nearly forty, Mordecai carved out for himself a kingdom which, though there never were treaties with neighboring lands to define its borders, may have measured as much as a hundred yards in length and breadth. He and his followers built a one room, one story castle of timber and thatch, and his men built a lodge of their own next to it. However, word of Alistair's anarchic order quickly spread, and the few souls whom he convinced to pay him tribute in exchange for protection abandoned him for Alistair's protection, whose terms they found much more to their liking. It did not take long for him to detect the course of events, and his instinct was to attack Alistair, an instinct stayed by, among other considerations, the memory of a pectoral tattoo. While he deliberated, his kingdom lost most of its population, many of whom contracted with Alistair and all of whom felt the pull of open land to the south, land which they could homestead and call their own and there be ruled by no one.

Enraged, Mordecai declared to the fourteen men who remained with him his intention to attack Alistair, who had only four other warriors. He was dissuaded by the timid observation that Alistair had over one thousand subscribers, most of whom pledged, in exchange for a discounted price, a certain number of days of military service should it become necessary. In the end, he saw only one chance, and that was to form his own company of protection and arbitration services. However, forced to compete with Alistair's rates, he found he could not afford to keep all fourteen remaining followers on the payroll. He agonized over the decision, wanting to keep an army as large as possible but feeling the new temptation of profit, which would have to be sacrificed if he were to pay to keep more of his men. In the end, having only a couple dozen customers, he kept only two.

So fell Mordecai's kingdom, small and short lived, done in not by barbarians or warfare or inflation or plague, but by market competition. In its place arose an extremely modest security firm Mordecai called The Shield. The owner grasped at a crown but wound up with a pencil and a ledger, with two employees amid a populace that, in reaction to his bullying, were reluctant to trust him with their protection when Ashley Security & Arbitration was available. Many an evening Mordecai glared at the Great Hill, saying nothing, just watching it darken as the sun escaped to the other side of the world. In the end, hampered by his reputation, he abandoned his castle and moved to the south side of the island in search of a new start and customers yet to form an impression of him.

∾∿

"Alright, let's get this over with," sighed Alistair.

Taribo, seated near the railing serving as the hut's perimeter, his arms folded over his chest, suppressed his mirthful chuckle, though he could not prevent a smile from forming. Alistair was seated at the long table, hands folded and resting on the table as he leaned forward, making eye contact with no one. He was flanked by Giselle on his left and Santiago on his right. The latter sported a skeptical frown on his face. Giselle betrayed no bias or emotion but merely held her pencil ready over a sheet of parchment. At opposite ends sat Miklos and Ryan, the former with a haughty and triumphant expression, the latter with one to match the expression on Santiago's face, save that it had a large dose of hostility.

Making no effort to mask his disapproval, Alistair said, "Miklos, what is the nature of your complaint?"

"Trespassing."

Ryan snorted.

"Please give us the details."

Miklos shifted in his seat and scratched his wide jowls. "He trespassed on my property," he said in his languid way, nodding his head at the small structure built for him to sleep in. "I told him not to come in and he came in anyway. Trespassing is a crime. You said so yourself."

"I built that damn hut," Ryan protested.

"But you gave it to me. You built it because you were kicking me out of this one."

"Because you snore like a pig."

"That doesn't matter. The hut's mine."

"Ryan," interjected Alistair before the two men could get themselves riled up, "did Miklos ask you not to go on his property?"

"Yeah, but he lost my hatchet."

"I didn't lose your hatchet; I gave it back to you."

"I let him borrow my hatchet a couple days ago—"

"And I gave it back."

"—and he never gave it back. He told me he didn't have it but I didn't believe him so I checked his hut."

"And I specifically said he could not come in."

Both men seemed satisfied with their end of the argument, so they folded their arms across their chests and stared at each other across the table. They could hear the soft scratching of Giselle's pen as she struggled to record the relevant details as rapidly as they gave them.

"I can do little about the hatchet," said Alistair. "In the future, Ryan, if you can't trust the people you are lending to, I suggest you get a receipt, and have the other party sign upon receipt of the object and its return. Without proof one way or the other, there is nothing I can do. As for you, Miklos, this isn't really what I had in mind when I founded an arbitration company."

"My understanding is trespassing is illegal."

Wellesley rolled his eyes.

"What sort of damages are you claiming?" asked Santiago with the tone of one who wishes to expedite.

Miklos shrugged. "Whatever damages are involved with trespassing. He invaded my space, destroyed my privacy."

"OK. I'm ready to make the pronouncement. Ryan," said Alistair while looking at Miklos, his tone that of a school teacher addressing a young child, "please do not go on Miklos' property when he asks you not to."

"Orders," corrected Miklos. "I ordered him not to."

"Get stuffed," said Ryan.

"I'm asking for damages."

"Are you kidding me?" asked Ryan and rolled his eyes again.

Miklos only leveled a serious stare at Alistair.

"Damages," repeated Alistair. "OK. Ryan, to compensate Miklos for the damage you have done to him, you will fetch him a cup of water. That will be all."

Alistair did not wait another moment to rise from the table and leave the hut.

Ryan also stood up, saying, "Fucking ridiculous. I'll get you your damn glass of water."

"I'm not thirsty yet," said Miklos and he stood up and trudged out of the hut, his chin triumphantly in the air.

Ryan watched him leave, his face a mixture of disbelief and irritation. Miklos did not look back and Ryan finally, with a shake of his head, took his own path out.

Immediately having left the hut, Alistair went to the camp fire where small tablets of wood, serving as plates, held a filet of fish, still steaming, and a cooked potato, withered from age and dotted with the remains of sprouted roots. Alistair grabbed the rough wood of a tablet and, having bartered with someone to make the trip to the coast to acquire the fish in the first place, helped himself to a serving and a wooden cup. He winced as he bit into the fish, for it was still quite hot, but swallowed his bite with the help of some water. Both the fish and the potato were unseasoned, but the plain fare was good enough for his protesting stomach, and his pallet was accustomed now to simple meals like this. Hunger, real hunger born of physical labor and a missed lunch, did more than any spice to make the meal appetizing.

His employees and a few others gathered around to eat, and by the time he finished they were chatting together while Alistair, eschewing conversation, sipped at his glass of water and stared off at the western horizon, nearly black now. While he thus gazed out, aware of the conversation around him only as a buzz in the background, he saw a solitary figure, tall and nearly gaunt, pop up above the edge of the hill and stride into view. The long, blonde beard and uncommon body frame revealed the identity of the traveler. Rising, Alistair went out to meet him, and conversation among his friends died out as they noticed his leaving and watched to see where he was going.

"Good evening, Odin," said Alistair to the pale, haggard face before him. Framed by darkness, the pallor of the former tribal chief stood out like a ghost.

Odin nodded, coughed once, and with his Mandarin accent said, "Good evening Alistair." He paused for a moment to survey the camp site. "It seems you won."

"Were we competing?"

"You know we were." Odin coughed again. "I never thought…" He shook his head. "My plans have been altered, it seems. But I'm not angry. I was staring at the ashes of my city this morning and I felt free. I was enslaved so slowly I never realized it. But no longer. I came to thank you."

Inept at accepting such implicit apologies, Alistair merely nodded and said, "Gregory can take a look at you if you're feeling sick."

"No, no, I'm—how do you say it?—on the mend? Yesterday I needed a doctor. Today I need an occupation."

"Are you…do you want to work for me?"

"No, but thank you. Duke, Caleb and Wei Bai have started their own security services. They asked me to do it but I don't want to. I never really wanted anything of what I got for the last…twenty years? How long have I been here? I really just came to set your mind at ease and to say thank you."

"What occupation are you looking for?"

Odin softly smiled, a smile muffled by fatigue and a little melancholy. "I have some plans. Plans interrupted in my youth, but maybe not dead. That's for another day. For right now, I was thinking it would be nice to have access to resources on the mainland."

Alistair slowly nodded, wondering what he intended to do.

"I think there are some great beasts of the deep that need to be exterminated."

"Are you serious?"

"I'm going to find a way to clear some shipping lanes." He nodded to Santiago, who had come up behind Alistair to join the conversation. "Good evening."

"Odin. Is there anything we can do to help?"

"I'll let you know." Turning to go, he paused to leave them with one suggestion. "Some of my men…used to be my men…some of them are settling on the north coast."

"I expected as much," said Alistair, not seeing his point. "Good timber up there."

"This island is ignored by the Gaians. They believe it is impossible to get here because of the krakens. Word of our disappearance will be spreading and they are bound to find out about it from Issicroy or Ansacroy. Even if they don't, when they pass by the south coast of the mainland, they may turn an eye to our island."

Alistair nodded in understanding.

"Every structure we build here is forbidden. If the men build on the north coast they can be seen, which will draw attention. We do not want to tangle with the Gaians. The outcome of any such battle is a forgone conclusion. It would be a modern army attacking a Stone Age tribe."

"That's something to think about," replied Alistair, scratching at his beard while he mused.

By way of goodbye, Odin merely nodded and set himself in motion. A gust of wind accompanied him on his way out, tossing his beard and hair about as he retreated back down the hill.

"He has a good point about the north coast," said Santiago after a few moments of silence.

"Yes he does."

"But what can we do? Do we have the right to prevent them from settling the land? Under any circumstances?"

"Hopefully, if we get down there before they have too much invested, it will be a fairly simple task of explaining the danger. They will be the first ones to come under attack, after all."

"And if there is resistance? What right do we have to stop them?"

"We need to find the right principles. I have no right to, say, drill on my land if it will result in an earthquake that destroys yours. You would be right to prevent me from doing it."

"I think so."

"Well, what's true of an act of nature is true if the repercussion comes from human agents. What if my drilling created only a 50% chance of an earthquake? Would you be right to stop me then?"

"Certainly."

"What about at 20%? 10%? 1%? At what point does risk become great enough to make intervention legitimate?"

"I don't know," conceded Santiago. "But I think the risk they pose by building on the coast is great enough to warrant intervention there."

"Then we'll go tomorrow, and hope a little reasoning is all we need."

65

At the southern edge of the northern forest, scores and scores of men hacked at the tree trunks. Two great arboreal pillars had fallen and lay pointing south. Like ants on a carcass, men swarmed over the fallen giants and stripped them of their branches. With so many hands at work, it was a matter of minutes from the time the tree fell to when it ceased to be a tree and became a log. The sound of so many tools impacting against the lumber carried well up the hill, each thud mixing with the manifold others so that it was as distinguishable as the plop of a raindrop hitting the earth during a storm.

When the rays of the sun first peaked over the eastern horizon, revealing a drab, gray sky and a misty ground to match it, Alistair and Taribo, well armed, left camp, which the residents of the area, by some common consent, referred to as home but which Alistair insisted on calling camp. Now, an hour later, a diffuse light weakly lit the land but made no shadows, and a sprinkle of rain fell upon them. Srillium the planet was still somewhere in the sky, invisible behind the clouds, having begun to set late as its moon progressed through another revolution. They were spotted by the workers long before they reached them, but no one came out to give a greeting nor took much notice save to pause for a moment between ax strokes. Alistair was wondering exactly how to initiate the proceedings and with whom when he spotted Duke and Caleb emerging from the trees to his left and making their way towards him. He altered his course to meet them.

"There was a time when I expected my next sighting of you would be with you bound hand and foot and delivered for justice," said Duke by way of saying hello. He was unarmed but his companion bore a tremendous ax in his massive right hand.

"Punishment, you mean," replied Alistair. "It would not have been justice."

They stood in the tall grass, which reached Duke's chin as it rustled in the breeze, and regarded each other.

"Well. You are to be congratulated on your coup," the Englishman finally managed. The words, bathed in a strained British accent and sallying forth as they did from a jaw that scarcely unclenched its teeth to let them out, were tinged with a resentment he was at equal pains to hide and display. "It's all the rage now, your security firms. Everybody's doing it. Including me."

"Perhaps I should thank you for the flattery of your imitation." To his right, Alistair spotted one he had seen before, with his nearly bald pate graced only by a black pony tail on the top of his head, leaving the forest and heading for them.

"Don't bother. At any rate I don't expect it to last for long. To what do we owe the extreme honor of this visit?"

"We spoke with Odin last night."

"Very well."

"We wanted to know what was going to be built with this lumber. More to the point, where it was going to be built."

"I would say that is very little your business."

The nearly bald man joined them and stood next to the towering Caleb.

"If I build a house on that hill," said Alistair, "and you wish to build on the slope above me, it is very much my business inasmuch as I need to be sure your foundation is strong so your house won't come tumbling onto mine." Duke folded his arms across his chest and tucked his chin downward. "My point is our thriving on this island requires us to remain out of sight of the Gaians. My understanding is that they pass by the north coast with some frequency. The last thing we need is to be building on the north beaches. I figured this was in all our interests."

Duke glared at Alistair with an impenetrable look before answering. "Well, you must think we're bloody idiots."

"We appreciate your concern, Alistair," said the Oriental man, preferring to speak in his native Mandarin. *"Understand we value our privacy here as much as you. You have no doubt noticed we are chopping down the trees on the south side of the forest for this very reason."*

"Alistair, this is my business partner, Wei Bai," said Duke.

"Excellent. So our understanding is that no construction will occur in view of anyone in the channel north of here? That any effort to settle and build in those areas will be forcibly stopped if necessary?"

"Thanks so much for stopping by," said Duke with a cold grin buried beneath his mustache. He turned on his heel and left, not bothering to speak over his shoulder, perhaps not caring if they heard. "Please don't hesitate to come by again if the mood should strike you. We're always pleased to see you."

"We have an understanding," Wei Bai assured them, his smile a mixture of bland, perfunctory politeness and humor at Duke's treatment of them.

"Feel free to leave now," Caleb said, staring down at them with bold, unfriendly eyes.

Alistair, his objective achieved, was on the point of doing just that but Taribo, who found himself the direct object of Caleb's stare, stood his ground. The muscular African's face split into a toothy smile and to the half-Persian, half-European he said, "I was actually going to advertise for my company."

"Maybe not a great idea," suggested Caleb and he hefted his ax.

"My fellow citizens!" Taribo called, holding his arms out as if he meant to embrace them.

Alistair winced, wishing the earth would swallow him whole and take him away from all those gazes turning in his direction.

"Allow me to offer you the services of Ashley Security & Arbitration."

Caleb charged at Taribo, who brought his spear into a defensive position, but was intercepted by Alistair, who grabbed Caleb under his arms and drove him back, a drive Caleb arrested with an exertion of his strength against Alistair's. At that moment, the Aldran wanted nothing as much as to leave in peace, unnoticed, but he felt compelled to defend his friend. *Besides,* he thought, *this is an important precedent to set. We have no government. No firm's customers are off limits to competition.*

"You don't own these people," Alistair was forced to hiss as he struggled against Caleb, whose power he found, with not a little disappointment, to be equal to his own. Each pushing into the other, they reached a static point where all the exertion of muscle resulted in a strained immobility. "If they want to hire us, or if we want to make them an offer, it doesn't concern you."

"These men have already hired Duke," Wei Bai informed them.

"And they are free to stay with him," Alistair groaned in Mandarin, his voice straining only a little less than his limbs. *"But they are just as free to change their minds and hire us, or anyone else."*

"You can find us at the top of the Great Hill," Taribo proclaimed, his smile at Caleb a taunt. "We would be delighted to do business with you."

Alistair and Caleb finally separated with a last, mutual push. They breathed with great heaves of their chests.

"Go now," ordered the half-Persian.

"You need to get used to the new paradigm," said Alistair, noting with approval that his own breathing calmed before Caleb's. Picking up the spear he dropped, he walked away. "These men are free, and so are we. You don't give orders anymore."

"I do give orders, and I notice you are following them," Caleb shot back at their receding forms, as close as they had seen him to an outburst.

"You could tell us to keep breathing and we would do it, but not because of your command," Taribo, mirthful, called back.

When they reached the slope of the hills, the elevation provided them with an opportunity to look over the land, and to the southeast they noticed a crowd gathered nearly a mile distant. It was difficult to say what they were about, but most were packed together in the shape of a crescent, facing the same thing, whatever it was, while a few strays wandered about, now rejoining the crowd, now separating again. Many were on their knees or flat on the ground, and more than a couple were passionately gesticulating.

By common, unspoken consent, Alistair and Taribo, having paused to observe, shared a glance and changed course. By the time they reached the throng, it was half again as large as when they spotted it. The packed bodies still described a crescent with all sightlines converging on a tree. A buzz of conversation permeated the air. It was a subdued hum, or perhaps a restrained one, holding in check a certain excitement that revealed itself in nervous twitters, suppressed shivers, tense gestures accompanying pronouncements delivered with wide-open, fervent eyes. Those not in the crowd were generally prostrate on the ground, faces down and spread eagled in the preferred Gaian position of absolute submission to Nature. Their lips moved in silent prayer, their exhalations occasionally blowing dirt or grass out to the side, and their eyes were closed. They reacted to nothing and no one while they concentrated on the object of their worship.

"Alistair!" called a man whom Alistair vaguely recognized as one of his subscribers. "It's a sign!" he proclaimed, his eyes lighting up. He pointed at the tree.

Without replying, Alistair strode up to the crowd and, Taribo at his side, inserted himself into the mass of bodies, eventually working his way to the front. Three men stood separate, out in front near a tree which, as far as he could tell, displayed no quality that should be responsible for such intense interest. One was the Beseecher, and he was sitting in his usual position, a small pile of fruit at his side. The second was the Druid, the fingers of his right hand, with their long, gnarled nails, clutching a staff. His beard flapped idly in the soft breeze and he turned his bald pate from side to side, scanning the crowd with an air of expectance and approval while water from the drizzle trickled down his hairless dome. The third and last man, though Alistair could not clearly see his face due to his prostrated position on the earth, he knew was Clyde Oliver Jones.

"Why are we staring at the tree?" whispered Taribo to a man at his side.

The man's roughened, bass voice came as if rumbling up from the depths of the earth, full of awe and respect. "Gaia has shown herself."

Alistair could see no sign of Gaia. Clyde, apparently not entirely oblivious to his surroundings, shifted and caught sight of Alistair and Taribo. For the briefest of instants, a span of time so vanishingly small that Alistair could not with complete confidence declare it happened at all, Clyde blanched. Or maybe he just had a facial tic. Whatever it was, if it was anything at all, it was gone almost as soon as it appeared, engulfed by the warm, beatific smile that lit his face from chin to forehead as he rose from the ground to come greet the two new arrivals.

"Alistair! Taribo!" he exclaimed in a half whisper, and several men nearby, seeing the welcome they received from such a figure as Clyde, gave to the two recipients of the warm greeting respectful nods. "It's a blessing you are here."

"Good to see you too," Alistair managed to reply.

"Gaia has revealed herself here, as he said. This is holy ground."

"Holy ground," the man with the bass voice reverently repeated, nodding in satisfaction.

Alistair pursed his lips, as if fighting back a belch. "Revealed herself how?"

Clyde turned and, with sublimely gentle smoothness, swept his hand along until it was pointing at the tree. "In the bark of the tree."

Alistair stepped forward to get a better look. "Where?"

One from the crowd drew near to the tree and, reverently stopping short so he did not come in contact, gingerly pointed a finger at a place in the bark about three feet from the ground. Alistair's skeptical look prompted a clarification from Clyde.

"It is the face of Gaia," he said with the smooth falsetto of one who wishes to sound sublime.

Tilting his head to the left and furrowing his brow, Alistair studied the bark's pattern. Then he tilted his head to the right. Then back to the left. Having looked at it from every position save for that of a handstand, he decided, *It looks like a caterpillar humping a goat.*

Seeing the result of Alistair's thoughts displayed on his face, Clyde himself approached the tree to point out features to him. "The eyes...the nose...the chin...the whole circular swirl here is the face."

"OK. I think she has a gigantic tumor growing on her forehead."

At this pronouncement there were mutters of disapproval from the crowd. With a nervous laugh Clyde went to Alistair and laid both hands on his shoulders.

"Alistair, it's an image rendered in bark. The bark is there, but focusing on it is like looking at swirls of paint from close up, rather than the image the swirls form."

"OK."

Clyde smiled and dropped his hands to his sides. "This is holy ground, mate," he said with an expectant look. "Gaia has shown her face to us."

"It's been positively identified as Gaia, then?"

Clyde's eyes widened and he gritted his teeth. Placing his hands on Alistair's thick arms, he guided the Aldran away from the crowd, leaving behind some disgruntled muttering and a few withering looks. Taribo trailed behind them, though his attention was riveted on the image in the bark and he fingered one of his dreadlocks in his left hand.

"Alistair, this is a sacred place and time for Gaians. Please be respectful. For us."

"I merely asked if it had been positively identified as Gaia."

Clyde gave Alistair a look with a tilted head, as if he expected him to hear the same naïveté in the question that he did.

"In all seriousness. How do you know it's not Genevieve?"

"Who's Genevieve?"

"Exactly. Are you sure it isn't random swirls of bark that happened to form themselves in a shape your brain interpreted as Gaia, a woman you have never seen?"

"Gaia is more than a woman," said Clyde, and he placed a hand on Alistair's chest where his heart was. "If you listen to your heart, she will speak to you, and that will be all the signature and identification you need."

Alistair shrugged in response. "My heart pumps blood." Before Clyde could raise a protest, he continued, "I'm glad you found some bark to make you happy, Clyde. I know how long you've been a Gaian and have been looking for something like this." Clyde's face assumed an impenetrable impassivity. "Would you like me to register it for you?"

"This is sacred land, designated so by Gaia's manifest wishes. I would not presume to own it."

"Was it you who discovered the...image?"

"It was me."

"You will be its caretaker?"

Clyde considered the question. "I will, I think."

"Would you like me to register that for you?"

"I suppose we can do that. Yeah." Clyde smiled and Alistair managed a fleeting one of his own.

"Stop by my offices any time you like."

"I'll think about it."

Nodding, Alistair said, "Well...Taribo and I are going to head back now."

"Actually, Alistair, I think I am going to stay here for a bit."

This declaration surprised Alistair, but he shrugged his shoulders and said, "Suit yourself. Just remember I need you on the west coast this evening."

"I remember."

"That's a five mile walk from here. Over the hills...we're talking three hours."

"I have plenty of time. I will be there."

"Alright then." With another nod goodbye, he grabbed his spear and walked away, heading for his camp.

❧⁓❧

"There are three witnesses who have sworn the mallet belongs to Mr. Djorovich," said Santiago. "They identified it by the notch on the handle. Furthermore, Mr. Djorovich has testified he has not transferred title of the property to anyone. That is sufficient for this arbiter to declare that the mallet belongs to Mr. Djorovich and must be returned to him."

The Oriental man across from Santiago frowned, drawing his eyebrows down over the tops of his sockets and gripping the wooden table with his hands, causing them to go livid. "I paid with a length of rope for the mallet. That makes it mine."

Giselle finished scribbling on her parchment and waited for the next bit of information.

"Mr. Zhou, please let me explain," said Santiago with a reasonable tone. "The question here is who holds the title to this bit of property. Mr. Djorovich, backed by three witnesses, claims his hammer disappeared a few days ago. You turn up with it, but claim it was sold to you by one Zachary Fielder. Zachary either stole the hammer from Mr. Djorovich or found it lying somewhere and improperly took possession of it. Unless Mr. Fielder can demonstrate he rightfully acquired title to the hammer, the hammer is not his. Therefore, not possessing its title, he cannot have transferred it to you. What Mr. Fielder did was steal your money. This is something my agency can help you with, but it is no reason not to return Mr. Djorovich's property to him."

"But I'm out my rope!"

"Mr. Zhou, there has been a theft. Someone is going to be out something until the thief is found and made to compensate his victims. Either Mr. Djorovich is out a hammer, or you are out a length of rope. Since Mr. Djorovich is the title holder of the hammer, it is correct to return his property to him, unless you two can come to an exchange agreement."

"I'm not paying for this twice!"

"Then we are going to insist you return it to Mr. Djorovich. As you are a subscriber to AS&A, we will make sure we find Mr. Fielder and he will compensate you for your loss. But since you have never acquired proper title to this hammer, you must return it to its owner. When you purchased the hammer without verifying who owned it, you took a risk. This time, it was a bad risk, but rest assured you will be compensated by Mr. Fielder for the trouble he caused you."

Giselle was scratching at the parchment as rapidly as she could move her makeshift pencil. Mr. Zhou was still glaring, but was partially mollified by Santiago's assurances. With a frown that was not entirely skeptical, he produced the mallet in question from a sack at his feet and gave it to Mr. Djorovich.

"Our agents will track down Mr. Fielder immediately," Santiago assured him.

Alistair arrived in time to see the result of the meeting, and Mr. Zhou extended to him his hand as he was walking out.

"I hope you can find Zachary soon," said the recent defendant.

"All efforts will be made."

Mr. Zhou nodded and turned to go, but then changed his mind and hesitated on the top of the four steps leading outside.

"On Earth the police do not even bother to investigate crimes like this. The small ones. The ones they do investigate can take months or years."

"And you still don't get your restitution until you pursue a separate civil suit," said Alistair. "Meanwhile you pay for the criminal's stay in prison."

Mr. Zhou nodded. "This is good, Alistair. This is very good." With that pronouncement, he completed his exit.

No sooner was he gone than Giselle placed herself directly in front of Alistair with a thoughtful expression on her face.

"What sort of statute of limitations is there for crimes?" she asked.

"None."

"None?"

"What is the point of a statute of limitations? If someone commits a crime against you and goes a long time without paying for it, that is a reason for them to pay more, not less. In reality a statute of limitations is just a way for a government to cut back on their responsibilities. If a case goes long enough without being solved, the government just forgets about it."

"And what about double jeopardy?"

"A crime is a crime, regardless of whether or not a previous court came to the wrong determination. With a government I suppose I can see the point. It prevents some prosecutor from hounding you from court to court until he gets the verdict he is looking for. But in our system we have to please our customers or lose their business; we have no incentive to retry a case unless there is good reason to believe the wrong verdict was passed the first time. No one would trust us if we behaved unscrupulously, and the other security firms wouldn't allow their customers to be so treated, and that's exactly where people would go: to other security firms."

Giselle responded only with a nod and a squint of her eyes as she considered what Alistair said.

"Why do you ask?"

"Just…curious is all."

The Arcabelian beauty, born before Alistair's grandparents, moved away with her sheaf of parchments. He caught himself watching the outline of her butt underneath the animal skin she wore, somewhere between loin-cloth and skirt. He blinked once to break the trance and turned his attention to Santiago, who was tearing into some bread and cheese where he delivered his verdict moments before. Taking a seat, Alistair gave him a nod promptly acknowledged with a like nod. It was ample communication for them: more praise and encouragement than Santiago required, more thanks than Alistair needed in return.

"We need to insure our customers," said the Argentinean.

"That's a difficult proposition…" Alistair began as he rubbed at his forehead.

In response, Santiago reached down into a small bag at his waist and tossed its contents onto the table. The metallic disks, thin and no larger than a man's eye, clanked together.

"Darion has minted coins from iron," Santiago said. "You can bet this currency is going to spread…at least until someone finds gold or silver. We'll have prices and that means insurance is less of a headache. We need to insure people."

Alistair's eyes were riveted on the handful of coins, and a smile of delight threatened to sprout on his lips. "Money," he said simply, with relief.

"Mr. Zhou could have been insured, which means he could have walked out of here already compensated for the theft," Santiago explained and tossed a chunk of cheese into his mouth. "We could then go after Zachary ourselves. Those men who claimed the shaft…they could take out insurance against another claimant coming for his property. We could—"

"We can do all sorts of things. I know, Santi. It's a great idea and we're going to do it. But we can't just jump into it. We want to make sure we offer the proper terms. Without actuarial tables, that will be difficult. We also need to see the exchange rates these coins have against everything else. It's one thing to have coins; it's another to establish prices."

"The one follows the other. As soon as possible we need to offer insurance."

"We will."

Suddenly, the earth shook.

Accompanied by a rumble, it rattled everything, from Alistair's body to the floor beneath him. Alistair rattled down while the floor rattled up while the table rattled sideways, and everything crashed together dozens of times in the space of a few seconds. One moment, he was seated across from Santiago and the next he was staring up at the ceiling. Shaking his head to clear it, he fumbled at the stools around him when the rumbling stopped. He pulled himself up and, as his eyes rose above the surface of the table, saw Santiago was doing the same.

"What the hell—?"

"Earthquake," Santiago said and, without fuss, brushed off breadcrumbs and took his seat again. He bent over to retrieve the coins.

Taking his own seat at the table, Alistair asked, "How often does it happen?"

"Once or twice a year," he said with his head below the table top. He popped back up and deposited the coins on it. "They are not usually too bad. I suppose I would recommend against building over a few stories."

"We're near a fault line?"

"Maybe. We're also near a gas giant."

"Ah…" Alistair said. "Like Io."

"The tidal forces from Srillium can't be too large or the ocean tides would be enormous. Maybe it's just a fault line, or maybe Srillium contributes to it. Just like Jupiter does to Io."

"Any other geological or climatological occurrences I need to know about?"

Santiago thought a moment. "We have one or two solar eclipses every year. They last for a few days."

Alistair nodded while he considered the new information. "Speaking of insurance…"

"Speaking of insurance?"

"That sort of thing is good to know."

66

A faraway drone found Alistair's ears and inserted itself there, like a tiny, incessant drill that eventually lifted him out of slumber. His mind incorporated the noise into his dream, and when he finally passed through the layers of unconsciousness to awareness, it remained as the dream dissipated. Lying on his side, he opened his eyes to the dim pre-dawn light finding its way through the slots in the wall of the communal bedroom. Someone's foot was inches from his face, the hairy leg it was connected to disappearing under a thin blanket. Gregory had spent the night elsewhere and Miklos was relegated to a separate building, but Taribo and Ryan were there, as was Santiago, whom, for the first time he could remember, Alistair preceded in rising. He rolled onto his back and sat up, focusing his attention on the whirring in the distance.

With a great yawn, he rose and, less nimbly than he might, stumbled to the staircase and went down to the lower level, his plodding steps making the boards creak but not waking anyone. The air was warm and still and nothing moved save him and a thin wisp of smoke that yet rose from the ashes of the previous evening's fire. Srillium still dominated the western horizon, its ruddy swirls standing out amid the somber grays of the early morning but its power to gently illuminate vastly diluted now that the vanguard light of the sun had arrived.

He filled a cup with water and sipped from it as he strolled around the grounds, listening to the drone and scanning the sky. The damp grass, beaten down by the many feet that roamed over it, was soft under his bare soles. Shirtless and wearing only what amounted to a loincloth, he turned in circles, still perplexed at what might be making the noise, waiting for something to emerge.

Downing the rest of his water, he went back to the basin and tossed the cup next to it. He then went to the food stores underneath the hut and produced another loaf of hard bread, wrapped tightly in dried leaves and growing mold on top. The cheese he found was no less moldy, and he spent a few minutes scraping it off before he set the victuals on the table and took his seat on a stool to have his breakfast. His pallet was not pleased by the meal, but his stomach was at least satisfied.

Cotton seeds, he thought with disgust as his teeth broke the hard bread into crumbly bits. *I should have told Henry to bring me garlic. And oregano. And pepper. And sage. And thyme.* He accompanied the thoughts with a sigh, and he wondered for a moment what Henry was up to. And how old he was.

When he finally spotted a black speck in the sky to the west, transiting across the face of Srillium, he came to his feet. It was a distant speck, miles to the west, flying above the ocean, so that even his vision could detect no details, but there was no doubt it was a flying craft, was likely the progenitor of the noise, and was something surely only the Gaians could be in possession of.

In no more time than it takes an eye to blink, he darted for the stairs and, stomping like a bull, bounded up until he reached the lookout tower. As he passed through the second story he called out, "The Gaians are here!" and Ryan, Taribo and Santiago, jolted awake, started. Once up in the lookout tower, he relocated the speck. The sky was a shade or two lighter than when he had risen, but he discerned no more details. As he watched, the speck finished a transit across Srillium, pulling farther south and framed now by the dark blue sky, almost disappearing in it. Then it described an arc in the heavens until it turned ninety degrees and headed east, towards the island.

The stairs creaked beneath him as someone from below climbed up. It proved to be Santiago, who stood next to him as he knelt on the bench. His face was a mottled red and white, the skin branded by the folds of the blanket he had lain on, and his hair was a twisted mess on the right side of his head.

"What's that noise?"

Pointing at the black dot in the sky, Alistair replied, "The Gaians."

Santiago considered the aircraft. "Why is it making noise? It needs a new CSS." He was referring to the countercyclical sound suppressor that muffled engine noise.

"We've been found," said Alistair. He spoke with the grim acceptance of a condemned man.

The craft accelerated and headed almost directly towards their camp, its drone growing louder every second. Taribo and Wellesley were on their feet one floor below, peering up the stairs and waiting for some kind of explanation. Outside, faces were popping out of doorways and scanning the sky. For a moment, Alistair took it all in, then raised his eyebrows once in an expression of resignation, said, "Well," but attached no conclusion to it, and turned to descend the stairs.

"Where are you going?" asked Santiago as Alistair's head sank below the floor of the tower.

"There's work to do. A hovercraft in the sky doesn't change that. Nothing we can do about it."

"Shouldn't we prepare our defenses?" asked Ryan as Alistair went by the second floor.

"Preparing our defenses consists of hefting a spear or placing an arrow on a bow string. If that craft is armed it would have about the same effect as an ant attacking an elephant."

The last part faded in volume as he reached the bottom of the stairs and left the hut. Men and women were coming outside to gawk. Alistair spied Layla and Gregory leave the women's lodge together, their hair mussed but their eyes not so full of sleep that the alarm did not show through. Gregory walked with a protective arm over Layla's shoulder as he looked into the brightening sky. In contrast to the others milling about the common area, Alistair moved like he had a destination. He grabbed an available ax and chopped at a recently felled tree on the outskirts of the camp. A few looked at him questioningly, surprised by the casualness of his behavior, but he took no notice.

As the craft continued to do loops over and around the island, the novelty wore off and the onlookers came to be convinced by Alistair's way of thinking. Though conversation was continuous and glances towards the sky abundant, the others eventually realized the flight over their home did not signify a holiday from the demands of the human body. One by one they set about working towards those ends, beginning with breakfast. This further depletion of the dwindling food stores was followed by the day's labor. A couple of men came to work with Alistair to make fuel for future fires. By this time he was covered in a sheen of sweat, and before long his two companions were in a similar state and the three of them had the tree broken down into manageable logs.

Alistair gently ran his thumb over the edge of the axe and discovered it had become quite blunt. A quick check of the other two axes led him to the same conclusion. He hoisted the tools in his arms and, carrying them to the hut, dumped them on the ground at the foot of the steps. The sound of them falling caught Giselle's attention as she sat scribbling at the table.

"Can you see that these get sharpened?"

"Will do."

At that moment the drone from the hovercraft changed in pitch as it swerved and, slowing to a near stop, came to float directly above them. A shiny silvery color, it was the shape of a triangle with rounded edges and had no discernible features. Alistair gave it a dark look and Giselle rose from the table and came to join him at the bottom of the steps. The engine of the craft was loud enough that Giselle needed to raise her voice to be heard over its hum.

"Why doesn't it do something?"

"It's probably just scouting. We can expect trouble soon. Have you seen the Gaians before?"

Giselle nodded. "They sent an emissary to meet with Issicroy a couple times a year. And once I got to watch them destroy a ranch someone built. You see them flying around every so often."

"You and I will have to talk, then. I'll need to know what you know."

"I don't know much."

"Every little bit helps."

As he left, heading for the path down to the lake, the hovercraft moved away, not yet leaving the island but apparently finished observing their camp. By the time he made it to the bottom, it was somewhere over the north coast and heading towards the mainland. *A successful defense will determine whether this little experiment of ours can work or not,* he thought as he waded into the cool water. When he made it to a depth that brought the water up to his waste, he spread his arms wide, fell backwards, and allowed the lake to give him a quick bath.

67

The capacious bay between the two southern peninsulas held four islands, none larger than a square mile, clustering together near the tip of the western peninsula. The water was shallow, consisting of one large sand bar of which the islands themselves were elevated extensions with a layer of soil and vegetation on top. Though a couple islands were as much as two miles off the coast of the peninsula, a tall man could, on a still day, wade out to them and never get his chest wet.

The four islands had a couple dozen men working on them, breaking up soil with their crude hoes, turning the land into a moist, muddy brown. Already, the largest of the islands was entirely worked over and a handful of men were planting seeds there.

Wellesley waded out to the largest. He reached the west beach and trudged through the sand, passing a couple rafts and, after cresting a small slope marking the edge of the beach, a copse of trees until he was given a view of the interior. There were few trees and the ground was flat so he could see clear to the other side. Skirting the edge of the plowed land, he came to a narrow path of packed earth running through the softer soil and took this to another stand of trees near the middle of the island. Two men were resting in the shade there while the three continued walking the paths, reaching into sacks at their waists and tossing seed into the soil. The two resting men were leaning against a wooden tub surrounded by wooden crates, many of which had been opened, emptied and tossed to the side.

As Wellesley approached, one of the two rose to his feet. His curly hair was black with a few strands of gray, like his beard. He was dirty from his labors, with dirt and dust caked on his face and darker soil packed under his fingernails, but his eyes shone with a merry glint and his rough lips stretched into a smile as Wellesley drew near.

"How can we help you?"

"I've been sent for Darion Chesterton."

"You found him. Alistair send you?"

"That's right."

Ryan was standing face to face with Darion now, and the latter grabbed a wooden ladle from the edge of the tub and dipped it into the water it contained. He passed it to Wellesley who eagerly drained the contents, smacking his lips when he was done.

"Take as much as you like," Darion offered, and Ryan spooned a few more loads into his mouth. The water was warm, but that mattered little to a thirsty man in clothes soaked with salt water and wet moccasins covered in sand and dirt. Between the ladles of water and the evening breeze sweeping over the island, he started to feel a little refreshed. The grass around the copse of trees swayed and rustled in the wind.

"Did you see the hovercraft?" Ryan asked, setting the ladle down and turning back to Darion.

"Yeah, we seen it," said the other man who was still sitting on the ground, chewing on the end of a long blade of grass. "Gaians."

"Gaians," agreed Ryan.

"Is that what brings you here?" asked Darion.

"Alistair told me to tell you not to build any buildings. Keep planting but don't build anything likely to get blown up soon."

"And what is Alistair planning?"

"He's having a meeting tonight. Probably going on right now." Ryan added with a trace of bitterness, "I guess I wasn't needed."

"We're just planting wheat and corn here, along with a little cotton Alistair smuggled." Darion nodded to a stake planted in the ground. "All the cotton on the moon is in that soil right there. The other islands, one is going to be an apple and orange orchard. The other two will have tomatoes, potatoes, barley, wheat, corn, soy…you name it. Alistair traded for the seeds. He's going to own the islands, we get the proceeds of the first harvest."

"Sounds like a good deal."

"Yes. Normally, I'd be paying these workers but…there's not enough capital on the island to start up a proper business. Not of this size. So the workers are doubling as investors. They're giving up their wages now in exchange for a bigger share later on."

Shaking his head, Ryan cut in, "Alistair's always talking about capital, too." He said it with a dismissive tone meant to end the discussion. "I'm going to sleep here tonight and go back tomorrow."

"You can sleep right under the trees with us."

Darion's companion came to his feet, spitting out the grass in his teeth, and said, "I've got a little more planting I can do before it gets dark."

Ryan took out some bread and strips of dried meat, carefully wrapped in cloth, from the pouch he wore at his waist. As Darion walked away, Ryan stopped him with a question.

"I remember when you got arrested in Arcarius," he said, and Darion turned an inquisitive look on him. "What were you guilty of?"

A smile played at the corners of Darion's mouth. "Same thing I'm doing now."

Ryan frowned at the answer but Darion said nothing more, with a wink leaving Wellesley alone with his meal of stale bread and meat.

There was a storm brewing in the north, where thick, black clouds brought a premature darkness to the land. Over Odin's Island the sky was partly covered with unthreatening, fluffy cumulus clouds whose western edges were colored rose and orange by the spectacular sunset. In contrast, the angry clouds to the north, black as coal, were occasionally outlined by the silver flash of a lightning bolt distant enough that its attendant thunder, when it finally arrived, came as a grumbling so faint that a trace of breeze could almost cover it. A ring of torches, attached to poles eight feet high, were set in the center of camp, spacious enough that the two-score or so settlers of the Great Hill could comfortably fit inside, along with a handful of others. Though the sun still hung low in the sky, the torches were lit, the flickering flames ready to hold back the tide of darkness soon to drown the land. Santiago sat on a chair in the middle, having been asked by Alistair to conduct the meeting. Alistair, Taribo, Miklos, Gregory, Layla and Giselle sat around Santiago, and around them the other attendees were gathered, some sitting on the ground, others standing, arms folded and with grim expressions. Alistair, looking at Gregory and Layla, who were holding hands and sitting with the nearness and comfort of lovers, turned his attention to Santiago when the Argentinean cleared his throat.

"We have to prepare to defend ourselves," he declared.

There were several earnest nods while they waited for Santiago to continue.

"It is certain the Gaians will come and demolish what we've built."

"What happens if they come?" asked Gregory.

"They knock down every structure they find, and there is little we can do about it."

"No, exactly how do they do it? If we want to make plans we need to know what we are facing."

"I built a shed once," offered a man of African descent. "For my tools. Tried to disguise it, hide it next to some trees but they found it. They came on one of those hovercraft and blasted it with some…I don't know. Some weapon."

"Describe the weapon," said Santiago.

"It was…almost like a spotlight. There was a sudden pressure…and it hummed. Then the wood of the shed just exploded like a grenade hit it. But there wasn't no fire. Nothing but an exploded shed. Then they left."

"And they didn't harm you?" asked Greg.

The man shook his head. "No. They don't if you don't attack them. I heard about one guy attacked them and they fried him right where he stood. But they don't give you no punishment for breaking the rules, they just destroy your building."

"It will be the same thing here," said Giselle. "If we don't resist, they won't harm us."

"But they'll control us," mumbled Alistair, staring at the ground, his forearms resting on his knees. Only a few heads in his vicinity turned to acknowledge the comment; the rest did not hear it.

"That is the decision we are here to make," said Santiago.

A lively discussion began. Many were too busy talking to worry about listening, simply casting their opinions out like fishermen in the hopes that someone would latch on and listen. Many claimed to prefer to fight, but a gentle reminder of the Gaian technological superiority never failed to subdue, if not entirely defeat, their courage. Some suggested letting the Gaians have their way and starting over until it was pointed out that the island would be closely monitored from then on. Every possible idea in between was proffered and vetted, and the discussion moved like a raft on a stormy sea: always kinetic, but along no path, with no locomotion other than what the wind and waves chanced to provide.

A gust of wind swept through the camp and the flames from the torches, flickering now horizontally, hissed and sputtered.

"This island cannot support the thousands who moved here," Alistair said, almost mumbling and still staring at the ground. Gregory and Giselle heard him, and a couple others, and they turned their attention to him. "Not without the improvements we've begun to make. Our stores are almost out and a few crops have only just sprouted." A widening circle of silence fell over the group, as more and more men and women were drawn to hear what was softly said. "We came to this island to escape the fighting and starvation of the mainland." Almost imperceptibly, the crowd pressed in on Alistair, those on the outside straining hard to hear what he said. "I don't see the point in living when life is nothing but a desperate struggle to feed yourself with no hope that hard work and saving might make your life better tomorrow. I'd rather not die, but I am not going to sit still and let the Gaians destroy what is mine. However many they send, there are ways to deal with an opponent with a technological advantage, especially a complacent one, who thinks we won't raise a hand against him."

The crowd was silent when Alistair stopped speaking.

"Attacking the Gaians is foolhardy," Gregory finally said. "Fighting of any kind is foolhardy, as much for the winner as the loser. We are where we are, and I think we have to accept that."

The debate was taken up once again. Alistair said no more, but he had said enough, and his speech, so diffidently delivered, carried enough weight to determine the course of things. A very few minutes later, those in favor of passivity were few in number.

As there would doubtless be little time before the Gaians came for them, a coordinated defense of the island was impossible. Santiago charged them to spread the word they intended to fight, and everyone could contribute to the best of their abilities should they choose. Alistair promised nothing other than to resist, but underneath every conversation was an implicit confidence that the Aldran and his men would find a way if there was a way to be found, and most of those at the meeting were sure to shake Alistair's hand, or give him a friendly squeeze or pat on the shoulder before they left.

Night arrived, interrupted only by the glow of torches and the white flashes of light to the north. The storm clouds were camouflaged now against the obsidian sky, their outlines revealed only for brief instants. The breeze became a wind and dropped several degrees in temperature. Gregory, Giselle, Layla, Santiago, Taribo and Alistair were all that remained of the crowd, and they stared to the north at the ominous rumblings there, their clothes and hair tossed about in the streaming air. Layla shivered once and hugged herself, and Gregory was immediately at her side to hug her to him. The sky above was immaculately black, and above the steady whoosh of wind, thunder rumbled low in their ears.

"We have done a terrible thing," said Santiago as he stood next to Alistair.

Alistair did not speak but turned an inquisitive look on his companion.

"We have dared to hope."

"I still haven't stopped."

"Neither have any of these," said the Argentinean, sweeping his arm to indicate the camp, or perhaps the entire island.

"Should they?"

Turning to leave him, Santiago called back, "This is a dead man's planet, Alistair. I knew that when I came…you know it now even if you won't admit it. Man is what he is, and fine sentiments won't change that." He walked away and disappeared into the darkness of their hut.

Alistair felt a strong urge to shout back, but he could think of nothing suitable to say. Instead, he grimaced as the wind tore at him. Taribo, passing by his boss, slapped him on the back and, shouting over the wind and thunder, said, "Come, Alistair. I will help you put out the torches."

He lingered a moment longer, staring at where Santiago disappeared into the hut, surprised his words bothered him so. Finally, he moved to help with the torches. From above, another rumble of thunder came to their ears, and they felt the first few drops of rain sprinkle down.

68

Through the entire night the sky emptied its discontent on the island, flashing lightning and growling thunder. The rain abated for a time in the earliest hours of morning, when the sun cast a touch of gray on the night's ebony, but a second wave of storms came with terrific fury, winds ripping at trees and houses, lightning striking like the fangs of a serpent. It was manifestly impossible under such conditions for a human being to fall asleep. In every slit and crack dripped water, now in droplets, now in streams. The imperfectly built hut that housed Alistair and his men allowed enough wind and water through that the bedroom was nearly converted into its own miniature hurricane.

The poor soaked men huddled together, wrapped from head to toe in soggy blankets, sitting against the walls of the second floor, or perhaps lying on their side, clutching at the covers to keep them tight around their bodies. Occasionally they would drift off, but always were brought back to wakefulness, whether by a blast of thunder, a gust of wind, or the unpleasant conditions in general. When morning came with the abatement of rain, a couple hours of miserable sleep were had, but as the rain grew in intensity once again, they decided that, the morning light having arrived, they might as well get up.

Alistair found himself alone in the lookout tower, trying to peer through the sheets of grayish rain, his face a perfect reflection of his bad humor. His breakfast was a chunk of foul smelling cheese and an onion with sprouted tubers, both drenched before he could bring them to his mouth. In such a rainfall, no work could be performed, so he remained in the tower, abandoning himself to the cause of his discomfort.

It was not long before he spied lights on the ocean.

With the nearly impenetrable rain, his view of the sea was such that he only spied the lights, not the craft itself as it drew near to the north shore. The lights moved at a high speed until slowing down near the beach. The craft now visible near the shore, it idled for a few moments, perhaps scanning the area, and Alistair, tense, upright and alert now, hollered that the Gaians had returned. He was not sure his call was heard over the rain and was about to shout again when he felt the shakes announcing the presence of a body on the stairs beneath. A moment later Taribo was at his side with Santiago only two steps behind.

"Where?" asked Taribo loud enough to overcome the elements.

Alistair responded by extending his arm and forefinger.

"I see it," said Santiago, taking up position on Alistair's left side.

"Do you see that!?" Alistair exclaimed, his calm abruptly shattered. "Do you see it!"

"You mean besides the lights?" asked Santiago, and both he and Taribo squinted hard into the rain, using a hand like an umbrella to shield their eyes.

"The white figure? Don't you see it?"

From the craft, a blur even to Alistair, a white smudge appeared and hopped over the side of the ship and into the water. It waded to shore, traversed the beach, and disappeared a few seconds later into the foliage of the northern forest. The blue lights dimmed, almost as if the ship were snoozing.

"A dreadbot," Alistair said, and in his skin he felt a chill for which the rain was not responsible.

"I didn't see anything," said Santiago.

"You have the eyes of an eagle, my friend," declared Taribo. "Was it only one dreadbot?"

"That's all I saw."

"I've never seen a dreadbot," Santiago said.

"I've only fought *with* them," Taribo said.

Alistair's thoughts were many hundreds of trillions of miles away, on his homeworld and the last few hours he spent there. "No man is a match for a dreadbot. No fifty men are a match for a dreadbot."

Their optimism, a specious optimism, the artificial byproduct of determination, was swept away and their courage wilted. They stared to the north with a sense of profound helplessness. It was Taribo who gave voice to the idea that occurred to all of them.

"We don't have to resist."

Though it was Taribo who said it, Alistair turned his gaze on Santiago when he replied. "If we don't resist, it means we have given up hope and submitted." He let his stare linger for a moment longer on the Argentinean before he went down the stairs to the bottom floor.

A couple dozen men and women congregated at the foot of the stairs.

"Get the weapons," Alistair ordered and pushed through the crowd to the storage spaces outside.

Before he grabbed the first weapon, there were men at his side, opening the doors and pulling out the various mallets, axes, spears, maces and daggers they had accumulated. Alistair grabbed for himself a spear, two daggers, and a wicked looking axe with a granite head a normal man would hesitate to try to lift. The daggers, rare and made from iron, he placed on each hip. The axe he slung from his back with a leather sheath made for it, and the spear he held in his hand. When he was finished with his armament, he looked up and saw staring back at him the dozens of similarly armed men, their jaws set and gazes hard.

He forced the words out of his mouth. "I only need a few men for what I'm going to do. A large group is too many. The rest of you can do what you want, but you will not defeat a dreadbot with axes and spears." When he pronounced the word dreadbot, a murmur swept through the crowd. "From what I understand, resistance is not looked upon kindly. Make your own choices."

"If you can't defeat a dreadbot with axes and spears…"

"What are you doing?"

"I'm not going after the dreadbot. Not yet." The declaration had an invigorating effect on the despondent and desperate people as they guessed what Alistair was after. The murmur in the crowd became more energized, more optimistic. "Taribo, Santiago, Miklos…are you with me?"

"Armed and ready," said Taribo with an exuberant grin, and he slapped his muscular chest with the shaft of his spear. Santiago was armed too but did not answer the entreaty, instead merely watching Alistair without expression. Miklos, hammer in hand, managed a nod, the usual bored expression on his face gone, replaced by something Alistair recognized well from his time on Kaldis: the creeping fear that soldiers try to quell in the presence of their comrades but which does not recede until the adrenaline of battle overtakes it. Alistair had the same insistent feeling in the pit of his stomach.

He swallowed once to lubricate his vocal chords. "Then let's go."

As the men strode out of camp, the shouted encouragement of the others accompanied them.

৵৹

A swimmer in the ocean goes with an awareness of danger. Beneath him there is a vast and deep realm from which a creature may swim to pluck him from the surface and drag him to the depths. He feels an ever-present tingle in the toes that scrape at the edge of the deep and dark waters. This same feeling was what Alistair and his men felt as they went north in the downpour, moving from woods to woods, glade to glade and hill to hill. At any moment, they knew, a featureless figure in pure white could step out from behind a tree, or rise up from a clump of tall grass, or emerge from the bottom of a ravine.

Without any direction, they fell into a diamond formation, with Alistair at the front, Taribo and Miklos in the middle, and Santiago at the rear. In setting the pace, Alistair settled for a compromise between his urge to reach the hovercraft and his need to avoid the dreadbot. They saw no one, coming across nothing more than two plowed fields, each partially ringed by flat stones stacked two high. There was a small house at the edge of one of the fields, in truth more of a shed, dilapidated from the moment it was born. When Santiago knocked to advise the occupants of the predicament, there was no response.

After traveling under the pelting raindrops, the party entered the relative protection of the northern forest. The roar of the rainfall changed tune, falling now on the leaves above them, producing a less immediate, less insistent sound, giving them a feeling of some space. They crossed several trails Alistair disdained to follow, preferring to continue due north. A mile later they emerged from the soggy ground of the forest onto the edge of the beach, though their view of the sea was blocked by tall dunes. Alistair paused, and his three companions gathered around him.

"Shall I have a look?" offered Taribo from underneath the canopy of leaves, a cascade of water a couple feet in front of him.

Alistair shook his head. "Stay here."

Leaving the verdant umbrella, he stepped into the downpour and, dropping to all fours, clambered up the side of a sand dune, perhaps ten feet in height, finally dropping down to his belly when he reached the top. After a moment spent scanning, he signaled with a wave that they were to follow. When all four were lying on the summit and the ocean, with its furious waves and jagged white caps, was visible, Alistair pointed to the west. There, not half a mile away, was the unmoving silver form of the hovercraft, perhaps sixty yards from the shore, its blue lights dimmed.

"You brought us almost right to it," commented Taribo. The West African coughed, having inhaled some of the rain as it splashed on the sand only inches from his face.

"Do you think it is..." Santiago struggled to find the right word, "...alerted to our presence? Is it on guard?"

"If it is, this is going to be a very short operation," said Alistair.

"You have a plan, right?" prompted Miklos.

"We're going to swim out a ways and circle around behind it. If they have a computer system monitoring the area it won't matter where we come from, but if they don't, they'll probably be facing the island. We'll sneak on board…" He did not feel the need to finish the rest.

"They are complacent," said Taribo with confidence. "They have settled in for a long wait. They surveyed the island, they know how big it is, they know how many live here… They have come ready to spend three or four days. They're probably watching threedies right now."

"Gaians aren't supposed to watch threedies," said Miklos.

"They're not supposed to operate hovercrafts either," Alistair pointed out. "These are not orthodox Gaians."

"I don't see any windows," said Santiago, anxious to get back to the task at hand. "If they can't see us, we can save a lot of time by just walking up to it."

"If they made it with vidrilium we won't be able to tell if they have windows or not," said Taribo.

"When we circle around," said Alistair, "don't let anything more than your heads come above water. And no chatter."

He got to his feet and, crouched over, traversed the width of the beach. Dipping into valleys and rising over the peaks of dunes of wet, packed sand, Santiago, Taribo and Miklos followed close behind, finally gaining the flat expanse at the edge of the sea before splashing into the water.

❧ ❦

Gregory's first urge, upon hearing of the impending threat, was to alert the other citizens of Odin's Island. To this end he set out after packing a small lunch, a task he accomplished within a minute of Alistair's departure. Layla and Giselle were eager to accompany him once they learned what his intention was, and the trio hustled over the soggy ground to the various nearby hamlets. In two of them they recruited another to head in a different direction to spread the news, though most were reluctant to venture out with a torrential downpour and a dreadbot to contend with, and they furrowed their brows and grimaced at Greg with the hard, angry stare a man learns from time in a penal system.

They were approaching the another hamlet which sat at the peak of a steep hill, and lost sight of it when they reached the slopes of the hill. A group of three men and a woman burst into view, descending the hill, one of them losing his footing on the wet grass and tumbling for a few feet before collecting himself and getting back up. When this other group saw the trio, they waved them away.

"There's a robot here!" screamed the woman, nearly falling. "It's attacking! Stay away, stay away!"

Gregory cupped his hands over his mouth and called out, "How many people are left?"

They either did not hear or did not care to answer, as they continued to hustle down the side of the hill as fast as the treacherous footing would allow.

"We have to help out," Gregory insisted, and he pressed upward.

The summit was similar to the Great Hill, with a reasonably flat expanse of ground dotted with trees and bushes. There were about a dozen dwellings, most little more than a lean-to, and three were broken into kindling and scattered on the ground. A few individuals were running about in panic while a figure in white, its form vaguely female with the faintest hint of facial features, was leveling thunderous blows at the support beams of a one room cabin. Each blow snapped a piece of timber in two, sending chips and splinters of wood flying. Gregory stopped as if he had run into a wall, his mouth agape as he watched the thing destroy the structure in a matter of moments.

"Don't resist it!" he cried out when a hapless man, hefting a simple log, moved to attack.

With a speed surpassed by lightning and little else, the right hand of the dreadbot swept in an arc that intercepted the log and sent it flying from the man's hands. Before an eye could blink, the left hand snapped in an equal and opposite arc and struck the man in the head with such force, the poor fellow was lifted off his feet and sent flying several yards to the side, his heels sailing high over his head. The sickening thud of the blow reverberated in Gregory's mind as the man landed in a disorderly pile and never moved again.

"Don't anyone resist it!" he called out again over the screams and yells of those who witnessed the atrocity. "It's here to raze the buildings. Don't resist and it won't harm you!"

Having given this instruction, he moved in a circle around the dreadbot, stopping at the crumpled man in the mud. As another man, standing on the outskirts of the hamlet, screamed his frustration at the machine, Gregory felt for a pulse, though he knew it was in vain before he tried it. The part of the man's skull he could see from underneath his torso suggested a neck bent at an unnatural angle, and that part of the skull was fractured and bashed inward, leaking what it had formerly contained and protected.

Hearing a gasp, he turned and looked up to see Layla covering her face and turning away. Giselle grabbed hold of her and buried the terrified girl's face in her neck, though she herself was pale. Standing up, Gregory was about to put his arms around Layla when he spotted Mordecai standing at the edge of the hill and holding a large bow to which he was affixing an arrow.

"What the hell are you doing?!" Gregory yelled.

Mordecai drew back the string and let the arrow slice through the rain until it struck its target, hitting the dreadbot in its back, just below where the right shoulder blade would be in a human. The arrow, giving a low thud on impact, rebounded several feet, its shaft shattered, and fell harmlessly to the ground. The dreadbot did not respond; a man bitten by a mosquito would take more notice.

With the speed of a whip, another arm flew out, and the sound of the impact with the timber produced another thud and crack. Another blow did the same, and a third, and then another cabin was tumbling to the ground where the dreadbot, despite two more bolts Mordecai shot at its back, stamped them into chips and pieces with an almost comical rapidity, like some macabre dance at twice regular speed.

When it was finished, without an instant's pause to consider, the dreadbot turned to Mordecai. One moment it was stamping out wood chips, the next, as if a switch were thrown, it was advancing on the former Issicrojan slave, who faced the frighteningly swift and smooth progress with cool impassivity. Dropping the bow on the ground, Mordecai hefted a great hammer and readied it to strike a blow.

"He's mad," said Giselle, and Layla, still embraced in Giselle's arms, peaked over her shoulder to stare at what was about to occur.

"He's dead," said Gregory with grim finality.

When the dreadbot drew close, Mordecai squatted down and grabbed hold of a rope before plunging backwards as if into a swimming pool. The rope pulled taut as a lasso caught hold of the dreadbot's ankle, and the machine had its leg swept out from underneath it. It fell to the ground with a thud and slid towards the lip of the hill. As it passed over, two men, theretofore concealed on the downslope, stood up and, raising their axes high, brought the ponderous weapons down and struck terrible blows to the midsection and neck. The axes rebounded as the arrows had, almost carrying the men over backwards with the momentum.

Gregory, Giselle and Layla found themselves in a group of a score or so who were peering over the edge of the hill, watching Mordecai, lying with his back on a flat board, slide down the slick hillside while a white humanoid tumbled along, unable to arrest its descent.

"Who the hell was that?" demanded a man, breathless with excitement.

"It was Mordecai," answered another, his tone bestowing reverence on the name.

"That crazy sonofabitch!" exclaimed a third in what was fully a compliment.

Near the bottom of the hill a group of perhaps a dozen men waited at the edge of a pond. When Mordecai sped by them he released his grip on the rope, and before the dreadbot came to a halt the men charged it, some with mallets and axes, others with nets weighted with stones. The machine was soon entangled in a mass of twine wrapping around it tighter and tighter, and every time it managed to tear one bit of rope, another replaced it, and all the while blows from heavy weapons rained down on what came to look like a spool of thread. When it was thoroughly enmeshed in netting, its movements hampered like a fly wrapped in a spider's webbing, two men carrying part of a tree trunk between them and wielding it like a battering ram rushed the dreadbot and knocked it off its feet and back several yards.

Landing on its back, the dreadbot, in the way it shook its limbs, gave the impression of a turtle overturned. It was quickly surrounded by its assailants who proceeded to bind its already bound form to the battering ram. This entire bundle was lifted with a supreme effort and hurled over the pond, but before it plunged into the water, the dreadbot, with what little maneuverability was left to it, reached out its hand and grabbed a hold of one man's long hair. The unfortunate pitched forward and the two figures splashed into the water together. This produced a cry of dismay from the watchers on the hill, until then on the edge of euphoria. Four men immediately dove into the water, but only three reemerged a minute later. There was nothing left for them to do. They grabbed what gear they had and quickly made their escape, descending into a ravine, popping back up on the other side, scaling a hill and finally disappearing over the crest, Mordecai, still bearing his makeshift sled on his back, at their head.

"Water doesn't hurt a dreadbot," said a voice from the crowd on the hill.

Gregory heard someone, in Arabic, invoke the name of Allah. Following suit, a Christian asked God to bless the fallen, and another, in Russian, appealed to Gaia.

The first voice spoke again. "We better be gettin' a move on," he said. "Sooner or later that thing'll untangle itself and...we don't wanna be nowheres near it."

This advice was promptly followed by most. Gregory remained where he was, his features couched in a deep despondency as he stared at the pond far below.

"That was pointless," he muttered, knowing only Giselle and Layla could hear him. "Two men are dead, and the houses on this hill are going to be destroyed anyway."

Layla sidled up next to Gregory and held his left hand in both of hers, resting her chin on his shoulder. Giselle laid a hand on his right shoulder.

"They made a choice to fight," said Giselle. "Some prefer to die standing rather than live on their knees. They knew what they risked."

Gregory gave no response, and when Giselle peered at his face, she saw his eyes were closed and his lips moved in silent prayer. Feeling intrusive, she removed her hand from his shoulder and stepped back, bowing her head in sympathy. When the doctor finished, he indicated with a nod that they should go. No one was left to watch by the time two bodies broke the surface and, unmoving floated. Moments later, the white figure surfaced and clambered out of the pond.

ॐ ॐ

The swirling winds stirred the sea, the waves they created crisscrossing each other and forming transitory peaks and valleys that closed with a clap and a splash, each one pockmarked by the multitude of momentary craters made by the rain. Normally deep enough only to reach a man's midriff, the water now rose high enough to cover even Alistair's face and then plummeted down to his knees while water from the heavens poured down and water from the sea's surface, struck by the hurtling drops, was ejected upward and then, caught by the wind, slung sideways. It was a tumult such as he imagined existed in the center of a star, or perhaps within an atom, unpredictable, kinetic, unrelenting and frenzied.

The hovercraft was in front of them, silver and sleek with water running down its sides in a series of miniature waterfalls pouring diagonally into the ocean. The vehicle had the vague shape of a shoe and was twelve feet high from its flat ovular base to its deck at the top, ringed by a guardrail. Front to back it measured twenty feet, and another ten from side to side. The seamless sides rose up gently at first, then became steeper before reaching the deck, which measured twelve feet front to back and seven side to side.

If there was any crew that spotted them, there was no sign of it. The four men approached until they stood at the edge of the craft hovering above the water, high enough that the highest waves could not quite disturb it, leaving it's bottom edge mere inches above their heads. As the wind whipped water into their faces from above and below, Alistair considered the sleek sides of the vehicle. He turned to Miklos.

"If you can lift me—"

He pitched forward and his words were choked off by a wave as it passed over his head. He resurfaced spluttering and gasping for breath, which the next two waves made more difficult. Finally having cleared his lungs of salt water, he roared over the noise of the storm.

"Miklos, give me a lift on your shoulders and I can climb to the top."

Miklos turned his back to allow Alistair to climb on. The Aldran handed his spear to Santiago and clambered up the back of the tattooed man until he was standing on his broad shoulders. Miklos grunted, and every now and then a wave would pass through and leave him spluttering. Santiago and Taribo held up a hand to shield their eyes from the rain pellets while they observed Alistair's progress.

He was bent over, leaning into the side of the vehicle as he straightened his legs out. He lifted a leg, let it waver for one moment in the air between Miklos' shoulder and the edge of the hovercraft, and then brought it down on the craft. He gave the slickness of the vehicle's body the ultimate test by raising his other foot off of Miklos and putting all of his weight on one foot. In response, the craft almost imperceptibly dipped down but made the tiny correction required to right itself. He set his second foot down and clung to the slippery and wet side of the vehicle.

With utmost care, he slid up the side until it became too steep. As the treacherous streams of water poured down, brimming over from the deck above, he inched up until he was perhaps a foot above the bottom of the craft. His hands, were he to stretch them out above his head, would still have been a few feet short of the edge of the deck, so he reached behind his back, over his shoulder, and pulled the axe out of its sling and reached up as high as he could, just enough to slip the back blade, a thick piece of obsidian rock, over the edge of the deck, like it was a grappling hook.

From there it was a matter of climbing the axe, hand over hand, his feet doing little to assist. With his muscles bulging, he worked his way up until his left hand grasped the edge of the deck. The overflowing water ran down his arm in rivulets as he struggled to where he could grab one of the posts of the guardrail. Moments later he threw a leg over onto the deck. When he bent down to reclaim his axe, he saw Taribo was just leaving Miklos' shoulders and stepping onto the side of the vehicle. He left the axe for his comrade who clambered up the side, getting a helping hand from Alistair for the last part.

The twelve by seven oval deck was an inch deep in water with a serrated metal floor to afford better footing. At the front there was a hatch, and next to it a computer terminal set in the floor entirely submerged in water.

Buffeted by the elements, Alistair and Taribo sloshed through the water to the front of the deck and Alistair bent down, grabbed the handle of the hatch with both of his beefy hands, and pulled up. The hatch popped open with a slurp and the water poured down the hatchway. A surprised face appeared underneath the hatch. It was framed by long hair and a long, straggly beard, unkempt in the strict Gaian fashion, and its owner wore plain robes of green. The quizzical look had only a moment to turn to alarmed shock as Alistair's axe hit his head. The Gaian was knocked unconscious and collapsed in a heap on the floor, hitting it only an instant before Alistair, who did not bother with the ladder.

The single room interior was also an oval, and most of it was lined with computer stations whose monitors and glowing buttons provided the only light in the dark interior. There were three chairs at the back affixed to the wall, and another green robed Gaian gave the appearance of having just jumped out of his. In a wide legged stance with his mouth wide open, the older man gave a cry when he saw the intruder and immediately rushed to a computer station nearby. Grabbing a handgun of some kind, he turned it on Alistair, but Alistair had not waited for him to complete his move. With all the considerable speed at his command, he charged and, just as the weapon was turned on him, ducked to the side. The gun went off, firing a concussive blast that did the fleet Alistair no harm but which hit the front computer, producing sparks and a cacophony of noises.

The craft pitched forward and Alistair and the Gaian came crashing into each other, a collision out of which Alistair emerged better off. A quick twisting of the Gaian's wrist had the gun out of his hand, but a moment later, as the incline of the ship approached forty-five degrees, the two men were thrown forward and fell to the front. The impact of the fall caused Alistair to squeeze the trigger and another concussive blast was fired, this one hitting the storage bin above and causing some more sparks to jump. Then, the ship righted itself as the back end fell. Alistair was back on his feet before the Gaian, who had fallen on top of his comrade, recovered his senses.

"Taribo!" Alistair yelled, but heard no response.

Rain from the open hatch fell in between them, landing on Alistair's gun and then trickling to the floor. The old man, with one hand raised as if it would protect him, haltingly spoke in an unknown language. His jaws shivered as if he were cold, and he seemed to stutter.

"I don't understand you," said Alistair, neither gentle nor rough, but loud enough to be heard over the sound of the wind and waves outside. "Do you speak English?"

Despite his fear, the man summoned an insolent expression and snapped his jaws shut. Alistair was certain he had understood.

"If you don't speak English, there is no sense in keeping you alive."

"I speak English and Mandarin," the man declared, though Alistair knew by his accent neither was his native tongue.

"You speak German?"

"I speak German," he answered with a native speaker's ease and fluency.

"What was that language a moment ago?"

"Gaian," he answered as if he was not impressed with Alistair for having to ask the question.

"What else do you speak?"

He gave a look like he was not sure why Alistair cared at that exact moment. *"Spanish, Portuguese, Russian, Swahili and Oromo. I was a missionary for a long time before coming here."*

"Those languages will get you around most of the colonized galaxy," said Alistair, switching back to English.

"I'm aware of that."

"Do you have a name?"

The man hesitated. "Call me Bert."

"Bert? Good enough. Bert, how many dreadbots are on our island right now?"

"Two."

"How many hovercraft then? Two?"

"No. Just this one."

"So you and your friend released two dreadbots to destroy what we have built?"

Bert was mastering his fear by this point, and he looked at Alistair with a clenched jaw concealing what fright remained. He did not attempt to say a word in answer.

"I'm afraid that shows, at best, a blatant disregard for property rights."

Bert seemed genuinely stupefied by the comment.

"We're going to play show and tell, now, Bert. Do you think you can manage that?"

Alistair heard a noise above him and he looked up to see Taribo's face hanging over the hatch. He was sporting a broad grin as a stream of water poured off his chin and into the hovercraft's interior.

"We are not hovering anymore. We have landed in the ocean."

"We'll see if we can't take care of that. Bert here is about to teach us a few things."

꿈꿈

The wind that lashed at them at last performed a favor and carried the rain away. It left behind a still air filled with the soft taps and plops of water drops dripping off of leaves and landing on multifarious surfaces. Had the sun been at its zenith, it would have boiled the stew of grass, mud and roots beneath it, but the yellow orb was nearer the horizon from where it lit the surface through a nearly cloudless sky, the objects standing in the way of its rays leaving long shadows like tracks in a solar pathway.

The hunt for the dreadbots was carried out with crude measurements, each one giving nothing better than an approximation. A rumor garnered from an untouched hamlet; a pointed hand from a fleeing man; the distant sound of lumber snapping; screams piercing the air; all these indications moved them in the right direction but imprecisely. The hovercraft had a tracking system, but it was damaged by the struggle. Also damaged was a communication system.

They were fortunate to salvage some weapons and ammunition. Alistair bore the injured and unconscious Gaian to the beach, where he left him and a bound Bert in the hands of Santiago and Miklos. Taribo and he then set off on separate paths, each with the task of bringing down a dreadbot.

By degrees the telltale sounds grew louder, and the harried looks on the fleeing faces were fresher. In proportion as he imagined he drew nearer to the machine, Alistair stepped with more trepidation, expecting an encounter every time he turned a corner or crested a hill or in some way opened up a new area to his view. After he passed through a small woods and emerged into a clearing, the report from a rifle rolled over the land, rumbling like thunder, each successive echo fainter than the last. The sound froze him in place, and he looked west, hoping it was Taribo who took the shot. He waited a few moments but no second shot was fired. Praying this meant the African had felled his prey with efficiency, he squeezed the heavy plastic of his own rifle once and continued.

Halfway up a hill, careful not to lose his balance on the treacherous terrain, he tread on a narrow footpath crisscrossed by the long shadows of every stone and weed protruding from the ground nearby. The path wrapped around a large boulder just ahead of him and continued to the right, behind a shoulder of the hill, out of his line of sight. As he approached the boulder, a shadow appeared on the path from around the corner. He met the shadow with an immediate sense of foreboding, somehow certain it was no man, so that by the time the pale humanoid machine rounded the corner he already had his rifle's butt on his shoulder and his eye to the scope.

A dreadbot is human-like only in shape, not behavior. It does not startle or hesitate. New data is received and interpreted and a decision made with speed bordering on instantaneous. When the machine rounded the corner, already aware a human was on the path before it but unaware that this particular human was armed, it went from a determined stride to a rapid charge in the same amount of time Alistair needed to blink. But Alistair had space between them, so despite the swiftness of the dreadbot, he pulled the trigger and a second shot rang out with a second series of echoes rolling over each other.

There was little kickback in the modern rifle, and the bullet hit the dreadbot in the middle of its torso, exploding on impact and sending the thing flying backwards, tumbling down the side of the hill into a deep, half bowl-shaped depression at the extreme edge of which Alistair now stood, watching the machine through his scope. It reached the bottom where it grotesquely twitched, attempting to rise and finally doing so, though its innards spilled out and its movements were jerky, syncopated and unsteady. Its rubbery skin, impervious to axe blows, was now torn and jagged, blackened at the edges, punctured first by a projectile and then rent outwards by the explosion the projectile produced.

Cradling the rifle in his large hands and kneeling down, Alistair studied the readouts of distance and wind speed the scope provided him. When he gently touched the trigger with his finger, a red dot appeared in the scope's screen, indicating where he should place the crosshairs if he wanted the bullet to hit the target the crosshairs were trained on. He paused only for a second, reveling in that moment before victory is achieved but when it is guaranteed, and then finished pulling the trigger. The bullet hit the head of the figurine and another explosion sent it flying. The curved shape of the depression mixed the echoes of the explosion together into an amorphous lump of sound until, like waves on a pond, they dispersed and the air cleared once more. This time, when the dreadbot hit the ground, it did not twitch.

He rose to his feet, letting the rifle drop from his shoulder until the butt came to rest on the ground. He surveyed his work with a grim nod, noting the small fire burning in the stomach of the machine, and then he eyed his rifle. It was made of some composite material; he was not sure which. The elements of this material could be found scattered around a planet as pebbles, drops of liquid, or fumes of gas. The same elements which composed the rifle could be gathered together in a single wheelbarrow and be no more useful than so much sand. But manipulated by man, they changed into something with new properties, new capacities, and this wheelbarrow's load of material, a pittance, would give him the power to remake a planet.

69

The encampment on top of the Great Hill was razed. The buildings were wood chips with a few lengths of timber left somewhat intact. The residents of the erstwhile village, when they finally regrouped, contemplated the desolate ruins with torpid stares. They did not return to a few repairs; they did not face the prospect of starting over; they were behind where they started when the first foot stepped on the hilltop. Tools crafted on the mainland and transported to the island were now splinters. Nearby trees had been used for sheds and hovels which were now shattered, leaving their building materials farther away.

Among the few dozen homeless citizens of the hilltop, none could witness the destruction and proceed without pause, like a dreadbot, to rebuild. Some looked at the scene in utter despair. Others hung their heads and kicked at the woodchips, knowing they would find the strength to restart but needing time to mourn. Men and women embraced in mutual sorrow. Giselle, summoning all the wounded dignity she felt within her, walked with her head held high to where the entrance of her lodge had been. There, by the torn earth marking the outline, the stiffly stoic woman melted, collapsing onto the ground, prostrating herself face first as if pleading with some unseen magistrate.

She made but one sound, a choked sob, and lay unmoving, spread-eagle on the wet dirt and grass. Some looked at her perplexedly, unsure whether to try and comfort her or leave her alone with her grief. Others looked almost frightened, and they tiptoed around her as if she were a sleeping dragon.

Below the summit, near the edge of the lake and in full view of the cliff face on its western shore, Alistair and Gregory stood before a mound of freshly turned earth. They were sweating and dirt covered their arms to the elbows and was streaked across their shoulders and foreheads. A small shovel, untouched during the recent violence, leaned against a tree. The two folded their hands in front as they contemplated the grave, Gregory with closed eyes and bowed head, lips fluttering.

"Should we mark the grave somehow?" asked Gregory when his prayer was finished.

Alistair shrugged. "Gaians don't use graves. Bodies are left in the forest to rejoin nature. I don't know what would be appropriate. I don't really care either."

"I suppose a cross would be offensive to his religion," mused the doctor, briefly rubbing at the short, nappy beard on his chin.

"Give him a cross then."

Gregory gave Alistair a dark look. "I don't like his religion either, but a modicum of respect for the dead seems decent."

Alistair gave a mocking, cavalier frown and shrug of the shoulders.

"Not your first kill, eh?"

Alistair's face clouded over. "I didn't mean to kill him."

"You hit him on the head with an axe. His brain swelled like a sponge in water."

"I didn't mean to kill him. But I'm not going to shed tears over it. Gaianism…I hate Gaians. No other species but humans produces members who consider their own species a cancer."

"Not all Gaians think that way."

"The real zealots do. They lobby for laws prohibiting colonization of new worlds. They lobby for laws prohibiting development in established colonies and on Earth. They lobby to outlaw new technologies. The worst are the ones who don't bother to lobby, they just set off a bomb. If Gaians had their way, every planet would be like Srillium, with humans living hand to mouth." Alistair spat on the mound of earth, which made Gregory wince. "I have more than my share of regrets, but I'm not going to mourn for him. If you don't want to get hit on the head, don't destroy people's property."

He left while the last pronouncement hung in the air. Gregory, appalled, stayed behind and said another prayer, an apology to the deceased.

When Alistair returned to camp, he saw a host of familiar figures waiting for him. Odin was there with his predictable retinue including Duke, Wei Bai and Caleb. Also there was Mordecai with a few of his toughs while Santiago, Wellesley, Taribo and Miklos stood as if in confrontation with them. Those of the Great Hill were arrayed around them on all sides, like spectators at a fight. The look of relief on Wellesley and Taribo's faces when they saw Alistair told him exactly what sort of meeting this was.

"Good afternoon," said Duke.

"What can I do for you gentlemen?" asked Alistair as he drew close.

"You destroyed the dreadbots with rifles you took from the Gaians," said Odin.

"You're welcome," interjected Taribo, who was standing with his feet apart, arms folded.

"We want you to share your salvage," said Mordecai.

"For the good of the community," added Wei Bai.

Alistair spent a moment looking at them and then shook his head. "No deal," was his soft reply. Unlike the others, he was not speaking so the audience could hear.

"May we at least see what you salvaged?" asked Odin.

"I've sent most of it on to my business associate," Alistair replied, staring at his feet and leaning on the shovel. His voice was still soft and a faint blush colored his cheeks, but he managed to affect a casual air nonetheless. "We stripped the hovercraft and dismantled the hull. The materials are going to be stored until such a time as they can be used. The weapons are being held elsewhere."

"Where?" asked Mordecai.

"Elsewhere."

"What about the Gaians?"

Alistair nodded over his right shoulder at a tree in the distance. "Bert is tied to that tree. I just finished burying the other one."

"We should interrogate the Gaian," said Mordecai.

"Correct," Alistair replied, still looking at the ground.

"We need a plan of action," said Duke. "We can't just wait for the Gaians to hit us again."

"Correct," said Alistair.

Duke's voice betrayed frustration. "Damn it, Alistair! Now we have the weapons to do something!"

"Correct. Although I could quibble over your use of the pronoun 'we'."

"So what are we going to do?"

"I can only speak for myself."

"Bloody particular. Fine then: what are *you* going to do?"

"I'm going to destroy the Gaians."

Whether it was the words or the matter-of-fact tone that carried them, the pronounce-ment was followed by a deep hush. The Gaian control of Srillium was absolute, their rule remorseless and implacable. The Gaians were no more open to persuasion than was gravity, and from their perspective, gravity was an easier foe to overcome. It was as if Alistair an-nounced he was going to wrestle a tidal wave. They looked at him like a man who blasphemed in a church in which they did not worship, but they expected to see angry parishioners any moment.

"That's..." Odin could not think how to end the sentence.

"Have you thought this——" started Duke.

"I'm coming with you," declared Mordecai. "You're not going to do it alone."

Alistair was about to form a caustic reply but Santiago held up a restraining hand and drew close. Placing his lips next to Alistair's ear, he whispered to him in Spanish.

"It might be a good idea to let them come along. If we leave them here while we go hunting...who knows what state the island will be in when we get back?"

"They just want to get their hands on the guns. Once we give a gun to Mordecai, we're not likely to get it back."

"Are you regulating who has the power now?"

Alistair gave Santiago a direct stare. *"No, just my property."* To the men before him he softly said, "Alright."

After acquiescing, he made for the bound Gaian. The rest followed, and he looked like a shepherd leading a flock. Bert, becoming aware of the approaching throng, sat up on his knees and regarded them with a foreboding look. When Alistair reached him he turned with an irritated look at the crowd.

"This doesn't require an expeditionary force."

"We wanna watch," replied an indignant man from the crowd, and he defiantly folded his arms.

Alistair ground his teeth but turned his attention to Bert. The man was trying his best to remain impassive but his beard was shaking and his eyes were wide, drawn to the shovel in Alistair's hands.

"You're going to help us out," Alistair informed him.

"And if I don't?" he asked, mastering his voice.

"No point in discussing that. Purely hypothetical."

Ryan Wellesley untied just enough of Bert's bonds to allow him to come to his feet and grabbed him by his hair to get him to stand. While the former rebel was engaged in this Alistair spoke to the others.

"I'm going to leave a couple men here with weapons in case the Gaians come again. Mordecai, Odin, Duke and Wei Bai, you may come along."

"I'm taking Frank with me," Mordecai insisted, resting his right hand on the shoulder of a large youth of no more than twenty years. Tall and thick with long blonde hair but almost no beard, he folded his arms and raised his chin, looking Alistair right in the face as if daring him to say no.

"Then bring Frank. I'll take Taribo and Wellesley. Bert will be coming too. That's nine."

A few voices were raised in protest, as men demanded to take part.

"We don't need anymore than nine…" Alistair trailed off, waiting for the outburst to subside.

"We need people here too," Gregory called out, having returned unnoticed from the gravesite. "We can't all go attack the Gaians." The voices died down as the men listened to the doctor. "We have farming to do and things to rebuild. We don't have a lot of weapons and we don't have a lot of food." He paused, and when he spoke again it was in his customary soft voice. "Alistair was trained in the marines for missions like this. If he wants nine to go, then nine will go."

"You said we are free to now do what we want," a man from the crowd pointed out, his Hindi accent making his speech difficult to understand. "If we want to come, what will stop us?"

Before the murmurs of agreement could crescendo, Alistair answered him, "You are free to go where you will and do what you want. But I am asking you to let me handle this. One free man to another."

"We will have to build another ship," said Odin, making his way to a nearby boulder and sitting on it with a sigh.

"Nothing fancy," said Santiago. "Just to get across the strait."

"We'll need supplies," Mordecai said.

"Alistair's got plenty of those," said one of Mordecai's men.

"Are you volunteering my property?"

The question, and the note of irritation in it, stopped the man short. "I just meant…" he mumbled. "You know. Give back to the community. You're rich."

"Give *back* to the community, or give *to* the community?" The man blinked once, and all the rest, save for Santiago, stared at him in wonderment. "I don't remember taking anything from the community."

The hurt innocence of the crowd quickly became annoyance.

"You got a lot from us," said one.

Another said, "You've got more than any man on the island."

"I only have what you decided to give me," said Alistair, his features turning crimson as he faced his audience. His words came out in a forced manner, as if the gears of his voice box were grinding. To his horror, a slight stutter crept into his speech, but the harder he tried to clamp down and control the words, the greater became the stutter. He felt their gazes as tingles all over his body. "You gave it to me in exchange for what I was offering, and I haven't failed to provide the promised services."

There was an immediate outburst in response to this, as men gesticulated in the direction of the destroyed buildings.

"I provided as much defense as I was able! I didn't see any of you taking out the hovercraft or destroying the dreadbots!" Alistair swung an arm behind him in the general direction of where the hovercraft had idled. "I was as faithful in my end of the bargain as I could be, which is more than I can say for a few delinquents who haven't bothered to pay for what they ordered!" He was angry enough that his eyes stung and embarrassed at what he considered the childish weakness of his stutter. Seeing no way to bow out gracefully, he said, against the tide of noise directed at him, "Anyone who wants to come can supply themselves," and stomped away through the wide channel created as the men and women made sure to move far out of his path.

The recently obliterated village was not an ideal place to walk off in anger. There were no doors to slam, no rooms to retreat to, and not much else with which to occupy oneself. Not wanting to be seen running away from them, he stopped at the edge of the cliff and, as he calmed his breathing, folded his arms and gazed out over the lake. Santiago was at his side a few moments later.

"How many customers did that cost us?" he asked, but his tone was gentle.

"I would have been fine supplying the expedition!" Alistair exploded, and his arms were shaken loose from his chest. He refolded them a moment later and calmed his voice. It was easy to master himself with only Santiago there. "Just ask nicely. Don't do business with me and then claim I am morally obligated to give your payment back."

"I am the choir, Mr. Preacher."

"It's the implication. I've worked as hard as anyone here—"

"Harder."

"—to establish a peaceful place to live. Then they try and tell me I've been taking from them and need to give back what I stole. That's the implication. And then we take out the dreadbots and they try and pretend I've been shirking my duties!"

He felt another presence, and then a hand on his right shoulder. He looked and saw Giselle giving him a diffident smile. Suddenly sheepish about his emotions and his loose expression he gave her a faltering smile of his own.

"Of course I'll outfit the team. But that's the type of shit I heard all the time on Aldra. A society will not work better than the people in it." The ex marine spat over the side of the cliff. "No society can thrive if it hates the ones who make it better. I'd rather not do business with any of them if that's how they feel. They think I'm stealing from them, not doing my job? Fine. To hell with them!"

Giselle slid her hand down Alistair's arm and grabbed his hand, giving it an affectionate squeeze, which had the effect of startling him. Santiago patted him on his other shoulder with a sigh.

"Alistair, my friend, you are not a businessman. I am not reproaching you; I say that like I say I am not a *fútbol* player. It is time for you to do what you do best, and we all need you to do it." He gave him a reassuring squeeze on the shoulder and left him with Giselle.

"Alistair, I want to go with you," she said after Santiago left. As Alistair started to give what was going to be a negative response, she continued, "It might come in handy to have a female along. All nine of you are men and there are some things, especially on Srillium, that might require a woman." He looked at her uncertainly. "Come on. It can be your way of giving back to your workers."

The comment elicited an unwilling smile from his lips. Seeing this and taking it for assent, she smiled and gave him a quick kiss on the cheek, causing him to blush as furiously as when he was arguing with the crowd.

70

Odin and his men had a wealth of experience building boats. Putting together a craft to carry them across a narrow strait was the easiest obstacle to overcome. It was a shoe that wanted tying on a mountain climber standing before the Himalayas. With plenty of hands at the task and a surfeit of idle lumber in the wake of the dreadbots, a boat that would hold together for the job asked of it was swiftly built. It would handle moderate waves and wind, bear the weight of a crew and its supplies, keep enough water out to stay afloat, and move fast enough to make the journey in a day. It would not, however, withstand a single blow from the great beasts, the krakens, patrolling the straits.

They would rely on the newly acquired weapons. There was no doubt the creature could be stopped by bullets and grenades; the true concern was whether they would have warning to fire before the creature shredded their little craft. None of their attacked ships survived, nor had a single passenger from those ships, nor had any debris or cadavers washed up on shore. No one they knew had encountered a kraken and survived the meeting, including the original inhabitants of the island. They were in a state of nearly complete ignorance, knowing only that this time, with a solitary ship trying to pass, they were certain to encounter one. Should the kraken mode of attack consist of a rise to the surface from the depths, directly beneath the boat, it was not something they could prevent.

The trip was to be made by ten men—Odin had convinced Alistair to allow Caleb to come—and a woman, armed as well as any modern marine platoon, but riding on a boat at which a Phoenician would scoff. The weapons they took with them consisted of four rifles, each with a range of several miles, whose projectiles were explosive; a rocket/grenade launcher, which looked like a thick, stubby rifle; and one automatic side arm apiece, which fired concussive blasts rather than a physical projectile. The ammunition was less plentiful and made Alistair uneasy. The concussive guns would cease to function only when the battery ran out, but they were old models. Though they were fully charged, he could not say how much juice they had in them. Each of the comparatively newer rifles had twenty rounds, and the rocket/grenade launcher had four rounds of convertible ammo.

The morning of the launch, Alistair was with Giselle, rummaging through their belongings, making sure they packed everything they would need. The newly risen sun heated the land, and sweat dripped from him as he moved. Intent on his task and running a hand over his brow to keep the sweat from the corners of his eyes, for a moment he forgot Giselle was with him until she spoke.

"Frank is scared," she said as she, satisfied they had everything and only waiting for Alistair to reach the same conclusion, sank down onto a tree stump. To her comment he responded with an absentminded grunt. She went on, "The louder he boasts, the broader he grins, the harder he slaps his mates' shoulders…I can see that he is scared."

The words penetrated deeply enough into his mind to distract his concentration, reaching that part of his conscious thoughts that recalled Giselle would likely appreciate some sort of verbal response.

"He's never done anything like this before," was his generous reply.

"You noticed it too?"

Alistair, who had never considered it before, hesitated with the response. "I suppose."

He had just set his mind back to his task when she interrupted him with another idle observation.

"Odin isn't afraid. Odin is determined. He's seen too much, been too close to death too many times to be afraid." When he did not immediately respond, she continued, "He's as determined as you are. Probably for different reasons."

"Did you pack the flint?"

"A long time ago."

She smiled to herself as Alistair, after a nod of acknowledgement, returned to his appraisal. She understood his inattention to her was entirely innocent, a product of his concentration and not disinterest.

"Wei Bai and Duke aren't scared either. But they're not driven like Odin. They have other motives."

"What about Mordecai?" asked Alistair, feeling obliged to participate.

"Mordecai is scared, but not of the krakens."

This halted him, and he looked at Giselle, who crossed her right leg over her left and placed both hands on her right knee.

"What is he afraid of?"

"You."

Alistair furrowed his eyebrow in an expression of pure skepticism.

"It's true."

Furrowing his brow even further and giving a doubtful frown, he scooped up a travel bag and slung it over his shoulder. "We're ready to go. Why the hell would Mordecai be scared of me?"

"Alistair, do you ever look at people?"

"Of course I look at people," he said with a tone of protest as she walked past him. He fell into step with her, his skeptical expression changed to one of complete incomprehension. "How the hell could I avoid looking at people?"

Giselle only grinned. "Do you need me to carry anything?"

"I've got it."

"Can I ride on your shoulders?"

"You don't have enough money."

"I didn't say which way I'd be facing."

He gave her a quizzical look, then turned beet red when he figured out the geometry of her suggestion. His tongue was suddenly too thick to shape the sound issuing from his mouth into a clear reply, and the last thing heard on the hilltop was her laughter.

৵৹

What soothed into languid slumber a tourist sunbathing on a beach now provoked shivers in the men who heard it as a ceaseless, taunting, ominous whisper. Many a glance was shot at the ocean's waves as the boat was dragged into place on the beach. The grunting, struggling figures, their sweaty skin baking under the morning sun, approached the water with the sail boat in tow the way a man takes a saddle to a wild bronco. Word of their plans had spread, so a few score individuals came to see them off, as excited and awed as circus goers watching a tight rope walker and just as relieved not to be a part of the act.

There was a mild breeze rustling the leaves and churning up waves, and a few large, white, billowy clouds floated above, taking their time about passing overhead. As Srillium the moon neared its eclipse with Srillium the gas giant, the angular distance between sun and planet narrowed. Presently, Srillium, as a crescent, preceded the sun in rising, a great predator leading a smaller prey, preparing to swallow it.

When the boat was brought to the edge of the water, now on wet sand, now embraced by a wave expending itself, the Druid stepped forward with Clyde Oliver Jones just behind. The ten men and one woman paused in their labor and, heads bowed in most cases, turned to face the religious leader. He extended his right hand with its long, gnarled fingernails and began a sing-song chant in the Gaian tongue. Alistair, impatient for the ceremony to end, allowed his gaze to wander. He exchanged a glance with Wellesley, who raised his eyebrows in a mocking expression, and Alistair gave him a sympathetic grin. Mordecai stood still, staring at the Druid, but gave no indication of pious thoughts. *Is he really scared of me?* thought Alistair, but he detected in the man no indication either way, and with a skeptical frown concluded neither Giselle nor anyone else could either.

After the prayer, Alistair was ready to finish loading the boat, but first Duke and then Wei Bai felt compelled to give speeches, the former in English and the latter in Mandarin, so alike in form and substance as to make at least one of them unnecessary. Alistair, more out of a desire to be unobtrusive rather than polite, postponed his task and stood still to listen. Then, not wanting to seem subordinate, Mordecai took a turn with his own extemporaneous speech, which turned out to be a less graceful rehashing of the previous two. No sooner had the applause died down than Clyde stepped forward and launched another, and this proved more than Alistair was willing to bear.

Grabbing a length of rope, he said to Giselle, "Would you mention to these gentlemen the sun is not pausing to listen to them blabber and if we find ourselves on the water at night we will most likely be something's dinner?"

Duke and Wei Bai both gave Alistair sharp looks, but the Aldran did not acknowledge them. Taribo and Caleb also heard and, almost sheepish, began to assist Alistair. When the others saw them return to work, they at first hesitated, but apart from Duke and Wei Bai, quickly passed from indecision to action and also resumed loading the boat. The result was that Clyde's charismatic eulogy was directed at a group of people, the majority of whom gave him only passing nods and infrequent smiles while they spent most of their attention on the boat. Undeterred, Clyde smoothly switched his target, in mid-sentence, from the eleven of them to the audience and betrayed not the slightest sign of being nonplussed. When Clyde ceased talking, Alistair considered it a small mercy no one stepped forward to succeed him.

When the boat was loaded, the luggage secured and Bert, his hands bound, brought forward to hop on board, the throng of well wishers pressed forward to push the boat the final short distance into the ocean. When the sail was raised, a great cheer went up, and a hundred hands were raised in goodbye. Best wishes were shouted. Only the Druid remained stoic and motionless by the water's edge.

The main body of the boat was little more than a large canoe, displacing little water and giving only just enough room for two people to sit side by side. There were four benches which had to be stepped over if one were to move from one end to the other, and luggage was stored in both the front and back. In the middle was the mast with its brown sail, filled with wind, tugging at it. At the top of the mast was a lookout tower at which someone was permanently stationed, either Alistair or Mordecai. The height of the mast necessitated design alterations to keep the boat from tipping, and Odin chose pontoons, attached to the boat on either side by three planks. Each three foot wide pontoon had a seat in the middle, allowing it to serve as a perimeter defense in addition to a stabilizer. At all times two men sat on the pontoons, rifles tied to the chair by a short length of rope and ready to fire.

They waited for their confrontation with a predator, knowing not when nor how the attack would come, only that it would. They felt that unsettling mix of feelings that comes from dreading an inevitable consequence yet being desperate that it should occur and end the terrible wait. Alistair took the first turn in the lookout perch. Silent, his only purposeful movement was to turn in circles, constantly scanning the waters, afraid that a mere blink could provide the margin of difference between eliminating whatever it was and being eliminated. He was the kind of alert that can only last for so long, that saps one's energy; the kind of tensely vigilant adopted only when one knows one's post will be relieved soon.

Taribo and Caleb, both former soldiers, were stationed on the pontoons, Taribo on the left and Caleb on the right. The West African faced his task bravely, but not stoically. He spared a hand to tug at his dreadlocks. He bit his upper lip. He bit his lower lip. He wiped sweat from his brow and shifted in his seat. His face was set with a determined expression, but it was clear he sought relief from the churning in his guts through fidgeting. Caleb, on the other hand, only swayed when the boat moved beneath him. His rifle was at the ready, gripped in both hands, and he slouched in his seat, his long legs splayed out but bent to keep his feet out of the water.

Alistair suffered through dozens of false alarms, his eye tricked by the waves reshaping the light, occasionally seeming to make a flicker of solidity out of coalescing shadows. When the actual attack came, it arrived with an unyielding certainty as distinct from those ephemeral teases as a tornado from wisps of fog. A great form rose from the lightless depths, a grayish torpedo perhaps fifty yards to port, as large as a small submarine. Its great bulk, and the frightening speed at which it moved, combined to stir the surface of the water above. Alistair yelled an incoherent warning whose naked ferocity tore at his throat, escaping before his lips and tongue could move to shape words out of it, but his hands were trained in a way his voice was not. Even as his hysterical yell startled his companions, his rifle was brought to his shoulder, the scope to his eye, and his finger to the trigger.

Below, poor Taribo nearly tumbled from his seat when Alistair screamed but managed to keep from plunging into the water. Everyone else was on their feet, looking in the same direction as Alistair. Odin spotted the creature and pointed, letting out a cry of surprise, a cry repeated in some form by every passenger when they finally saw the monstrously large shape coming their way. Through the scope, as the creature drew nearer the surface, Alistair got his first clear image of what they faced. It rolled a bit to its side and he saw the pitiless, terrifying profile of a shark, its lifeless black eyes trained on its target, its maw full of teeth longer than a man's forearm and as jagged and sharp as flint.

He pulled the trigger several times, and Taribo followed suit, his first shots overlapping with Alistair's last. The tiny bullets, hardly more than slivers, sliced through the air, plunged into the water and pricked their target like a bee stings an elephant. What saved them were the explosions that followed, explosions occurring in the skin because the bullets did not penetrate far into the thick hide, especially after passing through a few feet of water. Though shallow they were, they shredded the skin near the head in nine successive blasts before the great expressionless shark plunged into the depths of the sea to escape the barrage. Alistair fired six times; Taribo got off five shots of value though he wasted a few more rounds after the beast went too deep to hit.

"It's under us!" shouted Duke, frantically peering over first one edge and then another, hopping about as if his feet were on hot coals.

"It's passed under!" called Odin, reverting to his native Mandarin.

Everyone, Giselle included, grabbed a gun, and now four rifles and six concussive hand-guns were aimed at various points in the water, many of them shaking in unsteady hands.

"Alistair! Let me come up!" demanded Mordecai, and when Alistair returned a nod, the lithe half-Chinese hopped on the mast and climbed until he was on the lookout perch. Only when he reached it did Alistair swing a leg over the side to descend.

"What the bloody hell was that thing?!" demanded Duke when Alistair reached the bottom.

Alistair did not even bother to shrug. Instead, he pointed his rifle over the side where, unless the shark doubled back, he expected to find his foe.

"Megalodon," breathed Odin as he came to Alistair's side.

"What the hell?" asked Wellesley, who was nearby. The Aldran kept his puny handgun aimed at the water, jerking it back and forth as he fought his panic.

"Megalodon," Odin repeated.

"What the hell is Megalodon?"

"I don't want to be out here anymore!" called Taribo from his pontoon.

"A shark that went extinct almost two million years ago," said Alistair with an appropriate reverence in his voice. "The biggest ever known to exist."

"Extinct?" demanded Ryan in an angry tone. "It doesn't look very fucking extinct from here!"

"How backwards is Aldra?" demanded Duke.

"DNA from extinct species can be resynthesized," explained Alistair in a less confrontational manner, his searching eyes never leaving the water. "There are usually gaps that need filling with educated guesses. That creature probably has DNA similar to the Megalodon."

"It was a hundred feet long!" Ryan almost squeaked.

"I'd say sixty," corrected Odin. "They must have made some changes to the DNA. Megalodon hunted whales and dolphins. These creatures attack ships on the surface like they were designed to patrol."

"Not only attack ships, but rip them to shreds and kill every last soul on board," added Alistair. "Sharks don't pursue something that doesn't meet caloric requirements. An original Megalodon would be unlikely to attack a ship, but if it did, one bite into the hull would have been enough to send it on its way."

"How the hell do you know so much about sharks?"

"Why don't we change the pontoon guards?" Taribo called out. "Anyone who wants it."

There was no immediate reaction to the suggestion, but after a moment, Frank ventured out to relieve Taribo. As Wei Bai moved to relieve Caleb on the right side, the rest relaxed a bit from their tense postures. Odin returned to the rudder and Ryan and Duke sat down on the benches, still nervous but allowing their muscles to uncoil a bit.

After gingerly shuffling down the plank, a process interrupted by several waves that, though they only tipped the boat slightly, still induced a halt to movement lest the men fell into the unthinkably dangerous water, Frank and Wei Bai finally reached their respective pontoons. Careful to maintain their balance, Caleb and Taribo ceded their seats and effected their own trip down the planks. Alistair sat on the bench immediately in front of the mast, and Taribo joined him. The young Aldran, after his time spent in the perch, his mind in a heightened state of attentiveness, his muscles ready to spring into action, and after the rush of adrenaline from the shark encounter, felt fatigue grip him. His body was like wax going soft under a hot sun. He initially struggled against the sleep that came upon him, but eventually found himself persuaded. His eyes closed to narrow slits that eventually shut tight, and he tucked his chin into his sternum and slept.

The next he knew, Taribo was leaning across him, grabbing the end of his rifle. Alistair jerked fully awake as the West African guided the rifle's end until it pointed out to sea, away from the boat.

"You had Caleb dead to rights while you slept."

Rubbing at his eyes, Alistair said with an annoyed grimace, "That was stupid of me."

"Your safety was on."

"That doesn't matter. That was sloppy of me. How long was I asleep?"

"We're a mile from shallow water," said Taribo, and he turned in his seat to point behind their boat. "There are two of them now, trailing us."

Alistair abruptly stood up to get a view of their pursuers.

"Can't see them well from here," Taribo explained. "Mordecai is watching, but they haven't made a move to attack. They're in firing range, but..."

"No, if they're not attacking let's not waste the ammo."

"If they figure out to come at us from underneath..."

"It's a shark. I'd be surprised if they had that sort of problem solving skills."

"It's a modified shark."

"If they haven't figured it out yet...I doubt they'll deviate from their natural attack pattern."

"The water's changing color ahead!" called out Mordecai from above them. "Shallow water in five minutes!"

There were some long sighs and inchoate exclamations of joy and relief, and Ryan and Giselle embraced.

"We made it," said Taribo.

"Across the strait," Alistair clarified.

Frank rose from his seat on the pontoon, let out a whoop of victory, and shuffled his way back to the main part of the boat. Alistair frowned at the premature celebration but declined to protest since Mordecai was still in his place with his rifle ready.

"Let's get the baggage ready to disembark," suggested Duke, and not needing a second prodding, they set about doing exactly that.

71

They were soon inland. What had felt like a warm day, invigorating, turned into a sweltering one without the ocean breeze. The sun cooked them and in the stagnant, humid air they sweated and chafed with their rough clothes. The two Arcarians were the most affected, but even African Taribo had moments where he paused, took a deep breath, and wiped the trickles of sweat off his brow.

They were in an open country south of the foothills and walked in an order established hundreds of thousands of years ago, when the genus homo had pronounced brow ridges and prognathic faces: the men walked the perimeter, and the women, or in this case the lone female, walked in the center. Alistair walked in front with Taribo and Wellesley, Mordecai walked in back with Frank while Odin, Duke, Caleb and Wei Bai flanked Giselle and Bert, hands bound behind his back, in the middle.

Presently they came into view of a pair of horsemen, though both had dismounted and were engaged in something the nature of which was not immediately apparent to the group. Whatever it was, they stopped upon spotting the eleven travelers. At some point as the group neared them, they must have spotted the weapons that, on Srillium, only the Gaians should have but were calm enough to remain put, knowing full well that, if the band intended them harm, escape was hopeless by then.

The two men were dressed like warriors and seemed solid specimens. One was bald with an ugly, twisted face whose many scars were an improvement inasmuch as they gave one something to look at other than the features Nature had so maladroitly formed. The other, a man with a head of salt and pepper hair, looked as if he were in pain.

"I do not know you," said Taribo. "I expected to recognize any we came across here."

"You are from Issicroy?" demanded the bald man with some kind of Slavic accent, his voice as unlovely as his face.

"No, Ansacrojan. Not anymore. It seems to me you have wandered off your land and are trespassing." At this both men shifted uncomfortably, glancing once again at the weapons. "Not that I mind," Taribo added. "Like I said: I am no longer of Issicroy."

"Lords Issicroy and Ansacroy have signed a peace treaty," explained the bald man. "We are just coming from Issicroy."

"Another peace treaty? May this one last a full week."

The bald man seemed on the point of saying something, but thought better of it. Instead, he said, "Give me a moment."

In response to Taribo's nod, he picked up an arrow from the tall grass at his feet. He held a slender string in his other hand, and this he tied to the tail end of the arrow. Setting the missile back down, he took hold of the other end of the string and approached his miserable-looking companion. The other opened his mouth and the first, sticking his grimy fingers inside, tied the string around a tooth, which action provoked a round of half-stifled moans and fully expressed grimaces. This having been accomplished, the Slav took up the arrow and the bow with it. While his suffering companion tensed, balling his hands into tight, livid fists, the bald one placed the arrow, drew it back, aimed up and away, and let it fly.

There was a sound unlike any Alistair had ever heard when the string pulled taut and ripped the tooth from its moorings, followed by a familiar pained wail. As the arrow shot off, a stream of blood trailed after it, spattering the ground. The older man sank to his knees, clutching his mouth as more blood streamed from it, and doubled over. The amateur dentist casually slung his bow back on the saddle of his horse and turned his attention once again to the band of travelers.

"That's an infection risk," said Alistair as he nodded at the collapsed man. "If you don't burn it, at least swish salt water around in the mouth."

"Yes," said the other with a hint of the patient tone of one who receives unnecessary instruction. "I believe there is an ocean just south of here."

"Here's hoping for a speedy recovery," said Odin in his incongruent Mandarin accent.

For the first time the bald man gave him some scrutiny. A look of recognition crept into his expression. "I would be...disappointed with myself later if I did not ask you now how you got those guns," he said as his companion rose on unsteady feet.

"We took them from the Gaians," said Duke, pleased to include himself in giving credit for the deed.

The Slav fixed a skeptical look on them.

"We are on our way to take some more," declared Wei Bai, but from the expression on the Slav's face it was apparent he did not speak Mandarin. Wei Bai rolled his eyes and did not look at the man again.

"He says we are—" began Duke.

"We're on our way to Issicroy," Alistair interrupted. He was loud and forceful enough that it must have been apparent to the Slav that Alistair did not want him to hear the translation. "We need to purchase some horses."

"Purchase?" asked the man with a quick glance at the guns. "You look like you are going to take some horses."

"If that were the case we would not be having this conversation," Taribo pointed out.

The man nodded and glanced at his steeds. "I'd sell you ours...for the right price...but I am afraid Dmitri is not fit to walk very far right now." He accompanied this with a rough slap to Dmitri's back. Dmitri looked ready to vomit, and some blood spilled out between his lips and covered his chin. Then, gravely and with a significant look at Odin, the bald man added, "I would be careful going to Issicroy right now. One of your companions might be mistaken for a man with a price on his head." From the wry expression on his face, it was quite clear what he intended to convey.

In response to this, Taribo hefted his rifle. "We do not much fear Issicroy, my friend. But I appreciate your advice."

৯৫৬

Heading north, they came to the road they had taken from Issicroy what seemed a long time ago. Thereafter their going was easier, and they made what Alistair considered acceptable time, although their harmony was disrupted by Duke and Wei Bai demonstrating they were not to be commanded. The result of this was frequent disputes over the smallest suggestions. Mordecai was of a similar bent, and made sure to disagree with Duke and Wei Bai frequently enough to make it clear to them he was vassal to no man. Alistair was eyed warily by all three but, like Odin, kept quiet, ordering no one, expecting no compliance with his wishes. Eventually, a compromise plan for the various details of the hike was fashioned. After Mordecai, Duke and Wei Bai were satisfied it had been amended sufficiently to show their influence, a general agreement was reached as to how Bert was to be treated, how he was to be tied, with whom he was to walk, how often they would switch positions in the march, how frequently they would stop to eat and rest, when and how many times they would fire if attacked and things like that.

When dusk arrived they were within sight of the forest at whose northern edge Alistair and his companions caught up to Santiago the night of their escape. There was a brief argument about whether they should camp there or press on until they reached the forest, and when it was decided they would press on a simmering Mordecai trudged along behind, grumbling to himself.

When they were just inside the woods, they finally dropped their burdens and, wincing at sore shoulders and aching feet, sat down to consume a brief, cold meal. Little was said, the ultimate goal being to fall asleep. Giselle slept next to Alistair. The big Aldran marine lay down on a patch of grass and Giselle, as blithely as if she were sitting next to him at a kitchen table, lay down on her side, her back pressed against his chest. She wiggled once or twice to find a comfortable fit and, contentedly sighing, arranged his arm so she might use his bicep as a pillow.

He was not particularly bothered to be lying next to her, in fact he had imagined the scenario more than once, but facing the reality he was not sure how to respond. Her forwardness was quite beyond anything he had seen in a woman before, and she said nothing, taking liberties with his body as if by well established custom. On such a warm night, he could not credit his body heat as being sufficient reason for her actions. A different creeping explanation left him too flustered to think. He desperately wanted her to say something, to make the situation less awkward, but by the pace of her breathing he guessed she was falling asleep, oblivious to his discomfiture. The longer he said nothing, the more awkward he felt, and the more awkward he felt the less apt he was to say anything. In the end, he took a long time to fall asleep, lying with Giselle, his eyes wide open, his body tense and his nose filled with the aroma of her unwashed hair, which was for him, in such a place, quite wonderful.

࿎ ࿏

It took them almost the entire next day to pass through the forest and reach the slopes to Issicroy. With Srillium hulking overhead, they trudged on until they met another pair of horsemen. The two men, armed with spears, bouncing lightly on their trotting horses, approached with arrogant, hostile expressions that abruptly evaporated when they spied the group's guns. They spun their mounts around and galloped in the opposite direction, the steeds kicking up clumps of dirt and sod in their hasty retreat.

"We won't be reaching the city with stealth and surprise," surmised Odin as he watched the fleeing figures.

"We don't need stealth," was Mordecai's reply.

Several of them were intimately familiar with the area, but Mordecai proved the most keen to lead, and he urged them along with an eagerness to match a leashed dog aching for a walk. Knowing they would be expected now, he chose an open path with little opportunity for ambushes. They went with two rifles in front—Mordecai and Frank—and two in back—Alistair and Taribo. The rest had their handguns, and if they fell short of the vigilance displayed on the trip over the strait, it was not by much.

Eventually, given the topography, they were forced to walk an enclosed path between hills with a few turns in it. Mordecai proceeded with a sort of frantic caution. Trained well, he took his time and made sure every turn was safe before continuing, but his impatience to reach the city was etched on his every feature, expressed by his every curse at the smallest inconvenience, radiated from his every impatient twitch and jitter. The path they walked, a sort of small canyon, deepened by degrees and as they passed farther over the rough ground, the sky seemed to shrink above them until, in looking up, they saw only a small sliver of it, turned to a deep blue by the time their path ran into the canyon where the river flowed.

It was only a short walk to the city, and as they neared it, Giselle took hold of Alistair's hand and, with the exertion of a bit of pressure, indicated she wanted him to fall farther behind the group. He glanced at her, and her return glance told him to be patient. When Taribo, who had been with Alistair at the rear of the party, was finally several yards ahead of them, she spoke to him in a low voice.

"Mordecai is going to get us into something."

"What?"

"Look how anxious he is. Lord Issicroy humiliated him for years, used him as a footstool, made him go naked everywhere...When Issicroy took me to bed he would make Mordecai stand there holding towels so he had to watch, but forbade any woman to ever touch him." She gave him a significant look. "Now he has a gun."

"Goddammit," hissed Alistair. "Goddammit."

He quickened his pace to catch up with Taribo. Laying a hand on the African's shoulder, he leaned in as close to his ear as the dreadlocks would permit. "Mordecai is planning something." Prompted by a curious look, he continued, "Look how anxious he is to get back to the place where he was a slave. Now that he has a gun."

A look of understanding bloomed on Taribo's face. "Do you want to help him or stop him?"

The question surprised Alistair.

Taribo shrugged. "It might not be a bad idea. Issicroy would crush us if he could."

Alistair's voice, when he responded, was hard as steel. "We're going to purchase some horses and leave as peacefully as we can."

With another shrug, Taribo said, "Whatever you say, boss. It's all the same to me."

Alistair notified Wellesley about Mordecai's likely intentions, as well as Odin and his former subordinates, none of whom were enthusiastic about pushing a confrontation with Issicroy just yet. By the time the canyon widened to create the great river valley, Mordecai and Frank were being followed by suspicious men and one woman.

The Gaian evening ritual was over. The valley was in darkness; only a few torches burned in cave entrances and on the rope bridges spanning the canyon. Only two men did they see near the river, stragglers busy replacing a fence post and determined to finish before ending their work for the day. The men peered through the darkness at what were to them the indistinct forms of Alistair's party, not overly suspicious, no doubt figuring nothing more than that a hunting party was returning late.

Near the base of the canyon wall was the market, but the various tents and stands, struck for the night, were in a different arrangement. Alistair figured this sort of thing was continual, like sand dunes in the desert that displayed a new pattern after every windstorm. Two men, an African and an Oriental, sat smoking on a wooden bench in between a bare wooden frame that tomorrow would be covered by a canvas. Two orange dots waxed and waned in the darkness as the men inhaled the smoke from their cigars, relaxed and idly chatting before turning in for the night.

As the group approached, the two fell silent, the Oriental man folding his arms over his chest. The African uncorked a canteen and took a swig from it, then replaced the stopper and set it back down on the bench beside him. It soon became apparent they were content to watch without speaking. The Oriental took a long pull from his cigar, and the burning end cast a faint, orange glow on his face.

"We wish to buy horses," Duke finally said, his tone gruff.

"That can be arranged," said the Oriental, his accent British. Neither he nor his companion moved.

"We wish to buy them now," Duke added. "So, start arranging and we'll make it worth your while."

Taribo jingled his money pouch. The two looked at each other, shrugged, and finally the Oriental stood up and, unhurried, headed for one of the ground level caves. The African took a pull from his cigar and another swig from his canteen but said nothing.

Mordecai pulled away from the group and Alistair exchanged a look with Wellesley, who nodded in understanding. The half-Caucasian, half-Oriental, rifle in his grasp, stood facing the façade of the complex of caves. With the faraway waterfall as the only other sound, the crunch of Alistair's moccasins on the crusty dirt and gravel must have alerted him, but he did not react, even when Alistair stood shoulder to shoulder with him to take in the view of dark façade punctuated by torch light.

Turning his head to look at the former chieftain, Alistair said, "It would be suicide to attempt it."

Mordecai blinked once, and one corner of his mouth turned up in a snarl.

"I'm not saying you don't have some revenge coming, but now is not the time. Not if you want to live through it."

Frank came to stand on the other side of Mordecai, and he gave Alistair a defiant look. Mordecai himself did nothing. Satisfied he had the willpower to resist his urge, and realizing he was not going to get a conversation out of him, Alistair left the two of them alone.

A few minutes later, the Oriental returned, accompanied by a handful of men, each leading a few horses attended by assistants busy saddling the steeds as they walked. While the Oriental man sat back down on the bench next to his companion, the various horse merchants introduced themselves to the group, a few making nervous but polite comments about the rifles and handguns, and haggled over prices. Since no clear leader with control of the purse strings was presented to them, each merchant latched on to a different member of the party, extolling the attributes of his mounts and hoping he was speaking with someone of importance.

The decision making process was inevitably comprised of bickering, a bickering on the outskirts of which the merchants hovered, ready to intervene with the right suggestion or observation, diffidently proffered, to sway the result in a direction more favorable to them. In the end, they bought a horse for each to ride on—including one for Bert—and three more to carry equipment. The immediate result of the purchase was a significant lightening of their load, as nearly all of the iron coins they brought with them were turned over to the merchants. All parties left pleased.

The merchants retired to their abodes, dropping, before they left, a few coins in the hand of the Oriental man. Alistair's band took to their mounts and headed east, following the river through the canyon, eager to put some distance between themselves and Issicroy. The two smokers remained on their bench, as placid and unperturbed as before, finishing their cigars and booze, exchanging the occasional comment as if nothing at all had interrupted.

☜☞

After taking the relatively flat ground of the canyon floor a ways, they bedded down for the night, a moment Alistair faced with no small amount of anxiety. He could not have explained why he felt so nervous. The illogic of it confounded him, but despite a great effort spent reasoning with himself, pleading with his jittery muscles and sweaty palms, when the time came to lay down he found himself as tense as any spring, for some reason dreading yet also desiring Giselle's presence. This she bestowed on him like the previous night, lying down in the crook of his arm after flashing him a smile he fumbled to return. Again, she failed to explain herself, merely resting her head against his shoulder, as calm as she could be. Again, Alistair lay in agony, fervently desiring at least some verbal exchange to acknowledge the new arrangements and frustrated with the way his mouth dried out whenever he considered broaching the subject.

The next morning, they rushed through breakfast and continued their journey. Having extracted information from the resigned Bert, they used what he told them to plan their route north and accordingly turned in that direction after the canyon gradually whittled itself down to a ravine. Passing out of Issicroy, they entered tribal territory but saw no one. They saw signs of inhabitants but it soon became apparent they were being avoided. They came upon meager habitations—little more than lean-tos—and small patches of farmland. Most gave the impression of a recent presence, like when one walks into a room and finds a rocking chair still moving back and forth. In a land dominated by nomadic tribes who little tolerated each other let alone individuals or small communities who did not swear fealty, their reticence to be seen by a band of heavily armed warriors was understandable.

After two days of hard travel north, the land flattened out and trees became more common. They met no one, and saw no greater sign of the tribes than a series of hoof prints, days old, sweeping east. From the summits of hills they could see the dense forest to the north, its tree tops wreathed by mist in the mornings, the occasional bird skimming over the leaves and letting out a cry to break the stillness. It was a matter of opinion where exactly the forest began. Like a planet's atmosphere slowly grows thicker as one descends to the surface, the trees became more numerous and grew closer and closer together.

Alistair, who had experience in the wilderness from Kaldis, noticed signs of greater animal habitation the denser the trees grew. Their first full day in the woods, during their midday break, he broached the topic of a hunt and some scavenging. Their stores were not critical, but were beginning to dwindle, and Taribo and Wellesley agreed to the idea and repeated the suggestion to the others.

Ryan approached Wei Bai and Duke, both of whom were seated on the ground, their backs to the same tree. Wei Bai was engaged in a short nap, his arms folded and his head tilted back against the bark, while Duke, his moccasins off, was busy giving himself a foot massage. Without preamble, Ryan addressed them.

"Alistair thought it would be a good idea to replenish some of our food supplies. Do you…have hunting skills? Or know about plants and stuff?"

Duke gave no indication of having heard, but Wei Bai opened his left eye and considered Ryan for a moment.

I have hunted since I was a young boy. I have often hunted on this moon as well." The left eye closed again.

Ryan, uncomfortable, blinked once and shifted his stance. With a shake of his head, he said, "I only speak English."

"I only speak Mandarin," replied Wei Bai, this time not bothering to open his eye.

"Listen, guy, I know you understand English. So…" He made a gesture meant to prompt the Mandarin to speak. "How about speaking in a language I can understand?"

"If you wish to talk to me, why don't you learn a civilized language?" Both eyes remained closed.

"I just told you I can't—"

"He has hunted since he was a child," said Duke, dropping his left foot and focusing on the right. "He's hunted on Srillium too."

"And he can't tell me himself? In English?"

"English is a quaint language. And ugly."

"I've asked him that myself," said Duke, groaning as he worked at the sore muscles in his right foot. "I've told him no language can match English for universality." He paused in his massage to stare directly at Wei Bai. "More people speak English than any other language."

Like a wagon on a well traveled path whose wheels fall into the habitual ruts, Wei Bai, eyes flashing open, plunged into the debate.

"Whether you concede the point or not, it is a well established fact that Mandarin is the most spoken tongue in the galaxy, and little wonder."

Duke snorted. "It's a monosyllabic bunch of pings, pongs and nonsense noises. Entirely unfit for modern speech. If we hadn't rescued you with a Latin alphabet you'd still be waiting to use your first typewriter! And it is manifestly not the most spoken language in the galaxy. English claims that honor and your desperate denials don't change that."

Wei Bai chortled with unconcerned amusement. *"Gaia save us if English should ever boast of more speakers than Mandarin. The quality of a man's thoughts is limited by his language. I would fear for progress itself should the galaxy come to be populated by inhibited men, condemned to brutishness by a language that smothers intellect."*

"Shall I list the great English-speaking thinkers for you?" asked Duke, raising a hand as if preparing to count on his fingers. "The artists? The philosophers? The inventors? The scientists?"

Wei Bai pretended to look at a watch on his wrist. *"I have ten seconds. Tell me twice."*

"We'll break for dinner in the middle."

"So, basically," interjected Ryan, "he can hunt, but don't pair him up with someone who can't speak Mandarin?"

"You can pair him with me," said Duke, dragging his gaze from Wei Bai and looking at Wellesley. "He can go ming-ling-wong-hong-songing through the forest while I catch us some dinner."

"Ming-ling-wong-hong-song," repeated Wei Bai with a bemused expression. *"An improvement over English!"*

Three pairs of hunters left camp. Alistair left with Giselle, Duke with Wei Bai, and Mordecai and Frank formed the final pair. Left in camp to guard Bert were Caleb, Odin, Taribo and Wellesley.

Armed with a concussive gun, set for a wide range at the cost of some force, Alistair stalked the forest, accompanied by Giselle who was not armed at all. Her presence was, as far as the hunt was concerned, entirely superfluous, for she had no way to fell prey and Alistair was more than fit to carry home the kill. Her chatter was the only sound loud enough to cover the crackle and snap of twigs and branches she broke underneath her feet. He would have considered her presence wholly counterproductive, except he had the remarkable insight that she offered to accompany him for motives unrelated to catching dinner. The mere thought, a sort of inchoate realization, caused him to break out in a sweat that felt like tiny beads of ice on his skin, the result being that Alistair, an indifferent conversationalist under the best of circumstances, was well nigh mute.

With her hands unburdened, Giselle was free to pick at stalks of grass or flowers she came across, tearing off petals and leaves and letting them flutter to the ground to create a sort of floral wake behind her. This she interspersed with chatter of a non-demanding nature, little thoughts and observations requiring no response. Occasionally she would look at Alistair, often caught him looking at her out of the corner of his eye, and always shined a sweet smile on him. If she caught his gaze square on, he returned the smile with a fleeting one of his own. If he managed to avert his gaze soon enough that he might plausibly argue he did not see her smile his way, he returned no smile at all.

In his altered state, he would have been sore pressed to find an elephant if one had been roaming about. His attention was fixed on Giselle, the only forest creature he saw. When her brazen amiability forced him to look away, he ceased to notice anything at all. In those moments he saw only because his eyes were open, but he observed nothing, instead turning his concentration inward, but she waited for him there, too.

Mammal species subject to predation adapt by evolving eyes on the side of their head, which bestows a more ample field of vision. Alistair could have made do with just such a help right then. He lacked also the light swiftness of a gazelle and the thick hide of a hippopotamus. Camouflage was quite beyond him. The former concubine, as she prowled around the defenseless ex marine, moved smoothly, confidently, a lioness without competition who could choose the moment when she brought down her prey. Alistair was left with sweaty palms and a dry mouth, and eyes that widened whenever she gave the slightest indication she was going to make a move.

"Alistair, did you leave behind a girl on Aldra?"

Alistair cleared his throat and swallowed. "You mean…a girlfriend?"

"Or a wife."

"No. I didn't…I didn't have…no. No one."

"No one claims you as her own?" She tossed her flowers on the ground.

"It would be a moot point, anyway."

"I suppose so."

For all his nervous alertness, and for all the noise she had been making, the short conversation distracted him, so that he was unaware of her approach until she was right behind him. Suddenly, there was a hand on his shoulder, gently urging him to turn around. He obeyed though the weakness in his legs made him fear he would collapse. Then both her arms were around his neck, tugging him down even as she stood on her toes to press her lips against his. They were rough lips, long worn by weather and lacking products that soften skin, but he could not have imagined a more wonderful, albeit terrifying, feeling.

The rush of blood to his head threatened to make him faint, so he did not take an active role in the kiss. She released him with a smile, and he stood like a novice actor on stage, lines forgotten but too inexperienced to extemporize, though he knows the unbearable silence is probably worse than anything else he might do. Giselle, equal parts fascinated and touched by his extreme gracelessness, took pity and rescued him with another kiss. This time, he shuddered and exhaled heavily through his nose. She suppressed a laugh and gave him another smile.

"Alistair, have you ever done this before?"

He might have managed a verbal answer had she not slipped her straps over her shoulders and pushed her clothes down to her ankles. This new assault left him without the power of speech. It was all he could do to stiffly shake his head no. A feeling of infinite pity welled up in the breast of Giselle, no stranger to men and the intensity of their needs, and the sensation manifested itself on her face. She grabbed his hand and placed it on one of her breasts. Alistair, the valiant soldier, marshaled enough nerve to paw clumsily at it, at which point Giselle took his face in her hands and, pressing her naked form against him, delivered a knock out kiss that ended with him sitting on the ground and her straddling his lap.

Finally, tardily, he wrapped his arms around her and pulled her to him as a familiar feeling built inside, a feeling that this time went unaccompanied by frustration.

"You don't mind doing this with an eighty year old woman, do you?"

He laughed at the absurdity of the question, a laugh that, tempered by the receding but still present nervousness, came out as a strangled giggle. Infected by the silliness of it, she laughed too, until simultaneously, their laughter died out and they were left staring into each other's eyes, noses nearly touching.

With one more kiss, she stood up in front of him, placed a caressing hand on the back of his head, and with her left leg stepped over his right shoulder, bringing his face into her where her hair tickled him. He was engulfed by sensations for which nothing could have prepared him, and these produced the most fantastic head rush he had yet felt. He kissed her, ineptly but sincerely, and she purred more for his benefit than her own. He kissed her all the way back until he was lying on the ground, and while she perched on his face, he kissed her some more. His arms fell limp and outstretched, and his legs, loosely bent, lay on the ground.

She gently grabbed at his hair, fondling his scalp, prepared to move slowly from station to station so he would get his fill. Willing and compliant, the massive ex marine, so powerful, let Giselle guide him, and all thoughts of catching dinner were forgotten.

A man recently fulfilled is not an object of admiration among his less fortunate mates. Instead he attracts their scorn and they laugh at his faults. This was even more true on a prison moon where women were outnumbered more than nine to one, and the evidence of Alistair's guilt was abundant. He returned from the hunt happy, rather than serious and with nothing more than a stupid grin on his face. His sleeping arrangement with Giselle had not gone unnoticed, and his new demeanor and habit of blushing when they shared a smile led to an instant realization among the others, who took to snickering.

"He's grinning like a goddamn virgin," muttered Frank, not seriously believing how close he was to the actual truth.

Even Ryan and Taribo, inclined to be happy for their friend, were nevertheless toughened men, veterans of combat and crime, and had to concede that his mawkish display was unbecoming. Alistair himself never noticed anything amiss among his mates.

Over the next three days, Alistair and Giselle had no opportunity to renew their dalliance. Alistair was limited to daydreaming with a tiny smile at one corner of his mouth and Giselle, when she saw this, looked away with a pleased smile of her own. There was some grumbling among the others, complaints that Giselle had distracted and therefore ruined him for the important work about to be done, though in truth it may simply have been a convenient excuse of reproof for a woman who discriminated against them in conferring her favors.

Near the end of the three days, they came to a slope rising slowly at first and then increasing in steepness. At its top the hill became rockier, and vegetation less abundant. The horses' hooves clattered on the hard ground, and it was decided they would dismount and walk. As the evening sun was immersing itself in a ruddy and purplish light, they came to the comparatively flat summit of the stony hilltop and were greeted by the silhouette of a man standing at the precipice marking the hilltop's abrupt end. Behind him was an expansive valley, densely forested a few hundred feet below the summit of the hill. Beyond it was another series of hills leading to snow-peaked mountains, and encircling the entire valley was the same precipice with its curved wall.

The party stopped several yards from the stranger, at the tip of his shadow, and he, calmly and deliberately, turned to inspect them. He was dressed in a white robe with a black sash tied around his waste. The robe had a hood but it was hanging from the back of the neck. He wore sandals but no other garment. His black hair receded far from his forehead, leaving much of the top of his head bald. His eyebrows, as if compensating for the loss, were thick and unkempt, and the features of his dark face were sharp, almost menacing, so that he seemed to glare at them without trying. His well weathered face belied the age suggested by his uniformly jet black hair, and Alistair guessed him to be near sixty.

"My name is Shukri," he informed them without preamble, speaking easily in Mandarin but with a thick accent of a native speaker of Arabic. *"We have watched you coming for the last few hours."*

"Who is we?" demanded Wei Bai.

"My fellows and I."

"He's not Gaian," said Duke in a low voice.

In the interim wherein they regarded the man—and he them—in silence, a horse snorted. Another shifted on the rocky terrain; the clop of its hooves interrupted the silence.

"If you want to tell us something, be quick about it." Mordecai finally said.

"You carry Gaian weapons but you are not Gaians. This interests us. You are also traveling towards Floralel with these Gaian weapons. This fascinates us." When the man called Shukri mentioned the Gaian city, he turned and swept his arm across the immense vista behind him, and in the center of the valley forest they saw the shimmer of a translucent hemisphere, like a bowl turned upside down. Through the shimmer one could just make out the rope bridges going from tree top to tree top, or a wooden platform built around one of the colossal arboreal giants. A few soft lights illuminated different areas within the shimmering force field, and there was even a building in the center of the city whose top they could spy.

Casting his scrutiny on the area, Alistair asked, *"Is this Srillium's Birth Crater?"*

"It is. And none but a Gaian is permitted entry."

"Is that what you came to tell us?" demanded Duke.

"I came to invite you to dine with us tonight. And to talk." When the party gave him dubious looks, he continued, *"Surely you do not intend to enter the Gaian Valley right now, as the sun is setting? Please come with me a short distance. I believe you will be glad you did."*

He did not linger to watch them deliberate. Alistair was sure he would not have waited a moment for them if they opted to decline his invitation. They did not decline, his offer being too enigmatic and therefore too tempting to forgo. Hardly had Shukri reached the steep slope of the hill when the eleven party members, ten volunteers and one prisoner, were leading their horses after him.

72

Shukri led them down the steep slope to a large outcropping of rock situated at the point where the gentle part of the slope ended and the earth took a more severe turn upward. In a dark nook, there was a tall but narrow opening and he headed for it, assuring them their horses would fit. He was proved correct, and they followed him down a man made passage that turned into the hill. Before them in the widening tunnel was a black curtain and a soft white light spilled out around it.

Putting a hand to the curtain's edge, he turned to them and explained, *"The curtain is a precaution."* With that, he drew it aside.

At the point where they entered, the cavern did not have a wall that formed a neat ninety degree angle with the floor. Instead, the ceiling slanted down to meet the floor. This meant their passageway sliced through the ceiling of the cavern until the latter, in slanting up, achieved sufficient height to be a proper ceiling. They were therefore obliged to move forward several feet to fully view the cavern.

The most salient feature was an electric light affixed to the ceiling maybe seventy feet above. This simple and crude apparatus, hearkening back to the Dawn of Technology, was, in a place like Srillium, so arresting that they stared at it with mouths agape. The glass of the bulb was thick and irregular, blown into an ovular shape a bit larger than a rugby ball. An imperfection, a large bubble in the glass, caused a distortion in the light and cast a faint but permanent shadow on the wall. Also affixed to the ceiling, and running from the base of the light bulb into a dark tunnel on the opposite side of the cavern, were a pair of naked copper wires.

The stalactites were gone, leaving behind squat, jagged stumps on the ceiling, but many of the stalagmites were left in place. Most of these were encircled by levels of shelves and served as conical storage units, holding sacks and boxes and crates and bottles of blown glass filled with liquids of various colors. In the far right corner there was an irregularly shaped pool. It was impossible to say how deep it was, but from front to back and from left to right it was around fifteen feet. On the left side of the cavern there were a number of wooden structures. A few of them were small, box-like things Alistair supposed were just large enough to be sleeping quarters. Another of the structures was a dining area built like a gazebo. One long, rectangular table dominated the floor of this squat building, situated next to a long slit carved out of the left wall of the cavern which he realized was an oven from whose hot interior a few aromatic odors were wafting.

Also on the left side, but closer to the front, there was a great fissure in the wall forming another passageway. It was filled in with sand and gravel, but was wide enough that a series of pens fit in it and these pens contained a number of chickens, a handful of pigs, two horses, a bunch of sheep and a few cows all recently brought in for the night. The odor of the animals was apparent, even over the smells of cooking, and their snorts and grunts and other noises filled the air.

The cooler temperature of the cavern was a pleasant sensation after so many days of tropical heat. Apart from that, the only other thing to attract their attention was the muffled roar of what must have been an underground river somewhere down the lightless passage across from the entrance. Alistair suspected this was used to generate the electricity for the light bulb.

There were four others already in the cavern, dressed like Shukri with white, hooded robes and a black sash, and all were advanced in age. Two shared the same hair color and dark olive skin as Shukri, another was an indiscernible mix of races resulting in the same skin tone, while a fourth was Oriental. Two were women and two men, and one of the women wore a sleeveless white robe, and Alistair realized she had lost her arms all the way up to the shoulders. None of the four registered anything like surprise when the party entered, and they stopped their work to gather around the group and be introduced.

"This is Amina Abdirahman," said Shukri, his arm extended and the hand held palm up, pointing to a woman of about the same age as himself. "And this is her sister Faisa Abdirahman," he continued, indicating the armless woman about the same age as Amina. Pointing to the Oriental, Shukri said, "This is Akihiro Sawagato." The apparently Japanese man, older than the rest, bowed his hoary head. "And this is Raja Gulyanov." The last of them, with the mixed ancestry, a Hindu name, a Russian surname and easily the youngest at around forty years of age, nodded with a serious smile. "I, as you know, am Shukri. Shukri Abdiaziz. You are all welcome in our humble home."

"Shukri Abdiaziz," Alistair repeated, testing the name.

"Abdiaziz means servant of God." A smirk appeared on Shukri's face. "Which is proof, if proof were needed, that there is nothing of importance in a name. I serve a very different master."

"But not Gaia," said Alistair.

"Not Gaia. Although like Gaia, and Allah, and Yahweh, the master I serve does not exist. Unlike them, he will exist one day. One day soon."

Directly the words left Shukri's mouth, Alistair knew he was a Singulatarian. "And you want to know if we are going to fight the Gaians," said Alistair in English, well aware of the animosity Gaians and Singulatarians felt for each other.

Shukri smiled. "We have many questions for you, but we would not want to be such poor hosts as to demand answers before offering you as fine a meal as we can cook."

Nodding, Alistair said, "We thank you for that. There is a member of our party who does not speak Mandarin. Would it be impolite to request that we speak in English?"

"We can speak English," Shukri said, his accent in that language as strong as in Mandarin.

"About goddamn time," Ryan muttered behind Alistair, who, suppressing a wince, prayed none of their hosts heard the comment.

The meal they were served in the gazebo was lavish by Srillium's standards. They began with an excellent salad of lettuce, apple slices, oranges, nuts and a tangy dressing, and to drink they had apricot juice chilled in the cold water of the underground river. Slices of leavened bread were served right out of the oven, and the white, homemade butter they spread on it melted on contact while steam rose from the sliced interior. The main course was a seasoned and succulent venison stew with potatoes and chick peas, and it came with a red wine served

503

in stout glasses with the imperfections of homemade glass. Their plates were glass as well, with a blue tint, and the silverware actual metal. The dessert was bread pudding with raisins and cinnamon and a sugary icing on top. All of it had the rich texture and freshness of a meal made right on the farm where the food is raised. Alistair could not remember having ever eaten so well.

There was little conversation during the meal, for the guests were famished and, used to dry, stale victuals, gave the meal their rapt and unceasing attention. The hosts were sensitive to their condition and did not pester them with chatter. Faisa attracted some notice as she ate, for she grasped the silverware with her toes and fed herself that way, bringing her foot up to her mouth and gripping her fork, spoon and glass with nearly as much dexterity as they had with their hands. After it was over, as the clinks of silverware on plates died down, Alistair and his party slouched in their chairs, hands on stomachs, and stared into space with the satisfied smile of one who has fulfilled a basic need with style and artistry.

"The meal was to your liking?" asked Amina, her English excellent and her accent hardly noticeable. It was apparent she had studied in England, or at least under English tutelage, for the British tones in her speech outweighed the Arabic ones.

"A finer repast was never served," said Duke. "We are in your debt."

"Your home here is amazing," commented Odin.

"We do what we can with it," said Shukri by way of acknowledging the praise. "The closer one lives to the Gaian city, the farther one finds oneself from the violence of the tribes."

"But you hide from the Gaians," said Odin.

Shukri shrugged. "The Gaians know we are here. Whether they know what we have here in the cave…We take precautions just in case."

"The Gaians tolerate Singulatarians?" asked Alistair with a penetrating gaze, and several of his party gave him a sharp look, wondering how he had discovered the religious convictions of the white robed hosts, or whether he knew what he was talking about.

Their hosts smiled at this, save for Faisa whose expression was never far from dour.

"The Gaians have their instructions from the company," said Akihiro, the accent coloring his venerable voice confirming his Japanese heritage. "They are to patrol the moon and prevent permanent structures to keep us from advancing as a civilization. If we do not bother them, they take no action against anyone. Even Singulatarians."

"If they ever caught us in the Birth Crater they would kill us," said Faisa in the flat tone. Her accent was as polished as her sister's, and she looked at her guests with a bitter smile. "You are too polite to ask, but I don't mind explaining to you. My arms were taken from me on board The Incarcerator. That was twenty years ago."

"Twenty-two," said Amina.

"Why did they take your arms?" asked Ryan, his voice angry, touched by the injustice of it.

"No one can come to Srillium with implants of any sort," explained Shukri. "If the implant is vital to the survival of the prisoner, the prisoner remains on his homeworld. If it is not, the implant is removed before the prisoner is transported here."

"My arms were enhanced," said Faisa in a dead tone.

"Enhanced?" prompted Wellesley.

"I added improvements to the flesh I was born with. In time I added so many, and replaced so much frail flesh, that the arms could not stand alone. They deemed my implants non-vital, and removed them." She gave a bitter smile. "Imagine going into hibernation and waking up with your arms gone."

"It was…a difficult time for Faisa," said Akihiro.

"What are Singulatarians?" asked Wellesley.

"Robot worshippers," answered Taribo without thinking, but he became embarrassed at his response. "I'm sorry…I…"

Shukri patiently smiled. "We do not worship robots. We recognize the next step in the evolution of intelligence. Carbon life has reached its limit. Organic matter cannot become more complex and still gain benefits, but silicon…The human race is the height of animal evolution, but intelligence can be passed on in a superior form. Minds that can conceive and understand the deepest mysteries of the universe, can think in extra dimensions…the human mind did not evolve for these tasks; we have reached the limit of what we can understand."

"Some would dispute that," said Alistair, his gentle reminder indicating he was one.

"But whatever the limit is," countered Akihiro, "it is certainly well below what a computer's mind can achieve. You can see the beauty of the system. The carbon based molecules of life have, after billions of years of evolution, produced a species capable of investigating the universe. A species whose more gifted members can build a superior intelligence that can go beyond anything they could ever do."

"Our duty is to do just that," said Shukri. "Though governments have forbidden it."

"And what happens to humans afterwards?" asked Alistair.

"I see no reason why the Singularity should not allow us to go on," said Faisa with a hint of sarcasm. "As long as we do not get in the way."

"Faisa and Amina are Fusionists," Akihiro explained. In response to Ryan's lost look he continued, "They believe the human body and mind can be the vessel for the greater intelligence. By a process of conversion."

A look of understanding crossed Ryan's face. "Is that why you were…" He faltered and nodded at where Faisa's arms should have been, "…doing the thing with your arms?"

"The thing?" she asked.

"The…improvements. Enhancements."

"Yes, that is why I was doing the thing with my arms."

"And our religion," began Akihiro, "although it is not really a religion…but our beliefs were the cause of our incarceration. Earth is in the grip of the Gaians, like most systems, and a number of years ago there was a great purge. Amina and Faisa's brother Mukhtar enhanced himself more than Faisa. His life depended on his improvements."

"So he could not be sent to Srillium," said Amina.

"Either that or they removed his enhancements and it killed him," said Faisa in a flippantly cynical tone, like what one uses to cover a stronger emotion.

"The moral of the story is you hold no love for the Gaians," Odin concluded.

Shukri smiled again. "We were enthusiastic to see a party of non Gaians approaching the Birth Crater with weapons, a Gaian captive," Shukri pointedly said with a wicked grin at Bert, "and a very determined air about them."

"I am a Gaian," said Taribo. "But not an extremist."

Shukri gave Taribo a tolerant smile of the kind a polite host will give to a guest he believes has just embarrassed himself.

Taribo grew insistent. "I believe in the sanctity of a planet and its ecosystem. I believe man has a place as the head groundskeeper of a planet's life. These are good things. Every religion has adherents who stray too far, who take good ideas and…and…"

"The extremists, as you call them," said Akihiro, "were the religion's founders, though perhaps I should call it a superstition. You are, if you will permit me a moment of candor, simply someone who cannot live by the pure doctrine but still wants to derive benefits from the belief system. So you dilute and soften the dogma and call yourself a believer. I don't mean to make you angry," Akihiro quickly said when he saw Taribo's jaw set and his eyes fill with resentment, "but the Gaianism you practice is a watered-down variety. The original Gaians, the ones who made the religion and gave it a name, were far more extreme than you. In fact, they would have imprisoned you for the lifestyle you have led."

Taribo plainly was not pleased with the remark, but he could offer no rebuttal or excuse.

"These particular Gaians outside your door aren't exactly purists," Alistair commented.

"Indeed they are not," scoffed Shukri, the disdain evident in his voice. "The meteor that wiped this moon clean of life is an anathema to the real Gaians, who would have us leave the universe alone. I cannot imagine a true Gaian, even if forced to live here, choosing to reside in the very epicenter of what he considers blasphemy." Shukri delivered the pronouncement with a steady crescendo of passionate derision, his thick eyebrows bunched over his eyes and his knuckles rapping the tabletop. He now relaxed and spoke more calmly. "They live in a Birth Crater; they enjoy a city powered by electricity generated…who knows how. They ride on hovercrafts. I'd wager my last Credit they eat red meat."

"They sold their little Gaian souls when they agreed to be shepherds here," Akihiro agreed.

"So…" said Faisa, "…what are your plans for our Gaian masters?"

"They are going to be exterminated," said Mordecai.

It was impossible not to notice the grim satisfaction this pronouncement gave their hosts.

"Can you help us?" asked Odin.

"Yes we can," said Faisa who, of the five Singulatarians, seemed the most pleased. "We can take you farther into the tunnels and show you a way into the Birth Crater. You can avoid detection if you don't come down from the rim. We can give you a partial map, even a little intelligence on what to expect."

"Tomorrow the sun will not rise," said Shukri. "Srillium will eclipse it sometime tonight, on the other side of the moon, and there will be no dawn. If I were inclined towards superstition, I would say this is a fitting time for Floralel's downfall."

"Are there other Gaian cities?" asked Alistair.

"Yes," said Faisa. "We believe they are in communication with each other."

The implied threat hung in the air for a moment.

"Do you still wish to declare war?" she prompted.

"It has to be done," said Alistair while the others uncomfortably shifted in their seats.

"Success," said Raja, his first word since they arrived.

"Success," agreed the other four, more or less in unison.

The large table was carried out of the gazebo to give the party a place to sleep. When their belongings were arranged to their liking, Shukri took Alistair back to the lip of the crater to show him the lights of the city and explain its layout. Mordecai, within earshot when Shukri offered to take him, insisted on coming along. Night had claimed the sky by the time they left, making their rocky path up the steep outer rim of the crater an uncertain one. When finally, after much stumbling and scraping their shins and knees, they reached the top and stared out over the vast depression in the earth, the city of the Gaians stood out. The shimmering defensive dome gleamed, and underneath it they glimpsed other lights of various colors, some of them in motion, some of them flickering and flashing. The dark mass of foliage below, indistinct, roiled and hissed like an agitated sea as a night wind rushed over it.

"We guess there are two thousand living there," said Shukri, standing right on the edge, his white robes flapping like a flag on a mast. Tucking his chin into his chest and folding his arms, he stared at the hated place, his sharp features and thick eyebrows, faintly illuminated by the distant city lights, accentuating the threatening glare he gave it.

Alistair and Mordecai stood a few inches farther back in respect for the vertical drop.

"We should get as much information as we can from Bert," suggested Mordecai. "After that he is no longer any use to us."

"We're not going to kill him in cold blood," Alistair said. "His usefulness might extend well beyond the battle tomorrow."

Shukri turned his head to Alistair. "Leave him with us if you don't want to get your hands dirty."

"I'd rather not. Thanks all the same."

Shukri made an expression that often accompanies a shrug and stared back out over the Birth Crater. "You will be a king, Alistair?" The words, cast out to the void before Shukri, were tossed about by the wind and brought back less distinct.

"That's not precisely my plan. What will you do with the Gaians gone?"

"I don't expect too much will change right away."

"I expect it will. That electric light you have…a nice piece of work, but about as far as you can go by yourselves. Imagine what can happen when people are free to own property and improve it. Imagine the division of labor being extended. Instead of manufacturing the electric light yourselves, a score of different companies each manufacture one part of it. They specialize in one aspect and become good at it. Imagine how far a free people could advance in no time at all."

Shukri looked back at Alistair. "You are some sort of Capitalist Fundamentalist?"

"That has a derogatory ring to it. I believe in the Free Market. Entirely and without reservation. I am what was once called a liberal, then a conservative, then a libertarian, then a Freimann, then a liberal again…it has gone under many more names. "

"But you'll need a king to keep your Free Market safe."

"A king is the greatest danger to a Free Market. There will be no States on Srillium, just free individuals cooperating on their own terms." He paused a moment before continuing. "I'd like to hire you to work for me. You were scientists on Earth, were you not?"

"We were."

"Come work for me and you can be scientists again. Instead of living in a cave, you can live in a mansion. Instead of making electric lights like Thomas Edison, you can make... whatever you want."

Shukri almost imperceptibly nodded his head while he mulled over Alistair's offer. "More than anything right now, I would like to know why we are alive on this moon."

"How do you mean?"

"We are in orbit around a gas giant. Srillium must have a magnetosphere...unimaginably strong, with deadly radiation belts. The only organisms native to this moon were a few hardy forms of bacteria tucked away deep under the sea and buried underground. So why are we alive and healthy on its surface? That is what I would like to find out."

"Come work for me and you can study anything you want."

Shukri stared over the Birth Crater for a few more seconds before turning from it.

"We will work for you, Alistair, under the right terms. But let's not think too far in the future. You have a battle to win tomorrow. Attend to that first."

"That's my specialty. God forgive me for it."

"You believe in God?" asked Shukri as he descended the slope once more.

Alistair and Mordecai fell into step behind him, carefully balancing themselves on the rocky incline with all of its loose pebbles.

"I don't know," he finally answered, though he said it so softly he was not sure whether Shukri heard.

73

The next morning the light was switched on without warning and Alistair, whose eyes were open, squinted against the glare. Rubbing his tired orbs, he sat up while the bodies around him stirred and made groans of protest. Bert sat nearby, outside the gazebo but tied to it, and his bleary, red eyes told of a night with no sleep at all. Breakfast consisted of some biscuits, butter and cured ham with chilled tea to wash it down. When they finished their meal, the Singularians wished them luck, and Shukri, carrying a torch, led them deeper into the cavern. Alistair at first tried to convince Giselle to stay behind, but even invoking his authority as her boss did not secure her compliance, so she came with the rest, weapons and ammunition bouncing and clicking as she walked.

When they emerged into the bottom of the Birth Crater, they found themselves in what seemed to be the dead of night. The dew that would not be chased away by a sun covered the ground and glistened from the light of Shukri's torch. Stars twinkled in the sky as a soft breeze gave cool kisses to their skin. Above, there was a soft but constant moan, indicating the wind was stronger above. At the floor of the crater it could barely be felt, but the tops of the trees swayed under its influence. Near the horizon there was a patch of starless sky and a faint trace of a circle of light they knew to be Srillium.

"Can you navigate your way to the city?" asked Shukri, speaking to Alistair once again in Mandarin.

Pointing to a part of the sky where he could see a ghostly glow, Alistair said, *"That has to be from the city lights."*

"Then you know where you are going. We await your return."

Shukri bowed his head to them and retreated back into the tunnel, leaving them on the forbidden bottom of the Birth Crater, now wrapped in nearly complete darkness.

"I never did get used to these Srillium nights," said Duke, glancing about. "At home the cicadas would be singing an opera right now."

It was as much of a send off speech as anyone cared to compose. They crept into the dark woods while the branches rustled overhead, fanning out but staying close enough to provide support to each other. Alistair, Mordecai, Taribo and Wei Bai carried the rifles, while Caleb held the grenade launcher. There was enough military experience in the group that they fell into an easy rhythm of movement and communication. Odin, Giselle and Wellesley merely attempted to be as unobtrusive as possible, while Bert was just tugged along by Mordecai, who had been more than satisfied to take charge of him.

"There are no lookouts?" Mordecai asked of him at one point. *"No radars? Scanners? Sensors? Nothing?"*

"I told you once," replied the Gaian with excellent Mandarin. *"We have our defensive field. There is no fear of the prisoners within the safety of Floralel."*

"But the craft sent to destroy the island…it is long overdue. That will not cause them worry?"

Bert shrugged as best he could with Mordecai tugging at the leash around his bound hands. *"I cannot say for sure. This has never happened before."*

It is uncertainty that most accentuates fear; the unseen monster is the most dreadful. In that forest, every tree was a hiding place, every step a potential trigger for an alarm. They went in ignorance, not knowing if their bodies were registering right then as red silhouettes on some heat sensing system whose operators were chuckling in pompous derision at their approach. Though Mordecai promised to cut the tether keeping Bert's head attached to his body if he were caught in a lie, there naturally were still grave doubts about the veracity of the information he gave them.

By degrees as they proceeded, the whitish haze in the sky grew brighter. Once, they halted to allow Mordecai to climb a tree and when he returned they made a small correction in their direction. Before long, rays of artificial light were filtering through the foliage, given an amorphous quality by the thin mist through which they passed. Alistair spied the defensive field about a hundred yards away and gave a signal to halt that, with reasonable efficiency, was passed along their formation. While the others held their position, Alistair moved down the line until he reached Mordecai and Bert.

"We've reached the city," he said. "It's probably almost noon."

"The procession will start soon," Bert promised.

"If it doesn't…" threatened Mordecai.

"I've told you everything I can and as truly as I can. We make a procession to the clearing during every eclipse and a ceremony continues through the entire event until we see the sun again. If the procession is not held this time, it will be for no reason I can think of."

"And the shield is lowered for the procession?"

"How else could they exit the city?"

Alistair and Mordecai exchanged glances.

"Take us to the clearing," ordered Alistair.

It was a short trip, and they stopped well short of it for some acolytes were already there, setting up torches around the edge and an altar in the middle. The hooded acolytes worked in silence, using only nods to acknowledge each other on those occasions when their paths crossed. This Alistair witnessed through his rifle's scope, and after a few moments of observation he nodded, satisfied.

"Let's get Caleb into position."

The position turned out to be a large tree with a stout branch on which to perch. It was several yards closer to the city than the clearing, and Caleb, grenade launcher loaded, clambered up the giant oak and readied himself.

From the tall grass of his own hiding spot, Alistair studied Floralel. It was a city whose inhabitants lived largely in the trees, and long plank bridges went from enormous trunk to enormous trunk, while dwellings of all shapes and sizes nestled among the leaves. On the leafy paths along the ground, each one lined with soft white lights, were the communal buildings of Floralel. On the outskirts of the city, right next to the protective shield, was the hangar, Alistair's target, not a hundred yards from where he crouched. Constructed of something like white adobe and with a garden growing on its roof, the building was shaped in the Gaian style, with no edges or corners. The doors were made of some artificial, plastic like substance that blended in well with the walls.

Beyond the hangar, barely glimpsed between the thick tree trunks, was another building of the same white adobe which, based on Bert's descriptions, Alistair took to be the Town Hall. It was several stories with terraces and roofs all over its irregular exterior, and light of various colors poured out of its open windows, sometimes flickering, sometimes constant. Behind and to the left of it was a structure fashioned from numerous living trees bent and wrapped around each other into the vague shape of a European cathedral, though smoother and more irregular. There was no mortar and no nails of any sort, merely trees bent under the will of the builders.

It was a peaceful city, and beautiful in an alien way. Fountains dotted the landscape, and hedges and other plants, carefully tended, wrapped around the bases of trees and spread out. A brook ran softly through, and bridges spanned it at various points, each one looking as if the earth itself, rather than man, had decided to form them. It was hard to imagine it as the provenance of the attack on the island, and Alistair experienced a moment of sharp regret at what they were about to do.

His thoughts were interrupted by Giselle who, crouched in the tall, damp grass with him, leaned in to whisper in his ear.

"Be careful of Mordecai tonight…or today," she breathed.

Alistair flashed her a look.

"Why?"

She shook her head and peered off to the north, to the general vicinity where Mordecai was hiding. "Beware friendly fire." At Alistair's furrowed eyebrows she continued, "He would shed no tears if you were to die. This is an opportunity to get rid of you he may not want to pass up."

A chill ran up and down Alistair's spine as he considered her words.

"You may want to get him first. Before he goes after you."

He was ashamed to realize that there, on the verge of battle and with a rifle in his hands, he was tempted. He shook his head, though his resolve was less firm than he represented it to be.

"I've got no right."

"Alistair—"

"I couldn't even get my finger to pull the trigger." It was a lie, and he blushed when he told it. *I've pulled a thousand triggers,* he thought with disgust. *I've committed greater crimes than killing Mordecai.*

"There isn't a warrior on this planet with a right to complain if he were shot," said Giselle, and there was a fierce bitterness in her voice, but she said nothing further.

With his attention returned to Floralel, though with his thoughts now much perturbed, Alistair realized his clothes were growing damp from the dew of the high grass. Every minor gust of wind raised the hairs on his arms and legs and once even caused him to shiver. By Arcarian standards it was still quite balmy, but having accustomed itself to the intense, wet heat of his current latitude on Srillium, his body reacted as if to a fall breeze.

Leaning back into Giselle, he whispered, "How cold does it get during the eclipse?"

"On the last day there will probably be a snow storm."

His eyes widened. "I didn't—"

"I packed you some winter clothes."

His relieved grin was cut short by Taribo.

"I see the procession," he hissed.

Yanked back to attention, Alistair searched for and quickly found the long line of the processional, just coming into view from behind the Town Hall as it wound through the city's obstacles. The foremost three Gaians each carried a pole with a green flag outlined in white and with a red circle at the center. Behind them walked a man whose green robes stood out from the others for the intricate design of gold leaves and vines nearly covering the entire surface of the otherwise simple clothing. Walking in front of him, but facing him and stepping backwards as they went, were two short acolytes, probably children, each struggling to hold aloft one half of a great tome from which the man with the ornate robes read aloud. Behind these six came the great throng, moving in something less than a practiced, tight formation, though it retained a basic serpentine shape.

Coming part way out of his crouch, Alistair caught Caleb's attention with a signal which the tall man returned from his perch in the tree.

"Don't waste ammo," cautioned Alistair when he was once again tucked away in the grassy undergrowth. "No unnecessary kills. Send them running if you can. Kill only if you have to."

The only movement came from the tops of the grasses and weeds swaying in the slight breeze or when they exhaled. Their anxiety was made almost unbearably acute when the procession neared the defensive shield, plodding along at an unhurried pace. Finally, the long line of Gaians came to the edge and stopped, the flag bearers nearly touching the shield with the tips of the poles. The ambushers felt like a rubber band pulled taut.

When the shield opened, it was only a small section that slid apart like a pair of automatic doors. There was, of course, no actual door opening up, but it seemed that way as first a narrow slit appeared and then widened. No more than eight feet high and perhaps ten feet wide, the aperture gave Caleb, who was well above it on his branch, no angle from which to destroy the generator farther back.

They all realized the dilemma at the same time, but it was Mordecai who acted first. Jumping up from his hiding place, he raced for the tree where Caleb was sitting in indecision. When he reached the base of it he called for the grenade launcher, which Caleb dropped down to him. Like a man in the middle of a deep plunge on a roller coaster, Alistair groaned through clenched teeth as the launcher plummeted, picturing a disastrous explosion. Instead, Mordecai neatly snatched the weapon out of the air, ran the ten or so steps to the middle of the path between the processional and the clearing and, while the Gaians paused and uncertainly pointed at the figure in front of them, launched a grenade.

With a high pitched whoosh it flew through the air, and just as it hit its target and exploded, a second grenade was launched, followed by a third, though the defensive shield was down before the last found its mark. There came the sound of crackling as the shield disintegrated, being first reduced to shooting lines of bluish light running over its hemisphere and finally disappearing altogether.

"Forward!" cried Mordecai, and as his companions jumped into action he launched a series of grenades at the processional.

The grenades hit and exploded at several points along the line of worshippers. Bodies flew into the air with chunks of earth, and fires burned on the ground. Those Gaians still of sound body scattered in terror, and Mordecai sent a couple more grenades flying their way, sending up sod and flesh as if from a geyser and causing more of the forest to ignite.

"God damn him!" yelled Alistair as he ran behind Taribo.

The forefront of the panicked wave of Gaians reached them, and Alistair, setting his concussive gun for a wide range, fired off shot after shot, knocking dozens to the ground. Dazed but uninjured, they moaned as Alistair, Wellesley, Taribo and Giselle weaved through and jumped over them. Those not knocked to the ground yielded to Alistair's persuasion and flew in another direction, leaving them unhindered in their dash to the hangar.

A detachment of a dozen Gaians with the wherewithal to collect themselves amid the chaos made a break for the weapons depot. Not a cohesive unit, they moved as individuals who separately had the same idea. Most were flung into the air with a well aimed grenade from Mordecai, who was slowly advancing on Floralel as he pumped the explosive charges. A couple of the Gaians managed to reach the weapons depot, but Duke, Wei Bai and Caleb, now deprived of his grenade launcher but still armed with a concussive gun, entered moments after.

As Alistair neared the hangar, he saw the double doors open and two terrifying white forms emerge. Both were armed and, immediately detecting the threat, turned their guns on the four armed ambushers running at them. Alistair's rifle was already aimed, however, and before the dreadbots could, he fired several shots even while his heart skipped a beat. The explosive rounds, hardly thicker than needles, sliced into their prey and detonated inside the bodies. The skin of the machines burst outward with a tiny flash of light, and as smoke poured out of the craters left behind, the dreadbots collapsed, twitching on the ground in a macabre parody of a human expiring. When he reached the double doors, Alistair, signaling for his team to stop, put a round into the skull casing of each.

"Ryan and Giselle, on my go I want you to open the doors."

Giselle was breathless and looked dazed, but the words reached her and she nodded, taking up a position opposite Wellesley who, a veteran now of a handful of battles, looked more collected than she. Alistair and Taribo lay flat on their stomachs in front of the doors, rifles ready to fire.

"Go."

They flung the doors open while Taribo and Alistair's tense fingers perched on their triggers, but there was no immediately obvious threat inside. Alistair swept his rifle back and forth, carefully scanning the many shadows, but if there were other dreadbots their presence was not apparent.

When the four of them were inside and the doors closed, there was an abrupt, disconcerting quiet. Mordecai had finished launching grenades and the screaming mass of Gaians was scattered. Whatever noises were left were muffled by the building's walls. Inside, there was ragged breathing from the four and a low hum underneath, which may have come from the dim electric lights above.

There were several different models of flying craft parked inside, casting shadows like puddles with the dim lights directly above. A gloom like twilight enveloped everything. The floor was a smooth concrete, and in each corner of the hangar a set of stairs led to a balcony, one at the front and one at the back. Beneath each there were double doors, and at the opposite side of the hangar there was a large, sliding door big enough to permit the various craft to exit. The structure's main central room was larger than a rugby field.

Alistair lay flat on his stomach to peer underneath the aircrafts, his rifle still held ready to fire. The other three stood still, slowly regaining control of their breathing. A drop of sweat fell from Taribo's chin onto the floor. After a couple long minutes of careful searching, he rose.

"I'll take the north end if you take the south," said Taribo, his voice, along with his breathing, more relaxed.

Alistair shook his head. "I'd rather not separate."

Moving to the north end, they ascended a set of stairs and searched the balcony above, but there was nothing there save a few computer stations. Alistair gave these a cursory inspection and, though he could not read the printed Gaian, was moderately confidant he could figure out how to operate them. There was a moment of tenseness when they stood before the double doors below, but this dissipated when the opened doors revealed a small locker room as empty as the rest of the hangar.

A trip to the south end of the building, with Taribo stationed as a sniper on the north balcony, revealed it to be similarly unoccupied. The computer stations there seemed to be redundant, but the room underneath, past the double doors, was a control room. Emerging into the large hangar room once more, Alistair signaled for Taribo to rejoin them, which action the African accomplished with alacrity.

"There are only two exits," said Alistair.

"That we can see," cautioned Taribo.

They heard what sounded like firecrackers popping outside, in rapid succession, and in response, from farther away, came another series of pops with a higher pitch. Silence followed.

"We're going to lock the doors we came in," Alistair continued with an uneasy look in the direction the sounds came from. "Giselle and Taribo will stay to guard the hangar." He indicated one of the balconies with a nod and continued, "Take position up there and don't let anyone in. Ryan and I are going to make sure the weapons depot is secured. If they can't get firearms they can't take the hangar, and if they can't take the hangar the city falls."

With a slap to Ryan's shoulder, Alistair headed for the exit.

In the darkness outside, with the doors locked behind them, Alistair and Wellesley considered the scene. A few fires burned around charred craters in the earth. Inert forms and rent body parts lay like ejecta from a meteorite. A few agonized moans and whimpers were heard, and one bloodied Gaian, his robes burnt and torn, was feebly attempting to crawl across the ground. To their left, many yards distant, the torches flickered in the clearing, some of the light making it through the gaps and interstices in the foliage. There was no sign of anyone else; all able bodied Gaians had fled and Alistair's companions had penetrated the city.

"That's the weapons depot, right?" prompted Wellesley.

Alistair absentmindedly nodded, scanning the area one last time before falling into a slow trot across the ground. Passing by the stout trunk of a gigantic tree around which wrapped an intricately carved staircase, the two of them made for an archway marking the entrance to the weapons storage facility. The sliding gate that served as the front door was partway open, and through it they could see a hallway lit by small lights set in the floor, one row on each side. There were larger lights in the ceiling, but these were turned off, leaving the interior, much like the hangar, in a sort of twilight.

Alistair entered and Ryan followed as surely as if a rope bound them together. The building was not overly large and it was not difficult to find the main storage room, which comprised half the building. The door leading to it was shot through from both sides, its window shattered, and a large scorch mark stained almost all of what remained.

"Squad one coming in!" Alistair barked.

"Squad two reporting!" called back Duke's voice.

He relaxed his hold on the rifle, stepped through the door and was presented with a storage hall with a roof nearly thirty feet overhead. The concrete floor was a dark gray with multiple stains, and the metal support beams were a dark red. There was a walkway above circumscribing the chamber and row after row of shelving reaching almost to the ceiling. Duke and Wei Bai were standing next to a pair of Gaian bodies and looked to be in the middle of dragging them somewhere. Duke's face was blackened, and his mustache and eyebrows, along with the bulk of the hair on the front of his scalp, had burned off. A little smoke wafted out of the singed ends of what remained on his head, and already there were blisters forming on his scalp and forehead. The blisters were sullied by the soot Alistair guessed was hair not long ago. Looking to his left, he saw Caleb lying face down in a pool of blood, silent and motionless. One outstretched hand lay next to his gun.

"We're minus one," said Duke.

"No casualties," Alistair reported with respectful sobriety.

"Three more bodies in the back," continued Duke with a nod of his head towards the labyrinth of shelves. "None escaped."

"How many exits?"

"We haven't had a chance to look yet," said Wei Bai. "This should be the only way in or out."

"One would think," added Duke.

"Confirm that for me, Ryan," said Alistair.

His companion hesitated a moment, and Alistair remembered he had not understood Wei Bai.

"See if there are any more exits."

Ryan nodded and readied his gun before entering a row and heading for the back.

"The hangar is secure; Taribo and Giselle are guarding it. We took out two dreadbots; that leaves two unaccounted for if Bert was telling us the truth."

"Fine," said Duke.

516

"I'm going to leave Wellesley here with you. If we can maintain control of the guns they're not taking back the city."

"Don't keep us waiting long," said Wei Bai.

☙❧

The way to Floralel's Town Hall was not obvious. Alistair felt as if he were in a labyrinth of hedges impeccably trimmed into amorphous, rounded shapes; sculpted rocks; and paths of soft dirt and leaves. This by itself would have sufficed to frustrate his efforts, but his difficulties were compounded by his slow pace and the attention he gave to corners and shadows. Furthermore, the steadily dropping temperature coaxed an increasingly opaque fog out of the humid air.

The Town Hall was always in sight, its upper story visible over the hedges, even if the route to it was unknown. The room at the top with a dome of glass was the only room in the building whose lights were still on, and he was finally able to reach it when he came to the base of a massive tree trunk with a spiral staircase wrapping around it. The staircase and its banister were composed of varying colors of wood melded together, smooth and irregular, as if Nature, random and dispassionate, had chanced to fashion something resembling a human creation, like a cloud that recalls a castle. When he stepped on it, it felt as solid as granite, yielding nothing under his weight, despite its delicate appearance.

It was forty feet from the ground to a landing that gave way to a walkway spanning the distance between two great trees. He raced around the tree several times before reaching it. Once on the landing, he swept his rifle over the area, knowing he would be easy to spot above the fog. With his right foot he tested the walkway and, finding it to be as solid as the staircase, darted over a city as still and cold as a sarcophagus. When he reached the other end, he felt relieved to descend the opposite staircase and wind up mere yards from the Town Hall's front door.

To gain this front door, one had to climb an earthen slope and cross a roofed patio with four irregular stone columns at the corners. At Alistair's approach, the front doors slid open and the muscled Aldran passed through. Another twilit interior greeted him. He took only so much time as he needed to confirm he was safe before pressing deeper into the building. As he moved farther in, he became aware of a trace of something, a sound too faint to distinguish. It hovered in the air around his breaths when he paused and the echoes of his footsteps faded away, filling in the quiet intervals like mortar between bricks.

This was all he heard until he reached the second story. There, he detected the sound of feet treading on the tile floors and looked around for a likely hiding place. There was a door, oval in shape, set a couple feet into the wall and Alistair made use of the small alcove it created, tucking himself in behind the rounded corners just as two men rounded a bend in the hall.

They were Gaians, robed in green and armed with hand guns. Their long beards swayed from side to side as they moved with haste. He watched their grim faces until they passed, then leapt out with the deadly end of his rifle pointed right at one of their heads. When he addressed them, his voice was loud and aggressive, as he had been trained.

"Drop the gun and put your hands on your heads! I will splatter your brains on the floor if you don't drop those guns now!"

The Gaians spent their years on Srillium as the uncontested masters of a populace that could do no more than throw stones at them but dared not. Alistair's shouted commands shook them as much as a grenade. Their guns were on the floor in an instant, followed by whimpered entreaties for mercy as they placed their quivering hands on top of their heads.

"Kick the guns down the hall and get on your knees!"

These commands were obeyed with no less alacrity.

"Lie flat on the floor!"

Again they obeyed, and he moved closer to search them.

"How many more in this building?"

"I don't know," stammered one, his faltering voice doing as much as his thick accent to make his speech difficult to understand. "There are...we were running from the...the..."

"The command center," finished his companion with the accent of a native English speaker. Alistair guessed he was Terran, American or Canadian. "They've taken control of it."

"How many other Gaians in the building? If you lie to me I'm going to kill you."

"We escaped the command center. The only others we know of are captives up there."

Alistair finished patting them down and then recovered their guns.

"Up. Walk in front of me and stay ten feet away from each other. You make a sudden move and I pull the trigger. Now take me to the command center."

As they neared the center it became apparent the faint sound Alistair heard was the mix of noises coming from it. Different machines hummed and whirred as they ran, footsteps crossed and recrossed the floor, men spoke, and punctuating it all was the desultory rhythm of some sort of series of impacts, a thumping of some kind. Before he could ponder what this was, they reached an intersection where several hallways merged to form an irregular chamber. At the far end the wall was round and convex, and Odin stood guard in a doorway, half looking in and half looking out. The former chieftain tensed when he spotted the Gaians, but their body language, with hands on their heads, was unthreatening, and when he saw Alistair he relaxed.

"How goes it?" Odin asked.

"Hangar and weapons depot secure. Two dreadbots down, two unaccounted for. Caleb's gone."

Odin accepted the news with a slow nod. "Frank took a round in the chest. He's dead. The other two dreadbots, Mordecai shut them down from the control center."

There was a great thud and a wail of pain. Alistair gave Odin a questioning look.

"Take these two," he said brushed past him into the command center.

The room was circular, sixty feet from side to side and brightly lit by a multitude of lights, to say nothing of the glowing buttons, switches and 3D displays. There was blood over much of the floor, most of it in long streaks where bodies had been dragged. These streaks led to a side of the large, conical room where several Gaians were piled one on top of the other. Frank's cadaver lay to the side of the haphazard pile, composed in the traditional position with hands folded on chest. The flesh of his chest was torn open and a large hole yawned where much blood clotted.

As many Gaians as lay dead knelt in another part of the room, their hands on their heads, some sporting bruises and gashes on their faces. Mordecai, covered in blood but seemingly unharmed, had hold of a final Gaian who was half lying on the floor, raising a feeble hand to ward off the blows raining down on him. His face was bruised and bloodied, and the fingers of his left hand were smashed and jutted out at unnatural angles. Alistair did not hesitate to intervene.

"That's enough, Mordecai," he said with something less than a shout but which did not lack for firmness.

Mordecai, startled, paused for a moment to regard him. With a derisive curl of his lips he turned back to his victim and once more smashed his face with his fist.

"I said enough! Mordecai!"

Mordecai turned back to Alistair, weighing his options. Though Alistair's weapon was not pointed at him it attracted his glance and perhaps decided the issue. He dropped the beaten Gaian onto the floor and glowered.

"It's done," said Alistair. "The Gaians have scattered; their weapons and ships are ours."

Despite his look, Mordecai's voice was well moderated. "We need to find the ignition keys for the aircraft. Then we can take complete control of the city. And the planet."

This response gave Alistair a feeling of unease, but before he could formulate a reply, a familiar voice from among the Gaians addressed him.

"The ignition keys are safe and secure." It was Bert, kneeling with his hands on his head like the rest. "You can take them at your leisure. The launch codes are on the computer. But there is a power station outside the city that is open to attack. If it is taken out the city will be crippled. I can take you to it. Simple enough. Just to make sure it is not attacked."

"I know right where it is," said another Gaian with dark skin and indeterminate heritage. "I will help take you there."

Alistair and Odin exchanged glances. The Aldran noticed Bert gave the second speaker a nervous look, caught Alistair's eye for a moment, and looked at the floor. The rest of the Gaians exchanged furtive glances.

"We're not concerned about them crippling the city," Alistair finally said. "Sit there and keep quiet."

"I only thought you would want to preserve what you have taken," said Bert without looking up from the floor. "If the station is taken out..."

"We can all help you," said a third Gaian. "We'll take you there and show you how to defend it."

"What the hell is going on here?" demanded Mordecai, and he grabbed his gun and pointed it at the captives. "Why didn't you tell us about this power station before?"

"I didn't...it never occurred..." Bert began, but then fell into an awkward silence.

More than one of the Gaians was glancing at the 3D displays. Alistair went over himself to inspect the equipment. The script was in the Gaian tongue, and he could not discern what each computer was for, nor what it was that drew so many furtive glances. He turned back to the Gaians.

"Mordecai asked you what the hell was going on. I want to hear the answer."

"There's nothing...going on," said Bert, but his breathing was rapid and shallow, and the sheen of sweat on his face thickened, producing drops that ran down his face. His usual pallor was more pronounced, and a couple of his companions, their eyes squeezed tight, seemed to be in the midst of silent prayer. Another looked ready to vomit.

Moving forward, he placed the barrel of his rifle against Bert's forehead, threatening to knock him over backwards.

"If I don't get a convincing answer the bullet in this chamber is going through your skull."

As surely as if he had turned a dial, Bert's heart and breathing rates accelerated, and his lower jaw chattered. Despite this, he forced a reply out of his mouth.

"They're going to destroy the city."

Another captive barked something at him in the Gaian tongue.

"Shut up!" yelled Alistair. To Bert he said, "Who is going to destroy the city?"

Bert gave a nervous look at the man who had yelled at him. "The other Gaians." With a nod to the 3D displays, he continued, "There is a missile on its way for us right now."

With a curse, Alistair grabbed the back of Bert's robes and hauled him to his feet.

"Show me."

Bert pointed at the 3D display and Mordecai and Odin, forgetting the prisoners, bunched in around them. The German Gaian typed a few strokes on the keyboard and some script appeared.

"It will be here in eighteen minutes."

"How many?" asked Mordecai.

"Just one."

"Can you call it off?" asked Odin.

Bert shook his head. "Once the signal is given the city is presumed lost. My brothers got here before you. We should already be dead but...this has never happened before. The other cities did not respond quickly."

"I can take the missile out," said Mordecai. At Alistair's inquisitive look he said, "I was a pilot."

Shaking Bert for emphasis, Alistair said, "Get him the ignition keys!"

Alistair's thick hand, gripping Bert's robes, was replaced by Mordecai's, who hauled him out of his chair and out of the control room. Alistair turned to the captive Gaians.

"I need to be in communication with Mordecai. Someone needs to help me understand these computers."

There was a pause before one of the Gaians answered, "We are prepared to die."

There was conviction in his voice to match his statement, but one of the other Gaians spoke up.

"Will you let us go? Afterwards?" she asked.

"I'll at least let you live."

The Gaian slowly rose from her kneeling position, her expression uncertain as if she were waiting to receive permission. When Alistair did nothing, she nodded and went to one of the computer stations. She stroked a couple keys and a new display popped up, including a 3D image of the hangar.

"I don't know yet which craft he will use," said the woman with excellent English. There was a faint trace of a Latin accent.

"But we'll have communications with him when he's in the craft?"

"Yes we will."

Behind them, the same voice spoke once more in the Gaian tongue, rumbling low and steady. One did not need to understand it to feel the remonstration. With a growl of impatience, Alistair turned to the group, whom Odin was now watching over, and aimed his rifle at them.

"There will be no more talking unless we ask you a question." Turning back to the Hispanic Gaian, he commanded her, "Tell me what he said to you."

Ashamed, the Gaian tucked her chin into her chest and, blushing, replied, "He asked me if I was going to help you rape the planet next."

Alistair could not suppress a chuckle. "A strict Gaian would accuse this entire community of raping the planet."

"We've saved this planet from pillaging. To do that we are forced to use technologies—"

Alistair let out a short but loud guffaw and exclaimed, "That's always the excuse! Every Gaian who ever ate meat found some way to justify it!"

"I don't eat meat."

Alistair laughed. "It's an expression. On Earth 'eating meat' meant doing something prohibited. Like driving autos, using modern medicine, buying a computer…you know, the sort of thing 99% of all Gaians do. A true Gaian, if he could be found, would call you a carnivore. Of course, no religion has ever been faithfully followed by more than a small handful of adherents. Gaianism is no different."

The woman shook in her seat, and her knuckles went livid from gripping the edge of the desk. The keyboard even rattled on its holder, but she did not reply, finally mastering her emotion. A moment later, one of the aircraft floating in the 3D display before them blinked red. The Gaian touched it with her finger and the display changed, giving them a view of the cockpit where Mordecai and Bert were sitting. Bert's hands were bound to his sides.

"Can you hear me, Mordecai?"

"Roger."

"Take off on your go."

A wobble of Mordecai's head was the only indication the craft was put in motion.

"How long do we have?"

"Eleven minutes."

"They got to the hangar pretty fast."

She shrugged. "If you know the way, it doesn't take very long."

"Let me see a map of the area. I need to see where the missile is and where Mordecai is."

She complied with a few keystrokes.

"The missile's coming in from west northwest, Mordecai."

"Copy. I've got it on my display. This is an old model. Handles funny."

The sound of concussion fire broke out, several shots startling Alistair enough that he lost his grip on the rifle and only the strap over his shoulder kept it from falling. A shower of sparks from a nearby computer station erupted, and the overhead lights flickered for a moment before coming back.

He spun around as the sparks rained down. Two Gaians lay twitching on the floor, the concussive force of Odin's gun, set to a fine point, having torn into their flesh just like a bullet. One of the Gaians had charged Odin while another charged at Alistair. Odin downed them both, though one of his shots missed and took out a computer station which buzzed, popped and hissed with tiny flashes of light. Alistair viewed the carnage without comment. The damaged computer crackled one more time and fell silent.

"Take them into the hall," said Alistair. "And have them lay down on their faces. Five feet of separation between each one."

"What the hell happened in there?" demanded Mordecai.

Odin marched the Gaians outside and Alistair returned his attention to the 3D display.

"Minor uprising. Nothing to worry about." To the Gaian he said, "What's the missile's ETA?"

"ETA?"

"Estimated Time of Arrival."

"Eight minutes."

"Time to intercept?"

"Three and a half minutes."

"I confirm. Three and a half minutes."

Alistair grabbed a nearby chair and collapsed into it. "How many hours do you have in the air?"

"None. I did space flight."

"Well that explains why you thought it handled funny!"

"Stop your worrying. It's not much different than space flight. Just a little drag from the atmosphere."

"How many hours in space did you have?"

"Stop worrying."

Alistair ceased his pestering, leaving him nothing to do but sit and leave sweat stains. As time passed, the dots on the map, one representing Mordecai's craft and the other the missile, drew closer and closer. Every so often the Gaian would update the time to intercept, and Mordecai would confirm it.

Many dozens of miles away, Mordecai stopped the acceleration driving him and his passenger deep into their seats. Even from the height of a mile over the ground, the land moved past in a blur of different shades of green. Then the blur became a deep blue, and Mordecai, checking his windshield which doubled as a computer display, confirmed he was now flying over the ocean. He passed through a cloud, to him nothing more than an ephemeral blink of white.

When a green light flashed on his windshield, he confirmed for the command center that he was nearing striking distance. Then the light turned red. Mordecai prepped the laser and the computer had it aimed and ready to fire. His thumb hovered over the button, and for a moment he felt he would let the missile slip by, let it continue to the city while he flew away. He pictured Alistair's burning, mutilated corpse; he pictured his entire private security system burning with it. But there were other Gaian cities, other Gaians who would come for him. He knew this, knew he needed everything they could take from Floralel. He even recognized he needed Alistair, at least for now.

Grimacing, almost snarling, Mordecai pressed hard on the button. The red light instantly stopped flashing and there was a small explosion in the sky ahead. A dark cloud billowed, expanding from the center of the explosion. It grew larger in his windshield until his craft passed through, resulting in a dark gray blink almost too fleeting to notice.

Over the communication system, he heard Alistair demanding confirmation the missile was down, but he did not reply. Instead, he dropped a lazy finger over the switch to the com system and turned it off. Eventually, he turned the craft around and headed back to Floralel.

74

In the end, many more missiles were launched at Floralel. The attacks were not well coordinated, but Mordecai was kept busy for some time, picking off one attack after another. It was an act of trickery that stopped the assault. Bert took Alistair to the main power station and Mordecai allowed one last missile to approach the city. Just when it crossed the border of attack range, Alistair killed the power at the same moment Mordecai downed the missile. To the other Gaian cities, it appeared Floralel was obliterated. While frost claimed all surfaces and snow fell in the long night of the eclipse, they raided the Gaian stores and equipment. Mordecai and Ryan, who, at Alistair's insistence, received some training from Mordecai, made many trips to transport their new materials.

What took them days to traverse now took them minutes. What was a journey of sweat and saddle soreness with nights spent on hard ground was now a brief flight in a cushioned seat, little more inconvenient than a man's trip from his living room to his pantry. It was the difference between the Bronze Age and the Space Age. Alistair, Giselle, Taribo and the five Singulatarians, after hours of ransacking and finally detonating a bomb to destroy Floralel, rode in the back of a craft piloted by Ryan, bursting with pride such that Alistair wondered how he had gotten the restraining straps to fit over his chest.

Ryan flew no more than half a mile above the ground. Following Alistair's instructions, he accelerated for the first half of the trip, driving them back into their seats to the limits of their ease and comfort, and then decelerated for the second half, at which point the seats of all but the pilot swiveled around and they were again driven into their seats. It was practical flying with no flourishes. There were control and guidance systems that made it a relatively easy matter to fly, so Ryan learned the basics in a short time. Their accompanying craft, piloted by the more experienced Mordecai, swept into a wide arc over the north beach of their island home, then, at the end of the arc, descended almost to the surface of the sea and skimmed over it, tearing at the smooth water and throwing up spray before finally coming to an abrupt stop in a field south of the beach. The gathered crowd was delighted by the display and a great cheer arose.

As Alistair looked out the window, seeing two rows of aircraft neatly lined up in the large clearing, he felt fingers scratch the back of his head and he turned to smile at Giselle. Having availed himself of the Gaian facilities, he was freshly shaved and his hair was buzzed short once more. Giselle had only just developed the habit of twirling his hair; now she turned to scratching it instead.

The guidance system on the aircraft cushioned the landing so that their return to earth was like settling into a pile of pillows. The soft whir of the engine, which Alistair had ceased to notice, briefly elicited his attention by going quiet and was replaced by the more insistent buzz of the walk ramp being lowered. The eight passengers—Singulatarians included—and one pilot unclasped their restraining straps and moved down the carpeted aisles to the exit.

When the door was lifted, the sounds of the crowd hit them, and they walked down the ramp to a renewed gust of applause and cheers.

Santiago, rifle strapped to his right shoulder, was at the bottom, unable to contain an approving smile. Seized by a surge of affection, he and Alistair embraced with a few rough slaps on the back, and they allowed themselves a coarse and hearty laugh.

"For three hundred years this moon was a prison planet," said the Argentinean. "Never has there been a victory over the Gaians in all that time."

"It's just the beginning," Alistair promised.

Giselle elbowed in to receive a welcome hug and kiss on the cheek, and Miklos met Taribo and gripped his friend's shoulders before delivering a slap to both. Amid the mirth, Alistair glanced at the other craft, which landed a couple hundred feet away, and saw Mordecai and the rest descending from their walk ramp. *Time for another struggle,* he thought, steeling himself.

To Santiago he said, "Is Darion here?"

"I told him you were arriving this morning. He said he would be here."

"And Gregory?"

"Busy."

Taking the information with a nod, Alistair signaled to Giselle and his men to follow him and headed towards Mordecai's craft. As he went, like a satellite tugging at the water of the planet it orbits, he drew the crowd with him so that a sort of high tide of bodies gathered near him and Mordecai. Mordecai turned from greeting his men to face Alistair, and Duke, Odin and Wei Bai, who were similarly engaged, turned as well. Alistair addressed them without preamble, in a voice loud enough for his targets to hear but without regard to others listening in.

"We can divide up the goods now and go our separate ways."

"This instant?" asked Duke.

"No time like the present. Giselle and Shukri compiled a list of what we have and what crate it was stored in. The equipment and the aircraft...we can get this over with quickly."

The crowd stirred as they strained to hear what was going on.

"You want to start now?" Mordecai asked in disbelief.

"We can meet tonight to divide it. Right now you can survey the lists and plan what you would like to take. I propose each team get credits and we'll bid for the different items with them."

"I have no objection," said Duke, "but I should like to talk with some of the scientists first."

"The Singulatarians work for me. They'll be busy working with Mr. Chesterton in preparation for the bidding."

This pronouncement was met with angry glares.

"It is bad form to snatch everything up for yourself, Alistair," said Wei Bai. *"You take everything: the hovercraft that brought the dreadbots, the weapons it carried...now you claim the Singulatarians—"*

"The Singulatarians have consented to work for me. I am paying them. No one owes you their advice, their knowledge, or anything else. If you lack something and wish to get what Nature has not freely provided for you, then you must come to terms with someone who can help you. Nothing is owed to you that you do not earn. You have earned a right to a share of the spoils…but if your knowledge of the equipment is wanting you must clear that up on your own. Neither I nor anyone who works for me owes you this service free of charge."

"It seems to me," said Mordecai, "that your talk of freedom and anarchy is not backed by any substance. You want to grab power for yourself."

"That is more absurd than I care to respond to," Alistair replied, and indicated the conversation was finished by turning away.

During the gathering, Darion Chesterton appeared with a jaunty step, sporting an ornately carved cane that, as far as anyone could tell, served little practical purpose. As he lightly bounced along the ground he twirled it, or carried it on his shoulder like a rifle. Occasionally he would press the end of it into the ground but he leaned little weight on it. His spry and energetic legs did not require support. A manservant followed close by, carrying a torch. As he strolled through the crowd with a cheerful smile, he nodded at bemused onlookers when he was not gazing about with a self satisfied air. Upon seeing Alistair and the rest he bowed elegantly and came over to meet him.

"Well met and happy returns."

"You mean our return or an investment's returns?" asked Alistair.

"Why does it have to be one or the other?"

With the spoils of their conquest spread out around them, with the curious and eager crowd gathered to celebrate their success, with the prospects of prosperity in the forms of the goods and the talents of the men and women there, with Darion's breezy cheerfulness infecting him, Alistair felt exultant. When Floralel was taken he felt relieved and in need of rest. With the details of the looting of the city pressing down on him he felt strained once again. Now, for the first time, he felt almost giddy and could not suppress a smile.

"Darion, allow me to present to you Shukri Abdiaziz, Amina and Faisa Abdirahman, Akihiro Sawagato and Raja Gulyanov. Ladies and gentlemen, this is Darion Chesterton of Aldra, my homeworld."

The Singulatarians nodded and Darion executed another bow, deeper than the first, that finished with a flourish of his cane.

"Very pleased," said Darion.

"You'll be working with them to survey the goods, and then I'll need you with me tonight when we have the auction."

"Excellent. But let's have some lunch first."

So saying, he clapped his hands and three men, burdened with baggage, rushed forward to prepare a sort of picnic there on the ground. One laid out what on Srillium passed for a fine tablecloth, while the other two set out the serving dishes, plates and silverware. Darion could not help but notice the expression on Alistair's face as he regarded the servants, the bemused expression a man exudes when he is not precisely uncomfortable, but not in his element either.

"After a man raises himself out of the dirt, his first order of business is a good bath," Darion explained. "Then, he must find his style. Ah! By the way, our cotton plants are surviving."

"They are?"

526

"Most. They are a tad withered but they'll make it through, I think. I dug a moat around them and filled it with burning embers. There is nothing I can do for sunlight, but at least they won't freeze."

"Get rid of the seeds of the ones that did not survive."

"Cull the herd?"

"If we want a cotton harvest on this rock we'll need the plants to adapt to it."

"A first rate idea. But right now let's get some sustenance. We have an auction tonight!"

As if waiting for Darion's pronouncement, Srillium began to change. Its edge continued to grow brighter, and a ray of sunlight, bright and powerful, peaked out from the side, and immediately they were touched by it they felt the warmth grow on their faces. The snowflakes glinted as they passed through it. The land brightened to the level of dawn, and short shadows jumped out everywhere. As the sun began its job of attacking the snow, Alistair felt Giselle embrace him, and again he smiled.

࿇ ࿇

The boulder was pushed aside, and once again the shaft in the hilltop exposed. Long shadows returned with the setting sun, and on the bare top of the hill the Singulatarians, Miklos, Taribo, Giselle, Gregory, Layla, Darion, Santiago, Ryan and Alistair, who was the new owner of the shaft, cut dark figures into the pink and orange and purple sky. Miklos, with feckless curiosity, leaned over the shaft and spit into it. Apparently satisfied with the result of the experiment, he stood up straight again.

"That's deep."

"I expect it is," said Darion, more amused than appalled.

"Raja is the youngest of us," said Shukri to Alistair. "He is eager to explore. However, unless my guess is wrong, he will not be able to solve this for us. That will have to wait until we can get some of the equipment running."

"Which means batteries," said Alistair.

"Which means industry," said Santiago.

"Which means capital," finished Darion. "No one man can make a battery."

"I will go until I cannot," said Raja, the halting English passing through his smile, and he produced from his white robes a small stick with an orb of crystal at the end. With a squeeze he set it glowing and then fastened it to his rope belt. His four companions gathered around, giving him encouraging squeezes on the shoulder or, in Faisa's case, a touch of foreheads.

"This will be a while," advised Shukri as Raja stepped to the edge of the shaft and, like a boxer in his corner before the bell, prepared to begin. "Say goodbye and go to your meeting. We will wait here."

"The other guy said he thought he made it maybe half a kilometer down before he gave up and came back," said Alistair.

"Raja will go farther than that," said Amina.

Akihiro strapped on Raja' backpack, which held a few tools for climbing as well as a sack Raja could attach to the metal rungs to rest. In addition it held three meals and plenty of water. Lastly, a communication headset was fixed to his head to keep him in contact with the others. Akihiro, upon finishing the preparations, stepped away from Raja, as if giving him room to launch.

"On your way, my friend," said Shukri, and the others all produced a goodbye after their own fashion.

Then Raja disappeared into the hole. No more than five seconds gone, his voice came through the speaker of Shukri's communicator.

"Testing equipment," he said in Mandarin, a language he spoke only a little better than English.

"We read you," returned Faisa.

This acted as cue for the others to go. Alistair enlisted them all for the evening's auction, an event he fully expected to last until the sun appeared on the opposite horizon the next morning. As he moved to descend the hill, he peered out over the lowlands to the north. There, torches were stuck in the ground, recently lit. A large table was built for the occasion in a location Mordecai considered sufficiently neutral to suit him. This task seemed a lavish waste of time to Alistair, who was just as happy sitting on the ground or a tree stump, but the event took on a life of its own beyond his ability to control. Even now he spotted a procession led by a man he knew must have been the Druid, with Clyde by his side. The young Aldran was pleased to arrive only after the Gaian blessing and consecration.

"We can't just divvy up the loot," he muttered. "We've got to try and add some mystical significance to it all."

"You'll find humans are like that," said Gregory, walking by Alistair's side. "We often need more than just the practical fact of something. It's in our nature, and this is a significant event."

"Not significant enough by itself, apparently," Alistair replied, though in a tolerant humor. "We have to pile some mysticism and ceremony on it."

Gregory patted his friend on the back, and they left the hill.

75

The narrow channel between Odin's Island and the main continent was now little more an impediment than a puddle. So long as their fuel lasted—water purified to an extreme level of limpidness—it would remain so, though they were without means to purify more. Thus, most made the decision to return to the mainland, leaving behind only a few who preferred to continue the work they deemed most profitable. Among such work was the farm with which Darion was charged, though Darion himself returned to the mainland.

No sooner had he set foot on soil than he was hiring prospectors to search out new locations for mines. It was long a commonplace that the best locations for the really interesting resources were the craters of meteors that brought heavier elements to the relatively light crust of a planet. Srillium, held in close proximity to a gas giant whose gravity was a great magnet for space debris, was the victim of far more meteorite impacts than a typical terrestrial planet. Darion was drooling to get at them.

It was also a commonplace that money was the lifeblood of an economy, but any serious reflection reveals this metaphor is not entirely fitting. Money was more like lubrication, facilitating the exchange of goods, allowing the shoemaker to buy fish even when no fisherman desires his shoes. The true lifeblood of an economy is its energy, its power source, that which drives actual work. To this end a powerplant was planned directly they discovered a suitable source of moving water.

The labor for such an undertaking proved readily available. Indeed, so many of the barbarian tribes came flocking to them that Alistair purchased the services of his workers at prices that scandalized Gregory, who immediately protested. Red in the face, he came storming up to Alistair as soon as he heard about the situation.

"It seems the pharaohs have returned," he growled while Alistair was looking through a stack of papers with Giselle. Startled, they looked up at Gregory and, unable to form an immediate reply, blinked. "I just got the most unbelievable news that my friend was resorting to slave labor for the powerplant."

"The pharaohs didn't use slave labor," Alistair replied. "That's a common misconception."

"I don't give a damn about ancient Egypt! Is it true what I heard about their salaries?"

"Probably. I'm not paying them very much."

"I don't fucking believe it!"

"But they're not slaves. They agreed to work for the wages I'm offering."

"That's a technicality! It doesn't matter they're not actually slaves."

"I think it does, since that was your charge."

"Goddammit." Gregory collapsed into a nearby chair. "Alistair…"

"I forgot this was going to be a problem with you." Alistair sighed, dropped the quill in his hand and leaned back in his own chair.

"How can you expect a society to be healthy with salaries like that?"

"You know, Greg, they are getting paid with money Darion and I coined. There was no such thing as a salary until we came and offered them one. We don't owe them a damn thing, but we offered them a job because we wanted labor. They agreed to work for it; I can only presume they prefer a salaried job, however slight the salary, to the tribal barbarism they lived under until just a day ago."

"You're not giving them very much."

"They're not giving *me* very much. Their tools are hardly better than what *Homo erectus* used. They don't produce much, so they don't get paid much. And there are a lot of them. Too many of them."

"So take advantage of them?"

"So earn as much of a profit as I can and make my position more attractive and theirs less. We have more labor than we need; we need more businessmen and entrepreneurs. The cheaper labor is, the more workers will decide to try their own hand at starting a business. The higher the price of labor, the fewer workers will try to strike out on their own. And I need workers to strike out on their own. I need tools. I need nails. I need screws. I need I-beams. I need all sorts of things a bunch of men in animal skins, working in tents, can't make. If labor is paid well when there is too much of it there is no incentive to change. But if men start making their own businesses..."

"Yeah, yeah, yeah," said Gregory, rising from his seat and making a gesture as if dismissing him. "You've got an answer for everything."

"If I've got an answer for everything that might mean something!" he yelled as Gregory left.

Giselle gave him a kiss on the cheek.

"Women can do those things too, my dear," she whispered.

"What?"

"You said you needed men to start businesses."

"Oh, don't start," he said but a smile broke through.

More difficult than the labor was the technical know-how. The Singulatarians were invaluable in this endeavor. Upon first arriving at Srillium, they were at a loss as to how to go about building from scratch. Though not specialists in the field, they went back to their basic scientific knowledge and designed a miniature power plant in their cave near Floralel, rethinking fundamental ideas in an effort to build something so rudimentary. With this experience to build on, they now designed a grander powerplant to drive more than a homemade light bulb.

In the end, progress was delayed while Darion hunted down new mines and searched for new minerals and chemicals. This too was delayed while food was found to sustain the men who were out prospecting. Giselle remarked several times how difficult it was to get the project underway, that she had figured it to be a matter of hiring workers and building. Alistair muttered a reply about the importance of savings, that no such project could be accomplished without it.

With the design finally resolved, and labor available, the last remaining problem was funding. Alistair, Duke, Wei Bai and Darion each put up capital for the project, but hesitated to sink too much of their own money too early. What remained unfunded would be solved, they decided, by issuing bonds, and these they set about marketing. There was no regulatory board before which they had to present their plan for a stamp of approval, there were no politicians to be bribed, no monopoly privilege granted to prevent their entry into the market. The four men held a meeting, decided how much they wished to raise in bonds and according to what schedule, agreed upon an interest rate, and hired a few salesmen. If the bonds did not sell, it was a swift and simple matter of adjusting the terms.

☙❧

When Alistair and his men approached the tribes with their offer, extending promises of property protection to all paying customers, an offer they made while gripping weapons the primitive tribal chiefs could not hope to match, the tribes disintegrated in a matter of minutes. The wide open lands that frequent warfare made too dangerous to plow were homesteaded at a dizzying pace. Farms appeared overnight, and each day the cultivated areas expanded, stopping only at the hastily erected stone walls, usually only ten inches high, demarcating the borders of property.

Not every tribesman, of course, elected to hire Alistair. Duke and Wei Bai's firm, called Bedrock, attracted many, and Mordecai's The Shield also took a good share. Some small communities formed and took care of their own problems without outside help. A few chose to risk no protection at all. New firms sprang up, far from the transformation's epicenter, and cultivated their own client base. Within a single week the entire area was being farmed or used for some other productive purpose, and the effect spread much like falling dominoes, and almost with the same rapidity.

Alistair's arrival and announcement touched off a storm that flew out of his control. Each new tribe, upon hearing the news and the firepower in possession of the new security firms, broke apart, all exhortations by the tribal chief notwithstanding. Upon observing the inescapable trend and seeing so much land to be claimed for the mere price of settling down and working, men deserted their tribes, driven by an impulse most had never felt before. The phenomenon extended beyond Alistair's ken. He truly had no idea how large an area, on any given day, was affected by the revolution.

He made it clear all disputes could be resolved without outside interference. This was surprisingly effective, and even Gregory remarked at how little conflict there was between homesteaders claiming land.

"This is no surprise," he replied. "For the fireworks display on Foundation Day, do you ever remember a fight breaking out on the lawn when we gathered to watch? Everyone brings a blanket and lays it out, and everyone has an innate sense of how much space should be allowed for that purpose. The first to arrive are the first to choose their space, and everyone respects that. Simple and natural."

"I think claiming property is a bit different from gathering on a lawn to watch fireworks for an hour," Gregory countered.

"It's not fundamentally different. We all naturally accept the principle that the first to arrive has first claim. We have at least a basic idea of how much land should be allotted for a given purpose. Conflict is minimal, as it would have to be for any society to function, government or not."

For the purpose of farming, a certain amount of territory was allotted to each home-steader as soon as he worked the land for that purpose, but even Alistair was surprised to discover it was not he and his business associates who determined what acreage to allow per farm. A general determination evolved on its own through the interactions of the homestead-ers. It being different than their original determination, they quickly changed their standard to conform to the market, and Alistair chided himself for having presumed to set a standard to begin with.

Bottom up, not top down, he reminded himself. *Always.*

∂~∽

The price of labor paid to those who longed to hold some sort of coin in their hands, and quickly, soon rose as other jobs sprang up and demand for workers increased. With land as cheap and accessible as it was, Alistair had to make his wages more attractive lest his workers decide to become farmers, or work for any number of other fledgling industries, or become entrepreneurs.

The result of the limited productivity of their society was that certain jobs did not get done, or were long delayed. The greatest desires were satisfied first. This meant that, idle aircraft being relatively abundant for Ashley Security and Arbitration, no offices were constructed, nor any dormitories in which to sleep. Giselle's office was in the cargo space of a box-like craft not unlike the one that brought the dreadbot to Odin's Island. There she stored her papers and files as well as met with clients. Her working conditions were almost luxurious compared to what she had grown accustomed to. Even after several days the novelty of her new position was still keen. She counted herself fortunate, felt like royalty when she worked, and faced each day with glee, even when working with former warriors.

There were muddy tracks all over the floor, and without proper cabinets she had to improvise her filing, which left her papers somewhat vulnerable to the elements. These ele-ments invaded the craft with regularity because, to conserve energy, the exit ramp was left down, thus leaving the entrance covered only by a hanging animal skin curtain. The clientele laborers who showered only when it chanced to rain, and never with soap, did little to improve the surroundings.

The specimen in front of her was a typical example. His skin glistened with sweat in the hot and humid air and bore dark smudges of dirt, most of them streaked where perspira-tion trickled down. His red hair was long, like his beard, and both were gnarled and frizzy. In his mouth were at least two gaps where teeth once were and two prominent scars adorned his warrior's face.

"It's a bit complicated," said the man in front of her after wistfully rubbing his jaw.

"I can help you with any questions," Giselle offered, quelling her distaste and plastering a serviceable smile on her face.

"Why can't I just pay my fee and have done with it?"

"We feel our price structure offers you advantages," she replied, but then remembered Alistair's strict order of absolute honesty. "The truth is it's better for us too. It's good for us both."

"How?"

"In a lot of ways. It's to our advantage, not just yours, that you not be the victim of a crime. It's less work for us, so we offer rate reductions for any self defense classes you take with Taribo. If you own a weapon and demonstrate you can competently use it, this reduces the likelihood of you being a victim of crime. Naturally we offer a discount for that. In the future, certain danger areas might develop that we prefer you avoid; we'll offer incentives for you to do so. We have what we consider a more than acceptable defense force, but may need to raise an army some day, so we offer a reduction for a promise of military service. You can volunteer ten, twenty or thirty days of service per year, and the rate reductions increase commensurately. We offer a payment for graduation from a one week boot camp with Taribo."

The man frowned as he tried to process all the information she flung at him.

"You don't have to decide today—"

"I want a lot of reductions."

She did her best to make her smile genuine. "Let's sign the papers."

Ten minutes later, Thomas O'Leary of Ireland, Earth, was a client of Ashley Security and Arbitration and a reserve soldier with an obligation of military service not to exceed thirty days per year. Having sworn an oath of good conduct, he enjoyed a rate reduction for the weapons he owned and was on his way to see Taribo about boot camp. When he left, Giselle, seeing he was the last in line and no other waited for her, took advantage of the lull to clean her office, starting with a thorough scrubbing of the floor and grimacing at the thought of the dirty brute who had just been there.

The site chosen for the Gaian Temple was only a few miles from where the powerplant would be built. The ground-breaking was largely symbolic, for no work followed for a period of weeks, but Clyde Oliver Jones immediately set about raising funds. Alistair met the news with a predictably stoic expression and a noncommittal shrug. To most it seemed he did not care. Only Giselle, who was coming to know him better, and Gregory detected the faint note of uncomprehending derision. This attitude became more and more evident, and morphed into hostile contempt, when Clyde's project came to conflict with Alistair's.

More than a few times Alistair's bond salesmen returned with disappointing results, each one of them citing the Temple as a prominent cause of their difficulties. Charitable donations given to the Temple left less for the financing bonds essential to supplementing the original capital for the powerplant. No religion ever bested hunger in a straight fight, but when the farms, both new and old, began to produce, many men turned to their beliefs. Each time a bond went unsold, Alistair thought of the Temple. Each delay in the arrival of supplies caused him to curse the emerging foundations only a few miles from his embryonic electric plant. One day, he stormed into Giselle's office, tracking mud, and launched into a tirade with no notice of Gregory and Layla, who had stopped by to visit.

"I don't understand the need to worship," he proclaimed in a voice that reverberated in the confines of the aircraft. "What good comes from pretending there is some greater deity, or system, or entity or power and submitting yourself to a will you yourself invented?"

He paused only long enough to take a breath.

"We've got so damn far to go and one of the first things they want to do is build a goddamn Temple! What the hell use is it?"

He finished his outburst with a roar and, deflated, leaned on a nearby crate. It was a moment before Giselle, exchanging surprised glances with Gregory and Layla, ventured a reply.

"I thought everyone was free to pursue their own ends."

"They are free to pursue their own ends. But what the hell do they want to waste good time and resources on a fucking Temple for? We're starting from damn near scratch here. Build a Temple later. Right now we need to work on more useful things."

"There's no point in explaining religious convictions to you, Alistair," Gregory softly declared. "But most people have them. You don't need to understand it; you just need to tolerate it. I believe I've heard you say the same thing a few times."

"Honey, you told me value was subjective. They're building a Temple because they want to build one. It doesn't have to serve your interests."

He had no reply to the logic he fed her and which she now gave back to him. He stood silently a moment, leaning on the crate and looking at nothing in particular, before Giselle spoke again.

"We'll finish the plant. You say we have a long way to go…but to what? There's no final destination."

"Are you sure?"

Giselle looked confused. "We just keep working to make things better. Like you told me, we all have to cooperate to achieve more. Cooperating means allowing people the use of their property. Right?"

Alistair sat down in a chair, his temper under control.

"Do you know how he's raising money? He's having séances. Reading people's palms. Performing magic tricks. Predicting the future. There are just enough drooling idiots out there to keep him in business, and when he tells them their dead grandmother still loves them or the spirit of Gaia is with them, they pour all the money they've earned in his hands."

Gregory shrugged. "If they're dumb enough to fall for that crap…"

"I ought to arrest him for fraud. I seriously mean it. He's committing fraud."

"You think all religion is fraud."

"Religion is silly. But when you take people's money in exchange for putting them in contact with their dead relatives—"

"But he doesn't do that," Gregory interjected. "He reads them their future and then accepts donations. He is not technically selling anything. That's not fraud according to the definition you read me when I signed my contract with Ashley Security & Arbitration."

"Besides, if you try to arrest him you'll lose every Gaian client you have, which is most of them," reasoned Giselle.

Alistair glared darkly at the floor. "I don't want any Gaian clients," he muttered and left the office.

৯৽ ৺৾

The first thing Mordecai did upon returning to the mainland was order the construction of his new house. Having fewer funds than Alistair, he was forced to sell pieces of salvaged equipment in order to pay for it, an act he committed with the utmost agony. No king ever grieved more over the loss of a territory. When these funds ran out and he had to sell a couple more pieces, he felt as if his empire were unraveling.

The audacious structure was made of lumber and stone and progress was measured in inches per day. Part of this was due to the lack of good tools, but also contributing was Mordecai's insistence that his home stand on the top of a large hill, and all the materials had to be dragged up the mount by the toil of underfed workers. Some of these were chronically undernourished former slaves who, despite the improvement in their position, had yet to regain their former vigor, and some were former warriors who, though well fed until recently, were showing signs of want now that food was purchased, not apportioned, and there simply wasn't enough yet to make the entire population hale and hearty.

When the ground level was livable with the floor of the second story acting as roof, Mordecai made do with a converted living room as the master bedroom. He received his visitors in what would be his banquet hall when his table was finished. He placed an order for it but the best offer he could find was from a farmer who promised to finish the piece as soon as his field was in a satisfactory state. Seething with impatience, he cursed this voluntary society and Alistair, the man who forced it on him.

He sat in his banquet-hall-to-be at a small desk with a wooden stool. The interior was bare and unfinished, giving the appearance of a shed more than a dining area. With his arms folded and his chin tucked into his chest, he did not distinguish the polite knock on the door from the bangs and wallops of construction coming from above. Finally, diffidently, the visitor entered and gingerly crossed the floor to stand before Mordecai at his desk.

"*Are you finished?*" grumbled Mordecai.

"*Yes, sir,*" was the reply in a heavy Russian accent.

"*Then out with it.*"

The nervous little man fumbled with some papers which he finally put into the desired order.

"*There is no possibility of supplying weapons for the troops in the next three months, and probably not for the next three after that.*"

"*God damn it.*"

"*There was, uh…it seems the tool makers are making farm tools right now. I offered good money for swords and arrows but…*" the small man winced before he delivered the next bit of news, "*some of them outright refused to make weapons. A couple said they would accept but…the prices they are charging…*" He gave a weak smile and waited for a response from Mordecai. When none was forthcoming he continued. "*At any rate, even if we could get weapons we probably wouldn't have much of an army to use them. We are having difficulty charging our customers enough to cover an army. Alistair, Duke and Wei Bai have a light security force—*"

"*Which is why we can strike them if we can raise an army!*" Mordecai bellowed, and the startled man in front of him jumped back.

The obsequious and nervous smile quickly returned and he continued. "*But that is also why they are charging so little for their services. In order to stay competitive we have to adjust our prices… it seems we have little discretionary room. Furthermore, and I hesitate to bring this up…you did authorize me to alter the terms of service to stop our subscribers from going over to Alistair…*" Mordecai only stared blankly at the man, so he continued, "*Our clients are no longer obligated to give military service. Now*" it's an option we offer in exchange for reduced rates." Mordecai looked as if he were ready to explode so the man hurried to continue. "We were forced to! We were losing clients because they liked Alistair's offer better. Some of them have agreed to military service, but only for defense. And they are getting reduced rates for it. We simply are not taking in enough money to raise an army."

"Then borrow!"

"I tried. There are few with that kind of capital, and they all asked to see our books and wanted to know what the loan was for. No one wants to finance a war, and no one thinks your earnings prospects are worth the risk of lending you the amount of money we would need to raise an army. An army that will be without weapons for at least the next half year."

The report finished, the man laid the papers on the desk in front of Mordecai. He stood with his arms at his sides and waited for a response, but at first Mordecai only rubbed at the bridge of his nose.

"It's like trying to climb out of a sand pit," he finally said, his voice soft and weary. "Every time I reach up I slide down, and I can't make any headway."

"Perhaps this is the way things are going to be."

"You may go now."

The man nodded once and began to leave but stopped before reaching the door and half turned to say one last thing.

"Two of the pilots you trained left. Alistair hired one and Wei Bai the other."

He spoke the two sentences in the manner of a man who reaches out to grab the handle of a frying pan whose temperature he does not know. When Mordecai did not explode with rage, did not even respond, he sighed in relief: the handle was cool to the touch. Not wishing to press his luck, he opened the door and made a hasty exit.

かいか

There was one large aircraft Alistair acquired from the auction. It seemed to have been a diplomatic vessel, a capacious affair with sleeping chambers, board rooms, antechambers and just about anything one would expect from an embassy. He used it as his headquarters, and it had flown only twice since he acquired it: once from Floralel to Odin's Island, and then from Odin's Island back to the mainland.

It was circular, with an outer hallway running near the perimeter. On the outside of the hallway was the cockpit as well as several private chambers. Inside was a large meeting room with a polished, mahogany table, a plush carpet and cushioned chairs, all done in the Gaian style of swirls, rounded corners and asymmetry. It was there Alistair chose to hold his weekly meetings.

Darion Chesterton always attended, though he was not technically a part of Ashley Security & Arbitration. The Singulatarians, as science and technology advisors, were there, as were Taribo, Wellesley, Santiago and the indispensable Giselle. They gathered one day around the table, underneath the irregular green ceiling with the recessed whitish patch that glowed when turned on, giving the impression of a sun shining through a canopy of leaves. Alistair entered late and was greeted by the soft murmurs of hushed conversations, the occasional throat clearing, the rustle of papers. When he sat down and tapped his stack of papers on the table top, it sliced through the hum of background noise.

"Let's get this started," he said as he fished out a couple sheets of paper from his stack.

"Should we do a roll call?" asked Shukri with an inoffensive delicateness, referring to a decision from the previous meeting that Alistair was forgetting.

"It doesn't seem…" he began but trailed off. "I think we can keep things less formal."

"It can be helpful to have a thorough record of these things," suggested Santiago as he rattled the table top with his fingertips.

"Giselle can note who attended in the minutes," pronounced Alistair with a tone of dismissal. "Now, first order of business: supplies."

"Yes," said Faisa, "we have much to discuss about supplies."

"We are concerned we are not going to be given the proper time to work with what we salvaged from Floralel," said Akihiro with a polite but firm tone.

Amina and Shukri lodged similar grievances, the one on top of the other. Darion, leaning back in his chair and fingering the top of his cane, was not affected by their complaints. Indeed, he gave no indication he was even listening until the Singulatarians were finished and everyone turned their gazes to him. At that point he spoke but did not take his eyes from his cane.

"We have such a mountain of things…we simply can't use it all."

"If you give us enough time…" said Shukri and then he turned to the company head. "Alistair, we need more time. There are all sorts of projects we can undertake—"

"But not enough labor to undertake them all," Alistair interjected. "We can take advantage of the expertise out there, sitting idle right now. You are scientists. You can tell me what a particular device can do. Darion is a businessman. He can tell me the most profitable course of action. All I need you to do is explain the equipment to Darion and he will decide whether it is best for us to keep and use or to sell to the highest bidder. That way, we allow anyone who thinks they can make use of something the opportunity to use it. We can't do everything. We don't have business interests in every field of human endeavor. It doesn't make sense to hoard everything in a vault until we get around to using it."

"But how can you know whom to sell it to?" countered Shukri. "Finding the right man, making sure he uses it in a way that furthers our—everyone's—interests…"

"We don't need to do that," said Darion, still intent on inspecting his cane. "I have sent out men far and wide announcing an auction. We will sell anything to anyone who pays the right price. We don't need to know what they will use it for; if they put up the money to buy it I assume they have an idea in mind for it and are welcome to it. For the right price, I will sell every last piece we have."

A roar of protest went up from all five Singulatarians, but Darion did not flinch.

"You have to learn to let go, to trust and use the market," said Alistair when the shouting died down. "By selling off this equipment, we allow it to go to where it is most valued."

"But no one else has the facilities you do," said Faisa. "No one else can put it to such use."

"For any single piece of equipment, I agree with you. But we have thousands of items. After the first few dozen, their value to us falls based on the simple fact we don't have time to get to it. Even if we sell it to someone who lacks our capacity to use it, the fact that it's their primary piece of equipment means it is at the top of their list and will receive their utmost attention. This puts that piece of equipment in a better position."

"How will they recharge the batteries?" asked Akihiro, but his tone was weak, like one who is almost ready to give in.

"When the powerplant comes on line, there is already someone who is looking to recharge batteries," said Darion. "He is going to purchase some of our equipment and is already building a little shop right next to the powerplant. A recharging station. It will be difficult, but if he succeeds, and he seems confident, then we may not have to worry about the equipment running out of power…at least not until the batteries themselves degrade."

"And maybe by then we'll be producing our own," finished Alistair. "And that's something we are going to be working towards: production. The knowledge is out there to produce higher technology."

"But we're light years away from having the equipment," added Darion.

"We will have to build up gradually. The tools we have today we use to make better tools, which we use to make even better tools, and so on, until one day…we're making HD drives, superconductors, nanobots, femptochips…a journey that first took thousands of years. But we are starting out with the knowledge already extant. Most of the scientific discovery won't have to be redone."

"So if it took humans tens of thousands of years the first time, how long does it take us?" asked Amina.

"I hope not long," said Alistair.

"Two decades," predicted Darion.

"But until we advance farther, I am grounding all flights except for emergencies. The fuel for the aircraft is water. To get the fusion needed the water has to be purified to a degree we can't manage, and impure water would destroy the engines. So we don't fly for a while.

"Now, Darion said it would be twenty years before we become a modern society. We need to talk about strategies to shorten that time span. There are no children here, and that is bad news for us."

Ryan Wellesley snorted. "That was the one nice thing about this place."

"That's bad news for us," continued Alistair, "because it means the savings rate will be lower. An economy grows when you produce and shrinks when you consume. If you earn money, meaning if you create something and put it in the market, then you get paid for it and can use that money to draw something else out of the market and consume it. When you earn the money but do not draw from the market, you have saved that money."

"And this saving can be lent to a businessman like me," said Darion. "And these loans allow me to buy equipment to expand productivity."

"Spending simply consumes what has been produced," Alistair resumed. "My concern is people here are going to consume what they produce and not save enough to expand production. We need to preach savings. With a bunch of Gaians whose creed is to leave the earth alone, this won't be too hard."

At this point Giselle stirred in her chair, looking uncomfortable. "But you just said there are no children here. If people decide not to save…it makes sense in a way. Why spend your whole life working and not enjoying the fruits of your labor when you can't even leave your savings to loved ones. I mean…you said value is subjective. If people want to consume, who are we to tell them to save?"

"We're not forcing anyone to save if they don't want to. But we are perfectly free to encourage savings. It's the only way to modernize in a reasonable span of time. Let's try to instill some civic pride in saving and not spending. Make it a creed."

"I would expect you to want to leave people alone to do what they want," said Giselle, a frown clouding her features.

"I'm all for leaving people to themselves," said Alistair with a note of exasperation. "But I think it's important to modernize. After all, at some point the Incarcerator will be back and they will probably notice something amiss. It won't take them long to find our busy little society. The more modernized we become, the more chance we have of defending ourselves, or negotiating some sort of treaty."

"That's a good selling point," said Taribo.

"Any ideas you may have…" Alistair concluded, and then proceeded to the next point of business. "Now, the shaft on Odin's Island…"

"We have stopped exploration," said Shukri. "Raja went down as deep as he could." Raja nodded in confirmation. "He made it down, we estimate, eight miles. There was no sign of a bottom, and it became too hot. Until we can manufacture some protective suit, we cannot continue."

"Was there a change in the shaft?"

"None," said Akihiro. "But we have a strong suspicion we know what it is for."

"Go on."

"It probably leads to a station far below. Right on the edge of Srillium's mantle."

"I told you before we should all be dead on this moon," said Shukri.

Akihiro continued, "There are grooves along the sides of the metal rungs. I believe there was once a platform that could take one up and down faster. We speculate the station was one of many used to inject an artificially fabricated metal into the core to create a field for the planet which protects us from Srillium's radiation belts. There are certain artificial compounds which could do it."

"It's our best guess," said Shukri.

"And nothing more can be done for now?"

"Raja saw no sign of the station at eight miles down," Faisa replied. "If it is much deeper, it would be too hot for a human to survive. We would need a protective suit to explore any farther."

"Well," said Alistair, "that project is closed for now. Next order of business."

"There has been a murder," said Santiago. "What we do about it is going to have—what are they?—ramifications." Unfamiliar with it, he said the last word slowly. "One of our subscribers murdered one of the former warriors of the tribe he was a slave in. The warrior took his wife and used her as a concubine for the last six years. He took advantage of his chance for revenge. The man he murdered was a client of Duke and Wei Bai. We're going to meet with the other firm and set the groundwork for a trial. The negotiations will set the standard for future cases.

"This planet is filled with men from the warrior class who have committed many crimes against others."

Giselle interrupted with a snort, as if she considered it a gross understatement.

"Their defense will be that they were forced to survive in the system as well as they could."

"That's shit!" Giselle burst out. "You can't hide behind that. A murder is a murder and a rape is a rape. He's not going to hide behind that excuse."

This outburst made Taribo turn decidedly uncomfortable.

"We were all placed in a difficult situation," he began, but Giselle cut him off.

"Yeah, it was real difficult for you!"

"When a man must kill or be killed, you cannot blame him when he kills!"

"That doesn't absolve you from responsibility!"

Alistair laid a gentle hand on Giselle's shoulder, and he quieted Taribo with a look. Giselle, tossing her head back, spun her chair around and crossed her arms, presenting her back to Taribo.

"This is exactly the issue we are going to be dealing with," said Alistair. "We can't escape from our history. Half the population are women who were forced into white slavery and men who were forced into general slavery. The other half were picked to be soldiers, to be part of the upper class. Had they rebelled they would have been killed and eaten like all the others who didn't survive their first day on Srillium. We have to find the point where just compensation mollifies the first class without going too far against the second."

"If that point exists," muttered Santiago.

"There is a half of our new society with a very severe, very real grievance, but an aggrieved class does not often stop at a reasonable point of retribution. And if the old warrior class feels threatened…We are here to provide services traditionally monopolized by a State. As a private firm, we will provide them better and more efficiently, but that doesn't mean we live in a healthy, happy, peaceful society. This issue, this murder, presents a danger for everyone. Society is a cooperation of individuals; we have to make enough of them feel that justice has been done. Absolving the warrior class of all guilt won't do that, nor would it be actual justice, and allowing the former slaves to deal out vengeance to the extent of their hatred won't work either. We have to find the right balance or we won't survive as a society."

The ugly expressions on the faces of Giselle and Taribo did not fill the rest of them with any optimism.

Alistair was moved to speak further. "We will find that balance."

This had no effect on the African and the woman from Arcabel. Alistair, seeing this, shook his head and mumbled a dismissal, dismayed but resolute. The meeting thus concluded, Taribo rose from his chair and shuffled out of the room. Giselle refused to budge from her position until he was gone.

܀

In the time when no houses were permitted, when no castles were built, when no structures of any kind graced the land, the tall canyon walls of Issicroy and the many interconnecting steps carved into them, and the narrow rope bridges spanning the canyon, were imposing and awe-inspiring. Now, for a man who had destroyed Floralel, who now flew above the city in formation with five others, it seemed puny. The grandeur was gone, but the hatred Mordecai felt for it remained undiminished. A multitude of tiny dots poured out of the canyon walls to stand with those at work in the canyon, all gaping at the sky above. Mordecai malevolently smiled as he was gawked at. Never had so many Gaian craft come at once, much less so boldly zoomed over the canyon in formation.

He circled back, leading his flying mates and, tilting down, streaked towards the canyon floor. The tiny dots at first did nothing, but as the craft drew closer without veering away, they scattered. Mordecai was no more than eight feet above the ground when he and his group tore through and the wind kicked up by their crafts knocked many of the fleeing forms head over heels. Horses panicked and bolted; carts and tents were overturned and trampled.

By the time he circled around for a second pass, the crowd was gone, having taken refuge in the city caverns and leaving behind only the mess their panic wrought. Left without a tempting target, he ceased toying with the beleaguered Issicrojans. Settling his craft in the canyon, no more than fifty feet above the ground, he faced the wall. The Gaian flag at the temple entrance fluttered in the weak breeze. Lord Issicroy's flag did the same, and the sight of it caused him to squint and grind his teeth.

Insulated from the sounds and smells of Issicroy, ensconced in his air-conditioned cockpit, he fixed his sight on the flag he so abhorred. He pulled a trigger and a projectile shot out of one of the cannons recessed in his craft, flying straight and true to its target. There was no question of aim: the sensors on the inside of his windshield read the light bouncing off his eyes and the cannon fired at what those eyes focused on. The projectile left a small trail of wispy smoke and an explosion shredded Issicroy's flag and sent fragments of rock into the air.

Immediately, a barrage of like shots pummeled the city, and like bees from a hive knocked to the ground, the city dwellers poured out of the caverns, spilling onto the canyon floor. For several minutes the barrage continued. The canyon walls collapsed in large chunks, and a cloud of smoke and dust billowed out, filling the canyon and spilling over the sides onto the land above.

Finally, Mordecai landed his craft and extended his exit ramp from the rear of the vehicle. Dust assaulted his eyes as he exited, and he coughed when the stuff got into his lungs. The bulk of the escapees were gone, running down or upstream according to whichever impulse seized them. Only a few stragglers staggered nearby. As the dust slowly cleared, he spotted a dark silhouette wobbling towards him. It was a man coughing terribly, and he lurched forward one more time before falling to his knees a few feet in front of the city's destroyer.

"*Mordecai...*" he breathed, and he stretched his arms out sideways as if in supplication.

"*Giuseppe,*" Mordecai replied, startled.

The man with the Italian moniker was a light brown color, his heritage drawn from all races. His hair was disheveled and of medium length, reaching the top of his shoulders, and a short beard, well trimmed, covered his cheeks and chin. When he pronounced Mordecai's name, it bore an Italian accent, but when he next spoke in Mandarin, there was no indication he was not a native speaker of that language.

"*You won,*" he said, marveling.

"*I won. I won and you were wrong.*"

"*You won. You beat them.*"

There was a moment when neither one could think of anything to say. Mordecai folded his arms and looked down on the man as a king on a subject.

"*You are a chief again?*"

"Yes," he declared with no little pride. *"Soon,"* he quickly amended.

"Do you want me to work for you again?"

The question hung in the dirtied air and Giuseppe coughed after asking it. Mordecai observed the man for another moment before turning his back on him.

"Ansacroy is next," he simply said.

Giuseppe, conversant in the language of Mordecai's mien and posture, rose to his feet and followed after as confidently as if he had said, "Come!" Both went up the ramp and disappeared into the aircraft, which moments later was in flight again, heading towards the coast.

76

After several months the electric power plant was completed, a squat and solid structure made to withstand earthquakes. Around it several different shops sprouted up. Darion and a few competitors mined the areas nearby, and Darion sent a team of prospectors to the Birth Crater, banking on a rich supply of raw materials to be had there. A gold mine was established, and the iron coins disappeared, replaced by gold ones as the iron was put to different uses. The resources from the mines and the forests flowed into the shops around the power-plant, and in the powerplant the moving water turned the wheels and sent electricity flowing. Out of the shops flowed a stream of goods, most of them capital goods. This stream sputtered and coughed a lot at first, and some of the goods produced there were shoddy, but as time went by the artisans improved in their crafts, and the stream of goods became a torrent. The farms filled up with them, as did the logging and construction teams.

The first harvests brought down the price of food, and the populace began to lose their gauntness. Ships were built and traders explored. Hundreds and even thousands flocked to the area, settling down within easy reach of the shops and the electric plant powering them. Other electric plants were planned, and all of it happened quite out of any one person's control. Alistair ventured to guess that never in history had any population advanced so far so quickly from such humble beginnings. Even the first colonists to new systems had started with far more, and though it was true that much of what they were doing was retreading a path already well defined by others, and though they were helped along by devices taken from the Gaians, Alistair considered their accomplishments truly marvelous.

Satisfied with how things were progressing and finding his coffers full of gold, he paid for the construction of a house. Several miles up the river from his electric plant there was an inland lake of five hundred square miles. Near the southern edge, his modest home was built. The top story was the bedroom, perhaps nine hundred feet square, and the veranda affording a view of the lake. The first story had a living room, a dining room, a kitchen and larder, and guest quarters. He never saw the place when he worked, but every so often he would take a few days to relax and inevitably went there, and Giselle went with him.

He permitted himself one exorbitant expense, and that was the costly windows composing the entirety of the wall facing the lake and the veranda. Two sections of this windowed wall were now open, and a cool night breeze came through and caressed him as he lay with Giselle on the softest bed on the moon. The sound of waves tickled their eardrums, and the ruddy glow of Srillium filtered in and made fuzzy shadows with the furniture. They were both naked and a sheen of sweat was evident on their skin, though it dried as the breeze cooled them. Alistair lay on his back, right arm thrown back with the hand under his head. Giselle lay on her side, snuggled against him with her head on his shoulder and her left hand playing with the hairs on his chest. It was such a time that a person can't help sighing, and since no single exhalation of breath could quite sum up one's contentment, another sigh was sure to follow.

"I'd never met an anarchist," whispered Giselle as she stared over Alistair's chest out the window. "Before you."

"There aren't many of us."

"Santi?"

"He never said if he was fully an anarchist or not."

"Why...I mean, what made you an anarchist?"

"My grandfather was, I think. When I was a boy he used to read to me all the time, until he moved south to escape the cold."

"You lived in the north?"

"A very cold north. My grandfather was something of a political agitator. I don't know if he was an anarchist or not, but I read a lot of his books, and some of the authors were. My grandfather understood economics, more than anything. Something almost nobody else does."

Giselle sighed. "It's working. It's actually working."

"We'll see," said Alistair. "In two days we are going to rule on the murder trial. If we fail, we'll fail the day after next."

"How is the jury going to rule?"

"Tomorrow I am going to submit my brief, and Duke will submit his. The jury will decide."

"Thousands of people will show up to hear the verdict. Not the verdict really, the punishment. That's what they want to hear."

"That's a pretty big fight if things get ugly."

"Who is on the jury?"

"Four former slaves and four former warriors. Duke, Wei Bai and I were careful about that."

"It's funny how things work out," she said after a short pause. "I wonder if your grandpa had any idea when you were on his lap that he was shaping the mind of the leader of a revolution. What would have happened if he decided to play frisbee with you instead?"

"What's frisbee?"

"It's a game from Arcabel."

Alistair shook his head, staring all the while at the ceiling. "He died while I was off on Kaldis."

The last sentence elicited a solemn silence that Giselle held for a full minute. Her fingers stopped their play with his chest hairs, and she bit lightly at her upper lip.

"What was it like on Kaldis?" she finally, tentatively asked.

Their speech, at first whispers under the spell of the lake breeze, had grown louder with each successive reply, but now fell back into soft murmurs.

"Kaldis was a lot of things."

She felt a spring of infinite compassion for Alistair, for she could read from his face every emotion in his breast. She felt his dark reluctance, and the myriad emotions it covered, and in this state where their emotions were exposed and raw, she slipped into her native language, Italian.

"You can speak to me when you feel ready."

He turned his head for the first time and, with the ghost of a smile, said, "Honey, my Italian is pretty terrible."

She smiled back at him but declined to repeat it. Rolling over to his side, Alistair faced Giselle and placed a stroking thumb on her cheek.

"Will you tell me your last name?"

"La Triste."

"I mean your real last name. The one you had before."

Now it was Giselle's turn to roll onto her back, her left hand flopping down on the mattress, and she stared at the ceiling.

"I will never pronounce that name again."

Her words were gentle enough not to hurt, but firm enough to stop the inquiry. Alistair sadly stared at her and felt disappointed, forgetting his own impenetrability. What was to have happened next, however, will never be known, for at that moment there was a knock at the door. Alistair tore himself from Giselle, tossed on a few scraps of clothing and went downstairs to see who was visiting at that hour.

He opened the thick wooden door at the back of his cabin to reveal Gregory. Srillium's red orb was directly overhead and its light bathed the top of the doctor's head, leaving only a small puddle of a shadow at his feet. He offered Alistair a tentative smile, and Alistair grasped his friend's shoulder and guided him inside.

He took a few moments to fumble in the dark with a bulky contraption that served as a lighter and he soon got some sparks to catch on a piece of parchment he used to light the wick of a candle. The blackness of the bottom floor was pushed back a few feet by the dim light. Moments later they were sitting at the kitchen table, each with a wooden cup of water and a pineapple split open between them. While they conversed they sliced off pieces and popped them in their mouths around sips of water.

"I didn't mean to come so late," began Greg with the tone of an apology. "I didn't realize how far north the lake was."

"Wouldn't worry about it. We've got guest quarters here. You can stay as long as you like."

"I came to ask a favor…" Gregory paused, almost wincing as he formed the next sentence in his head. "I don't know if this is something you would want to do. I came to ask if you would donate to my hospital."

"Why don't you let me invest in it instead?"

"I don't want to run a capitalist hospital. And I'm not criticizing you." Gregory leaned forward and his manner became earnest. "I have to admit something to you: I'm amazed by what you've accomplished here. I admit…it works. I never thought of courts and police without government, but…really they're just services, and they can be provided on the market, and we're doing it."

"We're not the first."

"I know, Ireland, Iceland, Kaldis…but it's one thing to hear you tell stories about anarchist societies. It's another thing to actually live in one. The Law is straightforward. There are hardly any lawyers, no Byzantine legal codes only they can guide us through. Policemen are friendly. There are no taxes…things are working well. I mean that. You deserve to hear it, especially after how many times you've been ridiculed. But…I want to provide medical care for free. At least for the poor."

"Almost everyone here is poor right now."

"This is important to me. Maybe health care isn't a right, but I want to provide it for people cheap. I don't want to charge like a profit seeking company."

Alistair considered his friend. "Thank you for what you said about our law system. I wish you could see profit as something other than dirty and exploitative."

"It's not that I think it's dirty…"

They became aware of Giselle who came down the stairs and stepped into the light of the candle, her bare feet making soft whispers on the wooden floor. She wore only a robe and with a friendly smile for Gregory she sat down next to Alistair at the table. Drawing her brunette hair behind her ears, she leaned forward and rested her elbows on the table, curling her legs under her backside.

"Hello, Giselle."

"Hi, Greg."

"Greg," said Alistair, "you're participating in the market. That's unavoidable."

"I know that. I—"

Alistair raised a hand to quiet him. "No one can build and run a hospital by himself. You need the talents and resources of other individuals to build it for you, to supply you with your medical equipment, such as we have right now, and you need others to help staff it and run it. It's a market situation without question."

"I know that."

"Well, everyone who donates something to your hospital has to forgo donating that something to someone somewhere else. It's called opportunity cost. If I give you a heart monitor, supposing we get to the point where we have heart monitors again, it is made of materials that cannot be used now for something else. And the labor that goes into manufacturing it cannot be used for something else. Resources are scarce, and we have to be careful about allocating them. How are we to decide what should be allocated to your hospital? Or if it even makes sense to build it in the first place?"

"I think a hospital is unquestionably worth building."

"If you use donations to run your hospital, it will use up resources in relation to the goodwill of the people who donate. Your hospital will grow in proportion to our friendship. But what is your hospital for? Are you building it to give me something to feel good about or to serve the sick?"

"To serve the sick."

"Then I think your hospital should grow according to the needs of the sick, not the goodwill of your friend. So charge the sick according to their desire to pay. If your hospital is free you will get overrun with people using medical services they don't need. If you charge them, they will come only if they want to pay for their medical care. You raise the price of your services until the number of patients who come in equal your ability to serve them. Otherwise, you won't be able to help everyone who wants it, and your low prices will keep other people from starting hospitals to help the sick. You remember the waiting lines on Aldra."

"Yes I do," said Greg softly, thoughtfully. "But what about people who can't afford to pay?"

"You can charge different prices for different customers," suggested Giselle.

"Something which the law prohibited on Aldra," said Alistair.

"Well, what about an endowment for the poor?"

"Will you let me invest in your hospital and also make an endowment?"

"Yeah, Al. I guess that makes some sense."

"Excellent. I'll have Darion look into it tomorrow when I get back."

"And then the big trial the day after," said Greg and he slipped a piece of pineapple into his mouth. "A lot of former warriors are calling for an execution."

"There will be no executions on Srillium," Alistair firmly said.

Their conversation was interrupted by another knock on the door. Alistair looked at Greg but Greg merely shrugged his shoulders. Rising from his seat, Alistair went to answer. Giselle and Gregory, through the pitch black of the hallway leading to the door, saw a sliver of red light that widened into a rectangular shape. Alistair and another's black silhouettes stood out and a hushed conversation followed. A moment later the figure entered and the door was closed and then Alistair reappeared in the candle light, an unknown young man in tow.

"Greg, you are welcome to stay here for the night. I have to be going."

Giselle and Gregory were both out of their seats.

"What happened?" asked the doctor.

Alistair cut off one last piece of pineapple and downed the water in his cup. "The Incarcerator is back."

☙❧

Only a few months before there was a stone tower on the plain, a marker indicating a drop off site, but it was torn down and its material used elsewhere. Now there was only the open plain. The first transport ship to drop, appearing at first as a speck of fire in the sky, arrested its fall from the clouds a couple hundred feet above ground and lingered there.

"They're fussin' over the tower," muttered a man near to Alistair, and there were a few murmurs among the group.

Alistair stood with Taribo, Miklos and Ryan as well as a handful of other men, some of whom he hired to be salesmen for his firm and some of whom had their own business. Duke and Wei Bai were a few yards away with their own group, and Mordecai came as well, arriving late with his contingent. They were a few kilometers removed from the drop off point, but the wide open plain gave them a perfectly good view of things. A few dozen pegs were driven into the ground where they stood, spread out over a large area and stuck in the dirt in groups of four in the shape of rectangles measuring twenty feet to a side.

Duke wandered away from his group and drifted towards Alistair's.

"They're taking a long time about it."

"They're waiting for instructions," said Taribo. "The tower's disappearance has puzzled them."

A soft wind rustled the tall grass around them, save for the more rigid stalks found inside the rectangles described by the posts. Upon closer examination, these stalks proved to have been painted green and were not living material like the grass around them.

"We should have done something about saving the tower," muttered Alistair as the transport continued to hover in the air, completely undisturbed by the wind around it.

"You can't anticipate everything," said Duke. "What with so many people suddenly on their own. Can't think of everything."

"That's sort of my motto," Alistair replied.

The soft chatter among the men faded as they grew uncomfortable. Silence turned to restlessness, but eventually the transport completed its descent. Almost immediately, a line of naked prisoners jogged out of the exit portal and down the ramp. It looked as if the ship were leaking some mottled liquid forming an ever expanding puddle over the ground. Eventually, the drainage stopped, the portal doors closed as the exit ramps were retracted, and the ship fell upward.

Three more times this process was repeated as the sun tracked over the sky, and each time the puddle grew larger. By early evening, when the hot air lost its edge, there were a few thousand new inhabitants milling about, waiting for something to happen. Alistair had long since taken a seat on the ground and, his evening meal of bread and strawberries recently finished, was contemplating his skin, grown a few shades darker since his arrival.

Wei Bai caught him in mid contemplation when he approached to make a suggestion.

"Four loads is the typical limit. We believe the mother ship stays at high noon over the planet. We are approaching sunset now and the transport ships will look for closer landing sites."

"Let's wait a bit longer," suggested Alistair. *"That crowd isn't going anywhere and I'd rather not risk running into a fifth transport."*

They waited until the sun was low on the horizon and casting a pinkish glow before they stirred. The stakes were pulled from the ground and the painted stalks of grass, which proved to be the covering for some tarps, were pulled away. Underneath were several pits. Inside each was an aircraft whose top rose nearly to the level of the ground above. In all, nine were concealed in the earth and their top hatches were now opened and men disappeared into them. Moments later the drone of engines was heard, followed by the silver forms rising out of their holes. Skimming mere feet above the ground, they accelerated.

The vast throng regarded the oncoming vehicles with trepidation. The specifics of the situation on Srillium were mysterious to most, but it was generally known what they were witnessing should not be happening. In their already unsettled state, a disconcerting event such as that struck a panic in some, and that contagion spread until, when the airships got to where the crowd had been, it was no longer there. Remaining to observe the crafts approach and touch down and to see the occupants come out and give a friendly salute were a handful of brave souls, resigned souls who figured they were no match for an aircraft anyway, and a few others who simply lacked the wherewithal to run. Some of the panicked herd looked back and discovered the stragglers were not immediately slaughtered and in fact appeared to be having an amicable discussion with the pilots. These few stopped running, and those that noticed them also stopped. In this manner the stampede was arrested by degrees. The rapid flow out, as if a meteorite displaced the water of a pond, turned to a cautious trickle back in.

Alistair was the first out of his craft. Next came a man from China, half Negro, who was looking for labor for his new clothing factory. After him came a representative of a worker's commune looking for new members to come live and work with him and his fellows.

Third after Alistair was another fledgling industrialist, a blacksmith, also in need of labor. The other eight hovercrafts bore men like them who were paying for a chance to get first crack at recruiting the new exiles.

The men Alistair hired swiftly moved into the crowd, still largely dispersed, and began to make their pitch. Each carried loads of clothing and food and kept an eye out for potential workers for AS&A. To each was given some clothing and a small, cold meal; if they contracted with AS&A for six months they were given more food. Within minutes a large group of subscribers gathered around Alistair's contingent, newly dressed, hunger attenuated. In short order they boarded his transports, most having already contracted to work with other industrialists, a few preferring to strike out on their own. Their first order of business was to fly back to the heart of civilization and sign with Giselle and be briefed as to how things worked in their corner of Srillium. From there some would set out on foot while others were destined for another flight, their final stop determined and paid for by the entrepreneurs who hired them.

They saw no horse riders and they saw no butchery. They chose their path rather than be forced down one. The lowest and meekest was better fed and clothed, within an hour, than the chosen warriors after previous drop offs, and all who desired were gainfully employed before finishing their first meal.

There was an important commodity the new exiles brought with them, apart from their ability to work, and that was news. It could not be determined exactly what date it was, but the new exiles knew at least the date of their own embarkation. Since the Incarcerator ships made numerous stops on their long, circuitous journey through the civilized galaxy, it turned out some of them were placed into hibernation even before Alistair, Greg and Ryan. Others they found who were shipped off six full months after the Aldran trio, and it was from them they got the most interesting news.

An older man named Angus proved to be the most loquacious. He was Negro with roughened and wrinkled skin the color of coal and puffy hair the color of chalk. His toughened hide had been beaten, scraped, rubbed and blasted in countless factories. His English was native but with an accent Alistair did not recognize, and he looked like he would be most at home on a bar stool, wearing sturdy denim and leather, with a mug of ale in one hand and a cigar pinched between his stained teeth.

"The Kaldis war all over but the shoutin'," he informed with the air of one who is pleased to be imparting news to eager listeners. He took a moment to prod at a tooth with his tongue, perhaps to dislodge a bit of food from his recently devoured snack, and then continued. "The occupation...yes, that the problem we have now. 'Cause the killin' ain't stopped just on account o' the Terrans sayin' it over. But that hardly the worst of it. The last Kaldis kingdom to fall...well they don't go quiet. They shoot off a Juggernaut in the last hours; slip it right through the blockade. Last I hear it out there, somewhere, and nobody knows where it headin'. Maybe a year away, maybe two; maybe just a month. Nobody knows."

The news brought a depressed hush over the listeners. A Juggernaut was the greatest weapon of destruction ever created. They were enormous unmanned vessels laden with nuclear weapons and capable of traversing the entirety of the civilized galaxy from one extreme to the other, a distance of about one thousand light years. Upon entering a targeted system, the ship braked into orbit around the star and launched an armada of smaller, unmanned craft that spread out at sub lightspeeds, and each launched its own nuclear missiles at the targeted homeworld. Some Juggernauts could launch a mere thousand nuclear missiles, while the greatest of them could launch a hundred times as many. Once the mother ship itself dropped below lightspeed, it could be detected within the system, but unless a station was near enough to detect it quickly, it was nearly impossible to stop the swarm that scattered from the mother ship. That these launch vehicles would then trail their own missiles and defend them from attack only made the situation more hopeless for the targeted world.

Once the missiles were launched, they glided through space at an ever increasing rate. Launched from, for instance, Neptune, they would reach Earth within three or four days, pelting it with missile after missile and effectively destroying the planet. None had ever been launched except in test attacks on unoccupied worlds, but it was considered doubtful whether any system, even Terra, could completely defend itself from a Juggernaut. Once the button was pushed, it was a death sentence for the target, a delayed sentence but a near certain one. Prospects were made even bleaker by the fact that transmissions were still constrained by the speed of light. If the Juggernaut were fast enough, it would reach its target system at about the same time as the messengers sent to warn of its coming.

"And you heard this news on your planet?" asked Duke, his voice somber and his head down.

"I hear this news on Tantramon," replied the man. "Everyone hear it."

"Tantramon is…" Duke came up with a quick estimate, "…two hundred light years from Kaldis? The fastest ship ever built would take five months to reach you just in the hyperjump. When did you hear this?"

"It broadcast about a week before I board the Incarcerator."

"And you had to be at least two or three months in hibernation before you got here? Ladies and gentlemen, whatever happened with the Juggernaut, wherever it was going…the thing's done. Or will be soon. Unless they miscalculated their launch, some system has been destroyed."

They spared a moment to feel shocked before they fell to speculating over which system was targeted. Some assumed it would be the Terran system, the strongest and principle aggressor in the War on Kaldis. Others flatly denied it, insisting no one would destroy the birthplace of the species. Under cover of all this conversation, Alistair approached Angus.

"What happened to Mar Profundo?"

Angus frowned and shook his head. "Don't know it."

"It's a city on Kaldis."

Angus shook his head again. "Oh, well then. Kaldis in a bad way. A very bad way. I don't think much of anythin' left standin' thereabouts."

A tide of interrogators carried Angus away, but Alistair had nothing more to ask. He discredited the notion that little was left standing on Kaldis. That struck him as an exaggerated rumor concocted in the mind of someone with little war experience. What actual condition the city was in he simply could not know, and he left the matter there.

He kept an ear out for Aldran accents, being ravenous for news of his homeworld, but as passenger after passenger filed by, all under the ruddy glow of the Srillium night, his hopes of finding another Aldran faded. The crowd was half processed when he felt someone prod his shoulder and turned to see Taribo standing behind him, and behind the African was someone Alistair took to be Mordecai. A moment later he noticed his clothing, the kind passed out to the new arrivals, and a mild corpulence the toned Mordecai did not have. Then he noticed the face, while remarkably similar, was not identical.

"I think we have your twin brother here," he said after he finished staring at the man.

"You probably have several of them," the man replied, his voice and light Mandarin accent matches to Mordecai's but his buoyantly flippant tone a decided contrast. "At last count I had four hundred and seventy eight siblings still alive. My mother was a Petri dish and my father a spatula."

Alistair's lips parted. "Four hundred seventy eight?"

"Maybe less now."

"And your name?"

"A/175," he said with a wicked smile. "I like to call myself John."

"What's your last name?"

"My mother was a Petri dish and my father was a spatula."

"You never bothered to find out which company manufactured the spatula?"

The retort made John smile, and he bowed his head back and let out a guffaw. "It was probably Kregel LLC," he chuckled. "I choose John Kregel, since I'll never find out for sure."

Alistair grasped him by the shoulder. "John, why don't you take a trip back with me? There are a few things I would like to discuss with you."

77

John Kregel took no less delight in the aircraft serving as AS&A's headquarters than he did in the invention of his last name. Before he could be convinced to take a seat in a small private office, he insisted on wandering around and marveling. A few minutes turned out to be enough to take the edge off his curiosity, and Alistair finally got him and Santiago in his office chamber. John helped himself to a comfortable chair and Alistair sat in another. Santiago, arms folded, leaned against the wall. The office had electric lights, but they dared not waste their limited lifespan on anything trivial. A window allowed the rays of the morning sun, hitting a spot on the wall, to bring some meager luminance to the interior. Specks of dust glinted as they passed through the nearly horizontal column of light; the rest of the room was nestled in soft shadows.

"You want to talk about my hundreds of twin brothers," John guessed as he cast a scanning glance along the ceiling of the office. He sat back relaxed in his chair, his legs splayed out and his arms resting disordered on the chair's arms.

"I want to learn more about Mordecai," said Alistair.

John sat up only a little straighter in his chair, and to the same extent assumed a more serious attitude. "You'd be surprised how good I became at distinguishing my brothers. Small things like the nose: one would grow one way, and another differently, with the same DNA code directing things. These differences become more pronounced over time. A man is more than his DNA code…but that's a cliché. But it's true. A man is also his history, and this affects his body. I became interested in the subject for obvious reasons. We still don't entirely understand it."

"Who is Mordecai?" asked Alistair, like a tug on a dog's leash or a horse's reins.

"I believe he is B/452…that would be my guess. It's been a while since I've seen him. He looks a bit like B/017 too, but I know him to be dead. I watched him die, in fact."

"Who *is* he?" Alistair repeated.

Distracted for a moment, John ran his hand through the shaft of light and set the dust motes wildly spinning around.

"He is one of a thousand genetically identical engineered soldiers incubated from January 6, 2733 to February 18 of the next year." John took his gaze from the dust motes and laid it on Alistair. "You know they incubate us longer than a woman's womb would? It's easier to take care of us in an incubator so they keep us in there. Eventually, of course, we must be taken out so our muscles will grow."

"And you were raised to be soldiers?" asked Santiago.

"Raised to be soldiers, designed to be soldiers, trained to be soldiers…forced to be soldiers." He pulled aside his new shirt and showed a familiar tattoo to Alistair. He had one star over the points in the circle. "That is what led to my exile here. I escaped from the army. I and a few others…we were on Kaldis and got ourselves smuggled to Tantramon. It's a newer colony, not a big population…we figured we'd hide in some remote little frontier town or something." John's eyes looked into the distance, far past the walls of the office. "A lot of them would mark themselves. Brand themselves, scar themselves, tattoo themselves. Everyone was trying to establish his own identity. Some grew their hair out; some dyed their hair."

"You didn't," observed Santiago.

John shrugged, brought back to the present by Santiago's interruption. "What's the point? A tattoo doesn't change anything but the surface. I'm my own man." The last bit he insisted with some heat.

"And they found you and condemned you to life on Srillium," Alistair guessed.

"Yeah."

"Are any other of your brothers here?" asked Santiago.

John shrugged again and stared at the floor. "I don't know if they caught them or not. I was alone when they took me."

"Which government was it?" asked Alistair. "That carried out the project?"

John's head popped up. "Terra. We were incubated in Hong Kong, trained in Beijing. Then shipped out to Kaldis. Over half of us died there before I decided to desert. How many are left in all, I don't know."

Alistair and Santiago shared a glance.

"Have you met with Giselle, yet?" he asked.

"Just this morning. I start orientation later today."

"Welcome to Ashley Security & Arbitration."

"Thank you." He grinned from ear to ear and shook his head, as if he still couldn't quite believe what was happening. "It's a…funny little system you have here."

"We think it works well."

John shook their hands and left, whistling some unidentifiable tune. Santiago and Alistair were left to ponder the meeting for a bit before Santiago stirred and roused Alistair from his reverie.

"Time to go?" asked Santiago.

"Time for a verdict," Alistair confirmed.

ஃ•ଌ

Alistair could greet the multitude gathered around the tent that was to serve as a courthouse with no better than a grimace. Standing at the edge of a downslope giving into a wide open valley fenced in by rolling hills and distant mountain peaks, he gazed at the multifarious camps that sprouted up around a large, circular tent. The anxious crowd spread out over the valley and up the slopes of many hills, and he felt a powerful foreboding.

Santiago stood at his left and Giselle at his right. Behind him were Greg and Layla. Taribo, Ryan and Miklos wanted to come, but Alistair, citing the potential for a crime spree and doubling the strength of his patrols, placed the three disappointed men on duty during the trial. Seeing the many groups of men gathered, some former warriors, others former slaves, and listening to their frenzied chanting back and forth, he regretted the paltry number of guards he assigned to the location.

"This is worse than I expected," he muttered.

A few of the men camped on the slope noticed him, and they shouted encouragement. Warriors and slaves both, they applauded, a contest to curry his favor. He blushed like the planet Mars and tucked his chin into his chest.

"Santiago, would you please go say something nice to them," growled the ex marine, and then he plunged forward, giving the impression of a man walking headfirst into a gale.

If Alistair was interested in something other than throwing out a distraction, he might have thought for a moment and chosen someone other than Santiago to perform a neutral dance for the crowd. The gruff Argentinean had proven himself a keen businessman, but had never been one for pep talks. His first reaction to Alistair's request was to frown, his second was to wonder what exactly Alistair wanted him to say, and his third was to pass by the men and deliver a few extemporaneous phrases that carried all the charm and inspiration of mildew. Nevertheless, a strong enough fire can use almost any fuel, and his damp words were snatched up and consumed.

No sooner did Alistair put the first wave behind him than he ran into the second, which grabbed the notice of the third, fourth and fifth, and soon a throng gathered along his route to chant and cheer, each side equally convinced he would take their part. Duke, Wei Bai and Mordecai, having arrived a few minutes earlier, received the same greeting. They and their retinue were already seated in the tent when Alistair, desperate, finally arrived at the flap serving as the front door.

He was met there by two men who had stopped Duke and Wei Bai a few minutes earlier. One was large with multiple scars on his barrel of a chest. The other was much slighter, though no less indelicate. Neither was in possession of a full set of teeth, nor had seen the inside of a bathtub for a long time. They both sought to grab Alistair's attention first. Alistair, who was as uncomfortable as if a drill were brought to bear on one of his teeth, looked at neither, but halted with a sigh of impatience when they interposed themselves between him and the tent.

"I have nothing to do with the matter any more," he informed them, before they could complete their simultaneous hailing.

"We are confident justice will be done today," said the man, obviously a former slave.

"We were all placed in a difficult situation," proclaimed the former warrior. "We all did what we could, given the circumstances."

"I have nothing to do with the matter any more. Duke, Wei Bai and I agreed on the composition of the jury, we agreed on the instructions they would be given. It's in their hands now."

"If I could, just for a moment..."

"Mr. Alistair, I think that if you listen..."

They talked on top of one another, but Alistair was saved by Giselle, who grabbed him by the arm and thrust him, inasmuch as she could actually manipulate his bulk, into the tent. The two delegates did not turn off their spouts, but rather redirected at each other, without so much as an instant's pause, the message they had prepared for Alistair and with no more of a persuasive effect.

The great tent was Odin's when he was a chieftain. It had a diameter of approximately forty feet, and the ceiling rose to a central point at least the same distance above the ground with a wooden pillar in the center. At the far end of the tent was a long, rectangular table behind which sat the members of the jury, eight men and one woman of varying ages but none young. There were a few chairs and stools in front of the table, and on these sat Duke, Wei Bai, Mordecai and their retinue, as well as the accused and his counsel, who faced the jury quite removed from the rest. There were a couple dozen others in the tent, but these were forced to sit on the ground behind the wooden chairs and stools. There were two torches in the tent, placed directly under flaps pulled aside to create an exit for the smoke. The open flaps did not carry out the smoke as efficiently as a chimney, so the air carried a hint of murk in it, and the smell of smoke was thick, partly from the accumulated soot of years of gatherings just like the present one.

In three seats on the left, next to one of the torches, sat Giselle, Santiago and Alistair, only just recovering his ease after bearing the assault of public scrutiny. Gregory and Layla were privileged to witness the proceedings but took their places on the ground behind the seated attendees. Having returned a few nods of greeting, Alistair gave one last one to the jury foreman, signaling they were ready for the verdict. As the foreman stood, Alistair's glance fell on Mordecai, seated on the opposite end of the row of chairs, and darkened. News of the destruction of Ansacroy and Issicroy had spread, and it was no secret who was responsible. Few expressed outrage at what occurred, and many, especially of the former slave class, spoke well of Mordecai. Alistair, however, could only picture crushed bodies rotting in collapsed caves.

The jury foreman who now stood before them was an aging man of Hindu descent. His roughened skin and knotted knuckles were just beginning to show the first signs of slipping from vigor into hoary decrepitude, which likely made him one of the oldest men on the moon and conferred upon him an estimation of wisdom from his younger fellows. Alistair's revolution had come just in time, no doubt, to save him from a swift decline and early demise. It was a testament to his robust corpus that he survived long enough to venture a few steps into elderliness.

"The heads of the security firms have asked me to request no one leave the tent and spread the news of the verdict until such a time as we decide how best to disseminate the information." The speaker's English was excellent, slightly accented with British and Hindu. His voice was in the same condition as his body: still serviceably strong but fraught with hints of blemishes and unsteadiness. "Therefore, as you can see behind you we are posting two guards at the exit. If you do not wish to be held in here past the reading of the verdict, you should take the opportunity to leave now."

The privilege of being among the first to hear the verdict proved to be well worth the inconvenience of remaining, at least as those present adjudged it. Not a man or woman so much as leaned towards the exit.

"We met in private to determine the guilt or innocence of a man who admits to having committed manslaughter. Our decision today will reverberate throughout the entirety of our society. We are not blind and deaf to the crowd waiting outside this tent, but our purpose here today, as given to us by the two parties who hired us, is to search for justice, not expedience and not convenience. If a wrong has been committed, we are to require the guilty party to make amends. If no wrong has been committed, we recognize we have no right to commit a wrong ourselves simply to placate an angry crowd.

"The facts of the case are not disputed. Iñaki Etxeberria, formerly of Bilbao, Earth, killed François da Silva Dos Santos, formerly of Beltrán, Trillian. François da Silva Dos Santos was a warrior and second in command under Zeus, while Iñaki was a serf in the same tribe. Iñaki's wife, Raquel Etxeberria, formerly of Madrid, Earth, was François' concubine, during which time Iñaki and Raquel were prohibited from living as man and wife.

"Iñaki's defense is that it was a justifiable killing in retribution for the crimes François committed against both him and his wife, involuntary servitude and white slavery. The prosecution contends that a killing in retribution for a rape is too extreme, and that François was simply surviving in a system he had no control over."

The foreman paused to draw breath and collect his thoughts, while the audience shifted in their places, eager to hear the verdict. Only Iñaki did not look at the foreman, instead folding his arms and glowering at the floor.

"A man may do damage to another man's property without criminal intent or negligence. He is not a criminal, but must make the injured party whole again. He may also do intentional damage, and so he is not only obliged to make the other party whole, but the other party has the option, even after compensation has been paid, to repay the aggression in kind. For instance, a man may accidentally elbow another man in the face. Unless the injured party be found at fault of negligence that led to the elbowing, the first party is responsible to the second. The first party must pay any medical bills as well as an amount to compensate for the injured party's suffering, an amount a jury considers reasonable. However, the elbowing may have been an intentional act of aggression, in which case the guilty party is still obliged to make the injured party whole, but in this case, after compensation, the injured party also has the option to commit the same act against the guilty party, or to hire someone else to do it for him, or to accept further compensation from the guilty party in exchange for forgoing his physical retribution.

"This right to retribution we base on so firm a foundation as reason itself. If a man does not respect the rights of another, then he is left without objection if others do not respect his rights. He gives permission to do unto him by embracing that very code of conduct. If a man commits theft, then to that same degree his property can be taken from him. If a man commits an act of unjustified violence, then to the same degree may violence be done to him.

"In the case of Iñaki and François, there are four possibilities. The first is that François was within his rights to take Raquel as a concubine and condemn Iñaki to serfdom, in which case Iñaki has committed an unjustifiable homicide. The second case is that François, to one extent or another, has violated someone's rights, but Iñaki has gone farther in his retribution than justice permits. The third case is that Iñaki's retribution is commensurate with the crime or crimes committed and the matter may be dismissed from the courts. The fourth and final possibility is that François' crime has still not been satisfactorily punished, and Iñaki may take further steps to bring justice to the issue.

"According to the agreement between the three security firms, an unjustified killing is considered the greatest crime a person can commit. We may therefore dismiss possibilities three and four, since François did not kill Raquel or Iñaki. It is an unavoidable conclusion that Iñaki has gone—"

There arose in the tent a disturbance, as some men muttered approval while others grumbled. Iñaki himself finally looked at the foreman for the first time, and he ground his teeth and scowled at him. The foreman raised his hands to quiet the crowd, and Alistair noticed Giselle was angrily fidgeting. Finally, a shout from Mordecai brought some order back to the proceedings and the foreman continued.

"Iñaki has gone too far in his retribution. Apart from signing an agreement with AS&A in which he agreed not to take the law into his own hands, he has punished François beyond the point of François' alleged crime. The only thing left to determine is whether François was entirely innocent—"

Here the foreman was interrupted by a shout from the defendant, whose veins stood out in his neck and whose face turned a deep red as he cursed in his native Basque, which no one else understood. Iñaki's legal counsel grasped him by the arm and whispered in his ear, and he finally calmed down enough to stop shouting and returned to staring daggers at the foreman.

"...whether François was entirely innocent," continued the foreman, "or whether he too was guilty and therefore Iñaki was guilty only in a portion of what he did.

"We the jury find François was guilty of white slavery. He was not bound to take a concubine, and would not have suffered any danger to his person if he had chosen to eschew taking one. He stands guilty therefore—"

More shouting erupted, but this time the factions switched, with the former grumblers now voicing approval while the other side bellowed their discontent. Again the foreman raised his hands, and again Mordecai restored order with a yell. When the foreman spoke again it was with a louder voice, and his agitation was apparent until he was back in the flow of his speech.

"He is guilty of coercion into white slavery. As to the charge that he enslaved Iñaki, we find there is some substance to this. François was not in a position to free all the serfs of his tribe, and would have been cast out or even put to death for trying to free them. We do not require that a man risk his life for another. However, after extensive interviews we can find no record of François doing anything to oppose the practice of slavery, not even so much as a suggestion to Zeus that the practice should be stopped. He could have escaped from his tribe and lived on his own, as others did. Instead he stayed and climbed to the penultimate position in his tribe, a position he obtained by enforcing its codes with enthusiasm. We therefore find François guilty of slavery and white slavery. The only question—"

For a third time a din broke out in the tent, and men and women took to their feet and shouted. Fingers pointed, spittle flew and even Mordecai could not calm them down. Giselle was on her feet shouting, and Alistair at first responded by covering his face with his hands. He spared a glance at Santiago and saw that the Argentinean, imperturbable as usual, was leaning back in his chair with his arms folded. Perhaps his features were touched with disappointment, but other than that he was unreadable and a non-participant in the emerging fracas.

Standing up, Alistair put what he hoped was a soothing pair of hands on Giselle's shoulders. She seemed not to notice at first, so he bent his lips to her ear and whispered, "Please don't get involved like this. Not like this. Not now."

Giselle spun about and faced him with a look of righteous indignation.

"He gave that fucker what he deserved! He's our client and we need to protect him!"

Alistair gently squeezed her shoulders. "Please don't get things riled up."

"I'm not riled up! You'll see riled up unless we get a better verdict. I'm not going to sit here—"

"Giselle, please!"

At these first harsh words from him, the Arcabelian's eyebrows shot up. With a savage twist she ripped her shoulders from his grasp but ceased her shouting. Instead, she stomped away from him, going to the fabric of the tent wall and, facing it, folding her arms and standing there. Having demonstrated her current opinion of him, she was content to stay put.

While the shouts of the angry mingled with the shouts of those demanding silence, Alistair began the laborious process of addressing individuals and politely asking them to return to their seats and allow the proceedings to finish. By these discrete degrees the tumult diminished. Eventually a few others simply ran out of steam, and then those shouting for quiet realized they were responsible for most of what noise was still being made. A few sweating debaters were breathing rapidly, but quiet and order did finally reign again in the tent.

"The question of compensation is a difficult one," resumed the foreman. "François is dead, but he named his heirs in his contract with Bedrock, so the receivers of the compensation were determined before the crime was committed. What has yet to be determined is how much compensation is due. How much should a man be made to pay if he takes another's life? What is the compensatory value of a murder? And what of rape? What is the compensatory value of a murder minus a rape? The question of the death penalty for murder has yet to be determined here, but the death penalty for anything besides murder is surely too much. We hold that Iñaki Etxeberria is responsible to the heirs of François da Silva Dos Santos to the extent that murder exceeds rape.

"We therefore present our opinion of what justice must be in this case, and let future juries consult it as a non-binding precedent. A murderer should be made to spend the rest of his life paying compensation to the heirs of the slain, allowing one day per week as a day of rest and permitting him to keep only so much as he needs to stay alive. For François' crimes, we would demand that three days of every seven be spent laboring to pay off the debt. By this reckoning, Sr. Etxeberria owes three days of labor, for the rest of his life, for the crime of excessive retribution, unless he and the heirs of Sr. da Silva Dos Santos come to a different agreement on their own." The foreman looked now to the heads of the two representing firms. "Is there further business from Ashley or Bedrock?"

Santiago rose from his seat to address the jury. "We accept the decision. Mr. Etxeberria has violated his contract with our firm and we decline to provide services for him in the future."

With this simple pronouncement given, Santiago sat back down. Next, Wei Bai rose from his chair and spoke.

"*Bedrock is satisfied with the verdict. Pursuant to our contract with the deceased, we will assume all debt obligations to the heirs of Mr. da Silva Dos Santos in the event of Mr. Etxeberria's escape or untimely death and therefore shall undertake to be vigilant against such.*"

There was some rumbling in the tent as the jury gathered themselves and prepared to leave. The lawyers from both sides met to finish business, and Santiago leaned in to whisper in Alistair's ear.

"That is something we should be offering our clients," he almost hissed. "We need to offer more options like that. Our current contract options are becoming less competitive every day."

"We'll go over the contract sometime this week."

"We should have gone over it a long time ago."

"I've been busy, as you may have noticed."

"You've been busy with Darion and the Singulatarians, but not busy enough with your firm."

Santiago sat back and fixed a disapproving gaze on Alistair that carried all the weight and gravitas of an older man. Blushing, Alistair now leaned in towards Santiago.

"We can do some preliminary work tonight, if you like. Do we have any other business?"

"One item. Miklos has filed a complaint against Ryan Wellesley for splashing him with the cup of water he owes him. Ryan is countersuing for noise pollution."

"Noise pollution?"

"Miklos' snoring."

"Jesus fucking Christ. Are you joking with me?"

In Santiago's impassive face Alistair found his answer.

"We'll dispose of that in five seconds. Then we'll work on the contract. OK?"

Santiago nodded, and Alistair imagined his stoic expression meant he was mollified. He had no more time to think on the topic, though, because he was called to come discuss with Mordecai, Wei Bai and Duke the issue of releasing the verdict to the public.

78

Alistair's house on the lake shore did not stand for long before his business partner Darion Chesterton built a far larger, four story cylindrical tower two hundred yards away, on the crest of the next hill, and had it painted in such a striking way as to ensure any passing eyes would be drawn to it. When it was complete, Darion invited a small group of guests to participate in a ribbon cutting ceremony which, Alistair was heartened to discover, only lasted about fifteen minutes. Afterwards, Alistair, Giselle, Gregory, Layla, Santiago and one of Darion's business associates, a West African named Emmanuel, followed Darion to the second story of his tower.

The second story was open to the warm air and measured a hundred feet in diameter, with a ceiling fifteen feet above the floor. It was a great dining room, dancing hall and smoking room all in one. Four stout pillars at its edges kept the third story from becoming the second story, and an enclosed staircase on one side traversed it from floor to ceiling. Crouching underneath the diagonal wooden stairwell, which twisted once upon itself as it went up, was the kitchen, and this was separated from the dining area by a few thin partitions. Darion's maid and butler were hard at work there when the guests arrived, and the smells wafting from the partitions gave a favorable report of their progress.

The dining table was dwarfed by the room it was in, but was easily large enough for the party of seven. Giselle and Alistair sat there while Emmanuel, who knew a great deal about the details of the house, and Darion were showing off the woodwork of the various end tables, stands and other bits of furniture to Gregory, Santiago and Layla. At one point as they strolled from piece to piece, Emmanuel's hand entwined itself with Darion's, and Alistair, noticing this, reacted as if splashed with cold water. A moment later a look of realization crossed his face, and Giselle, who could look at him and read his thoughts as if by cue cards, laughed. He was startled by her mirth and could not repress a sheepish grin.

"I didn't know."

This only made Giselle laugh harder, with her chin resting on the palm of her right hand from which position she had been observing him.

"You knew?"

She nodded, no longer audibly laughing but still with an amused twinkle in her eye. He was quite cognizant of how much it pleased him to be the cause of that twinkle.

"He never told me."

"He never told me either," she replied and giggled again, her smile peering over her palm.

As the sun retreated from the sky, a warm, soothing breeze swept unimpeded through the second story, causing a flickering of the flames of the torches Darion's butler was lighting. A couple of Giselle's stray hairs fluttered in the stream of air, and Alistair reached out a thick hand and tucked them behind her ears. The wind carried the other five to the dining table to join them, their footsteps making almost no noise on the smooth wood of the floor, which absorbed sound and created a hushed environment. The gentle tap of Darion's cane as it descended from an ostentatious arc announced they were returning.

"I hear a brewery is being built," he announced as he pulled out a chair across from Alistair for Emmanuel to sit in. Gregory did likewise for Layla. "For our next dinner together we may have a greater choice of beverages. Naturally it will be twenty years before any good wines can be had."

"A good ale will be nice," said Gregory as he took a seat next to his partner.

The butler finished lighting the torches and candles spread around the vast circular hall, and the maid appeared with the first course, a platter of fruit baked in some crusty bread coated with a sweet glaze. A couple of clay pitchers of chilled juice were placed on the table next to the platter. Several pairs of hands reached for the food and drink, and soon plates and cups were filled.

"Alistair," said Emmanuel with the same musical accent Taribo had, "I am interested to hear your opinion of the verdict." He, like Darion, was dressed in the finest clothing currently available. There was, so far as anyone knew, no silk on Srillium, or they surely would have worn it. Instead, they contented themselves with the next best thing, dyed and sewn in an intricate style at an expense a typical worker could in no way have afforded. The West African slid a corner of a pastry into his mouth and bit off the end. Some banana and strawberry oozed out the side. "You instructed them on the principles by which they were to make the decision. Was the result satisfactory to you?"

"The verdict was an injustice," said Giselle.

Alistair pondered the question a moment, staring at the tabletop, before he answered. "I think their reasoning was sound. There are a couple details I might take issue with."

"Such as?"

"Well…I don't agree with sentencing Iñaki to labor for the rest of his life. It's counterproductive and even if it weren't I don't think it approximates justice."

"Approximates justice?"

"There are times when justice cannot be completely served, or perfectly known."

"Really?"

"How do you compensate someone for the loss of their life? How much money should go to their heirs? How do you fix an amount of gold to something like that? In these cases we do our best to approximate justice, but we may never know what it is exactly."

"So justice is not a human invention," said Emmanuel, genuinely intrigued. "It exists on its own and we need to find it."

"I think so."

Emmanuel nodded and cast his glance about the others. When his gaze came to rest on Santiago's stoic expression, he asked, "And how do you feel about that?"

Santiago shrugged. "It doesn't matter. Whether justice is real or not, our 'approximation' to it will always be our own invention. It will be subject to whims and passions and prejudices for as long as humans have them. A jury's verdict is so much wind unless it is carried out, which depends on people willing to do it and the rest of us not interfering."

"So it does not matter whether we have a government or not…ultimately the success or failure of a society depends on the people in it?"

"Our success depends on us," said Alistair, "but the question of government matters quite a bit. When we act in a system of voluntary consent, we get different outcomes from those of a system based on power and domination. This point is crucial…but yes, we will rise or fall based on our own merits."

"And might the fall be a fall back into government, then? Maybe that will be the nature of our failure."

"No. Free people will not choose a government once they have tasted freedom and seen it work."

"Their passion for freedom might still be outweighed by a passion for vengeance," said Santiago with a quiet tone. "And we should not discount the possibility they can be led back to government and not know it…that government may be upon them before they realize it."

"It will be our task to dispel naiveté," said Alistair.

There followed a moment of quiet, and then Emmanuel spoke again.

"Please forgive my questioning…in Lagos I was put in prison for asking questions like these. It feels good to be able to ask them again. If I may pursue another course…? You said Iñaki's sentence was counterproductive and does not approximate justice. Could you expound on that?"

Clearing his throat, Alistair took a sip of juice and complied with the request.

"It's counterproductive because, what incentive does he have to produce wealth on those three days? Now, the jury was simply hired to render an opinion. The actual details of the sentence will be hammered out by Duke, Wei Bai and myself, and I am sure we will agree to make his payments a percentage of what he earns, rather than make certain days debt days and certain days free days. But even that is not entirely satisfactory, and I am going to try to get Bedrock to agree to a different deal."

"Why is it not satisfactory?"

"Because whatever François' life was worth, it is a fixed amount. Even if we can't honestly know what that amount is, we still try to guess. By giving François' heirs a percentage of Iñaki's wages over the course of his life, we are saying the amount to be paid, the value of François' life in this case, is dependent upon what Iñaki earns. That's nonsense. If I break a vase in your shop, I must pay you the amount of the vase, not a percentage of my wealth. I compensate you specifically for the value of the vase, to the extent it can be determined."

"I'm uncomfortable with that," Gregory interjected. "If a man is wealthy enough, he can commit murder and simply pay a fee?"

"Restitution for a murder can never be made," said Giselle, her voicing rising and taking on an angrier tone. "If a man punches me, I am entitled to restitution…some sort of payment…but also retribution. That's according to our own contract. I can punch him back or hire someone else to do it. But if that punch turns into a murder, retribution is taken out of the equation? You're treating murder differently from other crimes."

"Murder is different from other crimes," said Alistair.

"Yeah, it's worse!" said Giselle. "There ought to be more retribution, not less."

"We cannot build a healthy society which condones the taking of human life," said Alistair.

"That's the best thing Alistair has done, is stop the killing," said Greg.

Giselle half rose out of her seat to deliver her next speech.

"The man who killed my husband...it's not your business what happens to him. It's mine. You're imposing your unprovable beliefs on me. Building a society which executes its murderers makes a lot more sense than one which lets you murder if you can pay the fine!"

Alistair's quiet explanation came after the brief pause that follows an outburst. "We do allow for physical punishment for murders, but not a killing in response to a killing. Restitution is the primary focus of our justice system, and we will collaborate to come up with an appropriate amount for a murder."

"That's something we should leave to the people to decide," said Santiago. "If we would actually move forward with my proposal, we could insure all our clients against murder, and pay out the sum they choose to their heirs should they ever be murdered. The amount to be paid will depend on how much we are willing to pay out, and how much the client is willing to pay in a premium. We can then go after the murderer for the sum we paid out; the sum our client chose." Santiago gave Alistair a significant look but Alistair avoided his gaze.

"But buying insurance like that costs money," Layla protested, and Gregory nodded encouragement from his seat next to her. "A monthly fee at least. Poorer workers will insure themselves for less."

"Which makes it easier to murder a poor man than a rich one," added Greg.

"Which is why there should be retribution for a murder as well," said Santiago. "A man who does not recognize the right to life in others can hardly be said to have it himself."

"How will you go after the murderer for insurance compensation if you put him to death?" demanded Greg.

"We may not," Santiago conceded. "This too can be chosen by our client. If they want their murderer put to death right away, they will pay a higher monthly premium to cover the risk we take in making a pay out and not getting the money back. Or they can allow a five year wait until the murderer is put to death, allowing us a chance to recoup some costs and them a lower premium. Or they can make no demand for an execution and pay an even lower premium. It should be left up to the clients."

"All academic," said Alistair. "We are not going to execute anyone, save for in self defense at the moment there is actual danger."

"I don't know why you think you get to make that decision for everyone else," muttered Giselle, and she would not look at Alistair.

"It is good to be able to have discussions like these," said Emmanuel, and he raised his glass. "That is a true achievement, to have an open society where people are allowed to disagree. Here's to freedom."

They dropped their disagreement and raised their glasses.

"And here's to our first hospital," added Darion, with a nod to Gregory.

At that moment the maid and butler returned, the former clearing the table of the now empty platter and the latter bringing a ladle and a deep wooden bowl filled with a meat soup. He poured some into their bowls and conversation was postponed while they sampled the second course.

Five courses were served in all, and before the fourth was finished Alistair leaned back in his chair to feel the evening air, fresh and warm, as it flowed through the open second story. He had eaten his fill but not beyond, and knowing full well he would take it too far with the final course, he resolved to enjoy a moment of satiation and comfort before proceeding to torture himself with what would surely stuff his stomach. He gazed out at the land, at the black silhouettes of trees normal eyes could barely discern against the dark purple background of a sky on the cusp of night, and felt a profound peace.

This harmony was interrupted by the butler, who approached Giselle and whispered something in her ear, whereupon she, with a fleeting smile for Alistair, rose from her chair and went to the stairwell, accompanied by the butler. Gregory and the two hosts did not notice, being lost in conversation, but Santiago saw, and so did Layla, who observed the exchange with a serious expression. A minute later Giselle reappeared and ran to Layla, whispering something in her ear. Layla rose from her seat and Giselle came to give Alistair a kiss on the neck.

"Layla and I have been called away," she said, carefully regulating her voice to seem regretful. "Darion, the house is wonderful and so was the meal. Thank you for a wonderful evening."

"We absolutely love your home," agreed Layla. "Unfortunately, something has just come up and we have to excuse ourselves."

Darion and Emmanuel were out of their seats while Gregory and Alistair were busy staring at their dates with incomprehension.

"My dears," said Darion with a fluid bow that nearly brought his forehead to the floor, "we are honored to have you here and the door will always be open for you."

The two women disappeared, and neither so much as looked back over her shoulder. Alistair looked to Greg, who wore a frown, but the doctor just shrugged.

The Aldran ex marine rose from his chair and left the table, walking to the circular edge of the second story and a small railing. Grasping it in both hands, he leaned on it and stared at the dirt path leading from Darion's new home to a larger trail to the south, by the side of the river. There was almost no light left, as Srillium had yet to rise, so Alistair viewed the forms below in shades of gray. He spotted the female figures of Layla and Giselle rapidly walking down the path with a half dozen male forms and a dark feeling of resentment welled up in his breast. For the rest of the evening his thoughts returned to that image, of Giselle leaving in the company of men who knew her plans, which she had declined to tell him.

Later, after the meal was finished, the five men gathered seats into a small circle near the edge of the room, inside the glow of a stand of torches, and sat in discussion. Pipes were passed around which Gregory and Alistair politely declined, and the butler stood by the kitchen partition, waiting to attend to any whim. Their voices were hushed, better fitting the hazy, soft, yellow torchlight and the darkness outside, and the conversation was desultory, pausing often when small ideas came to dead ends, during which time three smoke stacks would send clouds towards the ceiling.

"If I had been enslaved…seen my wife made a concubine…I would commit murder too," said Santiago after a lull. He followed his pronouncement with a puff on his pipe.

Alistair had a sense the comment was meant for him, but he said nothing. It was Emmanuel who responded.

"You don't think Iñaki went too far?"

"He went too far," Santiago conceded, his mild Spanish accent almost undetectable when his voice was near a whisper, as it now was. "I don't think he should be made to pay half of what he earns for the rest of his life…but yes, he went too far. I am only saying what he did is understandable. There are many among us who understand it, many who agree with it and are angry at his punishment."

Still Alistair said nothing, so Santiago, keeping his lure in the water, spoke again.

"A wronged man is seldom satisfied with a mere just punishment, and a criminal inevitably thinks himself ill used by it. This does not bode well for our society. There will be no peaceful, reasonable, just agreement."

"I disagree with you, Santi," Alistair finally said.

"Do you think the punishment is too harsh?"

Alistair did not directly answer the question. "We are going to adopt your insurance idea. People can decide things for themselves, and their premiums will be set accordingly."

"But in this case, the amount of a rape and enslavement must be subtracted from the price of a murder. Do you think they were too harsh?"

Alistair stared unblinking for many moments at the flickering flame of a torch before he finally, torpidly, shook his head. "I don't know."

"Most of the people outside these walls do not bother with uncertainty. Half of them are certain of one thing, half of the opposite, and no argument, no matter how reasonable, is likely to change many minds. What happens if we find a just verdict, but it satisfies no one?"

"I don't know."

"People are segregating themselves, and some are ready for violence. Mordecai has positioned himself as a champion of the former slaves, the one who destroyed Issicroy and Ansacroy."

"And probably murdered who knows how many slaves and servants in the process."

"That's not the tale they tell on the streets," Santiago countered. "Bedrock, almost by default, is positioning itself as the defender of the warriors. It is time to take sides in this."

"I hardly think it fitting for a security firm to cater to one kind of client. The very idea of justice requires neutrality with respect to race, sex, class…religion. These things have nothing to do with dispute resolution and criminal justice."

"But this is what I am asking you, Alistair. What happens when justice and practicality are not compatible in the society you live in?"

"I don't know, Santi. Like I said before: I don't know. Maybe we are about to find out. A society that cannot manage to be just will not manage to thrive either. Maybe there are too many old wounds for us to live through. Maybe everything is going to come crashing down around us. All I can do, or at least all I am willing to do, is offer to help interested parties discover justice, and to help administer it. If we take sides in a fight where neither side will accept a just outcome, then we are simply turning back into a government. If the ex slaves and the ex warriors cannot live in peace, then one will come under the domination of the other. It means this society was diseased, and things wouldn't be any better with a government, they'd be worse."

Darion, Emmanuel and Gregory were like spectators at a tennis match, turning their heads back and forth as they followed the play of the dialogue. After Alistair's speech, Santiago was silent and the others sat blinking, waiting to see if it was over or not. Alistair, who had slowly come to sit upright at the edge of his seat, now sank back into it, a position from which Santiago had not stirred. Three more clouds of smoke went billowing towards the ceiling.

"I am not saying you should abandon justice," the Argentinean offered after reflection. "I am just saying these are things we need to consider in the coming days."

᪶᪶

A little village sprouted up on the banks of a river, a quiet affair with dirt paths and houses of timber, some with a stone chimney, and Alistair went there to see it for no other reason than that it was there. Nothing like a city had emerged on Srillium, but around the town that grew around the powerplant, called Freetown by common consent, several satellite hamlets could now be found. Alistair guessed forty people lived in the present one. Other than the various lodges in which groups of five or six men would cohabitate, it sported a rickety dock for the small boats trafficking up and down the waterway. It lacked a Town Hall or Municipal Building, but at its center was a tavern doubling as a brothel. Every one of the emerging villages in the area had a brothel; indeed, a brothel was a seed from which a village was sure to grow if one but planted it in any random location.

The residents of this hamlet, without a name Alistair had discovered, were mainly farmers and herders with land nearby. The herders housed their animals at night in pens built on the outskirts of the settlement. There were a handful of merchants in the hamlet, men who took in feed and wool and meat and timber and whatever else was being sold and in exchange passed out the newly minted gold coins. Then, the merchants loaded their goods and materials on boats and headed downriver, or upriver, or loaded the goods on wagons. They left with the goods and returned with more gold, ready for a new round of exchanges.

This particular evening, as he strolled through, Alistair cut across the long shadows of a village whose residents, with their flushed faces and animated but dying conversations, gave the impression of having been recently stirred up. On the porch of the tavern two prostitutes reclined. A man a few yards away looked to be repairing a section of his lodging house. Naked from the waist up, he knelt down and sawed at a section of wood, oblivious to Alistair's passage. Nearby a group of three men, all former slaves, paused in their discussion to turn suspicious glances on him.

As he passed by the tavern, he spied a piece of parchment, which was still expensive and uncommon, affixed to one of the wooden posts supporting the porch's roof. Stopping to read what someone took time and a good deal of expense to advertise, he saw it was a poster proclaiming the virtues of Mordecai, defender of the little man, destroyer of the slave cities of Issicroy and Ansacroy, who spent long years as a humiliated slave himself.

"It wouldn't interest your kind, warrior," said a hard, raspy female voice.

Alistair only glanced at her out of the corner of his eye and then turned from the parchment. The two women snickered at him as he left. His ears burning, he left the prostitutes behind and headed out of the village, following a path north which took him to another hamlet. This one too exhibited the aftereffects of a great to do, but this time the populace still swirled around the streets, with people moving from one conversation to another, carrying with them their heated opinions and fiery rhetoric. They all seemed to be of the same opinion, for there were no arguments, just a lot of nodding and handshaking and black-slapping. He endured more suspicious and even angry glares from these former slaves.

A third hamlet he reached while its populace was still together, gathered around a grassy knoll outside, being infused with energy before release. A few dozen people, mostly men, gathered around a pair of speakers, both female. One stood by and nodded while her companion incited the crowd with energetic gesticulations, and her voice carried in the humid evening air only just enough to be detectable from where he was. Curious to discover the reason for this gathering, he continued towards it for a few more steps until the speaker turned and he got a better view of Giselle.

Now uneasy, he jogged until he was close enough to distinguish her words, putting him several yards still outside the throng. What she told them was a compliment to the poster he had just read. She did not mention Mordecai, but she waxed on about the dignity of former slaves, of how it was their time to seize the opportunity for justice and settle accounts. She spoke of Iñaki, the injustice done to him first by François, then by the jury. The audience reacted with approval, filling in her pauses with encouraging cheers and delivering a resounding roar after her climax.

There is no way for a disheartened listener in a crowd to make his feelings known. An angry man may yell, and a happy man cheer, but a dispirited man only deflates and shakes his head. As the crowd pressed in on the two ladies, the muscular former marine, now suntanned but otherwise the same as the day he left the corps, turned around and shuffled back to the hamlet, looking only to take the beaten path back to Freetown.

79

A red body, sometimes as a full orb like a completely bloodshot eye glaring at the surface, other times as a slender scimitar slicing across the sky, stained with the juices of lives it had claimed, dominated Srillium's sky. There was a bloody scythe in the sky when violence broke out below, just the sort of coincidence that leads some to believe the human story on the ground is governed by the happenings in the heavens. By the same lengthy process of accretion that produces a planet, a mob formed. A few members congregated, and their chanting and howling, which grew in hysteria in proportion to the size of the throng, acted like gravity to attract more members who, with a squawk and a yelp, contributed their own mass and decibels. It was not a solid body that formed, but a roiling, seething, fluid mass of clenched fists, bared fangs, sweaty skin and primal wails. After bubbling and fizzling for a time, some critical limit was reached, inertia defeated, and the mass poured down a beaten path and finally drained into a small camp of a dozen former warriors.

It is an obvious fact that a crowd is composed of individual and autonomous units. Each member makes his own decisions and any pangs of conscience he suffers are also his own. If a conscience, at least for some, is a mere fear that someone may be watching, then the behavior of individuals cloaked in a crowd's anonymity is already half explained. Throw in a volatile issue and a rousing speech and the mystery is entirely gone.

The tumult heralding the mob alerted, but did not at first alarm, the former warriors. When the noise was distant and indistinct it roused only a mild curiosity. When the nature of the provenance of the sound became clearer, the men paused in their tasks but still there was no concern in their expressions. The mob finally found them standing, facing them with tools in hand and blinking eyes. It was only just before the tide swept into them, in that moment immediately prior to impact, that the men of the invaded camp realized what was about to befall them. The slaves overwhelmed the warriors through numerical advantage. Once battle was engaged, the outcome was never in doubt.

A wave that crashes onto shore must inevitably recede back into the sea. If it is large and violent enough, the shore from which it retreats will not be the same one it crashed into. When the angry mob slipped away, the camp ground was torn up, as if a rugby game had been played there. Weeds were trampled and ripped from the ground, and where the ground was bare, packed dirt before it was now kicked up, as if some gardener made a half-hearted attempt at it with a hoe. The two tents and wooden lean-to comprising the only structures of the camp were demolished. Five bodies lay on the ground, bloody and with joints twisted at unnatural angles. The face of one cadaver was pressed deeply into some soft mud. From two trees nearby, two bodies were suspended, ropes tied around their necks, still rocking back and forth from the blows with sticks and fists. One of the knots was tied by a prisoner with some competence in the matter; his victim was lifted seven feet above the ground by men standing on a pile of logs and when he was dropped, his neck snapped and he instantly lost consciousness. The other was less fortunate: a rope was tied around his neck with no more care than that given to a shoelace, and rather than dropped he was hoisted up from the ground kicking and flailing. He suffocated while his legs were shattered like a piñata by the men standing below him.

Five of the warriors managed to break free and escape. The mob left in the opposite direction, their chanting and jubilant cheering eventually fading until the only sound was the soft, rhythmic creaking of the two ropes as they swung back and forth, rubbing against the branches they were tied to.

ॐ ॐ

When Santiago answered Alistair's request to come see him, he found the ex marine with his hands clasped behind his back, pacing about his conference room with a bounce in his step indicative of good humor. Alistair did not at first notice Santiago, who leaned against the door frame at the entrance, the automatic doors being left permanently open. The Argentinean eyed him as he sauntered about the room, examining walls like he was at an art gallery, except there was nothing more interesting to see than a few Gaian designs he had seen many times before. Santiago finally cleared his throat to announce his presence, and Alistair turned to him with a pleased expression, his lips hovering on the edge of a grin.

"Santiago. Thank you for coming."

"I had a few things I wanted to discuss as well."

They sat down at the table and Alistair leaned back, clasping his hands behind his head and resting his right foot on his left knee. Santiago remained in a more formal posture.

"The steam engine is almost finished," Alistair said.

"That's good."

"The tracks between the mines and the foundry will be finished about the same time."

"Excellent."

"I wish my brother were here to see it. Not to gloat, I just want him to see it. There are three hundred men working to transport materials from the mines right now. In a couple weeks all but a handful will be out of a job...but Darion and I are going to hire them as miners and increase our output from the mines. That's how progress is made. Almost ninety percent of the population are farmers. They just need more capital, then ten percent, or five percent, or one percent will be able to grow the same amount of food that requires ninety percent right now. The rest can go on to do other things."

"I believe the expression is 'preaching to the choir'," said Santiago with a faint grin covering an underlying tenseness which, had Alistair been more observant, he would have noticed. "I am here right now for saying that kind of thing too often, too loudly and to the wrong people."

"To the right people," Alistair corrected him. "They were the ones who needed to hear it."

Rather than disagree, Santiago gave him the same faint smile.

"I have the finished report on the most recent shipment of prisoners," he told his boss. Alistair demonstrated his interest by sitting up in a more formal fashion. "It's hard to tell what to expect. According to Bert every Incarcerator ship that arrives makes routine contact with each Gaian city. The last ship must have confirmed the destruction of Floralel. That ship will be..." Santiago paused a moment to run a rough estimate in his head. "...over halfway back to Earth."

"There's no reason for them to be particularly alarmed," reasoned Alistair. "They would have been told by the other Gaians there was an insurrection, but they ended the insurrection according to protocol. At worst, a few escaped and some equipment is out among the prison populace. The last ship would probably just head back to its next planet, alert their branch manager there. That takes a couple months or so, depending on where their next stop is. That branch sends a ship for the main offices on Earth…another nine months, give or take. Their likely decision will simply be to rebuild Floralel, so they assemble a team, launch a ship and nine, maybe ten months later it arrives. They'll have a security force, of course, but nothing too formidable. At that time we either choose to ambush them, or let them go without any knowledge of us."

Santiago picked up the thread. "The main problem will be having a Gaian city in the vicinity once again. When the Incarcerator construction team leaves, we'll have to take it out again." He leaned forward and assumed a conspiratorial tone. "We should attack the other Gaian cities before the construction team arrives. We have about a year to do it." Alistair began to shake his head so Santiago hurried on. "Just listen a moment. These are religious zealots who want us living a hunter-gatherer existence. They have agreed to maintain a system where petty thieves and political prisoners are exiled to a planet that is overloaded with so many people the land cannot support them all. This forces the population to turn to slaughter and cannibalism. There are incurable murderers and rapists here, yes, but most of the prisoners are guilty of selling specnine, or stealing an auto, or voicing unpopular political opinions. What do we do when a man steals?"

"He is forced to pay back twice the amount he stole, and more for the emotional trauma he caused, plus any expenses incurred in his arrest and trial, plus more for any interest that accrues."

"But he is not thrown in jail."

"Of course not."

"Because that would be kidnapping, which is far worse than stealing."

"Without question."

"It is absurd and offensive to resort to a jail every time a crime is committed. Some crimes…no, most crimes require nothing more than compensation. And most things that are considered crimes by governments are not even crimes. Darion was sent here for importing goods the government decided he should not import. How much worse is it to go beyond kidnapping and send the person to Srillium to either be slaughtered within hours of arriving or forced to live this sort of existence?

"The Gaians oversee this. They are murderers, and when we fought back, they tried to murder us. We know when they discover us, they will attack. They are bound to. Peace cannot be negotiated. We are fully justified, both for past offenses and the certainty of future ones, in destroying them. What's more, this is not a situation where an innocent civilian populace will be killed as collateral damage. Every Gaian here comes knowing full well what they are coming for, and they come eager to do it.

"We need to develop a plan of attack. We need to capture what cities we can, and destroy the rest. Enough time has passed that their guard is likely to be down. We have a year or so to do it, so…what is your phrase?…let's get to it."

Alistair had his arms crossed and his right hand cupping his chin. Long after Santiago finished speaking he was still staring at the floor.

"I'll consider it," he finally conceded.

Santiago reacted with stoicism. He received neither the answer he longed for nor the one he feared, but rather the careful one he expected. "I will formulate a plan. We can talk more later."

"I'm not saying I'll do it."

"I understand." There was a moment's pause before Santiago continued. "I spoke of the last shipment of prisoners. There were some men from Aldra in it."

This instantly tore Alistair out of his brooding state.

"It sounds like they were collected by the Incarcerator almost exactly a year after you were…I guess you call them cycles. There was no one from Arcarius, but the entire planet was in civil war. The government at Rendral reliably controls only a parcel of territory around the city; most everything else is either seceded or changes hands from week to week." Santiago fixed a pointed gaze on Alistair. "Every one of them recognized the name Oliver Keegan."

Alistair's expression was like dark clouds threatening a storm. "Is he a king or a president?"

"Unclear."

Nodding once, the Aldran changed the topic. Though everything in him yearned to ask more questions, even the same ones again for no other reason than to continue talking about Aldra, resisting that temptation felt like a victory over Oliver.

"What of the Juggernaut?"

"No news. As of the last date of embarkation, no one heard anything new."

A light rapping on the door frame drew both men's attention to Giselle, who smiled a greeting and, not concerned with formalities, entered and sat next to Santiago.

"Did you start without me?" she asked as she took a seat, but before any answer was returned she continued. "Santiago and I were talking, and we wanted to discuss a few things with you."

Alistair detected in her voice some impending criticism, and he folded his arms as if to shield himself.

"We are concerned about the company, about where it's heading," said Santiago.

Giselle continued, her comment overlapping Santiago's, "I think we need to consider how we are doing business."

"We started with a tremendous advantage in market share," resumed Santiago. "But we are getting fewer and fewer of the people who move here, or of the shipments of new exiles. And we are losing existing members at a greater rate than we are recruiting new ones from other firms."

"Santi and I think we have identified a few problems; easy to fix."

These statements, made calmly and assertively by Santiago and passionately and breathlessly by Giselle, induced no reaction from Alistair. Neither spurred on by encouragement nor dissuaded by a scowl, Giselle allowed only a moment to quietly pass before she related the details to her boss and lover.

"Our clients are murdered at a higher rate than Bedrock's and The Shield's. There is no likely explanation for this other than the fact that Bedrock and The Shield execute murderers. And they continue to demand we turn over the three convicted murderers we are holding who murdered their clients. That's something we'll have to resolve."

"And it will be resolved," said Santiago. "They can charge more for their services because they are advertising the fact their clients are killed less frequently than ours. They will either drive us out of business or, to stay in business, we'll have to change our practices and turn over the convicted murderers."

"No one is under any illusions about what kind of population we have here," said Giselle. "They are a bunch of horny men who get laid, at most, once a month and then only by spending a king's ransom…and many were violent offenders in the first place. We have yet to see a convicted murderer not plead for his life rather than face the death penalty. That means he prefers the other punishment, which means the death penalty increases the cost of murder, and an increase in cost will lead to a decrease in quantity demanded. I believe it was you who taught me that."

Alistair was impassivity itself before the avalanche of her words.

"Also, the fact our society is divided into ex slaves and ex slave masters is unavoidable, and right now reconciliation seems far away. Bedrock is attracting all the former warriors, and The Shield has become the champion of the slaves. That doesn't leave us with a whole lot. I know you preach neutrality for a security firm…we thought maybe we should try to attract the religious…the Gaians. Maybe…"

Giselle trailed off and looked for a reaction from Alistair, but he gave her nothing.

"Another thing: we have to change our sales pitch. We're too brutally honest. A Bedrock salesman sits down with a client and tells him about how Bedrock is committed to his well being, that nothing could ever break the bond between them, that Bedrock employees take delight in making their customers happy…none of which is necessarily false across the board but…When we talk to a potential customer, we tell them the only way we can make a living is by serving them, that we try to hire only committed employees, but that this dependency is an extra insurance against bad service from us. And we always give them a long lecture on the wisdom of saving instead of spending, which really is irrelevant to our business…Alistair, people don't want to hear the naked truth. I'm not saying we should lie, but we can dress the truth up nicely…that's what advertising is for; that's what makes a good sales pitch."

"A business is supposed to make money," said Santiago, his calm voice a foil to the pitch to which Giselle's had risen. "It's not an instrument of social change, for improving people. A business caters to customers. It does not guarantee those customers have reasonable desires; it merely satisfies those desires. If everyone were as rational and logical as you, they wouldn't be persuaded by a flashy presentation, or a well turned phrase. They would look at the heart of the matter, dispense with the unnecessary and that would be all. But not everyone is like you, and a business operates in the real world, a world with people who want to be told niceties, who want rhetoric to cushion life's sharp edges, who aren't willing to deal with pure, cold logic and reason.

"Alistair," here Santiago turned his hands palms up in supplication, "a single man cannot remake a society. You've done so much. You've done more, I think, than any one man ever has. But you're not going to be able to remake everyone. Some men are born murderers; you can't educate that out of them. Some are thieves, and you can't help them either. Some men don't like the market, or don't like freedom, or don't like that other people have freedom. You're never going to completely change this. A business must make money, and yet we're always steps behind the other security firms while you are playing with the Singulatarians. A business has to accede to people's wishes, not remake them. You're not a businessman, Alistair, you're a crusader. Giselle and I have worked hard for this and we don't want to see Ashley Security & Arbitration fail."

Alistair held up a hand and Santiago fell silent.

"I have said my peace on the death penalty. Killing in self defense is justified, but never in cold blood. After my time on Kaldis I have sworn never to kill again unless I have to, and when a murderer has been caught we don't have to execute him."

"It isn't even consistent with your philosophy of punishment," muttered Giselle, but he held up his hand again.

"We are not going to sell ourselves as a Gaian security firm. I have spoken with our subscribers and I know many of them appreciate a neutral firm. Not everyone is ready to split society up into factions and live only with his own kind. And even if I didn't believe in neutrality, I would never cater to Gaians." Alistair made the word sound pejorative. "I am even considering adding a clause to our contract in which our subscribers must renounce hard line Gaianism."

"Please tell me you're joking," said Santiago, while Giselle's jaw simply dropped open.

"As for our sales pitch, I don't deny for a second I am hurting business by preaching. I can't preach myself…I can't speak in front of crowds…you know this. But I can pay people to do it for me, and suddenly I have the money to do it. Darion and I have brought numerous business ventures—successful ones—into being and after contributing so much to the market I am now entitled to consume. This is me spending money on me. I don't know if I can remake society, but I am going to try."

"What's the point of banging your head against the wall like that?" demanded Santiago, and for the first time his voice rose and color tinged his cheeks. "What good comes of these farsighted plans that have the slimmest chance of coming to fruition but only after you are dead?" He collapsed back into his chair, coming as close as Alistair had ever seen him to outright sulking. "Better to make the most of anything you do have. Get along quietly and enjoy the time given to you."

"Or else get sent to a prison planet," said Alistair with the tone of a man who has just had an insight.

"*Yes!*" Santiago abruptly hollered in his native tongue. "*They send you to Srillium and your son grows up without you! And never knows you! And all the good you tried to do is laughed at while you're doing it and forgotten the moment you're taken away!*"

Santiago winced as if immediately regretting his outburst. The tension drained out of him and, hanging his head to look at the floor, he shook it like a ballplayer who has just committed a senseless error.

For his part, Alistair was as careful as a guest in a foreign temple, afraid what he was about to say would be sacrilege. His voice was hushed and infinitely gentle.

"And yet, here on Srillium, you chose to continue the fight."

Despite his precaution, the words were an incitement. Santiago tensed up once more and slammed the top of the table with his open palm. The stout wood absorbed the blow without so much as a shiver, and Santiago grimaced as he stood up. Casting the chair aside with a violent swing of his arm, the Argentinean stormed out of the room, leaving behind a trail of curses and the thuds of stomping feet.

Alistair stared at the door through which Santiago left until he could no longer hear him and then turned his attention to Giselle.

"I need you to stop agitating."

"Agitating what?"

"You know very well what. You heard about the mob that killed seven men the other day?"

"I had nothing to do with that!"

"Of course you didn't! But you're stirring people up."

"People are already stirred up. And they have a right to be."

"I don't need you adding to the discontent," said Alistair, and then hurried on when Giselle made as if to protest, "Not if you are working for Ashley Security & Arbitration. We're neutral. We're on the side of the Law." She snapped her mouth shut, folded her arms and started to spin around in her chair, but he grabbed hold of the arms and held her in place. "Giselle, please. I don't need any histrionics. I'm not saying I don't want to be with you. I'm not saying you're right or wrong; I'm not even really telling you to stop. What I mean to say is you can't be a leader in the cause of the ex slaves at the same time you are serving ex warriors as clients, especially when the service is justice and arbitration.

"If you want to be a leader of this cause, that's your decision. But I will not allow my workers to participate in that sort of thing. It is not fair to half of my clients who are paying me money to represent their interests."

She did not looked convinced but took the information calmly.

"I don't know what I prefer to do. I'll have to think about it."

He frowned at her answer, and she at his demand. They exchanged a pair of polite goodbyes and then she was out the door. With her chin tucked into her chest, she walked right by Santiago without noticing him. Only when he called to her did she pop out of her reverie and lift her stare from the ground.

"You seem out of sorts," he offered after she returned his greeting.

"I just…" She rolled her eyes rather than complete her sentence.

"I was thinking, Giselle…maybe we should leave and form our own security agency." Her eyebrows shot up.

"It's a free market. Alistair is…a remarkable man. But he has no head for business. I don't even think his first concern is his business anymore. I think he yearns for the day when a factory turns out an HD Engine. He wants to leave. You and I could put together a better firm, a more profitable one. I'm tired of the sloppy way this one is run. Why don't we…"

He trailed off when he saw the answer in her eyes.

"I'm not leaving Alistair."

"I'm not asking you to leave him, just to join me on our own business venture."

576

She shook her head again. "I don't want to leave AS&A, Santi. I'm flattered you came to me, but I'm not going." She smiled a humorless smile. "Alistair just gave me an ultimatum: either stop holding rallies or leave AS&A. I told him I'd have to think about it but I've already made my decision."

He accepted this with good grace, giving her a somber nod and turning to gaze at the horizon.

"Alistair is a good man. I can work for a good man, even if he makes me crazy." He stared in silence for a moment before adding, "He's not the only man who sees a way off this planet."

80

Bedrock, The Shield and Ashley Security combined their fleets, and the scores of workers attending to the last minute preparations took to calling it the Armada. This lasted until Alistair told them the famous Spanish Armada had been obliterated. After that, the name The Second Thousand took hold, a reference to The Thousand, the great space fleet of the defunct Solar Empire. Alistair pointed out that fleet was used to enslave colonies and maintain power, not to free men as theirs was meant to do, but either the men were tired of looking for names or that particular point did not impress them because The Second Thousand remained its moniker.

The mechanics and loaders and other workers of the fleet bounced as they walked, almost giddy with the excitement of those who live in interesting times but feel sheltered from the forces that make them interesting. After Alistair issued to them every order he could think might be useful and spent some time directing traffic, he made his way to the center of the makeshift launching pad, nothing more than the flat ground of a nearby prairie, and turned in a slow circle to survey the entirety of the project. Overhead a noon sun shone down on a ring of guards surrounding the fleet, holding their rifles and allowing none to pass who did not have proper clearance. Beyond them several separate throngs gathered to gawk. Inside the ring of guards was the chaos of an ant colony, with workers doing everything but crawling over one another as they moved about.

While Alistair was in the center of the maelstrom, Duke's short form strode across the turf to meet him. His expression was as serious as it always was, his brow as furrowed.

"If I could have a moment of your time, Alistair," he said and did not hesitate before taking that moment. "When our operation is complete I thought we might have a sit-down with Mordecai to discuss some items of importance."

"Is this your idea or his?"

"His. Giuseppe's, actually. Though I quite agree with him and might have proposed it myself."

"Proposed what?"

"Mordecai has come to me with an idea for a treaty."

"We can't do it."

"You haven't heard the details yet."

"A treaty is something governments sign. We'll have to make it a contract."

Duke deeply inhaled and his brow furrowed more. "Technicalities aside, Giuseppe has proposed a contract for us to sign."

"I can imagine how enthusiastic I am going to be about this."

"Just listen for a minute. We are going to form a network in which we standardize procedures and policies and punishments. It will facilitate cooperation between our firms, smooth over some rough spots. No security firm not part of the treaty and admitted by our three firms will be recognized as a legitimate security agency."

"No."

"Hold on a second! Now the slaves and the warriors are already splintering apart, segregating themselves and many are forming their own little security firms. Who knows what sort of nonsensical laws they'll enforce? We've got an established reputation and method, and no firm that docs not meet our standards should be permitted to practice. It's not safe."

"Duke..." Alistair began, ready to start his rebuttal but instead broke down in a sigh. "Duke, what the hell would give us the right to do it? We offer security services already; if someone is being abused by one of these firms they can hire us and we'll help them out. Negotiation is what should develop a system of law, not force. Is this a preemptive measure against something Mordecai dreamed one night? It sounds like a solution in search of a problem."

Duke folded his arms and said nothing more than a low, "Hmmm."

"This network you describe is not very different from a government."

"I'm not opposed to having a government," Duke replied. He hastily added, "That's not to say this isn't working. In fact I've been pleasantly surprised by it. But we're seeing the danger of people running amok—"

"No one is running amok."

"Maybe not running amok, but everyone's unsettled. There is no end to the former slaves who want to blame all their past troubles on people like us."

"But that is true whether we form this network or not."

"True, perhaps, but...there's no sense in risking it."

"Risking what?"

"Well, what if fighting breaks out?" Duke demanded, furrowing his brow. "I mean fighting on a larger scale?"

"If fighting breaks out Ashley Security & Arbitration will do everything in its power to protect the lives and property of its clients."

"That's not what I'm...Damn it, Alistair! Stop being difficult. If fighting breaks out, it's something our network might have prevented."

"You're talking about forcibly putting down any security firm we deem to be a rogue firm. That's not preventing violence, that's initiating it."

"An ounce of prevention is worth a pound of cure. We would be stopping greater future violence."

"What we would be stopping is the negotiating process. We would begin a process where our network imposed its will. But what if we're in the wrong? What if these rogue firms are representing clients with legitimate grievances? If the ex slaves are this worked up about things, there is probably a good reason for it. Why not try to reach an agreeable settlement rather than impose our will?"

Duke tapped his chin while he considered Alistair's arguments. "Something to think about," he grudgingly said. Then, his demeanor changed and he vigorously shook Alistair's hand. "Good luck today. Come back safe. We can talk more after we get back."

"Good luck and stay safe," said Alistair, and then Duke left him for his airship.

Alistair flew in the large craft he had been using as offices. With him went the pieces of a missile launcher, a computer station, a portable power source and a large team of men of barely adequate training whom he was counting on to pull the operation off. This team consisted of a gunner's crew for the launcher, two communications men, four mechanics to set up the power station, a company of forty troops led by Taribo, and two pilots, one of whom was Ryan Wellesley.

In the central conference room of the ship, he sat with Taribo and the two communications officers. Occasionally another would enter to confer with him, but the room never filled up and little was heard above the level of hushed mumblings. There were overhead lights available but these were left off, meaning the room was lit by the sunlight coming through the window in the ceiling and by the lights from the computers. Apart from the shaft of light from the window hitting the center of the conference table, the dusky light in the room was soft and encouraged whispers and more delicate movements, which Alistair preferred.

They flew low over the surface and employed every means at their disposal to scramble and cloak their signal. The sky streaking over the window above was devoid of features, a mere average of the colors they passed under and a testament to the great velocity of their craft. One of the 3D displays showed a section of the globe with four white dots representing Alistair's ship and its convoy. Their continent roughly had the shape of a top heavy crescent, tilted a bit, whose lower portion dipped just below the equator. The section of the globe on display now showed only a portion of the west coast of the crescent, and the four white dots were well out over the sea.

There were two smaller continents on the other side of the globe, one in the arbitrarily defined northern hemisphere and one in the southern. The southern continent, whose lowest extremity plunged into the polar region and whose broad northern coast fell well short of the equator, was their destination. A third of that continent was locked in ice without interruption. Not a single acre escaped snowfall in the winter, but there was a band running along that northern coast where farming and herding could be done, and along that strip of settled land there were four Gaian cities hundreds of miles apart. It was their intention to simultaneously attack them, plunder them, and leave behind smoke and rubble.

At a certain speed, heading west as they were, they could have remained in eternal noon, but they were moving far too fast for that. Even when the 3D display was set at a scale of hundreds of miles the white dots made perceptible progress across it. Noon became morning, morning retreated to sunrise, and sunrise gave way to predawn gloom. Overhead the color of the sky streaking by lost vibrancy until it faded to black speckled with white stars blinking in and out of existence when clouds passed between them. Even the stars, at that startling speed, crawled across a black tabletop, moving from one edge of the window and arriving at the other some minutes later.

An expansive ocean, the equal of Earth's Pacific, separated the continents so that for a while the four white dots were surrounded by blue. Every so often an island appeared on the display and provided a sense of movement as it tracked from left to right. Passing deep into the night side of the moon, they eventually moved into a storm and the black clouds extinguished the stars. Apart from that, there was little sense of being in a tempest: the ship's compensators cancelled out the effects of the wind so that even the strongest of gales felt like little more than a soft shudder, and the sounds of the storm were similarly muffled. There were frequent but fleeting flashes of light, little wills o' the wisp that to the craft's passengers were lost in the blink of an eye but outside must have been great streaks of lightning.

The conference room was much darker now, lit only by the computer displays, and this with the constant hushed murmurs of the communications men nearly hypnotized Alistair. On the dark wood surface of the table he had a crude pencil, such as they had used on the island. It was thicker than a crayon, and its lead composite was dirty and given to leaving smudges and crumbling when it scratched the surface of a parchment. Next to it was a sleek modern pen, pilfered from Floralel, which used neither lead nor ink but whose tip would leave a precise, black mark on any paper it touched. The desired thickness of this line could be adjusted with a simple turn of the pen's other end. It was smooth and light and it glided over paper like an ice skater in a rink. There was an inch of space between the two instruments, but as he stared at them he wondered how many years were in that inch.

Presently, one of the communications men announced they would begin to decelerate, and a moment later Alistair felt it like an insistent tug drawing him out of his seat. The pen and the pencil slid across the table, out of his line of vision. It was the click of Taribo's seatbelt that finally brought him out of his reverie, and when the deceleration increased and the tug of inertia became more insistent, the head of AS&A sat back in his chair, bracing himself against the floor, and secured his own seatbelt.

After several minutes they slowed to a stop and the aircraft landed. His brooding lethargy dissipating, he was out of his seat and winding through the corridors, joined first by Taribo, and then by the men of his company as the exit ramp lowered to the ground. His booted feet were on the ramp even before it touched down, and the men were close behind him.

The air outside was cool but still, the storm they had gone through having passed by a short while before. They were in thickly forested territory, and a good number of the trees were pine and spruce and evergreen. Water still dripped from leaves and pine needles, and the softened earth held puddles hidden by weeds and tall grass. The smell of pine, the crispness of the cool air and the appearance of their breath in the form of white mist had a jolting impact on him. The smell was not exactly the same, but it was close enough to remind him of home, and he pictured his parents.

"Let's get moving," he said, his voice hard, but the company of troops was already in action.

Communications were established with adequate promptness, though it was another few minutes before the other teams were on line. They first confirmed the other three ships in their convoy were in position around the city before confirming the other convoys had surrounded their targets. While the teams erected the artillery, the communications officers passed scrambled messages back and forth.

Alistair had little to do during the preparation. He erected himself a command center composed of a chair and a table next to the aircraft's exit ramp and sat down to observe. There were several minor problems, and a few of those went unsolved, but for the most part the operation started smoothly. He spent minutes at a time regarding the trees which stared down at the outsiders trespassing on their land.

Not until he was informed they were ready for action did he pop out of his chair. He ordered his men to their positions and told them to remain alert. He demanded confirmation from the other teams that they were prepared to launch the assault, and in a matter of moments it came through. Next he wanted to hear from the other convoys, and after a few minutes word came through that they were all prepared.

Before the austerity of the dark forest there was little chatter beyond a whisper or two and only between men sitting close together, but the communications officers had kept up a steady rhythm of talk and this now ceased, and the eyes of every man turned to Alistair, little white orbs interrupting the night's black and gray canvass.

"Issue the countdown," was his command.

The missile launcher resembled a scorpion, with six legs piercing the turf, a central body resting on the ground and a pipe from which the missiles launched. The body was five feet high, the pipe reached eight feet beyond that and from one end to the other it measured twelve feet. When the countdown reached zero, they heard a hollow, metallic pop, but between extreme speed and lack of light no one saw anything other than a brief blur shoot out the end of the launch pipe. Powered by the same system as the aircraft, there was no trail of smoke, no fire at the back end, and therefore the missile was invisible to all but the detection system built into the body of the launcher.

"All four missiles away," confirmed the operations officer at the launcher, his face and chest lit by his computer terminal.

"Time to arrival?"

"Thirty seven seconds…thirty six…thirty five…"

"Resume countdown when you reach ten; launch second missile."

The second missile popped out of the launch pipe, and twenty five seconds of breathless quiet followed. Someone shifted his weight and his boots slurped in the mud.

"Ten seconds," said the officer, and he counted down from there. When the countdown was complete he paused a second, then said, "Four confirmed missile hits, defensive barriers still up."

"Launch missile three."

A third pop sounded, followed almost immediately by, "Four more confirmed hits… barrier down!"

This produced a cheer from the men. Alistair turned to his right, to a group of twelve troops seated on four Torpedoes. Three to a machine, they grasped them between their legs and grabbed at the handles. The forward most of the three held small handlebars and ducked his head below a slanting windshield.

"Raiders away!"

The four raiders lifted a few feet off the ground, bobbing slightly like a hot air balloon whose tethers are lengthened, and then shot forward, rising over the tree tops and skimming over them towards the besieged city.

One of the two communications officers said, "City number three has lost its defensive barrier. Still waiting to hear from the other two."

This was followed by the operations officer saying, "Four more confirmed hits. Power is out and city hall destroyed.

"Last two barriers down!" said the other communications officer. "Targets one, three and four have lost power...Target two has lost power!"

More cheering followed, but Alistair cut through it with a query.

"Is there any indication of a response from the Gaians?"

The team waited while the two officers of communication scanned the area.

"Negative. We hit 'em in their sleep, took out their power...they're sitting ducks for the raiders."

"Time to raiders' arrival?"

"Forty seconds."

From there, a familiar story was repeated: the city fell, caught off guard and invaded by warriors with better equipment than the Gaians ever expected to find themselves up against. Each team sent a dozen raiders on four Torpedoes. Each team had good maps and established targets. The Gaians were blinded, crippled and not good soldiers. They came to tend a zoo, not to suppress rebellions when the monkeys escaped their cages. Having forgotten Floralel, they preferred to imagine themselves once again masters of the moon, unchallengeable, immune, quite out of danger.

The air buzzed with incoming and outgoing transmissions filled with updates, progress reports, queries, answers and, increasingly as the rout became clearer, banter. The weapons centers were secured, though there was a firefight at one for the unlucky reason that they launched their attack during one of the infrequent inspections and thus a few Gaians were able to arm themselves. He listened to each report which added to the list of secured areas until, one by one, an 'all clear' was issued from every city.

"Send the air defense," he commanded.

Twelve of the sixteen aircraft were promptly in the air, forming a perimeter around the cities, ready to stop the inevitable missile attack. Alistair's aircraft and the remaining three, all larger vehicles, were close behind, traveling to the cities themselves and preparing to make off with loot. The cargo aircraft, when fully loaded, then departed for the south, for a valley near the northern tip of a rugged chain of mountains whose southern extremity reached the south pole. In that dark, quiet valley they left the cargo and a small detachment of guards before lifting off and heading back for more booty.

The response from the other Gaian cities, sluggish and tardy, did finally come. The first wave of missiles, consisting of only five was easily dispatched. The second wave forced them to tighten their defenses. Abandoning two of the cities to total destruction, the twelve defensive crafts converged on a smaller area and managed to save the other two. This gave them enough time to send out a second shipment of goods to their secret valley. They returned as dawn caught up with them again, and simultaneously the third wave of missiles was launched.

Every Gaian city participated in this final attempt at destruction, each sending multiple missiles in an unceasing avalanche of death. The displays of the tracking computers lit up as their operators called out the news, and once again they cut their territory in half, abandoning the third Gaian city so the defense craft could converge on one area. For this third attack the other Gaian cities must have coordinated their efforts, because the speed of each missile was such that it would bring it into the vicinity of the last two cities at approximately the same time as every other missile launched. They were due to reach the city in just under fifteen minutes.

Desperate to have one last load of cargo, Alistair reorganized the perimeter. After the communications officer relayed his defense directions, he made a quick calculation and with great timidity said to his commander, "If any of those faster missiles slip through the last line of defense...we'll have thirty seven seconds to get beyond the blast radius."

"Nonsense," Alistair returned. "We can tell as soon as they slip through the second line whether or not the last two ships will be able to intercept them. We'll have about a minute."

If Alistair's intent was to relieve the young man, he failed.

"Just get me another few minutes."

"All the missiles that get through are coming at the same time," said the man. "We've either got all the time we need or we've got twelve minutes."

It was not enough, of course. Nearly one hundred and twenty long range surface to surface missiles were launched, sixty per remaining city. The first four aircraft managed to intercept nine missiles. Of the remaining fifty one, the second six aircraft took out twenty three of them. Twenty eight missiles were more than the last two goalkeepers could possibly handle; the issue was over.

The cargo craft lifted off and shot across the sky. The sound of their departure died down, and for a few final seconds the Gaian city was quiet. The sound of the trickle of water from the creek on which the city was built gently rolled over the neatly tended paths and rebounded off the walls of the buildings and the bark of the trees. If one could turn one's back to the charred scars still billowing smoke and view only those sections untouched by the assault, it seemed an idyllic place to live. It was a moment in time, impossible to keep, existing now only in memory: the city in its last moments. Then, if one had known where to look, one might have spotted a dot in the morning sky moving almost too fast to follow. By the time one managed some sort of reaction, however, it would already have been too late.

81

When the Singulatarians touched down on the hill's summit, they were nearly the only souls for a few miles in every direction. With the threat of the Gaians and warrior tribes gone, most of the populace opted for the vaster stretches of open land on the main continent. A handful of hermits lived in the forests and hills, and in the south, where cotton grew, a community established itself in a little port town visited once or twice a month by a ship now that Odin, by use of Alistair's aircraft, had eradicated the Megalodons. On top of the hill where Alistair once lived there was nothing to indicate anyone had ever called it home, not even ruins.

Raja and Shukri made for the rock covering the opening of the shaft and, with some effort and a long pole, their aging limbs managed to shift it to the side. Amina bore a box which she set down a few feet away from the rock. Faisa walked with old Akihiro, who went now with a cane, a concession he made only after his legs and back repeatedly made it clear they would require assistance.

When the rock was pitched over and the shaft exposed, Raja turned his attention to the box Amina brought and from it produced a body suit cobbled together with bits and pieces of loot from the Gaian cities. Akihiro, in his younger days, would have at least assisted him in donning it, but now he rested his weakened legs, taking a seat on the rock and leaning both hands on the cane while he panted. Instead, Amina and Shukri went to his aid. The body suit was full of straps and buckles and had several instruments sewn into it, as well as a head piece not unlike what a deep sea diver would wear, and this made putting it on a complicated process.

Shukri and Amina spent ten minutes testing the instruments while Faisa tested the communicator, and only when they were satisfied did they give Raja some space. He turned to them each, nodded and got salutes in return. Then he hoisted a backpack carrying, among many tools, meals and other instruments, a sleeping bag. It had two holes through which his legs could slide, and thus seated and hanging in space, he could stop and rest. At the hole's edge he stretched his shoulders and took a deep breath. Putting his feet on the top rung of the shaft, he spoke one last goodbye through the communicator, gave a salute, and disappeared into the hole.

❖❕

It was a full week before Alistair and the others returned from their conquest. Some of the time in the southern valley was spent cataloguing and dividing their spoils; the rest was spent lying low, scanning the skies, and waiting until Alistair felt sufficiently comfortable to venture forth again. Mordecai, who Alistair suspected was anxious to engage in some aerial combat, was seething by the end of the last day. They agreed to remain in the valley until Alistair, Mordecai, Wei Bai and Duke all decided it was safe to leave. Mordecai was ready within hours of the strike. Wei Bai and Duke were ready the day after the loot was divided.

The Aldran commander, fully immune to Mordecai's ill-mannered grumbling, finally capitulated to an entreaty by Wei Bai. Mordecai was in the air within minutes.

AS&A's portion of the booty was delivered to several spots flung far over the continent. Alistair and Darion had joint mining interests in increasingly remote areas, a lumber company rented some equipment in advance and some of it was put up for auction and what remained would be left at the disposal of Alistair's science division. The head of AS&A made sure the right equipment was on the right craft and sent to the right destination, and then headed for home.

There was advance warning of their return, and to Alistair's dismay there was a crowd waiting for him when they touched down. With a sigh he resigned himself to a conqueror's parade but when he came down the exit ramp he was treated to a different atmosphere. While not outright hostile, the throng played a note of discontent, and he was taken aback by it for a moment until Giselle came running to the ship and met them at the bottom of the ramp. Breathless, she gave him a look of excited determination.

"I found him!"

He had only an instant to look perplexed before she continued, her excitement becoming exultation.

"I found the man who murdered my husband!"

She grabbed him by the sleeve and tugged, although rather than a horse drawing a cart, the effect was more like a child pulling along a consenting parent. There was a small wooden building some yards away, and it was there she directed him. As he went, he picked out some of what was shouted as people pressed closer to him. Most were demanding execution.

Santiago was waiting in the reception room when Alistair was ushered inside, and Wellesley, Alistair's pilot, followed shortly after. The Argentinean sat behind a table at the far end, out of the direct sunlight, and his face looked solemn as he nodded at Alistair. Miklos and another man stood guard at a door leading to holding cells.

"He was part of a merchant caravan passing through," Giselle resumed, still breathless, as she pulled up a pair of seats opposite Santiago.

She took a satchel off his shoulder and set it on the ground next to the chair to which she guided him. Alistair, looking distinctly wary, sat on it and made it groan. Wellesley, eager to observe what was about to transpire, retreated to a corner of the room and leaned against the wall with folded arms. Outside, some in the crowd sang an organized chant, though with so many voices and wooden walls in between it was difficult to understand exactly what was being shouted.

"Where is he now?" asked Alistair.

Santiago made as if to answer and looked irritated when Giselle cut in.

"He's back in those holding cells."

"Arrested?"

"Yes," she replied, as if the question were absurd.

"Who ordered the arrest?"

"I did."

"I signed the order," said Santiago before Alistair could point out Giselle was not a part of the enforcement division and did not command that kind of authority.

"Ladies and gentlemen," said Alistair, "we do not make arrests here before a trial. A false arrest is the same as kidnapping—"

"He was part of a merchant caravan and was going to leave the next day," Giselle interjected. "An arrest of a guilty man is perfectly acceptable."

"You better hope he is found guilty."

"He's the one," she said, and her nostrils flared. "He killed my husband. I couldn't mistake him for anyone else."

"What does he say?"

"He denies it," said Santiago.

"He's lying," Giselle insisted.

"What tribe was this?" asked Alistair.

Santiago made sure to speak up quickly lest Giselle take over his duties. "We have found two others who were in that tribe at the time, a warrior and a concubine. The former concubine obviously wasn't there at the drop off to witness any killing, but she did confirm that Henrik—his name—was a warrior in the tribe at the time. The other former warrior refuses to speak."

"Does he have a security company?"

"He's with Bedrock."

"Bedrock's got the same clause we do: he's required to cooperate with all investigations."

"I've already contacted Bedrock," Santiago assured him. "They will either produce a statement from him or he'll be blacklisted from all coverage until he cooperates."

"Those fucking cocksuckers are thick as thieves," said Giselle, and at a look from Alistair added, "The warriors, not Bedrock."

"What's your sense of it?" asked Alistair of Santiago.

"He's the one. I know when a man's lying to me. And the look on his face when he was confronted with Giselle was proof all by itself."

Alistair leaned back in his chair and allowed himself a moment to mull it over. He cast a glance at Wellesley who shrugged the carefree shrug of one without any burdens in the matter.

"Well, that's that. It'll go to trial and we'll get a verdict one way or another."

"He needs to be executed," insisted Giselle, and she bore her teeth like fangs when she said it.

"Giselle—" Alistair began.

"I am going to slice his throat just like he did to Gianluca—" She stopped short, her throat constricting on the name. "I am going to see him dead."

Short of submerging a hand in boiling water, Alistair could not have looked more pained and distraught.

"Honey, we're not going to handle this any different from any other case. Even if I did believe in the death penalty, a case like this is different. People were bound to die at the rate they were dropped off here. That doesn't give anyone the right to kill, but it does change their culpability a little. He will be made to pay off his debt to Gianluca's next of kin, which is you, correct?"

There was a pleading quality in his tone and a distinct strain as well. Giselle glared at him for a full minute. Then she rose from her chair, walked calmly but stiffly to the door and left, making sure to slam it shut behind her.

"God damn it," he muttered as he stared at the door.

"Be careful how you handle this one," Santiago advised.

Alistair looked at him with a hard stare. "I'll handle this one the same way as all the others."

ले॰ ॰ले

Raja Gulyanov lost track of the time on his way back up. On the way down he lost contact with his friends on the surface, an occurrence they expected, and when, on the way back, Amina's voice broke through the rhythmic but muffled sound of his hands and feet making soft clangs on the metallic rungs, his semi-hypnotic state was interrupted and he realized with a relieved smile that he was nearing the surface. With renewed vigor he continued his ascent, feeling less alone now that he could chat with the others, and about an hour later he emerged from the shaft into the red tinged landscape of a night on Srillium with a full planet.

Once back on the surface, the Singulatarian with a Hindi first name and a Russian surname let his baggage fall to the floor, unlatched his helmet and, giving it a twist, lifted it off his head. His filthy hair was matted and damp, with drops of sweat hanging off the tips. He sported smudges of dirt on his face and his breath, though he did not realize it, was appalling. There were dark sacs under his eyes but those orbs contained a glint of triumph.

"I made it to the bottom," he declared as soon as he drew his first breaths of fresh air.

"Is it what we thought?" demanded Shukri.

Raja nodded and struggled over to the rock to sit down.

"My feet have never hurt this much in all my life." For a moment he enjoyed the sensation of not having his weight bearing down on metal rungs. "I stopped to rest twice. I had the idea to count the steps down but...I abandoned that plan early on. Suddenly, instead of another rung, my foot hit a solid floor. It was pitch black, of course, so all I could see were the readouts on the screens inside my helmet and the reflection of my face in the face plate, but I had the sense I was in an enormous cavern. When I got the light out of my sack and turned it on I was proved correct, because the light was not bright enough to illuminate the other side. I could make out some dark hulk of a machine many yards away, and I could tell I was on a platform of some sort, and the floor of the cavern was very far below me...too far to see it. The platform was at the top of a series of platforms and ladders built against one wall of the cavern, and there was an army's worth of old computer stations.

"I think the place has been undisturbed for the last three hundred years. I didn't dare try to turn anything on. I did take down notes on the script I saw, which I did not recognize."

Raja paused to fish out of his zippered pocket a few sheaves of paper, and Amina took these to examine while Faisa looked at them over her shoulder.

"It's Old Korean," said Faisa, and Amina nodded her agreement.

"What does it say?" asked Shukri.

"I don't read Korean, I just recognize the script."

"The Incarcerator does all its transactions in Mandarin and English," said Akihiro as he thought over the new information. "Srillium was terraformed by a power company. I don't know which...but centuries ago a lot of the smaller languages were still using their old scripts."

"Old Korean is still used in a few backwaters," said Shukri. "I'm sure we can find someone here who can read it."

"Whatever it says," Raja continued, "twenty five miles below us there is an Aradnium station, or a precursor to Aradnium. I spent some time exploring those platforms, finally made it down to the cavern floor. It was at least half a kilometer from the shaft's entrance. There were pressurized and temperature controlled workers' quarters, all empty. Lots of computer stations. All very old equipment, but all in very good condition, considering. The dekinetics must still be working, still diverting stress shocks.

"All the while on that platform I could see that great dark shape reaching up to the cavern's ceiling and, as I figured, all the way to the floor. When I finally made it to the bottom I crossed over the stone floor—maybe two hundred yards—and inspected the thing. It is still humming, faintly, after all these years. Some of those old machines, I hear, are four hundred years old and still working. It's obviously not a new model, but it's stirring Aradnium or a close cousin to it, I'd stake my life on it.

"It's too hot down there to open my helmet to eat, and I was hungry and thirsty like you can't believe. I didn't cross over to the other side...I figured we had what we came for. I climbed back up the platforms, a couple miles up the shaft and got some water in me. I fell asleep...I don't know for how long... then I started up again. I took two more breaks on the way up...you know the rest."

"Are you hungry or thirsty?" Amina asked him.

Raja shook his head. "I ate a couple hours ago. I need to sleep more than anything."

"There's a cot in the aircraft waiting for you," said Shukri. "You can sleep for a week."

ॐ ॐ

Clyde Oliver Jones' face was flushed with self satisfaction as he walked through the dimly lit interior of the Temple, a pouch at his waist jingling as he went. The corridor he was in, more like a tunnel with its rough-hewn stone walls and irregular path, led to a reception area just inside the front double doors through which the majority of Gaian worshippers were required to enter. The reception hall had a thin, removable ceiling to allow sunlight for the bushes and small trees surrounding the oasis at its center, though at night the ceiling was generally in place, as it now was.

At the other end of the reception hall there was another set of double doors guarded by two nearly naked men with flowing, vine-like runes of green and brown tattooed all over their bodies. When Clyde moved in their direction, they opened the twenty foot tall doors for him and he gave them a solemn nod as he passed and entered the Hall of Worship. A grin returned to his face once he was inside, but quickly disappeared when he looked down the long aisle between the rows of benches and saw the Druid, back to the doors, kneeling at the foot of the dais that held the altar.

The doors shut behind him and the noise echoed for a long time in the hall of stone and marble, only recently completed. A few torches cast meager light, mostly near the altar. The temple still being new to him, Clyde gazed at the carvings on the walls, benches and statues dotting the room as he walked through it. Upon reaching the dais he looked to the Druid and waited to give him a nod should that one decide to favor him with a glance, but the Druid did not react to his presence so Clyde skirted the edge of the dais and finished crossing the hall. At the other end he entered a small antechamber, built with more forgiving wood and carpet, and deposited his newly acquired coins into the coffer there with a smile of self-satisfaction. A minute later he was back in the immense Hall of Worship kneeling next to the Druid.

While the sound of soft trickles from the several small fountains tapped at his ears, Clyde cast an uneasy glance at the holy man. It was never a pleasant greeting with the Druid, but he always tried to coax a nod out of him. It was reassuring to know he would deign to nod at him; it signified Clyde was still in his good graces. When he didn't get his nod, he felt uneasy, even guilty and paranoid. He suppressed a shudder when he looked at the long fingernails wrapping around like corkscrews, every one rough, contorted and discolored, and stared instead at the ceiling far above. Sitting on top of this temple to nature, right above the spot where his gaze fell, would be the Beseecher, on his small pad, contemplating nature and begging forgiveness for Mankind's sins for another hour or so before turning in for the night. When he took his gaze from the ceiling, he saw the Druid had tilted his head to the side just enough to glare at him out of the corner of his eye.

Clyde managed a smile as he said, "Eighty two ounces of silverweight today."

The Druid gurgled a growl and bore the fangs of his sharpened teeth. Clyde realized there were tear tracks down his cheeks. Before such an awful sorrow and those knowing eyes, he did not dare effect his usual cavalier attitude and easy smile. Feeling like a scolded schoolboy, he instead endured the gaze until the Druid chose to return it to the altar. A wave of relief flooded through him when he did, but before he could cobble together some sort of speech or query, the Druid spoke.

"They murder Nature," he said, his voice rumbling from the depths of his chest.

The Druid's utterances were infrequent enough that his voice always surprised Clyde, who did not think such a voice fit the man it issued from.

"They murder our brothers."

Only a firm conviction that silence was not the safest option compelled him to compose some sort of response, which he delivered with all the smooth grace of a stuttering man trying to control his speech impediment.

"I have…I heard about it…I—I prayed."

A period of agonizing silence followed before the Druid leveled his gaze on Clyde yet again. The holy man's breathing was becoming labored, and his lips were still curled in a feral snarl.

"We…are caretakers."

The Druid experienced a strange sort of convulsion, and it was a moment before Clyde realized he was choking off a sob.

"We *are* caretakers," Clyde whispered, surprised to discover he actually felt some of the sympathy he expressed.

"A blight. A blight." The Druid was staring at the floor now, or staring through it, seeing something about which his short sentences gave hints. Then the convulsions subsided and his breathing came more easily. Letting out one cleansing sigh, he stood up, rubbed his face with his palms and shuffled his feet until he had turned around. "We will talk to the faithful," he said with the tone of a promise. "We will be caretakers."

Clyde relaxed in proportion as the Druid walked farther away. Even after he left through the double doors, he, Gaian soothsayer and spiritualist, stared in wonder at the place he last saw him. Straightening out his robes, which twisted around his legs, Jones came to his feet. He was unsettled by the raw emotion of the encounter.

"What about Floralel?" he whispered, his breathy speech enmeshed in the sounds from the fountains, almost undetectable. "He gave his blessing to them for that."

82

Giselle disappeared. She did not show up for her scheduled shift the next day, and the day after both she and Santiago skipped work. Alistair took the first opportunity to go to his cabin on the lake, but she was not there and her belongings were gone. Also missing were a few items Alistair did not consider hers to take. Feeling a chill, he spent no more than a few minutes in the home he built with Giselle in mind as much as himself. It was enough time to scout the area, confirm that Darion and Emmanuel were not at home and leave the now inhospitable abode.

Bedrock sent him a message containing the sworn statement of the ex warrior from Henrik's tribe. After his situation was explained to him, he confessed to witnessing Henrik commit the murder of Gianluca, Giselle's late husband. He remembered the act, he claimed, principally because of Giselle's hysterical display of rage, something rarely witnessed because of how uncommon it was for close friends or relatives to be together on the Incarcerator. The verdict was delivered and punishment imposed. The only thing left to do was inform Gianluca's heir of the arrangement.

A week later Santiago reappeared on Alistair's doorstep, or exit ramp, as the case was. A rapping on the side of the aircraft through its soundproofed walls was not enough to awaken him, but the Argentinean waited patiently in a drizzling rain for Alistair finally to come out. The two men shared a cold nod of greeting, and after a short staring contest Alistair invited Santiago inside. He informed his former boss that he and Giselle had formed their own security firm. As part owners of AS&A, the equity they earned as part of their salaries they wished to cash out in the form of some of AS&A's capital.

Alistair did not betray a hint of emotion, neither anger nor resentment, and Santiago was his match for stoicism. They worked out a deal that satisfied Santiago, coldly shook hands, and then the Argentinean left. Fighting a strong urge, Alistair, rather than watch his retreating form, shut the exit ramp behind him and withdrew into his aircraft. He had also successfully fought the urge to inquire about Giselle, or ask where the two of them were staying.

His morning was spent brooding in a dark and empty craft when a second visitor, a messenger, delivered a letter to him. His mood further darkened when he read that Mordecai called for a conference to discuss the field of law and law enforcement, and that Bedrock agreed to send representatives. He crushed the parchment in his fist and tossed it to the floor where the crumpled paper began to open like an arthritic hand. He glared at it but, after a few moments of glowering, rose out of his seat. When he left the room, he stepped on the sheet, but even this second attempt to close it was not successful, and once again the paper began to unfold.

❧ ❦

Feeling he might be able to steer the conference to a more adequate conclusion if he put his hand on the wheel with all the others, Alistair assembled a delegation consisting of Taribo and a small detachment of guards; Gregory, who had agreed to help Alistair in a clerical/support role Giselle would once have filled; and Odin, who surprised Alistair by showing up one morning to offer his services during the conference. Alistair asked him to speak for the AS&A delegation after a short conversation confirmed for him that Odin was convinced by the system he had seen work. John Kregel, now one of Alistair's security guards, requested to come along, but Alistair, moved by a vague presentiment, declined.

The man who surprised Alistair by his lack of fierce resistance to the revolution, who seemed relieved to lay down the burden of leadership and authority, was hardly recognizable to the Aldran, who had not seen him for months. Odin had shaved off his beard, revealing a lean, almost gaunt face and skin still not darkened enough to match the bronze of the rest. The somber eyes were the same, but the brow less furrowed, and the lips sometimes displayed a tremulous capacity to grin, which either was not there before or was hidden by the beard. The hands were still strong, like the slender limbs, and under the fingernails there was a trace of dirt and grime no washing completely got rid of. This dirt under the nails was the mark of work, in Odin's case construction.

As he told Alistair in his Chinese accent, "I was studying to be an architect when I was arrested and imprisoned. Caucasians on my homeworld are a minority and not well treated. I was convicted of a rape that not only did I not commit, it did not even occur. But there are architects on this world, and now instead of enslaving them I am learning from them. I am an older man but I will be an architect yet."

The conference was held under a gigantic tent with a roof, a multitude of poles holding it above the ground, and no sides at all, allowing whatever breeze nature might provide to pass through and cool the delegates. There was a dais at the center holding a large, round table and it was surrounded by several small tables where the ancillary attendees could be seated. Surrounding the tent at a distance of twenty or thirty yards was a ring of guards composed of a small portion of each delegation's retinue, and Taribo duly directed a few of his men to join their ranks.

Having arrived only just in time, Alistair and Odin, upon entering, immediately took their seats at the main table, while Gregory, Taribo and the rest of the retinue of guards sat down at one of the smaller satellite tables. The contingent from The Shield, consisting of Mordecai and Giuseppe, sat ninety degrees away to Alistair's right, and to his left was the contingent from Bedrock, consisting of Wei Bai and Duke. Mixed in between these giants in the field were various smaller security details, some of them small companies, others nothing more than voluntary collectives from neighborhoods and villages. It was the contingent sitting directly across from Alistair that gave him his great shock. Santiago and Giselle took their seats at one of the four cardinal points of the table.

If Alistair was looking forward to staring at Giselle and causing her to avert her gaze, she deprived him of that satisfaction. She met his glare with one of her own, unflinching and unrepentant. She seemed freshly angry, as if they had just quarreled minutes ago. Santiago was less determined to meet Alistair's stare, but he did not avoid it either, showing neither contentment nor displeasure.

"*Thank you, my friends, for joining me today,*" said Mordecai with a speech that startled Alistair out of his staring contest. "*We are here to discuss the future of our business, the business of Law and its enforcement, perhaps the most important business there is. It is the business that holds all others together, the business without which no other business would be possible."*

"Objection," said Alistair softly to Odin. More at home in an arena that called for less subtlety and maneuvering, he was still well aware of the old lawyer's trick of continuously objecting. Odin understood at once and rose from his chair.

"If I may raise a small objection. I think we can recognize the importance of our own endeavors without belittling those of others, like the farmers, whose work is also one without which no other business would be possible."

This interruption caused a mild stir among those assembled, as if satisfied at this confirmation the proceedings would not be dull.

Mordecai bowed his head to Odin and smiled amicably. *"We meant no offense to the farmers. Or to anyone else. But I think we can recognize our field is distinct from the others."*

Odin sat down and Mordecai replied, but after Alistair whispered in his ear he stood back up.

"I object to your use of the 'royal we' when you speak. If you meant no offense, then say it, but I do not believe you should speak as if for an entire nation. That is a pretense we would do better to avoid."

Mordecai looked nonplussed, but Odin continued without pause.

"I also disagree that our field is distinct to any greater degree than any other field. This has been the statist thinking for centuries, but if Alistair has demonstrated anything to us, it is that protection and arbitration are services and, in their essence, not different from any others. It should be supplied within a voluntary framework. All that is required is a common agreement on what constitutes a crime, something all societies from time immemorial have, to a great extent, agreed upon."

Mordecai was on the verge of a retort, but Giuseppe, whose manner was comfortable and smooth, a diplomat in his element, stood up and spoke first.

"We thank—I thank delegate Odin for his insight. There is truth in what he says. But I insist that law enforcement is distinct from agriculture in some very important ways. A farmer sells his produce to a willing buyer and both men go home happy. Our field deals with times when coercion has been used, when someone has forced his will upon another. What is to be done when the aggressor's firm won't allow a punishment the victim's firm has promised to deliver? And surely justice is something that ought to be uniform at all times and all places. Why should justice between company A and B be different than the justice between company A and C? Surely this service we provide cries out for a standard. That is what we aim to do today: to make sure any firm seeking to supply justice services conforms to a standard we can agree on here."

The words chilled Alistair's heart, but he had time for no more than to exchange a grave glance with Odin before Giselle rose and, in a Mandarin as immaculate as a native speaker's, said, *"We agree with the delegates from The Shield. We look forward to reaching an agreement that satisfies all parties, and to making sure justice is uniformly applied according to a consensus standard."*

The last words were spoken with a pointed glance at Alistair.

"Bedrock is willing to explore the idea," announced Wei Bai.

After the preliminary comments, the parties broke into smaller groups to discuss the proposition, occasionally sending intermediaries between them, and the tent was filled with the rumble of chatter. Over the course of a few hours they reconvened the discussion at the central table three times only to break up again. Towards evening a thunderstorm erupted and a nearly windless downpour drenched the land around them. The meeting went on as if no one noticed, and the storm lasted only a short while and left the land cooler than it found it. When the sun's light was extinguished and the red glow of the gas giant bathed the land, when torches round the tent were lit, they reconvened one more time at the main table.

Alistair participated little after the opening comments. Odin and Gregory he sent around to get a feel for how things were progressing, but it was apparent the idea proposed by Mordecai and Giuseppe was popular and some version of it was going to be adopted. Suddenly, he had little fight in him. He was relaxed, contemplative, unconcerned, lost in thoughts he kept to himself. The time he spent with Odin was dedicated to developing one final plea, and that night, after the storm, when all were gathered again, Odin stood and delivered it.

"At Ashley Security & Arbitration, we hold to one truth above all others: that all relationships should be voluntary, that no man should be compelled to deal with those with whom he does not wish to deal, and no man should be prohibited from dealing with those with whom he wishes to deal and who agree to deal with him. This ideal informs every action we take, and we will resist any attempt to impose a different one.

"There is merit in the idea of a standard of justice. We agree there is one; indeed, AS&A has always insisted there is a standard of justice, and that it must be discovered, not invented, not legislated. But how are we to discover it? We can think of no better method than allowing the marketplace to weigh ideas and actions and allow a standard to develop. When a man shows preference for one firm over another, he takes part in developing this standard. When two firms agree to rules and procedures with each other, they take part. When a philosopher writes a treatise and throws it into the public sphere to be debated, he does likewise. By this argument we are already in the process of this discovery, and if the market has not rendered a final judgment yet, this should make us hesitant...no, this should make us loathe to reach a conclusion here and now.

"But even this need not be a cause of great concern. If two firms can sign a contract with each other, there is no reason why three or a dozen or all of them might not come together and do the same. AS&A does not object to the idea of a standard we might agree on tonight. But let us be humble enough to admit we might not have the final answer. Let us allow for dissent. If the men and women who hire us do not like our arrangement, let us allow them to form their own firms, or to subscribe to different firms. By requiring rival firms solicit entry into our organization, we have introduced the element of coercion, and that, someday near or far, will be our downfall.

"Society is built on the relationships of its individuals, and introducing coercion changes the nature of those relationships. A relationship based on consent is one where both parties, to achieve their desired ends, must respect the other party. A relationship based on coercion is entirely different; it permits one to feed off another, to abuse another, to use another for his ends without thought for the good of that other. The proof of this can be seen right here, in this land of criminals, where in these last months not a single complaint of police brutality has been filed anywhere. The nature of the relationship between the police and the people is one of consent, not coercion. I need hardly mention the behavior of the police on other planets. I am sure many of you were mistreated by them on your way here.

"You now propose to introduce coercion by forcibly preventing some firms from operating, and by forcing others to continue to conform to standards we develop. This will change the nature of our relationships to the ultimate detriment of all. Where before our behavior was regulated by the ability of any client to withdraw his subscription and go without, or seek a firm that suited him better, you now propose to close this escape valve. *Now, the standards we develop will be done with more thought to our convenience, and less thought to the good of society, because we will have stifled competition. And this is but the first step: once coercion is introduced, what further steps are to come?*

"*If you have an argument to make, make it. If you think justice can be done better, than do it yourself. And be patient, because time is required to find the right answer, and there is no remedy for that. And be willing to accept the market's verdict, be humble enough to accept you might be wrong. But do not introduce coercion into relationships that up to now have been voluntary. If we do not yet have one overarching standard of justice for all, it is because there is no consensus yet on what that is, at least not in the fine details. Let us not risk imposing the wrong standard simply to have it done more quickly.*

"*Ashley Security & Arbitration will not participate in any such course of action. Neither will we submit an application and ask permission to operate. Neither will we countenance any initiation of coercion on your parts such as you have proposed today.*"

Odin stopped speaking and cast his stern gaze over all assembled before him. His audience, just as stern as he, looked back. To his speech he merely added, "*Now you know how we feel.*"

ڡ۲

It was nearly midnight before Alistair returned. His retinue dispersed, headed for their own abodes, and he, having used his home and office to transport them, stayed behind. He did not retire for the night, however. Instead, he permitted himself the luxury of lighting a lamp and brooded in one of his small offices. At times he sat with his arms folded; at times he paced the floor, moving in and out of the halo of diffuse light incompletely streaming through the lampshade.

He heard the exit ramp being manually lowered, then heard the door at the top being opened. One pair of heavy footsteps trod on the carpeted hallways, opening first one door, then another. Knowing the visitor was looking for him, he did not feel helpful enough to call out. Instead, he sat down in a chair, on the edge of the lamp's light and facing the door, folded his arms and waited until the searcher finally happened upon the right door.

It turned out to be Miklos, who gave Alistair a tense nod upon entering. His normally lethargic expression was replaced by one of acute worry.

"Gregory is asking to see you," he said, then added, "You should come quickly."

"What's the matter?" asked Alistair, impressed enough by this rare display of vitality on Miklos' part to rise out of his seat.

"It's Ryan."

Alistair followed Miklos into the fresher night air. Though it took them several minutes to arrive at their destination, he knew from the moment they started where they were going. At the front façade of Gregory's two story hospital, which reminded one more of an overbuilt log cabin than a proper hospital, Miklos looked back to cast another troubled glance at his boss but did not hesitant to enter. He led Alistair to the back of the building and down a flight of steps to the basement.

Gregory and Layla were both in the dark, stone cellar. A single electric bulb on the ceiling provided just enough light to read by. Scattered about were several cabinets, tables, beds, carts and other supplies. A few areas were curtained off, but in one the curtain was drawn back, and there Alistair saw the body of Ryan Wellesley lying on a morgue cart.

He reacted as if a blow landed on his gut. He half doubled over, placed his hands on his knees and breathed unevenly. The others hung their heads and folded their hands.

"There were eight of them," Gregory softly said when he deemed it appropriate to speak. "Layla has been preparing their bodies all day."

Alistair glanced at Layla and for the first time in a long while she smiled at him, though it was a sad smile full of pity. She held his gaze only for a moment before staring at the floor again.

Straightening up, Alistair finally approached the body. It was clean and composed, but there was no hiding the marks of violence, nor the pallor claiming his skin. Whoever killed him made a point of violating the entire corpus, not even respecting the most private regions, and the cadaver was in ruins. Even the face was damaged to the point where it was not an easy matter to identify him.

"Was a thorough examination done before it was cleaned?" he asked, stone faced, as he stared down at the body of his friend.

"I did it myself," said Miklos. "I can tell you who did it. The Gaians. They stuck twigs and branches in his body, and rubbed dirt all over him, and branded a circle on his chest, and scraped his—"

"I'll read the report," said Alistair, interrupting the crescendo of emotion.

Poor, loyal Ryan, he thought as he placed a hand on the corpse's hair. *So many chapters end so abruptly. And so violently.*

"If all the work has been done you may bury him," he mumbled.

"First thing tomorrow morning," said Gregory. "He was Christian, right? Did he have a burial preference?"

"He wasn't Christian," said Miklos. "Not practicing anyway."

"If he had a desire for his burial it'll be recorded in his file," said Alistair. "If not we'll cremate the body."

Without waiting for further deliberation and not bothering with a goodbye, he was on the stairs and out of the basement morgue a moment later.

స

Alistair risked a trip on a Torpedo to a cave system he had homesteaded for his company. There he found Shukri and Amina still awake, surrounded by trinkets and gadgets and tools and hunched over another pile of the same, their light provided by the same bulb from their cave by the Birth Crater. When they heard his footsteps they stopped their work and twisted their bodies to face the entrance, apparently not expecting any visitors at that hour of the morning. When they saw who it was they looked both relieved and curious.

"Alistair," said Shukri by way of greeting.

Alistair absentmindedly nodded as he strolled over to their pile to catch a glimpse of what they were working on. "How long until we can make advanced circuits and superconductors?"

"A long time," said Amina, more perplexed than before. "That is years away."

"We have to build the machine that can build the machine that can build the machine that can build it," said Shukri. "And we have to build the machine that can build the machine that can extract the materials needed to manufacture all the compounds. If we stopped everything right now and dedicated all our efforts to it, which we could only do if we stopped needing food, shelter and clean water, it would still be many months, maybe years away. I've told you this. Why do you ask?"

"We're limited to what we salvage from the Gaian cities," said Alistair, an understanding more than a question.

"Correct," said Shukri.

Alistair bit his upper lip as he thought for a moment. "Build me a spacecraft. Make it your highest priority."

"The aircraft you have now can make it into space," said Amina. "I assume you want an HD Drive?"

"The best you can give me. When can you finish?"

"Alistair," began Shukri with a note of irritation. "If we can do it at all, and that depends on what remains from what has been salvaged...Two months."

"Two months." He nodded, staring through their workbench and seeing something they could only guess at. "Fine. Make it happen. Work on nothing else until you finish it."

As Alistair turned to leave, Shukri said, "We got the Old Korean translated. It's an Aradnium system like we thought. It's making a protective shield for the moon—"

"I'll read the report," said Alistair, and then he was gone.

83

Having left no instructions as to the care of his cadaver, Ryan Wellesley was cremated. Gregory took charge of planning the observance, which surpassed in ceremony what Alistair considered proper but he endured it. There was a respectable turn out, and many well wishers came who had not known Ryan but wished to express their condolences to Alistair. Nature, always indifferent to Man's sorrows and joys, turned out a beautiful morning that had better accompanied a wedding. When the ceremony was finished, Alistair retired to his aircraft and shut himself in, alone, and there was finally able to say goodbye in a solitary and quiet manner that suited him.

About a week after the cremation, a man came to see Alistair about applying for his permit. Santiago and Giselle formed Justice Enforcement, and together with The Shield, Bedrock Security and a number of smaller entities formed The Law Enforcement and Arbitration Network, demanding anyone presuming to provide arbitration and security services submit an application and comply with certain standards. Alistair, seated in a chair with his hands resting on his belly, listened to the man. When he was finished speaking, Alistair continued staring at him, as if still listening, to the point where the man grew visibly uncomfortable.

"What is your reply?" he finally asked.

"What happens if I don't apply for my permit?"

"You need a permit to operate."

"My question was what happens if I don't apply."

"You need a permit to operate."

"I understand that. What happens if I refuse to apply?"

"No one will be permitted to operate without a permit," the man said again, drawing himself up to his full height and sticking his chest out.

"You will shut me down?"

"Your operations will be shut down if you have no permit."

"Shut down how?"

"Does it matter?"

"I want to know."

"Well, I don't have that answer. Now, may I give you the paperwork for the application?"

"What if I insist on operating without a license?"

The man rolled his eyes and shifted his stance. "Why would you do it? All that is being done is…we are applying a standard. So everyone gets the same justice, dealt in the same way."

"What if two people have different ideas about justice, and how it is to be dealt? Should they not have different options? And if some differences must be resolved, why should it not be resolved through cooperation between firms?"

"That's what we are trying to do."

"No, you are forcing me to shut down if I do not apply and agree to certain standards. That is not cooperation. So please answer my question or get out of my sight: how will my operations be shut down?"

"I already told you I don't know that."

"Presumably they will send troops."

The man clenched his teeth. "If you force them to."

Alistair tossed his head back and barked a humorless laugh. "That's rich! I am forcing them to do nothing. *They* are forcing me to comply or be shut down. Don't you think that's awfully rich? For the aggressors to try and blame the victim for their crime?"

The man stammered and spluttered for a moment before Alistair cut him off.

"Do you agree I should be forcefully shut down if I don't have a permit?"

The man's pitiful efforts at speech abruptly ceased. Once again he drew himself up to his full height. "Yes," was his even reply. "This is for everyone's good and if you can't see that, we are not going to bother arguing with you about it. Now, may I give you your application papers?"

Alistair smiled without genuine merriment and faintly nodded his head, as if mulling something over. Rising from his chair with a casual air, he then sprang like a bear trap, striking the messenger in the abdomen with a fist. His breath escaped him in a rush and he fell to his knees, at first silent, a few seconds later wheezing to get air back in his lungs. Alistair stared down at him.

"Get out of my sight," he ordered with a tone brooking no dispute.

As soon as the man's legs regained enough strength to support him, he was on his way.

⊱⊰

The investigation of the murder of Ryan Wellesley and seven others was quickly taken as far as possible. It was clear a group of Gaians had attacked, and Alistair figured he already knew why, at least in a broad sense. Finding the particular Gaians responsible for the crime was another matter.

Activity at their temple had recently become more frantic, but no one from any of the security agencies was allowed within shouting distance of it. There was a din of chanting and dancing and wailing and banging of instruments with crescendos and diminuendos but which never completely ceased. At night Alistair would sometimes go up to the roof of his aircraft to star at the sunset, or the stars, or at Srillium, and contemplate the state of affairs, and he could hear the distant cacophony. It was just enough to buzz at the edge of his consciousness while he marinated in his melancholy. Unsure how to proceed, whether to attack the Gaians if they refused to cooperate or to allow the horrible crimes to pass unpunished, he was caught in a permanent hesitation from which he felt incapable of extricating himself, and he feared only an outside impetus would bring the affair to some form of resolution.

He periodically would check in with the Singulatarians, observe them for a few minutes, ask a couple of questions to determine how far along they were and then leave. They calmly weathered his repetitive interrogations for the few minutes he was there. Even the grimace he inevitably gave when they told him how much longer they would take they endured with aplomb. If, in his impatience to have an HD Drive, he inclined a bit towards the ungrateful, or lacked proper appreciation for their wonderful work, they were willing to forgive. They liked Alistair, enjoyed the freedom and the salary working for him entailed, and when one day they informed him the drive was nearly ready, that all they needed was an ignition key, his thankful smile was compensation enough for his earlier behavior.

The five of them, having expected his regular visit, awaited him behind their creation with the pride of a peacock. Even Faisa could not help but grin. It was vaguely box shaped, with several compartments and tubes and wires protruding. Its most salient feature was the bluish crystal dome at the top, a dome Alistair knew would glow when demands were made on the engine. He almost knelt in its presence but, remaining on his feet, took to circling the creation.

"Now, this isn't the fastest engine in the galaxy," said Akihiro, who was hobbling on his cane in Alistair's footsteps as the Aldran described large circles about the equipment. "Not much faster than the first HD Drives."

"It *can* reach supraluminal speeds, correct?"

"You can be sure of it," said Faisa.

"When you reach your top speed," continued Akihiro, "you'll travel a light year in about four days."

This caused Alistair to pause and Akihiro nearly plowed into the back of him.

"That would make Aldra, at a straight shot…almost two years away."

"And you won't have any hibernation technology," the old Japanese man reminded him.

Looking a little nervous, Alistair slowly nodded. "It'll do." Then he more convincingly said, "It's marvelous. It really is a marvel."

"You're welcome," said Shukri, his bushy eyebrows bunching up as he smiled.

"We couldn't make an ignition key for it," said Akihiro.

Alistair shook his head as if it were of little importance. "Darion's got a few of those in his drills in the mines."

"And we'll need a week to install it in your aircraft."

Alistair finally tore his attention from the motor and turned his smile on his five scientists. "When I get back…I don't know…I'll make a donation to the development of artificial intelligence."

"Just blow up a Gaian temple," said Faisa, her smirk equal parts camaraderie and malevolence.

Akihiro came around to face Alistair and grasped his arm with his free hand. "I did my best work on this, Alistair. We all did. But engines can break down, things can go wrong. If you get stranded out there…"

"I understand."

"Why go? Why risk it? You have a life here now. We have a society. And you're in a better position in this one or you never would have been sent here in the first place. Why leave?"

Alistair grasped Akihiro's arm in response. "Let's just say I have the urge."

☙ ❧

A detachment of six troops arrived sometime later, a delegation from the other security firms, demanding to speak with Alistair. They informed Taribo they had a cease-and-desist order to deliver to the head of AS&A. The West African sent a man to relay the information, and when he returned it was to say that Alistair would permit only one of the six to enter his aircraft and deliver the order to him. The head of the delegation informed Taribo this would not be satisfactory, at which point Alistair's head of security shrugged his shoulders and returned his attention to where it had been before the delegation arrived.

After a minute of deliberation, a peeved leader of the delegation told him he consented to Alistair's conditions, at which point he was permitted to enter the aircraft. Only a minute later the door reopened and Alistair came out, carrying the leader of the delegation by the hair on the back of his head and the seat of his pants. The papers of the cease and desist order had been crammed into his mouth and a trickle of blood flowed from a cut on his eyebrow. The great muscular Aldran heaved the hapless man into the air, but not far enough to clear the entire exit ramp. Instead, he fell face down onto the end and half bounced, half rolled into the dirt beyond it.

With the clipped and frantic motions of a furious man, he sprang to his feet, ripped the papers out of his mouth, spat, adjusted his clothes and returned to his detachment with a face red from anger and embarrassment. With a movement of his hand like he was slicing something with a dagger, he motioned for his men to follow him and, not looking back, vacated the premises.

"Tell Mordecai I said hello," said Taribo without bothering to look at them. He received no response.

～◦～

Alistair and Gregory met one night in Alistair's aircraft and sat down to a couple drinks of a golden ale that had recently become popular. Alistair had taken to staying up later and later, and to more and more seclusion, and Gregory made a point of keeping him company once in a while, no matter how surlily he responded to the doctor's appearances. This surliness manifested itself in a frown and a grunt when Alistair opened his door to see Gregory, but it evaporated soon thereafter, becoming an even but not unpleasant taciturnity, something to which Gregory was accustomed. It was the transition, more than anything, which evoked grumpiness in Alistair. Settled in his solitude, he was irritated by disruption but quickly recalled the company of a friend was a pleasant thing after all.

Touched by the ruddy light of Srillium and the soft glow of the three candles Alistair lit, Gregory's face was like a receptacle where all the exhaustion of his many hours of work was deposited. However, he came with a smile, and if there was fatigue on his countenance there was also tranquility. In his left hand he carried a flask, and in his right two cups. Moments later both cups were full.

He unleashed a steady stream of chatter, most of it about the hospital, and for a time Alistair did little other than listen and nod. When halfway through his second cup of ale, he lost focus of what Gregory was telling him and, driven by his own thoughts, interrupted his friend.

"I am probably going to leave Srillium."

Gregory, who stopped speaking as soon as Alistair cut in, blinked once.

"Probably sometime soon."

"How?"

"In the very aircraft you're sitting in. The Singulatarians installed an HD Drive. There's no hibernation equipment so I have to preserve and stock a whole lot of food. And gold. I'm going to convert everything I own to gold."

The revelation moved Gregory to silence. He tapped his empty cup with a few of his fingers.

"Are you stocking right now?"

"Not yet."

"So…you aren't sure you're ready to leave."

Alistair winced but nodded. "If I knew I had a home to go back to it would be an easier decision. You have a free ticket to come back with me if you want it."

"I'll think about it. I don't know if I can take Layla to Aldra. It wouldn't be fair for her. And I can't leave her. I'll think about it."

"I can't not see my brother again," Alistair whispered. "We left things…And Oliver. And Katherine."

Neither mentioned Giselle's role in delaying, or perhaps provoking, Alistair's departure.

"I guess I'm surprised you want to leave. Isn't this the society you've always wanted to live in? I…I'm enjoying myself here. It's simple but…free. You know we have penicillin now?"

Alistair nodded.

"It's exciting watching the progress. Being a part of the progress. And things are easier, simpler without a government." Gregory seemed like he had a lot more to say but, after a moment of deliberation, settled for, "I'm a convert, Alistair." He broke into a boyish and almost guilty smile. "I'll bet you've been waiting to hear me say that for a long time."

The corners of Alistair's lips turned up in a grin. A lull followed in which he refilled both cups, and as he leaned back to sip at his ale, staring out the window in the ceiling, he noticed something flash across the sky. His sudden change of posture and expression alerted Gregory, and that one sat his cup down on the desk.

"Something the matter?"

"Someone's flying overhead. Two!" exclaimed Alistair after he saw another flash across his window. "What the hell is going on?"

No sooner did he ask the question than they heard the sound of feet treading the hallways. Alistair leapt up and ran to the open portal. Around the corner of the hallway he spied a flickering glow and called out to announce his location. Three men, one of them Taribo, came jogging to him. Their faces were etched with the kind of concern that, in a less trained and disciplined mind, is easily nudged into panic.

"The Incarcerator's back," Taribo announced. "This time they know about us."

The sounds the aircraft's soundproofing kept from Alistair's ears were revealed to him when the hatch opened. Men dashed across the ground, hustling from building to building. Voices of every sort were heard, from shouts called out to the buzz of private chatter and many grades in between. The whoosh of aircraft slashing through the atmosphere mixed with the other sounds, and many lights, similar to the stars, crawled or sometimes streaked across the sky. Some of them passed in front of Srillium and appeared as little black bugs before, the transit complete, they entered the darkness of the sky and once more were detectable only by their navigation lights.

Gregory called out a farewell and, not waiting for a response, made for his hospital. Alistair did not even notice his departure as he, breaking into a jog, took the lead and made for another aircraft serving as a communications hub. When he arrived, the communications equipment was being offloaded into a small hut nearby. A generator inside gave power to the hastily arranged assembly, transferred to the hut to allow another aircraft to be used for patrolling. The men inside, not quite frantic, gave him a salute and one stepped up to deliver a report.

"We caught them on our scanners about ten minutes ago. There are four large mother ships and…we're not sure how many smaller ships. As soon as we detected them we got a transmission." The man allowed himself a smile as for an inside joke. "They're demanding to speak to our leader."

Alistair reciprocated the smile.

"Mordecai was the first to answer."

Alistair's smile disappeared. "Of course."

"It's a gamble," said Taribo of Mordecai.

"I know someone else who took the same gamble," Alistair whispered. Then, more loudly, he said, "Paint the picture for me."

"They're demanding our surrender; giving us twenty four hours to comply. The mother ships are in orbit, about two thousand miles from the surface. A few smaller craft entered the atmosphere but retreated when our aircraft went up. They outnumber us about twenty to one, and that's disregarding the mother ships. Our aircraft…the ones from the other agencies too…our aircraft are flying defensive routs and all surface to air weapons are locked and loaded and pointing to the sky."

"Make sure none of our craft get above fifty miles altitude."

"Already taken care of, sir. There have been no more communications after the Incarcerator issued its ultimatum. Mordecai and Bedrock both tried again but there was no response. Bedrock contacted us, though. They're calling another meeting and want you to attend."

"A friend in need is a friend indeed. When does the meeting start?"

"The others are already on their way."

Alistair leaned back to whisper to Taribo, "Send someone to get the Singulatarians. And put together a security detail to accompany us."

With a nod, Taribo was out the door.

Alistair turned back to the other man and said, "Get me a couple pilots."

There was no time to set up a tent. The leaders of the security firms gathered on the slope of a hill in the middle of the night, blown by a breeze and guarded by their security details. They gathered in a group, those who thought to bring a chair sitting and those who lacked that foresight, such as Alistair, standing. Akihiro alone chose to sit on the ground, upslope a bit from the group, looking tired by his nocturnal exertions but still solemn and alert.

Alistair's eyes were drawn to Giselle, but she resolutely avoided looking at him. Giuseppe, turning circles around his boss, who sat in a chair with his arms folded and his chin tucked into his chest, was pleading with them to listen to his version of reason. He passed by Santiago and Giselle, moved on to Duke and Wei Bai, and finally passed Alistair and Taribo, flanked by the rest of the Singulatarians, all the while his voice falling on them like a silk sheet tossed over a mattress.

"We have to come together now or this little experiment of ours is done. Finished. It'll never happen again. The Gaians won't be so careless as to let arms fall into our hands again. We cannot afford to be divided. We need a leader to see us through this, if we are to get through it at all. I propose we invest Mordecai with authority to lead our defense forces until the threat is over."

"Wouldn't that just be the culmination of your dreams," said Alistair, his revulsion overcoming his habitual timidity.

The comment stopped Giuseppe, whose features first registered surprise but then slid into a smooth smile.

"We see Alistair has come to help us. We thank him for that. We must remind him, though, that until he has been approved, he will not have a vote on this council. Nor a voice in it either. Our matters are our matters—"

"If you give this man that authority you're a bunch of damn fools."

Giuseppe considered him for a moment and then, deciding it was not worth the effort, went back to his beseeching.

"This defense affects us all. Everyone benefits from our services, so everyone must contribute to the defense. This is a simple matter of fairness. We can talk about the future after this is over. Right now, everyone contributes their fair share and let's worry about the here and now."

Alistair tilted his head back and looked at the dance of lights in the sky, the mobile dots of the aircraft moving around the fixed ones of the stars and cutting across the giant planet dominating the sky into which it thrust itself. A low aircraft flew past and the whoosh of it reached his ears under the drone of Giuseppe's talking. *Not even two years,* he thought. As the thought flitted through his mind, his eyes sought Giselle again, but she spared him no attention.

He interrupted the speaker, saying, "As you said, Giuseppe, I am not part of your group, so forgive me if I prefer to handle other business and leave your power grab for later. I'm not interested a bit in your vote, but I do have an interest in the Incarcerator. We believe we have a way to tilt things in our favor."

Alistair nodded to Shukri and he stepped forward.

"My name is Shukri. In another life I was a fluid physicist at the University of Singapore. Here, I am as much of a scientist as I can manage. My companions and I," he continued with a nod of his head to the others, "have determined the core of this world has been infused with Aradnium. How much I don't know, but based on some data I can calculate an upper and lower limit. There is an Aradnium stirring station not far from here; at least, traveling to the entrance is a matter of hardly any time at all. The station itself is miles below the surface. We have made three suits to withstand the temperature that far down, and Raja visited the station once.

"Aradnium produces a powerful field depending on its rate and pattern of flow. That field is what is keeping Srillium's radiation belts from killing us all. But this pattern and rate of flow can be manipulated, changed to produce different results. What is a harmless protective field now could be turned into something else. An Aradnium field can cripple the electronics of an aircraft, for instance."

Mordecai was on his feet now.

"You can disarm the other aircraft?"

"Not all of them. Probably not. But some of them, yes. The mother ships are maintaining a distance of two thousand miles from the surface, and I doubt the station could create a field strong enough that far out. But after their twenty four hour deadline passes, they will presumably launch an attack. If our ships are on the ground, they will be deactivated but undamaged and can regain their power within four or five hours. The Incarcerator ships will presumably be in the air when we do it."

"And will crash to earth," said Santiago.

"But if it's the flow rate and pattern..." began Giuseppe, "...I'm guessing you can't turn this on like a switch."

"We can increase the rate a good deal more before it would even cause any concern. When we reach that point..." Shukri shrugged, "We can deliver a crippling blow within two or three minutes. Many of their craft will crash to earth; some will be lifeless in orbit. Only those that get out beyond...I will guess...two hundred miles will escape."

Alistair continued with the exposition. "We will send a coded signal to land all aircraft. It'll be on my mark. Sometime in the next few hours we'll deliver the code to you."

"It leaves a lot to be desired, Alistair," opined Duke. "Our craft will be disarmed too. Yes, they'll be on the ground, but the Incarcerator can send in a second wave then..." Duke shrugged in dismissal.

"They can send in another wave, yes," replied Shukri, "but we can deliver another blow."

"But how long can you continue to do this?" asked Wei Bai. *"You have only three suits. How long can you stay down there?"*

The wind picked up and clothing rustled and flapped. Akihiro spoke to them, reverting to Mandarin as prompted by Wei Bai's speech and staring down on them from higher on the hill like a prophet of old, the breath of some god moving his hair and clothes as he spoke.

"Raja said there are living quarters down there. If we can regain power through the entire station and reclimatize them...we could go on indefinitely."

"And if not," said Mordecai, *"it will take you almost until the deadline is up just to get there."*

"Raja can get there faster than that," said Shukri. *"The team will still be able to eat a few miles above the station. They can climb back up the shaft in shifts if they need to eat and drink again. We can maintain this for some time. And maybe we'll get lucky and get the living quarters climatized."*

Mordecai frowned and gave a doubtful, *"Hmmm."*

"It's all we've got," said Akihiro. *"If we can't get it to work..."* he shrugged once. *"I guess you get to fight."*

"Why won't this Aradnium field disable the stirring equipment?" asked Giselle.

"The equipment would have to be insulated against it," Shukri replied. *"The odds are small that The Incarcerator has insulated its ships in the same way."*

"Who will be going?" asked Duke.

Shukri nodded his head towards Raja. "Raja is the youngest of us and can make it down the fastest. We have one who reads Old Korean, unfortunately a necessity down there. He is young too and can descend quickly."

"Taribo will be going as well," said Alistair, and the West African registered surprise to hear it. "In case you need some muscle."

"And you're sure you can do this?" asked Mordecai.

Shukri shrugged again. "The machine was built before my grandfather's great-great-grandfather was born. If it fails, we are in no worse a situation than we are in now."

There was much glancing around as the different heads of security tried to sound out the general feeling for the idea by watching the expressions of their colleagues. This glancing around eventually morphed into so many nods of assent.

"Do as you wish," said Mordecai. "Now, if you'll excuse us, Alistair, we have business to attend to."

For the first time, Alistair caught Giselle looking at him, and he had never gotten a harder glare from an enemy. The growing breeze drew strands of hair across her face, but even with the dim light it was not enough to cover the anger, or the haunting, bloodshot eyes. The Aldran held her gaze for a moment only before leaving with his entourage.

☙ ❧

The aircraft was nearly empty as it streaked through the sky. Two pilots sat in the cockpit; a single communications officer manned his post in the central meeting room; and Alistair, the Singulatarians, Taribo and one other rode in the same room. The other was a young man, almost a boy, who spoke no English and only passable Mandarin. His inclusion was due to his ability to speak Korean and read its old script. He sat by himself, away from the main table, in a chair in the corner of the room, his hands fidgeting in his lap as he ogled the ornate wooden ceiling. Taribo was donning one of the protective suits the Korean speaker already had on.

The acceleration of the craft was like an insistent push, gently driving one deeper into one's chair. When someone got up to walk around, they leaned into or against their walk, as someone on a steep hill. The Singulatarians were busy making calculations, affixing their papers to the tabletop with their hands lest the acceleration cause them to slide off. Alistair approached Shukri while the latter was scribbling.

"You're going to get there with just over twenty two hours left."

"I don't require an encouraging speech, though I appreciate the sentiment. As you can see I am preparing things for Raja."

Taking a seat next to Shukri, Alistair said, "You can control the shape and intensity of the Aradnium field?"

Shukri wrote for a moment longer before he dropped his writing hand on the table, both a sign of resignation and a hint to Alistair that his patience was finite. "Correct."

The force pushing at them abruptly ceased. A moment later it was replaced by an equal force tugging at them.

"Then I want you to leave me an escape route."

He saw the understanding in Shukri's eyes, and they shared a silent nod conveying more than speech could. A moment later, the impatience returned to Shukri's demeanor and tone of voice.

"This will mean recalculating, of course," he said and crumpled up a paper riddled with pencil marks. "It will be easiest to leave you some space at the poles. There will still be an increase in the field in those areas, but we can make it so it won't disable your craft. The brunt of the field will fall nearer the equator, which is where they will be coming to attack us." Shukri paused with his pencil over a clean sheet of paper. "You have your ignition key?"

"Not yet. It's a few minutes' installation. Not to worry."

Nodding, Shukri began his calculations over, and Alistair went back to his chair in the corner.

When the craft reached Odin's Island, it posed on its summit for no longer than a minute. The Singulatarians came down the exit ramp according to their various states of physical vigor, while Taribo and Alistair bounded down it and, going to a storage bin in the underbelly of the craft, pulled out two Torpedoes, each capable of carrying three men. A smattering of other instruments and equipment was deposited on the hillside, a quick goodbye called out, and then Alistair was back in the craft. As it lifted off, the Singulatarians seemed already to have forgotten it.

Eschewing company, Alistair left the communications officer to his duties and retreated to an old office he used as a bedroom. A spacious couch where diplomats used to sit was his bed and, enervated, he tossed himself on it, abandoning himself to the quiet ambient sound of the room and the soft glow that trickled in through the window from the sky.

The acceleration pushed him into the couch as he stared out the window. The hectic events transpiring outside—in orbit many miles up, on the hill slope not far away, in a long slender shaft leading under the crust—intruded on him only in the form of a subdued tingle in his stomach, an after effect his listlessness could not entirely extinguish. Apart from that faint reminder, it might have been an ordinary evening of introversion and melancholy. He saw the faces of the people who had marked his life but who now seemed lost to him. Santiago's serious countenance appeared; he saw Oliver Keegan, then he saw him with a black eye; Katherine and Gerald nodded at him, his sister with a wistful smile; his eyes watered when he saw his parents, then closed shut to ward off the unbidden sight of their death masks. Finally, he saw Giselle, and his mouth opened and his chest shuddered with repressed sobs. There was an ache in his throat as of a raw nerve, and then, as he was tugged now to the edge of the couch, it all faded. It was a matter of a man soaking in the emotion each face brought and then, as if some purpose were satisfied, the images dissipated, and with it his enervation. Somehow, when the aircraft was back on the ground, he had again the energy to go on.

John Kregel and two others were waiting for him when he came down the exit ramp.

"No changes since you've been gone," Kregel reported, stepping forward and delivering a salute.

"Send someone to Darion," said Alistair, immediately walking past Kregel and obligating him to turn and move with him. "Tell him I need to close matters tonight."

Kregel gave a curt nod to another of the two walking with them and that one, returning the nod with equal brusqueness, moved off to see to the matter.

"Send someone with a purse to purchase some preserved food. All kinds: meat, dried fruits, bread…it'll have to be unleavened. Enough for thousands of meals. Fill the aircraft with it. Just leave me the cockpit, my bedroom and the hallways. And fill the storage tanks in my craft with water. In fact…" Alistair stopped walking and pulled a scrap of paper out of a purse strung through by his belt. "Here is the list of what I still need. Get it done."

Kregel snatched the paper and handed it to the other man who grabbed it and then left them.

"Anything else?

"One more thing," said Alistair as he faced Mordecai's look-alike and men scurried around them, still frenzied as they ran. "Take a map and a Torpedo and load it with weapons and ammo. Choose a few different sites and bury them. Then bury the Torpedo, not too far from here and not too near, and then report back to me."

"What about you?"

"Me?" Alistair gave a cavalier expression with a smack of his lips. "I'm going to sleep."

84

It was a ray of sunlight shining on his face that woke him, leaving him to feel he might have rested a bit longer but, when the memories of the previous night sprang into his consciousness, he was entirely unable to roll over and fall back into slumber. He rubbed the sleep out of stinging eyes and sat up, cherishing a moment more of inactivity before he launched himself off the couch. It would be late morning if the sun was up high enough to peek into his window, meaning about half the grace period had elapsed.

Several crates, canisters, flasks and a few jars were stacked outside the ship, forming a tunnel around the exit ramp. Squinting against the bright light of morning, he glanced over his food supply and noted with some alarm how small it was. With a grimace he turned from the food and tracked down Kregel, who was back on duty after what must have been a short sleep. He found him near a small cannon, haranguing a mechanic who apparently was having difficulty fixing whatever was wrong with the gun. Alistair pulled him aside to question him.

"Is that all the food you bought?"

"Yes."

"Did you spend the entire purse?"

"Yes, I did. Alistair, people know what's going on. As soon as word got out you were buying in bulk, and buying preserved food, prices went through the roof. Some people aren't selling for any price." He hesitated and looked at Alistair tentatively, out of the corner of his eye, as if preparing to avert his gaze again. "Is it really going to be that bad? Is that why you're buying preserved food?"

Alistair took a measure of Kregel, but decided against full disclosure.

"You never can tell."

"You want me to buy more?"

Shaking his head, Alistair said, "No. Not if prices are like that." *I'll make a stop somewhere and buy where it's cheaper. It'll prolong the trip, but...* "Did you get the weapons stored?"

"Yeah. I buried the Torpedo too. I just got back."

Kregel said the last bit with a weary sigh, handing a map of the buried treasure to his boss. For the first time Alistair noticed the lines and shadows of fatigue on his face.

"Have you slept?"

"Just got back an hour ago. Haven't had a chance." Glancing at the mechanic, he said, "There's so much..." He finished with an impotent shrug.

"How much longer until the deadline?"

"Around thirteen hours."

"Then get some sleep now. And don't bother with repairs on something that's going to be knocked out of commission anyway."

"Knocked out of commission?"

"All part of the plan. I'll see you later."

They parted with a handshake and, on Kregel's part, an inquisitive look. From there Alistair made his way to the rustic hut in which there was now so much advanced equipment. The frantic rushing about had given way to a jittery stillness. The men finished their preparations and those not sleeping were bunkered down at their stations. Inside the hut there were three men, two seated in front of some equipment and a third standing behind them, directing. They all saluted when Alistair entered.

"Updates?" asked Alistair.

"Silence from the Incarcerator. Mordecai has been pretty constant, trying to hail them, but it's like hailing a brick wall."

"They meant what they said. What about from our science team?"

"They've been giving us hourly updates. Taribo is placing a small, communication relay every few miles and so far it's working. They've still got contact with him. The other two are making better progress, of course, and don't have the communicator so we can't be sure exactly where they are."

"How far down is Taribo?"

"We think close to the bottom. We figure the other two have already made it."

"Good. I need my supplies to be loaded. Store them carefully. Leave the cockpit and my bedroom free. And don't block the path to the engine room underneath because some of the stuff needs to be refrigerated. You know: use common sense."

The man nodded but gave Alistair a suspicious look.

"You planning on taking off?"

"I'm moving our supplies around, hiding a lot of it." It was the truth but it avoided the question and felt like a lie. He hoped he was not blushing as hard as his burning cheeks made it feel. "We have to prepare for a phase two if phase one doesn't go our way."

The man accepted the explanation with a nod. "Anything else?"

"Just get the food loaded. And if Darion comes calling for me let me know right away."

It was not Darion who came to see Alistair, but Gregory and Layla. They came at a sprint, or at least the best facsimile of a sprint Gregory could manage while encumbered by Layla's weight. Their hair was disheveled and their skin sweaty and covered in soot. He had dozens of cuts and scrapes and minor bruises, while a large gash in her scalp drained blood down the side of her face. Alistair looked at them with mouth agape but sprang into action and helped get Layla into a supine position on his aircraft. It was only when he took Gregory's burden that he noticed a trail of smoke in the sky.

"She's going to be alright," said Gregory as they laid her on the couch serving as Alistair's bed. "She's a little dizzy from the blow and the running."

"Do you need anything?"

Layla let out a faint moan.

"I'm going to check her over. She could use some cleaning up."

No sooner had the words left Gregory's mouth than one of Alistair's employees entered with a wet cotton cloth and a glass of some juice. Gregory was already lifting Layla's eyelids and asking her to focus. Alistair accepted the towel with a nod of thanks and, discreet, the man left them. A couple of men loading the supplies waited outside the door, and Alistair dismissed them with a gesture. When Gregory assured himself Layla was in no serious danger, he sat back on the floor. Alistair stood back to allow him space, leaning against the wall with his arms folded. The doctor turned his face towards Alistair.

"The Gaians destroyed the hospital."

Alistair felt an anger well up inside his breast, and he ground his teeth.

"What about the patients?"

"Dead. I fought. Layla fought. But the hospital's gone. And our penicillin!" Gregory said the last bit in shock, like it just occurred to him. He was back on his feet but found he had nowhere to go nor anyway to change what happened. He stood in place and fidgeted. "What the hell has gotten into them?"

"It's always been there. It's just coming out. There are members of our species that are cancer cells, and they turn against their own kind. They want nothing more than to destroy the human race, or reduce it to an animal existence. What set them off now? We're making progress. We are distancing ourselves from the existence of a common animal. We're using more and more of nature to suit our ends."

"We attacked the other Gaian cities," said Greg with a haunted expression. "Alistair, this is all coming undone."

"It's not coming undone," he said with a bothered tone. "The Gaians are easily handled. They're a bunch of tree worshippers with nothing to fight with."

"Not nothing."

"Little enough."

"And the Incarcerator?"

"What about it?"

"And the ex slaves and the ex warriors?"

"What about it?"

Gregory shook his head. Layla, having recovered her senses enough to sit up, put the cup to her lips and took a couple small swallows. Greg knelt at her side and kissed her cheek.

"How's your head feel?"

"If you've been hiding any aspirin this would be the time to pull them out."

The response relieved Gregory. Layla, taking one more sip of juice, lay back down.

"How many Gaians attacked you?"

"About twenty. I..." Greg seemed about to say something more but instead closed his mouth and stared at the floor.

"Are they still at the hospital or where did they go?"

"They left."

Alistair cursed. "This is the last thing I need right now."

"Alistair, I...I killed one."

"One less to take care of."

These were the rough words of a soldier. After they left his mouth, he noticed the stare in Gregory's eyes. His expression softened and he spoke in a low tone, like one uses to sooth a spooked child.

"You were defending your property, Greg."

"I hit him in the head with…I don't remember what. I felt his skull break in." He shuddered.

Alistair squatted next to his friend, grabbed his shoulders and gave them a squeeze. Outside the room, two men lumbered by, their heavy footsteps pounding the hallway as they struggled with a crate.

"They're murderers. You defended yourself and your property."

"You should have killed ten," Layla weakly said from where she lay on the couch, her eyes closed and a forearm thrown over them.

"And you should have done it long before now," said a voice from the doorway, and Greg and Alistair turned to see Darion standing there. Layla, immobile, was satisfied with the report from her ears and did not bother looking to confirm.

Standing to greet the newcomer, Alistair said, "I've been waiting for you."

"It took some time to wrap things up."

"Are you two OK in here?" asked Alistair of Gregory who nodded.

With a twirl of his cane, Darion was back out in the hallway and Alistair followed. They skirted around a couple more men coming on board with cargo and then were out under the sun. Alistair happened to notice Darion's clothes, always as fine as any to be found, and more ostentatious. The stitching of some of the embroidery seemed, at least to Alistair's inexpert eyes, to be well done and of high quality. *You can follow the trail of our progress through Darion's clothes,* he thought.

"I bought you out myself," said Darion, and with his cane he pointed at a couple boxes at the foot of the exit ramp. "At half the price you requested." At Alistair's look, he went on, "With The Incarcerator up there, demand for your company is down. I gave you the best price you were going to get."

Alistair nodded. "Thank you. And I'm going to need an ignition key from the mines."

"I suppose I can spare one."

In his quiet moments of repose, Darion had an air about him like the world amused him. When he was at work, he was exhilarated. This was absent now. He was calm, not sad but serious.

"Do you really want to stay?" Alistair asked him.

Darion sketched an abstract design in the ground with his cane. "What are our chances here?"

"Not great. But at this point the cat's out of the bag. There are pieces of high tech equipment scattered all over. Weapons. I've had several hidden myself, which reminds me." Alistair grabbed from his pocket the map Kregel had given him. "Here are a few treasures. As head of Ashley Security & Arbitration you might be interested."

"I'll have to decide on a new name."

Alistair's expression darkened for a moment, but he shrugged it off. "Anyway," he continued and cleared his throat, "we'll put up a fight here and then scatter. We may have to rebuild, but it's only a matter of time. More Gaian cities will fall. Eventually the Incarcerator won't be able to suppress it anymore. The cat's out of the bag."

"And you don't want to be a part of that?"

"No. It's going to be a life struggle. If I made it to seventy I might see its success. You want to spend the rest of your life struggling?"

"I prefer to look at it as a project, one that never ends. We never see the beginning, we never see the end. You work on it, make it the best you can and enjoy yourself while you're here." Darion glanced a moment at the aircraft overhead. "This situation sounds less dangerous than the one you're returning to. Earth is probably a smoldering ruin right now. Oh yes, let's not be naïve. That Juggernaut was launched at Earth; it makes the most sense. What passes for an economy in the galaxy just got the biggest shock it's ever had. Almost half the population lived in the Terran System, and most of that on Earth. I hate to think about what's going on elsewhere right now. You are headed for Aldra, I presume?"

Alistair nodded.

Darion shook his head as if reconfirming his opinion. "No. Aldra is probably half ripped apart by civil war. And all those black market goods smuggled in, the ones that kept our population on life support, now that Earth is gone…Here," Darion held out a hand to indicate his new home, "we have something. If Earth has been destroyed the Incarcerator is going to find itself short on resources to fight a war with us. And everyone here has seen a possibility. People will remember. We'll build something again." Darion tried to smile but it seemed more of a frown. "Why don't you stay? Instead of risking your life and sanity on a two year voyage whose destination…you don't even know what state Aldra is in."

The question brought to the surface all the feelings Alistair struggled with deep down. He needed a moment to master himself. "There are people I have to see. And I want to return to a planet I was banished from and show them they couldn't get rid of me."

"And then?"

"And then…I don't even know. I want to see what's left of my family, at least. I think I'd like to study something and…I don't know. Watch a movie. Read a book. Go to a concert. I spent four cycles of my life preparing myself to fight, but now I'm sick of it. Why should everything have to be a struggle just to be free? I just want to enjoy the life I have."

"I think there is someone here you want to leave."

"Maybe."

Darion thoughtfully nodded. Then he extended a hand which Alistair took.

"Best of luck to you, Alistair Ashley."

"And to you, Darion Chesterton. I hope I'm not making a mistake."

"Me too."

Darion gave Alistair a bow and sauntered away. The destruction of their civilization was in orbit above them but this only went so far in affecting his unflappable aplomb.

Alistair spent the rest of the morning and afternoon planning his voyage, wracking his brains for anything he forgot that would be useful, or even indispensable. Gregory approached him to ask if they could accompany him to Aldra. He immediately accepted, and if he inwardly blanched at taking two more on board it was only for a moment. He already knew he would have to make a stop to restock.

Finally, a young worker came and announced Shukri's team had reached the bottom, communications were still open and they had control of the machinery and were fine tuning their calculations. When he finished his report, delivered in halting but comprehensible Eng-

616

lish, Alistair thanked him and told him to alert him as soon as the calculations were complete and the Aradnium field increased. The man gave a salute and returned to his post.

If Time's passage is swift before a dreaded deadline and dawdles before a desired one, then Alistair must have been anxious to leave. Even the many tasks he gave himself could not distract him. It seemed Time's hourglass must be partially clogged, that the grains counting the seconds were stuck together and refused to fall through. The sun was a continent in a blue ocean and drifted like it, always in motion but budged only imperceptibly by currents beneath it. When evening approached and shadows grew longer, a great stir was caused in the camp by the arrival of Santiago. He came on a Torpedo at such a speed, and executed such an abrupt stop, that he pitched forward over the handlebars and nearly tumbled onto the ground. Not bothering to lament his lack of decorum, he called for Alistair and, spotting him before anyone responded, rushed over to the ex marine who was carrying a wrapped bundle in the direction of his craft.

"*You're going to be attacked!*" he cried, reverting to his native tongue.

"*By whom?*" Alistair demanded, finding his Spanish easier than his Mandarin.

"Giselle," he replied and suppressed a look of guilt. "The attack is five minutes away. Maybe less. She planned it without me...I only found out by accident."

Alistair dropped his bundle and sprang into action. He called out the alarm, ordered the men to arm themselves and sent them to their battle stations. He waved his arms as if he might speed the men up, though they were already moving with the speed nascent panic brings. Gregory appeared at the top of the aircraft's exit ramp, holding his hands up inquisitively, but Alistair did not have time to give him an explanation. When he was satisfied things were moving on their own he returned to Santiago.

"What the hell is this about?"

"She wants her husband's murderer. That's why she left you, and that's what she's back for. And I think Mordecai is in on it. He's taking the mines—"

"God damn it!" Alistair let out such a loud curse that Santiago started. "Santiago, I have to go. This is Darion's firm now; I'm leaving. I have an HD Drive and I'm going back to Aldra. I can't take the chance it will be damaged."

"I'm going too. I had my own HD Drive built."

Alistair gave him a surprised look as bodies flew past all around them.

"Shukri and the others are not the only scientists on this moon. I'm going back to Earth. I'm going to look for my son."

While the world raced around them in panic, while men shouted and grunted and strained as they prepared for battle, Alistair held out his hand and Santiago grasped it.

"I'm sorry, Alistair," he said, and it was clear he meant more than just regret for Giselle's attack.

"I was wrong. I should have let her have her vengeance."

"Yes. His punishment was her business, no one else's." Santiago gave him a sad smile and moved back to his Torpedo. The space between them quickly filled with hectic workers and soldiers.

Alistair headed towards his spacecraft, then stopped. "Don't try to leave now, Santi!" he called above the din. "You won't make it through the blockade."

"Alistair, the pulse is going to disable our ships before long!"

"Go to the north pole!" They stood on their toes to peer over the tops of heads. "Wait for the pulse to disable the ships and take off from there! The pulse won't affect you at either pole!"

Santiago waved goodbye, but before Alistair could return it he felt rough hands grabbing his shoulders and he turned to see Miklos.

"We have to protect the equipment," said the big man.

"Call down one of our ships and load it," said Alistair. Miklos nodded and turned to go but Alistair grabbed him. "Miklos, this is Darion's firm now. I have to take off; I can't let my aircraft get damaged. You are in charge of the defense. If you can't hold this position, retreat. And get that equipment set up somewhere else."

Miklos' face registered the frustration of a man who has many questions and no time to get his answers. He nodded and went running for the hut. An instant later Alistair was running up the exit ramp where Gregory was still perched. Gregory had his mouth open to say something but Alistair cut him off.

Pointing towards a long, low building of logs a few yards removed from everything else, Alistair said, "I need you to go to that building and get John Kregel."

"Who?"

"Just ask for him. He's Mordecai's twin. Go get him and bring him with us. I've got to get the ship warmed up."

Not waiting to see his orders obeyed, Alistair charged into his space vessel and, taking the curving corridor to the front, turned right, jumped down the small incline in the floor and, racing past navigation computers, came to the cockpit doors. These he kicked open and a split second later hopped into one of the pilot's seats in the black cockpit. His training in flying was sparse, and several times he tripped over the startup procedure but, after a couple minutes, did manage to get the aircraft humming. The multifarious knobs and dials and buttons, many unknown to him, glowed, and on a monitor he saw several blinking lights nearing his position. Looking out the one-way transparent metal that served as a windshield, he still could not see the approaching vehicles, but he estimated they were only a minute away.

Outside the cockpit, he passed Layla in the hallway, ignoring her questioning look. She spun around as he passed her and followed him to the top of the exit ramp. He was about to leap to the ground when he spotted Gregory with Kregel. He waved them on and their jog turned into a sprint even as a drone to the west built. Kregel was armed, but he had the look of a man who had thrown himself together at the last moment. Alistair gave him a nod and returned to the cockpit. All three passengers followed.

"What the hell is going on?" demanded Kregel, sitting down next to Alistair in the copilot's seat.

"We're being attacked. And I need you for a special mission."

"You mean The Incarcerator?" asked Greg.

"Rival firms."

The blips on the monitor showed the attacking party was almost on top of them. Alistair flipped switches and turned dials, raising the exit ramp and closing the exit door. A moment later they came free of the ground and fell into the sky with enough rapidity that

Alistair and Kregel were pushed deeply into their seats and Layla lost her balance and stumbled to the cockpit floor. Alistair let them fall until they were about forty yards in the air, above the tops of the tallest trees and then, while gunfire broke out below, shot forward. Layla, just regaining her feet, stumbled forward and pitched onto the dashboard.

Irritated, Alistair grabbed her with one hand and lifted her off, saying, "If you're not in a seat you need to be out of the cockpit!"

Gregory put his arms around her and shuffled out, leaning forward so the acceleration would not sling him back in.

৵৶

The trip was short. They did not accelerate for long before Alistair decelerated. Gregory left the cockpit door open so they could hear two bodies stumble and fall to the ground with a curse. When they came to a stop, Alistair lowered the craft and set it on the ground in a clearing. There was a bit of a jolt when the novice pilot landed, but nothing serious. Next, Alistair extended the exit ramp and, stopping only to grab a handgun, was there before it finished extending.

Outside there was a long and slender pile of freshly dug earth, and Alistair was in it up to his elbows in short order, heaving clumps of it to the side. Kregel joined him a moment later.

"I'm glad I spent an hour burying this."

"Unforeseen circumstances. I have a mission for you. It might be a dangerous one."

"Go on."

Alistair paused a moment to look over his shoulder, in the direction of some hills and the darkening eastern sky.

"Darion has a mine about a mile in that direction. There, look at the ships!" Alistair pointed and Kregel was able to make out a couple of ships parked on the slopes.

"Mordecai is trying to seize the mines and I need something inside."

"Go on."

Alistair reached down and his fingers met with resistance. It was a tarp used to protect the Torpedo from the wet earth.

"I need you to order the ships to leave. Don't give them anytime to think, just get them out of there. Accept no excuses."

"Just march up and tell them to leave?"

"Those are Mordecai's men."

Kregel's eyes widened and he tilted his head back and parted his lips. "No fingerprint identification. No retina scans." Kregel nodded his head. "You couldn't get away with it anywhere else."

"We need to get away with it here." Alistair saw Kregel was looking with apprehension at the hills behind him. "Are you OK with this?"

His only response was a slow nod. After they dug out the Torpedo and made sure it was functioning, Alistair went back on board his spacecraft and told Gregory and Layla to stay put until he got back. Then he returned to Kregel, mounted the Torpedo behind him, and they took off.

The way Kregel handled the Torpedo bespoke experience. He slalomed through the trees and underbrush with the calmness of a skier on an unchallenging slope. When they fully accelerated the trees whizzed by almost as a green and brown blur. The mile or so between the spacecraft and the base of the hills was traversed in seconds.

Before exiting the foliage, Alistair jumped off. Kregel idled for a moment, allowing the soft hum of the bike to play, before twisting his torso around to look at Alistair.

"Here goes nothing."

"It'll work."

"Thanks for the job. I was expecting something…a whole hell of a lot worse when I got here."

"It's been a pleasure, John."

"I'll see you soon."

Alistair had to force out a response. "Sure thing."

Kregel nodded once and then darted up the hillside, the sound of his engine fading to silence as he disappeared over a small arm of the hill. Alistair was left alone in the darkening forest edge. The preternatural stillness of Srillium's forests struck him again, and he thought of the chirping crickets and buzzing bees to which he would return. The only sound around him was the soft rustle of leaves in the gentle evening breeze and an occasional snap of a twig when he shifted his weight.

He grew impatient. The sky got perceptibly darker and still there was no indication Kregel succeeded. Thoughts of the many possible ways the plan could fail ran in his mind and, frustrated, he clenched and unclenched his fists, unsure what to do. He almost decided to go up the hillside when three metallic disks rose above the hill. Letting out a deep sigh of relief, he let them get smaller in the sky before he started up the slope, taking it at a jog.

When he was within sight of the mine entrance, he was startled by a powerful whoosh overhead, and a breeze buffeted his body. Squinting against the dirt and other particles kicked up, he lifted his gaze and saw, to his horror, a magnificent dance of lights in the sky. The population of lights had more than tripled, and in the western sky, which still clung to a hue of lighter blue, he saw the silhouette of a larger craft, not a mothership but far larger than anything he possessed. It was slowly descending towards the surface, and around it, like hornets, buzzed craft from both sides, locked in a dogfight. The sound of distant gunfire reached his ears, and this served to get him running again.

The shots, presenting themselves with a diffident tapping at his eardrums, presently grew louder until he rushed into the mouth of the mine, at which point the sounds receded until they were no longer audible. It was only after he was several yards in and his enhanced sight turned the blackness into gray that he realized how foolish he was to charge in. There might yet be some of Mordecai's troops inside the mines, plundering Darion's equipment. He stopped his headlong rush and, after a moment to control his labored breathing, quieted down and listened. He heard some amorphous sound from deeper in the mine. Taking his handgun out and cocking it, he stepped more cautiously, even though his guts churned inside in anticipation.

The soles of his moccasins crunched the loose gravel of the mine. Being uncontested by other noise, these reports of footfalls seemed almost deafening as his feet tossed them out into the darkness. Many times he stopped, abruptly, to listen for any indication he was not alone, for any crunching coming from other feet, but he heard nothing. Then, as he plunged still farther into the bowels of the hill, the rock around him vibrated, and it was accompanied by a deep rumble, as a distant explosion. Pebbles rained down, and sand and dust billowed and formed a sort of smoky haze in the air as the rumbling faded. A moment later a second such occurrence took place, and the pebbles, hitting his head, tumbled down his face or past his ears, onto his shoulders and back and chest, and finally onto the ground, making a thousand little pizzicato clicks.

He coughed once, then stifled a second. No third portentous rumble assaulted him; quiet and stillness reclaimed the mine. He was familiar with the layout and knew the shaft he was in, the main shaft, went back and down into the hill more or less directly, with a multitude of branches stemming from it. There were, however, some minor bends and twists and coming around one of these he was presently greeted with a splash of color intruding on his gray vision with the familiar ripples like heat waves.

With his normal vision he saw a light source spilling into the main tunnel from one of the side shafts. After holding still and silent for a minute or two, he heard a soft sound, as of someone shuffling around, and then a loud clank followed by what sounded like a hushed discussion. Another clank sounded and the discussion built into a brief crescendo that, by degrees, ebbed into silence once more. With a reassuring grip on his gun, he crept towards the junction of the main shaft and the branch. Each foot he settled on the ground with the delicate care one uses in placing an infant in its cradle. Each foot was lifted with similar caution. A spider, if it were careless, had made more noise.

He crept up against the wall of the main shaft when he reached the branch. Both hands he placed on the hewn stone wall, bracing himself against it, and cast his body to the left but slowly and only slightly, just enough to bring his left eye past the edge of the wall. He allowed himself a quick glimpse and then pulled back, undetected. The glimpse was enough to appraise the situation: the light source was a lantern placed on the ground, and it showed him four figures nearby. A great drill, a patchwork of equipment salvaged from the Gaian cities, was there, and it would have the ignition key he sought.

He leaned out past the wall one more time, but this time his hands held his gun. The four figures did not notice. Taking careful aim, he lined the gun up with the lantern and inhaled until his lungs were full. Still, the men took no note of him. Holding his breath, he pressed the safety latch and a click sounded. The four men started. He could not know how much they saw or whether, accustomed to the lantern's light, they could see him at all, but it made little difference. He pulled the trigger.

The lantern exploded in a shower of sparks. The sound of glass shards and other bits falling to the floor mixed with the reverberations of the gunshot. Four voices called out and four figures scrambled to hide behind boulders or equipment or whatever offered itself as a likely shield. Once more, Alistair saw everything in gray.

"Who's there?" demanded a voice in the darkness, and the walls threw the angry shout back and forth, breaking it up until it was no more.

A response on Alistair's part would have done nothing more to reveal his location than his gunshot had already done. He might have given them his name, height, weight and occupation for all that it mattered from a practical standpoint, but a human voice would have been a solace, if for no other reason than it confirmed the very walls of the mine had not decided to cast them out or some such fear which, in the dark, tickles the brain of even a skeptical man. Alistair denied them that minuscule measure of comfort.

"Who's there?" the same man called out again. The same echoes followed.

A third tremor shook the mine and rained bits of rock down and it served to remind Alistair he did not have the luxury of time. He stepped into the middle of the branch shaft and, letting out a magnificent bellow, pulled the trigger several times, unleashing a volley of bullets that sparked against the shaft walls, floor and ceiling. Two of the men jumped out of their crouches and scampered farther down the shaft. The other two only tucked themselves tighter into the niche in which they hid, but when Alistair shot at the wall just above their heads, when the sensation of a bullet's near passage shook them, when splinters of rock ejected from the bullet's crater pricked their skin, these last two ran after the first pair. The result was four men cowering several yards farther down the shaft, howling for mercy and leaving the drill abandoned.

Alistair ran to the drill, holding his gun in the waistline of his pants, and dug into the motor.

"If you come any closer we'll shoot!" screamed a new voice.

Ignoring him, Alistair opened hatches, unhooked parts, detached wires and worked his way down to where he knew the ignition key was. A glance down the shaft showed one of the more intrepid of the four venture out from behind a pile of rocks. Alistair paused for a moment to grab his gun and fire another shot, sending the man scurrying back behind the pile. A few moments later he had the key in his hands. Gently cradling the precious bit of equipment, he fired four more shots, inducing another series of wails, and went back the way he came.

Moving more quickly now, he was back outside the mine and in the warm night air. The sounds he heard as he neared the entrance prepared him for the view that greeted his eyes. In the north a vast fire burned, coloring the sky a deep orange and outlining black aircraft crossing in front. In the sky, lights of aircraft weaved in and out of the lights of gun and laser fire. Every so often there was a burst of light, revealing the body of a vessel which would, like a meteor, plummet to the ground and cause another explosion. The noises of battle were unrelenting. Explosions, gunfire and the screech of aircraft moving at incredible speeds rushed over him like a tidal wave.

He stood on that hillside at night, surrounded by that display of violence, and felt shame wash over him. He felt no fear, no anxiety, not even anger, but rather a stinging shame, as if called upon to give an account of his species before some universal court and, faced with such a damning exhibit, he could not. His body, like a wax figure on the verge of melting, slouched, and for a moment he had an urge to chuck the ignition key into the forest, cast himself on the ground and let everything disintegrate around him.

This urge he conquered and he ran down the hillside and into the forest. It occurred to him he was not familiar with the area, and he was glad Kregel took a direct route to the hill so he could find his craft again. After a few minutes, when he figured he must be getting close, he felt a sudden sharp pain in his ankle and he pitched forward and fell face first onto the forest floor. A stick on the ground gashed his forehead and some rocks scraped his right hand.

His first reaction was to grab at his ankle, and he discovered nothing was broken despite the formidable pain he was feeling.

He was some minutes in recovering the ignition key, which flew out of his hand and which, lacking his special vision, he would never have found. When the key proved to be undamaged, he thanked whatever god might be listening and limped through the forest. Desperate to get back to his vessel as soon as he could, he fought through the pain in his ankle, permitting himself no sign of weakness greater than a wince, an occasional grunt and a limp.

When he finally reached the clearing, he found Gregory and Layla at the top of the exit ramp, holding each other and staring at the sky. They looked down when they heard Alistair's footsteps on the ramp. Their expressions changed from one of helpless resignation to sharp concern, and if he could have seen his bloodied visage it would have been apparent why. Gregory went halfway down the ramp to meet his friend and help him the rest of the way up.

"Are you alright?"

"Fine."

"You took forever."

"I got the key."

Inside the craft, Alistair flipped a switch and turned on the lights lining the hallway on the floor and ceiling. Leaning on a struggling Gregory, he made his way to the cockpit.

"Are we going to make it?" asked Layla, trailing behind.

"I don't know," said Alistair. "They came a few hour before the deadline. I don't know when the Aradnium field will be ready, or even if we are still in contact with the team down there."

Now in the cockpit, he knelt between the two pilot's seats, pulled up a panel of flooring and began to install the ignition key.

"Anything I can do?" asked Greg.

"Can you fly?"

The question needed no answer.

A flash lit up the inside of the cockpit, and Layla gasped. Looking out the windshield, Alistair saw the aftereffects of an explosion within a few tens of yards, its sound unable to reach their ears. Redoubling his efforts, he let out a shout of triumph a moment later, hobbled into the pilot's seat and started the engine.

"I suggest you take a seat somewhere else," he said.

Instead, Gregory moved into the copilot's seat and Layla sat on Greg's lap.

"The key," said Alistair as the craft dislodged itself from gravity's grip and slowly fell into the air until it was above the tree tops, "is to make an exit without attracting notice. I think we'll head south first."

They crept along, almost brushing the tops of the tallest trees, their exterior lights off. They would not escape detection by any instruments, but it would hide them from the human eye. Increasing speed, they were alternately lit up by flashes and cast back into gloom. With the soundproof walls of the craft, their escape was like passing through a muted threedy. All they heard was their own tremulous breathing and nervous swallowing in the dark cockpit, but a light display played for their eyes. Alistair pressed a button to light the dashboard and produced a readout display in 3D.

"The Aradnium field is increasing."

"Do we have time?" asked Layla.

"Unknown."

Eventually, the forest gave way to fields, the ground blurred and the battle fell behind them. Not long after, the ground became pitch black, flat and smooth and they knew they were over open water. Alistair turned the craft west, continuing to pick up speed. A few minutes later they were out of sight of land and he turned the craft north. He continued to fly low, a hundred feet above sea level, but now moved with greater speed than a bullet and still accelerated. He struck a few more buttons and the 3D display became a globe of the moon with a dot of light representing their craft.

'I don't know if we have an hour, five hours or five minutes," he said. "I'm going to up the acceleration. One of you should find a better seat. And when we break…hold on tight."

Gregory and Layla made their way to Alistair's bedroom, the only room free of cargo, and strapped themselves into chairs. He gave them a minute to get ready and then, his hand on the lever, increased the rate of acceleration. Before long, it was almost painful. Still they increased speed, and despite the design of the craft he knew they would be trailing smoke and fire behind them. He could see the flames from the compacted oxygen fluttering in front of the craft.

Finally, he stopped accelerating, allowing himself a moment to catch his breath before he squeezed the handle of a lever and twisted it around, rotating the ship. The Aradnium field was steady. He began to decelerate. Now facing the other way, the deceleration caused the same sensation as the acceleration had done: he was driven with ever more power into his seat. He withstood the extreme pressure for a couple minutes before, through his squinting, bleary eyes, he saw they were going to fall short of their target and slowed the deceleration.

The sun was creeping over the northern horizon. The ocean below was more white than blue, and as it streaked by it showed in the light hue of blue it produced. Alistair stared at that southern horizon for a time, the horizon of his home for many months, the horizon of a grain of sand in a colonized strip of galaxy measuring a thousand light years from end to end, a backwater moon in a backwater system. For a time, it had been pleasant, even exciting. He knew he would never see it again, and the thought both thrilled him and produced a melancholy regret, a nostalgia for what had almost been and an excitement for what might yet be.

He did not allow his musing to distract him for long and decelerated again. By the time he reached the vicinity of the northern pole, they were going a mere thousand miles per hour. His computer detected another ship nearby, on a gigantic flow of ice, and he approached until he could see it through the windshield. Setting his vessel down a rugby field away from what he knew was Santiago's craft, Alistair unfastened his seatbelt and pressed the intercom button.

"We're on the ground."

A glance at the readings indicated the Aradnium field was still holding steady. He rose from his chair, making sure to first set an alarm to warn him when the field changed, and limped to meet Gregory and Layla at the exit.

"Want a taste of home?" he asked and pressed a button on the wall.

The door slid open while the ramp extended. Frigid air poured into the craft, cold enough to make even Alistair blanch. Layla withdrew with a cry of distress.

When the door was open and the freezing wind had free rein to whip at them, Alistair, dressed for the tropics, stepped out onto the exit ramp, took a deep breath, and tossed an arm into the air to wave goodbye to Santiago. He never knew whether Santiago saw him or not, for his alarm went off and he went back inside, pressing the button to close the exit, and back to the cockpit. Layla and Gregory joined him a second later.

"Look!" said Layla, pointing out the windshield. "The other ship is blinking its lights!"

"He probably can't communicate with the increased field."

"I thought the field wouldn't reach here."

"It reaches here, but it's weaker."

He found a light control switch in his own cockpit and blinked his lights a few times. When the other vessel stopped, so did he.

"How much longer?" asked Layla.

"I don't know. Hell, they could lose control of the equipment and not be able to stop it."

"But we can still leave, right?"

"Sure, as long as we stay in the pole until we are far enough away."

"So we can go now?"

Alistair considered her point. "Any last words for Srillium?"

"Goodbye," Layla said decisively.

"We hardly knew ye," said Greg.

"Here's to a long trip home," said Alistair, and then they lifted off the ground.

Santiago's spacecraft, a good deal smaller than Alistair's, was off the ground only seconds later. They fell into the sky, impelled by gravitophotons, becoming black dots beyond the clouds and, finally, disappearing altogether.

☙ ❧

There were five people amid the ruins, a mix of burned log cabins and the twisted metal of crashed aircraft. Long, charred gashes in the earth still smoked, but there were no longer any bodies strewn about. Two of the figures were probably men, but as they were dressed in battle gear, it was difficult to say. With the miniature cannons mounted on their helmets they kept watch over Miklos who, arms bound behind his back, knelt on the earth. A woman, dressed in a business suit with pants, wearing high heels that kept sinking too far into the soil and carrying an electronic clipboard, surveyed the scene while Angus, hobbling on a crutch due to a wounded leg, stood nearby.

"When we finally landed our battalions on the surface they were fighting each other," the woman remarked as she inspected some wreckage. She apparently expected an answer from Angus, because after a slight pause she turned from the wrecked aircraft and gave him an expectant look.

Angus shrugged and tried to think of something to say. "People always fightin' each other."

"But why were they fighting?"

Angus shook his head and looked down at the ground. Seeing she would get no answer from the man from Tantramon, she looked to Miklos, who gave her a defiant stare.

"Why were they fighting?"

"It's not your business. Just consider yourself lucky, or you'd never have won."

She became interested in her clipboard and only gave half her attention to Miklos when she responded. "You were outnumbered twenty to one; I don't think anything was going to save you."

"My people whipped the Persians at Marathon with worse odds than that," he growled with all the pride of a prisoner who refuses to submit.

After a moment more at her clipboard, she looked up. "It was Thermopylae. And you lost."

"It was Marathon."

"I'm not going to argue with a convicted war criminal. So obviously you somehow raided Floralel and used what you stole to take out other Gaian cities. Then you divided into four kingdoms and, being a bunch of rapists and thieves, immediately started fighting over territory. Is that about it?"

"You're a piss-poor historian," said Miklos and spat.

The woman was unperturbed. "Who was the head of the kingdom here?"

"We didn't have kingdoms. Like I said, history's not your strong suit. There were three, well, four main security firms. Everyone lived where they wanted and did what they wanted. If you needed protection or arbitration, you could hire a firm. They sold insurance too."

"Where were the borders?"

"There weren't any boundaries. They were businesses. We looked for customers wherever we could find them."

"Four warlords all sharing the same territory? No wonder you were fighting. You are... Miklos Papadopolous? Which of the four did you fight for?"

"I was with Ashley Security & Arbitration."

"Alistair Ashley 3nn. Can you tell us where he is? Where he would be hiding?"

"I have no idea."

The woman typed for a moment on her clipboard and then nodded at the guards. "You can take him away."

As the guards seized Miklos and half dragged him back to a detention cell, Angus felt the impulse to speak to the woman. "Things work well for a while."

The woman, in turning around, stepped out of her high heel shoe lodged in the mud. Grumbling, she reinserted her foot and did not hear what Angus said.

"When I first come here, everythin' fine," he repeated.

The woman spared him a quick glance and said, "Paradise was short lived."

"Oh, I don't think you can blame Alistair for that. Things hard on Srillium, no matter how you live. Conditions always gonna be hard here. And people hurtin'. But when I come here, I put down naked and hungry, like a million people before me. In an hour I have a job and a meal. If I come here two years before, I get sacrificed and eaten, no mistake on that."

She considered his words with a skeptical look. "I still don't understand exactly what was happening on this rock, but whatever experiment you were running, it failed. Even if we hadn't been here to put it down, you were at each other's throats."

"People always at each other's throats on Srillium. Like I say, people here hurtin'. There old wounds that don't heal. That somethin' anybody has to deal with, president, king, anarchist. You talkin' to a man alive because Alistair's system better. As long as I live you won't hear me say different."

"Interesting. Nevertheless, it fell."

"It falls. But anythin' gonna fall when you come. While it lasts, it works. Alistair says any system limited by the people in it. Well, I tell you, we got people angry, hurtin', wantin' revenge. If you don't come maybe they work it out, maybe they don't, but only Alistair gives 'em a chance to. He the only one who believes in it for a while, and he tries to make it spread with people who don't believe, not ready yet. But they start to believe, a little at a time. Maybe not quick enough, but that not his fault. But his mistake, he stubborn and makes his woman angry. He tells us to work things out, cooperate, but on one issue he tries to impose himself. But it a good system. I know cause I live in it."

The woman clearly did not follow Angus' speech, and not following it, she dismissed it as nonsense. She took down one more serial number from the side of a downed aircraft and then made her way back to her camp. Angus, unmoving, watched her go.

"But Darion gets away," he said. "And your biggest client probably wiped out by the Juggernaut. So maybe you strong, but maybe you don't last. Maybe this fight not over yet. Maybe somethin' just startin' to wake up."

This last private speech delivered, Angus hefted his crutch and hobbled away, moving in the opposite direction.

End of Part II

PART III

85

Stars in the G category, like the Terran sun, had proved to have the planets most propitious for human colonization. They are a good deal larger than the majority of stars in the universe. Driving an auto through the center of a G class star—if one could accomplish such a feat—at a speed customary to the average highway and never pausing once for a break or to sleep, a person could spend well over a year getting from one side to the other. If such a star were shrunk to the size of a period on a page, the nearest star, in that zone of the Milky Way colonized by humans, would be several miles away. Like the atom, the galaxy is mostly empty space.

Only a sailor on a submarine experiences anything akin to what a traveler in interstellar space feels, and even then it is but a weak version of it. Such a traveler finds himself in a tiny bubble hospitable to his needs, surrounded by a vast emptiness inimical to them. In the deepest oceans of the galaxy, the submarine is never more than a few miles from the surface, but the spaceship is often, from the nearest star, at a distance one describes as immense, or enormous. Such words, though, were invented for different uses, when an enormous distance meant the width of the Atlantic Ocean, when immense meant the prairie between the Rocky Mountains and the Mississippi River. It is best to call space inconceivably huge and there let the matter rest.

A man may say that Rome is far from Berlin, having made the journey, and rightly claim to know what far means. Space travel is entirely different. No winds buffet the vehicle, no scenery streaks by, even the stars exhibit parallax at a glacier's pace. Without the instruments in the cockpit, one has absolutely no sense of movement, cannot distinguish between a ship at rest and one speeding at a light-year per day. Consequently, though a man may travel from one star to another, he still cannot conceptualize, cannot feel or imagine the distance he has traveled. He can read that another man is six feet tall and have an idea to go along with the datum. He may learn that a train travels at three hundred kilometers per hour and have a sense of what that speed entails. If he reads that Tantramon is 2.4 quadrillion miles from Arcabel, he has only the number and, if he is wise, a profound sense of humility.

When the ship left Srillium's gravity and slowed to an easier acceleration, Layla unstrapped herself and went to an antechamber filled with supplies. Crawling over, around and through the many crates and sacks, with her back nearly scraping the ceiling, she came to a window at the back and pressed her forehead against it. She could see a wedge of Srillium the gas giant stuck in the corner of the window, but her eyes were drawn to the blue and green dot, with a splotch of white in the middle: Srillium the moon, as seen from above the north pole. The expression on her face as she watched it shrink was something like a wife's watching the departing train carrying her husband to war.

When Alistair rotated the ship, the view from Layla's window changed and she lost sight of the world that was her home for several years and all her adult life. It was a hard world and treated her cruelly, prematurely forcing her into adulthood and enslaving her, but it was what she knew. The world waiting at the end of a two year journey was unknown to her, and even Alistair and Gregory were unsure in what state it would be if they managed to return.

An interstellar trip is accomplished in three stages: acceleration, hyperspace and deceleration. The Heim-Droescher Drive converts the photons of electromagnetism into gravitophotons, carriers of one of the three forces of gravity. This gravitational force moves the ship without propellant. After a period of acceleration, the gravitophotons combine with gravitons to reduce the mass potential of the ship, but since momentum must be conserved, the reduction of mass is accompanied by a concomitant increase in velocity. With enough of a mass reduction, the speed of the ship goes past the speed of light, at which point the vessel is forced into hyperspace and the second stage begins. Finally, the HD Drive is cut, the mass of the ship increases, bringing the velocity down, and the ship falls out of hyperspace.

The optimum amount of time spent in stages one and two depends on the length of the trip. The longer the trip, the greater the benefit of a prolonged acceleration. For a trip between planets in the same system, a few hours of acceleration, followed by mere minutes in hyperspace and a few more hours of deceleration will make for the shortest trip. For a journey between a planet and its moon, the hyperspace jump is not even used. For interstellar trips, acceleration of the equivalent of one g of gravity was the norm, but Alistair chose a slightly higher acceleration, shortening their trip by nearly a week. After about a month, they reduced their mass potential and slipped into hyperspace, going at about a quarter the speed of a standard interstellar liner.

The oppressiveness of the void was omnipresent, like the soft, constant hum of the engine that may recede to the back of the mind but leaves a residue in its awareness. Under their feet was a solid floor, to the touch indistinguishable from a mountain of granite and yet it seemed a tenuous thing keeping them from floating free in the nothingness. The temperature was pleasant, but every view through a window was a reminder that a mere few inches held back an implacable frigidity.

Confined, lonely, isolated, one mechanical malfunction removed from death, they did what most humans would do, what they needed to do: they grew close. This happened by degrees as Layla realized Alistair would not bite, then that he could be civil, even pleasant, and finally affectionate after his own fashion. She first stopped casting suspicious glances in his direction. Next, she exchanged words with him. Before long she found he could make her laugh, not from a genuine joke such as a comedian might tell, but from the generous laughter friends give each other but which strangers cannot elicit. Finally, she could stay in the same room with him when Gregory left and not feel uncomfortable.

There was very little to do during the journey. The cockpit was open, but due to its disconcerting view, Layla avoided it which meant Gregory avoided it. Alistair would occasionally go there to check on the systems or to lean back in the pilot's seat and stare at the stars. With the cockpit door closed, it was a dark room illuminated only a little by the red and blue glows coming from buttons, knobs and displays. Sometimes he turned off even these lights to allow himself to be surrounded by the brilliant points of light which, in space, do not sparkle.

Alistair's bedroom, which became Gregory and Layla's bedroom too, was used only infrequently when they were awake. With only one couch, they fell into the habit of sleeping in different shifts. Gregory and Layla slept together, and afterwards Alistair slept by himself. The third of the day they were all awake they spent wherever they pleased, but when one was sleeping they mainly kept to the hallway. Alistair used it for exercise; Gregory and Layla were less active and usually sat together, talking away the time. Sometimes they strolled around the circle, and each day they made love and made sure to take an hour doing it.

The engine room below had a small cooking area and a freezer in which a grown man could fit. Next to it was a small area with a drain and a faucet with a hose. Though intended for machinery, it worked as a shower and all the water they used passed into the drain and was cleaned and recycled. The area was poorly lit but clean, without the stink and stains of burnt oil and only a soft, permeating hum for noise. The engine was a hemisphere roughly twenty feet in diameter, though many wires, tubes, crevices and such marred its roundness. The HD Drive the Singulatarians installed looked like some protruding mechanical growth. There was a blue light leaking out of the engine from inside, and it faintly pulsed in perfect synchrony with the slow rhythm of the hum. There were other lights in the engine room, but other than the ones above the kitchen they rarely turned them on, so the entire subfloor was usually in shadow with splashes of azure.

The first few days they ate well, dining on fresh fruit, bread, cheeses, eggs and meats, the finest Srillium could produce. After that, they resorted to the freezer and the meats stored there and, with bread they baked themselves, got along for another few weeks. After that, they were left with dried fruits, salty meats and tough, unleavened bread which by monotony quickly made eating a chore. A few months into the trip, when tedium had long ago set in, they found mold on some of the food. This they could at first brush off, but later an increasing amount of food was inedible. Layla and Gregory were alarmed, but Alistair assured them they had enough food despite some of it going bad. A second bedroom was cleared of supplies as they and the mold consumed more and more food. This allowed Gregory and Layla their own bedroom, and when they moved into it, they synchronized sleeping schedules.

One day, while they sat in Alistair's bedroom, in the midst of a lull in a wandering conversation, the lights of the spacecraft turned red and blinked on and off. Gregory and Layla were alarmed, but Alistair was unconcerned. Rising from his chair, he made his way to the cockpit with his two friends in tow. On one of the displays a timer was counting down to zero. Flipping a couple switches and turning a couple knobs, he kept his eye on it until it reached zero, at which point he flipped open a small lid and pressed the button underneath. In response, the ship popped out of hyperspace, rotated about so its bottom was facing where the top had just been, and began to decelerate.

"The first leg is almost done," said Alistair, and that was the end of the excitement for that day.

They stopped the deceleration weeks later when they slowed to thirty thousand miles per hour, a snail's pace. Alistair turned off the navigating computer and took control of the ship. They were still in interstellar space with nothing to see but stars, but on the metal wall acting as both windshield and computer screen there were some readouts and he steered according to these.

"Strap yourself into a seat, Layla," he said.

The young woman pulled down a panel on the wall behind the pilot seat and revealed the other side to be a chair. No sooner did she strap herself in than Alistair began an intense deceleration. Since they were moving backwards now, the deceleration drove them into their seats, and this they endured for about ten minutes. Their breathing sped up and Gregory, blinking and searching the screen, saw they were moving at four thousand miles per hour. Alistair rotated the ship along its north/south axis so they were moving forwards instead of downwards. He then initiated a gentler deceleration and Gregory watched as the velocity lowered into the three thousands.

On the computer screen/windshield there was now a blinking red dot towards which Alistair flew. For a little while this was all they saw, but gradually a form appeared and grew larger so he turned the dot off. The shape on their screen was something like an auto's tire but measuring a quarter mile in diameter and a tenth of a mile in height. Myriad lights, some on the outside, others shining through windows great and small, illuminated the space station. They shivered with excitement as they approached this island in the middle of an infinite ocean.

Like remoras around a shark, many small craft skimmed over its surface, some on their way to a docking bay, others carrying workmen bound for repair duty. They passed such a work crew engaged in extra-vehicular operations as they entered the docking bay to which they were directed. A few larger spacecraft, too large to be accommodated by the docking bays, were clustered outside, their passengers and crew having taken ferries inside. Alistair eventually set the craft down on a landing pad, and then all three rushed to the exit, yearning for some time off the confining craft in which they spent the last year. As Alistair hit the button to lower the ramp and open the door, he reached behind a panel in the wall and pulled out a small sack that jingled. Then the exit was open and they raced down the ramp to stand on the metal docking bay floor.

The artificial gravity was set to match Earth's, one g. There was a difference in smells, the docking bay having an at once metallic and sweaty one, distinct contrast to the odor of their own vessel they long ago ceased to notice. Layla even wrinkled her nose in aversion.

Since Aldra was an outlying colony, they had been making their way to the edge of colonized space and thus to less trafficked areas. The docking bay was not bustling with the same activity that buzzed in other space stations, but it was yet filled with the clangs and pounding of blue collar men at work. A man, more interested in his hand-held computer/clipboard than in the new arrivals, approached them with the swift, bold strides of a busy worker. His skin was brown and his features a mix of many races. Giving them a glance and a frown at their primitive clothing, he made his best guess as to which language to use.

"You have your docking fee?"

His English was American and flawless. Alistair held up his pouch and jingled it.

"Minted where?" The man now stood next to them and came to a halt.

"Private mint. New one. It's a gold and copper alloy."

The man typed a couple things into his clipboard. "We don't recognize numismatic value unless it's from an established mint. Just metal content."

"I understand."

"Have you posted bond?"

"No."

"We'll have to search and catalogue your ship, then. Unless you want to post bond."

"Not this time."

"You a subscriber?"

"No."

"Do you want to?"

Alistair considered it a moment. "I'll look into it."

The man typed for a moment more and then yanked a plastic card out of the clipboard and handed it to Alistair.

"Take it to that guy," he said with a nod towards a man seated at a desk near the docking bay exit, and then moved past them.

"Subscribe to what?" asked Gregory as they moved towards the indicated worker.

"They send out rescue ships to sweep the area, looking for stranded spacecraft," Alistair explained. "If you subscribe ahead of time, the rescue is free. We could also give them our route before we leave so they are aware of the need to run through that area."

"What's the bond for?" asked Layla.

"If you post bond they let you through without searches to look for dangerous materials. If they find anything objectionable they are going to confiscate it."

"Do we have anything objectionable?"

"No. But some smugglers carry things that explode. They won't let it in here unless possible damages are paid for in advance."

Having arrived at the exit, Alistair presented the card to the bored worker, slouched in his seat. The man took the card and slipped it into a slot in his computer.

"Not posting bond?" he asked as he looked at the information on his 3D display, never bothering to sit up straighter.

Alistair shook his head.

"How long are you staying?"

Alistair looked at his companions, and Gregory and Layla, looking at each other, shrugged.

"Three days," he finally said.

"How are you paying?"

He laid the jingling pouch down on the counter and the man overturned it to get a look at the coins. One by one, he placed them on a small pad where they were scanned.

"Three days' docking plus a search."

When he had taken enough, he typed in a code on a small safe at the edge of his reach, moving only those parts of his body that were absolutely necessary, and dumped the coins in it. He fished around for a moment before depositing a few silver coins on the counter. Alistair took the silver coins and, along with the remaining gold ones, dumped the disks back into his pouch and put the pouch in his pocket. Finally, the man handed the card back to them.

"Enjoy your stay," he said without enthusiasm.

Passing through the docking bay exit, they came into a dimly lit open mall whose ceiling, hundreds of feet above them, was the ceiling of the space station. Across from them, at a distance of perhaps a rugby field, was a grandiose escalator which, splitting in two, swept up

in two spirals past the many landings of the many stories of the station. These stories had rail-
ings at the edge and were subdivided into several hallways whose great width made the ceiling,
from afar, seem low though in reality it was twelve feet high. A great multitude could have fit
in that mall, though the current crowd numbered hardly a hundred, and many of the establish-
ments along the edges were closed and dark. There was little noise apart from some shuffling
feet, a couple hushed conversations and a bit of music coming from some bar or other.

They went to the nearest open bar, a shoebox open at one end, and sat at the counter.
Only one other patron sat inside and he cradled a beer in his lap while, leaning back in his
chair, he stared at a 3D display on the center of his table. The only bartender was sweeping the
floor as they entered, but he dropped his broom and stood behind the counter, greeting them
with a nod and awaiting their order.

"I'll take a beer," said Alistair.

"Water," said Layla.

"Do you have any wine?" asked Greg.

"No wine."

"Gin and tonic?"

"No gin. No tonic."

"What do you have?"

"Beer."

"Beer, then."

The man set about filling the orders.

"We need to get some new clothes," said Alistair.

The bartender shook his head as he filled a mug. "Not here. Not now."

"No clothing stores?"

The man snorted. "Ain't gonna be *anything* soon enough." The man set a mug down in
front of Alistair. "This whole place'll be shut down less than a year. Way things are goin'." He
set a glass of water in front of Layla and then ran his gaze up and down the three of them. "I
agree you need new clothes, though."

"What's the matter with the way things are going?" asked Greg.

This made him pause as he reached for another mug. "How long you been out there?"

They looked at each other almost guiltily, as if a professor had demanded an answer
they should have known.

"Earth's gone."

They froze, as if shocked by electricity. Knowing Earth might have been the target of
the Kaldisian Juggernaut did little to lessen the impact of the certainty. The bartender had
already done his mourning, however, and without sympathy or remorse he filled one last mug
and set it in front of Gregory.

"It's still there, obviously," he amended, "but I doubt too many people are living
there."

So saying, the bartender left them and returned to his sweeping. Alistair immediately
thought of Santiago and the son he was trying to find. If Santi's ship was as fast as his tortoise,
which he doubted, he would still be far away from home.

"Good luck, *amigo mio*," he whispered.

This sentiment, given voice, provoked his two companions to raise their glasses, and they shared the most solemn of toasts. Afterwards, Gregory and Layla spoke a little, but Alistair said nothing. Instead, he stared out across the mall. Standing up, he mumbled something indistinct, and left. Gregory and Layla watched him cross the mall's open court and it soon became obvious he was going to a brothel.

"Oh," said Layla, a little surprised. "I didn't think..." she shook her head and let the sentence trail off.

"Didn't think what?"

"Giselle said he was a virgin before he met her. I'm just surprised he would go there."

Gregory shrugged. "Once you've had it...It's been a year. And it's going to be another year before we get back."

Only after they went through several cups did Alistair return, and he came back with the air of satisfaction and pleasant fatigue a man has after a workout at the gym. He said nothing but merely pulled back a chair at the table his companions had moved to and collapsed into it.

"Did you get it worked out?" asked Layla with a raised eyebrow. Alistair blushed.

They sat for only a few more minutes, enough time for Alistair to have another cold beer, and then they got a room to stay in. It consisted of a bed only just large enough to fit the three of them, a bare linoleum floor of the same sort found in the hall outside, nondescript white walls and ceiling, a single chair in the corner and a globe of light partially recessed into the ceiling. The bed was a thin mattress with no sheets or blankets, and Alistair was forced to make a trip back to their ship to get some. Being tired, and Gregory and Layla being the greater part of inebriated, they did not go back out once Alistair returned. One blanket they laid as a protective layer between them and the mattress, another they used to cover themselves in a station that, upon ceasing activity, they noticed was a bit chilly.

They had no way of knowing how long they slept. The station had no day and night, and it made little sense to effect such a phenomenon in a place without consensus as to what constituted a proper length for a day, or what point in that day it ought to be when people arrived. In the past, the station was brightly lit, a cheery and active inn for the weary space traveler. Now, with docking revenues declining, it was kept in a somber but less expensive twilight.

After waking, Alistair checked on the ship and looked for provisions. It turned out food had risen in price such that, considering he had lengthened their journey to go to the station, he might have been better off buying more food on Srillium and going straight to Aldra. Nevertheless, it was preserved with more advanced techniques and they stocked the rooms with a greater variety of foods and spices. Along the way, he had compiled a list of items they found wanting, and some of these he found shopping around the station. Despite the bartender's pessimism, they did find clothing, though not much and for exorbitant prices. He also found products that had not occurred to him during the trek but which struck him as desirable once spotted. Not least among these were some soil beds, twelve of which he installed in the circular hallway of his spacecraft. Over each soil bed there was a lamp designed to propitiate photosynthesis, and he, Layla and Gregory spent a few hours preparing their garden. Alistair also spent a large sum of gold in purchasing a special incubator. Fed with their own waste products, some phials of amino acids and proteins, and primed with the proper DNA, the incubator could grow body parts over a period of a few weeks. Alistair purchased lamb and bovine DNA and looked forward to fresher food during the second leg of their journey. An impressive rack of liquor and wine also found its way into the ship's engine room, an expense which further depleted his now dwindling gold stores but which made the prospect of twelve more months on board seem less unpleasant.

These provisions were bought, loaded and installed over a period of two days, or at least two intervals between sleeping. During this time, their engine was given a tune up, though Alistair lacked the funds to upgrade their velocity. After these preparations were complete, they decided to extend their stay, an extension which itself was extended until they spent nearly two weeks on the station. An hour each day was given to watering and tending their new garden, and they made sure to cultivate a leg of lamb in the incubator, but most of their waking time was spent in recreation. The station had tennis courts and bowling alleys, a couple dance clubs, even a threedy theater, all of them in shoddy condition and nearly empty but they were wonderful for the three escaped convicts. Had Alistair no concern for his supply of coins, and had they not felt the lingering urge to finish their journey, they might have spent a couple months dining and drinking, shopping and playing, with Gregory and Layla visiting dance clubs and Alistair visiting brothels in the station's last weeks in operation.

Eventually, they reached the end. Alistair tucked away a reserve of gold and silver coins in a safe built into the wall of the ship, leaving a few more for their enjoyment. When these ran out, they left. The prospect of being cooped up for another year was daunting, but their new supplies and purchases heartened them enough that they boarded in a mood that, if not ecstatic, was at least optimistic. They took positions in the cockpit, and when they received word, Alistair conducted the ship out of the docking bay and back into space. Moving at a slow acceleration, he rotated his craft so they moved backwards and, in the dark cockpit, could face the space station as they left. They said nothing, but Layla waved a goodbye to their oasis, and then Alistair turned the ship around and they faced the desert.

86

After another deceleration, their interstellar ship came to a near stop within a hundred thousand miles of Aldra. The three pairs of eyes in the cockpit watched it appear and grow. When they were traveling at a mere forty thousand miles per hour, Alistair flipped the ship so what they knew to be the north pole was up and the south down.

"There isn't much land on Aldra," commented Layla from her seat in the back of the cockpit.

"Most of the land is on the other side," Gregory replied. "There's only one main continent."

They came around to the night side of the planet as they continued to draw closer, and Alistair brought their speed down to a few thousand miles per hour. The eastern edge of the main continent was peaking into the light, getting brushed by sunshine. The rest was difficult to see, and this disturbed the two men. Many of the familiar population centers were dark; most of the rest, with the exception of Rendral, were reduced in scope.

"Aldra is sick," said the doctor.

"Avon is completely black," said Alistair.

"Arcarius has some lights."

"Not many."

"What month is it?" asked Layla, who had heard many stories of Arcarius and wondered if the season might explain the dearth of illumination.

"Hell if I know."

The planet enveloped their view screen and they lost all sense of its spherical shape. As flames licked at their ship, the main continent spread out beyond their vision, and after that they saw only a coast, a channel north of it, and another coast north of that. This unfolded before their eyes as the flames receded and disappeared, and finally they reduced their speed to zero and hovered a couple thousand feet over Alistair and Gregory's home.

"Should we try to contact someone?" Greg asked.

"There are lights near the mines in the north. Let's go there."

He descended until they were a few dozen feet above the tops of the buildings while at the same time moving north. Uncertain what state the planet was in, but not comforted by what he saw so far, he preferred not to alert any hostile authorities to the presence of his ship. Thus far, there was no sign they were being monitored. He found the ruins of a building whose cement floor was intact and whose walls still reached high enough to enclose his craft. Roofless, it made a serviceable landing pad and, after two years speeding through the interstellar void, they touched down on Aldra.

Alistair and Gregory let out a sigh as soon as the ship settled. Unclasping straps, all three rushed to the exit whereupon Alistair lowered the ramp, opened the door, and in the blink of an eye they were out. Gregory breathed deeply and held out his arms, as if drinking in the cool air through his skin.

"It's late summer. Almost autumn."

Layla was already holding herself and snuggling up to Gregory. They were far enough north not to hear the ocean's waves, but the breeze was strong enough to make a soft whoosh, occasionally whistling over the jagged edge of ruined property, a broken wall or shattered window. It was almost pitch black, so Gregory and Layla could see vague shapes but little else. Alistair made a quick scan of the area and decided they were alone and clear to proceed. He unsnapped the holster underneath his jacket and, seeing this, Gregory did likewise with his. Then the trio left the ruined building and went north.

They walked past lifeless buildings and vacant streets. Somewhere along the way, they became sensible to the sounds of machinery which stood out over the Arcarian wind. Not long after, they entered an area of steep incline into which some of the glow of the workmen's lights filtered. Finally, rounding a bend, they saw a pair of lights on a couple mobile towers shining down so brightly it seemed like afternoon on a cloudless day in the ring of light they made. There was the open maw of a black tunnel, and a vehicle was emerging from it, its motor growling, burdened by equipment it carried in an open bed.

Several workers approached to unload it. On the edge of this activity Alistair spotted an idle worker, dressed in neon orange like the others and wearing a protective helmet. He made his way to the man and gave him a nod when spotted.

"You in the mood to make some money?"

The man looked him up and down and spared a glance for his two companions. A cautious look crept onto his features.

"You're tin," he accused.

Drawing forth a few silver coins, he held them out to the man who did not at first react.

"What's your order?"

"What happened to Oliver Keegan?"

By the look on the worker's face, it was clear he was keen to ask a few questions of his own, but the silver now in his pocket procured his discretion.

"Nothing, far as I know."

"He's leading the rebellion?"

"Naw, he's putting down the rebellion. Is that all you wanted?"

Alistair only half heard the question because he and Gregory were sharing a look. He turned back to the man.

"I need to see a directory on the Comlat."

The man grew uncomfortable. "We're not supposed to—"

"That's why you're being paid."

He hesitated a moment, looking again at his coworkers, none of whom were paying attention. Sighing, he turned and, with a nod of his head, indicated they should follow. He took them to a mobile office set to the side.

"You'll need a few more coins," he said as he opened the front door and entered.

Inside, there was a corpulent man sprawled out on a couch and enjoying a cup of something. Alistair gave him only enough regard to toss a few coins in his lap and say, "Keep quiet."

Startled, he quickly recovered, set his drink down and gathered up the coins, giving the three strangers furtive looks between ogling his money.

Alistair took a seat at the computer while the man he originally bribed kept a lookout at the window. Gregory and Layla came to stand behind him while he typed at the keyboard.

"Marty, get me some of what you got," said the first worker without looking away from the window.

The second worker, the fat one, gave the first an indignant look but finally, with a groan, got to his feet to prepare a cup. Alistair continued his work.

"Everybody's in Rendral," said Gregory as he studied the 3D display.

"This is gonna be quick, right?" asked the first worker.

"We'll be gone in a minute," said Alistair.

Marty brought over a steaming cup to the first man and returned to the couch where he turned his attention back to his coins.

"A lot of this is old information," said Alistair after a bit of quiet.

"Yeah, it doesn't get updated like it used to," said the first man and he took a sip from his cup.

"It didn't get updated all that well before," said Gregory. "Alistair, look up my sister."

After a moment, Alistair said, "Still in New Boston."

"As of five months ago."

"Doesn't get updated like before," said Marty.

Alistair typed in a couple more things and then shut the computer down.

"Gentlemen, thank you for your time."

"Is there anything else we can help you with?" asked Marty.

"Have a good night," said Gregory since Alistair was already outside.

The first worker took one more sip, set the glass down and left. Already the trio were several yards away and a minute later they turned a corner and the city's cadaver swallowed them.

87

Alistair had already decided to look far outside the metropolis of Rendral for a place to park the craft when he was accosted over the transmitter by a severe voice demanding to know his destination and his business. Upon delivering a partially honest reply, Alistair was informed that unauthorized craft were not permitted over the city and if he wished to go to Rendral, he would have to dock at a spaceport outside the restricted zone and come in another way. By the time he turned around, there was already an escort of two other craft on their way to meet him. They never caught up to him, though, for they stopped at the edge of the restricted zone and waited until his craft was well on its way to a new destination.

A short while later they touched down in a field that once grew crops but looked like the scene of a recent battle. There were great smoldering gashes in the ground, and it looked as if large chunks of earth had been scooped up and whipped around. Plants were uprooted where they were not mashed into the soil. The other fields around it were generally in better condition and a few were growing crops. The only buildings in the flat expanse of land, broken only occasionally by copses of trees and ditches and dirt roads, were an old farmhouse and three ramshackle barns, one whose roof had collapsed.

Two men, one elderly and one Alistair and Gregory's age, came outside and met them. They were dressed in the typical rustic style of poor farmers. The old man hobbled a bit and used a cane for support, while the other was hale and hearty but suspicious. Both were sweating profusely and dirt from the fields covered much of their skin.

"Was there a fight here recently?" asked Alistair in as pleasant a tone as he could manage.

"Not much of a fight," called the old man in the accent of Rendral.

"An attack," said the other. "The resistance."

"Who's resisting?" asked Gregory.

"There's always somebody resisting. Can't ever seem to stamp it out." The two parties now came to stop a few feet away from each other. "Why they went after my field I can't say."

"They're after the food supply," muttered the young man, although it was clear the field had not been planted when it was hit.

"What brings you here?" asked the old man with the tone of a change to a more important topic. "By your accent I'd say you're from Avon."

"I saw you were missing a roof off one of your barns," Alistair said with a nod towards the indicated structure.

"Got it that way. Haven't had a chance to repair it yet."

"We'd like to park our craft there for a few days. Maybe a couple weeks. We don't have any Credits—"

"You've been gone for a while," said the young one.

"Credits are gone. No more," said the old man. "If you want to use my barn you got to have some real money."

Alistair produced from his pocket several small coins of a golden color and handed them to the grandfather.

"That should buy me a month at least."

"You've got yourself a landing pad," he acknowledged, impressed with Alistair and the coins in his hand. All suspicion and cautious reserve in their conduct evaporated.

After Alistair put his craft in the barn, he and Gregory covered it with a large tarp and went into the farmer's home to conduct another transaction and there met several others, some of them family to the old man and some of them migrant workers. While gold was not illegal anymore, it was required that Aldrans hold their gold at one of the five approved private banks. The result was that gold coins were not legally spendable, only bank notes. The farmer agreed to exchange some of Alistair's gold coins for bank notes, saying he had a friend who could melt the coins down so he, pretending it was former jewelry, could turn it in to a nearby bank for more notes.

The farmer, who made out rather well on the exchange, agreed to give them a ride to the nearest train station. The three travelers piled into a dilapidated auto that rolled off an assembly line around the time Alistair was born and had been patched up and reworked many times since. They bounced over country paths and then, drawing near to a town, bounced over pot holes. The town the farmer took them to, while not teeming with activity, at least boasted a healthy population. Each man and woman moved with a purpose but nevertheless the mood was somber, and the strangers were eyed with suspicion.

The old man left them at the train station with an amicable goodbye, and an inquiry at the ticket booth got them the arrival time of the next train and three tickets to Rendral's central station. As far as food was concerned, there was little selection but what there was could be bought relatively cheaply. The trio bought a snack and some drinks and settled down in the station.

When the train finally came a couple hours later, as the sun was nearing its zenith, they boarded along with a few taciturn travelers and, in the insulated quiet of a carriage, had their pick of seats. The boarding lasted no more than a couple minutes and then the train, hovering over the magnetized rail, slid out of the station with hardly a sound, leaving behind only a single ripped portion of a poster fluttering in the artificial breeze.

Over flat territory they glided, whizzing by farmhouses, many of them abandoned, and over the occasional brook or ditch. They approached the ghastly corpse of a destroyed town and rushed through without stopping, catching only glimpses of the pale, gaunt faces of looters and scavengers streaking past their window. In the distance, they spotted the tops of some towering spires and from there the land became less and less devoted to agriculture and more and more to habitation.

After some time on the train, Layla lifted her head from the window and looked about. She looked at the two other passengers in their car, then at the landscape outside, then at Alistair and Gregory and all with an air of having awakened and been surprised by her circumstances.

"It's just noon now," she declared.

Alistair and Gregory nodded.

"This planet has a fucking long day." Dispirited, she laid her head back down on the window.

"We usually take a four hour nap about now," said Gregory.

"I'm not likely to fall asleep with the sun shining on me like this."

Despite her words, she nodded off, her head sliding forward on the glass and her chin nearly coming to rest on her breastbone. She awoke with a start when the train came to a halt at a station in the outskirts of the city. The carriage now carrying more passengers, there was more bustle as the train exchanged one set for another. When they started moving again, they passed through a residential area. In front of the train, just visible on their side, were the enormous skyscrapers of the downtown section of Rendral, perched on the lip of the Birth Crater, towering over a city sprawling throughout the crater and extending outside the bounds of the impact's imprint.

Presently, their train reached the rim and, not pausing to acknowledge it, angled down. For an instant they found themselves on the edge, their carriage hanging over the lip. Behind them was the outer city, before them a long drop and a cityscape extending for miles. Like a great wave on the ocean, the buildings grew steadily in height until reaching the western wall of the crater where the tallest stood, nestled around the base of the tallest skyscraper of all, the one that climbed the wall of the crater and continued past until piercing the sky. It was there, at the western wall of the Birth Crater, that the heart of Aldra's government lay. Traffic moved on the streets and in the air, weaving around buildings, the sun glinting off windshields. Rendral's power station shone a constant white, without the dark portions to which Arcarians had become accustomed a few cycles ago. After their moment on the lip, they joined the traffic in the air, descending towards the main train station in the center of the city.

There were myriad clouds, white and unthreatening, scattered about the sky. Though the ordinary Aldran was not aware of it, his home was one of the cloudier ones in the civilized galaxy. This was by design. Though planets were abundant, there were none on which, untouched, a human could live as on Earth. Adjustments had to be made, and even then, there were no planets whose living conditions could be maintained as on Earth, by biological intervention alone.

In Aldra's case, the excessively long day made for some challenges. In those latitudes hit by direct sunlight, the planet heated up to an extraordinary degree during the day. At night, given such a long time to radiate the heat back into space, things became quite cold. Planetary engineers had, however, hit upon a solution which attenuated the highs and lows of temperature, though tropical Rendral was still given to hot days and cool nights.

One of the principle keys to regulating the Aldran climate, and to artificially making it more like Earth, involved water vapor and highly charged particles. This water vapor, produced by great oceanic humidifiers, held in heat, keeping temperatures from getting too low on the night side. Other factories spewed charged particles in imitation of the cosmic rays of supernovae which roamed the galaxy and occasionally pelted its planets. These artificial rays were seeds for low forming clouds, whose net effect was to cool the planet, thus keeping temperatures from getting too high on the day side. These interventions provoked other quandaries, side effects, which were dealt with by more interventions, and all of it required advanced machinery with parts manufactured in diverse systems. Every colonized world was kept habitable by an interconnected net of planetary maintenance, even Aldra, whose government had always made an exception for itself and imported key parts from other planets.

When the three travelers finally stepped off the train and exited the station, in the middle of the commotion of Aldra's largest city, it was underneath a partly cloudy sky. Alistair was anxious to find the apartment where his sister lived, but Layla felt sorry for those cabdrivers who were hitched to a sort of wagon they pulled through the streets, and she insisted they give their patronage to one of these poor souls rather than to one who drove a regular taxi. Alistair consented, and they squeezed into a small wagon made for two. The lean cabbie was so thankful for the banknote placed in his hand, he never blanched at the weight of an extra body. In the end, due to stop lights and traffic jams, the pedestrian cabbie got them to their destination in about the same time as a motorized taxi.

After a short trip through some small streets and alleys, which took them to the center of a residential area a few blocks removed from major thoroughfares, they came to the building where, according to the directory, Katherine Ashley lived. One of the mail boxes at the front door bore her name and suffix code. There was an intercom so a visitor could announce himself and allow his host to press the buzzer and open the door for him, but the door was ajar already so Alistair did not bother calling. Inside, the building was in about the same shape as the exterior: worn by use, a little grungy between cleanings, but not in disrepair. It took them only a minute to take the elevator up three stories and seconds later they stood in the gloomy hallway, in front of Katherine's door.

"I hope she's home," said Alistair and his knuckles rapped the door.

They heard footsteps, then the click of the lock and finally the door opened. Katherine stood on the other side and when she saw Alistair she started as if hit in the face. Tears welled up in her eyes. No greater look of astonishment ever wracked the features of a human being. With a gasp, she covered her mouth with both hands and for a moment was immobile, as if afraid to test her vision and discover she had been tricked. Then she was embracing her brother and sobbing, and he sobbed in his turn. Contagious, the tears welled up in Gregory and Layla's eyes too.

The embrace in the hallway lasted for many minutes and was mixed with sobs and laughter. When Katherine, her cheeks soaked, finally pulled away, she saw Gregory and gave him a warm hug. Layla received a handshake and then a hug, beneficiary of a joyous moment. When this was accomplished, Katherine ushered them inside and closed the door.

They found themselves in a comfortable living room with a 3D display. On the opposite side there were sliding glass doors leading to a small balcony. Sunlight streamed through these partially opened doors, allowing a breeze to sweep in and rustle the translucent white curtains. At the back left corner, the rectangular shape of the living room was marred by the imposition of another room overlapping there: a dining room whose table held the remnants of Katherine's unfinished meal. This they observed in a moment, and as soon as the door was closed she was urging them to sit down as she rushed to the kitchen to prepare them drinks.

"How did you do it?" she asked when finally they each had a glass in hand and she was sitting next to her brother on the couch, turned slightly to face him.

"I looked you up on the Comlat."

"No, how did you get off Srillium?"

Her three visitors shared looks as of someone who has just been overwhelmed.

"That's a long tale to tell," Alistair answered.

"After we've slept some," said Gregory with a tired smile.

"Of course," she said with an apologetic tone. "We have a guest room…Alistair you can use my bed. Eddy won't be home until—" Katherine stopped short and looked at her brother. "Eddy's back," she said, her expression somehow agonized and radiant at the same time. "But you know that. He told me he saw you."

"Right before I was arrested."

A shadow passed over her radiance and, clasping her hands until the knuckles turned white, she swallowed once and looked her brother in the eye.

"Mom and Dad passed away, Al."

Katherine's face seemed ready to break down in fresh grief for her brother, who she thought was just getting the news. Instead, he nodded somberly.

"I know."

Katherine was perplexed but did not ask how he found out. "We lost contact with them. Gerald finally tracked them down. Apparently, they made it to Trenley but because of everything they couldn't contact us. There was an influenza epidemic in Trenley and…"

She trailed off with a shrug of her shoulders. For his part, Alistair slowly nodded, fighting to compose his face so his perceptive sibling, always able to read him, would not detect anything amiss. Too engrossed in her own memories, she noticed nothing.

"Apparently they were cremated and…Trenley got leveled during the fighting." A solitary tear poured over the rim of her right eye and made tracks down her cheek to her jaw. With a sniffle, she wiped the tear away and with it her gloom. "Your revolution was a success. Oliver…" Katherine paused to shake her head. "Oliver Keegan is the president. Can you believe it? I still…" Katherine could do no more than shake her head again. "Gerald works for Oliver now. He can take you to see him." Alistair shifted uncomfortably in his seat, but his sister continued without pause. "If you go to see him, there's, uh…If you could do me a favor." She picked her glass up from the coffee table and took a sip of water. "I've been trying to get Oliver to fund a mission…this is classified information, by the way…Oliver thinks it's not worth it right now with all the problems with the resistance."

Katherine sat forward, bringing her face within a few inches of her brother's, and leaned her elbows on her knees.

"We discovered something a few cycles ago, before the Realists fell. Alistair, we proved our theories about the Overlay. Do you remember…?"

He nodded.

"We proved its existence. But we discovered a signal someone was sending through the Overlay. We eventually traced it to its source…" She turned a significant gaze on her guests, as if preparing them for the awesomeness of what she was about to reveal. "Whatever was sending the signal was about fifty thousand light years away."

Her guests hung on her words, leaning forward as she did, enraptured.

"No human vessel has ever gone that far," she reminded them.

"The Galactic Survey Fleet—" Gregory began.

"None of the vessels that returned made it farther than forty thousand light years. And none of them were capable of sending signals through the Overlay. Christ, it was an automated fleet; the Overlay hadn't even been conceived of back then. Whatever sent the signal was fifty thousand light years away when we finally traced it...at least for a while."

Her guests leaned farther forward, snagged by another hook.

"The source came closer, moving faster than any known vessel."

"So it wasn't coming from a planet?" asked Alistair.

Katherine shrugged. "Within one cycle it was only twenty light years away."

"Fifty thousand light years in less than a cycle!?" said Gregory amid the general exclamations.

"Whatever it is, it took a position four cycles ago and, as far as we know, hasn't moved since. We won't even be able to detect it by conventional means for another sixteen years. It still sends us signals through the Overlay, and we responded to it for a while with no result."

"Soooo...?" prompted Alistair, unable to get a sentence out.

Katherine shrugged again. "The Revolution interrupted things. Oliver took over the Overlay program to use in the war effort. Every once in a while he gives me a little time with the equipment. Three weeks ago, the signal sender was still twenty light years away. That's all I can say. Oliver doesn't want to send a mission out there."

"We've got a small ship," said Gregory with a look to Alistair. "It got us here from Srillium."

Katherine looked hopeful.

"We could get to this signal sender in eighty Earth days."

Katherine did a quick calculation in her head. "About...thirty Aldran days or so. It's a really small ship, then?"

"Pretty small," said Alistair.

She frowned, her hope extinguished as soon as it was lit. "It would hardly be worth it without equipment."

"And dangerous too," added Layla.

At that moment, they were interrupted by a knock on Katherine's door. When she opened it, Alistair spied his brother on the other side. Gerald's pleasant greeting for his sister was interrupted by her demeanor. A moment later he looked over her shoulder and spotted Alistair. Astonishment swept over his face, and he shuffled past Katherine into the apartment, dropping the plastic sack he was carrying.

Alistair stood and uncertainly looked at his brother. Gerald's face was older, developing wrinkles. A handful of gray hairs were scattered around his scalp and his hairline was thinning out, preparing to recede. From twenty feet he looked the same as the day he rescued Alistair from execution, but from three, the tracks of five cycles were evident.

The repatriated exile dropped his guard, his careful reserve shielding emotional vulnerability, and rushed to embrace the brother to whom he owed his life. However, Gerald's astonishment never evolved into a merry greeting. Instead, he continued to stare at his brother past the point when it felt awkward for the others.

Finally, disentangling himself, Gerald nodded, held out a hand and said, "What a surprise. Welcome back."

Alistair, dismayed, managed to shake his brother's hand. Katherine, not comprehending Gerald's reaction, moved towards the kitchen after picking up the sack Gerald dropped.

"I'll get you a drink," she said, dropping the groceries on the kitchen counter and opening up the cupboard.

Looking uncomfortable for a moment, Gerald finally found an unoccupied chair and sat in it, and Alistair sat down as well.

"Good to see you, Gregory."

Gregory, from his seat, shook Gerald's hand.

"I understand I owe you a lot. This is my partner, Layla."

Gerald stood to shake her hand and Layla gave him a charming smile.

"A pleasure to meet you," she said.

"You're...not from Aldra?" he asked when he heard her speech.

"She was with us on Srillium," Alistair explained.

"Oh," said Gerald, and his demeanor became chilly as he regarded the former convict. He sat back down in his chair as Katherine brought him his drink.

"You have a niece and a nephew," announced Katherine as she patted Gerald on the shoulder and sat down next to Alistair. "Kyle and Kelly."

"I'll introduce you to my wife sometime," said Gerald, his tone tepid, nothing more than polite.

Alistair nodded, unable to express the joy he would have preferred and uncertain how to take his brother's behavior. When their drinks were finished, Katherine showed Gregory and Layla to the guest room. Layla declared she was going to sleep for a week, and as they disappeared down the hallway, the last thing Alistair heard was Gregory gently suggesting she take only a nap and try to get her body used to the Aldran schedule. Alistair found himself with his brother on the balcony, the sun still brightly shining overhead and the gentle murmurs of an unperturbed city below. The third floor balcony was halfway up their building, and an eight story building was just across the way, close enough that Alistair thought he might almost have jumped from one balcony to another. They leaned on the railing, their drinks refilled, making a pretense of ease and comfort while they tried to think of something to say.

"I didn't expect to see you again," Gerald finally managed, staring at the brick wall on the other side of the alley.

"I owe you a hell of a lot."

"Yeah," said Gerald, and a moment of silence passed. "Mom and Dad died," he said with a sniff and took a sip from his glass. "Got the flu. They were down in Trenley—"

"Do you know how they really died?"

Gerald was startled, but recovering quickly, his face became hard and he stared into his brother's eyes. With savage intensity, he snarled, "Yes!"

With that response, with the granite hardness of it incompletely masking the heat underneath, Alistair suddenly understood his brother's deportment. He considered making a plea to Gerald, to explain things, but discarded the idea. Instead, taking another sip from his drink, he turned from his brother and stared at the brick wall several feet away. Gerald took up the same posture.

"I'd like to see Oliver, if you can arrange it."

"The last time I took you into a government building you killed his predecessor."

"*Oliver* killed his predecessor."

Gerald took another sip. "I can probably take you tomorrow," he said and then left Alistair on the balcony.

88

The Civil Palace at the Birth Crater's western wall was a city unto itself, the result of thousands of years of human engineers being instructed to outdo what had been done before, upping the ante with every new capitol building. It recorded the threshold of grandiose and imposing as it was understood three centuries ago. Occupying the equivalent of several city blocks, and wider than it was tall, its exterior was a composite of pillars and façades, spotlights and landing pads, terraces and balconies, domes and stain glass windows. On the top was projected the 3D image of the Aldran flag, larger than any flag ever made, waving in an imaginary breeze.

Upon arriving at the Civil Palace, after nearly an hour's jaunt on Rendral's crowded public transportation, Gerald took Alistair to the Palace's own internal Metro system. A brief ride on this, followed by a short walk, a trip up an elevator and another walk down a long, narrow cylindrical tube—all made possible by Gerald's identity badge—brought them to a less trafficked section. There, the almost manic ruckus of busy bureaucrats was absent, replaced by the hollow quiet of marble, which gave the sparse footsteps and whispers an indistinct echo.

They reached a section of suites and approached the secretary working at the entrance. Gerald showed her his badge and, while Alistair exchanged hard glances with the two armed Guardsmen on either side of the hallway, explained his purpose to her. She nodded and indicated he and his brother should take their seats in the waiting area.

They sat in silence for a few moments before Alistair finally asked, "Do you have a picture of Kyle and Kelly?"

With the look of a man who has been approached for spare change, Gerald reached into his back pocket, took out a wallet, and from it produced a series of 3D photographs he handed to Alistair.

Eyeing the pictures with a wistful smile, Alistair asked, "Do they know about me?"

Gerald seemed irritated at the question. He took the photos out of Alistair's grasp and put them back in his wallet. "They're still young."

The sound of footsteps on the marble floor, wrapped in their own echoes, preceded the appearance of a man impeccably dressed in dark blue with red trim and sash. Stiff and formal, he walked up to Gerald and bowed his head, displaying his nearly bald pate. This induced Gerald, and then Alistair, to rise from their seats, whereupon the man executed a turn on his heel and, never saying a word, led them deeper into the section of suites. Coming to a door at the back, he opened it and stepped aside.

The capacious room on the other side had a large, ovular table with as many as thirty seats spaced around it. Beyond the table was a stone floor with a relief map of Aldra carved into it. The ceiling was ornate and thirty feet over their heads, with recessed lighting. The back wall was one gigantic window, floor to ceiling, with a view of the crater wall not two hundred feet away. That particular section of wall was full of the carven busts of former presidents, prime ministers, dignitaries and other historical figures. At that moment a team of workers, standing on hovering platforms, were busy with a new bust, still in its embryonic stages and as of yet unrecognizable.

When Gerald and Alistair entered, their guide closed the door and a bulky figure staring out the back window, hands clasped behind his back, turned to greet them with a smile.

"Alistair Ashley," said Oliver Keegan, raising his voice a little to be heard over the distance. "Welcome back."

His voice was as warm and friendly as a host greeting an unknown guest, and with the same reserve. With the large and bold steps of a man in his element, he strode across the room. Alistair, less confident, shuffled to meet him partway. Oliver held out both hands; one of these he used to shake Alistair's hand, the other was for a healthy slap on the shoulder. After a moment to smile at his old friend, Oliver turned to Gerald and gave him a more subdued greeting.

Alistair studied Oliver while that one greeted his brother. He had become portly in the intervening cycles. Though still young and not exactly fat, there was a softness to his middle and a fullness of the flesh of his neck not there before Alistair was exiled.

"I got quite a shock a couple minutes ago. I never thought—come with me!—I never thought I'd see the day." He was walking away, towards a small carpeted area with several cushioned chairs and a cabinet at the side. "I suppose I shouldn't be surprised. When you put your mind to something…"

Reaching the cabinet, he opened it, took out a crystal decanter and glasses, and into them poured a brown liquid with an orange tint.

"Ice?" he asked.

"None for me," said Gerald. "I'm due elsewhere."

"Ice for me," mumbled Alistair.

After handing Alistair his glass, Oliver shook Gerald's hand and thanked him. While Gerald walked to the door, Oliver took a nearby seat and Alistair gingerly sat down across from him, uncomfortable and suddenly not looking forward to the next few minutes. Oliver drained a good portion of the contents of his glass and Alistair took a small sip. The sound of the door closing after Gerald resounded in the room.

"So how did you manage it? How did you make it back?" asked the former rugby star. He wore the same wide yet distancing smile he had been flashing since the moment he turned to see them enter.

"Stole a ship from the Gaians," Alistair said, his expression mirthless and his tone flat. "Outfitted it with some other things I salvaged here and there."

"Gaians?"

Nodding, Alistair took another sip. "Srillium is watched over by Gaians."

If Oliver was waiting for more, he was disappointed. Finally, he made a face of appreciation. "Only you could do it."

He fell silent, indicating it was Alistair's turn to think of something to say. Uncomfortable under the weight of that unchanging smile, Alistair cast his gaze around the expansive meeting room.

"The ceiling's new. You should have seen it when we moved in. This is a real nice one."

"So what did I miss?"

Oliver spread his arms out. He might have been indicating the room, the Palace, the city of Rendral or the entire planet.

"We won."

"And now you're president."

His disapproving tone made Oliver chuckle, and he rose to pace.

"I envy philosophers," he proclaimed with a jolly bellow, and it was a couple seconds before the echoes subsided. "I envy idealists. I envy them for the position they must be in to be an idealist. No man in my position can hold onto idealism."

Oliver paused to regard Alistair, but he sat still, holding his glass in his lap with both hands, returning Oliver's look but saying nothing. Oliver broke into a knowing smile and resumed his pacing.

"We had excellent ideals when we were younger, didn't we? We knew liberty, knew what was wrong and how to fix it. There just weren't enough of us."

Oliver came to stand by the window again, a small figure in a giant frame, watched by the busts of presidents past and staring at a new bust being formed. With one tip of the glass he swallowed the rest of his drink, never taking his eyes off the workers on the hovering platforms, and Alistair never took his eyes off Oliver.

"Every man who closes his book and leaves his study, who goes out into the real world, has a compromise thrust on him," continued the Aldran Head of State and turned to walk back to his vacated chair. "Life demands compromise. Our ideals are a guide, a compass, not a set of laws. There are fleeting opportunities when we can put our ideals into practice, and we do the best we can. Other than that, we have to be realistic, practical."

Reaching his chair, he sat down again, setting his glass on an end table. When he spoke, his tone changed from relaxed reminiscing to an indignant, almost angry, defensiveness.

"I defy anyone to look at the Aldra of a few cycles ago and tell me we aren't better off now." The flash of anger left and Oliver relaxed again. "I opened up all that unused land, first come, first served. The Homesteaders dream was finally realized. Tell me that wasn't a victory for liberty."

"Gerald told me about that," said Alistair with a nod. He set his glass, still almost full, on an end table. "You only opened up the land around Rendral."

"There's still fighting going on. It's hard to defend a populace scattered all over the face of the planet. We have instituted policies to encourage people to congregate around the cities, especially Rendral. You can't believe how the farm industry has taken off...well, I'm sure *you* can believe it...but it's amazing. We went from starvation to plenty in the course of a single cycle. It's liberty at work, our ideals put into practice!" He had the enthusiastic tone of a salesman now.

"Why can't people own gold?"

"They can own gold," Oliver said with a note of exasperation. "They can't own or circulate gold coins. Jewelry, bars of gold...these are fine."

"Why can't they circulate gold coins?"

Oliver sighed and leaned back in his chair. "I didn't want to do it. I even got rid of the Credit and allowed private banks to print money."

"You gave five banks a monopoly privilege to print money."

"In exchange for their support. A support instrumental in ending the war here."

"So why can't people circulate gold coins? And why are these five banks printing five ounce-notes for every ounce of gold they actually have?"

"Those conditions..." Oliver shook his head, despairing of ever impressing Alistair. The mask he had worn was off. Behind the contrived smile and congeniality had been a grim realism which was nearer to sincerity. Behind that, nearer still to sincerity, was uncertainty and even guilt. "Those conditions were dictated to me by the other colonies."

"Why should the other colonies be able to dictate anything to you?"

"We got loans from them," Oliver replied like a man making a damning admission. "It was all part of ending the war. Twelve and a half million people had died, either from fighting or starving or disease. There was no end in sight. But the government developed Overlay technology. Naturally, the other colonies and Earth wanted it. We promised to sell it to them in exchange for their support.

"They lent us money, but we had to conform to certain standards if we wanted to join their economic community. Any mad rush into a stronger currency can set off hyperinflation in the currency being dumped. Some of those other currencies are inflated...they weren't going to risk things by making exceptions and we couldn't get their help without accepting their demands." Oliver glumly stared at the floor. "At any rate, it's had its uses."

"Banks can print five ounces worth of notes for every ounce of gold in their vaults."

"Yes."

"But the ratio used to be four to one."

"I lowered reserve requirements."

"And I can tell you why you did it, no explanation needed," said Alistair with a cocksure certainty of tone. "In exchange for guaranteed loans from the banks, probably under very favorable terms, you snapped your fingers and conjured twenty five per cent more money to lend out. Also, this will make prices rise, which means more tax money coming in to pay other loans that fall due in the next couple years. A debtor is always in favor of cheaper money, and with all the fighting you've been doing you must have enormous debts."

The silence that followed confirmed Alistair's understanding.

"You opened up trade with other colonies, but later imposed conditions, designating certain zones for foreign ships who are always under supervision."

"There is still a resistance, and if we got helped by smugglers then so can they."

"You lowered taxes, but you've raised them again."

"Debts fall due, Alistair. We have just fought a war and a Revolution must be paid for."

"You declared freedom of speech, but certain controls have since been put in place."

"The pen is mightier than the sword."

"You've restricted gun use."

"Only in certain areas where we can't be sure who supports us and who is fighting us. Enough!" Oliver roared when Alistair made as if to cite another imposition on liberty. "I also legalized specnine and streamlined the criminal justice system. The black market in specnine and all the crime and misery it caused are things of the past. Lawyers are no longer required to have a license…and let me tell you how much support it cost me to do that. I had a riot the next day."

"I'm sure you did. The legal system was so complex you needed an anointed guide to get you through it, and lawyers made a good living at our expense. When I left, nearly one in ten Aldrans was an attorney or working in the legal profession."

"It's about one in fifty now."

"Fine, but for how long? Taxes are getting raised again, speech is being curtailed, the money is being debased…pretty soon you'll need someone else's support and then—"

Oliver jumped out of his chair and said, "But how do you expect me to change it? I instituted reforms; things are better now. I'm sorry if I can't bring about a utopia single handed! If things do go back to how they were before, we at least had a brief time when they were better. I can't do it by myself!" The outburst concluded, Oliver fell back into his chair and a loud crack issued from it.

When Alistair spoke, his voice was soft and sad. "You should have been a teacher, not a leader." A sharp look from Oliver moved Alistair to speak further. "You should have convinced people of the ethics of liberty, taught them about freedom. Instead, you chose to lead them, and even if you wanted to lead them to liberty, a leader requires the consent of those being led. Authority is not yours; it is granted to you if people choose. When you lead, you must get people to grant you authority. That's when you start compromising principles, not when you close your book and leave your study, but when you command authority. That's when you grant monopolies to bankers: when you need a grant of authority. That's when you restrict speech: when you need to prevent others from undermining you. That's when you go into debt: when you need even more. You should have been a teacher."

"Someone was going to do what I did. If people believe in being led, someone is going to step up and lead them. Would you prefer someone else had done it?"

They sat in contemplative silence, and neither moved except to breathe. Finally, Alistair ended the stillness by reaching for his glass and taking another sip.

"Katherine wants funding for a voyage."

"I know. Are you here to ask for taxpayer funds?"

"I'm just relaying my sister's request."

"Now is not the time. We're in debt and still spending money…after the fighting is over." Oliver, in noticeable discomfort, shifted in his seat. "The old regime won't die, Alistair. When we took Rendral, we immediately saw the use of Overlay technology. We used it to end the fighting. We thought it was over, that we could put it behind us, but…Somehow they got their hands on it. Now the positions are reversed: we sit here exposed while they attack from the shadows."

There was a loud rapping on the door, which opened an instant later, and Alistair heard a familiar voice say, "There's another attack."

Though Oliver was on his feet the next instant, Alistair was at first too stunned to move.

"Come and see," said Oliver, his voice grim and, now that there was another observer there, as close to regal as he could make it.

Alistair lifted himself out of his chair and turned to see Stephanie Caldwell in Civil Guard uniform, more decorated than when last he saw it. His visage had the same effect on her as her voice had on him, as unsettling as a thunderbolt. Her hands, clasped behind her back when she delivered the message, came unclasped; her arms fell to her sides; her eyes widened and lips parted.

"I believe you two know each other," said Oliver as he strode out the door.

She managed the most hesitant and curtest of nods before turning to follow Oliver. Alistair hustled to catch up and finally reached them as they left the suites and came to a sliding electric door.

"This one's right here in the city," Stephanie was saying as she typed in a code on a keypad in the wall next to the door.

In response to the code, the door swiftly opened and revealed a transparent walking tube that, curving like a serpent many yards above the ground, connected the Civil Palace with Aldra's grandest skyscraper, the one that climbed the wall of the Birth Crater on its way to piercing the clouds. Stephanie did not wait, and Oliver and Alistair were right behind her. Looking down, Alistair saw they were walking above some extensive gardens tucked behind the Palace, between it and the crater wall.

"They've never attacked the city before," said Oliver while Alistair walked shoulder to shoulder with him. "They usually hit the countryside, sometimes small cities. We think they're trying to disrupt the food supply." Something in his tone indicated he was not entirely satisfied with that explanation.

When they were within a few yards of the other end of the tube, Alistair tilted his head back and let his gaze go skyward. The gargantuan skyscraper, sleek and black, loomed over them, reaching so far above, its top was like the point of a needle. Stephanie typed another code while the two men waited and once again the door slid open. On the other side were several others waiting for Oliver. Four armed Civil Guardsmen stood at attention, rifles in hand, while a gaggle of officials greeted the Head of State, their faces emanating the importance they felt in themselves.

Oliver was enveloped by the group of officials, and when the entire retinue finally fit inside a voluminous elevator, Alistair found himself standing next to Stephanie. The four Guardsmen focused on nothing but the door in front of their eyes, while the officials, when they bothered to glance at Alistair at all, spared only a brief, inquisitive look. For her part, Stephanie Caldwell eventually decided a conversation would be less awkward than ignoring the man standing at her side.

"Who rescued you?" she asked, her query barely audible under the loud discussion carried on by Oliver and his state officials.

"I rescued myself. When I left here, we were enemies."

"I was thrown in prison. Oliver realized he had a nation to run and needed personnel to do it."

"It's kind of hard to tell whether you switched sides or he did."

The elevator passed into the middle stories, and the back wall became transparent so that they were given a view of the entirety of Rendral as they, picking up speed, rose higher and higher above the city. The morning sun hung over the eastern edge of the crater, several miles away. The attack was immediately apparent, consisting of a swirling cloud periodically illuminated by great flashes. Hanging over the southern part of the city, it belched out sparks and balls of electricity, and when it passed over the tops of buildings, they disintegrated, like a sand castle in a windstorm, and what was left of their material was sucked into the cloud.

Though the Civil Guard did not lose their discipline, the state officials crowded to the back of the elevator, those nearest to it placing their foreheads up against the back window. A hush fell over them and all stared at the terrible display. They rose several dozen stories higher before a woman finally made an awed remark which Alistair, farthest from the back of the elevator, did not hear well.

"It'll be years before the damage is fixed," said a man in a louder voice.

"Why did they wait so long to attack the city?" asked another woman but received no answer.

Up they went, closer to the sky. The buildings in the crater looked like children's toys by the time they reached the upper levels. The back wall of the elevator shaft became opaque and they lost their view of the city. However, a moment later the elevator stopped, provoking the familiar feeling in the pits of their stomachs, and the doors opened.

At that dizzying height, the air was cooler and there was a brisk wind. Several aircraft were parked on the flat roof and there was even a small flight control tower at the center. The size of their party immediately doubled as several more officials and Guardsmen were waiting for them at the top. Alistair and Stephanie fell back from the group, making their way to the railing at the building's edge at a more leisurely pace.

At the edge, they saw the same scene witnessed from the elevator, only now they heard cracks and rumbles of something like thunder. Gripping the railing, Alistair ignored the attack for a moment and looked down over the edge of the building. He was struck, like so many times before, with the grandeur of the skyscraper. He thought of all the great cities he had been to: Rendral, Mar Profundo, New Boston, New York, Londinium, Tokyo, Whitehall, Sao Paulo. He thought of what an amazing feat it was to build something as superlative as a skyscraper. The enormity of the task and the quantity of toil involved inspired awe. Then, he looked at the attack, at the effortlessness and remorselessness with which it disintegrated so much work.

"I thought maybe they were leaving Rendral alone because they wanted to take it back," said Stephanie as the wind whipped her hair, causing it to lash at her face and scalp. She took no notice. "Maybe they changed their minds." Her tone indicated indifference.

There was a flash of light and the attack broke apart. The murky cloud stopped swirling and turned to dust which was dumped on the city below. Moments later, an aftershock of the attack buffeted them in the form of a wind as of a hurricane, and it carried with it the screeches and booms and rumbles of a great battle. A couple officials stumbled and fell to the ground and everyone moved away from the edge of the building. Oliver, flanked by two men busy explaining something to him, paused a moment when he was about to pass Alistair.

"That's what we're dealing with!" he shouted over the noise as the wind tore at his clothing. He pointed an insistent finger in the direction of the attack. "Talk to me of ideals after the battle is won. Sometimes sacrifices must be made!"

89

When Gregory, Alistair and Layla went to visit Henry Miller, he was prepared to receive them because Gregory called ahead of time. They found him in a ground floor studio in the eastern part of the city on a wide and well-trafficked boulevard. He had drinks ready when they walked through the door, and he greeted them with an embrace and a genuinely jubilant smile.

The studio was littered with the kinds of supplies one needs for a political campaign. There were posters in stacks, some of them blank, some of them printed with anti-war slogans and pictures. Signs affixed to stakes, ready for planting in the ground, were scattered everywhere. Two computer stations in the back corners were like islands of tidiness in a sea of disorder, and in between them was another machine used for printing and laminating. It was difficult to say when the place was last cleaned; anything not covered in dust simply hadn't been there long.

At the right side of the studio, by the brick wall, was a couch, a coffee table and a few chairs on a rug that wanted sweeping. Already there, waiting on the couch, was a young boy of no more than two cycles whom Henry introduced as his son Jeremiah. The three guests greeted Jeremiah in unison and the toddler, after staring at them for a moment, turned his face into the couch cushions.

"My wife and I work full time here," Henry explained as he swept his arm across the scene. "We found some patrons who give us enough to keep us up and running. Some people drop by now and then to volunteer." He nodded his head as if, upon rechecking the operation, he was still satisfied with it. "I'm not going to get rich this way, but…"

"You might wind up saving some lives," Gregory finished.

"Let's hope."

They sat down, and while Gregory introduced Layla and gave a brief account of their incarceration and escape, Alistair ran his gaze over the room of his formerly politically apathetic friend. He caught Jeremiah peeping at him with one eye, but when he looked at him he buried his face back in the couch cushions.

"How did those cotton seeds work out?"

"They helped finance our trip back."

"So it was worth it. Oh! By the way!" Henry popped out of his seat, rummaged around in a pile of odds and ends, and came back with a small box filled with index cards. "Greg, your sister is in New Kensington," he informed the doctor as he flipped through the cards. Finding the one he was looking for, he handed it to Greg.

Gregory took a look at the card.

"She moved a couple months ago. Her law firm closed down but she found a new job. She's doing background investigations."

"Interesting."

"It's particularly hard right now, with so many records destroyed. There's a lot of lawyers looking for other work at the moment."

"So I've heard," said Alistair.

"When Oliver revamped the legal code…" Henry shook his head and gave a low whistle. "He won't do anything like that again. Cost him way too much. I guess you do what you can. Make the reforms you can make."

A moment of quiet passed. Jeremiah moved from his hiding spot to sit in his dad's lap. From there he watched the visitors out of the corner of his eye, always quick to look away. Henry gave his son a kiss on the head.

"Stephanie's working for Oliver," said Alistair.

"Yes," Henry confirmed. "She was in jail after the coup, but Oliver needed people to run the infrastructure." His visage grew somber. "Alistair, did you hear about your parents?"

Alistair nodded, color touching his cheeks.

"Did Gerald tell you how it happened?"

"I was shown their bodies before I left."

"Oh." He effected a sympathetic expression. "So you know the real story?" In response to Alistair's nod, he continued. "I just brought it up because Stephanie reminded me—when you mentioned Stephanie—her boss was the one who ordered your parents' execution." He flipped through a few more index cards and finally plucked one from the box. "Captain James Montague Travis."

Henry handed the card to Alistair. It had a picture of Captain Travis, whom he immediately recognized, and a small written portion detailing background information. The last line listed the date of his execution.

"Oliver made it one of his primary tasks when he took power. He found Travis, tried him, and had him shot the day after the trial."

Alistair felt no sympathy for the dead man, but nonetheless the circumstances of the death gave him a chill in his stomach just as strong as the grim satisfaction he got from knowing the would-be tyrant had been punished.

"What about Elizabeth and Jack?" asked Gregory.

Henry's face was grim again. "Elizabeth is in prison. She left Arcarius and married one of the government's rich industrialists in Avon. He was active in the fight to squash the rebellion. When Oliver took over, he was convicted and executed. Elizabeth was convicted as an accomplice."

There was no mistaking the appalled disapproval on Gregory's face. "How long is she in for?"

"Life."

Like deflating balloons, Gregory and Alistair sank in their seats. Layla, who knew Elizabeth by reputation, hung her head in sympathy.

"Jesus Christ, Oliver," Gregory half whispered.

"It's not a subject I would bring up around him, if I were you. I tried it once."

"What about Jack?" asked Alistair.

"No one knows. He disappeared. Probably he…died during the fighting. No one's heard from him since soon after you left."

"What a huge, terrible mess," lamented Gregory, and Layla, sitting next to him, hugged him close.

"To fallen comrades," said Alistair, raising his glass. "Dead and imprisoned."

"To fallen comrades," they repeated and took a drink.

No sooner had they set their drinks down than the front door burst open and a young man of about seventeen or eighteen cycles rushed in. His face carried an expression fit for some calamity and his breathing suggested a long sprint to reach Henry's studio.

"You haven't gotten the news?" he asked in disbelief.

Henry, setting his protesting son to the side and standing up, shook his head. The young man rushed to one of the computers, turned on the 3D display, and found a news station on the Comlat. The other four moved to watch. The newscaster, an older man sitting straight and looking suitably dour, was behind a desk giving the news. Sitting next to him was a high ranking officer from the armed forces, a younger man—most of the older generals were either in prison or a mausoleum—but just as dour and gruffer looking than the newscaster.

"—just reaching us now. With me today is General Bancroft of the Third Division. General, this has come as a shock to the rest of us. Was the government as caught-off-guard as we were?"

"We were prepared for some bad news. Obviously the size of the disaster we were unprepared for, but we had developed some Overlay communications and were in the initial stages of sending signals. When they went silent on the other end and never got back up, we knew something had transpired. What exactly we are just finding out now."

"There are some who feel this is the work of more resistance members."

"I think this is quite beyond the capabilities of any resistance."

"But the Kaldisian sun was a young star. Do we have any idea what went wrong?"

"That's not something I want to speculate on at the current time."

"How many Aldrans were lost?"

"I don't have the exact numbers."

"Do you have an idea?"

"It's not something I want to speculate on at the current time."

"But it was a sizable amount."

"…We had a sizable garrison in a couple cities. A few ships in orbit."

"Is everything…everything lost?"

"We have very few facts at the moment. A supply ship was headed for Kaldis and got hit by a shock wave. They turned off their HD Drive and decelerated…they were less than a light year from Kaldis… and they couldn't detect the sun. They did a sweep around where the sun ought to have been and found two other ships drifting in space. Farther in, they found no ships, no planets and no sun."

"So the star did explode?"

"That's the interpretation at this current time right now. It explains the shock wave and the absence of any detectable star."

"Could it have been something else?"

"Honestly, I don't know how much it matters at this point. Either way, Kaldis will not be habitable. If the star exploded then it was a quick death for billions. If it was something else…we'll find out if there are any refugees. Frankly, some of them would have beaten the supply ship back home, so I don't expect we'll get any."

"General, Professor Horace Templeton is the J.P. Whitworth Chair of Astronomy at the Science Institute. According to him, Kaldis was supposed to be a main sequence G-type star for another seven to eight billion years. It was young, still burning hydrogen...no indication of anything wrong—"

"Well, Jerry, this is a little outside my field of expertise—"

"But, General, Kaldis was experiencing the same kind of troubles with resistance we are. In fact, according to reports, the attacks were more frequent there and bore all the signs of Overlay technology."

"Again, Jerry, the current estimation is that the resistance does not have the capability to destroy a sun. Neither do we. It's really not something I want to speculate on at the current time."

Katherine and Alistair made it to the Civil Palace and Katherine's I.D. got them inside, but not far. Once there, she made a call on an intercom, and little by little got her call transferred higher and higher up the ladder until a Civil Guardsman came to escort them to the top level of the Palace. They were taken to an area neither had seen before and admitted to what looked like a large study. The right hand side was taken up by bookshelves reaching fifteen feet to the ceiling and were nearly overflowing with tomes and parchments. Twenty men and women were occupied with work at computers, or among the bookshelves, or were speaking with Oliver.

Oliver, sitting in a chair at the left hand wall, greeted them with a nod of his head, keeping half his attention on the woman speaking to him. Katherine tentative and Alistair in a melancholy stupor, they crossed the floor, waiting for her to finish. When she did, they edged closer. For a moment, Oliver gave them his full attention and they saw the hallmarks of a night without sleep etched on his face.

"Good evening," he greeted and seemed on the point of saying something more but was interrupted by another who came jogging from a computer desk.

Alistair and Katherine hung back and allowed the conversation to proceed. Oliver got out of the chair, his every movement and expression exuding a regal authority. He followed the man to his computer station, studied the 3D display for a moment, issued an order and returned to his chair. He landed in it with a sigh and rubbed his temples.

"There are days when I wouldn't wish this job on anyone."

"Difficult decisions to make?" asked Katherine.

"You could say that."

"Well, there's one decision that just became a lot easier." She paused, as if giving him time to guess. "It's time to send out a vessel to investigate whatever was sending those signals."

He did not react, save to drop his left hand to his jaw and hold his head with it.

"When was the last time we confirmed its location?" she asked.

"You think it was responsible for Kaldis?"

"I don't know. I do know there is no known reason why that star exploded."

"If it destroyed a sun why do you want to go anywhere near it?" he asked, patiently suffering their intrusions into policy, indulging them a foray into an area where they did not belong.

"Oliver, I don't know what it did or what it will do. It's been sitting at the edge of civilization for several cycles now. Why it would wait to attack, I don't know. I don't know whether or not it did anything. I don't know how it will react to us...I don't know what it is."

She moved closer to Oliver. "I only know the two most populous planets in the galaxy have been wiped out. It's a good bet Overlay technology has something to do with the second. This seems pretty important right now."

Oliver stared as if trying to penetrate the floor with his gaze. One of his ministers came to stand next to him, an uncertain expression on his face when he looked at Oliver, a cold and unwelcoming one when he looked at the two Ashley's.

"Like you said, Katherine, a whole hell of a lot of things have to be done. More than we have the capacity to do. One of the oceanic humidifiers broke down and we are trying to scrape together the men and parts to fix it."

"The other humidifiers can compensate."

"For a while," responded the minister in a flat tone, "but they'll wear out sooner. None of the humidifiers is in excellent shape."

"Neither are the cosmic ray generators," said Oliver. "The whole damn system…" He shifted uncomfortably in his seat, looking stressed. "Alistair," he said when his composure reasserted itself, "I'm surprised you are begging for a government hand out."

Alistair blinked once, as if coming out of a reverie. With sluggish lips he whispered, "I haven't said a word."

"But you're here."

He pursed his lips and then forced a little more volume into his speech. "Like it or not, the government has the tools. It's got the ships, it's got the scientific equipment, it's got the money. I'm not going to stay behind and let a tsunami drown me just because government owns the rescue ship. We need to make some sort of contact with this thing."

"And if it attacks your ship?"

"Then we'll end up like Mar Profundo."

Katherine squatted down so her head was at the same level as the President's. "Oliver, the ramifications of Overlay technology have been greater than we expected. There's a lepton not participating in the strong interaction. There are multiple bosons occupying the same quantum state, right now as we speak. We've found hadrons composed of two up quarks and a down quark, with masses almost two thousand times greater than the lepton…and yet that lepton can still annihilate a positron." Her voice as serious as her expression, she leaned in to emphasize her point. "God forbid it should ever acquire a fractional angular momentum. Oliver, you have to let us go out there."

Jargon sufficiently technical is indistinguishable from babble. She spoke with the quiet calm of authority, with reasoning invincible. Oliver and his minister looked, for all the world, as if they were giving due consideration to her argument. If there was something he did not understand, the leader of all Aldra gave no hint. His concession took the form of a movement of his free hand, resting on his knee, a mere lifting of that hand so the index finger could point to the ceiling. A moment he held the finger up, his forearm still resting on his thigh, and then it dropped back down.

The minister understood the signal. He nodded once and addressed Katherine.

"We will be in contact with you when the details are determined and the voyage arranged. If you'll please step this way."

He held out his left hand to indicate the door, and his right to indicate them. Without protest, the Ashley's allowed themselves to be ushered to the exit, Alistair giving his sister a quizzical look and Katherine sporting an unreadable expression. With a brief smile, nothing more than polite, the minister closed the door, leaving them alone in the still and quiet hall.

90

For the third time in his life, Alistair left Aldra. The first time he knew he might not return, but if he survived he would see his home again. The second time he thought never to see it again no matter how long he survived. This time he left with such ignorance that any expectations were pointless.

The ship Oliver provided for them was a science vessel with some limited defense capabilities. It could comfortably carry a hundred passengers and had two smaller craft docked inside. When the nature of the mission was revealed to the crew, their irritation at being interrupted evaporated, to be replaced by a full realization of the charge given to them and a grim determination to see it through.

The Captain of the ship, recently renamed The Spirit of the Revolution, was the head of a crew of seventeen. Under his command were three pilots, two cooks, a communications officer, a navigator, a medical officer, two nurses, three engineers and three mechanics. In addition, Oliver gave them a squad of ten marines—a sergeant, a corporal and eight privates—placed under Alistair's command. Katherine was made head of a scientific team of five, one of whom included Louise Downing, who was stunned to see Alistair. Oliver inquired as to whether Gregory wanted to serve as a medical officer, but at the same time that Katherine was pleading her case to the big rugby star, Gregory and Layla were riding a train to the west coast, there to board a boat for New Kensington's archipelago. All told, thirty three individuals were on board when The Spirit left its launching pad.

When Alistair met his squad of marines, it was plain to him the sergeant was neither impressed with him, with wavy locks longer than what was deemed militarily appropriate, nor especially thrilled about being his subordinate. Upon being introduced, the sergeant saluted with a skeptical frown garnished by a furrowed brow, and then presented to Alistair the men who would be under his command. Under the studious gaze of the sergeant, he ordered the men at ease, looked them up and down once, and without a speech quietly sent them on their way. He may not yet have won the sergeant's respect, but his unassuming manner at least neutralized a portion of his animosity.

The Spirit's crew knew their assigned locations for takeoff; the marines and the science team gathered in the small meeting hall and strapped themselves in. They had little sense of movement there, just an overwhelming thrust like an invisible force trying to flatten them. After a time, the ship reduced its acceleration, and Katherine quickly unstrapped herself, hopped out of her chair and ran out the door towards the cafeteria. Alistair strolled after and found her with her face pressed against one of the many large windows of the dining hall, craning her neck to watch as Aldra grew smaller.

She finally turned from the window and gave him a nervous smile, exhaling unsteadily.

"Don't get excited," he said in a calm tone.

"It's my first time in space."

Before she could break down into tears, he wrapped his arms around her.

"I don't know if I want to do this," she said with a quaver, but managed to turn the quaver into a laugh rather than a sob.

He was on the verge of replying it was too late to do anything about that, but at the last moment tact won a small battle in his brain and he realized she was just expressing understandable anxiety. She did not need a logical and obvious response.

The trip had, for Alistair, little in common with the one that took him from Srillium to Aldra. There was more room to move about and exercise now, more people with whom to speak, food stored and preserved with modern methods, entertainment in the form of threedies and access to the Comlat, though updates took longer and longer to reach them. Though he had dreaded another trip into space so soon after a two cycle sojourn, he soon discovered he was comfortable on the ship. In those moments when he forgot the tragedy of Kaldis, which so overwhelmed him that he scarcely considered the danger ahead, the time aboard The Spirit of the Revolution was not unpleasant.

Louise Downing avoided Alistair, her initial shock at seeing him being the extent of the notice and emotion she was willing to expend on him. Alistair, neither eager nor loathe to talk with her, followed her lead and made himself easy to avoid. It was not until, in a crowded cafeteria, he took one of the few open seats, next to his sister who happened to be sitting with Louise, that they were forced to exchange words. Katherine left them a few moments later with the excuse that she had work to attend to.

With Katherine gone, Louise sat erect and rigid in her seat, with a frosty air, saying nothing. Alistair, equally taciturn, was more relaxed, a fact that increasingly bothered Louise whose frequent and furtive glances in his direction confirmed for her his indifference. Finally, growing supremely uncomfortable, she was moved to speak.

"A fat lot of good your revolution did us."

Alistair moved only his eyes, just for a moment, to glance at her. Then he shoveled in another bite of food. "What revolution was that?"

The apparent inanity of the question frustrated her, and she snapped, "The one that put your buddy in charge of the planet!"

Alistair shoveled in another bite and shook his head. "That wasn't my revolution."

"You were fighting in it."

"Weren't you working for the Bureau of Transportation?"

"Obviously."

"Fat lot of good your *government* did us."

His counterargument caught her off guard, and she fell silent and picked at her food.

"It was just two sides fighting to be in control. After the way they both behaved, there's no sense blaming one more than the other."

"I lost my brother, my uncle and two cousins."

"I'm sorry for your loss," he said, but under the weight of her accusatory tone, he couldn't make it sound sympathetic. His response made her grit her teeth, and after a second of deliberation she stood up, the motion sending her chair flying back.

"I used to think I liked you," she hissed and left him dumbfounded.

They reached the inevitable point where the hyperspace portion ended and deceleration substituted for gravity instead of acceleration. Later, there was a moment of weightlessness when the ship finally stopped its deceleration. Alistair was in his quarters when he felt himself come loose of his mattress, and then, when the artificial gravity was turned on, he sank back down on it. He set down the book he was reading and set out for the bridge.

As head of their respective teams, Alistair and Katherine were the only non crew members to have access to the bridge on their own authority. There were two separate automatic doors by which one could enter the bridge, and they each came through one at almost the same time. The Captain was standing behind two pilots, while the communications officer and the navigator were seated at their respective stations. The wall across from the entrances was almost entirely taken up by a window out of which only stars could be seen. Behind the Captain was a command table projecting a 3D image of the surrounding area. There was a small image of their ship always in the center of the display and, towards the edge but crawling towards them, another tiny dot.

"Take a seat," said the Captain with a serious and professional voice, nodding towards a couple seats against the back wall of the bridge. His accent was from the sparsely populated eastern coast.

Alistair and Katherine sat down and strapped themselves in, and the Captain sat in his command chair. He pressed a button and spoke in a clear voice.

"This is the Captain, we are going to execute a rotational maneuver. Please get yourselves strapped in."

A moment later, the navigator said, "Eighty thousand kilometers and closing."

At this the Captain nodded, and he turned in his seat to look at Alistair and Katherine. "We'll be there in a little over an hour." Alistair and his sister shared a nervous glance and nod.

After pausing to allow passengers time to secure themselves, the Captain said, "Execute."

Upon his order, the ship rotated and they swayed in their seats while the pilots and Captain relayed messages back and forth until the maneuver was complete.

Once again, the Captain pressed the intercom button. "The maneuver has been successfully completed. Passengers may now walk freely." With that, he unstrapped himself and was out of his seat.

He came around to stand at the command table, and Katherine and Alistair joined him a second later. No sooner did they arrive than the lights of the bridge, programmed to imitate an Aldran day, dimmed to a twilight level. The colored glows of the displays and buttons stood out more.

"Raise the lights on the bridge only," ordered the Captain.

A moment later the lights were back to daylight strength. The Captain grabbed a small object resembling a pen and poked its tip into the 3D display, pressing a small button on the side of the pen as he did. A red light blinked at the pen's tip and the display changed, magnifying the area where the pen tip had been, the area around the object they were after.

"It's big," he said and he scratched at his close cropped beard.

"It's larger than any ship in the Aldran fleet," said Alistair as he studied the display's readouts.

The vessel on the display was a flat-bottom craft in the shape of a square, a platform with the compartments of a ship affixed to it. Its most salient feature was the round, almost semi-circular building—if indeed it was a building—wrapping around most of the edge of the platform like two pincers of an ant, leaving a gap at one corner where the pincers did not quite touch and an open central area.

"Is this in true color?" asked Alistair as he inspected the black vessel.

"Yes," the Captain replied, and he stuck the pen into the display once again and enlarged the ship so it almost entirely filled the view.

They saw that the pincers-like building had an irregular, almost lumpy exterior. In the flat area in the center there was a space where a ship might land, but the rest of it was filled with what seemed to be round obsidian pillars.

"That's not human built," said the Captain with a deeply skeptical voice, almost disapproving.

"It came from too far away to be human," breathed Katherine with the sort of religious awe a pilgrim might have in Mecca.

"Seventy thousand kilometers," announced the navigator.

"Should we hail it, Captain?" asked the communications officer.

The Captain, leaning with both palms on the edge of the command table, glanced up at the scientist and the marine.

"How do you hail an alien ship?" asked Alistair, giving voice to all their thoughts.

"The protocol established before take off was to hail it when we were within distance. Now...I don't know."

He was a man of some fifty cycles, every one showing in the color of his beard, the wrinkles around his eyes and the calluses on his knuckles. It was evident indecision was something he was neither used to nor comfortable with, but he had little prepared for an encounter of this magnitude.

"We're not going to sneak up on them," Alistair softly said after a prolonged period of silence.

A moment more only did the Captain hesitate. "Hail them."

After a couple minutes, the communications officer gave them an update. "No response," he said. "Dead silence. I'm running through all the hailing protocols."

"Sir," said the navigator, "I'm not getting any sign of activity. No electronics, no movement, no energy fields...The only sign this is more than a lump of metal in space is the interior temperature: it's just above the freezing point of water at normal pressure."

"What the hell are those pillars?" wondered Alistair out loud, his gaze fixed on the image of his inquiry.

Shrugging, the Captain said, "Missile silos?"

The ex marine was dubious. "That's an odd design. Why silos?"

"Sixty thousand kilometers," said the navigator.

"Commence breaking," ordered the Captain, and from the gentle tug on their bodies they knew the ship was decelerating again.

"Still no response to our hail."

"And no sign of life."

"Well," said the Captain, "something built the goddamn thing."

Katherine returned to her seat, looking pensive and nervous yet determined. The navigator soon announced their distance from the ship was fifty thousand kilometers. Alistair had not moved from the 3D display and rarely taken his eyes off it. The Captain went from station to station, overseeing the process of bringing the ship to a stop at a precise location. At the point when the planet of Aldra would barely fit between them and their destination, Katherine rose.

"I am going to prepare my science team. We'll be there soon."

Alistair absentmindedly nodded while the Captain did not appear to hear her. A moment later she was gone. The miles flew by more slowly and more time passed between the navigator's announcements, an effect accentuated by their anxiety. Alistair felt they must have been crawling through space.

The navigator finally called a distance of twenty thousand kilometers and Alistair felt a chill sweat break out on his forehead. A debilitating fatigue seized his legs at fifteen thousand kilometers, and with a thrill of equal parts fear and excitement cramping his innards, the ex marine returned to his seat and sank into it. At ten thousand kilometers he was gripping the seat's edge, and his breaths passed through clenched teeth. For all his physical prowess, he was helpless there on the bridge, subject to a thing that may have destroyed a star. No superb action nor clever plan on his part would save him. His life hung from a whim.

The others on the bridge, with not a day's worth of combat experience among them, were worse off than he. Jittery fingers pressed buttons basted with sweat. Voices cracked and quavered; knees shook. Then, shortly after the navigator managed to force his vocal chords to deliver the news of a distance of one hundred kilometers, the Captain ordered an increase in the rate of deceleration. Alistair pitched forward in his seat, held in place by the straps and staring at the floor. This rapid deceleration lasted for some seconds. When it ended and the ship came to a complete stop, he sat back, let out a long exhalation…and saw the alien vessel through the bridge window.

At first it was barely discernible, its presence hinted at by a black patch of space where no stars were seen. The attenuated light of the remote suns and of The Spirit of the Revolution only barely served to bring some details into focus, right on the edge of resolution. The Captain ordered the spotlights turned on, and those tremendous illuminators clearly revealed the spaceship to the naked eye.

All tasks were dropped and all duties forgotten. Seated men rose from their chairs; standing men sat down. Somehow, some sort of change of position, slowly and reverently carried out, seemed a necessary acknowledgement. Centuries ago the first proof of an alien intelligence was uncovered on Kaldis. In the intervening time no second such find was ever uncovered. They were only the second group of *Homo sapiens* to discover a hint that in all the limitless vastness of the universe, in all the hundreds of billions of known galaxies and their sextillions of stars, Man might not be alone.

Silence reigned on the bridge and everywhere else, and out of every porthole and window wondering and frightened faces stared. They could no more have marred the moment with speech than they could have belched in the face of God. The obsidian hulk imitated their silence, or perhaps they imitated it. It was still, and they dared not move. It patiently waited, and they postponed action. They could only contemplate the wonder of it across the half kilometer of space between them.

And then its lights turned on.

91

Without acceleration there was no sense of movement; an object in motion felt the same as an object at rest. After Alistair and his marines left the docking bay and gave their transport vessel a short burst of speed, they could not, merely through their own senses, claim to know it was they who were moving and not the alien spaceship coming to devour them. They lined the walls of the squarish pod—with Alistair and the corporal in the pilot seats—dressed in their spacesuits, their helmets set on the floor or perhaps resting on knees. Instead of the nervous shakes and jitters of those unfamiliar with danger and fear, they displayed the grim squints and folded arms of veterans.

"Still no response to our hail," said the corporal as he studied his instruments and listened to the chatter on the bridge of The Spirit.

After lighting up, the alien vessel showed no further signs of life. It was not a dazzling display, just a handful of well spaced lights shining not out into space or onto the human's ship, but rather illuminating the alien vessel itself. It was enough to make out the ship, but not enough to make it shine.

Alistair watched as the vessel grew until it expanded past the boundaries of the transport's windshield. "Take a pass underneath it," he said.

The corporal guided their transport pod downwards, and they went underneath the black alien ship, eyeing its featureless bottom.

"No obvious cargo doors or anything," Alistair heard the Captain say over the intercom.

"And still no response," repeated the corporal.

After the ship's bottom slid by, the corporal turned their pod around to skim the top. They were now presented with a more interesting terrain to view. The semicircular part that was the bulk of the ship was confirmed to be smooth but irregular, lumpy. The other three corners of the square platform peeked out from beneath it. The flat portion in the middle, dotted with pillars, was also uneven, showing smooth dips and humps much like wet sand on a beach. The pillars themselves displayed the same irregularity, better resembling, upon closer inspection, the crooked digits of some ghoulish hand. The lights of the alien vessel slowly rotated now, causing the pillars' shadows to sweep the deck at the same pace.

Katherine's breathless voice burst out over the intercom. *"Alistair, take your pod back a few yards, back to where you were."*

Alistair and the corporal exchanged concerned glances, but Alistair nodded to indicate the corporal should follow her suggestion. When their pod was brought to a halt, the lights stopped rotating. When they retraced their path, the lights rotated again, but in the opposite direction.

"The lights are following us," said the corporal.

"The lights are shining on the ship, not you," said the Captain. *"Why should they follow you?"*

"I'm just telling you what I'm seeing."

"*Go slowly now,*" said Katherine, and as they reduced their speed, the lights rotated more slowly. "*Be ready to stop on my mark.*"

The shadows crept along, mimicking the pace of their transport pod.

"*Stop!*" Katherine cried, exultant.

The corporal obeyed and they hung motionless over the vessel. Below, the lights, and consequently the shadows, stopped moving. The warped pillars necessarily cast warped shadows. The uneven ground necessarily twisted shadows cast on it. However, right at the point where they now found themselves, the twisting effect of the ground cancelled out the warping effect of the pillars and the shadows were straight as arrows. Exclamations came from several speakers at once.

"*But what's it mean?*" demanded the Captain.

"*Alistair, take your ship another inch or two forward,*" said Katherine. "*I think you're not quite at the sweet spot yet.*"

The requested maneuver once performed, the pod again floated motionless above the alien vessel. Suddenly, the open space among the pillars, a sort of clearing in the midst of a forest, glowed orange and before anyone could react beyond a gasp of surprise, a ray shot out and hit the transport pod.

"*Alistair!*" Katherine called out, and the Captain emitted an incoherent cry.

The ray did no damage but drew them towards the clear area of the platform, where they touched down with the gentlest of bumps and sat still and silent. The orange glow faded, but as it diminished they felt a growing gravity until they felt as if they were back on Aldra. Out the windshield, the pillars seemed like fingers trying to clutch the pod. A few of the lights, quite bright at that distance, shone right into their pod and Alistair squinted against the glare.

"Alright, suit up," he commanded.

The marines needed little prompting. Helmets were donned and weapons checked. When Alistair placed the helmet over his own head, his ears instantly noted the change of environment. The ambient sounds of the pod were exchanged for a hollow sounding hum, almost like when one put one's ear against a sea shell. The rustling of the troops' preparations was muffled almost to silence, but as they too donned their helmets, he could hear their breath in their microphones.

They waited in their seats while the pod doors opened and the air rushed out. Alistair heard only breathing, his own and his comrades', as they exited the pod and surveyed the landscape before them. The Spirit of the Revolution could be seen, a toy hanging in space half a kilometer distant. Above them the stars shone beautifully and steadily, some with hints of blue or red in their hue. The many shadows of the pillars crisscrossed over the marines, and as they moved around the lights blinked in and out as the pillars alternately covered and revealed them.

"*You're being scanned,*" the communications officer's voice broke out in their helmets. "*No indication of hostile intentions.*"

Alistair went to the base of a pillar, which towered several meters above him but was more slender than his torso, and laid a hand on its surface. It was smooth, made of a material that, though it did not correspond directly to anything he had ever seen, seemed more metallic than anything else. Looking back at his men, he saw several of them were inspecting pillars of their own.

"We're going to approach the main structure."

The sergeant formed the troops into a spread formation, and thus scattered they left their clearing and moved into the pillar forest, rifles making broad sweeps. Alistair noticed, out of the corner of his left eye, a soft bluish light mix with the harsh white ones. Looking up, he saw a large door sliding open near one end of the U-shaped main building, and from it poured azure light.

"Halt!" he called and pointed his rifle at the opening.

The eyes of his troops followed the line of his gun, and they turned to face the new development. Silently, the door finished sliding open, leaving a portal about forty feet tall and sixty feet wide.

"Hold your positions. Check in front and behind."

The material of Alistair's helmet's shield was resistant to condensation, for which he was grateful. From his heavy breathing, normal glass or plastic would have quickly fogged.

"No further movement," came the sergeant's voice.

Katherine spoke up. *"This whole thing feels like you're being invited. It doesn't seem danger-ous."*

"That's easy to say from your position," growled the sergeant.

"Alter course, sergeant," said Alistair. He swallowed a lump in his throat. "Let's move towards it. Slowly."

They crept along, soundless perhaps but easy to spot, even with the naked eye, in their white spacesuits. They drew close enough to the entrance to be able to see some of the interior. There was a dais with a structure on it, its top faintly illuminated by the blue light. When they reached the threshold, one of the marines stepped forward and scanned the immediate area inside, finally issuing an "all clear" signal.

"Still no movement," Alistair announced.

He could see the dais was a circle raised two feet from the rest of the floor. On it was a semi-circular altar, or something of that nature. The source of the blue light proved to be an irregular river of light suspended just below the lofty ceiling and running along its length until the bend in the building blocked his view. This river did not flow, but moved randomly. Drops would detach from the main river and then be reacquired, certain portions would thin while others expanded. Dips and bulges formed at its edges, only to disappear. To the right, towards the middle of the main structure, he spied another dais complete with its own altar, and then another after that, and another after that, continuing until the bend in the building hid the rest from him. If there were any hosts in that alien vessel, their presence was not evident.

"That's enough for now," said Alistair. "Let's bring in the science team."

෴

Alistair and his men took up positions around the opening while Katherine and her team stood at the threshold, the soft blue light illuminating the fronts of their space suits, the harsh white light shining on the backs. She was waiting only for her team to finish a few cursory tests before she entered. They detected a force field at the opening, but it proved to be one they could pass through without difficulty. It served, however, to keep an atmosphere inside.

"The air inside is breathable," said one of the men. *"Doesn't match ours exactly, but its got oxygen and nitrogen. No carbon dioxide."*

"No carbon dioxide," repeated Katherine. "Because CO2 is a byproduct we make; we don't need it to breath. It's welcoming us."

"Maybe," said Alistair. *"How does it know what our requirements are? It's likely just the atmosphere from whatever homeworld this species comes from."*

"I'm going inside now. It's asking us to come in."

"Keep your helmet on, all the same."

No true believer ever approached the idol of his worship with more awe than Katherine approached that alien dais, nor ever moved with more careful reverence through his temple. Upon crossing the threshold, she could hear, faintly through her helmet, her footfalls, the air inside permitting sound once again. In a matter of a few dozen steps the middle Ashley child was standing at the edge of the dais, trembling and sweating but determined. She saw a semi circle made out of a smooth, whitish, translucent material standing around eight feet tall.

When she raised her left leg and placed her foot down on the dais, the semi circle lit up white, startling her.

"Katherine, step back!" yelled Alistair, but she raised a hand to calm him down. Nevertheless, he was at her side a moment later.

"This would be a very strange and elaborate way to kill somebody, if that's what it wants."

Alistair gripped her arm through their suits. *"There is no way to know the intentions of an alien species. A little caution costs us nothing."*

Katherine turned to face him and put both hands on his shoulders. "Alistair, I'm OK. I'm going to get on the dais now."

Turning from him, she stepped up and walked towards the shining semi-cylinder. When she came within the ambit of its reach, images appeared on it, flashing by as if it were a computer screen, and a script raced about. Finally, one image appeared and held steady, reaching seven feet in height. It was an alien creature, naked, but Katherine knew from its gaze it was intelligent. She, the first human to lay eyes on another intelligent species, gasped, but not from fear.

It was a deep red color, hairless but for some soft down on its head, taller than humans and more slender. Its face was slightly prognathic, and its skull long, with the top of the head extending several inches beyond where a human's would stop. The mouth was turned down just a touch, not quite facing the ground but inclining a bit in that direction, and a single aperture she took for a nostril was just above it. It had two arms and was bipedal, but possessed a skeleton and musculature that could never be mistaken for human. Like a bear, it lacked a collar bone and therefore had sloping shoulders. There were vaguely pectoral muscles but no nipples. Its legs were long compared to its body, but were jointed much like a human. Its arms were, in relation to its body, more human-like in length and also jointed like *Homo sapiens*. The hands had four digits, one of them an opposable thumb, and the feet had four digits as well, though they were much less prehensile. Between its long legs was a small organ she took to be a penis. The image blinked, replaced by a different creature of the same species. This one had a small aperture at the crotch but no penis, more hair on its—her—head, and a single lump on the belly that Katherine decided was a mammary organ.

Her state of euphoric fascination was interrupted when the image disappeared, and she reached out with a hand as if to search for it, grab it and keep it from leaving. A moment later a new creature appeared, this one a hirsute, robust animal on four legs, vaguely equine. She watched as, like a movie, it began to play in front of her, showing her images of the animal eating, mating, running, sleeping. Then it changed…evolved. Its face grew shorter. It lost its body hair, revealing ruddy skin underneath. One of the digits became a thumb. The downward turned mouth moved up to the front of the face. Its arched back curved more and more the other way as the animal spent time in an upright position. Occasionally, the animal would divide into two identical creatures, and then those creatures would evolve in separate ways, one of them finally drifting off screen while the remaining creature continued to evolve. Finally, the remaining animal became the original one first shown.

Next, a planet appeared, blue and green like Earth but with a different configuration of continents. She saw images of the species all over the planet, some thicker and shorter, others with dark red, almost brown, skin while still others were a light pink in color. The creatures lived in tribes where the bearers of children were protected, while the other gender maintained more strength. They wielded spears and bows and arrows, wore clothing and developed technologies. Language evolved. They explored and reached out to other tribes of their kind. They worshipped strange gods and spirits, made music unlike anything she had heard before, and she took off her helmet to hear it better. They fought each other, they helped each other, they cheated each other and they loved each other.

Evolution, as on Earth, was inevitable, and any species arising from such a process is one whose individuals have a highly refined sense of self preservation. Community was an advantage for this alien race, just as with humans, but each individual was self interested, acted for his own benefit notwithstanding those moments when a helping hand was extended. Each member sought its own happiness.

As a living organism, each alien placed demands on its environment, needed to use the resources around it to survive and flourish. This created the potential for conflict among them, for sometimes two individuals had different ideas of how to dispose of a resource. The solutions for resolving this conflict, for determining who would be permitted to dispose of the resource and who would not, were remarkably similar among all the various cultures of the species. Indeed, their solutions were remarkably similar to those reached on Earth. The first to acquire a thing became its owner, and could do what he pleased as long as what he pleased did not affect another's acquisition in a way the other objected to. These acquisitions could be traded or abandoned, but until such a time, the original appropriator was its owner. At first, many of these property rights were held in common by tribes, but with time many were individualized, and it was these cultures which developed and advanced the fastest. Where these simple rules were not well established, or where they were ignored or violated, there was violence.

As on Earth, there were two basic relationships. One in which the various parties agreed to terms, and one in which one party forced its will on another. In the former relationships, the parties occasionally improved their situation by trading. Other times no trade was made because terms were not mutually agreeable, and the self interested parties did not permit themselves to be taken advantage of. In these cases, though no improvement in situation was achieved, neither did they find themselves worse off.

The other relationship was parasitic. From such came theft and assault and all their sundry subsets. In these cases, one party often benefited, assuming the defenses of the second were not enough to cause it too much damage, but the second party invariably was made worse off. At times the dominant party convinced the other its power was legitimate. Government was born and, in the minds of the dominated creatures, became hallowed by time and tradition. Forever after, the balance of power could shift, but the struggle was over how much power government should wield, or what precise form the government should take, not whether or not it ought to exist.

The type of being that came to dominate in government differed from culture to culture, depending on circumstances and cultural values, but there was one commonality. In a democracy, the government leaders tended to be affable, well spoken and power hungry. In a warlike culture the leaders tended to be physically robust, athletic, aggressive and power hungry. Even in a monarchy, where supreme power is passed down from parent to child and might conceivably pass to a beneficent one, the new king found himself surrounded by high officials who got to their position through cunning, back stabbing and scheming all driven by a hunger for power, and contests for the throne often disposed of meeker monarchs.

Eventually, the species left its homeworld, spreading out into the Milky Way. Katherine witnessed the growth of cities, and she recognized an architecture that was a match to what remained of The Ruins on Kaldis. It was as close to a confirmation as could be expected: this was the species that built an outpost on that planet three millions years ago, before *Homo habilis* fashioned his first tool.

The ability to move off their homeworld was initially a boon for those trying to escape from parasitism. As time went by, government tightened its fist, and the vibrant and free colonies, still too small to fend off the homeworld's State armies, succumbed in war after war. Generally, by the time a colony came to blows with the homeworld, it was already under domination by a parasitic State of its own. The warfare was a cancer for the species. Millions died, and much of what they labored to produce was destroyed. The end came in a manner whose resemblance to her own times gave Katherine chills. In the midst of many battles, when economies were burdened with choking bureaucracies and many struggled to feed themselves, a colonial world was destroyed.

A stable planet fit for colonizing was a rare thing. Even a homeworld of an intelligent species is kept in good condition through biological means, but other worlds needed more than that. Like Aldra, there were conditions on these worlds that had to be balanced out, compensated for, attenuated, amplified or nullified by intervention. This intervention required advanced techniques and expensive machinery, like the oceanic humidifiers and cosmic ray seeders on Aldra. Each planet required its own, special solutions, and such solutions required the input of many millions of beings producing all manner of parts and exchanging them across light years.

The shock of a colony being destroyed caused the system to collapse. Capital decayed and replacement parts could not be found. Even so, disaster might have been averted, but the State chose to take full control during these disasters, with the consent and clamorous pleading of the populace. That institution which had done nothing but hamper their progress was tasked with saving them when things were most dire. As more and more workers were diverted from other tasks and put to work producing the absolute necessities, fewer and fewer of those goods that make life more amenable were produced, and therefore became more expensive. Consequently, more and more colonists returned to the homeworld, where at least habitable conditions did not require a capitalized labor force to be maintained. These flights of colonists were also flights of capital, and it was not long before the great factories and machines making planets more livable shut down and the planets reverted back to their natural states, which were inimical to the colonists. All beings not able to return to the homeworld died.

The massive influx of immigrants produced predictable problems, and Overlay technology played its role. Such awesome power was used by the State of the homeworld to enforce control. Immigrants fought for a life of dignity; natives fought to fend off the incoming tide. Overlay technology was used to control both groups, but it produced side effects. Each use of the technology produced waves and ripples in the Overlay which would, occasionally, combine with the after effects from other uses. Where these waves met violent phenomena occurred, wreaking havoc.

The curvature of spacetime was responsible for the fundamental forces of physics, and it was this curvature of spacetime that served like gravity for these waves in the Overlay. Occasionally, the sun of the home system would pry some of these waves loose from the homeworld. Each time the Overlay was used, more waves were stolen by the sun. Eventually, after prolonged accumulation, the great ball of fire exploded, and the last of the species perished.

This story, told through images and sounds as well as feelings impressed upon the watcher through some mysterious mechanism, brought Katherine to her knees. A tale of billions of lives, so fundamentally like her own, played out before her, of beings with the same hopes and passions, the same insecurities in the same lonely universe. It was a tale of potential occasionally realized but often forsaken, a tale frequently joyous but ultimately tragic. From the basic stuff of the universe, from quarks evolving increasingly complex relations over billions and billions of years, a species with intelligence and the capacity to be happy and make happiness of profound intensity arose. They then proceeded to entirely wipe themselves out, disappearing from the universe, leaving the galaxy empty until another such marvelous species could arise.

She found herself weeping for all the lives erased, for all the stories never to be told. Then she became sensible to a presence at her side, and turning her head, saw her brother. Having witnessed the same story as she, his eyes were moist but his face was a carefully controlled mask. Like her, he breathed the air of the spaceship. Then she twisted to look behind, and she saw the rest of the science team and the marines, enraptured by the display, each having forgotten his duties, each in a process of slow, faltering, somnambulant migration towards the dais where she and Alistair stood.

The images disappeared, though the dais still shone. Too stunned to speak, Alistair helped his sister to her feet and, arm in arm, they left. When they stepped off the dais, it stopped shining. They were left with only the soft blue illumination of the strange light above them, and the faces of their comrades, ensconced in their helmets, were returned to shadow. No one spoke nor acted. It was the Captain, who saw the tale through the imagers present but who, removed from its immediate presence, was not shaken with the full impact, who spoke first.

"*It looks like…this is the last of their ships,*" he said, though his voice was full of uncertainty.

"No," said Katherine.

"There was more to that story than what you could see and hear," said Alistair.

"You had to be here," said one of the marines.

Without the impediment of a face shield, their voices carried through the ship.

"*Explain that.*"

The members of the scout team exchanged glances, as if trying to confirm they all had the same impression. It was Katherine who finally responded.

"I don't think they were the ones who built this ship."

"We're not going to find anyone else here," said Alistair as his still awed gaze roamed about. "If they were here, they would have greeted us."

Lost in her own reverie, Katherine was not paying close attention to him, but the sound of his speech prompted her to give voice to her related thoughts.

"This ship didn't destroy Kaldis."

Her brother nodded. "We did."

"And there are no resistors on Aldra," said Louise. "Just side effects of the Overlay."

The great chamber swallowed her words, and they fell into silence. The group stood before the next dais, twenty yards or so from the first. They deferred to Katherine and Alistair, standing a bit back and leaving the Ashley siblings alone at the edge. Alistair deferred to Katherine, allowing her to move out front. Like before, as soon as Katherine placed her first foot on the dais the display at the center lit up. Less nervous and uncertain, she moved directly to the display and, just like before, images began to appear and disappear on it.

Another intelligent being was displayed. The last stages of evolution leading to its birth were shown, leaving a creature most resembling a bipedal reptile. After that, in all the broad details the story was the same as for the ruddy species. A society came to allow coerced relationships to predominate, eventually institutionalizing that form of relationship. They colonized the Milky Way while the precursors of the ruddy species still roamed their planet on four legs, and while primates were only newly arrived on Earth. The difficulty of maintaining suitable conditions on unsuitable worlds came up against the pressure of economic crises fomented by side effects of the Overlay, war and other government intrusions. Artificial ecosystems decayed, leading to a flight of persons and capital back to the homeworld, leading to ecological collapse, leading to mass immigration. With the species now returned to its homeworld, dependent on a system of interstellar trade that no longer existed, strife reigned. Conflicts were, by an institution founded on violence, combated with violence. Eventually, through misuse and overuse of the Overlay, the star exploded and the species was no more.

When the images disappeared and they were off the dais and once again in low light, Alistair said, "This is a museum."

"It's a mausoleum," said Katherine. "A harbinger of extinction. It comes to collect our finger prints before we die."

"Horse shit!" cursed the sergeant, having nothing with which to rebut their deduction save for his earnest desire that it not be true.

When the echoes of the sergeant's curse subsided, Louise ventured a question. "Is this all we do, then? Not that it's not fascinating but…it's not what we wanted when we came."

"What we want doesn't carry a whole lot of weight," mumbled a man from the science team.

The despondent tone of his voice gave them pause. Some bit their lips, others stared at the floor. It was during this lull that they heard the sound of footsteps coming from deeper in the chamber.

Without conscious thought to do so, they closed ranks, withdrawing into a compact group. They spied a figure coming around the bend. Its soft, bipedal footfalls would have gone unnoticed had they continued their conversation. They saw it only indistinctly, and after a breathless minute of watching it advance, they realized it had no distinguishing features to see. It was a blank, grayish thing, not unlike a dreadbot except that, for all its broad similarities, it obviously was not patterned after the human form. It carried something in the shape of a square, something black like the color of the ship.

It approached them at an even, unconcerned pace, and when it drew within a few yards, turned and went to the wall. There was a missing section into which it slid its black square. After it shone a light over the area with a small tool in its hand, the new section of wall melded with its surroundings until it was impossible to determine that this section was only recently added. Its work finished, the figure left the way it came. The humans did not move until it rounded the bend and was out of sight, its footsteps no longer detectable.

"What in the goddamn hell was that about?" demanded the sergeant, looking through the scope of his rifle.

"It's a repairman," said Louise.

"Well," said Alistair, casting his gaze over the group and shrugging, "I say we follow it."

They had entered the chamber at one extreme. In following the repairbot, they came to its middle. Before arriving, they became sensible to a light source around the bend, and when they reached the middle they were greeted by the sight of an enormous machine. Emitting only the faintest of hums, it nevertheless pulsed and throbbed and its parts spun and pumped. Its appearance was akin to a mountain of metal boxes piled on one another, with various tubes and disks poking out of the jumble. Two repairbots were standing on it several levels up, but they gave the party of humans no notice. Their attention was drawn to some part of the machine.

At floor level, on the edge of the machine, was yet another dais with a display at its center. This dais was larger than the others, and its display towered fifteen feet high, encompassing far more space. The displays having proven safe, the other members of the team overcame their trepidation and gathered around its edge as Katherine stepped onto the platform. The display lit up and when she stepped forward, images began to play.

She was confronted with an enormous image of a spiral galaxy, majestic and beautiful. Surrounding it was the blackness of space and a few smaller dwarf galaxies caught in its orbit. The matter in the galaxy, almost entirely hydrogen, occasionally condensed and formed stars, most small ones living for many billions of years. A few were gigantic stars that lived far briefer lives. These gigantic stars converted much of their hydrogen into other elements: helium, oxygen, carbon and others. Then they exploded and flung the newly created elements into space, where they would mix with clouds of hydrogen until finally participating in another star birth. Through this constant recycling, the composition of the galaxy changed over time.

Eventually, the heavier elements became abundant enough that planets would form around a new star. They came in many varieties, and orbited at any number of distances from their host sun. The rocky planets closer in were bombarded with chunks of material from out in space, and these chunks brought water and amino acids. Eventually, this bombardment abated as debris in the young solar system was vacuumed by the gravitational pull of the orbiting bodies. After that, surfaces cooled, and the amino acids eventually configured themselves into a self replicating form, evolving on every world where the conditions were right.

There were certain, extremely rare worlds where conditions were such that the life forms would occasionally acquire greater complexity. This did not happen often, as the conditions required much fine tuning of parameters: planet size, composition, amount of water, a satellite companion of sufficient size, large gas giants in the system but in stable orbits. Also critical was the size of the star it orbited and its location in the galaxy: away from the densely packed center and metal-poor edges.

Even these conditions were not sufficient for intelligence to arise. What really caused fundamental changes in the evolutionary pathways was a planetary ecological crisis. A deep freeze of a planet hitherto in a temperate realm of the solar system put the kind of pressures on life forms that raised the survival threshold and thus, with fewer survivors of any given species allowing greater and quicker changes in the populations, produced radically new forms, often more complex forms. Often, the changes helping populations survive proved useful in all environments.

As Katherine watched, the Milk Way collided with another galaxy. This did not cause any planetary crises, for the distance between stars was vast and no two stars collided while their galaxies were merging, but it did set the stage. The collision caused the interplanetary dust and gas to compact, increasing the rate of star births. A few million years later, the biggest of these new stars died. With the increased rate of star death came an increase in cosmic rays shooting through the galaxy, which seeded cloud formation and cooled temperate planets.

With the collision of the two galaxies, however, it wasn't just one planet that cooled down. Every terrestrial planet at a distance from its sun permitting liquid water, and therefore Earth-like weather, became cloudy and froze. It was this precise sort of crisis that had, on Earth, produced its first eukaryotes. What had not been anticipated before, and what she and the others learned for the first time, was that this led not to the evolution of eukaryotes on just one planet, but every candidate planet which was temperate before, now became an icehouse, and eukaryotes made their first appearance in the galaxy on many planets at the same time.

She gasped at the idea, tearing her gaze from the screen and finding her brother, whose awestruck expression mirrored her own. Unable to look away for too long, she returned her attention to the display.

Eventually, the rate of star deaths slowed and the planets warmed up again, allowing the new eukaryotes to spread. Billions of years later, after the Milky Way swallowed and assimilated the other galaxy in a prolonged and complex dance, another galactic collision occurred. Once again, within a few million years the temperate rocky planets cooled. This time, two things happened. First, a second generation of eukaryotes arose on planets that had not yet had bacteria, or possibly did not even exist, during the first collision. Second, the first generation of eukaryotes, under pressures not normally present on their planets, formed the first multicellular organisms. Multicellular life arose during the second icehouse phase.

After the second collision, there were two generations of more complex life forms, one having just arrived as eukaryotes and the other having become multicellular life forms. In the older generation, the oceans became saturated with oxygen, a byproduct of the physical processes of most of its life forms. The oxygen accumulated in the atmosphere, a deadly phenomenon for many, but there were some who took advantage. A few animals used the oxygen to drive their metabolism. At this point, the stabilizing moon that kept the planets' climates from chaotically changing became a barrier to evolution adding more complexity. However, a few of them, despite the moon, tipped over, such as happened on Earth, provoking the Cambrian Explosion.

With the planets tipping during the course of a mere several thousand years, the phosphorite and other minerals buried in ocean sediment were released, due to changes in ocean currents, into the ecosystems of the worlds. Chance mutations allowed some organisms to take advantage of this, and the result was shells and skeletons. These developments allowed larger and more complex body structures, the kind requiring control by more complex brains that could be exploited for other purposes.

Intelligence finally arose in the Milky Way. On one planet, a species evolved and, through the now familiar process, destroyed itself. They had no extant neighbors, but discovered evidence of an earlier species that had died out. In an improbable coincidence, the homeworlds of the two species were within a couple hundred light years of each other. Consequently, when the second species colonized a new world, they frequently found the ruins of the first.

What they learned served as a warning, though not effective enough to prevent the process of decay and collapse. There was, however, one group that recognized the process when it began. Motivated by despair, a scientific interest in recording history and a desire to help—even though the help might be to another species in the distant future—they put together an army of self-sustaining robots and built a ship for them, and it was on that very ship that Katherine, Alistair and the others were now standing.

There were other ships that escaped destruction, other individuals and groups who delayed the day of their demise, but it was only a delay. The robots survived because their capacities were greater and their needs fewer. They worked without tiring. Life support systems were not necessary for them. Neither was leisure. Neither was gravity, the absence of which was detrimental to life. Every robot could be programmed to perform, at an expert level, the tasks of resource extraction, construction and repair. The robots spent their time replacing worn down parts and collecting raw materials from other worlds without breaks. For the living creatures, it was a simple equation: their ability to produce lagged behind the rate of decay. Small populations could not benefit from extended divisions of labor, reducing their productive capacity. Many of the conditions on the homeworld, conditions provided for billions of years at a time, had to be reproduced through labor. They were like sailors dumping out buckets of water into which a river was pouring. A new homeworld was the only chance of survival, but a search of the galaxy meant abandoning established mines; even more labor would need to be diverted, every time raw materials became scarce, to establishing new resource extraction sites. The lifespans of these last populations of intelligence were measured in decades, and when they went, the last of the species became extinct.

In a lonely galaxy the ship of robots wandered, exploring and recording. Left with a basis of technology and some hypothetical speculation from their makers, the robots found a way to use the Overlay to increase their speed of travel. Later, millions of years after the extinction of their creators, they detected a signal in the Overlay coming from the other side of the galaxy. They rushed to it, arriving to find a species in its last hours. Though they had explored for thousands of millennia, they had visited less than one percent of the stars in the Milky Way and had no way of knowing of the existence of that other race until they detected the Overlay signal. They arrived too late to save them, but they recorded the history of the species. Many millions of years after that, they detected a second signal and sped to that unexplored corner of the galaxy. They found another race on the edge of extinction, and they recorded its history too. A third signal reached them, and a fourth after that, but then a great calamity occurred.

There was a third collision between galaxies, and for a third time the temperate planets of the galaxy were plunged into frigid cold. A third generation of eukaryotes arose, while the planets with second generation eukaryotes saw multicellular life arise. However, on those planets with first generation life, the generation from which evolved the species that built the robot ship, the icehouse conditions no longer served to tease greater complexity out of evolutionary processes. Instead, the complex organisms died out, leaving only a few tucked away in warm oases of their worlds and setting them back to the first part of the multicellular stage. In effect, the first generation life merged with the second generation life, leaving in the Milky Way one stage of multicellular life composed of two separate generations, and another generation of merely eukaryotic life.

There was no longer intelligent life in the Milky Way. When the burst of star deaths finally diminished and the icy worlds became temperate again, there would be more opportunities for intelligence to evolve, but this was a question of many millions of years. The robot ship, in the meantime, left the Milky Way, visiting what would, hundreds of millions of years hence, be called the Andromeda Galaxy. Crossing the distance in mere decades, the robots found it to be a lonely place. Like the Milky Way, it had much bacteria, but little in the way of complex creatures. They discovered the galactic collisions which provoked increases in complexity in the Milky Way occurred with far greater frequency in the Andromeda Galaxy. While this provided ample opportunity for eukaryotes and multicellular life to arise, it also too frequently wiped out complex species. They would evolve again when their planets warmed, but another collision come too soon continually wiped out these species.

Over vast stretches of time, the robot ship visited the galaxies of the local cluster. Galactic collisions between large galaxies were common, and the Milky Way, through blind chance, experienced a paltry number of them. This paucity of galactic crashes left long intervals of time in which evolution could add complexity, and in a few rare cases this led to intelligence. No such lengthy and peaceful intervals were experienced in other galaxies, where one galactic crash was followed by another a mere hundred million years later. In all its vastness, the Milky Way had produced, as far as they could tell, a mere six civilizations, and it was the only galaxy in the local cluster to have produced any at all.

There was a risk to traveling between galaxies, for though a million years was not a terribly long period on the time scale in which they were operating, a decade was a fantastically long time for the machinery of which they were composed and on which they depended. A trip of decades or a century between galaxies was a trip over nearly absolute emptiness. It was not attempted without a thorough stocking of provisions and materials. A trip of a millennium between galactic clusters was out of the question. Had the robots been mortals, they might have cast a wistful gaze out over the universe, at the billions and billions of galaxies they dared not visit, in all probability could not visit, and wonder if there were any suitable galaxies out there, which had partially, though not entirely, escaped crashes and therefore might have produced intelligence. There was no way to know: even through the Overlay they could not, at that distance, detect any signals.

From the Milky Way, however, they could detect signals, and eventually one came to them. The first intelligent species after the third collision of the Milky Way arose. Like before, the robots arrived to find them in rapid decline. A few dozen million years later, they met the red species. Three million years after that, *Homo sapiens* emerged.

The marines and scientists tore their attention from the narrative to look at their surroundings with a new sense of respect. Just as with an adult's body, which contains none of the material present at its birth, the ship had no doubt been recycled many times over. Nothing of the original ship remained, yet there was a continuum of nearly two billion years represented there. The realization that the vessel was built before the emergence on Earth of the first multicellular organism produced a profound and reflective state in the passengers.

When the display finally stopped, Katherine stepped down and the light turned off. Nearly silent, the machine could not cover up their labored breathing, a product of the emotional impact of what they just saw. No one spoke at first. Some looked around at their companions, as if searching for someone who had an answer, or at least comfort. Others stared at something only they could see. The sergeant coughed, a tentative prelude to a speech, but did not go through with it. The two robots, having finished their jobs, closed a lid, sealed it shut and left, bound for some other duty in some other part of the ship. After the silence of the team grew uncomfortable, it was Alistair who finally spoke.

"Let's go home," was his cheerless suggestion.

92

The species displays had a universal interface, a cord with a gelatinous end that shaped itself around any plug and filled any outlet. Through this cord they downloaded the contents of the Comlat, essentially the entirety of human knowledge, and thereafter *Homo sapiens* had its own display in that two billion year old museum. Millions of years in the future, another intrepid boarding party would stand before it and discover the human race.

The ancient vessel's lights turned off while they were en route to their ship in the transport pod. Illuminated now only by The Spirit, it moved for the first time in cycles. It accelerated at a rate far in excess of one g and, in the interstellar darkness, disappeared in seconds.

Back on The Spirit, a weighty despondence seized the passengers who remained behind as much as the team on the alien ship. Nothing seemed worth saying. There was no good news, no bright side and no reason to dally. If the Captain needed time to collect his thoughts, explore his feelings or somehow mull over the experience, he found enough of it while the team made their way back. Directly the marines and scientists docked, the Captain cut the artificial gravity, rotated The Spirit so its roof pointed towards Aldra, and took off.

Alistair sank into a black humor. His spleen was in harmony with his customary taciturnity, but had nothing of its usual aloofness. Never devoutly opposed to companionship, he nevertheless often preferred some measure of solitude. Now, though he did not much interact, he sought company, or at least its periphery. He might have locked himself in his quarters; instead, he lingered in the cafeteria, usually seated alone at a table but near where others sat, or where one might expect them to show up.

One day, he came alive again. Walking into the cafeteria, he spotted Katherine and Louise sitting together. They eyed him with the sort of uncertainty with which a husband views his wife when he knows she is angry about something. He managed a weak smile and gripped Katherine's shoulder. When she stood up, he embraced her, and then he embraced Louise as well. All the tension and resentment drained out of her; she accepted his hug and returned it. When they sat down, it was with a sense of relief.

"We should spend our lives being happy, spend the only lives we'll ever have making each other happy. Why do we do…what we do to each other?" he wondered aloud.

The women could only shake their heads at first, but Katherine finally spoke.

"When a ball of gas collapses into itself, the pressure ignites the hydrogen, and for a long time equilibrium is reached. Gravity wants to destroy the star, the ignited hydrogen saves it. Eventually, the hydrogen runs out, and gravity makes the star collapse further until only the neutrons stop it. If there is enough matter, if the star was massive enough, even the neutrons are overwhelmed and the star collapses into a single metron. In its place is a black hole.

"Why does every star have to collapse?" She shrugged her shoulders. "It lived and then it died. It's the nature of things. The same nature that allowed it to live had another side."

Alistair slowly shook his head, in disappointment more than disagreement. "A molecule can't learn to disobey a physical law. A star will collapse, but why must a civilization? Humans can learn. So why don't we?" He directed his gaze out a window, into space, as if the answer he sought might be among the stars. "We have among us those who act to destroy society, but there are also some who act to save it. Maybe neither is fully aware of the larger picture, but that's what their actions add up to. Society dies when the destroyers aren't held in check, when those who know better are too few, too weak, or just don't fight hard enough." With a firm resolve and a delicate agony, he gave them his conclusion. "I must return to Srillium. All that is needed for evil to triumph is for good men to do nothing."

The acceleration was eventually completed, three weeks were spent in hyperspace and The Spirit decelerated. Upon returning to spacetime, they sent to traffic control a signal of their return. After nine hours, which should have been enough time for their signal to reach Aldra and an acknowledgement to be sent back, their radio was still quiet. Many days of silence later they were in orbit. On the night side they saw a dishearteningly sparse display of city lights. Only a fraction of yestercycle's electricity was being generated.

No orbiting space station replied to their incessant queries, and two that should have been visible to them were gone. They detected some sparse chatter on radio waves, nothing like the full, robust noise of a vibrant civilization, but rather infrequent whispers. None of the more powerful radios, designed to communicate over distances of lighthours, seemed to be operating. On the bridge of The Spirit, there was a brief deliberation over what to do.

It was Katherine who made the decision. With the cavalier shrug of one who fears no further consequence, she said, "We are free to go where we want. As a girl I always wanted to see Istaria." Alistair and the Captain gave her queer looks, and she shrugged again. "Why not? We're not going to miss anything."

The Captain, suddenly seized by a fit of humor, belted out a desperate guffaw at the incongruity of her suggestion, but also discovered he, too, feared no further consequence.

"We'll set down next to Istaria," he promised.

Istaria was Aldra's grandest park of attractions, boasting the greatest roller coasters, displays, restaurants, theaters and anything else one could imagine. A short while after their discussion on the bridge, The Spirit of the Revolution touched down just outside the famous gates where evening was setting in on the heels of the departing sun.

The park was deserted, a mausoleum for once great rides, where the skeletons of roller coasters and the empty husks of theaters waited to decay, where nothing breathed and nothing moved. Having taken, as its sustenance, the leisure time and spending power of a society that produces, however fitfully, it had long since starved to death. Sidewalks sported cracks through which weeds would soon sprout. The roller coasters, though resistant to rust, were yet coated with grime, and one theater's partially collapsed roof gave testimony to the vulnerability of even the most advanced materials. Rain spouts clogged, water pooled on roofs, a million particles carried by wind lashed at structures, wearing them down like waves wear down a rock. Nothing was permanent, and without upkeep it would decompose.

Most of the passengers lingered around the ship. Many remained on board. Confused, they scratched their heads and awaited the outcome of the excursion, indifferent to it.

Louise, Katherine and Alistair wandered for a time through the silent park. On Katherine's face Alistair could read the play of her thoughts as she imagined thrills and delights she would never experience. Eventually the autumn air grew chill and Katherine asked Alistair to build them a fire. He left to collect wood and grab a tool from The Spirit. When he returned, Louise and Katherine were sitting in one of the carriages of a Ferris Wheel.

"I brought some food," he said, but neither woman responded.

He arranged his logs and kindling and, with a laser garnered from The Spirit, set fire to the doomed pieces of wood. As the flames consumed them, the leaves limply hanging from the twigs began to wither. The wood turned black and popped. One of the logs toppled over and the resultant crash sent sparks into the air where a chill, dry breeze carried them away. The tiny flaming specks eventually burned out, became invisible, and thereafter it was impossible to say whither they flew.

THE END

Made in the USA
Charleston, SC
09 August 2010